Pamela Evans v   in the borough of Eali   dren. She has two sons and four grandchildren, and now lives in Wales with her husband.

A Song in your Heart

and

Always There

Pamela Evans

headline

A SONG IN YOUR HEART first published in Great Britain in 1998
by HEADLINE BOOK PUBLISHING

ALWAYS THERE first published in Great Britain in 2002
by HEADLINE BOOK PUBLISHING

First published in this omnibus edition in 2004
by HEADLINE BOOK PUBLISHING

A HEADLINE paperback

10 9 8 7 6 5 4 3 2 1

ISBN 0 7553 2671 7

Typeset in Times

Printed and bound in Great Britain by
Clays Ltd, St ives plc

Headline's policy is to use papers that are natural, renewable and
recyclable products and made from wood grown in sustainable
forests. The logging and manufacturing processes are expected to
conform to the environmental regulations of the country of origin.

HEADLINE BOOK PUBLISHING
A division of Hodder Headline
338 Euston Road
London NW1 3BH

www.headline.co.uk
www.hodderheadline.com

A Song in
your Heart

Chapter One

In the private functions room of a back-street pub in Fulham one Saturday in January 1957, a wedding reception was in progress. It was a small, low-budget affair, just a few close friends and relatives gathered together to celebrate the occasion.

'The ham's nice and tasty, love,' remarked the father of the bride, Hal Miller, to his wife Winnie, who was sitting beside him at a large communal table.

'Not bad for the price, I suppose,' she said, glad of a few words with her husband while their guests were chattering among themselves. 'The mashed potato's lumpy, though.'

'Mine's all right,' reassured Hal, a tall, amiable man with a ruddy complexion and dark, greying hair. His most notable feature was his unflappable nature, which was useful to him in his work as a bookings clerk at Paddington station.

'This is vastly different to the wedding I had in mind for our eldest daughter,' said Winnie, a dumpy woman whose anxious disposition tended to overshadow her warm heart. A pillar of respectability, she was staid in appearance, her mousy-brown hair set in tight symmetrical waves around a shiny, plump face which bore no trace of cosmetic embellishment. Still wearing her outdoor clothes because the room was draughty, she was dressed in her best tweed coat and a new red hat purchased especially for the occasion.

'It's only natural for you to want a posh wedding for both our daughters. Most mothers do,' Hal said, turning to her, his hand touching her arm in a comforting gesture, his warm brown eyes meeting her worried grey ones. 'But you've done ever so well to get this do organised at such short notice.'

'You think so?'

'Yeah, I really do,' he said, with strong emphasis because his wife's confidence was more fragile than her manner sometimes indicated.

'I suppose you get what you pay for – and lumpy potato is part of the deal when you do it on the cheap,' she said.

'Look, love, eating out is a treat for all of us here; no one is gonna worry about a few lumps in the mashed potato.'

'I hope not.'

'Just stop worrying and try to enjoy yourself,' he said, patting her hand.

'It isn't just the cheap wedding, Hal,' Winnie continued darkly. 'It's the tackiness that goes with it . . . the stigma.'

'He *has* married her, so there'll be nothing like that.'

'There'll be gossip,' she said sagely. 'Always is when someone gets married in a hurry.'

'If there is it'll all be forgotten by the time the baby's born, 'cause they'll be an old married couple by then.'

'There is that,' Winnie said, but she couldn't restrain a wistful sigh.

My daughter is worth more than a shabby do like this, she thought, casting her eye around the dismal room with its fusty miasma of stale beer, old cigarette smoke and boiled cabbage. The wallpaper was muddy-maroon with raised cream flowers turned beige with age, and the bumpy brown lino looked as though it had been there since the year dot. Gill should have got married in style, with church bells and bridesmaids and a reception in a big hall with dancing and a band. She would have, too – had it not been for Arnie Briscoe.

A pretty girl in her eighteenth year with an office job and music qualifications, Gill could have done well for herself. But what sort of future did she have to look forward to now? What kind of life would she have with an unskilled factory worker currently doing his national service in the army – a man who hadn't even had the decency to put an engagement ring on her finger before taking the sort of liberties that led to a cheapjack wedding with all the usual trappings abandoned for the sake of speed?

Mashing the offending potato determinedly with her fork, it occurred to Winnie that she could count the times on one hand that she'd eaten out – apart from an occasional doughnut with a cup of tea in Lyon's when she was shopping. It was only over these last few years, since Britain had finally recovered from the war and a new wave of affluence had given the working classes the money and confidence to broaden their horizons, that people of their class had been able to afford meals in cafés and restaurants on a regular basis.

Winnie and Hal preferred to stay at home of an evening, though, especially now that they were the proud owners of a television set. They couldn't afford to go out very often anyway, not on what Hal earned; and Winnie hadn't been out to work in all her twenty-odd years of marriage. It had never been an option either of them even considered, because they had grown up in an age when a wife automatically stayed at home to look after the family. Even during the war years, when Hal had been away in the army and married women were forced out to work by law, as the mother of young children Winnie had been exempt.

Although she was usually shy and inhibited, Winnie's primal instincts overruled timidity when it came to defending her family; and unfortunately, in the resultant masking of her natural shyness, she had adopted a formidable air which often created a false impression.

'I could cheerfully throttle that Arnie Briscoe for what he's done to our Gill,' she said to Hal under her breath.

'Shush, Win,' he admonished in a hushed voice. 'That sort of talk isn't gonna help anybody, especially today.'

'But a third-rate wedding like this for Gill . . . She should have had a white dress and time to collect a bottom drawer.'

'I agree with you, but this is the way it's worked out and

3

there's nothing we can do about it,' Hal wisely pointed out. 'We've done all our shoutin' and hollerin' – the recriminations are over. They're married now.'

'More's the pity,' said Winnie, who had actually been stalwart these last few weeks despite her bitter disappointment.

'Arnie isn't so bad,' said Hal, who usually managed to see the best in people. He'd been devastated when the news of Gill's pregnancy had first broken, of course, and had given Arnie a thorough trouncing – but he had now accepted the situation and decided to make the best of things.

'She could have done a lot better, though.'

'Maybe she could. But he's her husband now and we have to accept him as one of the family.'

'I know that.' Winnie sliced a piece of ham without enthusiasm. 'But they're both so young, and he doesn't have any prospects . . .'

'They'll manage.'

'Just managing isn't good enough for our daughter,' Winnie said.

'Give Arnie a chance, he might surprise us all.'

'I can't see that happening.' She paused. 'I never thought Gill would let us down, you know.'

'Nor me. But these things happen,' Hal said, careful not to speak loud enough to be overheard. 'And she's obviously dotty about the bloke.'

'Totally besotted with him,' declared Winnie, her voice rising with feeling. 'She'll do anything he tells her.'

'Keep your voice down.'

'No one's listening to us,' she said, casting a swift glance around at the babbling guests. 'They're all too busy yapping.'

'You can't be too careful at a do like this,' Hal warned. 'We don't want any arguments breaking out and spoiling Gill's day.'

'What is there to spoil at a do like this?' Winnie said glumly.

'Give yourself *some* credit, Win. We've put on the best reception we could possibly afford – and you're the one who's done all the work, getting everything arranged at such short notice.'

'I didn't have any choice, did I, as you're at work all day.'

Despite the way she was speaking, Hal knew his wife had been an absolute diamond. Once she'd got over the initial shock she'd comforted Gill, thrown herself into the wedding arrangements, offered the couple a home with the family in Maisie Road, and robbed her precious post office savings – a small nest-egg built painstakingly from years of careful housekeeping – for Gill's wedding outfit. Although Winnie's manner was often abrasive – poor Arnie had been on the receiving end of it on more than one occasion since Gill's condition had become known – beneath his wife's redoubtable presence beat a heart of gold.

'But look around you, love,' Hal said. 'They're all having a smashing time – especially Gill. And all thanks to you.'

Winnie glanced towards the head of the table where the newly-weds were laughing together, completely engrossed in each other. 'Yeah, I suppose you're right.' She shrugged. 'You can only do your best with what you have, can't you? If they'd got engaged in the normal way and given us time to save up we'd have given her the works.'

'Course we would and Gill knows that. She's as happy as a queen with what we've put on for her today. It might not be the wedding of her dreams but it'll still be a day for her to remember.'

Looking at her daughter, Winnie swallowed hard on a lump in her throat. Gill looked so young and vulnerable, her small face turned eagerly towards her new husband, dark hair worn short with a floppy, uneven fringe. It was true what people said about her: she did have a look of Audrey Hepburn, with those huge brown eyes and heavy brows dominating her slender face. Winnie had to admit that she looked radiantly happy too, her cheeks brightly suffused against her fashionable scarlet suit. The much-maligned pillbox hat she'd worn dutifully to the register office had been removed; it seemed hats weren't popular with young women of Gill's generation.

'They're just like a couple o' kids playing at weddings,' murmured Winnie, blinking back the tears. 'I hope to God they've got the stamina to cope with reality, because they'll have plenty of that when the baby arrives.'

'Let's worry about that when the time comes, shall we?' said Hal, turning his attention back to his meal and lapsing into thought. Winnie was a dear, but she was like a dog with a bone over this wedding. Personally, Hal thought Gill and Arnie had what it took to make their marriage work. Admittedly Arnie wasn't the husband they'd have chosen for their daughter – and Hal had been as much against his going out with Gill as Winnie was at the beginning – but he wasn't a bad lad. He'd been through a yobbish stage a few years ago, swaggering around the streets in teddy boy clothes with marauding gangs of louts, but that had just been youthful exuberance and he seemed over it now – partly due to the army, in Hal's opinion. And anyone who could perform on a football field like Arnie Briscoe couldn't be all bad.

'You enjoying yourself, Hal?' asked a voice from across the table that was only just audible above the conversational hubbub.

'Not half,' he replied to Arnie's mother Phoebe, a tall, busty blonde in a bright blue suit that matched her sparkling eyes. 'Are you?'

'I'm having a smashing time, thanks,' she said, smiling and glancing towards Winnie. 'You and Win have done us proud.'

Sitting next to Phoebe was her younger son, John, a lanky eleven-year-old with the same compelling brown eyes and curly hair as his older brother. The Millers and the Briscoes had lived in Maisie Road for many years. But although they had known *of* each other for all that time, they had never

6

exchanged more than a passing greeting – until a couple of years ago, when Gill had started going out with Arnie.

From what Hal gathered from local gossip, it hadn't been easy for Phoebe, bringing up two boys on her own these last ten years since her husband had died. She'd done a variety of jobs to put food on the table, apparently: charring, factory work, and she now worked on the sweet counter in Woolworth's.

And after all she'd done for Arnie, he'd brought shame on her by getting a neighbour's daughter into trouble. Not that Phoebe seemed ashamed; that wasn't her way. Unlike Hal's dear Winnie, Phoebe was a relaxed sort of person able to take things in her stride. From the little he knew of her, she was the gregarious type who liked nothing better than a party. She had a bit of a reputation with the men, as a matter of fact.

'Winnie must take all the credit,' he said to Phoebe. 'She organised everything.'

A roar of laughter erupted nearby, and Phoebe put her hand behind her ear to indicate that she couldn't hear. 'Later,' she mouthed.

Hal nodded, and Phoebe became immediately engrossed in conversation with a friend of Arnie's sitting next to her.

'What was all that about?' asked Winnie, who had been out of earshot.

'She was just being friendly.'

'That's her speciality . . . being friendly,' she said with strong disapproval. Because Phoebe's unwavering confidence made her feel inferior, Winnie was inclined to be uncharitable towards her as a sort of defence mechanism. To a reserved soul like herself, Phoebe's self-assurance didn't fall far short of arrogance. 'It's where Arnie gets it from. It's no wonder that boy is degenerate.'

'Now that isn't fair, Win,' Hal said, gently reproachful but determinedly firm.

'Oh, do me a favour,' she replied. 'Everyone in Maisie Road knows what she's like. If snowmen were around for long enough she'd try to get off with 'em.'

At that moment fifteen-year-old Carol Miller, who was sitting on her mother's other side out of earshot of her parents' conversation, gave Winnie a nudge.

'What's for afters, Mum?' she asked.

'Sherry trifle.' Winnie looked at Carol's plate. 'But you've not finished your dinner.'

'Don't want any more. The ham's fatty and the potatoes are lumpy.'

'That's a waste of good food,' tutted Winnie, still inclined to practise the habit she'd picked up during the long years of rationing.

'Too bad, 'cause I'm not eating it,' was Carol's petulant reply.

'Leave it then, dear,' sighed Winnie, who was ashamed to admit that she often gave in to her younger daughter out of sheer exhaustion. Unlike her sunny-natured older sister, Carol had always been a difficult child. She could bend people to her will by wearing them down to a point where they would agree to anything. She was also very sensitive and needed lots of attention. Her demanding nature had been exacerbated by the onset of adolescence, with its biological changes and heightened self-awareness, and now her head was full of romance and she always seemed to be lusting after some boy or other. She was extremely affectionate; sometimes it seemed to Winnie as though she had too much love for anyone to cope with. Having recently left school, she had a job as a filing clerk in the offices of a local shoe-polish factory.

Winnie's thoughts drifted back to the wedding arrangements – and she gave due credit to Phoebe, who had offered to contribute towards the cost of the reception because of the special circumstances. But Winnie wasn't having that! What, and have people say the Millers couldn't afford to do the traditional thing and pay for their own daughter's wedding reception? Not bloomin' likely!

In the end they had agreed for Phoebe to pay for the

photographs outside the register office, and to provide a spray of flowers for Gill and the buttonholes. As a wedding present Phoebe had booked the couple into a small hotel on the outskirts of the West End for tonight.

Although Winnie thought the gift somewhat frivolous in the light of the couple's impending responsibilities, she was secretly rather relieved. The thought of the newly-weds spending their first night as a married couple at home with her and Hal in Maisie Road was acutely embarrassing to her – even though Gill's condition made it obvious that there would be no bashfulness behind their bedroom door.

'Dead romantic, innit?' said Carol with an elaborate sigh.

'What is?' asked her mother, turning to look at her daughter who didn't resemble her sister in physical appearance at all. Carol wasn't exactly pretty, but she was growing into an attractive young woman with an exceptionally well developed figure for her age. In contrast to Gill's dark colouring, Carol had light-brown hair and a pale, freckled complexion. Her almond-shaped, hazel eyes lost something because they were always simmering with discontent.

'Gill and Arnie, o' course.'

Her mother shot her a warning look, terrified that Carol might see her sister as a role model. Winnie couldn't face the prospect of having to go through all this again with her second daughter. 'There's nothing romantic about having to get married, my girl,' she said.

'Getting married is romantic however it happens,' Carol stated categorically.

'It's more romantic to wait and have all the trimmings, though: the white dress and bridesmaids.' She threw Carol a look. 'Surely you wouldn't want to miss out on all of that.'

'Maybe not. But Gill and Arnie are happy together even though they didn't have any of that,' she said, looking at the couple and emitting another sigh. 'Ooh, Arnie really sends me. He's even more gorgeous than Elvis Presley.'

Winnie cast a studious eye over her new son-in-law who,

admittedly, did cut rather a dash in the livery of the Middlesex Regiment, which he was wearing because Gill had wanted him to get married in uniform. Yes, she supposed his clean-cut looks would have a certain attraction for young women. Having played football since he was so high, he looked fit and athletic, and he had a smooth complexion and greenish-brown eyes that sparkled with warmth and devilment. His curly, chestnut-coloured hair was cut very short, army-style, and his smile could be quite devastating. But what use was a melting smile to the mother of his child with no home of her own?

'She's so lucky having Arnie as a husband,' continued Carol, who thought her sister's recent scandal was the most thrilling thing that had happened in ages. It had certainly livened things up at home. And such fuel for her lively young imagination too! Carol and her girlfriends had had great fun speculating on when and where the deed had actually taken place. The girl felt quite weak with excitement at the thought of what had been going on. 'I wish I was the one who had just got married.'

'Good heavens above!' reproached her mother. 'You're far too young.'

'Gill isn't that much older than I am.'

'She's nearly three years older,' declared Winnie, keeping her voice low as the waitress cleared their dinner plates. 'Anyway, Gill's still too young to get married. She wouldn't have done so if the circumstances had been different.'

'Well I still think it's romantic whatever you say.'

Romantic, my eye, thought Winnie. Drudgery, poverty and council accommodation – that about summed up her view of what life had in store for Mrs Arnie Briscoe. Winnie thanked God the pregnancy had come to light when it had. A few days later and Arnie wouldn't have been around to do the decent thing – for he'd been posted to Germany and was leaving on Monday with his regiment. He was likely to be abroad for months, certainly until after the baby was born.

10

Although Gill was quite naturally dreading his departure, it was a positive blessing to Winnie. At least she would be spared having a relative stranger living in her house – until after he was demobbed, anyway. Heaven only knew how long it would be before they could afford a place of their own. They certainly couldn't set up home on Arnie's army pay, and his own mother didn't have room for them in her poky little flat in the pre-war block on the corner of Maisie Road.

Winnie wondered how their marriage would stand up to the trials and tribulations of everyday living when he came out of the army, especially with the added demands of a baby to cope with. It certainly didn't have the ingredients for durability, being merely an arrangement of necessity. Still, whatever happened in the future, the wedding would have served a purpose in preventing her first grandchild from being born a bastard.

Who would have thought one of her girls would have landed in trouble? She thought she'd protected herself against every mother's nightmare by giving her daughters a strict and moral upbringing, hammering decent values into them for all she was worth. Hal had left that sort of thing to her, since it was generally accepted that bringing up the children was a woman's job.

But then who would have thought Gill would have got mixed up with someone like Arnie? Until he'd come into her life she'd been a serious-minded sort of girl, diligent in her work as a clerk in an accountant's office and passionate about her musical hobby. Since she had shown an interest in the family piano at a very young age, Winnie and Hal had made their budget stretch to piano lessons for her, and she'd rewarded them by showing real talent and dedication.

Before she'd got friendly with Arnie most of her spare time had been spent at the piano. Practising had never been anathema to Gill; she'd passed exams with flying colours and competed regularly at music festivals. Winnie and Hal had been so proud.

11

Then she'd caught the eye of Arnie Briscoe and become a different person almost overnight. Her piano was forgotten in her eagerness to go with him to dance halls and coffee bars. Her taste in music changed from inoffensive ballads and sober classical pieces to crude and deafening rock 'n' roll.

Her style of dress had altered too. She now spent all her spare money on stiletto-heeled shoes with winkle-picker points, and tight skirts, or exaggeratedly full skirts with stiff petticoats and flat pumps. And as if all that wasn't bad enough, Arnie had bought her a portable record player for a birthday present, and the disgraceful Elvis Presley could be heard bellowing out some tuneless drivel about his blue suede shoes.

The amicable relationship that Winnie and Hal had always had with their daughter became fraught with arguments. There was constant tension in the house. But nothing could persuade Gill to give Arnie up. Times had changed since Winnie and Hal were young; these days youngsters were far more assertive towards their parents than they had ever dared to be.

Their disapproval only drove Gill more determinedly into Arnie's arms. There had been one dreadful scene when Winnie, in desperation, had simply forbidden her to see him again. She'd never seen her daughter so angry. Through tight lips Gill had announced that she would leave home rather than give him up.

'Just 'cause he dresses like a teddy boy doesn't make him bad,' Gill had said. 'They don't all go out smashing up cinemas and dance halls, you know. He just likes wearing the gear, that's all, and dancing to rock 'n' roll music . . . and so do I.'

After that Winnie and Hal had kept a diplomatic silence, hoping the affair would run its course and die the death. After all, he would be going away to do his national service soon – surely, they reasoned, that would put an end to it.

But it hadn't. They'd written to each other almost every day and spent every second together when he came home on leave.

God only knows where it will end, thought Winnie now, as the crockery was finally cleared away and the waitresses began serving dessert.

'I'd like to thank you all for coming to share our special day with us,' said Arnie, who was on his feet making a speech. He paused for a moment with a wicked look in his eye. 'Even though it was rather short notice . . .'

Oh, really, has he no shame? thought Winnie furiously, as the company erupted into laughter. How dare he embarrass Gill in such a cheap and vulgar way? But Gill was laughing, which spoke volumes about the power he had over her. Hal was chuckling too. Winnie gave him a sharp dig in the ribs with her elbow and scowled at him when he turned towards her.

'He's only bringing something out into the open that everyone knows about anyway, Win,' he whispered, unheard by the others beneath the gales of mirth. 'He means well.'

'He shouldn't talk like that.'

'Don't take everything so seriously, love,' he said quietly as Arnie began speaking again.

'We're all friends here, so I want to be honest with you . . .' Arnie glanced at his wife and then fixed his gaze on Winnie, in the hope of getting his heartfelt message across to her and easing her mind about this marriage. 'I'll admit that this isn't the way Gill and I planned to get married, and it's sooner than we expected. But I want you all to know that we would have got married sooner or later anyway, and we're both really happy that it's happened now.' He turned and smiled lovingly at Gill, then looked back towards the company again. 'I consider myself to be a very lucky man. This is the happiest day of my life.'

A communal sigh rippled through the females in the room, interspersed with some loud and saucy badinage from the men. Arnie could feel his mother-in-law's eyes piercing into him. She'd sent plenty of hostile vibes in his direction since he'd been seeing Gill, and had given him a real roasting when they'd told her and Hal about the baby. It was a predictable reaction and he didn't blame her. But knowing she didn't approve of him as a son-in-law made him feel uncomfortable, and he dealt with it in the best way he knew: by ignoring it and being friendly towards her, despite her coolness to him.

Thank God he was spared having to live with his in-laws – for a while, at least. Having to face his mother-in-law's disapproving stare over his corn flakes every morning didn't bear thinking about.

The very first priority on his agenda when he got demobbed was to find them a place of their own.

But that was a long way off and, although he loved Gill to bits and didn't want to leave her, he couldn't help anticipating his trip abroad with a certain amount of excitement. He was young and hungry for adventure. Since he'd been forced into the army for two years, he was glad to be given the opportunity to see some of the world at the government's expense.

It was traditional among the blokes to complain about national service, and Arnie went along with the herd in this respect. But once the torturous basic training had ended he'd begun to enjoy his service. He was luckier than most: his skill on the football field had not only got him a job as a PT instructor, it had also earned him a place in the regiment team. As well as being given time off work for football training, he also travelled all over the country to play in matches. It was a damned sight pleasanter than working at a machine all day as he'd done in civvy street.

'I'd like to thank my mother for all she's done for me all my life, and for her support this last few weeks,' he said now, looking at his mother who beamed at him in acknowledgment.

He turned again to Winnie and Hal. 'I'd also like to thank my mother- and father-in-law for all their help . . . and for giving us this smashing party today.'

A cheer went up among the guests, and Arnie raised his hands for silence.

'And most of all I'd like to thank them for letting me marry their beautiful daughter.'

That's a good one, since we didn't have any choice in the matter, thought Winnie, meeting his eyes and, much to her annoyance, finding that hers were brimming with tears.

'I must assure them that I shall look after her and do my very best to make her happy.'

'You'd better do an' all, mate,' shouted Hal jokingly.

With a broad grin, Arnie assured him again before sitting down to rousing cheers from the assembled company and a hesitant smile from Winnie.

He was convincing, she'd say that much for him. She rummaged in her pocket for a handkerchief. It was no wonder Gill had fallen for him – he couldn't half turn on the charm.

Despite not having all the trimmings, this was the happiest day of Gill's life. A white wedding would have been lovely of course, if things had been different, but the important thing was marrying Arnie. The rest didn't really matter to her. She was so happy and proud to be his wife.

'Well done,' she said as he sat down.

'Was it okay?'

'It was great.'

'Phew. I'm glad it's over,' he said. 'It was a bit nerve-racking.'

'Fancy coming right out with the reason for the wedding, though.'

'It was a sudden impulse,' he said, looking at her with a serious expression. 'As it's common knowledge among the guests even though everyone's keeping shtum about it, I thought I'd let them know that we really wanted to get married and haven't done it just because of the baby.' He paused, looking doubtful. 'I hope I haven't upset you.'

'No, course you haven't,' she said, touched by his eagerness to declare his feelings for her in public.

'I don't think your mum was any too pleased, though.'

'You know how reserved Mum is,' she said. 'Her bark's worse than her bite.'

'I didn't want to offend her 'cause she's been good to us,' he said.

'Yes, she has.'

'I was trying to reassure her about my feelings for you as much as anything.'

'I know.'

Through the mists of joy, Gill was aware of her mother's disappointment in her, even though she'd been wonderfully supportive. But the knowledge did little more than cast a slight shadow over Gill's mood because her happiness was so intense.

This didn't mean that Gill didn't feel bad about letting her parents down. She was permanently suspended between guilt and rapture. But, in all honesty, she couldn't regret marrying Arnie and carrying his child when it was all she wanted from her life, which had blossomed since he'd been a part of it.

She looked across at her mother and smiled affectionately. Winnie smiled back, a brave effort that twisted Gill's heart. Her mother looked older suddenly, somehow frailer and less stern than usual.

Tears swelled beneath Gill's lids as she realised that nothing would be the same again between her mother and herself. Her wedding day was a new beginning, but it also marked the end of an era.

Imbued with emotion, her thoughts lingered on all the good things her parents had done for her. As well as providing her with a loving family life, they had made sacrifices so that she could have piano lessons. And she had repaid them by bringing shame on the family.

But for all that she wouldn't change a thing. She was young and inexperienced, but she knew that she and Arnie were right for each other.

'It's your dad's turn now,' said Arnie, jolting her out of her reverie to see her father rising to propose a toast to the happy couple. Her eyes filled with fresh tears as he spoke from the heart, wishing them well in their life together. He'd been the only man in her life until she'd met Arnie, and she had failed him.

Does your own happiness always come at the expense of someone else's? she wondered.

Hal's toast to the newly-weds marked the end of the formalities and people began to get up from the table and mingle. As the host, Hal got everyone a drink from the bar and the atmosphere soon became thick with smoke and alcohol fumes, the volume of noise and laughter rising as the drinks flowed.

With a gin and tonic in her hand, Phoebe went over to Winnie. 'Well, it's all going with a swing,' she said, smiling. 'You did a good job organising it.'

'There were no major catastrophes anyway,' said Winnie.

Phoebe inhaled on her cigarette, looking at Winnie thoughtfully. 'Except the biggest catastrophe of them all in your book . . . the fact that your daughter has married my son, eh?' she said with a wry grin.

Winnie's stomach knotted with nerves but she felt compelled to stand up for herself. 'How would you feel if it was your daughter who'd got into trouble?' she asked.

'I can't answer that, since I don't have any daughters,' said Phoebe candidly. 'But I can't see that it's any worse than seeing a son get married before he's ready.'

'It's a different thing altogether for a woman,' said Winnie through dry lips.

'Different, but potentially as damaging to a man's future,' said Phoebe, in a tone that bore no malice and was merely her considered opinion.

'I don't see how.'

'Arnie's only nineteen. He's much too young to be tied down with a wife and kiddie to support. He needs freedom to develop, to work out what he wants to do with his life.'

'He should have thought of that—'

'I couldn't agree more, dear, but young people are fresh to what life has to offer and it makes them impulsive,' Phoebe said in an even tone. 'They don't always stop to think.'

'Arnie obviously didn't.'

'Arnie wasn't a solo player,' was Phoebe's answer to that. 'And I haven't heard young Gill saying anything about rape.'

Phoebe sipped her drink, watching Winnie as her mouth opened then closed again, scarlet patches staining her cheeks, her mouth set in a grim line. Phoebe felt rather sorry for her. She always seemed to have the worries of the world on her shoulders.

'Look, Winnie dear,' she said with genuine friendliness, because she was a very even-tempered person who spoke her mind but rarely fell out with anyone, 'the kids have got married and we have to accept it whether we like it or not. How *we* feel about it isn't important, and certainly isn't gonna make a scrap of difference to the outcome of their marriage. So all we can do is let Gill and Arnie get on with it in their own way and stop worrying about them.'

Before Winnie had a chance to reply, Gill appeared at her side. 'Glad to see that you two are getting to know each other,' she said.

'We thought we ought to make the effort now that we're practically related, isn't that right?' said Phoebe with a meaningful look in Winnie's direction.

'Yeah, that's right,' said Winnie, because she knew it would please Gill.

Phoebe turned back to Gill. 'So, what time is Arnie going back to camp tomorrow?' she asked.

'In the afternoon.'

'How about coming to our place for Sunday dinner then . . . when you get back from the hotel? It's the last time I'll be seeing my son for quite a while.' She turned to Winnie. 'As long as that won't put you out, love.'

'Not at all,' said Winnie politely. 'We can have what's left of the joint on Monday.'

'We'd love to come then,' said Gill, smiling at her new mother-in-law.

'That's settled then.' Phoebe wriggled her shoulders and grinned to indicate her pleasure in the arrangement. 'Have I told you how pleased I am to have you join our family?'

'Several times,' said Gill, who liked Phoebe very much.

'I'll say it again just for good measure,' she said, hugging her new daughter-in-law. 'Welcome to the Briscoe family.'

'Glad to have joined.'

Aware that her mother was excluded from this uninhibited display of warmth and friendliness, Gill turned to Winnie. 'Thanks for everything you've done for us, Mum.' She hugged her tight. 'You've been really great, and we appreciate it.'

'That's all right, love,' said Winnie, warmed and softened by these few words of appreciation. 'It was the least I could do.'

'Well, I think I'll go and do some socialising before the party comes to an end,' said Phoebe, and sauntered off.

Watching her swinging her hips as she walked, Winnie felt a stab of envy for someone of whom she had never approved. It wasn't Phoebe's way of life she envied. Working on the counter in Woolworth's because she didn't have a husband to support her must be purgatory – and she was as common as muck with her heavy make-up and bleached hair.

But her vivacious personality and exuberant attitude to life seemed highly desirable to Winnie at that moment. She knew she could never be like that herself because it wasn't in her nature – and most of the time she didn't want to be – but at that precise moment she would have given anything for a small measure of Phoebe Briscoe's casual confidence and indomitable spirit.

Although Gill and Arnie had become accustomed to partings since he'd been in the army, they had never got any easier for Gill. And the one she faced the following afternoon cut deeper than any before because he was going abroad. There would be no weekend passes to look forward to from Germany, she thought gloomily as they left his mother's flat and made their way past the grey Victorian terraces that made up the majority of Maisie Road, heading for Fulham Broadway station.

It was a bitterly cold afternoon, with a sharp wind and dark, threatening clouds rolling above the grey slate rooftops; the tiny front gardens were bleak at this time of year. Arnie was wearing his army greatcoat, while Gill shivered inside a camel-coloured duffle-coat over black tapered trousers. His kitbag was strapped to his shoulders and her hand was tucked into his arm. She was savouring having him near, their last minutes together ticking away as steadily as the beating of her heart.

'It's been the most wonderful weekend of my life,' she said as they progressed into North End Road, which was bathed in the quiet of a Sunday afternoon, the shops closed, the street empty of market barrows until tomorrow, the wind blowing dust and litter across the road.

Dusk was already falling, and lights were beginning to appear in the windows of the homes in the residential side streets, some of which had changed since Gill was a child and the bomb-sites were built over. Lots of the slum areas in the borough had been cleared too, many of them replaced by municipal housing developments.

'Yeah, it was really smashing,' Arnie said, looking lovingly at her face, her cheeks glowing with the cold, her dark fringe flopping out of her hood on to her forehead. 'Especially last night. Cor, I won't forget that in a hurry.'

'I'll never forget it,' she declared earnestly, thinking back.

The hotel was more of a guest house really, but it was spotlessly clean and the food was delicious. One of the things Gill had enjoyed most about it, though, was the feeling of anonymity, people coming and going unnoticed, which was such a novelty to Gill and Arnie.

Throughout the whole of their love affair they had wanted nothing more than to be alone, and had expended a great deal

20

of effort to this end, usually to be thwarted by family or neighbours or friends. Just one of the drawbacks of finding romance so close to home, Gill supposed. But at the hotel, with its dark, antiquated residents' lounge, creaky old lift and freezing starched sheets, no one had taken any notice of them at all. Immediately after dinner last night they'd gone to their room and stayed there until breakfast without raising so much as a flicker of interest. It had been bliss!

Now they were back down to earth with a bump. Arnie had said goodbye to the folks, and it would be a long time before any of them saw him again.

'I'll miss you,' Gill said.

'I'll miss you too.'

'I'll write often,' she said.

'Me too.'

'Oh, Arnie, I can't believe we're actually married,' she said, just the thought of it making her heart race. 'Can you?'

He halted in his step and slipped his arms around her, looking into her eyes. 'Ooh, yeah, I can believe it all right – and it's really great.' He gave her a wicked grin. 'I'm a bit choked about not being around to take advantage of the fact that it's legal, though.'

'Is that all you think about?'

'Men of my age think of nothing else,' he replied, teasing her. 'It's expected of us.'

She gave him a playful punch on the shoulder and said, 'As long as it's only in relation to me.'

'Of course.'

'I should hope so too.'

They walked on in silence for a while, each lost in their own thoughts.

'Do you realise that this is the last time we'll be together as just a couple?' she said. 'When you come home next time we'll be a family.'

'Yeah,' he said, his tone becoming serious. 'That's gonna take some getting used to.'

'It'll be different.'

'Me a dad. Wow!'

'You'll be great.'

'I'll certainly do my best.'

At the station, they stood huddled together in the draughty foyer, away from the crowds hurrying to and from the platform. Brimming with emotion, Gill was both dreading the parting and wanting it to be over.

'I'll be counting the days till you come home,' she said.

'Me too,' he said. 'I shall cross them off on my calendar.'

'You can keep your sexy eyes off the fräuleins out there in Germany too,' she chided playfully. 'I don't want you getting off with any German girl.'

'As if I would.'

'You'd better not.'

'What about you?'

'Me?'

'Yes, you,' he confirmed with forced laughter. 'How do I know you're not gonna take a fancy to some other bloke while I'm away?'

'Oh, yeah. As a married woman with a baby on the way I'm gonna have bags of opportunity to play around,' she said with irony.

It was all just meaningless chatter to ease the pain of parting.

'Love you loads,' he said, kissing her deeply on the lips.

'Love you too,' she said.

And after one last feverish embrace he was gone, making his way across the foyer with long, purposeful strides – a tall, athletic figure, his kitbag shifting slightly from side to side as he walked.

Gill waited until he was out of sight then walked slowly out into the cold street, now fully dark and lit by the yellow glow from the street-lights which she saw through a blur of tears.

It was a punishing wrench, but she had a feeling of elation

and confidence in the future too. With Arnie's wedding ring on her finger and his baby growing inside her, she felt invincible. Nothing could defeat the wife of Arnie Briscoe!

Chapter Two

Time passed slowly for Gill after Arnie's departure, as she waited out the long months until his return. But the feeling of inner strength remained with her, despite the constant ache of missing him, and his letters were a great source of comfort. She also began to look forward more eagerly to the birth of her baby as the time drew nearer.

It was as though she was in a curious kind of limbo. Although she felt married in her heart, from the point of view of everyday life it was as though she was still single, living with the family and staying on at work – which she planned to do for as long as she was able.

The pattern of her life almost reverted to the pre-Arnie days: calm and uneventful. Most evenings were spent at home, though she occasionally met up with girlfriends in a coffee bar for a gossip, and sometimes went to the cinema with her sister. With time on her hands, her interest in the piano returned, until eventually she became too enormous to sit comfortably on the stool and reach the keys and pedals.

'Wow,' exclaimed Carol, one warm summer's evening when the birth was several days overdue and Gill was trying to keep cool by lying on her bed. Even the tent-like proportions of her maternity nightdress could barely contain her bloated form. 'How can anyone be that huge?'

'It's all too easy, believe me,' said Gill with a wry grin.

'Not if you don't have a boyfriend,' said Carol wistfully.

'Give it time, kid,' said Gill. 'You're not even sixteen yet. Your turn will come soon enough. And in the meantime have some fun. Being pregnant isn't exactly a laugh a minute.'

'I'm longing to get married and have a baby,' Carol said.

'Well, it's too early for you yet, so you'll just have to make do with a niece or nephew,' said Gill, who sometimes thought her sister was unnaturally impatient for such things.

'I wish it would hurry up and get born,' said Carol.

'You and me both, sis,' sighed Gill, who was finding the heat exhausting in her inflated condition and was eager for the inevitable to begin. She placed her hands on her extended stomach and addressed the huge bump. 'It's time you showed yourself, kiddo. We're all getting fed up with waiting.'

The baby obviously had a respect for authority, because Gill's waters broke later that night and she was taken into the maternity ward of Hammersmith hospital, where she entered into a very long and difficult labour.

'I'll murder Arnie when I see him,' she was heard to utter at one point of intense agony. 'For putting me through this.'

But she soon forgot the pain, when Craig Arnold Briscoe finally made his appearance and she stared with wonder at his beautiful little face with its high forehead, plump cheeks and squarish jaw that was so unmistakably Arnie.

'Oh, Craig. Your daddy is gonna be so proud of you,' she said with tears of joy running down her cheeks. 'But I do wish he was here to share this fantastic moment with me!'

Craig was a few weeks old when Arnie came home on leave bursting with health and even more handsome than Gill remembered. His tough image was forgotten in the emotion of the moment, and he wept openly when he first saw his son. Gill felt highly charged too. Seeing them together for the first time was a deeply moving experience.

Their son was six months old when Arnie finally returned to England for his demob and he and Gill were able to begin their life together properly. Although Gill had never doubted that he would settle down to marriage and fatherhood, because of his youth and the circumstances of their marriage there were plenty of people just waiting for him to let her down and go off the rails.

Happily for her, Arnie surprised them all by being a devoted husband and father. Established back at his old job at the engineering factory, he rushed home from work every evening in time to see Craig before he went to bed. He cuddled him, comforted him and even disregarded his macho inhibitions and took him to the park in his pram at weekends. He was simply longing for the boy to learn to walk so that he could teach him to kick a ball.

'The thought of coming home to you and Craig keeps me sane in that bloomin' factory all day,' he confessed to Gill one night when they were getting ready to go to bed.

'Don't you like it there now then?' she asked in surprise, because he'd always seemed happy enough with the job before the army.

'Like it!' he exclaimed as though astonished by such a curious notion. 'I hate it! Putting rivets into lumps of metal for hours on end every day is driving me stark raving mad!'

'It never seemed to bother you before you went away,' she remarked in a low voice so as not to wake Craig who was asleep in his cot.

'It didn't seem so bad then, probably because I didn't know any different,' he said gloomily, getting into bed and leaning back against the pillows with his hands linked behind his head.

She was brushing her hair at the dressing table, looking at him in the mirror. 'Sounds to me as though the army has unsettled you,' she said.

'It's bound to, innit?' he said. 'I mean, you're living a completely different sort of life for two years.'

'But everyone hates national service and can't wait for it to be over.'

'Most of 'em do hate it – but at least you get a change of scenery.'

'Mm, there is that.'

'I had it cushy compared to most of the lads 'cause of the football,' he explained. 'I reckon my game must have improved no end 'cause I got so much practice playing for the regiment.'

'And plenty of time off for training,' she reminded him chattily.

'Yeah. It wasn't so much the time off that I liked, because I didn't mind the job I was doing,' he said. 'It was being involved with the game so much more than I am in civvy street that I enjoyed so much.'

'Really?'

'Mm. And even apart from the actual football, when you play for the regiment you're always in demand,' he explained. 'It made me feel as though I counted for something, you know? Now I'm a nobody again and I miss the buzz.'

'But you play on a regular basis for the Town Park Shooters,' she pointed out, referring to a local amateur team.

'Only on Sunday mornings, if they've managed to get a game fixed up,' he said. 'In the army there were plenty of matches and regular training. I felt like a professional.'

'So you're thinking of signing on as a regular soldier just to get more soccer, are you?' she said jokingly, getting into bed and snuggling up beside him.

'Not likely.'

'I'd have something to say if you were,' she said.

'It's just that the day at the factory seems so long and boring now compared to what I've been doing this last couple o' years.'

'Can't you look for another job?' she suggested. 'There's plenty of work about.'

'There's no point. Factory work will be just as deadly boring anywhere,' he said, 'and it's the only sort of work I know.'

'You taught PT in the army,' she said. 'Can't you do something along those lines?'

'No chance. I was just an army PT instructor, that doesn't

qualify me to do anything similar in civvy street.'

'Surely there must be something else you can do though,' Gill said with concern. 'Something a bit more interesting for you.'

'There probably is, but I'd have to take a drop in wages – at first, anyway – and I can't afford to do that now that I have responsibilities.'

'I'm sure we could manage.'

'No, Gill. The money's good where I am, and we need every penny for when we get our own place, for furniture and stuff.'

'True. But I don't like the idea of your doing work that makes you miserable.'

'I don't have a choice, babe.'

'Of course you do,' she insisted. 'I think you should look for another job. Even if the money is less, we'll get by.'

'It's a nice thought, but it wouldn't be practical.'

'Perhaps I could make up the difference,' she suggested with rising enthusiasm. 'I could get a part-time job.'

'And what about the baby?'

'Maybe I could ask Mum to look after him for a few hours a day.'

'Oh no,' he said emphatically. 'I'm not having that.'

'Why not?'

'Your place is at home with Craig, and it's my job to provide for you.'

'But I'd like to do something to help. I'd rather go out to work than have you doing a job you hate,' she told him. 'Just until you get yourself sorted.'

'You're a real diamond, do you know that?' he said, slipping an arm round her so that she was nestling into the crook of his neck. 'I shouldn't have said anything to you about the job. It's worried you, and there's no need for that.'

'I'm your wife, Arnie,' she said. 'I should know about these things.'

'I'll get used to the factory again in time. Don't worry,' he said, sounding positive to reassure her. 'So don't let's waste any more precious time talking about it.'

'Ooh, I love it when you're masterful,' she giggled, wriggling closer to him.

'I can be as masterful as you like,' he said, laughing softly.

Listening to the low sound of talk and laughter in the room next door, Hal said, 'Those two are as happy as anything, aren't they?'

'Yeah, they do seem to be getting on well at the moment,' agreed Winnie, who was putting curlers into her hair in front of the dressing table mirror. Reckless optimism wasn't in her nature. Being too certain of things was the surest way she knew of coming a cropper. 'But it's still early days; the novelty of his being back hasn't had time to wear off yet.'

'I think Arnie has settled down very well though,' said Hal, who was already in bed. 'It can't have been easy for him to adjust to family life after two years in the army, especially as he didn't have a chance to get used to being married before he went away.'

'Mm.'

'Living here with us can't help matters, either.'

'No it can't and I don't like it any more than he does,' she said. 'I mean, it isn't as if we really know him, is it?'

'We know him well enough,' said Hal. 'Arnie's all right.'

'Just because he can boot a football around a field, he can do no wrong in your eyes.'

'It isn't just his football. I think he's a genuinely good bloke . . . and he thinks the world of Gill and Craig.'

'Yes, that does seem to be the case,' Winnie was forced to agree.

'They need to be in their own place though,' Hal remarked.

'Definitely!'

'Perhaps the council will come up with something for them soon.'

'It won't be for a while yet, I shouldn't think,' Winnie said, her down-to-earth nature coming to the fore again. 'The housing waiting list in this area is a mile long.'

'True.'

'Anyway, they need time to get some cash together so that they can furnish the place when it does come through.'

'He earns reasonably good money at the factory, I think.'

'Not enough to put much by with a wife and kiddie to keep.'

'Probably not.'

'They've only themselves to blame,' Winnie said, her tone becoming brusque as she thought again how different things could have been for her daughter. 'If they'd shown a bit of restraint they'd have had time to save up and get something behind them before they started a family.'

'A lot of young people seem to be buying their own places these days,' Hal remarked casually. 'Not like our generation of renters.'

'Gill and Arnie will still be living here with us when Craig's grown up if they wait until they've got the deposit on a place of their own,' she said.

'Still, they're happy – that's the main thing,' he said.

'I hope to God it lasts.'

'Let's look on the bright side, shall we?' said Hal in a conclusive manner as Winnie tied a pink hairnet over her curlers, took off her red woollen dressing gown and climbed into bed.

In the other bedroom, Carol was also listening to the low murmur coming from her sister's room. Being of a generation who thought the over-twenty-fives were a sub-culture, never mind ancient relics like her parents, she didn't share their concern for the practicalities of Gill and Arnie's life together. All she could think about was the romantic side of things. And unlike her parents she didn't want them to move into a home of their own, because she enjoyed having them here. The place would be like a morgue without other young people to take the edge off her mum's and dad's old-fashioned ways. She was fond of little Craig, liked having Gill on hand to chat to, and thought Arnie was the sexiest thing she had ever clapped eyes on.

I hope they stay here for ever, she thought, turning over on to her side and settling down to sleep. Imagining that Arnie was lying beside her, she shivered with pleasure and snuggled deeper under the covers.

The match was in the final minutes and the score was still a draw. Arnie tore down the field towards the goal, took possession of the ball from a long pass, dribbled it past two defenders and took a shot at goal. It was in! He'd done it! He'd scored the winning goal just seconds before the final whistle. Cor, what a blinder!

He threw his arms in the air victoriously as the shrill sound of the referee's whistle filled the air. Arnie's team-mates were all over him, slapping his back and hugging him. It might only be amateur football in the Sunday league, but that didn't lessen the importance of the game to the players.

It was impossible for Arnie to describe to anyone, even his beloved Gill, how he felt when he was in action on a soccer pitch. Only then did he feel fully alive, his senses finely tuned, adrenalin pumping in top gear. Nothing else on earth gave him the same feeling of release and excitement. The thought of a weekend game kept him going during the loathsome week at the factory. Such was the tedium of the job, he even found himself dreading the end of the football season.

'That goal definitely calls for a pint, mate,' said one of his team-mates as they walked off the field towards the changing hut.

The sharp March wind whipped through their shirts but they were all glowing from the exercise and didn't even notice. It was a deceptively chilly day, glimpses of watery sunshine appearing intermittently through grey and white scudding clouds, the cold, earthy tang of the muddy pitch filling the air.

'Not half,' said someone else.

There was nothing Arnie enjoyed more than the camaraderie of a drink with his pals in the pub after the game. But he'd be well and truly in the dog-house with his mother-in-law if he arrived home late for Sunday dinner with the smell of beer on his breath. He'd discovered that to his peril on a previous occasion.

'You *are* coming for a drink,' said one of the chaps when Arnie didn't reply.

'No, I don't think so – not today,' he said regretfully.

'Under the wife's thumb, eh?' joshed another of the men.

'Do leave off, mate – this is Arnie Briscoe you're talking to,' he objected with typical laddish bravado.

'Why can't you come for a quick one, then?' challenged his pal.

'It isn't my wife who's the problem,' he explained. 'Gill's as sweet as a nut.'

'Who, then?'

'Her mother. She sets dinner for one o'clock sharp on a Sunday and she likes us all to be there. It's half past twelve now; by the time I get changed and cleaned up—'

'Dear oh dear, I wouldn't stand for that,' interrupted one of the married men with feeling. 'It's bad enough having the wife giving you earache if you're late home, let alone the mother-in-law an' all.'

'When you live with your in-laws you have to abide by their rules,' said Arnie.

'You wanna put your foot down, mate,' suggested the man.

'I can't do that,' said Arnie, standing his ground bravely.

'Why not?'

'It's their house, innit?' he pointed out. 'It's only right that I should fit in with their way of doing things.'

'Well, I wouldn't let a mother-in-law of mine dictate to me,' said the other man.

'She isn't so bad,' defended Arnie.

'Sounds like a right old dragon to me.'

'She's a good sort in her own way,' said Arnie, 'even though she can frighten the balls off you if you get the wrong side of her.'

'She needs putting in her place though,' said his mate.

'Not really,' said Arnie. 'She's been good to me and the wife. No point in upsetting her if it can be avoided.'

'Well, I wouldn't put up with it . . .'

As they approached the changing hut, the conversation was interrupted by the appearance of a stranger who drew Arnie to one side as the others walked on.

'Can I have a word?' asked the man, who was fortyish and wearing a light tan suede coat with a fur collar over a black polo-necked sweater.

'Sure,' replied Arnie, eyeing him with curiosity.

'Frank Fisher of Thames United Football Club,' said the man, extending his hand.

'Oh really?' Arnie shook his hand, both excited and intrigued. Thames United was a professional club – only in the third division, but it was in the FA league. 'So, what can I do for you, mate?'

Frank shivered against the wind. 'It's colder watching the game than playing, and my toes are nearly dropping off,' he said. 'It'll be a lot more comfortable to talk in the pub.'

'I was going straight home as a matter of fact,' said Arnie, Winnie still in mind.

'I think you'll find it worth your while to take time to listen to what I have to say,' said Frank with a half smile. 'And I'd rather say it somewhere warm. I don't have such resilience as you players and I'm freezin' to death out here.'

'Hang on while I get changed then,' said Arnie, and he hurried towards the wooden hut.

'I'm sure Arnie will be home in a minute, Mum,' said Gill, looking at the clock anxiously. It was nearly half past one and her mother was getting more upset by the second. 'He must have got held up somewhere.'

'No prizes for guessing where,' snorted Winnie. 'Sunday morning football is just an excuse to go to the pub, if you ask me.'

'That isn't fair,' denied Gill, instinctively defensive of her husband even though she was livid with him. She had no objection to his going for a pint with the lads after the game, as long as he didn't upset her mother by being late home. He knew how strict she was about lunch on Sundays and he'd promised Gill he would be back on time today. Admittedly her mother was irritatingly inflexible on this issue, but as she did the cooking she was entitled to make the rules. 'You know how important the game is to Arnie.'

'Gill's right, Mum,' put in Carol, who wouldn't hear a word against her hero. 'He'll only be talking to his mates and there's no harm in that.'

'The food'll be burned to a cinder,' said the perplexed Winnie, whose Sunday roast really was worth hurrying home for.

The three women were in the kitchen, a long narrow room painted blue and white with a grey mottled gas cooker and a walk-in larder. In a sunny spot by the window, Craig was sitting in his high-chair banging about with a spoon.

'Why don't we make a start without Arnie?' suggested Gill, who felt guilty on her husband's behalf. 'I'll serve his on to a plate and put it in the oven for him.'

'You know I like us all to sit down together on a Sunday,' said Winnie, who genuinely believed that Sunday lunch eaten together helped to keep the family spirit alive. She also disliked the muddle caused by people eating at different times.

The baby squirmed in his chair and began to sound fretful.

'I'll have to feed Craig anyway,' said Gill, lifting him out and holding him in her arms. 'I'll move his high-chair into the other room.'

Hal appeared from the living room, where he'd been

reading the Sunday paper and where the table was already laid for lunch.

'Shall we start our dinner?' he said. 'Arnie will be home in a minute.'

'I suppose we'd better,' said Winnie, going over to the oven. 'He'll probably not appear until the pubs close.'

They adjourned to the living room, a multi-purpose chamber which was surprisingly cosy considering the amount of furniture that was packed into it – a dining table and chairs and a sideboard at one end, with easy chairs and a sofa placed around the television set at the other.

Hal had just finished carving the meat and they were helping themselves to vegetables when Arnie breezed in exuding good humour and smelling of best bitter. Gill was spooning mashed roast lamb with veg and gravy into Craig's mouth.

'Well, well, so you've decided to come home at last then, have you?' said Winnie acidly. 'I'm surprised you didn't wait until they chucked you out, having stayed this long.'

'And have your delicious Sunday roast get dried up, Ma-in-law?' he said with one of his most winning smiles. 'I'm not that daft.'

'You know we eat sharp at one o'clock on a Sunday,' she said.

'Yeah, I do, and I'm really sorry,' he said, but he didn't look particularly contrite on account of his luminous smile. He moved around the table to Gill, who was determinedly ignoring her errant husband and concentrating on the baby, who was dribbling the food out of his mouth as fast as she was putting it in and finding the whole exercise a huge joke.

'Don't I get a kiss, then, babe?' said Arnie, bending over his wife and putting his face close to her head from behind.

'You're joking,' she said without even turning to look at him. 'I'm strictly off limits to people who break promises.'

'Ooh, dear. I'm well and truly in the bad books then,' he said.

'You certainly are, mate,' said Hal.

'So don't make things worse by messing about,' reproached Winnie, who couldn't help warming to his comical exuberance, despite herself. 'Sit down and help yourself before everything gets cold.'

'Craig isn't cross with me. Are you, son?' he said, making a funny face at the baby who chuckled loudly.

'Don't distract him when I'm trying to get him to eat his dinner,' admonished Gill, adding to her sister who had erupted into giggles, 'And don't you make things worse by encouraging my thoughtless husband.'

Carol was shaking with silent laughter. Arnie winked at his kid sister-in-law and turned his attention back to his wife.

'I'll feed Craig if you like.'

Gill turned to him, sighing eloquently. 'No, Arnie,' she said in a firm tone. 'You just sit down and have your dinner and stop upsetting everybody.'

'Leave the lad alone,' said Hal. 'He'll sit down when he's ready.'

'Typical male mateyness,' observed Winnie, pouring mint sauce over her meat. 'They stick together like glue.'

'It's just plain childish,' pronounced Gill in a worldly-wise manner that belied her youth.

'You're learning fast,' said Winnie.

'If I can get a word in,' said Arnie with a twinkle in his eye as he took his place at the table next to Gill with Craig between them in the high-chair, 'I've got something to tell you . . . and I think I'll be forgiven for being late when you know what it is.'

'I doubt it,' sniffed his mother-in-law.

'You scored the winning goal,' guessed Hal, slicing some more meat off the joint and putting it on a plate for Arnie.

'I did as it happens . . . but that isn't it.'

'It'll take more than a goal to get you out of trouble anyway,' said Winnie.

Gill shot Arnie a look. 'Let's hear it then,' she said. 'And it had better be good.'

Arnie treated his wife to one of his most melting smiles. 'Well, after the match I was approached by a bloke and taken to the pub—'

'Taken by force,' Gill interrupted with playful sarcasm. She had already forgiven him. She could never stay angry with him for long. 'You were completely overpowered.'

'When I realised it could be in my interest – and yours – to go with him, yes, I was overpowered, by curiosity.'

'So, who was he?' asked Gill.

'Frank•Fisher, a talent scout for Thames United Football Club.'

They all stopped eating and stared at him, waiting.

'He's seen me play on several occasions, apparently, and he wants me to go for a trial at the club,' he said excitedly.

'A *trial*.' Gill was impressed.

'Yep. And if his bosses like what they see, I'll be offered a contract with the club.'

'You mean you'll play football professionally,' gasped Gill.

'Well, I don't think they're gonna employ me to answer the telephone,' he grinned.

There was a hushed silence as the family digested this amazing news.

'Oh, Arnie, that's wonderful,' said Gill, leaning over and kissing him. 'I'm so proud of you.'

'Hey, steady on, I haven't even been for the trial yet,' he said, but his confidence was high and he couldn't hide it.

'You'll pass with flying colours, no doubt about it.'

'It's tremendous news,' said Hal with a broad smile. 'Well done.'

The excitable Carol leapt up and danced around the room.

'Wow! I'm gonna have a professional footballer for a brother-in-law.' She hugged Arnie from behind. 'Cor, wait till I tell my friends. They'll be green with envy.'

Arnie looked at Winnie. 'Well? Am I forgiven for being late?'

'Trust you to come up with something unbelievable to get

yourself off the hook,' she said, but she was smiling and her eyes were warm. 'But – yes, okay, I'll let you off this time.' She cleared her throat because it was difficult for her to show her feelings. 'And well done, son.'

'Thanks.'

'But don't build your hopes up too high before the trial,' she added, running true to form.

'Don't worry,' he assured her, 'I've got my feet planted firmly on the ground.'

'Good. Now . . . do you think we can get on with our dinner before it gets stone cold?'

Immediately after lunch Arnie went across to the flats on the corner to pass on the good news to his mother and brother. Later that afternoon, when Winnie and Hal were snoozing in their armchairs and Carol had gone to the pictures with her girlfriends, Gill and Arnie wrapped up in warm clothes and set off for a walk to Bishop's Park with Craig in the pram.

It was still cold and breezy as they passed Fulham Football Club and entered the park, occasional bursts of sunshine glinting on the blue-painted paddling pool, dry and deserted at this time of year. The trees were swaying in the wind, which was blowing so fiercely through the shrubs and flowerbeds that some early daffodils had been flattened to the ground.

'You must be thrilled to bits to get this chance of a lifetime,' Gill said as they walked through the riverside park, which was actually the outer gardens of Fulham Palace and had been opened to the public as a park at the end of the last century.

'It's a dream come true,' he said excitedly.

'I can imagine.'

'I always hoped to get spotted as a schoolboy 'cause I played in so many matches, but when it never happened I thought I'd missed the boat,' he said. 'But I'm still only twenty; I've a good few playing years ahead of me.'

'It's wonderful for you.'

He halted in his step and turned to her with a serious expression on his face. 'Not just wonderful for me, babe,' he corrected, looking into her eyes. 'If I get that contract things will be a whole lot different for both of us.' He looked at the baby who was sitting up dressed in a bright blue siren suit with white fur trimming on the hood. 'And you, little fella.'

Craig was more interested in some young boys kicking a ball about nearby. Arnie tickled his chin and was rewarded with a fat chuckle. They continued on to the riverside path, the Thames dark and choppy in the wind.

'They're only a third division club, but the money they'll pay me is three times what I can earn in the factory,' he continued as they walked on.

'Is it really?' she said.

'Yeah. Frank Fisher was quite definite about that,' he confirmed. 'I won't get the sort of dough that first division players earn, but it'll do us nicely. The council can stuff their waiting list if I get this job, 'cause we'll be able to get a mortgage on a place of our own.'

'Oh, Arnie, how thrilling.'

'And the best part will be not having to go into that ruddy factory any more.'

'It'll be brilliant,' she enthused.

'It isn't the money as such that's important to me,' he said.

'No?'

'No,' he said thoughtfully. 'It's being able to earn my living doing something I love to do and know I'm good at.'

'I can understand that.'

'And I'll be able to give you and Craig a nice life.'

'We have that already.'

'A more comfortable one, then.' He slipped his arm around her. 'You and Craig are everything to me, you know?'

'I know.'

'A beautiful wife, a fine son, and a dream job in the offing,' he said, tightening his arm around her. 'I must be the luckiest bloke alive.'

'I hope you always feel that way.'

'I will . . . don't you worry about that.' He moved away from her slightly, raised his fists in triumph and danced a jig that made Gill laugh and produced one of Craig's throaty giggles.

'You're crazy,' she laughed.

'Yeah, crazy with new hope, because we're on the up, Gill – you, me and Craig,' he said.

'You really think so?'

'Yeah. I can feel it in my bones,' he said, his eyes shining. 'The future is gonna be brilliant for all of us.'

Gill's happiness was piercingly sweet at that moment. But she must have inherited a little of her mother's realism, because a warning voice nagged at the back of her mind, telling her it was too good to last.

Chapter Three

It was a warm summer's evening – Gill's twenty-first birthday – and Gill and Arnie were having a family dinner to celebrate the occasion. Gifts had been graciously received, the wine was flowing, the main course was over and the host and hostess were in their kitchen preparing to serve dessert. Arnie, however, was distracted from the task in hand.

'You look lovely,' he said, running an admiring eye over his wife, who was wearing a close-fitting black dress which was perfect on her slim figure, the effect enhanced by her luxuriant dark hair, which was longer now and backcombed over the crown to give it fullness and height. Her wrist was expensively adorned with the gold watch Arnie had given her as a birthday present.

'Flatterer,' she said, grinning at him.

'I'm only saying what's true.'

'Thank you, darling.' She lifted her arm to have another look at her watch. 'It's beautiful. I shall treasure it.'

'Glad you're pleased, babe. I enjoyed getting it for you,' Arnie said, slipping his arms around her from the back as she turned to get the cream from the fridge. 'Ooh, I could eat you.'

'You'll just have to make do with food as we have company,' she said in frivolous mood.

'They won't miss us for ten minutes if we nip upstairs,' he said jokingly.

'That's an antisocial suggestion,' she said, turning towards him and pushing him away in a firm but playful manner.

'Quite the opposite, I thought,' he said with a wicked grin.

'You're insatiable!' It was a light-hearted admonishment.

'If I am it's your fault,' he replied, stroking her bottom. 'You shouldn't be so gorgeous.'

'Behave yourself when we've got guests.'

'It isn't easy with you looking like that.'

'Glad you like the dress.'

'I like what's underneath more,' he said, wrapping her in his warm, strong arms.

'Later,' she said, drawing back, feeling weak and heady. 'And in the meantime you can make yourself useful and take the trifle into the other room.'

'You're cruel.'

'Our guests are waiting, Arnie . . .'

'Spoil-sport.'

'Shut up and take the pudding in.'

As he walked towards the door carrying an enormous glass bowl containing the product of Gill's labours, she had a sudden thought.

'Oh, by the way, this seems like a good time to tell them the news.'

'No, not tonight.'

'But it's the perfect opportunity, while we are all together.'

'This is your night, Gill,' he told her solemnly. 'You're the birthday girl and I want you to have all the attention.'

'Don't be so silly,' she said, but she was touched by his thoughtfulness. 'I'm as thrilled about your news as you are and I'm absolutely dying for them all to know about it.'

'They'll be told in due course,' he said, and headed for the dining room where their guests were seated around a large table near the French doors opening on to a lawned garden bordered with summer flowers in full bloom.

When Gill appeared behind him, Phoebe said waggishly, 'We thought you'd gone out somewhere to buy the pudding.'

'Sorry we were so long,' Gill said, her flushed cheeks and ruffled hair leaving no one in any doubt as to the reason for the delay. 'We were just adding a few finishing touches.'

'And I was a guest at Princess Margaret's wedding,' laughed Phoebe, who was looking brashly glamorous in a low-cut crimson dress in crêpe-de-chine with satin edging.

'I bet they've been snogging,' said Carol, now an attractive eighteen-year-old with long hair, a shapely figure and heavily made-up eyes.

'Ugh,' expressed fourteen-year-old John Briscoe with boyish disgust. 'Not again. They're always kissing and cuddling.'

'What's wrong with a man showing his feelings for his wife?' asked Arnie.

'It's soppy,' said John.

'It's nice,' said Carol.

'The trifle looks delicious, Gill,' said Winnie, swiftly changing the subject for fear that this sort of talk might lead to smut. 'The meal must have taken you hours to prepare.'

'Not really – and I enjoyed doing it,' said Gill warmly.

'I intended to take you all out to a restaurant to save Gill the trouble,' said Arnie, 'but she wouldn't hear of it.'

'I wanted to have you all here on the actual day of my birthday,' she told them. 'There'll be quite a crowd at the birthday party Arnie's organised for me at the community hall on Saturday. This is a more personal way of celebrating. I'm sorry Craig couldn't stay awake long enough to join us, though.'

'Never mind, dear,' said Phoebe. 'It was thoughtful of you to invite us, and you've really done us proud.' She looked round the table. 'Isn't that right, everyone?'

During the enthusiastic roar of agreement, Gill's thoughts drifted back over the last two years or so since Arnie had become a professional footballer. It had been a very happy time for them both and they were more in love than ever. His dramatic increase in salary had enabled them to get a mortgage on this house in Danny Gardens, which was about fifteen minutes' walk from Maisie Road in a neighbourhood which, while essentially working class, was slightly more refined.

The property itself was unexceptional, an old style semi-detached with high ceilings and sash windows. What made it so special was the sense of homeliness Gill and Arnie had created, renovating it together with loving care. She had known it was the right house for them the minute she'd set eyes on it, despite the fact that it had needed a lot of work.

It comprised three bedrooms, a living and dining room downstairs, with a pleasant sunny room off the hall which they used as a playroom for Craig. Gill's parents had insisted that she have the old family piano, since she was the only one of them who ever used it, and it now stood in their living room where she played as often as she could find the time.

Because the house had been a creaking shell of a place, without a trace of Formica or fitted units, they had picked it up dirt cheap and subsequently invested time, money and effort into modernising it to their own taste. The result was light and airy walls in pretty pastel shades, abundant mirrors, deep pile carpets and sleek, contemporary furnishings and fittings.

Their standard of living was by no means excessive, but it had improved considerably since Arnie had worked at the factory. They could afford to run a car now and have decent clothes and outings.

Recalled to the present by the fact that all eyes were upon her, Gill said, 'Thanks, folks. I'm glad you're enjoying yourselves.'

The conversation became general. They touched on the recent death of the controversial Labour politician Aneurin Bevan, who was best known for inaugurating Britain's National Health Service. Carol, to whom politicians collectively were an unknown species, was more interested in talking about a horror film called *Psycho* that was currently causing a sensation in cinemas across the country.

'Talk about scary,' she said dramatically. 'There was this

scene in a motel shower. God, I was nearly wetting myself!'

'We'll have to go and see that, Arnie,' suggested Gill lightly. 'You can hold me tight so that I won't be scared.'

'It's the sort of film you need to see with a strong man to hold your hand,' said Carol. 'I went with a girlfriend, worse luck.'

'I wouldn't mind going to see that,' said John. 'I've heard a lot about it.'

'It'll give you nightmares, by the sound of it,' said his mother.

'Leave off, Mum,' he said with youthful affront. 'I'm not a kid.'

'You're not an adult either.'

'Almost.'

'You're not quite there yet, son.'

'I wanna see the film, though.'

'You won't be able to get in unless you're with an adult, and these days you wouldn't be seen dead at the pictures with your mother.'

'And have my mates think I'm a mummy's boy?' he protested. 'Not likely!'

'The film isn't suitable for you anyway, so you can forget about it,' said Phoebe, who could be stern and authoritative when necessary, despite her easygoing nature.

'But M-u-um,' he protested with a pained expression.

For some inexplicable reason, Phoebe found herself awash with loneliness at that moment. She'd never really adjusted to being on her own after Bill died. Oh, she'd coped well enough over the years; she'd learned to be practical and independent, and most of the time she was happy with her lot. She wasn't short of company – she still had John living at home, and not many days passed when Arnie didn't call round to see her. He often slipped her a few quid too, now that he wasn't pushed for cash. It wasn't loneliness for people, as such, that she was struggling with now. It was more a longing for someone of her own – a soulmate with whom she could share her life.

45

There had been occasional boyfriends over the years – which wasn't surprising since she was widowed at only twenty-eight. She enjoyed male company, liked the special chemistry which reminded her that she was an individual as well as a working mother of two. But none of the relationships had ever got past the starting post – firstly because her sons had always come first with her, and secondly because she never seemed to meet the kind of man who had permanence in mind.

It wasn't easy for women of a certain age to meet men of any sort, let alone the type who wanted to settle down. A man could go out to a pub or a club without raising an eyebrow, but if a woman did the same thing she was branded as 'easy'. Phoebe knew that this was how she was thought of by some people anyway, but she didn't really mind. Better to be talked about than ignored, in her opinion. She was forty-one now – a bit late in the day to meet anyone. But she'd get by on her own; she'd managed this far.

She was jolted back to the present by Winnie, who was saying, 'I can't say that *Psycho* is a film I fancy going to see.'

'We've not been to the pictures for years anyway,' said Hal, pouring cream over his portion of trifle. 'People don't go so often now that they have the telly to watch at home.'

'That's why so many cinemas are closing down or becoming bingo halls,' said Winnie.

'I hope they don't all disappear,' said Phoebe. 'I'm rather partial to a night out at the flicks.'

They drifted on to other things, everyone talking at once, the conversation interspersed with gales of laughter. Mentally standing back from the company for a moment, listening to the friendly chatter, enjoying the scent of roses drifting in from the garden, Gill felt an inner glow. She loved having the people she cared about gathered together in her home, even though her mother and Phoebe only just managed to tolerate each other. The fact that it was her birthday added lustre to the occasion and she felt quite sentimental.

46

Over coffee, she decided it was time to make the announcement. 'Listen, everyone,' she said, standing up purposefully, 'Arnie and I have something important to tell you. And, no, I'm not having another baby – not at the moment, anyway.'

'Gill,' admonished Arnie, 'I thought we agreed not to say anything tonight.'

'You said we weren't going to,' she reminded him, 'I didn't agree.'

'Don't keep us in suspense then,' said Phoebe. 'If you're not pregnant, what is the big news?'

Gill looked at Arnie, who nodded for her to continue. 'Arnie's been offered a contract with Borough Football Club for next season,' she said, swelling with pride.

There was a brief hiatus while everyone digested this news. Borough FC was a first division London club.

'Wow!' said John.

'Oh, Arnie, well done, son,' said his mother, getting up and going over to him to smack a kiss on his cheek, her eyes glistening with tears. 'You really are going up in the world.'

When the effusive congratulations had died down, Hal said, 'So it'll be tuppence to talk to you from now on, then?'

'Do me a favour,' was Arnie's swift response. 'You know I'm not like that.'

'You're really doing well, though, son,' said Phoebe.

'I'm not complainin'.'

'Are you gonna be famous from now on?' Carol wanted to know.

'Don't be daft.'

'He's already been on the telly,' Gill proudly reminded her sister. Clips of the matches Arnie played in were occasionally shown on sports programmes. 'What more do you want?'

'But if you blink you miss him,' said Carol. 'I wanna see him on there properly, being interviewed or something.'

'You'll wait for ever if you wait for that,' said Arnie.

'Not necessarily,' said Phoebe.

'You're all making far too much of it,' declared Arnie,

making a face. 'All I'm doing is changing clubs. It's no big deal.'

'I'd say that being offered the chance to play for Borough Football Club is a very big deal indeed,' said Hal.

'Yeah, don't be so modest, Arnie,' rebuked his mother laughingly.

'Will you be getting a big flash car?' asked John excitedly. 'I hope you get something that goes like a rocket.'

'You'll be moving to a posh house, I suppose,' said Winnie.

Arnie stood up suddenly and raised his hands for silence. 'Right! Let's get this thing into proportion once and for all,' he said in a firm tone. 'I'm joining Borough Football Club, which is an upward career move for me, and I'm well chuffed about it. And, yes, I will be earning quite a lot more money, which means we'll be able to manage a few more luxuries. But we won't be changing the way we live. We're not planning on moving house or anything dramatic like that. I'll still be the same old Arnie. So, let's have no more daft talk of posh houses and flash cars.'

'All right, keep your hair on, son,' said his mother.

'Yeah, stop spoiling it,' said Gill, smiling at her husband. 'This is the most exciting thing that's ever happened to this family.'

'Carol won't be long, Dougie,' said Winnie one day, about a year later, to the young man who had come to call for her daughter and was perched nervously on the edge of the sofa in the living room. Hal was reading the paper and Winnie was knitting a sweater for Craig for the winter even though it was still only midsummer. 'She's probably just putting the finishing touches to her make-up.'

'Yeah, I expect that's what's keeping her, Mrs Miller,' said Dougie Rivers politely. A regular caller at the Millers' house lately, he was an inoffensive twenty-one-year-old with a shock of fair hair and blue eyes, which currently had a worried look about them because he felt uncomfortable when he was on his own with his girlfriend's parents.

'Where are you thinking of going this evening?' enquired Winnie, who didn't think it could be anywhere special judging by the casual way he was dressed in tight jeans and a leather jacket. But there was no telling with young people these days because they were so much less conventional in their dress than they used to be.

'We might go ten pin bowling if Carol fancies it,' he said, 'or the pictures. Depends what Carol wants to do.'

'That'll be nice.'

Winnie was knitting furiously, which usually helped when she was finding a conversation difficult – and this one was impossible. She cleared her throat loudly to get her husband's attention, then appealed to him with her eyes.

'Oh . . . er, I understand from Carol that your father is a sales representative, Dougie,' Hal said, taking the hint at last.

'That's right,' the lad said. 'He works for a firm of printers.'

'That must be interestin' for him, being out and about all the time,' Hal prompted, desperate to fill the awkward silence.

'I suppose it must be, Mr Miller,' said Dougie, glancing desperately towards the door in the hope that Carol would appear and rescue him from this agonising situation.

'You didn't fancy following in his footsteps then?' asked Hal.

'No.'

'You're in menswear, aren't you?'

'Yeah. I work in a gents outfitters in Hammersmith.'

'Oh.'

'I went back to my old job when I came out of the army.'

'Does it have decent prospects?' asked Winnie.

'Yeah. I'm hoping to be a manager of one of the branches eventually.'

'As long as you're happy in the job, that's the main thing,' said Hal, trying to put the poor lad at his ease because he'd noticed a strawberry flush suffusing his face and neck.

'You're right, Mr Miller,' said Dougie, wondering just

how much longer Carol was going to be.

'If you like the job and there's a future in it, you can't go wrong, can you?' said Winnie, who couldn't help viewing every boyfriend of Carol's as a prospective husband.

'No, Mrs Miller, you can't,' was Dougie's dutiful reply.

Winnie was thinking that her daughter would be wise to hang on to this one. He seemed like a steady, decent type and he had a job with prospects. Carol's boyfriends never seemed to stay around for long, though. Winnie wasn't sure why, but she thought the girl's demanding nature might have something to do with it. Still, there was plenty of time – she was only nineteen.

Thinking in terms of the present, Winnie hoped Carol wasn't going to keep him waiting much longer because *Emergency Ward Ten* would be on the television in a minute and she didn't want to miss it.

As luck would have it, at that very moment the living room door opened and Carol swept in, wearing a skinny rib top with a short skirt.

'Sorry to have been so long, Dougie,' she said smiling sweetly at him.

' 'Sall right,' he said, standing up and looking relieved.

'Let's go then, shall we?'

'Sure.' He almost bounded to the door in his eagerness to get away.

'Enjoy yourselves,' said Hal.

'Don't be too late now,' said Winnie.

'No, Mum,' sighed Carol with more than a hint of irritation.

As the front door closed behind them, Winnie said to Hal, 'He seems a nice enough boy.'

'Yeah, not bad at all.'

'Seems very keen on Carol,' she added.

Hal nodded and turned his attention back to the newspaper.

Winnie got up to turn on the television set and glanced out of the window to see the couple walking down the street. Carol was hanging on to Dougie's arm and smiling up at him adoringly. Winnie hoped she wasn't being too eager. She did tend to get a bit clingy with boyfriends.

It would be quite a relief to see Carol settled with a nice fellow. Being so sensitive, she had had her heart broken several times already. But Dougie seemed genuinely fond of her and, if Winnie was any judge, he was going to be around for some time – permanently, she hoped – giving Carol all the things her sister had missed: the engagement ring, the church wedding . . .

With her elder daughter in mind, Winnie reflected pleasurably on the fact that her doubts about Gill's marriage to Arnie had proved to be groundless. Gill was happy and settled with a good life, free from financial worries.

Arnie had gone from strength to strength since he'd got into that first division team a year ago. In fact he was quite a celebrity these days. His name regularly cropped up on the sports pages of the newspapers and he was often mentioned by sports commentators on TV. A regular stream of fan letters was sent to him at the club, too, by all accounts.

He provided well for his wife and child. They had been abroad on holiday recently, the first members of the Miller or Briscoe families ever to do so. He'd even bought Gill her own little car. For all that Winnie was a no-nonsense sort of person, she had to admit to enjoying being related to someone with a touch of fame about them.

Nowadays people wanted to talk to her in the street because of her famous son-in-law. He was a hero in Fulham and his name meant something to football fans all over the country. After her earlier fears, Winnie now had no worries at all about Gill . . .

'I'm not going to bed till Daddy gets home,' pronounced four-year-old Craig in stubborn mood one Monday evening in the autumn, pressing into the back of the sofa as though to make himself invisible.

'Come on, love, don't give me a hard time,' said Gill patiently.

'Not going to bed.'

'You are, young man.'

His cheeks were flushed from the warmth of the room, his huge brown eyes heavy with tiredness and puffy from crying with disappointment because his father hadn't arrived home yet.

'Now do as you're told . . . please.'

'You said I could stay up till Daddy gets home,' said the boy, who was freshly bathed and wearing a bright blue dressing gown over his striped pyjamas, his brown curly hair shining in the subtle glow from the wall lights. 'Daddy said I could too.'

'I know we did, darling, but Daddy is much later than I expected and it's way past your bedtime,' Gill said.

'Why can't I stay up?' he whined.

'Because you have to be up early in the morning to go to nursery school.'

'Not going to bed,' he said again with petulance, desperately tired but fighting sleep to the bitter end because he so much wanted to see his adored father.

'Be a good boy and come upstairs,' she persisted, clinging to her much-tried patience. 'I'll read you a story.'

'Want Daddy to read me a story.'

Gill looked at her watch and her heart felt like lead. Arnie had said he'd be home at about five o'clock at the latest. It was now seven-thirty. Money and success of the kind he'd enjoyed since he'd been playing in the first division had changed him. Although Gill had kept it from the rest of the family, he was no longer the devoted, home-loving husband he used to be. These days he preferred London's night-spots to his own home.

But it wasn't like him to be this late without letting her know, especially as he knew Craig would be waiting up for him. How long could a charity lunch go on for, for heaven's sake?

Realising that Craig was about to doze off, she sat down

and lifted him on to her lap where he fell asleep almost immediately. After she'd carried him upstairs to bed and settled him for the night, she came back downstairs and tried to watch some television but was too tense to concentrate, fearing Arnie had had an accident. Her heart was beating in tune with her riotous imagination as she pictured him in a hospital bed or the mortuary.

At ten o'clock he arrived home in a taxi and swaggered into the house without a care.

'I've been worried to death,' she said.

'Why?'

'Because you're five hours late.'

'I wasn't aware that I had to clock in in my own home.'

'I thought something had happened to you.'

'Cor blimey, woman, I can't tell you to the exact minute when I'll be home,' he said condescendingly. 'You know what these things are like.'

'But where have you been all this time?' she asked, hurt by his off-hand manner.

'You know where I've been,' he snapped, frowning darkly at her. 'At the Hyde Park Hotel for a charity lunch.'

'That started just after midday,' she said spiritedly. 'It's gone ten o'clock now.'

He flopped down into an armchair and loosened his tie. He wasn't drunk, but he'd obviously had plenty to drink. His colour was high and his skin gleaming with a fine layer of perspiration.

'So, I got held up.'

'For all those hours?'

'Oh, leave it out, will you, Gill?' he said irritably. 'The last thing I want is an inquisition. I'm shattered.'

'You're shattered!' she said, her dark eyes flashing. 'You've been out enjoying yourself—'

'The lunch was work,' he corrected.

'Oh, yeah, wading through a six-course meal at a posh West End hotel with the wine and champagne flowing must be real hard graft,' she said, driven to sacrasm by the fear of losing him.

He was becoming ever more deeply immersed in his own glamorous world and increasingly distant from her. As much as she hated to think ill of him, there was no denying the fact that he had become extremely arrogant lately.

'You know damned well what I mean,' he said aggressively.

'Do I?' she said, smarting inside from his coldness.

'It was a professional engagement,' he said with seething impatience. 'I didn't particularly want to go. But I went because my being there helps to sell tickets, which helps the charity and is good PR for me. You know I have to do a certain amount of that sort of thing now that I'm a name, because it puts me in a position to help raise funds. As well as doing my bit for charity, it's good for the club. Anyway, it's expected of me.'

'I understand all that, Arnie,' she said in a softer tone, because she loved him desperately, 'but I was worried about you . . . and Craig was disappointed. I had a job getting him to bed because you promised him he could wait up to see you.'

He slapped his brow with his hand, showing the first signs of remorse. 'Craig, o' course,' he said, his manner becoming immediately conciliatory. 'I forgot I'd told him he could wait up to see me. God, I'm really sorry about that, babe.'

'I should damned well hope you are,' she said. 'Let me down if you must, but not a four-year-old child. You could have phoned to let me know you were going to be late.'

'I could have, but I didn't,' he said, irascible again. 'I've said I'm sorry, so will you please shut up about it?'

'Don't try to make me feel as though I'm in the wrong,' she said evenly, standing her ground despite the fact that she was aching inside and on the verge of tears. 'We all know you're a big man now, the famous soccer star who gets his picture in the paper and fan letters in the mail. But that doesn't give you the right to disregard other people's feelings, especially your son's.'

'Oh, I've had just about enough of this! I'm going to bed,' he said furiously, and got up and marched to the door.

She ran after him and pulled at his arm. 'Oh, no, you're not gonna just walk away from this one,' she said, her temper rising. 'I'm entitled to an explanation.'

'For God's sake,' he said, swinging round and glaring at her. 'All I've done is come home a bit late. It isn't a criminal offence.'

He was even more attractive in this slightly dishevelled state. His tie was loose, suit jacket undone, white shirt emphasising his light tan, the combined result of their summer holiday in Spain and his being out in the fresh air so much in the course of his work.

With his close proximity came a strong whiff of something that turned her heart to stone. She put her face close to the lapel of his suit and sniffed.

'You've been with a woman,' she said, buffeted by the shock. 'I can smell her perfume.'

'Don't be ridiculous,' he snapped. 'It's my aftershave.'

'Please don't take me for a fool, Arnie.' The thought of him being with another woman was physically painful to her. 'I think I know the difference between Chanel and Old Spice.' She moved away, looking into his face. 'How could you, Arnie? How could you?'

'I haven't been with a woman,' he denied hotly.

'Don't make things worse by lying to me,' she said, her voice shaking, tears welling up. 'I can smell her on you.'

Worried now, he moved towards her but she shrank back.

'Don't touch me,' she said, her voice dull with pain. 'I don't want you anywhere near me.'

'Oh, for goodness' sake,' he said, grabbing hold of her and looking into her face, eager to pacify her now that he knew he was in deep trouble. 'It isn't what you think.'

'Isn't that what all adulterers say when they get found out?'

'I'm not an adulterer.'

She struggled to pull away but he held her firmly by the

arms. 'Just calm down and let me tell you what happened.'

'I'm not sure I want to hear it,' she said, her voice breaking.

'Please don't cry,' he begged, letting her go, full of regret now. 'Just give me a chance to tell you what happened, why I was late home and why I smell of perfume.'

'Go on then,' she said wearily, sitting down in an armchair, looking at him.

'I've been to a nightclub in the West End,' he explained.

'And . . . ?'

'I danced with a woman there,' he explained. 'And I mean *just* danced . . . The perfume you can smell must be hers.'

'You must have been dancing pretty damned close,' said Gill, a feeling of hysteria welling up inside her. She had known her marriage was in trouble for some time, and this seemed to confirm it. Arnie had always been an attractive man, but success and fame were an aphrodisiac to some women. She'd seen the way they looked at him at the glamorous social functions they attended nowadays. He could have anyone. Beautiful, classy women – models and showbiz lovelies. There was no shortage of temptation.

'Maybe we were, I can't remember,' he said. 'I'd had a good few drinks. It was all just a bit of a laugh. But nothing else happened, I swear to you. All we did was dance.'

'Who was she?'

'Dunno, just somebody on a night out with some friends,' he told her. 'The blokes dared me to ask her to dance.'

'God, it's pathetic,' she said, but she believed him, and it was a relief.

'It was just a bit o' fun.'

'You were in some sleazy nightclub,' she said, shaking her head and leaning forward, 'when you were supposed to be at home with me and Craig. No wonder you didn't want to tell me where you'd been.'

'It wasn't sleazy. It was quite classy as a matter of fact.'

'But you shouldn't have been there, should you? Not when

you'd promised to be home,' she said. 'God knows, you have enough leeway. I'm not the sort of wife to keep you in chains. I don't stop you doing what you want to do, especially now that you're getting invitations to social functions which don't include me. But when you promise your son that you'll be here for him, then that's where you should be.'

Sighing deeply, Arnie sat down opposite her, leaning forward slightly. 'Look, I had every intention of coming home after the lunch—'

'So why are we having this conversation?' Gill interrupted, her voice thick with emotion. 'While I was trying to pacify our son because you weren't here, and imagining you'd been taken ill or had an accident or something, you were smooching around the dancefloor with some dolly bird.'

'Look, the lunch went on until well into the afternoon,' he said. 'There was this chap sitting next to me, a businessman called George Flowers who owns Flowers nightclub . . . absolutely rolling in money. He's a bit of a comedian, actually, had me in fits. I was glad of his company, because some of the others were a bit dry. Anyway, he suggested a few of us go on to his club afterwards, just to wind down.'

'And you had to go because he suggested it, of course . . .'

'I wanted to go,' he told her straight. 'The lunch had put me in a sociable mood and it seemed like a good idea at the time.'

'All you had to do was pick up the telephone, Arnie . . .'

'I honestly didn't intend to stay long,' he told her. 'I don't know what happened to the time. The club wasn't open when we got there so we had the place to ourselves. Then suddenly it was evening and the place was full of punters.'

'And there was dancing and you entered into the spirit of the thing?'

'Exactly.'

'Apart from anything else, you're not supposed to be overdoing the booze,' she reminded him. 'You agreed to that when you signed the contract.'

'It'll take more than a few drinks to upset my game,' he blustered.

'I shouldn't be too sure of that,' she said. 'It'll take its toll if you do it too often.'

'That's my business,' he roared, his temper flaring again. 'I don't need my wife to tell me how to conduct myself.'

'You're getting too big for your boots, that's your trouble,' she said, rising.

'Rubbish!'

'Being a football star doesn't make you God almighty.'

'All of this because I danced with some woman,' he said scornfully.

'That isn't how it is and don't be so damned patronising,' she said. 'All of this is because you broke a promise to your son . . . and to me.'

'All right, so I let my hair down and forgot to ring you.' He lowered his eyes. 'I'm sorry.'

Suddenly Gill was very tired. 'Okay, Arnie,' she said, deciding that enough had been said on the subject. She walked across the room to the door feeling weak and shaky, as though she'd just had a near miss in the car, relieved to have come through it but very much aware that it could happen again. 'Let's forget all about it. I'm going to bed.'

'Okay.'

'Goodnight.'

'I'll be up in minute, babe,' he said, watching her go then leaning back and closing his eyes.

She was right, of course, he should have come home straight after the lunch. But it was hard to leave when your presence was so much in demand, people wanting to talk to you and buy you drinks.

He hadn't exactly been lying to Gill about having only danced with the woman at the club; but he had given her an edited version of what had happened. He hadn't danced with the woman because of a dare. She had been sending out signals and he'd responded. What man could resist the come-on from a Marilyn Monroe lookalike with endless legs and a bosom that would unsettle the most married of men? Dancing with her had been a tormenting pleasure, if you could call what they'd been doing on the dancefloor dancing. It was no wonder he'd come home smelling of her perfume.

When she'd invited him back to her place, however, the warning bells had been so deafening he'd managed to drag himself away. As tempting as the alternative was, and as much as he enjoyed being fancied, he didn't want those sorts of complications because he was a happily married man.

Looking back over his life, he could see that he'd never played the field like most young men, had not got it out of his system. He'd only been seventeen when he and Gill had started courting, and there had been no one else for him since. But although he didn't want any other woman, he did enjoy the glamour and excitement of being out on the town, being fancied by women and envied by men.

Unfortunately, a bachelor lifestyle isn't conducive to a happy marriage, he thought, getting up and following his wife upstairs to bed.

Chapter Four

The next morning Gill behaved with determined normality, even though she'd barely slept and was still smarting from last night's altercation. She'd made her opinion clear; there was no point in inflaming the situation by letting the argument drag on.

Arnie was in repentant mood when he came down to the kitchen for breakfast.

'Sorry about last night, babe,' he said, sitting down at the table, looking disturbingly macho in a black dressing gown.

'I told you to forget it,' she said evenly, helping Craig to spread honey on his toast.

'Yeah, I know you did, but in the light of day I can see that I was right out of order.'

'Apology accepted,' she said, relieved that he seemed so keen to put things right.

'You turned your back on me when I came to bed last night,' he said with a hint of reproval.

'You didn't expect me to do otherwise, did you?' she said.

'I s'pose not, but I didn't like it.'

'Serves you right,' she said. 'But it's past history now . . . over and done with.'

'You're a diamond,' he said affectionately, reaching for her hand.

'And you've more flannel than an elephant's nightshirt.'

Having made his peace with her, he emptied some corn flakes into his bowl, poured milk over them and turned his attention to Craig.

'You going to nursery school this morning, buster?' he asked.

Craig nodded, munching his toast.

'What will you be doing there?'

'Driving the car.'

'Oh? Don't you usually do painting and drawing pictures?'

'Yeah, but I like driving the car best,' the boy explained, licking honey from his fingers.

'They've got a pedal car and all the boys fight over it,' explained Gill.

'And the gels,' added Craig.

'Ah, I see.' Arnie smiled and looked at his wife, enquiring chattily, 'So, what are you doing this morning?'

'When I've dropped Craig off I'm going to Hammersmith . . . to the music shop.'

'For anything special?' he asked in a pleasant, conversational manner.

'Yeah. I'm gonna give myself a treat and get the music of that lovely new song that's just come out called "Moon River",' she said.

'I like that one too,' said Arnie.

'Now that we have the record, I can't wait to play it on the piano.'

'It'll be a piece o' cake compared to some of the stuff you tackle.' Arnie admired his wife's musical ability and was often quite awestruck when she played difficult classical pieces. He wasn't gifted that way himself, but enjoyed the musical atmosphere Gill created in the house.

'It shouldn't be too much of a challenge,' she agreed. 'But it's fun to play light pop tunes now and again for a change.'

'I'll look forward to hearing it.'

Gill frowned. 'Which reminds me – I mustn't forget to give the piano repairer a ring,' she said. 'I've got a couple of duff keys. The strings have gone.'

'Again?' he said in surprise. 'It isn't long since he was last here.'

'It's an old piano.' She drank her tea. 'Fortunately he never keeps me waiting for long and he's good at the job. He's reckoned to be the best tuner this side of the river.'

Arnie fell silent, seeming thoughtful while he ate his cereal.

'Are you coming straight home after you've been to the music shop – or going shopping?' he asked after a while.

'I've only a few odds and ends to get from the shops, so I thought I'd pop over to Maisie Road and spend some time with my mum until I collect Craig at lunchtime,' she said, diligent in her filial duty. 'I haven't seen her for a few days.' She paused, wondering why he'd asked. 'Why? Did you want me to get you something from the shops?'

'No.'

'Why the interest then?'

'No reason,' he said lightly. 'I was just making conversation.' He gulped his tea and got up from the table, in a hurry suddenly.

'Why the rush?' she asked.

'I have to get ready for work.'

'Already?' said Gill in surprise. 'Is training earlier today?'

Seeming preoccupied, he didn't reply but hurried to the door.

'Arnie?'

'Yeah?' he said, turning.

'Why are you going to the training ground so early?' she asked.

'Oh . . . um,' he began with suspicious hesitation, 'the boss wants us all there early . . . some sort of a pep talk before training, I expect. He was miffed about last Saturday's result. He doesn't like his team to lose two weeks running and wants to make sure it doesn't happen again this week.'

'Oh, I see.'

A short time later he reappeared wearing a casual jacket over his jeans and carrying his team holdall. He gave his wife and son a preoccupied kiss and hurried out of the door like someone with urgent matters on his mind.

'Well, your daddy is certainly in a hurry this morning,' Gill said to Craig, puzzled by the swiftness of Arnie's departure.

Gill was surprised to find that her mother wasn't at home later that same morning, because Tuesday was Winnie's day for cleaning the upstairs of her house and she wasn't given to breaking her domestic routine. Gill still had a key, and had let herself in to find the place empty.

Going upstairs to find the vacuum cleaner in the middle of the landing and dusters on the small landing table, she was further puzzled. Her mother would never go out leaving a cleaning job half-done unless something really urgent had cropped up. Perhaps she'd run out of cleaning materials – which probably would be a matter of some urgency to her, Gill thought. But that explanation didn't carry much weight, because Winnie was far too well organised to run out of anything. So where the devil was she?

Gill made herself a cup of coffee and sat at the kitchen table to wait for her mother's return. To help pass the time she glanced at the newspaper, which carried reports of the massive Ban the Bomb demonstration that had taken place in Trafalgar Square on Sunday, at which over eight hundred people had been arrested, some of them prominent musicians and actors. It was an emotive issue that stirred passion in the most unexpected people.

Gill had just finished her coffee when her mother appeared, flushed from the crisp autumn weather and breathless from hurrying.

'There you are,' said Gill. 'I wondered where you'd got to.'

'Did you? Why?'

'Because you don't usually go out on a Tuesday morning.'

'I don't usually, no,' Winnie agreed, offering no explanation.

'So, where have you been then?'

'Er . . . I had to pop down to the market.'

Gill gave her a shrewd look, noticing the absence of a shopping bag. 'What for?' she asked.

'Oh, just a few bits and pieces.' She tutted and removed her headscarf. 'But why am I being interrogated?'

'Just interested, that's all.' Gill paused thoughtfully. 'If you went to the market, where's the shopping?'

'Changed my mind when I got there, didn't I?' she was rather too quick to explain. 'Decided I didn't need any veg until tomorrow after all.'

'It isn't like you to go out and leave a job half-done, Mum,' Gill said. 'You were in the middle of doing the bedrooms.'

Winnie shot her daughter a disapproving look. 'Since when do I have to account for my actions to you?' she asked sternly, but there was something phoney about her manner somehow.

'You don't.'

'Good.'

'Is anything wrong?'

'Wrong? What could be wrong?' she said briskly, removing her coat and filling the new electric kettle that Arnie had recently treated her to.

'You seem a bit . . . well, preoccupied about something.'

'You're imagining things,' Winnie said, plugging the kettle in and turning it on.

'That's all right, then.' Gill remained unconvinced. 'I'll have another cup of coffee if you're making some.'

'Didn't you ought to be getting off home?' Winnie suggested, going over to the larder and taking out a tin of Nescafé.

Gill looked at her enquiringly. 'No. Why should I?'

For some unknown reason, Winnie's face turned bright pink. 'I dunno . . . to put your shopping away and do a few chores before you collect Craig from nursery school,' she said. 'Isn't that what you usually do?'

'Yes . . . but not this morning, because I've come round here to see you,' she said. 'I thought you'd be pleased.'

64

'I am, o' course, but . . .' Again there was uncertainty in her manner. 'I have to get on with the cleaning as soon as I've finished my coffee.'

'Are you trying to get rid of me or something, Mum?'

'Of course I'm not, but I can't chat for long because I've a lot of housework to do,' said Winnie, pouring boiling water into two coffee cups.

'You usually enjoy a chat,' stated Gill, puzzled.

'I know I do, but it's been one of those mornings.' She handed Gill a cup of coffee and sat down at the table opposite her. 'So, we'll make this a short break and then both get on with what we have to do, shall we?'

'Okay,' said Gill, but she couldn't help feeling worried by her mother's peculiar attitude.

Driving home in the golden autumn morning, the hazy sunshine filtering through trees ablaze with colour, Gill was thinking about her mother's odd behaviour. That tale about her going to the market and changing her mind about buying anything didn't tally with her efficient nature. She had definitely been hiding something. An unseen hand drove into Gill's chest as she thought that perhaps the subterfuge had been to conceal a trip to the doctor's about some ominous symptoms her mother might have been keeping to herself. Oh, well, she'll tell me when she's ready, she thought, turning into Danny Gardens and parking her green Morris Minor outside the house.

Stepping into the hall, with its polished wood floor and vase of fresh chrysanthemums on a small round table beneath a gilt-edged mirror, Gill felt the soothing atmosphere of home wash over her, calming her nerves, which were still jangling from the effects of last night's quarrel as well as her mother's worrying behaviour this morning.

Hanging up her coat in the hall cupboard, she went straight into the kitchen to put the few sundry items of shopping away, stifling the urge to get cracking with her new piece of music until she'd given the kitchen floor a once-over with the mop.

Chores completed, she went into the living room and over to the piano, looking at the music as she went. Sitting down on the stool, about to open the lid, she blinked hard. Stared again. What was going on? The old piano, with the scratchmarks and circles left by years of teacups and tumblers, had gone. In its place was a beautiful new Steinway, its polished black surface gleaming in the sunlight that streamed through the window.

The framed photographs she'd always had standing on the top of the old piano had been transferred to this new model. Propped up against their wedding photograph in the centre was a scribbled note in Arnie's handwriting.

'Sorry about last night. Hope this will help you to forgive me.'

'Oh, Arnie, you fool, you wonderful extravagant fool!' she cried to the room, tears streaming down her cheeks as she opened the lid and stroked the keys that were many shades lighter than the yellowed ones she was used to.

The sound of the telephone ringing in the hall interrupted her thoughts. She knew who the caller was even before she picked up the receiver.

'It's beautiful, Arnie,' she said, her voice ragged with emotion. 'Thank you so much. But you shouldn't have . . .'

'Am I forgiven?'

'You were forgiven anyway,' she said softly through copious tears. 'You didn't need to spend all that money . . .'

'It was about time I fixed you up with a decent joanna anyway,' he said. 'The other one had just about had its day. I bought the new one on a sudden impulse. When you mentioned you needed the repair man again, I thought it was the ideal opportunity.'

'It must have cost you a fortune.'

'You're worth it,' he said. 'And I can afford it, thanks to the job.'

'How did you manage to arrange it so quickly?' she asked.

'I was at the music shop in Hammersmith when they opened this morning, having called on your mother on the way to give her the key to our house so she could let the delivery men in,' he explained.

'No wonder you went off in such a hurry this morning.'

'Yeah. Once I'd had the idea I couldn't wait to set it in motion.'

'I'm surprised you managed to get it delivered that quickly.'

'You'll be surprised how fast people can move if you flash enough dough under their nose.'

'That's why Mum wasn't in,' she said almost to herself. 'She was here seeing the piano in when I got to her place.'

'That's right.'

'And I suppose that's why she wanted me to come home right away . . . because of the surprise that was waiting for me here,' she said, relieved that the mystery was solved.

'Yeah.'

'Oh, Arnie, you're a lovely man.'

'Can I have that in writing?'

'You don't need it.'

She could hear someone calling him in the background. 'Look, I'll have to go, babe,' he said. 'We're in the middle of a training session. I managed to slip inside to the phone.'

'Okay. I'll see you later.'

'Oh, by the way, Gill, the old piano is going back to your mum and dad's place, but I've arranged for it to have an overhaul at the shop first.'

'Really?'

'Yeah. Your mum couldn't bear the idea of it going out of the family altogether.'

The thought of the old piano being back in her parents' living room made her feel sentimental, and she felt fresh tears forming. It was like hearing that an old friend was safe and well.

'I'm glad,' she said thickly. 'But thanks for the new one. It was a lovely surprise.'

'It was a pleasure.'

'Love you.'

'Love you too.'

Replacing the receiver she wandered back into the living room, an epitome of style and comfort with its cream walls, soft red carpet and pale orange velvet curtains. She sat down on the piano stool and put her new music in the stand, her joy and gratitude almost painful in its intensity.

But nagging away at her glorious sense of well-being was a speck of discomfort she couldn't quite identify. There was something about this excessively generous gesture of Arnie's that made her feel uneasy.

She pushed it from her mind and put her fingers on the keys.

One Saturday evening in March of the following year, Carol and Dougie were lovingly ensconced on the sofa in Gill and Arnie's living room, having come to visit for the evening. *Perry Mason* was on the television but no one was watching it because they were idly chatting.

'Why aren't you two young things out enjoying yourself on a Saturday night?' enquired Arnie lightly.

'We *are* out enjoying ourselves,' replied Carol.

'You know what I mean,' said Arnie. 'A young couple like yourselves, with no ties, should be out letting your hair down at a dance or a disco or something.'

'We like staying at home with you and Gill,' said Carol, snuggling closer to Dougie, to whom she had recently got engaged. 'Don't we, Dougie?'

'Yeah,' he said, but he didn't sound wildly enthusiastic.

'As long as we're together we don't mind where we are, do we, Dougie?'

Carol's tone made Gill's skin crawl because it was so embarrassingly possessive. Her sister's cloying attitude towards her fiancé was getting worse, and Gill was worried about the effect it might be having on Dougie.

'That's right,' agreed Dougie dutifully.

'Saturday night in front of the telly is for married couples with kids like me and Gill,' opined Arnie. 'You two ought to make the most of your freedom while you can and go out and paint the town red at the weekend.'

'We're saving up to get married,' Carol informed him loftily, taking Dougie's hand in both of hers and caressing it. 'We're not interested in going out to dances and discos.'

'If we'd known you were coming, Gill and I would have arranged to have a night out and left you two baby-sitting,' said Arnie.

'I'll make some coffee,' said Gill.

'I'd rather have a pint,' said Arnie, throwing Dougie a meaningful look. 'Fancy coming down the local for a quick one while the girls are chatting, mate?' He turned to Gill. 'You don't mind, do you, love?'

'Course not,' said Gill, who was used to Arnie's going out and knew he would go whether she objected or not.

'Dougie doesn't want to go out, do you?' said Carol, frowning at her fiancé.

'Well . . . er, I wouldn't mind,' he said, looking sheepish. 'Just for half an hour or so . . . It'll be a break from indoors.'

Carol stared at him with a thunderous expression. 'We're supposed to be spending the evening together,' she snorted.

'They won't be gone long,' Gill intervened, hoping to defuse the rising tension.

Glaring at Dougie, Carol said through clenched teeth, 'You do what you like. Don't mind me.'

'There's no need to get the hump, Carol,' admonished Arnie in the forthright manner that comes with long-term acquaintance. 'Surely you don't begrudge him half an hour out of the house with his future brother-in-law?'

She shot Arnie a contemptuous look. He went over to where she was sitting and looked down at her persuasively.

'I'll have him back here in half an hour – an hour at the very most, love, I promise,' he said, winking at her. 'So how about giving your big brother-in-law a smile?'

'Just go, for goodness' sake,' she said, but she did manage a watery smile because she still had a soft spot for Arnie.

'Fancy a biscuit, Carol?' Gill invited after the men had gone and she had made coffee. 'The chocolate ones are yummy.'

'No thanks,' said Carol sulkily.

'Oh, come on, sis, cheer up,' said Gill. 'Dougie isn't doing any harm.'

'I haven't said he is,' she said, her hazel eyes full of pique. 'It's just that he's meant to be spending the evening with me.'

'Why come round here to visit us if you want him to yourself then?' Gill said. 'Why not go dancing or for a drink or to the pictures or something, as Arnie suggested?'

'I've told you. We're supposed to be saving up to get married,' she said.

'Is it a good idea not to have any fun, though?' queried Gill.

'You don't have to go out to have fun, you know,' Carol said huffily. 'We don't need expensive entertainment to keep us amused.'

'Even so . . .'

'We're trying to get enough money together for the deposit on a house . . . and there's the furniture and things to pay for as well,' she said crossly. 'We'll never have enough if we spend it all on going out.'

Gill sipped her coffee, looking at Carol over the rim of the cup and seeing a smart, moderately attractive young woman of twenty dressed in a black polo-necked sweater and red short skirt, her hair heavily backcombed into an exaggerated bouffant. Because Gill loved her sister and cared about what happened to her, she felt duty-bound to come right out and say something that was not going to make her popular.

'You must be doing quite well with your savings as you're staying in so much,' said Gill, leading up to her point gradually. 'Going out now and again won't make that much difference.'

'It will.'

'But you don't want your relationship with Dougie to go stale because of too much togetherness, though. Do you?'

Carol gave her sister a sharp look. 'Meaning?'

Gill braced herself to say what she felt she ought to. 'Meaning that if you're going to make a scene like the one this evening every time Dougie wants to leave your side for a spot of socialising, he'll start to feel trapped.'

'Huh! You're a fine one to give advice on how to keep a man,' retorted Carol indignantly.

'What do you mean by that?'

'Don't play dumb,' said Carol, who was trembling with anger, 'everyone knows that Arnie is giving you a really hard time, that he's always out boozing and womanising. I'm amazed he was at home tonight when we called, as a matter of fact.'

'So he likes a good time and he can afford to have one,' said Gill, agonised by the thoughts this attack had evoked. 'It doesn't mean anything.'

'You've got no hold on him now,' said Carol. 'He does just as he likes.'

'How do you know all this?'

'Arnie boasts about it to the other blokes,' she explained. 'He'll be bending Doug's ear about it at this very moment, I should think. Telling him about the glitzy clubs he goes to in the West End, and how the most beautiful women in London want to go to bed with him.'

'Shut up, Carol—'

'Your marriage is heading for the rocks and you know it,' Carol said.

'And you won't get married at all if you don't give Dougie some space.'

'You're just jealous 'cause you can't hang on to Arnie.'

Gill winced. 'The state of my marriage has nothing to do

71

with my opinion of the situation between you and Dougie,' she said, managing to stay in control as she had had to do so many times in the past when dealing with Carol's emotional over-reactions. 'But it makes me cringe to see you being so clinging with him. I've been wanting to say something for a long time.'

'I dunno who you think you are,' said Carol, her eyes shining with tears.

'Oh, Carol . . . please—'

'You've always poked your nose into my business and tried to run my life.'

'I have not,' said Gill. 'If I feel compelled to say something now it's only because I care about you and don't want you to get hurt.'

'Yeah, well,' muttered Carol, her volatile temper evaporating as suddenly as it had flared up. 'You don't have to worry, because Dougie loves me and he wouldn't do anything to hurt me.'

'Yes, I believe he does loves you,' said Gill. 'But I do think you ought to give him more freedom.' She paused, looking grim. 'But, as you say, I'm a fine one to talk.'

Carol was immediately contrite at her sister's admission of a problem. 'I'm sorry for what I said about you and Arnie,' she said, her eyes brimming with tears. 'I was in a temper. I didn't mean it.'

'Don't worry about it.'

'You're not upset.'

'Not with you.'

'Sure?'

'Yeah.'

'Good.' Carol paused. 'Do I really go over the top with Dougie?' she asked, seeming very young and vulnerable suddenly.

'Well, just a bit,' said Gill with the hesitant candour of someone who genuinely cares.

'It's 'cause I love him and I can't wait to get married,'

Carol said with an air of innocent enthusiasm that twisted Gill's heart. 'I want a home of my own and babies . . . everything you have.'

'It'll come,' said Gill. 'Just take it easy on yourself . . . and Dougie.'

'I'll try.'

'Good girl.'

'I really didn't mean to say that about your marriage,' said Carol. 'Arnie's great. I'm sure the two of you will work things out.'

'I hope so,' said Gill.

But life with Arnie was becoming increasingly impossible, and she just didn't know what to do about it.

Chapter Five

Gill was sitting on a bench in Bishop's Park one Sunday afternoon a few weeks later, watching Arnie and Craig kicking a ball about on the grass. She was thinking how much like his father Craig was getting – the same colouring, the greenish-brown eyes, the thick brown curly hair, similar mannerisms. He was even beginning to walk with the same swaggering gait as his father, even though he was only just coming up to five years old.

She didn't mind being slightly set apart from them by their maleness. It was the natural thing, and it gave her a sense of family. The fact that father and son were bonding was important to her because she thought it was vital for Craig as he grew up.

'Come on, son, shoot to me,' Arnie was instructing him.

'Okay, Dad.'

'Give it all you've got . . . That's it, boy. Oh, well done!'

Dressed in a football strip in Arnie's club colours, Craig leapt in the air then turned towards his mother for her approval, raising his arms proudly, his hair blowing about in the light breeze.

'Well done, love,' she called.

'He's coming on a treat,' Arnie shouted to her. 'He'll be playing in a team in no time.'

Gill smiled and nodded. Looking around the park on this sunny April afternoon – at the children shouting and calling to each other in the playground area, the youths joshing near the lake, the families out walking by the river – she was filled with a sense of isolation. Ostensibly she and Arnie and Craig were an ordinary happy family. In reality, she and Arnie were drifting ever further apart.

They had been so good together in the early years; she'd thought it would last for ever. But incidents like the one that had caused Arnie to buy her a new piano as a peace offering had become commonplace. He was hardly ever home in the evenings now because he preferred to be out clubbing in the West End. Carol had been right when she'd said Gill's marriage was heading for the rocks. She could feel it slipping away from her, and there was nothing she could do to keep them together because Arnie no longer seemed to care about their relationship.

Maybe the smart thing would be to grit her teeth and let him get on with it, in the hope that it was just a passing phase. But she was too emotionally involved for clever tactics. It wasn't just the fact that he was always out; his attitude towards her when he was at home was painful too. Although he was rarely impatient with Craig, he made it blatantly obvious that Gill irritated the hell out of him. It was as though having a wife hampered the social life he had come to value so highly, and he resented it.

Their life together swung between bitter enmity and sporadic bouts of remorse and reconciliation, during which he swore that he hadn't been unfaithful to her. At these times there was tenderness and passion. He said he still loved her despite everything, but most of the time it didn't feel like that to her. This definitely wasn't the same man she had married. Ever since Arnie had tasted the West End night-life his marriage had been a burden to him.

Perhaps they had married too young. Maybe all this was happening because he hadn't got it out of his system earlier. The money and attention he now received so much of was enough to turn the head of any ordinary working-class boy; she made allowances for that. But she wasn't ready to give up on him, even though she sometimes didn't feel able to take another day wedded to the monster Arnie had become.

One of the worst things was not being able to rely on him or anticipate his reactions, as she once had . . . And she had absolutely no idea how he was going to react to the news she had been putting off telling him!

One afternoon about a month later Arnie was summoned to the manager's office at Borough Football Club.

'You wanted to see me, boss?' he said breezily, expecting to receive some sort of commendation because that was what he had come to expect.

'That's right, son,' said Jack Benson, who was seated at his desk. A big man with greying hair and sharp, dark eyes, he waved a large hand towards a chair opposite. A famous player in his day, Jack had made a name for himself in football management and was well known for his ability to be ruthless if it was necessary for the good of the club.

'Sit down.'

Arnie did as he was told. 'So, what's it all about then, boss?' he asked cheerfully.

Jack stroked his chin, his eyes resting unwaveringly on Arnie. 'I've been hearing things about you . . .'

'All good, I hope.'

'All bad – and I don't like it,' Jack said, his tone becoming hard. 'I don't like it one little bit.'

'Oh?' Arnie was taken aback. 'What am I supposed to have done?'

'Don't get clever with me, boy!' roared Jack, who was also known for his booming voice. 'You know bloody well what I'm talking about.'

'Do I?'

'Yes, mate, you do! Birds, booze and nightclubs until all hours.'

'Oh, that.'

'Yes, that,' confirmed Jack. 'It isn't the way for a professional footballer to behave. Not one of my players,

76

anyway. When you signed up with this club you agreed not to do anything that might affect your game or the reputation of the club.'

'I dunno who's been saying all this,' mumbled Arnie defensively. 'A bloke's entitled to a night out now and again . . .'

'From what I've heard it's a bloody sight more than just a night out now and again.'

'Who's been running to you with tales?'

'Don't be so childish, man. Nobody's been running to me with tales,' Jack said.

'How—'

'I make it my business to find out what my players get up to on *and* off the pitch, and you've made no secret of what you do in your spare time,' Jack cut in. 'Quite the opposite, in fact. You seem to like people knowing that you're out clubbing until the small hours with models and showgirls and any other bit o' spare you can pick up. You're always shooting your mouth off about the fact that you practically live at Flowers nightclub. You must have known I'd get to know about it sooner or later.'

'I didn't think, boss . . .'

'That's your trouble. You've forgotten how to use your loaf.'

'This is no big thing,' said Arnie dismissively. 'Okay, I admit I like to live a little. What's so terrible about that?'

'Nothing – if you don't mind losing your job and your wife,' Jack said bluntly.

'Oh, come on,' objected Arnie. 'That's a bit over the top, innit?'

Jack remained calm, doodling with a pen on his blotter. 'When I first saw you play I was excited,' he said without looking up. 'Because I knew I was looking at real talent. That's why we gave you a contract, and why the club pays you a lot of money.' He looked up and fixed Arnie with a steely glare. 'When you first came to this club you were a genuine bloke, dedicated to your game and to the club.'

'I still am,' pronounced Arnie.

'That's a matter of opinion.'

'That isn't fair,' objected Arnie. 'Have I ever missed a training session?'

'Not yet, but that'll start to happen before long if you carry on as you have been.'

'Never! I'm a dedicated player.'

'You're dedicated to Arnie Briscoe, superstar. Not Borough Football Club,' said Jack brutally.

'That isn't true.'

'I think it is.'

'No!' Arnie shook his head, his cheeks scarlet.

'You've let the money and the fame go to your head,' said Jack.

Arnie said nothing, just stared at the floor.

'I've been there, mate,' said Jack frankly. 'Admittedly football didn't have the glamorous image in my day as it does now, because we didn't have the television to give us fame, and the game didn't have the sort of money that television has brought into it these days. We didn't earn as much as your generation of players, but we had our share of fans and adulation. Oh, yeah, we had kids queuing up for our autograph and women wanting to sleep with us – 'cause being famous is sexy. The only trouble is, when people treat you like God's gift you begin to believe it yourself. I know just what it feels like.'

'I can't help enjoying it. I'm only human.'

'Enjoying it is one thing, letting it change you is quite another.'

'Yeah, I know,' said Arnie gloomily.

'I suppose your marriage is in trouble over this,' Jack said.

'Well, the wife isn't exactly overjoyed with things at the moment.'

'You can't blame her for taking a dim view if you've been putting it about.'

'I haven't been putting it about,' Arnie denied emphatically.

'No?' Jack challenged, brows raised.

'No.' Arnie was adamant. 'I've flirted a bit – that's all.'

'Whether you have or you haven't actually done the deed is beside the point,' said Jack in a worldly-wise manner. 'Your wife will think you have. Women always do. You're young, it's natural for a young man to chase women. Wives don't understand this because they're different to us—'

'I'll say they're different.'

'Anyway, your marriage isn't my business,' Jack continued briskly. 'But your game is – and if you carry on as you are you're gonna find yourself out in the cold before very long.'

'I scored twice on Saturday,' Arnie was quick to remind him.

'I'm not disputing the fact that you can play football, Arnie,' said Jack. 'But I *am* saying that you can't burn the candle at both ends and get away with it for ever. Your game will suffer if you carry on as you are now.' His manner became uncompromising. 'No one is indispensable, not even you. A professional footballer has a short enough playing life. Don't shorten yours even more by behaving like an idiot.'

'Are you threatening me?'

'No, I'm just warning you,' said Jack. 'And hoping that you'll take notice of what I've said.'

'Oh.'

'Now bugger off and think about it and let me get on with my work.'

At about eleven o'clock that same night, feeling sick at heart, Gill scraped Arnie's congealed dinner off the plate and on to newspaper and put it into the bin. God only knows how much food she'd wasted in this way over the last couple of years. She was a fool to keep food for him at all when it was nearly always thrown away. But she'd been hopeful tonight, because this afternoon he'd phoned her from the club to say that he would definitely be home early.

Although she still loved him, she was at the end of her

tether. It was all very well to keep trying to make their marriage work, but what sort of a life was it for any of them the way things were? Arnie was rarely home, and Gill's nerves were always on edge because of the way he was carrying on – which, in turn, must have been having an effect on their son.

She washed the plate and went upstairs to check on Craig, who had fallen asleep at last. It had taken her ages to pacify him because his daddy hadn't come home – yet again – after telling him on the telephone that he would be there in time to see him before he went to bed.

Back downstairs she sat down to wait for Arnie. She had given up waiting up for him long ago, but tonight was different. Tonight she had had enough, and she was going to tell him so.

He came in at about half past eleven.

'You waited up, then,' he said, mooching into the living room to find her sitting on the sofa.

'I was expecting you hours ago,' she told him stiffly.

'Yeah, sorry about that,' he said casually. 'I got chatting and forgot the time.'

'You're really not being fair, you know, Arnie,' she said.

'Oh, for God's sake, don't you start nagging again.' Arnie was still upset about the meeting with Jack Benson and had been drowning his sorrows in the pub. 'I've had a terrible day.'

She stood up and faced him with her arms folded in front of her. 'And I've had a terrible two years while you've thoughtlessly destroyed our marriage with your complete lack of consideration,' she said. 'Frankly, Arnie, I've had enough.'

'Oh, so you're threatening me now, are you?' he taunted, guilt making him aggressive.

'Not threatening,' she said through dry lips, 'but I am saying that I'm not prepared to carry on like this any longer, sitting here every night on my own while you're out living it up, sleeping with any dolly bird who takes your fancy for all I know.'

80

'I haven't slept with anyone,' he said – and it was true, though he'd had a few near misses.

'I'd like to believe that—'

'You can believe what you damned well like,' he said nastily. 'If you don't trust me you can do the other thing – I couldn't care less.'

'Don't tell me you don't chase women at Flowers.'

'You've got it the wrong way round, babe,' he said with an air of blatant conceit. 'It's the women who chase me.'

'And you sit back and think of me, I suppose,' she said.

'No, I dance with 'em, chat 'em up,' he said. 'It's all just a game.'

'A dangerous game for a married man to be playing—'

'Oh, stop moaning, woman. You do all right for yourself,' he stated. 'I provide well for you and Craig. You've got a lovely home, your own car, and I make sure you're never short of money in your purse.'

'I'm not denying any of that,' she said. 'But I'd rather be penniless and have you by my side.'

'I am by your side—'

'No you're not,' she said. 'Even when you are here, you're somewhere else in your mind.'

'Rubbish.'

'I want my husband back, Arnie,' she said. 'I want a proper family life again.'

'Bloody hell. First I've got Jack Benson on my back, now you,' he said, his voice rising along with his temper. 'What is it with you people? Why can't you let a bloke alone?'

'You've changed.'

'Of course I've changed,' he snapped. 'I've got money in my pocket now, I couldn't afford to go out enjoying myself before.'

'I don't want to stop you going out, Arnie – but every night . . . and coming home at all hours. It really isn't on.'

'Look, Gill. I don't want to stay at home gawping at the telly like some old geezer,' he said. 'I like going out on the town, I like the atmosphere of Flowers and other nightclubs. I want to come and go as I please. I'm only twenty-four, for Pete's sake! I'm just not ready to sit at home and do the pipe and slippers routine.'

'I wasn't suggesting you should sit at home every night,' she told him. 'But I do think you should behave a bit more like a responsible husband and father.'

'I'll do what I like, when I like, and you can't do a damned thing about it,' he heard himself say.

'In that case you can take your things and go,' she heard herself say.

'Go! Me? Don't be ridiculous.'

'Get out, go on!' she shouted, beside herself now with pain and exasperation, her words tumbling out almost of their own volition. 'And leave Craig and me in peace.'

'If anyone's gonna go, it'll be you,' he said, saying things he didn't mean in the heat of the moment. 'It's my house.'

'Okay, if you feel comfortable about forcing your wife and child out of their home, then I'll go,' she stated boldly.

'Good.'

'I'll take Craig and leave first thing in the morning.'

'Don't worry, you can have the bloody house.' He couldn't believe he had actually told her to leave their home. *His own wife*. What was happening to him? 'I don't wanna stay here for another minute with a nag of a wife like you.' He stormed from the room, shouting back from the front door, 'I'll be back to collect my things tomorrow . . . or sometime soon.'

Shaking so much that her teeth were chattering, Gill heard the front door slam. Frantic, she rushed out into the street after him. He was already in his car.

'Arnie, wait, we need to talk.'

'Not likely.'

'That's right, run away from your responsibilities like you always do!' she shouted through the car window as he started up the engine and revved hard. She was in far too much of a state to worry about her voice echoing in the night and disturbing the neighbours as she tried to make herself heard. 'And just to bring you up to date: before very long you'll have another responsibility to run away from. I'm pregnant.'

And without knowing if he'd heard her or not, she turned and ran back inside, sobbing uncontrollably as she heard him drive away at high speed.

Arnie didn't have any particular destination in mind. He was a trembling mass of emotions – anger, frustration, pain and remorse, which he vaguely realised were the combined products of guilt – as he sped out of London, screeching to a halt at each set of red lights, glad when there were fewer of them as he distanced himself from town.

Having his foot pressed hard on the accelerator gave him a welcome rush of adrenalin that he needed to help him release some of his pent-up aggression.

The trouble with guilt is that it tears you apart inside. Arnie was angry – with himself for wanting things he shouldn't want, and with the woman he loved for restricting him. He knew that Gill was right. He knew Jack Benson was right. But he didn't want to admit it, because to do so would put a stop to his current way of life.

The bright lights had become like a drug to him. He got high on the excitement of a nightclub, the glamour of being among beautiful women and well-dressed men, being one of the 'in crowd'. He loved the scented air that greeted you in an evocative cloud when you walked into Flowers club: the smell of expensive cigars and even more expensive perfume.

George Flowers made a great fuss of him, had introduced him to important people, made him feel special. That was what it was all about: being in demand and feeling like a somebody.

Although he would never admit it to the lads, Arnie hadn't actually been unfaithful to Gill. He'd come pretty close to it a few times, but had never actually gone through with it. Sex wasn't really what it was about; it was more of an ego thing.

Being strongly fancied by women who wouldn't have given him a second glance a few years ago, and being able to call the shots, was heady stuff.

But was all this worth losing Gill for? Gill and Craig, whom he loved so dearly? Oh yes, he might be confused about a lot of things, but he wasn't confused about that. No matter what he'd said or how badly he'd behaved, he had never fallen out of love with Gill. He had merely become disenchanted with the lifestyle of a married man.

It was true what they said: you can't have your cake and eat it. So what was he doing driving towards Heathrow at this time of night while his wife was worried sick at home? Something had to go, and he didn't want it to be Gill.

At the next roundabout, he turned back.

Homeward bound, he received a strong mental image of Gill shouting at him through the car window as he'd driven away. He'd only caught snippets of what she'd been saying because of the noise of the engine and his preoccupation with his own thoughts. What he had heard hadn't registered properly.

Something she'd said was bothering him, but he couldn't quite piece it together. He began to replay the incident in his mind, over and over again. She'd been saying something about another responsibility. That was it . . . another responsibility for him to run away from. My God, she must have been telling him she was pregnant!

He pushed hard on the accelerator in his urgency to get home and put things right. There wasn't too much traffic about at this late hour, and soon his foot was pressed right to the floorboards. The driving conditions were ideal, being a clear dry night with a bright moon.

Like a man possessed, he forced the needle ever higher on the speedometer, all respect for the law disregarded as the car moved through the night ever faster on the almost deserted dual carriageway.

All the signs were there to indicate that he was approaching the Hogarth roundabout, but he paid little attention. All he could think of was getting home to Gill to tell her that he loved her and was sorry for the appalling way he'd been behaving lately.

He didn't need to stop or even slow down as he approached the roundabout. He was Arnie Briscoe – in control and invincible!

The car hit the roundabout head on, throwing Arnie forward with such force that he was pushed half-way through the windscreen, where he was suspended as the car bounced sideways off the concrete barrier.

It rolled over into the middle of the road with the crump of metal and the splintering of glass. With the final bump, Arnie was thrown to the ground with a horrific crunch, where he lay perfectly still, oblivious to everything, a silent figure in the road beside a heap of mangled metal. Blood began to trickle from his mouth.

Chapter Six

'Why don't you go and have a lie down in the relatives' room, love?' suggested Phoebe to Gill. 'I'll stay here with Arnie.'

'I daren't leave him . . . just in case he comes round . . . or—'

'Don't even think about the alternative,' Phoebe cut in, her voice quivering emotionally despite her indomitable spirit. 'My Arnie's a fighter. It'll take something worse than this to finish him off.'

Looking at the unconscious figure attached to tubes and wires, both legs and one arm set in plaster, Gill wondered what could be worse than this. He was unnervingly still, only a fraction of his face visible through the bandaging.

'It doesn't seem like Arnie lying there, does it?' she murmured.

' 'Cause you can't see him through all the bandages?'

'I meant more that he isn't the sort of person you can imagine lying in a hospital bed,' said Gill through parched lips.

'That's true,' said Phoebe. 'He's usually so noisy and full of beans.'

'I don't suppose he's ever been so quiet for this long in his life before.'

'That's a fact,' said Phoebe.

Observing her mother-in-law across Arnie's bed, and seeing the ashen tinge of her skin and the eyes raw from weeping, Gill said, 'You look absolutely shattered.'

'So do you.'

'Yeah, I am.'

'At least I've been for a bit of a rest, even though I couldn't sleep,' said Phoebe. 'I think you should do the same. Even half an hour's break will freshen you up.'

'I'll stay here for a while longer,' said Gill, though she was light-headed with tiredness, her muscles aching with tension.

'Okay. I'll go and see if I can get us some coffee then,' said Phoebe, yawning heavily as she plodded to the door of the small side-ward that was used for emergency cases.

'That would be a life saver,' said Gill. 'I'm gasping.'

It was the morning after the accident, and Gill and Phoebe had been at the hospital all night. Because of the seriousness of Arnie's condition, they had been allocated a room for personal use.

Thinking back to last night, Gill recalled how she'd rushed to answer the doorbell full of hope, thinking it was Arnie come back to make up with her. Instead she'd been faced with everyone's most dreaded scenario: two policeman standing on the doorstep. They had been very kind and helpful, had even gone to Maisie Road to get her mother to stay with Craig while she went to the hospital. Gill had collected Phoebe on the way.

Now she was afraid to take her eyes off her husband in case he slipped away. The doctors said he had a slim chance of recovery, but it was touch and go because he had internal injuries as well as many broken bones. They didn't know yet if there was any brain damage.

It was a miracle he had survived the crash at all, apparently. The police had ascertained from the state of the car and the skid marks on the road that he'd been way over the speed limit when he'd hit the roundabout. If he did pull through he would probably face a charge of dangerous driving.

The parlous state of their marriage had paled into insignificance against the possibility of Arnie dying. His survival was the only thing that mattered to Gill now.

'Don't die, Arnie,' she whispered, taking his still, cool hand in hers, her tired eyes filling with tears. 'Please don't die.'

Because Arnie's condition was critical, people could visit at any time. Not surprisingly, there was a stream of visitors throughout the day. Winnie came while Craig was at school, Arnie's brother John took time off from the factory where he worked to pay a visit, Carol came in her lunch hour, and some of Arnie's team-mates visited with the manager, Jack Benson. And Arnie remained oblivious throughout.

By late afternoon Gill was dead on her feet and forced to take a break when she could no longer function properly. The clinically clean room they had been given was small and basically furnished with two single beds and a washbasin. It was permeated with the antiseptic smell of the wards, which made Gill feel nauseous.

She flopped down on the bed fully dressed. Yet, although she was bone-tired, sleep eluded her. Her nerves were painfully taut, her mind racing . . . If only Arnie had been driving his car at a safe speed he probably wouldn't be on the critical list now, she couldn't help thinking as she finally dozed off.

Waking suddenly and completely disorientated, she flew into a panic the instant she remembered where she was. Jerking upright, she dragged herself out of bed, realising as she did so that she had been woken by a sharp pain across her middle.

Sitting on the edge of the bed, clutching her stomach and rubbing her back, her heart thudded as the alarming implications of the pain registered. Sweating with fear, she hurried back to the ward, established that there was no change in Arnie's condition, told Phoebe she would be back in a minute, then rushed into the ladies' toilet. Emerging soon after, ashen-faced and trembling, she found a nurse.

'I think I'm having a miscarriage,' she said, her face screwed up in agony.

'Are you and Arnie trying to make Hammersmith hospital

88

into your family home or somethin'?' Phoebe forced herself to be cheerful when she visited her daughter-in-law in the gynaecology ward the next day. 'Both of you being in here as patients at the same time is a real turn up for the books.'

'It is, isn't it?' said Gill flatly.

'Handy for visiting, though.'

'There is that.' Gill managed a watery smile.

'I'm ever so sorry you lost your baby, love.' Phoebe's mood became serious. She took one of Gill's hands in both of hers and gave it a comforting squeeze. 'You're getting it from all sides at the moment, aren't you, duck?'

'It seems like it.'

'I had no idea you were pregnant.'

'Neither did anyone else.'

'It isn't like you to keep something as important as that to yourself.'

'I was going to tell you all, but you know how it is . . . if you make it generally known too early, the pregnancy seems to go on for ever.' Her skin was paper-white and her dark eyes bloodshot and swollen from weeping. 'I needn't have worried, as it happened, need I?'

Phoebe shook her head slowly, her eyes glistening with tears. 'Does Arnie know?' she asked grimly.

'I'm not sure. I did try to tell him just before he drove off in the car, but I don't know if he heard what I was saying.'

'Oh, I see.' Phoebe paused. 'I suppose it must have been the shock of the accident that caused the miscarriage.'

'There isn't much doubt about that, according to the doctor.'

'Well, I shall have a thing or two to say to that son o' mine when he does come round,' said Phoebe, who determinedly refused to believe that Arnie wouldn't recover. 'He shouldn't have been driving like a lunatic.'

'We'd had a row. He was in a foul temper,' Gill explained. 'Anyway, you know Arnie – he's a law unto himself.'

'This'll teach him to drive more carefully, though.'

'Maybe.' Gill sighed. 'No change in his condition, then?'

'No.'

'Is anyone with him?'

'Don't worry. John's sitting with him till I get back.'

'That's good. I don't like to think of him lying there on his own, even though he doesn't know a thing about it. I'll be able to sit with him again soon.'

'The doctor was saying that each day he survives makes the chance of recovery more likely,' said Phoebe.

'That's really good news,' Gill said, but she was too numb to feel anything much beyond the loss of her baby. Being pregnant had been a symbol of hope in her crumbling marriage. Her beloved son and the thought of a new baby had given her a reason for continuing as Arnie had grown ever more distant. What made the miscarriage even harder to take was knowing that it need never have happened. If Arnie hadn't stormed out in a temper and been driving so carelessly, he wouldn't be fighting for his life now and their baby would still be growing in her womb. It seemed wrong to blame him for anything at all, but she had wanted that baby *so* much.

'Look, love, I know how much you must be hurting, and I know it's what everyone says at a time like this because they don't know what else to say . . .' Phoebe was speaking with deep compassion. 'But you're still young, you can try again.'

Gill shook her head slowly, her dark eyes dull with pain.

'You mean . . . ?'

'When they gave me the routine D and C after I'd lost the baby, they found some damage to my womb,' she explained, tears burning beneath her eyelids. 'I can't have any more children.'

'Oh, Gill, love . . .' Phoebe moved closer and put her arms around her. 'I'm so very very sorry.'

At that moment some visitors headed down the ward towards them. Winnie and Hal with Craig, followed by Carol and Dougie.

'What's up?' asked Winnie, instantly perceiving that her

daughter was on the verge of tears. 'Has something happened? Has he taken a turn for the worse?'

'Don't panic. Arnie's condition is just the same,' said Phoebe. 'But I think the one person in the world Gill needs right now is her mum.' She turned to the others. 'Come on, you lot. Let's go and see Arnie and leave mother and daughter alone together for a few minutes.'

Experiencing a rush of gratitude to Phoebe for her sensitivity, Gill flung her arms around her mother, the tears finally falling.

At first it was nothing more than a slight flickering of his eyelids. Then he opened his eyes for just a few seconds before sinking back into unconsciousness.

Arnie's slow recovery began a few days later. Gradually and painfully, he was awake for longer periods and on the mend.

Although Gill was very low in health and spirits, she managed to fake a cheery manner for her husband. He was in a great deal of physical pain despite being heavily dosed with pain-killers. He had enough problems; she didn't want to add to them by telling him about hers.

When he was taken off the critical list she had to adhere to normal visiting times, but she was always there with a smile and a positive outlook. Arnie had no idea of the mental torture his wife was suffering as she tried to come to terms with the loss of her baby and the fact that she couldn't have any more.

On Wednesdays, visiting was allowed in the afternoon as well as the evening. Gill was often his only visitor then, because most people were at work. One such afternoon, a few weeks after he'd regained consciousness, Gill arrived at his bedside loaded with goodies.

'So, how are you feeling today?' she asked, leaning over to kiss him.

'Fed up with being stuck in here, babe,' he told her.

His attitude towards her was more like it had been in the

early days, before fame and fortune had taken its toll. The argument that had preceded his accident had been forgotten. One of the first things he'd done when he'd regained consciousness was make his peace with her about that. And because she wanted to stay married to him she'd been happy to forgive him and put the past behind them.

'Yeah, I expect you are – but there's no point in them discharging you too soon.'

'It's so boring.'

'Better to be bored than dead. You're lucky to be alive,' she said, emptying the grapes she'd brought out of the brown paper bag into a bowl on his locker, and putting a bag of his favourite toffees down beside them. 'So just remind yourself of that and be patient.'

'Easier said than done.'

'I know.'

'I want be up and about again.'

'All in good time.' She unwrapped a toffee and popped it into his mouth. One of his arms and both legs were still in plaster, but the bandages around his head had been removed.

'It isn't easy for someone as active as me to lay about all day,' he said, the toffee bulging at the side of his mouth. 'I'm dying to get back to playing football again.'

Gill's heart lurched. 'You've been very badly injured, you know, Arnie,' she said cautiously.

'I know it'll be a while before I'm actually on the field again, even after I get out of here,' he said, 'but it's the thought of getting back to the game that's keeping me going. That and coming home to you and Craig, o' course.'

'Mm,' she muttered non-committally.

'How's Craig?' he asked.

'Fine. He's full of the school sports day at the moment,' she said. 'He's entered for some of the races.'

'Ah bless him,' said Arnie, his expression softening at the thought of his son, who had started primary school after Easter and was in his first term.

'He has to get through the heats first though, or he won't be competing on the big day.'

'He'll do it,' said Arnie. 'He's a natural sportsman, that boy.'

'I hope you're right. God knows how I'll console him if he doesn't make it,' she said. 'He's set his heart on it.'

'He takes after me. I used to be just the same at his age.'

They chatted about Craig some more. Arnie ate a few grapes as they talked.

'Have some, Gill,' he said after a while.

'No. I bought them for you.'

'I know, but I want you to have some too,' he said. 'They'll do you good. You're eating for two now, remember?'

He'd told her a few days before that he'd realised what she'd been saying to him as he drove off, just before the accident. He had gone on to say how delighted he was at the idea of becoming a father for the second time – and she'd spared him the truth because he'd been so ill and in such terrible pain. She and her parents and Phoebe had previously agreed that she should wait until he was stronger before she told him about the miscarriage.

Now, though, she knew that time had come.

'I'm not eating for two, Arnie,' she said, her throat so dry and constricted that she could hardly utter the words.

'Not three is it?' he said jokingly. 'You're not having twins?'

'I'm not having a baby at all, Arnie,' she told him.

He looked at her with light-hearted puzzlement, as though he thought she was teasing. 'Not having a baby?'

She shook her head.

'You mean I imagined that you told me you were pregnant that night through the car window?' His expression darkened. 'Well, honestly, Gill. Why the hell didn't you tell me the truth instead of going along with me about it?'

'You didn't imagine it, Arnie,' she explained. 'I was more than three months pregnant. I lost the baby while you were unconscious.'

'What!'

'I didn't tell you the truth because I didn't think you were up to it.'

His face worked, the grape in his hand dropping to the bed and rolling on to the floor.

'Bloody 'ell, Gill.' He had turned very pale. 'That must have been a terrible blow for you on top of everything else.'

'Yes, it was.'

'Are you okay?'

'It was a huge disappointment, of course,' she said with feigned calmness. 'But, yes, I'm all right.'

'What caused it, do you know?'

She couldn't bring herself to reply.

'It was the shock of the accident, wasn't it?' he said, shooting her a look. 'That was what caused you to lose our baby.'

'No one can ever be really sure,' she said to spare him. 'These things happen.'

'It was my fault,' he said, looking stricken. 'If I hadn't had the accident, which was caused by my reckless driving—'

'Don't torture yourself,' she cut in, taking his hand. 'It just wasn't meant to be, that's all there is to it.'

'Oh, God!'

'We've an awful lot to be thankful for,' she said soothingly. 'You're alive and getting better, and we have Craig . . .'

'That doesn't alter the fact that you lost our baby through my fault and I wasn't there for you,' he said. 'You had to go through something as awful as that on your own.'

She put her arms around him and held him close. No matter how badly he'd behaved in the past, she was still in love with him. How could she tell him the extent of the damage she had suffered to her womb because of the miscarriage? He was feeling guilty enough already; it would be too cruel to throw something else at him now. It could wait until he came out of hospital.

'It's all over now,' she said. 'We have to look to the future.'

'Yeah.' He sighed deeply. 'I suppose that's all we can do.'

'It'll be lovely to have you home with us again,' she said to cheer him.

'I'm counting the days,' he said, brightening at the thought of going home.

'I bet you are.'

'I just can't wait to get back to work,' he said, a hint of the old sparkle shining in his eyes. 'It'll be so good to get those football boots on again.'

His total lack of doubt about returning to his career made her feel duty-bound to introduce a note of reality.

'Have you given any thought to what you'll do if you can't play football professionally again?' she asked.

'No.'

'Don't you think you should?'

'There's no need, because I'm determined to get back on the field.'

'But—'

'People have been more badly smashed up than I am and still got back into the game,' he told her adamantly.

'Arnie . . .'

'There's no question about it, Gill,' he said. 'It's simply a matter of determination.'

Gill was all in favour of the power of positive thinking, but it did have its limitations, especially when so many bones had been broken. But Arnie obviously wasn't ready to accept this salient fact – not for the moment, anyway.

Peter Attwood was putting away a delivery of sheet music when Gill called at the music shop in Hammersmith a few days later while Craig was at school.

'Hi, Peter.'

'Hi, Gill.'

'I've come for a browse through the music,' she said, glancing around at the selection of pianos, guitars and other musical instruments on display.

'Anything in particular?' Peter was about thirty. An arty

type with a look of faded boyishness about him, he had clear grey eyes, a prominent nose and fair hair that was long and wild. A good-natured man, casually dressed in a T-shirt and jeans, he always reminded Gill of a folk singer.

She had only got on to first-name terms with him from being a regular customer at the shop, and she knew nothing about him except that he played the guitar in his spare time. He'd been working here for about six months and seemed to be in charge, assisted by a trendy young girl called Wendy who was far more interested in selling records than musical instruments.

'Something that will appeal to children – but not nursery rhymes,' she explained. 'I've already got a good selection of those, as well as a lot of the pretty classical pieces kids play when they're learning. I saved all mine.'

'Do you give piano lessons?' he asked, pausing in what he was doing and looking at her.

'Oh, no,' she said. 'I just play for my own amusement.'

'It's worth learning an instrument so that you can do that.'

'It certainly gives me a lot of pleasure,' she said. 'I'd like my young son to learn eventually, but I don't want to force him – and I don't think he'll do it willingly because he's more interested in going out to play football.'

'Sounds pretty typical,' said Peter. 'Most kids are more interested in playing records than instruments these days, anyway.'

'He's a bit too young for that yet; he's only five,' she explained. 'It's for his fifth birthday party I want the music, actually. I thought a sing-song around the piano might keep them amused if things get out of hand when we've exhausted all the other entertainments.'

'More "That Doggie in the Window" than a Chopin polonaise then.'

'Definitely,' she said. ' "That Doggie in the Window" is a very good suggestion for the party, actually. Do you have it in stock?'

Nodding, Peter turned to the racks of sheet music at the back of the counter, pulled out the requested item and handed it to her.

'Smashing,' she said, getting her purse out of her handbag.

'Do you know anyone around here who gives piano lessons?' he asked.

'There's someone in Wallis Street,' said Gill thoughtfully.

'She doesn't do it any more apparently.'

'Really? I didn't know she'd given it up.'

'She got fed up with all the kids coming after school when she wanted to get the tea ready,' he explained.

'That is one of the drawbacks of the job.'

'What about the person who taught you?' asked Peter.

'She retired a few years ago,' said Gill. 'I know of people out of the area who give lessons, though.'

'No good, I'm afraid,' he said. 'The person who asked me, a customer here, wants someone local to teach her daughter. The girl's dead keen at the moment, apparently. Her mother wants to strike while the iron's hot.'

'Before she goes off the idea.'

'Exactly. She doesn't want her to have to travel out of the area, though.'

'Very wise.'

'I told her I'd ask around,' he said. 'I'll put a notice in the window too. There must be some qualified person needing to earn some extra cash.'

This struck a chord with Gill. She had the necessary qualifications to give private lessons. Although money wasn't a problem at the moment because the club was still paying Arnie, they wouldn't continue to do so indefinitely if he couldn't go back to work for a while – or if the worst happened and he couldn't go back to football at all.

It could take a long time for Arnie to find another means of earning a living within his capabilities. There was also the possibility of his receiving a hefty fine for dangerous driving. The few shillings she'd make from one pupil wouldn't make much difference, but at least she would be doing something to help.

And apart from the money, she liked the idea of doing something useful with her skills. At present she had time on her hands too, with Arnie being in hospital. Teaching could prove to be awkward when he came home, of course, with the television being in the same room as the piano, but that was a minor problem that could be easily solved with a little co-operation from the family.

'I wouldn't mind taking on the job myself, actually,' said Gill. 'I am qualified.'

'Oh, that would be great.' Peter smiled and handed her a pen and a piece of paper. 'Can I tell her to give you a ring?'

'You certainly can,' Gill said as she wrote down her telephone number, feeling quite excited at the idea of a new project.

The doctor in charge of Arnie's case called Gill into his office one day when she was on her way out after visiting.

'We'll be discharging your husband soon, Mrs Briscoe,' he said. He was a small, neat man with thinning hair and a moustache.

'That *is* good news,' she said with a warm smile. 'We guessed it wouldn't be long.'

'The thing is,' he said, obviously troubled, 'I don't think Mr Briscoe realises just how difficult life is going to be for him when he is back at home.'

'Oh?'

'Things are going to be very different to how they were before the accident,' he said, leaning back and putting his two forefingers under his chin meditatively.

'How different, exactly?'

'I'm afraid that you're going to have to be very patient with him until he adjusts to the situation,' he said, evading the question.

'My husband won't ever play football again, will he?' she

said. 'That's what you're trying to say.'

He tapped his chin with his pointed fingers thoughtfully. 'Miracles can happen, of course.'

'But you don't think one will happen in Arnie's case?'

'I think it's most unlikely. He'll definitely not play as a professional again.'

'Oh, God!' Although she had been trying to prepare herself and Arnie for this, it was still a crushing blow. 'Is there no chance?'

'Because his right leg was broken in so many places it is slightly shorter than the left one, as you know,' he explained. 'The limp he has been left with will be permanent. He won't be able to walk very fast, let alone run.'

Gill sighed, running her hand through her hair in agitation.

'Originally we thought we might be able to correct the imbalance, but we now know that isn't going to be possible,' he continued.

'Does Arnie know this?'

'He has been told, but I don't know if he's heard what we've been saying,' he said, frowning at her. 'We've given him the facts and told him to think in terms of alternative employment, but he doesn't seem willing to accept this.'

'No, he wouldn't.'

'He seems to think that if he's determined enough to get back into football, he can make it happen,' said the doctor. 'I don't know if determination will be enough for his employers at the football club, though.'

'I suspected this might be the case, and I've been trying to persuade him to view the situation realistically for some time,' she told him. 'But football is his life. He can't even bear to contemplate going on without it. Even when he wasn't playing as a professional he played regularly for an amateur team. For someone like Arnie it's going to be really hard.'

'He'll just have to get used to being a spectator,' said the doctor.

'Yes.' Gill brushed her brow with the back of her hand, her

thoughts racing. 'It isn't going to be easy for him to go back to working in an engineering factory after playing soccer for a living.'

The doctor's brow became even more deeply furrowed. 'He won't be up to such heavy work as that, Mrs Briscoe,' he informed her quickly.

'But that's all he knows, apart from football,' she said.

'In that case he'll have to retrain to do something else altogether,' he said. 'There's plenty of employment about.'

'Yes, I realise that, but persuading him to consider something else is going to be difficult,' she said.

'Worse things happen than having to change one's occupation,' he said in the way of someone who sees pain and disaster on a regular basis. 'At least he's alive and not brain-damaged.'

'Indeed.'

'Anyway, I'm sure you'll work it out between you.' The doctor stood up to indicate that the interview was over.

'I'm sure we will,' Gill said with false confidence.

Chapter Seven

Bracing herself for a scene, Gill went into the living room. Arnie was sitting in an armchair with his feet on the pouffe, staring blankly at a children's television programme.

'Mary will be here for her piano lesson in a minute,' she said.

'So what?' he replied, but he knew exactly what she meant.

'So . . . would you be a dear and go into the other room for half an hour?'

'No.'

'Can you turn the television off then, please?' she requested.

'No.'

'But I can't teach against that racket,' she pointed out. 'It'll be much too distracting for Mary.'

'Tough.'

'Please, Arnie . . .'

'Oh, for God's sake!' he blasted. 'Isn't a man entitled to some peace in his own house?'

'It'll only be for half an hour,' she said patiently. 'And I'm sure you're not really interested in *Small Time*.'

'That isn't the point.'

'Craig's in the kitchen having his tea,' she told him hopefully. 'Why don't you go and keep him company?'

He threw her a glare, his eyes dark with resentment. 'As if I don't have enough to put up with, being in constant pain and not having a job,' he said, steeped in self-pity. 'Now I have to get out of my armchair and have the noise of the bloody piano banging through the house, setting my nerves on edge and giving me a headache.'

'We could try to squeeze the piano into the dining room in time for future lessons, to save disturbing you,' Gill suggested.

'Don't be stupid,' Arnie said rudely. 'We won't be able to move with the piano in there.'

'I suppose not,' she was forced to agree. She felt so tense that her jaws ached from clenching her teeth and her shoulders were stiff.

It was the autumn. Arnie had been home from hospital for three months – three months of hell for them both. He sat around the house all day sinking ever deeper into despair, angry with the world in general because he no longer had a future as a professional footballer.

Gill's compassion and patience were being stretched to the limit, especially as Arnie made no effort to look for a job – mainly, she suspected, because he had lost confidence in himself. She truly believed that gainful employment was the cure to his depression, but whenever she suggested he look for work he flew into a rage and accused her of being heartless.

'I'm sorry my teaching upsets you so much, love, but it's too late now to cancel today's lesson,' she said with determined tolerance. 'Mary will already be on her way here.'

With seething irritation Arnie got up, slowly and laboriously because of the lingering pain from his injuries, the effort of his movements exaggerated to gain sympathy. 'You can tell her mother not to bring her again,' he ordered. 'I'm not having my life disrupted every Wednesday afternoon.'

Her heart was pounding. She knew she must stand up to him.

'I'm not going to do that,' she told him.

His frown grew darker. 'You are, you know.'

'No I'm not . . . for two reasons,' she said. 'Firstly, because I've made a commitment to Mary—'

'Someone else will have to teach her,' he interrupted.

'You're not the only person in London qualified to teach the piano.'

'And secondly,' she continued determinedly, 'because we need the money.'

'Rubbish,' he said dismissively. 'Our mortgage repayments are low because we bought the house so cheap. Anyway, we've still got some of the cash I saved when I was earning big money.'

'That won't last long now that the football club have stopped paying you,' she wisely pointed out. 'Especially as we had to pay your fine for dangerous driving.'

'That's right, have a go at me about it,' he said, immediately on the defensive.

'I wasn't—'

'Yes you were,' he said maliciously. 'You're always getting at me.'

'Not intentionally.'

'I'll get a job when something I know I can do comes along, and not before,' he stated firmly, as though she had accused him of something.

She took a deep breath and silently counted to ten. 'I'm not getting at you, Arnie, honestly,' she said. 'I realise how difficult life must be for you at the moment. I'm just trying to be realistic about money.'

'We're not exactly on the bread-line,' he said aggressively.

'No, but—'

'It isn't as though I don't bring money into the house,' he cut in gruffly. 'There's my disability allowance.'

'Yes, and it's a great help,' she said, 'but it won't be enough when our savings run out.'

'The little bit you earn from teaching isn't enough to make any difference.'

'It's a contribution.'

'Not much of one.'

'Well, I'm going to continue to do it, because I feel I must do anything I can to help with things as they are at the moment,' she said firmly. 'Anyway, I enjoy it.'

'You're lucky to have something you really enjoy,' he said miserably.

'Yes, I am – very lucky,' she said, and she meant it. Music was a joy and companion, especially now that Arnie was so difficult to live with. Her piano soothed her nerves and provided an escape from the constant pressure of his black moods. 'I'm really sorry you lost what you love to do.'

'Me an' all.'

The doorbell rang.

'So, are you going to co-operate with me on the question of Mary's lesson?' Gill asked.

'I don't have much choice do I?' he growled, and limped painfully towards the kitchen while Gill went to answer the door.

She greeted her pupil, who was accompanied by her mother. The latter was about to depart as Gill ushered Mary inside, when she turned back.

'Oh, before I forget, Mrs Briscoe,' she said, 'a friend of mine is looking for a piano teacher for her daughter. I've told her how good you are with Mary and she asked me to ask you if you might consider taking her daughter on too.'

Another pupil would double the trouble I have from Arnie, was Gill's first thought.

'She's the same age as Mary,' the woman continued when Gill didn't reply. 'And she's very bright and keen to learn.'

But it would also double her earnings, and they were going to need every penny if Arnie didn't pull himself together and get a job soon.

'Yes,' she said decisively. 'Can you tell your friend to give me a ring and we'll get something arranged?'

Despite all the problems this was going to cause, Gill was thrilled to have her teaching skills recommended.

'Wotcha, Arnie,' greeted Phoebe one afternoon a few weeks later when she happened to meet her son in North End Road market. 'What are you doing around here?'

'Just mooching about to pass the time away,' he said. 'You not at work today?'

'I've got a day off, love.' She looked at her shopping bag. 'I've just been to the butcher's for a couple o' pork chops for tea. Though I dunno why I bother as far as John is concerned – he rushes in from work, gets changed and goes out again without noticing what he's eating. I could put fried doormat on the table and he'd scoff it. Teenagers, eh? Who'd have 'em?'

'Is he still knocking around with Head-Butter Harris and his crowd?' Arnie enquired, referring to a friend of his brother's who was well known for using his head as a battering ram on anyone who upset him.

'Yeah, unfortunately.'

'That gang o' losers are bad news.'

'You're telling me, but John thinks they're the next best thing to the Beatles.'

'He should steer clear of 'em.'

'I know, but what can I do about it?' Phoebe said worriedly. 'He's sixteen and working and paying his way at home. I can't tell him who to go out with, and neither can you.'

'No, I suppose not,' agreed Arnie. 'But I don't like it. He'll end up in trouble if he carries on hanging out with them.'

They moved out of the way of the tangled crowds. People were queuing at a nearby fruit and veg stall which was bright with oranges and shiny green apples, and a colourful autumn display of carrots, swedes and parsnips just asking to be made into stew. They continued their conversation outside the baker's, near a stall selling army surplus clothing.

'Anyway, how are you, son?' asked Phoebe.

'Surviving,' Arnie replied glumly.

'Cor, you've got a face like a bunch o' leeks,' she said. 'Cheer up, for Gawd's sake.'

'What is there to cheer up about?' he asked gloomily. 'I've got no job, and I've been chucked out of my armchair again 'cause Gill's teaching some snotty-nosed kid the piano.'

'The fresh air will do you good on a lovely afternoon like this,' Phoebe told him. Indeed it was glorious autumn weather, with hazy sunshine and a sharp chill in the air which was fragrant with the scent of bonfires.

'Bloody nuisance,' Arnie grumbled. 'The house is being turned into a music school.'

'Gill's doing her best to help out, love,' Phoebe admonished. 'Anyway, she's only got about four or five pupils, hasn't she?'

'At the moment, yeah. But it won't end there, will it?' he said. 'Not now that she's building a reputation for herself. And she doesn't seem willing to turn anyone away.'

'You should be proud of her for having the gumption to earn a few bob, not complain about it,' said Phoebe. 'Anyway, if you weren't moping around the house all day you wouldn't be inconvenienced by the piano lessons.'

'Don't you start,' he snapped. 'I know I ought to be providing for my family—'

'Course you should.' Phoebe thought a spot of brutal candour might shake her son out of the doldrums.

'And it's that easy, I suppose – when half the bones in my body have been broken.'

'They're mended now, son.'

'After a fashion.'

'You've had a very bad time, Arnie, but you're better now,' his mother said gravely. 'Okay, so you still have a certain amount of pain, you walk with a limp and you can't do the sort of work you're used to. But you're not incapable. And it isn't good for you to sit about the house all day feeling sorry for yourself. I'm sure you'd find some suitable work if only you'd look.'

'Oh, yeah, they're crying out for smashed-up ex-footballers.'

Phoebe was about to tick him off for being sarcastic when the utter despair she saw in his eyes touched her heart.

'It was the only thing I was any good at, Mum,' he said.

'I know how much your football career meant to you, son,' she said, swallowing hard on the lump in her throat, 'but you can learn to be good at something else . . .'

'You can't know what it's like to lose something so important.'

'Look, why don't you come home with me for a cuppa?' she suggested kindly. 'A chat with your mum might help.'

Looking into her face, Arnie wanted to weep with love. There was pure kindness in those vivid blue eyes, feathered with lines now, her plump cheeks brightened by rouge and the nip in the air, her bleached hair short and backcombed into a bouffant. He wanted to bare his soul to her, and to luxuriate in the warmth and comfort of her unconditional love. The child in him cried out for her to take away the black depression that shadowed his life and controlled his actions, making him mean to his wife even though he hated himself for it.

How wonderful to be a boy again, to have his mother talk him out of the clinging guilt over his reckless driving. An action that had killed the child Gill had been carrying and robbed him of his career and confidence, leaving him incapable of providing for his family and even more weighed down by conscience.

His mother was right. He probably could find a job, and every day he intended to start looking. He studied the newspaper, the advertisements for storemen and light labourers; he even occasionally got as far as the door of the labour exchange. But he couldn't bring himself to go inside because he felt worthless and unfit to take up any sort of employment. As each day passed with an increasing sense of failure, his confidence diminished further.

'You coming then, love?' asked Phoebe, recalling him to the present.

The temptation to go with her was strong . . . but he was pathetic enough already, without turning to his mother. He knew he must find the strength for himself, to defeat the self-pity of which he was so ashamed but unable to dispel.

'No, I'd better be getting back home,' he said. 'We'll do it another day.'

'Just as you like, son,' Phoebe said amicably.

'Tata, Mum,' he said, kissing her cheek. 'See you soon.'

'See you, son. Give my love to Gill.'

'Will do.'

Watching him walk away with his dragging limp, she felt his pain as her own. Her son was obviously a very troubled man. As an adult he must work these problems out for himself, she knew that; but her maternal instincts made her want to go after him and cuddle him, make him feel better, as she had done when he was a boy.

One evening in January of the following year, after Craig had gone to bed, and Gill and Arnie were relaxing by the fire in the living room, Gill said, 'I think it would be a good idea for me to take on more pupils and build up a proper teaching business.'

'Oh, nice,' Arnie said with bitter irony. 'And I'm supposed to sit in the dining room or kitchen for hours on end while you do it, I suppose.'

'No. If I were to do this as a proper business we'd have to make some changes,' she said. 'We could turn the playroom into a music room and give Craig the spare bedroom for his toys. The playroom would make an ideal room for teaching, being downstairs and near the front door. Pupils could come and go without invading our privacy as much as they do at the moment.'

'But the piano is a part of the furniture in here,' he said, looking fondly at it.

'I wouldn't use this piano,' she said, glancing towards the shiny black Steinway and feeling a pang of regret at what she was planning to do. 'I'd use my old piano from Mum and Dad's.'

'Have two pianos, you mean?'

'No, sell this one and use the old one for the lessons,' she said. 'All it needs is a good tuning and it'll be perfectly adequate. I tried it out the other day when I was round at Mum's.'

Arnie looked grim. 'You want to sell the piano I gave you as a present?' he said, sounding very hurt.

'Of course I don't *want* to sell it,' Gill assured him. 'But we have to be practical, Arnie. We need the money.'

'We're not that desperate.'

'We're heading that way,' she said. 'Now that all our savings have gone things are going to get really dodgy. The fact is, we simply can't afford such an expensive luxury as a beautiful piano when I can use the other one as a working tool and for my own pleasure.'

'I do bring in my disability allowance, you know,' he reminded her, trying as usual to justify himself.

'Stop defending yourself, love,' she said with feeling. 'There's no need. You've provided for us well over the years. Now it's my turn to do something to bring in some cash until you find a job that's suitable for you.'

'I still don't see the necessity,' Arnie said. The idea of his wife being the breadwinner was abhorrent to him.

'If we don't address the problem now we'll start to run up debts,' she said. 'I don't want to have to tell Craig he can't have new football boots or the things the other kids are having, when I know I have it in my power to help us keep a reasonable standard of living. If I do well, we might even be able to afford to run a car again.'

Arnie grunted.

'Selling the piano will give us some capital while I build up my teaching business,' Gill went on. 'I've been turning people away because having pupils in the living room is too disruptive to our family life. If we make the playroom into a music room, you and Craig won't be inconvenienced at all and I can give lessons on Saturdays too. It'll take some of the pressure off you if I'm earning more money, give you time to find a job you feel happy with.'

Although he could see the wisdom of her plan, it heightened Arnie's sense of inadequacy. But there was a new radiance about his wife that made his heart turn over. However low he had sunk, and however badly he behaved towards her, she still meant everything to him.

'You really want to do this, don't you, Gill?' he said.

'Yes, I do.'

'I suppose we'd better get it organised then,' he said, smiling properly at her for the first time in ages.

'Oh, that's great.' She went over to him and wrapped her arms around him in a spontaneous burst of affection. 'I do love you.'

'I love you too,' he said, kissing her.

Such tender moments between them were rare these days. But when they did happen, Gill knew that no matter how bad things had got between them, they did have something special.

'Can I have some more apple pie please, Gran?' asked Craig one Sunday in March.

'Course you can, love. Pass your plate to me.' Winnie took his plate and glanced around the table at which her family were having Sunday dinner. 'Anyone else for seconds?'

'I wouldn't mind a bit more please,' said Dougie, handing her his plate.

'He never can resist your apple pie, Mum. Can you, Dougie?' said Carol.

'I'm hooked, I admit it,' he laughed.

'You can blame Winnie's pastry for my paunch,' said Hal.

'Well, Carol, now you know how to keep Dougie happy after you're married,' said Gill, grinning. 'Get Mum's recipe and give him apple pie and custard for Sunday afters.'

'And while we're on the subject of your getting married,' Arnie teased, 'isn't it about time you tied the knot?'

'It's funny you should say that . . .' said Carol meaningfully, smiling coyly and nudging her fiancé.

All eyes were on the couple.

'You've set the date at last?' Gill asked.

'Yeah. We've decided on a September wedding,' Carol beamed. 'So you've all got plenty of time to get fixed up with your new outfits.' She turned to Gill excitedly. 'I'd like you to be my matron of honour and Craig to be my pageboy.'

'We'd be honoured,' said Gill.

The atmosphere became charged with excitement as the family discussed the forthcoming nuptials. Winnie wondered how different this wedding would be to Gill's sorry affair. Carol and Dougie had been engaged for a year, which had given her and Hal time to save up, hoping to give their daughter a proper send-off. Winnie was really looking forward to making all the arrangements, having been unable to provide all the trimmings for her eldest daughter.

'So, your days of freedom are numbered then, mate,' joked Arnie. 'Well, it happens to the best of us in the end.'

'Enough of that sort of talk,' said Gill, giving her husband a playful slap on the arm. 'It works two ways. Carol is giving up her freedom too.'

'And I just can't wait,' she said, squeezing her fiancé's arm lovingly. 'I'll be happy to be enslaved to Dougie.'

Oh, if only she wouldn't be so obviously besotted, Gill thought, burning with vicarious embarrassment. Despite her warnings, Carol still smothered the poor boy with cloying lovey-doveyness. Her eagerness to get him to the altar worried Gill, especially as she sometimes detected a pained look in Dougie's eyes.

'What more can any man want from a wife?' laughed Arnie.

As her concern for Carol passed off, Gill felt warm inside at this happy family occasion. It was a treat to see Arnie so relaxed. Although she often found it hard to like him these days, she still loved him desperately and wanted the best for him. But she knew this affable mood wouldn't last. He was still a very tortured man.

Mary Mitchell was sitting very upright at the piano as she came to the end of *Für Elise*, which was one of the pieces in her exam repertoire. When she'd finished, she turned to her teacher expectantly.

'That's coming on very well, Mary,' Gill said encouragingly. 'There's still a few weeks to go till the exam and you're almost ready. Keep practising, and don't forget to go over the scales.' She looked at her watch. 'That's all for this week. I'll see you again at the same time next week.'

The child slipped off the piano stool and gathered her music. 'Thank you, Mrs Briscoe.' Mary was a thin, sensitive child with dark eyes and brown hair tied back in a pony tail.

'You're welcome.'

Outside in the hall, a nine-year-old boy called Matthew Tucker was sitting on a chair waiting for his lesson, alongside Mary's mother who had come to take her daughter home. Gill and Mrs Mitchell exchanged a few words before Gill saw them out and ushered Matthew into the music room.

It was June, and she now had twenty weekly pupils and a waiting list. This was a particularly busy time for her, as she was preparing entrants for the thrice-yearly exams which would take place here, in the presence of an official examiner from one of the London Colleges of Music.

She was enjoying the work more than she'd imagined possible. It was a good feeling to be part of a child's musical development, working closely with them and watching their technique improve. Some pupils were really hard work, though, especially those who took lessons only because they had been persuaded to do it by their parents. When Gill came across a child with no aptitude for music and even less interest – rather than someone who was just a bit lazy about practising – she told their parents she would rather not continue, preferring to spend her time on someone with a genuine wish to learn.

Determined that her family life would be disrupted as little as possible by her new career, she made a point of being organised. She got up early to keep on top of the household chores, prepared meals in advance, and made sure that the teaching didn't encroach upon any time she wanted to spend with Craig and Arnie.

Arnie didn't actively stand in her way now that she worked in a separate room. But neither did he take much of an interest. It was almost as though he was pretending it wasn't happening. She knew he thought he was failing her because she was making a substantial contribution to their family budget. No matter how often she told him that she enjoyed the work and would want to do it even if they didn't need the money, he still castigated himself. There were brief spells of harmony between them, but tension was always simmering just below the surface.

Although she wanted to help him more than anything in the world, she knew this was something he must solve himself. She still thought the answer lay in employment, which would give him back his self-respect. But while she could gently suggest that he might try harder to get a job, to come on too strong about it could be even more damaging to his self-esteem.

Her teaching took the pressure off him financially, but was stressful to him because of the guilt he insisted on carrying. But it was a crucial outlet for Gill; it made her less susceptible to Arnie's bad temper because she was busy teaching for several hours every day.

'Right then, Matthew,' she said to her next pupil, who was one of her most reluctant and not an exam candidate. 'I'd like to hear you play the scale of C major, please.'

A fat boy with a moon face and a mop of ginger hair and freckles, Matthew Tucker was daydreaming and didn't reply.

'Matthew?'

'Yes?'

'C major, please.'

He gave an eloquent sigh, put his fingers to the keys and produced a noise so punishing Gill had to ask him to stop.

'You don't enjoy your piano lessons, do you, Matthew?'

He turned scarlet and chewed his bottom lip nervously.

'You can be honest with me, I won't bite you,' she said.

'Well . . . it's just that I'm no good at it, miss,' he said, adding bravely, 'and I don't want to be either.'

'You have no interest at all, do you?'

He turned to her slowly, lowering his eyes shamefully.

'It's nothing to be ashamed of, you know,' she told him.

'Isn't it?' he said, sounding surprised.

'Of course not.'

His face lit up, as though she had physically lifted a burden from him. 'I thought . . .'

'Well you thought wrong,' she said. 'We can't all enjoy the same things. I expect you have other hobbies you're good at.'

'I'm good at drawing and painting,' he said.

'There you are, then.'

'But Mummy says I'll regret it later on if I don't learn to play now. My cousin is brilliant at the piano. He wins medals for it.'

That explains a lot, thought Gill, but she said, 'I'll have a word with your mother about your finishing lessons.'

'Cor, thanks, Mrs Briscoe,' he enthused, smiling properly for the first time since Gill had known him. It was like looking at a different boy.

'Are you saying that you don't want to continue teaching Matthew?' said the boy's mother, a matronly woman with an expensive but frumpish look about her.

'It isn't a question of my not wanting to,' explained Gill. 'It's just that it's a waste of my time.'

'Hardly, since I'm paying you.'

They were in the music room, Matthew now waiting outside in the hall. The late-afternoon sunshine shafted through the window, striking the corner of Gill's desk which was piled high with music theory papers to mark and other general paperwork.

'I'm not in business to force punishment on children who have no interest in the piano and who, therefore, are never likely to get to grips with it,' she explained.

'It's merely a question of perseverence,' insisted Mrs Tucker.

'But learning the piano is agony for Matthew,' Gill informed her.

'I didn't like mathematics when I was at school, but I had to do it,' was Mrs Tucker's answer to that. 'That's life. We all have to do things we don't care for. It helps in the process of character building.'

'Some things must be endured for success in later life, I agree,' said Gill. 'But music is a different thing altogether.'

'It takes a lot of effort, the same as anything else.'

'It also requires a certain amount of aptitude,' said Gill. 'I don't believe in forcing the piano on anyone. Children have quite enough compulsory subjects to learn at school.'

'He'll thank me later on.'

'It's far more likely that he'll never go near a piano again once he's of an age to please himself.'

'I shall get another teacher for him,' snorted Mrs Tucker.

'That's entirely up to you,' said Gill, irritated by the woman's lack of consideration, the blatant snobbery that made her want to indulge in one-upmanship through her child.

'It certainly is,' Mrs Tucker said and swept out of the room.

Standing at the front door, watching her march down the path dragging Matthew by the hand, Gill knew she had done the right thing in refusing to continue. But she pitied poor Matthew, who might not have such an understanding piano teacher next time.

'Do I *have* to be a pageboy at Auntie Carol's wedding on Saturday?' asked Craig one Sunday lunchtime in the autumn of that same year.

'Yes you do,' declared Gill with an air of finality.

'But M-u-m, all my friends will laugh at me,' he wailed.

'None of your friends will see you,' Gill reminded him.

'There'll be other kids around, though, won't there?' he complained. 'I mean, I'm gonna have to go outside in that stupid outfit.'

'I thought it looked quite smart,' said Arnie helpfully.

'It's very smart,' said Gill, looking at Arnie. 'He looks smashing in it.'

'I look like a pansy.'

'Don't be silly,' said Gill.

'Never mind, son,' said Arnie. 'You won't have to keep it on for long. As soon as the photographs have been taken you can get changed into your ordinary clothes.'

'Can't Auntie Carol get someone else to do it?' he whined.

'Certainly not,' said Gill firmly. 'You can't let her down now. She wants you as her pageboy and you should be honoured to be asked. Anyway, you might enjoy it when the time comes.'

'I won't.'

'I should forget all about it until Saturday if I were you,' Arnie said. 'And in the meantime, how about going over the park for a kick-about this afternoon?' Although he could no longer play football as such, he could still throw and stop shots for Craig.

The boy brightened considerably. 'Cor, yeah! That would be smashing, Dad,' he enthused.

'I fancy a walk too,' said Gill. 'So I'll come along with you.'

They set off, Craig running ahead and bouncing the ball, looking colourful in a Fair Isle sweater and blue trousers. It was a fine September afternoon, the low sun shining from a steely blue sky and gleaming on the privet hedges hung with spider's webs, the grey streets looking even dustier in the glare.

'God knows how we're gonna get him into his wedding clothes on Saturday,' said Gill as they strolled into Bishop's

Park and walked beneath the luxuriant trees, the neat paths banked on either side with fallen leaves. 'Velvet and satin isn't exactly his thing.'

'I'll threaten to confiscate his football if he plays up,' said Arnie.

'If anything will do it, that will,' she said with a chuckle, enjoying the rare moment of togetherness.

'He's growing fast,' Arnie remarked.

'Yeah. Six years old,' she said. 'It hardly seems possible.'

'It certainly doesn't,' he agreed heartily. 'Makes you realise that it's time he had a brother or sister.'

Gill went cold. Arnie had been too wrapped up in himself since the accident to think about increasing their family, and because he'd had such personal problems she hadn't had the heart to tell him that this was no longer possible. Now she knew she must.

Steeling herself for his reaction, she said, 'I can't have any more children, Arnie.'

He halted in his step and turned to her. 'No more kids?' he said, looking puzzled.

'When I had the miscarriage my womb was damaged,' she explained.

'Huh! Nice of you to tell me,' he said with withering sarcasm.

'I should have, I know,' she said, 'but you had so much else to cope with, I didn't want to dish out more bad news . . . and it's not as though we've been considering trying for another baby since the miscarriage.'

'Even so, I should have been told.'

'I'm sorry. I didn't want to—'

'Make me feel more guilty,' he finished for her bitterly. 'Because it's my fault . . . because of the accident . . .'

'No, that isn't the reason,' she said. 'I saw no point in telling you something I knew would upset you when it wasn't necessary.'

'Spare me the pity.'

'I was waiting for the right opportunity.'

'Oh, God,' he said. 'Will the long-term effects of that bloody accident never stop coming?'

'It isn't the end of the world, Arnie,' she pointed out.

'Feels like it.'

'We have Craig.'

'My fault,' he muttered as though he hadn't heard her.

Sometimes Gill had had moments of desolation on this subject herself; occasionally she had experienced rage when she considered the fact that it need never have happened. But it wasn't going to help Arnie or her marriage for her to tell him this. 'Try not to brood on it, love,' she said.

'How can I not?'

'I've managed to accept it,' she said. 'You must do the same.'

'Yeah, I know,' he said, but she knew he didn't mean it.

Craig was bouncing the ball excitedly and shouting to his father, so Arnie limped across the grass to join him. Gill walked over to a wooden bench near the gently undulating river, tinted green in places by the sun. The quiet presence of the Thames was achingly sad to Gill at that moment, as she sat down and watched father and son enjoying each other's company. Despite the happy scene before her, she knew another brief period of marital bliss had been shattered.

Gill and Craig travelled together in the wedding car to the church on Saturday. Arnie was one of the ushers, so had gone on ahead. The weather was fine, and Craig looked a picture in his red velvet jacket with black satin trousers and a white shirt with a lace ruffle, his face scrubbed and rosy, curly hair combed neatly into place. Although she knew he would never admit it, Gill suspected that he was rather enjoying the attention now that the show had actually begun. She was wearing a pale peach satin dress and carrying a posy of freesias.

Arnie and the other ushers were outside the church when

they arrived. 'The bridegroom hasn't arrived yet,' Arnie said in a low voice as he helped Gill out of the car into the sunshine.

'The best man?'

'Neither of 'em.'

'Oh, dear.'

'Probably held up in traffic,' suggested Arnie.

'I hope he isn't going to keep Carol waiting,' said Gill as they went into the cool, dim church and stood at the back to wait. 'He won't live to enjoy his honeymoon if he does.'

'He'll be here in a minute,' said Arnie, going back outside.

She straightened Craig's collar and patted his hair proudly, feeling the buzz of excited apprehension rippling through the pews as the guests waited for the main protagonists to arrive. Heads turned and people smiled in approval as they caught a glimpse of the matron of honour and pageboy in their wedding finery.

The expectant hush soon became a murmur of concern, however, when events didn't progress as expected.

Gill went to the church door and peered outside to see Arnie waving the bridal car on, indicating to the driver to go around the block again. And still they waited. She had a sudden chilling memory of the trapped look she had sometimes seen in Dougie's eyes when he and Carol were together.

My God. He isn't going to come, she thought with horror.

She was right. A few moments later the best man arrived with the awful news that Dougie wasn't coming. They were to tell Carol that he was very sorry but he just couldn't go through with it!

'Bloody 'ell,' said Arnie. 'What are we gonna do now?'

Chapter Eight

The stunned congregation trailed out of the church murmuring among themselves, the bride having been taken home without even getting out of the car. As it was too late to cancel the wedding reception at a local hotel, Winnie suggested the guests should go to it anyway.

'No point in wasting all that food and drink,' Hal told them, taking control because Winnie had gone home to look after Carol. 'You were all expecting a party, so a party you'll have.'

Dougie's relatives were too embarrassed to stay, but most of the guests on Carol's side went along to the hotel, their mood respectfully subdued. Arnie and Hal looked after things there while Gill and Winnie tried to console the heartbroken Carol.

'How could he have done it to me?' she wailed, lying on her bed in her dressing gown, her face tear-stained and streaked with mascara, her carefully chosen wedding dress in a heap on the floor where she insisted it stayed. 'I really believed that he loved me.'

'This doesn't necessarily mean that he doesn't,' said Gill.

'He's got a damned funny way of showing it if he does,' snorted Winnie, tactless in her rage.

'All right, Mum, don't rub it in,' sobbed Carol.

'It's marriage he's rejected, Carol – not you personally,' Gill said in an effort to revive her sister's shattered confidence. 'He'll have got cold feet about the responsibility. Some men are really frightened of that.'

'He certainly chose his time to back out,' declared Winnie

angrily. 'I'll murder the bugger if I ever set eyes on him again.'

'You won't have to if I get to him first,' said Gill.

She could have told her sister that she'd seen this coming and had tried to warn her. But it would only add to her pain, so was best left unsaid. All she could do to help Carol was to be there with moral support and friendship. Sadly, though, there seemed to be nothing anyone could do to ease her pain, and Gill felt frustrated by her own powerlessness.

As Christmas approached and the world mourned President Kennedy's assassination in November, Arnie sunk to a low personal ebb and took to drowning his sorrows of an evening in the pub with his mates. While Gill was all in favour of his having some male companionship, he made too much of a habit of it, and soon the cost of his drinking became an expense they couldn't afford.

But if she dared to comment on it he lost his temper and accused her of penny-pinching. The situation between them was becoming intolerable, and she couldn't see things improving unless he regained his self-respect. Unfortunately there was only one way to do that and he wouldn't make any effort towards it at all . . .

One morning in early December when she happened to be in Fulham Broadway, she saw something that gave her an idea. An empty shop was being refitted, and on the window was a notice announcing the forthcoming opening of a branch of Bex Sports. This was a reputable firm of sportsgear retailers with branches in various areas of London. Gill had often used their Hammersmith shop for stuff that Craig needed.

The proprietor of the company was a well-known West London entrepreneur called Len Bex who was a retired professional footballer. Gill didn't know him personally, but she'd heard a lot about him, as most Fulham residents had. He was a hard nut with a soft centre, apparently. If you crossed him you'd be made to regret it, but if you earned his trust there was nothing he wouldn't do for you.

Seeing some shopfitters working inside, she went in and asked how she might contact Mr Bex.

'He's usually at the Hammersmith shop,' said one of the men. 'The main Bex Sports office is over the top of it.'

'Thanks very much,' she said, and left with a spring to her step.

'So, what can I do for you, ducks?' asked Len Bex, a robust man of about fifty with a solid jaw, shrewd brown eyes, and a nose shaped like the jagged edge of a broken bottle. He had a shock of white hair and thick, riotous eyebrows of the same colour. Though his harsh features gave him a look of toughness, he exuded charisma by the bucketful. His mode of dress was smart if somewhat flamboyant: he was wearing a silver-grey continental suit, a shocking-pink shirt and a multi-coloured tie.

Gill had not given her reasons for wanting to see him to the person she'd spoken to when she'd telephoned for an appointment. She'd simply said it was a personal matter, and was now in his office over the shop in Hammersmith, talking to him across his desk.

'I think you and I might be able to help each other,' she said.

'Oh?'

'I'm Arnie Briscoe's wife,' she explained. 'He used to play for Borough FC.'

'I remember Arnie,' he said in a warm tone. 'I used to be a great fan of his.'

'You weren't alone in that.'

'I heard about his accident,' he said, looking concerned. 'He's a great loss to the game.'

'The game is a great loss to him, too.'

'How is he now?'

'Not too bad.'

'What's he doing these days?'

'Nothing very much,' she said. 'Being forced to come out

122

of the game at such an early stage really knocked the stuffing out of him and he hasn't found anything suitable in the way of a job yet.'

Len shook his head slowly and sighed. 'It's a bugger when that happens to you,' he said, sucking in his breath loudly. 'I know that only too well.'

'Really?'

'Oh, yes. I had to retire from the game early because of injury too. It took me quite a while to get back on my feet. It's a hard thing to come to terms with.'

'The thing is, Mr Bex,' Gill said, emboldened by her belief in what she was about to suggest. 'I've noticed that you're opening a shop in Fulham in the new year, and I think Arnie would be an asset to you as a member of staff.'

'You do?'

'Yes I do,' she said without hesitation. 'He knows everything there is to know about football gear and he's still enough of a name in sporting circles to attract punters into your shop.'

Bex leaned forward, his chin resting on his linked hands, observing her thoughtfully. 'I quite believe it, my dear,' he said. 'But if Arnie wants a job, why doesn't he come to see me himself?'

'Because he doesn't see himself as an asset to anyone,' she explained, 'so there's no chance of his applying for a job with you or anyone else for that matter. He thinks he has nothing to offer now that he can't play football. It wouldn't even occur to him that he could be useful to you, and he'd be furious if he knew I'd come to see you with the idea of your offering him a job.'

'Mm . . . I see.'

'He doesn't have any experience of the retail trade, but he has a good all-round knowledge of sport so he could converse intelligently with the customers,' she went on. 'And he'd soon get the hang of working behind a counter.'

'Would he be up to shop-work physically, though?' Len enquired. 'He'd be on his feet for a lot of the day.'

'I'm sure he'd be fine,' she said. 'It's just heavy work he can't cope with now.'

He stroked his chin, mulling it over.

'I'm not asking for charity,' Gill was quick to point out. 'I really do believe that if you were to give Arnie a chance, you wouldn't regret it.'

Len knew what she said made sense. Players of Arnie Briscoe's calibre were long remembered. He'd been a hero in his day and would be an attraction to the punters for years to come. He knew he couldn't afford to be sentimental when it came to business – he'd worked too hard for what he had to lose any of it by being soft – but giving Arnie Briscoe a chance could prove to be a really smart move.

'If you don't have any vacancies at the moment, maybe you could bear him in mind for later,' Gill was saying persuasively.

'Wait here a minute, ducks,' Len said. He left the room, returning a moment later with the woman who had been in the shop when Gill arrived and had shown her up to the office. He introduced her as his wife, Mary.

Shaking her hand, Gill saw a woman of about the same age as Len, with shortish white hair and warm brown eyes. She was plump and pink-cheeked and had a homely look about her, being plainly dressed in a navy blue jumper and grey pleated skirt. Her appearance was in total contrast to that of her flashy husband, but somehow they seemed exactly right together.

'I've been helping out in the shop,' Mary explained, sitting down at the other desk in the room. 'I quite enjoy a break from the office now and again. It helps to keep me in touch with the grass roots of the business.'

'Mary and I run the firm together,' explained Len. 'And I never make an important decision without talking it over with her first.'

Instinctively liking the other woman, Gill said, 'I see.'

'This young lady is married to Arnie Briscoe, love,' Len told his wife.

'What – the Arnie Brisco who used to play for Borough FC?' Mary asked in a soft, slightly husky voice.

'That's the one,' said Gill, proud of the instant recognition of her husband's name.

'Mrs Briscoe has come to put a proposition to us,' said Len, and he went on to tell his wife about Gill's suggestion.

'Sounds like a good idea to me,' said Mary, 'and we do need staff for the Fulham shop.'

'It would have to be for a trial period, though,' said Len.

'Of course,' said Gill.

'But tell me . . .' said Len, peering at her. 'If Arnie isn't going to come to see me about a job, and he mustn't know that you've been here, how am I going to take him on?'

'Hmmmm . . . You do have a point there,' Gill admitted.

But Mary had an idea. 'You could just happen to come across Arnie somewhere, Len . . . in the pub he uses, for instance,' she suggested, turning to her husband. 'You could say you recognise him from his playing days and get talking to him the way men do in pubs. When he says he isn't working, you can offer him a job as though the idea has only just occurred to you.'

Len gave his wife a crooked smile and Gill perceived real devotion between them. 'My wife is the brains of our operation,' he said, looking at Gill.

'I can see,' she smiled.

'So . . . tell me which pub your husband uses and when I'm likely to find him there.'

'The Big Bell in Fulham, and he's there most evenings, unfortunately,' she said.

'Right. I'll make a point of being there one night soon then,' he said.

'Thanks ever so much,' Gill beamed. 'This could be just what Arnie needs to put him back on his feet.'

'He's a very lucky man to have a wife who cares enough about him to go to all this trouble for him,' said Mary.

'Whatever you do, don't let him know I approached you

125

on his behalf,' she said to Len urgently. 'He won't even consider the job if he finds out I had a hand in it. He's fiercely proud.'

'Don't worry, my dear, we'll keep shtum,' Len promised.

'We won't breathe a word,' added Mary.

For the first time in ages there was a happy atmosphere in the Briscoe household in the run-up to Christmas. Arnie was in such good spirits; it was incredible the difference the offer of a job had made to him.

'Len Bex wants me to work in the new shop he's opening in Fulham Broadway in the new year,' he'd said excitedly, having told Gill all about his 'chance' meeting with the well-known entrepreneur in the Big Bell. 'But they can use me at the Hammersmith branch right away, with it being so busy just before Christmas. So I'm going there to help out and learn the job.'

'Sounds right up your street.'

'I do fancy working there, I must admit,' he confessed. 'I'd never have thought of it if he hadn't approached me. But he really seems to want me on the staff.'

'I should think so too, Arnie . . . You'll be good for his business with your wide knowledge of sport,' she said innocently.

'He's a really nice bloke,' remarked Arnie. 'We hit it off right away. We've a lot in common, both being ex-footballers.'

'I'm so pleased things are looking up for you,' she said.

There were times when subterfuge was permissible, she told herself, and this was definitely one of them.

December was hectic for Gill, with the piano exams to organise as well as the family's Christmas preparations. There was always a feeling of excitement in the house on exam days with candidates coming and going, usually accompanied by parents. Gill used her living room as a waiting room because there tended to be a build-up of people and the hall wasn't big enough. To make a special occasion of it, she filled vases with fresh flowers and dressed in something smart – as did most of the candidates, since looking one's best is a great confidence booster. The atmosphere was charged with nervous expectation, and Gill made sure she was on hand with praise and encouragement.

Once the exams were over she threw herself into the Christmas preparations, enjoying it all the more with the return of Arnie's good humour. They went to her parents' for Christmas Day and invited the Millers and the Briscoes to their place on Boxing Day.

After a traditional Boxing Day lunch of cold turkey and pickles, they lounged around chatting and eating sweets. When Arnie decided to take Craig to the park for some exercise and fresh air, Carol and John joined them.

'Carol still seems a bit down in the dumps,' remarked Phoebe after they'd gone.

'She'll get over it,' said Winnie, whose pride wouldn't allow her to admit to Phoebe how worried she was about Carol.

'It's bound to take time for the poor girl to get over a thing like that,' said Phoebe kindly.

'Mm.' Winnie nodded.

Gill was also worried about her sister. She never went out now except to work, and spent most of the time at home alone in her room. Gill had never known her to be so quiet and withdrawn. She had given her an open invitation to visit any time, but Carol had not been near Gill's place since that heartbreaking fiasco in the autumn. To help take her mind off things Gill had suggested that they go to see a show one evening together, or to the cinema while Arnie looked after Craig, but Carol didn't seem to want to do anything.

'It's still early days,' she said now to ease her mother's mind. 'Three months isn't long when you think of what she's been through.'

'True,' said Phoebe.

* * *

Curiously, Carol seemed to have undergone a transformation by the time they got back from the park. She was smiling and full of beans.

'What did you do to Carol when you were out to get her smiling?' Gill asked Arnie after tea when they were both in the kitchen.

'Nothing that I know of,' he said.

'Well, something seems to have cheered her up.'

'As far as I know, nothing out of the ordinary happened,' he said. 'I teased her a bit as I always have done. We all had a kick-about, if you can call what I do with a ball these days kicking. But that's about it.'

'Oh, well, not for us to reason why . . .'

'Perhaps the fresh air and exercise helped her to forget her troubles,' Arnie suggested.

'Could be. Let's just enjoy it and hope it lasts . . . for the rest of the day anyway,' Gill said, guessing that Carol's change of mood wouldn't be permanent.

When she went into the other room, Carol's problems were pushed to the back of Gill's mind by a heated argument that had blown up between Phoebe and John Briscoe. They were standing in the middle of the room shouting at each other while Gill's parents and her sister sat on the sofa looking embarrassed, especially Winnie. Craig was watching the quarrel with a mixture of fear and fascination.

'It's plain ignorant, to walk out of your brother's house when you've been invited for the day,' Phoebe was saying to her younger son.

'Give over nagging, will you, Mum?' John said. 'We came for the day and it's evening now. I'm meeting me mates.'

'Don't worry about us if you want to go out with your friends, John,' said Gill reasonably. 'We don't mind.'

'We do mind,' objected Arnie. 'Don't encourage him in his bad manners, Gill.'

'Be fair, Arnie. We all wanted to be out with our friends when we were his age,' she said. 'Not stuck at home with the family.'

'We didn't have mates like Head-Butter Harris and his crowd though, did we?' said Arnie.

'He's all right,' John defended. 'He's a good laugh.'

'Harris is trouble.' Arnie glared at his brother, at the leather jacket and tight jeans, the hair cut into a Beatle fringe. 'And if you hang about with him and his mates for long enough you'll be in trouble too.'

'You know nothing about them,' John defended hotly.

'Everybody in Fulham knows about Head-Butter Harris,' said Arnie. 'He spent more time in the juvenile courts than he did at school.'

John let out an expressive sigh. 'I don't pick holes in your mates, so don't criticise mine,' he said angrily.

'You've no cause to criticise mine 'cause I don't go around with scum,' said Arnie.

'Oh, I've had enough of this,' said John huffily. 'I'm going out.' And he marched out of the house leaving a resonant silence behind him.

'The young bugger,' said Arnie, making as though to go after him.

'Leave him,' said Phoebe commandingly. 'The more we disapprove of his mates the more determined he'll be not to give 'em up.' She turned to Gill. 'I'm sorry he was so rude, love, after all your hard work and hospitality.'

'Don't worry about it.'

'That boy is a real pain lately.'

'He'll grow out of it,' said Gill.

'If he had something to interest him besides those yobs he goes about with, I'd feel more hopeful about him,' said Phoebe glumly. 'But he hates his job at the soup factory and he's got no hobbies. He hasn't even taken an interest in football since he got in with Harris.'

'I think I'll have to try to get him a job at Bex Sports once

I'm established there myself,' said Arnie. 'So that I can keep an eye on him.'

'I wish someone would straighten him out,' said Phoebe. 'He's driving me round the bend.'

'Arnie will get it sorted, don't worry,' said Gill, realising that there were other people here to be entertained. 'And in the meantime let's all have a drink and enjoy the rest of the evening.'

'Yes, let's do that,' said Phoebe.

Gill and Carol emerged from Earl's Court station one Saturday in the spring, having spent the morning shopping in the West End. It was a fine day with blue skies and pale sunshine, a deceptively fresh breeze whipping around corners and flapping through the shop awnings.

'Well, are you pleased with your new clothes?' asked Gill, who'd finally persuaded her sister to go out on this shopping spree.

'S'pose so,' said Carol flatly as they headed along North End Road to their parents' house. Winnie, who was looking after Craig while Gill was out because Arnie was at work on a Saturday, was making lunch for them all. Lessons had finished for the Easter holidays which meant that Gill had a free Saturday.

'Don't overdo the enthusiasm,' Gill said with irony.

'Well . . . where will I go to wear them?'

'Out enjoying yourself, I hope,' said Gill.

'Who with?' was Carol's answer to that. 'I gave up all my friends for Dougie. They're all married or got steady boyfriends anyway, now.'

Gill could see the problem. But she felt as though she had achieved a minor success in getting Carol to buy some new clothes. At least she'd brightened up a little. 'You need a new man,' she said.

'Unattached ones don't exactly grow on trees, you know.'

'No . . . but they do go to dances and discos in the hope of meeting someone.'

'I wouldn't go to something like that on my own,' said Carol, horrified.

'I suppose not,' said Gill. 'I'd go with you myself to keep you company but I don't think Arnie would approve.'

'You're so lucky,' said Carol enviously. 'You've got everything . . . a husband, a home, a child.'

'And so will you have one day.'

'I don't think I'll ever meet anyone,' moaned Carol.

'You're only twenty-two, for heaven's sake,' said Gill.

'But everybody else is fixed up,' Carol wailed, 'and I'm never likely to meet anyone at work.'

'Someone will come along,' said Gill. 'Just give it time.'

'It's so lonely not having anyone of your own,' said Carol. 'You don't know what it's like, Gill. You never have. You didn't have time to because you started going out with Arnie at such a young age.'

If she only knew how lonely you can be within a relationship, Gill thought, but she simply said, 'I understand what you're saying. But perhaps you should stop thinking about it so much. Mr Right will come along when you least expect it.'

'I thought Mr Right was Dougie.'

'Dougie's past history.'

'I know.'

The market was in full flow and they had to elbow their way through the vociferous crowds thronging the pavements, queuing at stalls, standing in groups chatting, some just idly browsing through the goods on offer. Gill stopped at a fruit stall to buy some apples and oranges.

'Arnie's a really big fruit eater,' she remarked casually. 'He reckons it's the key to good health.'

'Must be why he always looks so fit.'

'Maybe.'

'I think he looks great.'

'You've always had a soft spot for him, haven't you?' said Gill lightly. 'Ever since you were a schoolgirl.'

'Yes I have,' Carol replied, though what she'd been feeling

for Arnie lately was more than just a girlish soft spot. Her sister would have a fit if she knew what passed through Carol's mind about Arnie sometimes, especially since Boxing Day in the park with him and the others, when she'd first glimpsed an end to the depression left by Dougie's rejection. Nothing had happened between herself and Arnie, but realising how much she wanted it to had made her feel better somehow. At least it proved that Dougie hadn't done any permanent damage and that everything was still in good working order . . .

Arnie was busy serving a customer late that same Saturday afternoon when Len came into the shop and went straight through to the manager's office.

'Are you hoping to get into the school team one day, son?' said Arnie to his customer, a young boy who was here with his father buying a pair of football boots.

'Yeah.' The lad looked at Arnie with blatant admiration. 'I bet you played for your school, didn't you?'

'I did, as a matter of fact.'

'What was it like playing as a professional?' asked the boy as Arnie laced the boots for him.

'Magic,' he said. 'Sheer magic.'

'Did you ever play in a Cup Final?'

'No, I never did make that,' said Arnie with a note of regret – but not the self-pity that had once been so prevalent in his attitude. He finished tying the boots. 'You can stand up and see what they feel like now.'

The boy walked up and down to check the fit of the boots. 'They feel great,' he said.

'Good.' Arnie turned to the boy's father while the lad sat down to remove the boots. 'It's a bit late in the season for new boots, isn't it?'

'The kids where we live play soccer all year round.'

'We used to too. Cricket was never really in the running.'

The boy handed Arnie the boots to be boxed and Arnie went behind the counter to complete the transaction with the boy's father, answering a series of questions about his life as a soccer star as he did so.

Other customers came into the shop and were eager to hear what Arnie had to say, remembering how famous he'd once been. Despite all the chatter, however, Arnie continued serving, managing to balance entertainment with efficiency.

Considering the fact that it was almost the end of the football season there was still quite a demand for boots and replica strips of the professional teams, but the sales in cricket gear were also beginning to gather momentum. Over the next half-hour or so Arnie did a brisk trade in cricket bats, billiard cues and golf balls, glad he'd always taken an all-round interest in sport because it enabled him to converse with the customers whatever their chosen pursuit.

He was in his element in this job. The shop had taken over from the football field as his territory, a place where he felt important and in demand. Apart from the manager, Arnie was the only full-time assistant, but they had several part-timers and a schoolboy who came in on a Saturday.

Len was still talking shop to Jack, the manager, in his office. Glancing though the glass partition into the shop, Len watched Arnie working, impressed with what he saw.

'He seems to be shaping up very well,' he remarked.

'He's a ruddy marvel,' said Jack, following his employer's gaze. 'He could sell football boots to legless seamen, that one.'

'Yes, he does have a way about him,' Len agreed. 'Do you reckon people come into the shop just to chat to him?'

'I'm sure they do,' said Jack. 'But they never go out empty-handed, Arnie sees to that. He's full of chat, but he's a real slogger. He can talk and work at the same time.'

'So I've noticed.' Len looked at his watch. 'Well, it'll soon be time to shut up shop. How about my buying you all a drink when you've cashed up? As it's the end of the week and the shop is doing so well.'

'Sorry boss, I've gotta rush off,' said the manager. 'The

wife and I are going out for a meal tonight and she'll have my guts for garters if I'm late home. But I'm sure the others would love to go with you.'

Arnie was the only member of staff who wasn't in a particular hurry, as it happened, and he welcomed the chance of a social half-hour with his employer, whose company he found he enjoyed.

Inevitably, however, they talked shop.

'Why don't we have an end-of-season sale of football gear?' Arnie suggested, leaning on the bar with a pint.

'The way you shift the stock, we won't need to,' said Len, holding a glass of whisky and puffing on a cigar.

'It'll slow down soon, though, when all the organised games finish – until the new season,' Arnie pointed out.

'True.'

'Don't worry, though, boss – I'm becoming an expert on cricket . . . tennis an' all,' he said with a wicked laugh.

His employer chuckled too. Arnie was a man after his own heart.

'You've got a good head for business, Arnie, and you're a natural with the customers,' said Len. 'Mary and I are pleased with the way you've taken to the job.'

'Thanks, mate. I'm glad about that,' said Arnie, grinning. 'I'm dead chuffed about the way it's turned out an' all. Cor, if I'd known I was gonna have a talent for the sportsgear trade I'd have come to see you about a job long ago.'

Len drew deeply on his cigar, feeling relaxed and happy. 'You wouldn't have been thinking straight when you first came out of the game,' he said. 'It makes you feel too sick at heart to want to do anything for a while.'

'You're telling me.'

'I was just the same when my football career came to a sudden end.' He sipped his whisky, relaxing even more, rather too much as it happened. 'As I said to your missus when she came to see me, it's a hard thing to have to come to terms with.'

'People don't understand unless they've actually been through it.'

'Course not,' said Len. 'How can they?'

Arnie looked suddenly baffled.

'What was that you just said?' he asked. 'Did you say my wife came to see you?'

'That's right.'

'Oh?'

'Good job she did as it turned out, innit?' said Len.

Arnie didn't reply. Only on seeing his thunderous expression did Len remember his promise to Gill.

'Oh, blimey,' he said, making a face. 'I was supposed to keep shtum about that. Still, as you're doing so well, I don't suppose it matters now.'

'My wife put you up to it, didn't she?' said Arnie through tight lips. 'My wife came to see you and asked you to give me a job.'

'Calm down,' Len urged. 'It wasn't like that at all.'

'We didn't meet by chance in here that night you offered me the job, did we?' said Arnie, looking stricken. 'Did we?' he persisted when Len remained silent.

'Well, not exactly, but—'

'The whole thing was a set-up, to give poor old useless Arnie a leg-up.'

'That wasn't the way it was at all,' Len declared ardently.

'That's exactly the way it was,' said Arnie coldly. 'Now, if you'll excuse me, I have to go.'

And he marched out of the pub.

'How dare you belittle me!' Arnie roared, storming into the kitchen where Gill was busy preparing the evening meal. Craig was out at a friend's so they were alone in the house. 'I could kill you for what you've done, you interfering cow.'

She looked round at him, startled, her hands encased in oven gloves. 'What *are* you talking about?'

'You went to see Len to beg him to give me a job,' he blasted.

'No I didn't,' she said, shaking her head vigorously.

'Don't lie to me,' he said, grabbing hold of her arm in his fury. 'I know you went to see him. He admitted it.'

'All right. I did go to see him, but I didn't beg him to give you a job.'

'It's a bloody conspiracy,' Arnie growled. 'He told me you asked him not to say anything about it. Luckily for me he forgot his promise after he'd had a drink, or I might never have found out the truth about the job.'

'It's true, I did ask him to keep quiet about my visit, but I certainly didn't beg him to give you a job.'

'Oh, not much,' Arnie said, beside himself with shame and fury. 'He told me it was all a set-up, him and me meeting in the pub that night, organised by you . . . you scheming bitch.'

Gill looked at him, knowing he was feeling wretched. His eyes were ice-cold, lips set in a grim line.

'The only way you would have accepted the position was if he approached you and offered you the job on a plate.'

'Bitch.'

'If you'll calm down, I'll tell you exactly what happened,' she said firmly. 'Now let go of my arm, please. You're hurting me.'

He released her, looking at his hand in puzzlement as though he hadn't realised he'd been holding her so roughly. 'Let's hear it then,' he said.

'I went to see Len Bex because I noticed that he was opening a new shop and I genuinely believed you would be an asset to him,' she explained.

He clutched his head with his hands dramatically, closing his eyes. 'Oh, God, I can hardly bear to think about it,' he said, his voice trembling with rage. 'My wife begging some-one to give me a job. It makes me want to crawl into a hole and die.'

'How many more times must I tell you? I did *not* beg him to give you a job,' she said wearily. 'I told him I thought you would be valuable to his business – and I was right, wasn't I?'

'He would never have offered me a job if you hadn't gone to see him, though, would he?' he queried miserably.

'How could he when he didn't even know you were available?' she pointed out. 'He'd heard of you from your playing days, but he wasn't to know that you weren't fixed up with work. All I did was bring the two of you together, and it's worked out very well for you both. You're enjoying the job and his business is reaping the benefit. So what does it matter how it all came about?'

'I don't need a woman to go out job-hunting for me,' he said.

'You weren't doing anything about getting a job yourself, though, were you?'

'I would have.'

'The longer you left it the harder it would have got.'

'You had no right—'

Suddenly Gill had reached the end of her patience. She was tired of pandering to his fragile ego, treading on eggshells around him and making allowances for his moods. All the heartache and worry he had caused her these last two turbulent years culminated in a blistering surge of rage. 'Now you just listen to me for a minute!' she ordered, her voice high and brittle. 'Okay, so you think I had no right to do something I truly believed would help my husband. But you had no right to put me through nearly two years of misery because you lost your football career.'

'You couldn't possibly imagine what it was like for me when that happened.'

'And you couldn't imagine what it's been like for me,' she said, hating him at that moment for causing her such pain. 'Living with someone so drenched in self-pity as you were, on my back the whole time, criticising everything I did and making no effort to drag yourself out of the doldrums. You were even perverse enough to make it difficult for me to bring in some extra cash through teaching when we desperately needed it. And all because I hadn't lost my ability to use my talent and you had.'

'That's right, turn the knife—'

'I had to do *something* to help you back on your feet, Arnie,' she told him. 'I couldn't just sit back and watch you become a vegetable with no purpose in life when you still had so much to offer. That's why I went to see Len Bex.'

'How do you think I feel now – knowing that I wasn't taken on on my own merit?'

'You *were* taken on on your own merit,' she insisted loudly. 'All I did was make Len Bex aware that you were around.'

'Huh!'

'If you've any sense at all, you'll be proud of yourself for making such a success of the job,' she said. 'They wouldn't keep you on if you weren't good at it.'

'I can't stay there now.'

Gill sighed in exasperation. 'Oh no, don't tell me you're going to pack it in,' she said.

'I'll have to.'

'*Why?*'

''Cause I feel such a bloody fool, that's why,' he snarled.

Now it was her turn to clutch her head. 'Oh, give us a break, Arnie, please,' she entreated. 'Don't you think I've had enough to put up with since your accident—'

'That's right, drag it all up again,' he interrupted through clenched teeth, his eyes dark with hatred because every time he looked at her he remembered how much he hated himself for failing her. 'You don't have to remind me that it's my fault you lost the baby and my fault you can't have any more.'

She felt his words like a blow to the heart. She'd had no idea he was still brooding about that, still blaming himself. 'That wasn't what I meant.'

'You said—'

'I was referring to your bad temper and lack of co-operation, which have made my life hell,' she cut in. 'Despite what you may think, you are not the only person in the world.'

'And don't I know it?'

'You're prepared to give up a job you need and enjoy just because of vanity?'

'Vanity?'

'Yes – vanity,' she said loudly and with strong emphasis. 'That's *exactly* what it is. You're so damned vain, you won't even stay in a job you're good at because somebody else gave you a helping hand.'

'You don't understand . . .'

She turned away and continued with the task in hand because she was sick of trying to communicate with him. She took a packet of frozen peas from the ice compartment of the fridge and emptied them into a saucepan of boiling water. 'You do what you feel you must about the job, Arnie,' she said, her voice quieter now.

'I will, don't worry.'

'I'm sure.' She paused for a moment. 'Craig will be home at any minute. His pal's father is bringing him back in his car,' she continued evenly. 'I don't want this quarrel to continue in front of him.'

'Give me credit for having some sense.'

'If you want to cut off your nose to spite your face and give up your job, then I can't stop you,' she went on determinedly. 'But do be aware of what you're giving up. It might be a very long time before you find another job you like as much.'

'Oh, give over nagging, woman,' he said and marched from the room.

Gill's hand was trembling as she stirred the gravy in a saucepan. Somewhere along the way she and Arnie had lost something precious. Was it that too many of the bad things of the past still stood between them – guilt on his part, and resentment on hers? Or was it just that he had worn her out with his demanding and difficult ways? Maybe it was simply that first love hadn't stood the test of time.

Was I wrong to interfere on the question of his employment? she asked herself, and couldn't in all honesty accept that she was. But she did accept the undeniable fact that there was something seriously wrong with her marriage, something she didn't seem able to put right. Her latest efforts had backfired on her. So what else could she do?

Chapter Nine

'You and your big mouth,' said Mary Bex reprovingly. It was Monday morning, and she and her husband sat at their desks, reeling from the shock of Arnie's resignation, which was to take immediate effect. Storming into the Hammersmith office to give in his notice, he'd told them he would rather lose a week's pay than spend another minute in their employ now that he knew the truth.

'What on earth possessed you to tell him when we both promised we wouldn't?' Mary asked.

'I didn't intend to say anything.' Len looked suitably shamefaced. 'It just slipped out when I was feeling relaxed.'

'When the whisky had loosened your tongue, more like . . .'

'Maybe that's what it was,' he freely admitted, lighting a cigarette. 'Anyway, I feel bad about it whatever.'

'I should hope you do,' she said. 'I could murder you.'

'What's done is done. There's no point in your going on at me about it.'

'True.' She put on her spectacles and flicked through a pile of invoices, but her mind wasn't on her work. 'I bet his wife has had a rotten weekend. He's bound to have given her a bad time.'

'I don't know why he's so upset about it,' said Len, tutting and shaking his head. 'I mean . . . what does it matter how he came by the job in the first place – as long as he's doing well now?'

'Male pride is a powerful thing.'

'It must be in his case.'

'He's obviously lacking in confidence, even though he's so chatty and full of himself,' Mary said. 'Some men can't bear to think that they might have a woman to thank for something other than having their supper on the table when they get home from work.'

'You banging the drum for women's rights?' Len said, drawing on his cigarette.

'No, just stating facts.'

'Not with me in mind, I hope.'

'Of course not,' she said with emphasis. She and Len were a team; he freely admitted her contribution to the business and made no secret of it to other people.

'Just kidding.' He paused, thinking about Arnie. 'Okay, so he's had his pride dented. Surely that's no reason to give up a job he enjoys.'

'He obviously thinks it is.'

'Silly young hothead.'

'You were just the same at his age . . . and you were impossible to live with for ages after you came out of football.'

'I've never understood why you put up with me,' he said, teasing her.

'For your money.'

'I didn't have any.'

'It must have been your body then,' she joshed. 'It certainly wasn't your refined manners.'

'Cheeky bitch.' Len paused, becoming sentimental as he was inclined to do when thinking about his marriage. 'We've come a long way since those early days, haven't we?'

'We certainly have. Nearly thirty years married, and six sports shops to our credit,' she said. 'Not bad for someone who had his football career cut short.'

'I couldn't have done any of it without you,' he said in a sober tone. 'And I couldn't manage without you now.'

'Oh, I daresay you'd muddle along if you had to.' She

leaned back, clasping her hands behind her head and staring meditatively into space. 'But more importantly for the moment, what are you going to do about Arnie?'

'He's a bloody nuisance, causing us all this trouble.'

'I agree with you,' Mary said, 'but he's also the best thing that's happened to this business in a long time.'

'Mm.'

'So what are you going to do about it?'

'What do you think I'm gonna do?' he said, meeting her eyes.

'That's my Len,' she said, winking and treating him to one of her warmest smiles. 'And don't be too long about it either, because they're short-staffed at the Fulham branch without him.'

'I guessed I'd find you in here,' said Len.

Arnie was standing at the bar of the Big Bell drinking a pint. Observing the other man gloomily, he said, 'What are you having?'

'It's my shout,' insisted Len, puffing on a cigar. 'You can't afford to flash your money about now that you're out of a job.'

'That's my business,' said Arnie, reaching into his pocket.

'Shut up and do as you're told,' commanded Len. 'I've had about as much as I can take of your nonsense for one day.'

'Why don't you push off back to Putney then?' said Arnie rudely. 'This is my local. I didn't ask you to come round here looking for me.'

Len threw him a hard look. 'That's quite true. But since I *have* taken the trouble to come over from Putney, you'll listen to what I have to say.' He spoke with such authority that Arnie didn't argue, but followed him meekly over to a table in the corner carrying the drinks.

'Right, I won't beat about the bush,' said Len, swallowing some whisky. 'I think you're behaving like a spoilt brat and I don't like it.'

A shrug of the shoulders was Arnie's reply.

'Not only have you let me down, you've let your wife down an' all.'

'There's no law that I know of against giving up a job,' Arnie said sullenly.

'Oh, don't be so damned childish.' Len looked grim. 'Your wife didn't come to me begging for a job for you. In fact, the way she put it, I was the one who should consider myself lucky to have the chance to take you on. And what she said made sense. Having you behind the counter in my shop is a winning formula.'

Arnie said nothing.

Len leant back slightly and stared at the other man. 'Okay, let's look at this another way. Just supposing your missus had come to me on bended knee pleading with me to give you a job. What difference would it have made to the fact that you're doing well and enjoying the work?'

'It's in here, mate,' said Arnie, pointing to his chest. 'Right inside.'

'Oh, yeah, very dramatic,' said Len scornfully. 'But it doesn't impress me.'

'That's up to you.'

'Personally I think you should be grateful that your wife bothered to do something to help you. In fact, you're damned lucky she's still with you at all if this is the way you treat her.'

Drinking his beer, Arnie remained silent.

'You don't deserve her, mate,' Len continued. 'And it'd be your own fault if she buggered off and left you. She's too good for you.'

'You're not telling me anything I don't already know,' said Arnie, his voice quivering with emotion suddenly. 'It's a recognised fact that Gill's too good for me.'

'It's up to you to make yourself good enough for her then, innit?' said Len.

'Gill's in a class of her own,' said Arnie in a deeply serious tone. 'She always was a cut above, even when we were kids living in the same street. She never raked the streets like me and the others. She stayed indoors practising the piano while the rest of us were getting up to all sorts o' mischief in Maisie Road. Now she's a successful piano teacher and I'm a broken-up football player.' And I keep hurting her, a voice screamed inside his head. I can't stop hurting her and it's destroying us both. I can hardly bear to look at her because of what I'm doing to her.

'Ease up on the self-pity, for Gawd's sake, Arnie,' said Len. 'You'll have me crying into my whisky in a minute.'

'Sorry.'

'I should think you ought to be sorry an' all,' said Len. 'You've got a lovely wife who takes the trouble to do something to help you, and you repay her by throwing it back in her face. And if that isn't bad enough, you've got the brass neck to mope about feeling sorry for yourself.'

Knowing that what Len said was true made Arnie feel even worse, so he blotted out the truth and defended himself by attack. 'She shouldn't have—'

'She was only thinking of you,' Len interrupted in exasperation. 'Anyway, only someone without any responsibilities can afford to be sensitive about that sort of thing. You've got a wife and kid to support; you need to be working to provide for 'em.'

'I'll go back on to benefit until I find another job,' he said.

'And what are you gonna do with yourself until you find a job you fancy, eh?' Len demanded. 'Sit on your arse all day while your wife works to put jam on the bread for you all?'

Arnie lowered his eyes shamefully. 'No, I'll go out looking until I find something suitable,' he said. 'A job that I'll apply for myself.'

Len lapsed into silence, sipping his whisky thoughtfully. 'How long is it since your accident?'

'Two years.'

'Don't you think that's more than long enough to be feeling sorry for yourself?' Len asked.

'Yes it is, and I'm not.'

'Phew, not much!'

'Oh, you think what you like,' snapped Arnie. 'I couldn't care less.'

'I always admired you as a player, and when I met you in person I took an instant liking to you,' Len carried on regardless. 'I thought you and I were two of a kind. I thought you were the sort of person I wanted to have working for me. Bright, tough, full of good ideas . . . I also thought you could be trusted. It just goes to show how wrong you can be about someone, doesn't it?'

'I've never had my hand in the till,' exclaimed Arnie with affront.

'I know that.'

'You implied I'm not to be trusted.'

'There's more to trust than dishonesty,' Len told him.

'Oh yeah?'

'Don't act thick,' said Len. 'I'm talking about commitment to the job, reliability and respect for your employer.'

'I do respect you—'

'You say you respect me yet you're willing to leave me short-staffed with no one to cover for you until I can find a replacement,' he said angrily. 'And not even willing to work your week's notice. You call that respect?'

There was nothing Arnie could say to that. He had dug a hole for himself and he didn't know how to claw his way out. Everything Len had said was true, and Arnie felt deeply ashamed. But pride wouldn't allow him to do what Len wanted.

'Anyway, if this is the way you conduct yourself the firm is better off without you.' Len finished his drink and stood up to go. 'No one's indispensable, mate. I'll have no trouble finding a replacement for you.' He stubbed his cigar out in the ashtray. 'You'd be wise to keep that in mind before your wife realises the same thing.' And without another word, Len marched across the bar and left the pub.

146

After only a few moments' deliberation, Arnie got up and went after him.

That same evening, just after Craig had gone to bed, Gill received an unexpected visitor.

'I've called round to see how you're bearing up,' said Mary Bex as Gill showed her into the living room and invited her to sit down. 'In the light of what's happened with Arnie.'

'That's very kind of you, Mrs Bex,' said Gill, warming to her.

'Mary, please.'

'I'm all right, Mary,' she said with a wistfulness in her tone.

'Are you sure?'

'Well, naturally I'm fed up about the way it's turned out for Arnie . . .'

'I should think you are. I could have murdered that husband of mine for spilling the beans.' Mary was wearing a plain navy-blue suit and white blouse which was smart in a matronly sort of way.

'I was mad with Len too, at first,' said Gill. 'But now all my anger is aimed towards Arnie. I mean it's so irresponsible to give up a job he likes for such a silly reason.'

'Is Arnie at the Big Bell now?'

Gill nodded.

'Good. Because Len has gone there looking for him to try to talk some sense into him,' said Mary in her gentle voice. 'We aren't prepared to let him go without a fight.'

'Ooh good,' said Gill, feeling a surge of new hope. 'It would be such a relief if Len could persuade him to change his mind.'

'If anyone can do it, Len can.'

Gill invited Mary to stay for coffee and she said she'd love to. Within minutes they were chatting like old friends.

'I suppose things will be difficult for you if Len can't talk him into staying on,' said Mary, sipping her coffee.

'We'll manage like we did before he got the job,' said Gill. 'There isn't much left over for treats, but we'll get by. Fortunately I enjoy my work, so being the breadwinner is no hardship to me.'

'It must be annoying for you, though, knowing that Arnie could make life easier.'

'His frame of mind worries me far more than the financial side of things,' said Gill. 'He's so bitter about my working, even though he knows we need the money.'

'Men, eh?' said Mary.

Gill threw her a look. 'Not Len?' she said in a questioning tone.

'Steady as a rock now,' said Mary, 'but we had our bad times when we were younger.'

'Really?'

'Not half. Len was cut up about having to come out of the game too. Impossible to live with for quite a long time – so I know what it's like for you. But once he set up in business he never looked back. He started off selling sportsgear in the markets.'

'The two of you seem to be very close,' remarked Gill.

'We are. We've been together for nearly thirty years,' she stated. 'We've never had any children, so we only have each other. You might say the business is our baby.'

'Does it ever get a bit much – working and living together?' Gill enquired.

'No, not really,' Mary said. 'We have our off days, of course, like everyone else. I'm not in the office full-time anyway. I'm one of these old-fashioned people who enjoys being a housewife; I like to have some time at home. I can usually manage to get done what I have to in the office and still have some time to myself. Unless we're short-staffed and I have to help behind the counter.'

'Sounds as though you've got yourself very well organised.'

'I'm happy with the way things are,' she said, smiling. 'But

148

what about you? I understand you're a piano teacher.'

'That's right.'

'It must be lovely to be able to do something like that.'

'I'm glad of it, I must admit,' Gill said. 'I don't know what I'd do without my piano.'

'I'd love to be able to play.'

'Well . . . it's never too late to learn.'

'I'm a bit too long in the tooth now.'

'Not at all,' said Gill.

'You teach adults?'

'I don't actually have any on my books, but all ages are welcome.'

'Maybe one of these days, after I retire . . .' Mary said, smiling. 'Life is a bit too hectic at the moment for me to take anything else on.'

'I can imagine,' said Gill. 'Running a home and a business doesn't leave much time for other things, does it?'

'It isn't only those two things,' said Mary. 'Both Len and I have our own separate outside interests. He's involved with several associations who organise various kinds of social events to raise money for charity.'

'Which means a busy social life for you?'

'Yes, we do go to quite a few dinners and so on,' she said.

'And what about your outside interests?' queried Gill.

'I'm closely involved with the Friends of St Theresa's.'

'St Theresa's,' said Gill, trying to place the name. 'Isn't that the children's home down Walham Green way? The one run by nuns?'

'That's right.'

'I've seen crocodiles of girls walking with the nuns around there.'

'Yes. The older girls go outside to the local school,' Mary explained. 'The little ones are taught inside the home.'

'What does being involved actually entail?' enquired Gill with interest.

'I'm chairman of the Friends of St Theresa's committee,'

Mary explained. 'We work closely with the nuns, organising social events and trips out for the girls.'

'What a lovely idea.'

'Yes, I think it's a worthwhile cause. The children are very well looked after at the home, though the nuns are quite strict. But these girls miss out on so many things that other children take for granted.'

'I can imagine.'

'Our aim is to give them something special to look forward to outside of the institution,' Mary went on. 'We can't give them what they want most of all – family life – but we can arrange for them to have a few of the treats other kids have as a matter of course. Seaside outings, cinema trips, that sort of thing. We organised a trip to the ice-skating rink the other week and they thought that was great fun.'

'I bet they did,' said Gill, intrigued.

'It all takes money, of course, so we are endlessly fund-raising.' Mary smiled her warm smile. 'People must dread meeting me in the street for fear I'll try to flog them raffle tickets or get them to take part in some kind of fund-raising event. You're quite safe tonight, though, 'cause I don't actually have anything to sell.'

'I wouldn't have minded,' said Gill.

'The days of the old-fashioned orphanage with grim dormitories and very little to eat have gone in this affluent society,' said Mary. 'But the girls need more than just food and drink and education. The nuns can't provide everything.'

'Of course not,' said Gill thoughtfully, a germ of an idea beginning to form.

They chatted for ages until Mary said she had to go.

'I've really enjoyed your company, my dear,' she said as she was shown to the door. 'We must get together again sometime soon . . .' She paused and looked at Gill. 'Whatever the outcome of Len and Arnie's meeting tonight.'

'Yes, I'd like that,' said Gill, knowing she had made a new friend.

'What do you think of the idea of Bex Sports sponsoring a local amateur football team?' Arnie suggested that same evening after offering profuse apologies to Len, who had reinstated him. The two men were buddies again.

'We have sponsored local teams before from time to time,' said Len.

'I was thinking in terms of a boys' team, though.'

'What exactly did you have in mind in the way of sponsorship?'

'Supply the team strips, have a list of the match fixtures in our window, that sort of thing,' Arnie said with enthusiasm. 'We could also try to get the local paper to cover their matches. It would be good for them and good for us.'

'Hmmm.' Len pondered the idea.

'Okay, so it'll cost the firm a bit to kit the team out. But the word will soon get round about what we're doing. And where will the parents go for their cricket stuff in summer and tennis gear and anything else they need?'

'To us.'

'Exactly.'

'It's a good idea,' said Len. 'You get it organised and the firm will cover the cost.'

'You're giving me the okay without speaking to Mrs Bex?' said Arnie in surprise.

'You're getting to know me a bit too well, son,' Len smiled.

'Not really – but I do know how important her opinion is to you.'

'We're a team.'

'She's a great lady,' said Arnie. 'Everybody likes her.'

'She's a soft touch with the staff, that's why they're so fond of her,' said Len jokingly. 'But seriously, I know she'll go along with this idea, so you can go ahead. I'll mention it to her as soon as I get home.'

'You'll square it with the manager so he'll be in the picture?'

'I certainly will, but this will be your baby, Arnie, your responsibility,' Len said. 'The business will put up the money, but it's up to you to do all the work.'

'No problem.'

'Good.'

This latest scheme of Arnie's convinced Len that he'd done the right thing in hanging on to him.

'I'll get it organised for the new season,' said Arnie.

Len moved the conversation on to something else that was on his mind. 'The Fulham shop is getting so busy, we could do with another full-time assistant,' he said thoughtfully. 'You don't happen to know of anyone who might be interested, do you?'

'I do, as it happens.'

'Really?'

'Yeah. My younger brother,' Arnie said. 'If anyone needs a new challenge in his life it's John. He's working in a factory and he hates it. I could keep my eye on him and teach him the job.'

'Would he be interested in our type of work, though?' Len enquired. 'Because that's my main concern when taking someone new on. Lack of experience can easily be rectified. But enthusiasm for the job is essential.'

Arnie wasn't sure how to answer this. John had used to be keen and knowledgeable about sport, especially football – before Head-Butter Harris and his crowd got such a hold on him. Now the gang seemed to dominate him completely. Lately, though, Arnie had got the impression that the novelty of hanging out with thugs was wearing thin with John, even though he had shown no real signs of breaking away from them. He denied it, of course, but Arnie suspected that this was the case. Maybe a new job was just what John needed to put him back on the right track. Arnie was certain that John's salvation lay in a new sense of purpose of some sort.

'I'm not absolutely sure, but I'll talk to him about it,' he said.

'Tell him to come into the office at Hammersmith to see me for a chat if he's interested in a job,' said Len.

'I'll do that.'

Arnie had a horrible suspicion that he would live to regret introducing his brother to Bex Sports. But he felt duty-bound to do it anyway, in John's best interests.

With Arnie settled back into the job, life fell into a pattern for Gill that summer. Craig had his seventh birthday and continued to take after his father, both in appearance and personality. He became increasingly football-mad with every day that passed. Arnie said he was a natural, and got him into a local team for the under-nines.

Beatlemania continued to sweep across Britain and abroad, as the group's popularity spread throughout the world. Gill thought their music was great and had fun playing their songs on the piano. She even encouraged pupils whose interest was flagging to play catchy Beatles numbers in the hope of reviving their interest. Even Craig loved Beatles music – but not enough to inspire him to piano lessons. The house was filled with music of all kinds, from classical to pop, from piano to record player.

Gill saw quite a lot of Carol, who still didn't have a man in her life and grew ever more despairing about it. She often talked about getting a flat of her own, but Gill doubted if she'd do more than talk about it because she was too comfortable living at home with Mum and Dad.

For all that Gill was fond of her sister, she couldn't deny the fact that Carol was becoming even more self-centred. Her desperation for love and marriage was still an obsession with her too, and was a constant worry for Gill and her parents.

Now that Arnie was working and more settled in himself, Gill hoped their marriage might regain its former unity. But although he seemed to get closer to Craig, he grew more distant from her. They acted out a normal relationship, and on the surface everything was fine, but there was an underlying coldness between them now. They were always just a whisper away from an argument which might flare up at the slightest thing.

They didn't talk about it, but they both knew that something was wrong. It stood between them, an unspoken mutual understanding they daren't confront, for fear it would lead to a parting of the ways if brought out into the open.

So they sidestepped the issue, going through the motions of married life from day to day, loving Craig but not each other – or that was what it felt like to Gill.

John Briscoe started work at Bex Sports in the early summer.

'The Briscoes are getting into your business in numbers now,' Gill remarked lightly to Mary one afternoon. The two friends were having tea outside on the tiny paved terrace in the sunshine. The small back garden, which was lawned and secluded by high walls and mature shrubs, was currently overrun by exuberant little boys as Craig and his friends made the most of the summer holidays.

'They certainly are.' Mary looked across at Craig, who was using the swing frame as a goal into which his friends were kicking the ball. 'Will Craig follow in his father's footsteps, do you think?'

'As a member of your staff?'

'As a footballer.'

'Not as a professional if I've got anything to do with it,' Gill said adamantly. 'I shall do everything I can to discourage it.'

'Really?'

'Oh, yes. Football messed up Arnie's life; I don't want it to do the same to Craig. Play for fun and recreation by all means. But not as a professional . . . up in the clouds one minute and down in the dumps the next.'

'It isn't like that for everyone,' Mary wisely pointed out. 'Some professionals have a steady career.'

'Even if it goes the full term, it's short by normal standards,' said Gill.

'Yes, but there's always the possibility of going into management later on.'

'For a few, yes,' agreed Gill. 'But still I'd rather Craig got qualified for something safer. There are many more chances for youngsters these days than there were when I was growing up.'

'It's a bit early to think about it seriously yet, anyway.' Mary had sensed she'd hit on a raw nerve and deemed it wise not to continue with that topic.

'Yes, it is.' Gill paused. 'Changing the subject, I've had something on my mind ever since you told me about your work for St Theresa's.'

'Really?' Mary shaded her eyes from the sun and looked at her friend.

'I've been thinking about offering free piano lessons to any of the St Theresa's girls who might be interested.'

'What a good idea.'

'Will the nuns approve?'

'I should think they'd welcome you with open arms.' She paused thoughtfully. 'You'd have to go there to teach, though, because the girls aren't allowed out unaccompanied and the nuns wouldn't have time to bring them to you.'

'I'd already thought of that, and it isn't a problem. I take it they've got a piano.'

Mary nodded, smiling.

'We'd have to work the details out,' said Gill. 'But I was thinking in terms of going there on Saturday mornings for a couple of hours. Craig usually goes to my mum's place at that time. If we think in terms of two hours, that's four pupils. There probably won't be a huge demand because lots of kids are put off by the idea of practising.'

'Sounds fine to me.'

'Can I leave you to mention it to whoever is in charge?'

'Sure. I'll call in there on my way home.'

'Providing we get some interest, I'd like to start lessons at the beginning of the new term,' said Gill excitedly.

155

* * *

Going through the gates of St Theresa's was like entering another world. The building, which was hidden from the road by high walls and mature trees, had been built in the early 1900s and was a huge, grey place with attic windows and wide stone steps sweeping up to double front doors.

Inside the entrance hall, heading for the mother superior's office to finalise the details of her forthcoming lessons, Gill was struck by the strong spiritual aura: there were religious statues and paintings everywhere; the whole place gleamed with cleanliness, and the sweet scent of polish from the glossy wooden floors pervaded everything. Gill's footsteps seemed to echo intrusively into the hushed atmosphere.

The mother superior was an elderly woman with kindly blue eyes and pale skin, scrubbed and shiny next to her starched wimple, which looked paper-white against her black habit. When the arrangements for the lessons were complete, she handed Gill over to a middle-aged nun called Sister Maud who took Gill on a tour of the orphanage.

As they walked through the building away from the awesome quiet of the entrance hall, the atmosphere changed startlingly. Hordes of girls piled noisily into the playground for their morning break. Gill was shown the dormitories, which were basic and spotless with wooden floors that the girls themselves kept shiny, she was told. As well as classrooms, the main building comprised an assembly hall, a refectory, a chapel, and a recreation room with a table-tennis table, a large cupboard containing indoor games, small tables and chairs, and a piano tucked away in the corner.

Set slightly apart from the main building were a group of newly built houses, each basically furnished but comfortable, and each containing, to Gill's amazement, a television set and a table laid out for tea.

'These are our pride and joy,' said Sister Maud, a softly spoken woman with an Irish accent.

'The children live here, in ordinary houses?' Gill asked in surprise.

'Only some of them.'

'Even so . . .'

'There are ten girls in each unit, with two nuns in charge,' she explained. 'We're hoping that all the children will live this way eventually. The plan is for the old dormitory system to be replaced by home units. But it will be some time before the whole project is complete.'

'What a wonderful idea.'

'Indeed. It gives the girls more of a sense of identity and family,' she said.

'They eat here too?'

'They go over to the refectory for main meals, but we have facilities for drinks and light snacks here,' Sister Maud explained. 'It makes it more homely for them in the evenings.'

'I'd no idea there had been such advances,' said Gill. 'One tends to think of children's homes as rather austere places.'

'Things have improved since the old days before the war,' the nun said. 'But we are still very strong on discipline here. We have to be, with so many girls to look after.'

'I can imagine.'

'Anyway,' she said as they moved on, skirting the noisy playground on their way back to the main gates, 'I've arranged for you to have the use of the recreation room from ten to twelve on a Saturday morning for your lessons. The other girls will be told to keep to the other end of the room.'

'Thank you.'

'Thank *you*, Mrs Briscoe; it's a fine chance for our girls,' she said. 'Sister Bernadette plays the piano in assembly and takes the music lessons for the little ones in the school here, but she doesn't have a spare minute to give individual piano lessons.'

'I wonder if there'll be many volunteers,' remarked Gill. 'The idea of piano lessons seems dull to some children, I know.'

'I think there'll be a lot more girls coming forward than you've time for,' said the sister. 'I shall allocate the places strictly on a first-come-first-served basis. There's sure to be some who are keen to start and will then drop out as soon as the novelty wears off.'

In the event there were more takers than Gill could fit in, so a waiting list was duly introduced.

'There's one volunteer who won't last beyond the first couple of lessons,' said Sister Maud when Gill arrived at St Theresa's for the first session in September.

'Really?'

'Yes. Young Cherry Betts . . . She's a child of the devil,' said the nun.

'Oh dear.'

'She's the naughtiest girl we have, and she'll give you a whole lot of trouble if I'm not very much mistaken.'

'Why would she bother to volunteer for lessons if all she wants to do is cause trouble?'

'For the sheer devilment of giving you a hard time, I should imagine,' said the nun shrewdly. 'Someone new to torment is a challenge to that one.'

'I see.'

'If hers hadn't been the first name on the list I'd have turned her down flat,' said Sister Maud. 'But I like to be fair.'

'What does she actually do that's so terrible?' Gill wanted to know.

The other woman shook her head and spoke to Gill in a conspiratorial whisper. 'She's rude, rebellious, disobedient . . . She's even run away on more than one occasion. She's caused more trouble than all the rest put together.'

'Is she . . . I mean, does she have trouble keeping up with the others?'

'Quite the opposite,' said the nun. 'She's one of the brightest girls of her age group. But she seems determined to make life as hard for herself as she possibly can . . . and for the rest of us too, in the process.'

'What happened to her parents?'

Sister Maud drew a shuddering breath. 'Her father walked out on his wife and child,' she explained. 'And her mother couldn't cope. She put Cherry into our care eight years ago when the child was two years old. The mother never kept in touch . . . not so much as a postcard.'

'That poor child,' said Gill.

'Yes, it's sad indeed. I only hope you can find it in your heart to be as sympathetic towards her after you've given her a lesson,' said the nun.

'I'll do my best.'

'You'll have to be very firm with her, Mrs Briscoe,' the nun advised. 'Don't take any nonsense from her at all. If she smells so much as a hint of weakness, she'll run rings around you.'

'I'll remember that,' said Gill, wondering what she had let herself in for.

Cherry Betts was a plain child with straight auburn hair and huge blue eyes. She was bean-pole thin and this was emphasised by a baggy grey jumper and shapeless grey skirt. Gill immediately felt the impact of the anger and defiance that exuded from every pore.

'Why did you put your name down for piano lessons?' she asked as the girl sat down on the piano stool, the eloquence of her sigh leaving Gill in no doubt that she was bored.

'I've as much right as anyone else,' she said, immediately on the defensive. 'Sister said the first names on the list get the lessons.'

'But if you don't want to learn, what's the point in coming for lessons?' Gill enquired, sitting down beside her and putting a music primer on the stand.

'Who said I don't wanna learn?' said Cherry abrasively.

'Well you don't seem very pleased about it,' said Gill.

'What am I supposed to do, dance a jig or somethin'?'

'Don't be so rude.'

Cherry flushed scarlet – which was strange for a girl with no conscience, Gill thought. 'The nuns have told you things about me, haven't they?' she said accusingly.

Gill remained silent.

'They've got it in for me. Always have done. I hate the lot of 'em.'

'Let's just get on with the lesson and stop wasting time, shall we?' said Gill firmly, guessing that this pupil wouldn't stay the course, yet liking her for some unaccountable reason. 'And I'll tell you at the end of half an hour if it's going to be worth your while continuing.'

'What do you mean by that?' Cherry asked sharply. 'Why wouldn't it be worth my while?'

'Some people don't have any aptitude to learn the piano at all,' Gill explained evenly. 'And I can usually tell within half an hour.'

'I ain't thick.'

'I'm not suggesting you are. Now, can we please get on with the lesson?' said Gill patiently. 'There are other people waiting.'

'Okay, I ain't stopping you.'

Much to Gill's surprise, there was a stillness about Cherry as she listened intently to her explanation of where the keys were on the piano and how they corresponded with the notes on the music. In a first lesson she didn't expect to do more than impart the fundamentals and get a pupil to play a few notes with separate hands. But Cherry was exceptionally quick to learn, and managed 'Three Blind Mice' right through without a mistake. Gill was thrilled, especially as the girl seemed to be enjoying it.

'That's very good,' said Gill.

'I told you I ain't thick.'

'Yes, you did.'

'They're stupid tunes we have to play, though, aren't they? Bloomin' nursery rhymes for little kids,' said Cherry with scorn.

'You'll soon progress to other, more interesting music,' said Gill.

Quite suddenly Cherry's mood changed. Gill was startled to see her banging her fists up and down on the keys, making a terrible racket, her face contorted with anger. Nevertheless she let her continue, perceiving a rage inside this child that needed an outlet.

When the noise finally abated and the girl sat still, silent and spent, she turned to Gill with tears glistening in her eyes, her face ashen with two spots of colour standing out on her cheeks. 'That's what I really think of your poxy piano lessons,' she said thickly, her face tight and grim. 'I didn't want to do them anyway.' She got up from the stool and stared at Gill as though waiting to be dismissed.

'I'm sorry you feel like that,' Gill said, looking at her gravely.

'Why?'

'Because I think you could be good if you were to persevere.'

'I don't care.'

'Okay. As you're obviously not interested, I'll cross you off my list.'

'Good.'

Gill was disappointed. She had seen genuine musical potential in this troubled little girl. Cherry was truly exasperating, but Gill suspected there was more to her than her difficult behaviour.

Guessing, however, that any attempt on her part to encourage Cherry to continue with lessons would produce a negative reaction while she was in this mood, she turned back to the piano and flicked the music book back to the beginning ready for the next pupil. 'Can you tell the next one to come in on your way out, please, Cherry?' she said.

Cherry walked to the door, her plimsolls squeaking on the polished wooden floor. She stopped suddenly and turned back to Gill. 'It isn't that I don't wanna learn, exactly,' she said.

'You could have fooled me,' said Gill, swinging round to face her. 'You've made every effort to convince me otherwise.'

'I mean, if you really think I could be any good . . .'

'I don't like time-wasters, Cherry,' Gill told her, remembering the nun's warning and staying firm.

'I've blown my chances of piano lessons then?' she said.

'Stop messing me about,' said Gill with authority. 'You either want to learn or you don't: it's as simple as that.'

'I do wanna learn.'

Gill looked at her doubtfully, half expecting her mood to alter again. She found herself actually wanting to teach her. 'If you're really serious about wanting to learn, I'll teach you . . .' she said.

'I do want to.'

'But I'm not prepared to tolerate the bad manners you have shown me here today,' she said in a strong voice.

'I won't do it again.'

'One wrong word and I'll give your place to the next one on the waiting list,' she told her. 'Is that clear?'

Cherry nodded. 'I'm sorry, miss,' she said, looking genuinely contrite.

'Why do it, Cherry – why behave so badly?' asked Gill.

'Dunno,' she said, shrugging her bony little shoulders.

'You really don't know?'

'No I don't,' she confessed glumly. 'Something just comes over me . . . I get in a temper and I've done somethin' bad before I can stop meself.'

She looked so forlorn and lonely, Gill wanted to hug her. The urge to get closer to Cherry was strong. But she didn't want to upset the nuns by making too much of one particular pupil, especially on her first day.

'Well, if you behave like that again you're out. Is that clear?'

'Yes, miss.'

Looking at her watch, Gill said, 'There's still five minutes

162

to go of your time – so how about another go at "Three Blind Mice"?'

The little girl gave Gill a smile which altered her whole appearance, her eyes lighting up, a dimple appearing in her right cheek. 'That would be smashing,' she said, and walked back to the piano to sit down next to Gill.

Chapter Ten

One Saturday afternoon in January of the following year, the staff and customers at the Fulham branch of Bex Sports were discussing the recent demise of Sir Winston Churchill, who had been buried that day.

'It's very sad,' remarked a woman who was buying a pair of football socks for her son with the assistance of Arnie. 'But the great man had a good innings.'

'Not half,' Arnie agreed, putting the socks into a bag. 'I wouldn't mind living to be ninety myself.' He picked up his pen to write the sales invoice. 'I wouldn't fancy the idea of having people file past me as I lay in my coffin, though. I'd sooner be out o' sight once I'm dead.'

'Don't worry, Arnie,' smiled Mary Bex, who was standing in at the shop today because everyone except the Briscoe brothers had gone down with flu. 'There's no chance of your body laying in state.'

'Oh, I dunno so much about that,' joked John, who was serving a boy with a goalkeeper's jersey in the colours of Tottenham Hotspur. 'We could put his coffin on the turf at Borough Football Club so that all the old codgers can come and pay their last respects.'

'Watch it, bruv,' admonished Arnie, grinning. 'Any more of your cheek and I'll be ordering your coffin prematurely.'

Laughter rippled through the shop. Many of the customers were regulars and enjoyed the cheerful banter between the Briscoe brothers.

Mary, who was working her way through a queue at the

other counter and had just been to the stock room in search of soccer boots, came over to Arnie. 'Are there any more football boots anywhere?' she asked.

'Only what's there,' he said, glancing towards a pile of boxed boots behind the counter, 'and in the stock room.'

'Mm. That's what I was afraid of,' Mary said, frowning.

Having explained to the customer that they didn't have what he wanted, Mary served those people who were waiting then went to the small staff room at the back of the shop to make some tea, leaving the Briscoe brothers holding the fort.

They worked well together, and she and Len were pleased to have them on the staff. John had been a bit surly at first, but once he'd settled down and got to grips with the job he'd proved to be an excellent counter hand. Like his brother, he had a natural way with the customers. They made an entertaining double act and were a definite asset to the business.

'The tea's made, boys,' she called into the shop to them. 'You can take it in turns to come in for your break.'

Arnie joined her as soon as he'd finished serving his customer, leaving John in the shop alone.

'Why is the stock of football boots so low?' Mary enquired as she and Arnie sat down with their tea.

'We've had a run on them.'

'But more should have been ordered in plenty of time – especially at the height of the season,' she said. This was a matter of some concern; Mary was a shrewd businesswoman. 'I've lost several sales today because we didn't have what the customer wanted.'

'It's annoying, isn't it?'

'It's more than just annoying, Arnie,' she said. 'It's bad for business and it shouldn't happen.'

'Nothing to do with me,' he swiftly pointed out. 'Jack's in charge of stock control. He does all the ordering.'

'Yes, I realise that.'

'He might have more on order,' said Arnie, 'I'm not sure.'

'I'll find out and get things moving,' Mary said. 'I shall

also tell Len to have a few words with Jack when he gets back from sick leave. We can't carry on like this, losing business just because of sloppy stock control.'

Personally Arnie thought the manager needed a rocket up his arse to get him moving, but he had no intention of being disloyal to his colleague by saying so. He liked Jack as a person but didn't rate him as a manager at all. Unbeknown to the Bexes, Arnie was always reminding Jack to do things and covering up for him because certain jobs hadn't been done. It was irritating, especially as Arnie was convinced that this shop could do even better with more efficient management.

They talked about business for a while longer, then Mary asked, 'How's Gill?'

'She's fine.'

'And how is the budding musical genius from St Theresa's?' she asked.

Arnie looked blank.

'The little girl who's doing so well with her piano lessons,' explained Mary.

Still no reaction.

'Hasn't Gill told you about her?'

He shook his head.

'Really,' said Mary in surprise. 'I thought she would have mentioned her because she's so pleased with the way Cherry's coming along. She's always been a very difficult child up until now, but she's a changed girl since she started lessons with Gill.'

'That's good,' Arnie said flatly.

'She must have found her forte, I suppose.' Mary giggled to ease the sudden tension. 'Oh dear, what a dreadful pun.'

'Yeah,' he grinned.

'Anyway, the nuns are delighted with what Gill's doing for Cherry.'

'Good for Gill,' he said with an edge to his voice that worried Mary. She liked and trusted Arnie as a colleague, and considered Gill to be a dear friend. And if she wasn't very much mistaken they were having serious problems with their marriage. It was a pity, because they were both such lovely people and obviously made for each other, despite their current difficulties.

'She was full of it when I last saw her,' Mary continued. 'She seems to have become very fond of young Cherry.'

'She doesn't say much about her work to me,' Arnie said, his conscience troubling him for not taking as much interest as he might. 'Probably because I'm tone deaf.'

'Most married couples find it helpful to talk about their work, I should think,' said Mary casually, sipping her tea and nibbling a biscuit. 'But not you two, by the sound of it.'

'Not to any extent, no,' he said. He didn't add that he and Gill never talked about anything these days. All they did was bicker and snipe at each other, except when they were putting on an act for Craig's benefit. They seemed to drift further apart with each passing day, and he wasn't able to put things right because his feelings towards his wife were in such turmoil.

'Seems a shame.'

'We just never seem to get around to it,' he fibbed. 'You know how it is – you start watching the telly in the evening and it's bedtime before you know it.'

'That's the trouble with television,' Mary said. 'It destroys the art of conversation.'

It was more than just the art of conversation that had been destroyed between Arnie and his wife. Every time he looked at her he was reminded of the bad things he'd done to her, which inflamed the guilt that had festered and grown over the years rather than diminished with the passing of time. The accident, the miscarriage and its consequences, the loss of confidence that had prevented him from providing for his family and made him so hateful – none of these things would have happened if he'd not let success go to his head. The events were all in the past, but his feelings about them remained as strong as ever.

Perversely, his own sense of self-loathing made him want to hurt *her*. And when he'd done that with a few cutting words and a cold attitude, he hated himself even more. Because deep in his heart he still loved her. No matter how hard he tried to be different, it just didn't happen. The whole situation was driving him crazy, which was why he spent so much time out of the house – if he wasn't at home, he couldn't hurt her.

The little girl from the home was probably a surrogate daughter to Gill, he thought bitterly.

Personally he didn't regret not being able to increase their family, because he was content with Craig. But he sensed that one child wasn't enough for Gill, whatever she said to the contrary. She always used to talk about wanting a daughter – years ago, when that was still possible.

'So they reckon,' he said now to Mary. 'But few of us want to be without it, do we? Not if we're really honest.'

'That's very true, Arnie,' she said. 'It's become part of the culture.'

Mary had perceived a definite change of mood in Arnie since she'd mentioned his wife. Despite their cheery manner, both Gill and Arnie Briscoe were falling apart inside and there seemed to be nothing anyone else could do about it.

Mary finished her tea and stood up with a purposeful air. 'Right, I'll go and cover for John so that he can have his break,' she said.

'Okay, I'll just finish my tea and I'll be back on duty.'

As Mary re-entered the shop, the customer John had just finished serving was leaving with his purchases. In the split second before John realised that she was there, Mary saw something that turned her to stone and put all thoughts of Gill and Arnie's marriage out of her mind.

Arnie stormed into Phoebe's flat that evening looking for his brother, whom he found sitting at the table in the living room with his mother, tucking into sausages and chips for tea.

'You thieving toe-rag,' Arnie fumed, dragging his brother

from his chair so roughly that John's knife and fork clattered to the floor.

'Here, what's going on?' Phoebe demanded, abandoning her meal and standing up with an anxious look on her face.

'Yeah, what's got into you?' asked John breathlessly.

'You've had your sticky little fingers in the till at the shop,' said Arnie grimly. 'That's what's the matter.'

'Oh, no, John,' said Phoebe with a sob in her voice. She was scrupulously honest herself and had always tried to raise her sons to be the same.

'No I haven't,' John denied.

'You bloody well have, you young tea-leaf,' said Arnie, holding him by the arms and shaking him. 'So don't lie to me.'

'Calm down, for Gawd's sake, Arnie,' said his mother, who didn't want to believe these allegations. 'If John says he hasn't done it, then he hasn't.'

'I'm sorry that you're having to hear this, Mum.' Arnie let go of John and looked at his mother. 'But I've just come from the shop. Len came over to the branch just before closing time and asked me to stay on because he had something to tell me.' He looked at his brother, his eyes full of fury and disappointment. 'He wanted me to know before he fired you because it was me who recommended you for the job. You're getting your cards first thing Monday morning, mate. Mary Bex saw you pocket the money you took from a cash sale instead of putting it through the till. She actually *saw* you do it, so don't bother to deny it.'

John was whey-faced and silent, staring at the floor.

Arnie sunk down heavily into an armchair, a grim expression on his face. 'This isn't the first time, is it?'

Silence.

'You've been milking the cash sales, haven't you?' said Arnie with a heavy sigh.

John didn't reply.

'Haven't you?' said Arnie, leaping up and staring at his brother.

The younger man nodded shamefully.

'How long?'

'Dunno . . . a few months maybe,' he said, looking utterly miserable.

'But why, for God's sake?' Arnie started pacing the room. 'Why do a thing like that? Why jeopardise a job you enjoy by stealing from a fair employer like Len? I mean, it isn't as though he doesn't pay us a decent wage.'

No reply.

'Len's a good bloke. He doesn't deserve this.'

Still John remained silent.

'Greed. Pure and simple!' Arnie roared. 'You'd put a good job at risk just so you can keep up with those thugs you hang around with.'

'That isn't why I did it.'

'Why did you do it, then?' asked Arnie. 'You just tell me that.'

'I can't.'

'You can't, I see,' Arnie said with withering sarcasm. 'Oh, that's wonderful, that is. My brother betrays my trust by nicking from the boss, and he can't even tell me why.'

The green tones in John's eyes looked vivid against his ashen skin as he stared at his brother. Suddenly perceiving terror lurking there, a possible explanation occurred to Arnie.

'Is someone leaning on you?' he asked in a softer tone.

'Course not,' said John, his denial too fast and emphatic to ring true.

'Did Harris and his mates put you up to it?' demanded Arnie.

'No.'

'I don't believe you.'

'That's up to you.'

Arnie changed tack, becoming more understanding. 'Look, bruv, if those louts forced you to do it, then tell me and I'll get them sorted,' he said. 'And Len might give you another chance . . .'

'You can't get 'em sorted.'

'So they *are* behind this?'

John stared at the floor.

'You must tell Arnie the truth, son,' Phoebe urged. 'So that we can get this thing cleared up once and for all.'

'You can't get it cleared up,' John insisted in a shaky voice.

'Oh no?' Arnie's tone was challenging.

'You don't know what Harris and his gang are like.'

'They've threatened to beat you up if you don't steal money for them – is that it?' asked Arnie.

'You think I'm scared of a beatin' from that bunch o' losers?' said John with affront. 'I ain't that feeble.'

'They've threatened to do something if you don't steal from the shop for them, though, haven't they?' said Arnie.

John's silence was answer enough.

'Is it me . . . or Gill or Craig?' Arnie demanded. 'Have they threatened to harm us if you don't do as they say?'

John shook his head, his eyes moving away from Arnie.

'Mum!' Arnie gasped in horror. 'They've threatened to do Mum over?'

Sinking weakly into a chair, John nodded. 'I thought Harris and his mates were great at first, a really good laugh. But I got bored with 'em after a while . . . sick of hanging about the streets looking for mischief. So I stopped seeing 'em and they didn't like that one little bit. They would wait for me when I went out and give me a good smacking. I had quite a few of those, but I still didn't go back with 'em. Eventually they lost interest and left me alone.'

'So why this, now?' asked Arnie.

'They got to know that I was working in a shop with access to money and they started leaning on me really heavily,' he explained. 'They said they'd beat Mum up good and proper if I didn't do what they said. They would have, too . . .'

'Oh, John, you damned fool,' said Arnie. 'Why didn't you come to me?'

'Because you'd have gone after 'em and got yourself hurt,'

he explained. 'There's too many of them; you wouldn't stand a chance. They're evil, I tell you. They'll kill me if they find out I've told anyone. And Mum won't be safe.'

'I'd like to see 'em try to harm any member of this family,' said Arnie determinedly. 'We'll get Head-Butter Harris and his mates sorted, don't you worry about that, bruv. But before we do anything else at all, we are going to see Len and Mary Bex to tell them what's been going on.'

'Now?' John asked worriedly.

'Yes, now,' Arnie told him. 'It can't wait till the morning. We'll go over to their house in Putney. I know where it is.'

'They probably won't be in,' John said, hoping to talk his brother out of it.

'We'll take a chance on that. I know Len well enough to know that whatever he's doing he'll want to hear what we have to say.'

'I can't face 'em.' John bit his lip.

'You're going to have to face 'em, whether you like it or not,' said Arnie. 'And you're going to do it *right now*.'

'All right, all right,' said John and went to get his coat.

On Phoebe's day off the following week, she caught the bus to Hammersmith and went to see Len and Mary Bex at their office.

'I just had to come and thank you in person, and tell you how grateful I am to you both for all you've done for my boy,' she said after introductions had been made. 'It's ever so good of you to give him another chance. He's been a damned fool.'

'He certainly has, Mrs Briscoe,' agreed Len.

'Everyone calls me Phoebe.'

'Then we'll do the same, Phoebe,' Len said, glancing towards his wife, who nodded.

'Thanks anyway for what you've done; it means a lot to me.'

'We decided to give young John another chance because we think that what he's done was stupid rather than criminal, and he does seem genuinely sorry.'

'He is, I promise you.'

'If he'd taken so much as a penny piece from here for himself, I'd have had him in court before his feet could touch the ground – and if he ever does anything like that again, that's what I will do no matter what the reason,' Len said in an adamant tone. 'I've made that very clear to him.'

'So I've heard.'

'But I think he's basically honest, if not very careful when it comes to choosing his friends.'

'You don't have to tell me that,' Phoebe said, smiling and looking very striking in a red coat with a black furry collar, her blonde hair beehived on top and taken back into a French pleat at the back. The passing years had been kind to her, and her trim figure belied her forty-six years. 'Arnie and I have been worried to death about John ever since he got in with that Harris and his crowd. Of course, we didn't realise he'd tried to break away from them.'

'When we found out what was behind his pilfering, it put a different light on the matter,' said Len. He paused, and a hard look came into his eyes. 'He has to pay the money back, though.'

'And quite right too.'

'We've worked out roughly how much he's taken and we're going to deduct something from his wages every week until it's paid off,' said Mary. 'I know he doesn't actually have the money, but we have to recoup our losses. The louts certainly don't have any of it left. All gone on drugs, I shouldn't wonder. We're hoping it'll teach John never to get involved in anything like that again.'

'It's only right and proper that he should pay the money back, and it's very good of you to be so understanding,' said Phoebe, flashing a warm smile from one to the other. 'It's a load off my mind to have John away from that rough crowd, I can tell you.'

'I'm sure it must be,' said Mary. 'It's all behind him now.'

'Yeah, thank Gawd.' Phoebe paused and directed her gaze to Len. 'I understand that you've taken care of Harris and his gang,' she said, meeting his eyes and feeling dazzled by his overwhelming physical presence. It was as though he alone filled the room.

'I certainly have, my dear. They won't be bothering John again,' he replied.

'They're a wicked lot,' said Phoebe. 'I hope you didn't get hurt.'

'I didn't go anywhere near them,' Len explained. 'My brawling days are long over. But I've plenty of contacts around here. I only had to pick up the phone and the matter was dealt with sharpish.'

'You didn't arrange to have 'em killed, I hope,' Phoebe said worriedly.

Len threw back his head and laughed, a deep booming sound that touched something deep inside Phoebe.

'Even if I felt they deserved it, I'm a businessman not a gangster,' he said, still smiling. 'You can relax. All I did was arrange to have 'em roughed up and sufficiently shaken to make sure they keep away from young John in future.'

'I think it's taught him a lesson,' said Phoebe. 'In being more careful in the company he keeps, if nothing else.'

'Let's hope so,' said Len, observing her with approval. She was good-looking in a brash kind of way – the sort of woman he might have fancied if he hadn't been happily married.

'Fancy a cup of tea?' Mary asked. 'We're just about to have one.'

'That's very kind of you,' said Phoebe. 'I'd love one.'

When Mary had left the room to make the tea, Phoebe said, 'I hope I'm not holding you up.'

'We'd soon tell you if you were, don't worry,' Len said. 'We'd have been taking a break about now anyway. I'm going over to the Acton branch when I've had a cuppa, while Mary gets on with the wages.'

'She does the office work then?'

He nodded. 'She works on the counter an' all if necessary. We both do. You have to be versatile when it's your own business.'

'I suppose you do.'

'You not working?'

'Yeah. I work in Woolworth's, but it's my day off today,' she said.

'Do you like it there?'

'Yeah, it's okay,' she said. 'I've done worse jobs.'

'Such as . . . ?' Len asked with interest.

'Factory work, cleaning shops and offices at four o'clock in the morning, charring in people's houses to make a few bob. Not to mention my share of war work. I had to do whatever I could find with two boys to bring up on my own.'

'You've done a good job with those two.'

'Thank you,' she said without false modesty. 'I like to think so.'

'So . . . Woolworth's suits you then?' he asked chattily.

'It gets a bit boring sometimes on the counter, but most of the time it's all right,' she said. 'I like dealing with people.'

'Must be where your boys get it from,' Len said. He had noticed in Phoebe the same casual confidence he'd seen in Arnie and John – especially Arnie.

'Could be,' she said. 'You've got to like people to do shop-work. The public can be infuriating at times when you're the wrong side of the counter, as you well know.'

'I'll say.'

'Some people get all high and mighty because your job is to serve them,' she said. 'A lot of the girls I work with get quite upset about it, but I don't have much trouble.'

'We'll have to bear you in mind next time we're looking for an assistant in one of our shops then, won't we?' Len said lightly.

'Oh, I dunno about that,' she said, surprised by his remark. 'I'm quite happy where I am.'

'A change is as good as a rest, so they say,' Len persisted, grinning and cocking his head.

'I have heard it said.'

'I bet you know a lot about football, as the mother of a one-time professional player.'

'Not half.' She threw him a shrewd look. 'But you're not seriously offering me a job, are you?'

'Not at this moment, but I might be in the future when a vacancy comes up,' he said, because even without seeing her in action, he knew Phoebe was right for Bex Sports.

She was flattered. 'We'll talk about that another time, then,' she said.

'Sure.'

'You'd have more Briscoes than Bexes if I were to join the firm,' she laughed.

They were both chuckling when Mary came in with a tray of tea and biscuits. Len told her what they'd been talking about.

'It'd be company for me to have a woman on the staff,' said Mary. 'It's always the men who apply for the jobs in our shops, which means I'm completely outnumbered.'

'Maybe I'll help to even things up one of these days,' Phoebe said casually.

'I do hope so,' said Mary with genuine enthusiasm. There was something about Phoebe Briscoe that made her want to see more of her. She was so warm and hearty you knew instinctively that she'd be popular with the customers.

When she'd finished her tea, Phoebe left the shop and walked along King Street to the bus stop, thinking what a smashing couple the Bexes were. Mary was a real dear. It was no wonder Gill was so friendly with her. And as for him . . . well, he was what Phoebe called a *real man*. He would probably be described as ugly by some people, with his broken nose and granite jaw, but his charisma sent shivers up her spine. And when those piercing brown eyes had rested on her she'd felt like a girl again, hungry for all the physical pleasures of love.

Even though Phoebe had had occasional boyfriends since she'd been widowed, it was years since a man had aroused her that way. Silly cow, she admonished herself, catching sight of her reflection in a shop window and seeing a woman long past her prime – the man is happily married to a lovely woman, so there's no point in your getting any ideas.

Anyone is entitled to their fantasies, though, she thought, and she had a faraway look in her eyes as she got on to the bus.

'That was very good indeed, Cherry,' Gill said as the girl came to the end of a short classical piece that was one of the pieces she was to perform in her forthcoming exam. 'You play to that standard on the day and you'll earn yourself a distinction, just like you did in the theory exam.'

'Can I start on the music for the next grade if I pass this one?'

'Certainly. As long as the nuns agree to your continuing with lessons, I'll have the music here ready for you at the beginning of next term,' said Gill.

'I can't wait.'

Gill had no doubt that Cherry would sail through the practical exam, as she had the theory, which she had taken in a local hall with all the other candidates from the area. Gill didn't expect Cherry's performance to be spoiled by nerves as happened to so many pupils during a practical exam. This child didn't have a nerve in her body when it came to performing to an audience. In fact, she became so absorbed in the music that she hardly seemed aware other people were present.

After that difficult first meeting last autumn, Gill had found her to be a delight. She still had her moods like any other growing child, and there were times when Gill had to tick her off for being saucy. But for the most part she was a joy to teach because she was so keen and had such a natural aptitude for it.

Music had given her a new lease of life, according to the nuns, who were finding her much easier to deal with. She was still cheeky to them at times – that was undoubtedly inherent in her nature – but apparently she spent every spare moment she could at the recreation room piano. She often did a practice session before school in the mornings when there was no one else around.

Whether or not Cherry would retain this level of enthusiasm in the autumn, when she changed schools and went outside of St Theresa's for her education, Gill couldn't be absolutely sure. If she was selected for the grammar school, as the nuns expected she would be, she would have homework to cope with. There would be new friends and pastimes to distract her attention whichever senior school she attended. But Gill doubted that Cherry would lose her interest in music altogether, because she was a born musician.

'Can I do that piece again, please, miss?' she asked now.

Gill looked at her watch. It was past time, but Cherry was the last pupil. 'Only if you go through the whole exam paper, including the scales and arpeggios.'

Cherry did a mock groan, then played the pieces with accuracy and feeling. It was a pleasure to listen to her.

'You'll do,' said Gill, smiling. 'Now I really must go. I have to collect my son from my mother's and take him to a football match he's playing in.'

'How old is he?'

'Nearly eight.'

'Are you teaching him to play the piano?'

'No.'

'Why?'

'He doesn't want to learn.'

'Can't you make him?' she asked with youthful innocence.

'I could do, I suppose,' said Gill. 'But I don't believe in using force – not when it comes to music, anyway.'

'Sister Maud says that doing things you don't like makes you a better person,' said Cherry.

'I'm sure she's right,' agreed Gill. 'But I think there are enough hated tasks in Craig's life to keep him on the right track. I'm sure it isn't necessary to add music to them.'

'What sort of things?'

'All the usual ones ... lessons he finds difficult like arithmetic, running errands for me when he wants to play, going to bed at a reasonable hour, eating his greens—'

'Oh, those.'

'You see, Cherry, I believe you have to have a feel for playing a musical instrument or it's pointless.' Gill stood up and slipped into her reefer jacket which she wore over a short skirt and high, shiny boots. 'Craig's passion is football. He has a real feeling for it.'

'He's lucky to have you,' said Cherry. 'I wish you were my mother.'

Swallowing a lump in her throat, Gill buttoned her jacket. 'That's because you only see me once a week,' she said, blinking back the tears. 'If you saw me all the time and I had to nag you about keeping your room tidy and washing behind your ears, you'd soon get sick of me.'

'I bet I wouldn't.'

'Well, that's something we'll never know,' said Gill, feeling suddenly quite emotional, 'so let's just enjoy being friends, shall we?'

'Okay,' Cherry agreed.

Noticing that she seemed set to stay at the piano, Gill said, 'Give yourself a break from the exam pieces over the next few days. Play something just for pleasure. Something from that book of pop tunes I gave you.'

'All right, miss,' she said, 'but I just want to go through this once more.'

Such dedication. This girl has what it takes to go far as a musician, Gill thought, as she left the building and made her way along the gravel drive to the main gates. It was a dull, chilly March day with a sharp breeze swinging through ancient oaks and plane trees burgeoning with new leaves. The trees creaked in the wind and there was a smell of rain in the air as dark clouds rolled across the mottled grey skies.

Outside in the street the noise buffeted Gill after the quiet of St Theresa's grounds, bringing her back to reality and the weight of her problems. Teaching was her escape. Because it was so absorbing her thoughts couldn't drift on to the parlous state of her marriage or the fact that things couldn't go on as they were between herself and Arnie.

He was hardly ever home these days. Since he'd been made manager of the Fulham branch, he worked later at the shop in the evening. He even went in on Sundays for a while, supposedly to catch up on paperwork but she suspected he went to escape the tension of being with her. If he wasn't at the shop he was in a pub somewhere.

About the only thing he came home for was to eat and sleep, and to see his beloved son. He certainly didn't come home to see Gill. His attitude towards her led her to believe that he had finally grown to hate her. Naturally she wondered from time to time if he was seeing another woman, but she never gave this any serious thought because she believed their problems stemmed from something far more sinister and complicated.

She was worried about the effect the bad atmosphere between them must be having on Craig. Although they tried not to argue in front of him, surely he couldn't help but be aware of the coldness between his parents.

Deciding to walk to her mother's rather than wait for the bus, she strode out towards Maisie Road, the wind smarting her face with spots of rain. But she was glad of the fresh air to clear her head. Passing through Fulham Broadway, she glanced towards Bex Sports. Her heart had once leapt at the possibility of seeing Arnie; now her stomach knotted with dread at the thought, because they could no longer communicate.

North End Road market was in full Saturday flow as she headed for her mother's. The rowdy clamour hammered painfully into Gill's head and grated on her overstretched nerves: the shout of spielers, the uneven chant of people talking, the traffic roaring and Roger Miller's 'King of the Road' blaring out at full volume from the record stall.

Gill saw several people she knew and exchanged a few friendly words, but she felt isolated and alone as long as the worry of her failing marriage hung over her. She stopped along the way to buy fruit, some sweets for Craig and a bag of her mother's favourite toffees.

Somewhere between the market and Maisie Road, with a sinking heart, she made a decision. She was going to bring things with Arnie to a head – tonight.

She had to wait until after Craig was in bed before broaching the subject, at which point Arnie departed to the pub. When he got back he settled into an armchair and stared gloomily at the television.

Inwardly quaking, Gill went over to the set and turned it off.

'What's going on?' he asked, scowling at her.

'We have to talk, Arnie.'

'Oh no,' he groaned.

'Oh yes. You know as well as I do that we can't go on as we are.'

He got up in an agitated manner and glared at her. 'Don't you ever stop nagging?' he said, knowing he was being unreasonable but unable to stem the flow of words. Powerless to change anything, he felt compelled to strike out and hurt her.

'It's difficult not to nag given the situation,' she said.

'I've got a job now; I'm paying my share in the house. What more do you want?' he said, evading the issue.

'I want my husband back.'

'I'm here, aren't I?' he said, deliberately misunderstanding her.

'Your physical presence is occasionally here,' she told him, managing against all the odds to stay calm. 'But you haven't been here with me in your heart for a long time.'

'For God's sake, stop going on at me,' he snapped, 'or I'll go out again. I'm not gonna put up with all this bloody hassle. Nag, nag, nag, every time I set foot inside the door.'

As he marched towards the door, Gill went after him and dragged him back with a strength she hadn't known she had. 'Oh, no, Arnie, you're not running away from me this time.'

He stared at her, waiting.

'This time we're going to sort things out once and for all,' she said, her voice ragged with emotion, her body trembling all over as she let go of him and moved back. 'It isn't going to get any better by pretending there's nothing wrong. It isn't good for us and it isn't good for Craig.'

'All right. Say what you have to say,' he said, his voice shaking too.

'I'm not prepared to live like this any longer,' she said, struggling to remain strong. 'Your never being here and us bickering if we're together for more than a few minutes, I mean. I've had enough of your moods and your bad temper. I'm sick of making excuses for you.'

'Oh, so that's what all this is about,' he said, dodging the issue again. 'Just because I like to go out—'

'*No, no, no!* That isn't what this is about and you know it,' she said, her voice rising. 'It's the reason you stay out that's bothering me.'

'Why do you think I stay out?'

'Presumably because you can't bear to stay at home with me, because all we do is quarrel, and no matter what I do to stop it it still happens,' she said. 'I no longer have a husband so much as a sparring partner.'

His eyes were dark with emotion, his skin pale and suffused with a fine layer of sweat. 'All right. You want the truth, so I'll give you the truth,' he said, his voice quivering. 'You're right – I do stay out because I don't want to come home. And I don't want to come home because I can't cope with the way

I feel and I don't know what to do about it.' He put his hand to his chest. 'There's so much pain inside here, and you are a constant reminder of how I've screwed things up and let you down.'

'In what way?'

'In every way,' he said. 'The accident, your not being able to have any more children – all of it. I'm sick of carrying a burden which I can't forget as long as I'm with you.'

'I've never blamed you for any of those things,' she said.

'Maybe not, but we both know it was my fault.' He put his hands to his head. 'I can't get away from the past when I'm with you, and I'm tired of it. You've become an albatross around my neck.'

The pain was so intense, she couldn't move or utter a word. Part of her wanted to throw herself at his feet and beg him to work with her to make their marriage work, to give it one more try. But she had tried everything she knew over a long period. She'd persuaded and coaxed and made allowances for him until she was weary of trying, and it had made not a scrap of difference. When she looked back on the punishing complexities of their life together these last few years, she knew she couldn't take any more. It seemed so long since they'd been happy.

'In that case I suggest you move out,' she said in a small voice, hardly able to bear the agony of uttering the words. 'The last thing I want to do is be a burden to you.'

He slumped into an armchair with his head in his hands, his body trembling, shoulders heaving. Knowing he was crying, she wanted to hold him and soothe away his pain. But it was too late for that. That would only delay the inevitable.

After a while he looked up and spoke, his words seeming unreal to Gill, echoing in her head as though she was dreaming. 'Yeah. I think you're right. It'll probably be best if I move out,' he said thickly.

'Oh.'

'As you say, we can't go on like this any longer,' he said.

'Apart from anything else it isn't fair to the nipper.'

'No.'

'I'll go tonight and stay in a hotel or something. I don't wanna turn up at Mum's place out of the blue at this time of night,' he said. 'I don't feel like answering questions yet anyway.'

'There's no need for you to leave right away,' she said.

'If I stay until the morning I'll only put it off . . .'

'Yes.'

'Right, then . . .'

'Craig will be sorry not to have seen you,' she said through dry lips.

'Tell him I'll come and see him in a few days' time, and I'll arrange to see him regularly after that,' he said.

'All that sort of thing will have to be worked out in due course.'

'Yeah, sometime – but not now,' he said.

'No, not now,' she agreed, knowing that neither of them could face the agonising practicalities of a broken marriage just yet.

'Just tell him I love him and I'll see him soon.'

'Sure,' she said, biting back the tears.

He went upstairs to pack a case while Gill sat rigid in the armchair by the living-room fire, hardly able to believe this was happening.

'I'll be off then,' he said, poking his head round the door.

'Right.'

'I'll come back for the rest of my stuff in a day or two.'

'Okay.'

'See you then,' he said, as though she was one of his mates.

'Cheerio,' she said numbly.

And he was gone. Just like that. They had parted like strangers. It didn't seem possible.

She went to the window and peered through the curtains into the murky night as he opened the door of his Ford Zephyr. The rain that had been threatening earlier had settled into a

184

steady drizzle and a mist clouded the glow from the street-lights.

He stood there in the rain, looking towards the house, a sad, wet figure oblivious to the weather. Gill's heart pounded as she stupidly hoped he would come back to her. But after a few moments he turned and got into the car.

Putting the curtains back into place with trembling fingers, she stood with her back to the fireplace, staring at nothing, too tense to sit down or shed a tear. Although the break was a shock now that it had actually happened, she knew that her marriage had been over for a long time.

Looking back on it, she could see that it had begun to head for the rocks when Arnie had got his big chance in football. Everything had changed then. The bad times had heavily outweighed the good ones if she was brutally honest. So what had happened tonight was all for the best.

But even though she knew that she and Arnie were no longer compatible, she still loved him and felt utterly bereft now that it was over.

Mulling it over as he drove into Central London to look for an hotel for the night, Arnie told himself he'd done the right thing in leaving. For Gill's sake as well as his own, he'd needed to be free from his marriage for a long time, but had been too much of a coward to bring it to an end. The constant bickering had been destroying them all.

He'd never wanted any other woman but Gill, and still didn't. And he loved his son. But what should have been a winning combination just didn't work for them.

The wipers beat a path across the rainsoaked windscreen with their plodding rhythm, the tyres fizzing on the greasy roads. His thoughts drifted back to the beginning, to the good times he and Gill had had. They had been so right together once – before life had become grim and disappointing, before love and passion had turned to resentment and pain.

Even though marriage had been forced upon him before

he'd been ready, he'd never felt trapped because Gill was all he had wanted in life. Not until after the accident had he felt the constant need to escape from the limitations that had been heaped upon him. Marriage had seemed like a prison then, because he'd been so hemmed in by his own sense of failure.

What had happened tonight was inevitable, and was the best thing for them all. Once you stopped being able to make a woman happy, it was time to get out of her life and leave the way clear for her to make a new start.

But if it was so right for them all, why was his heart breaking?

Chapter Eleven

'I guessed all wasn't well with those two,' said Winnie gravely a few days later. The Millers were having their evening meal, and the break-up of Gill and Arnie's marriage was now common knowledge. 'But I didn't think it would come to this.'

'Is it definitely all over between them?' asked Hal, cutting into a lamb chop.

'Sounds like it to me,' said Winnie, mashing some potato into her gravy. 'There didn't seem to be any doubt in Gill's mind when she said there's no chance of their making it up. Things have been really bad between them for ages, apparently.'

'It's a damned shame,' said Hal.

'There's been a terrible atmosphere between them for a long time,' said Winnie. 'I've felt uncomfortable in their company.'

'We all have.'

'Bearing that in mind, I suppose what Gill's going through now can't be much worse than living with all that bad feeling for so long.' Winnie sympathised strongly with her elder daughter, who she knew was broken-hearted despite her brave attempts not to show it.

'It's the best thing that could have happened in my opinion,' said Carol sharply.

'That's a bit hard, dear,' said her soft-hearted father.

'I don't see why,' she said briskly. 'If they're not happy, why stay together?'

'They've had a bad patch.' Hal liked Arnie, and was disappointed to lose him as a member of the family.

'Come off it, Dad,' Carol said in a mocking tone. 'It was a lot more than just a bad patch. It was like a war zone at their place when they were both at home.'

'You're wrong when you say it's the best thing that could have happened, Carol,' Winnie intervened. 'The best thing would be for them to work through their differences and stay together . . . for the sake of Craig, if nothing else.'

'That's a very old-fashioned attitude,' declared Carol.

'I am old fashioned, and I've never pretended otherwise,' announced Winnie. 'I was old fashioned about Gill being pregnant before she got married too, and I was proved right. This is what happens when people get married before they're ready.'

'Not necessarily.' Carol was finding both her parents irritating in the extreme. Apart from their suffocating homeliness, they were so out of touch with the modern world.

'They were just a couple of kids with no experience of life when they got married,' Winnie said.

'We don't know that's the reason for their breaking up, love,' said Hal, who always tried to be fair. 'It could have happened anyway. Marriage doesn't work for everyone.'

'People change and want different things, that's why,' said Carol.

'People don't work at it, more like.' Winnie was uncompromising because this was something she felt strongly about. 'Marriage is for life in my opinion.'

'That's what we think, dear, but attitudes towards marriage aren't the same as they were,' Hal pointed out evenly. 'Some people don't even bother to get married at all nowadays.'

'Unheard of in our day, all this living together nonsense,' said Winnie.

'Mm,' Hal murmured.

'And what about young Craig?' Winnie said, her mind racing with the far-reaching consequences of her daughter's

188

failed marriage. 'What's life gonna be like for him now? That little boy thinks the world of his dad.'

'He was always a good father,' said Hal, 'I'll say that much for Arnie.'

'And he still will be,' said Carol with seething impatience. 'He isn't leaving the country, for heaven's sake.'

'No, but it won't be the same for the child.' Winnie ignored her daughter's rudeness because she was used to it.

'Of course not. How can it be?' Carol said through clenched teeth. 'But if Gill and Arnie aren't getting on, they shouldn't stay together just because of Craig.'

'Plenty of parents do,' said Winnie, throwing her daughter a dark look. 'Many a marriage has survived because of the children.'

'It might have been like that in your day—' Carol began.

'And it still is today in a lot of cases,' said Winnie. 'All right, so you have the mini-skirt and the pill and free love and all the rest of it. But a lot of young people still believe in marriage. Even that bloke from the Beatles, Ringo Starr or whatever his name is, got married the other day. I saw it in the paper.'

'I know that. All I'm saying is that divorce isn't frowned upon these days,' Carol insisted. 'People do it all the time.'

'Hey, hang on,' Hal said with a deeply furrowed brow. 'Who said anything about divorce?'

'Well, I just assumed ... I mean, that's what people do when they split up, isn't it? They get divorced. There's no point in their staying legally married if they're not together any more.'

'I suppose not,' Winnie agreed with reluctance.

'Frankly, I think their breaking up was inevitable.' Carol pushed her plate away.

'Oh, you do, do you?' Hal evidently didn't like his daughter's attitude.

'Yes I do,' she confirmed heartlessly. 'You can tell they've stopped loving each other. That's been obvious for ages.'

'I wouldn't go so far as to say they've stopped loving each other,' said Hal.

'Why are they always at each other's throats then?' Carol asked.

'Things have been difficult for them since Arnie's accident,' he replied.

'Because they fell out of love, that's why,' Carol stated.

'It isn't always as cut and dried as that, love,' said Winnie knowingly. 'Marriage can be a very complicated business . . .'

'And I wouldn't know anything about that, of course,' said Carol acidly.

'Well . . . you can't speak from experience, can you, dear?' Winnie gave her daughter a shrewd look. 'Some things you have to experience personally to know what they're like. Marriage is all about everyday living as well as love.'

'Obviously,' Carol sneered.

'There's no call to get lippy,' Winnie rebuked.

'Oh God!'

'Don't you "Oh God" me.'

'Oh, for goodness' sake—'

'I'll thank you to watch your manners, my girl,' Winnie retorted. 'You're impossible to live with these days . . .'

'Perhaps I should move out of here then,' Carol threatened.

'You know where the door is,' said Winnie, but she knew that the only way Carol would move out of the family home would be by getting married. She was far too fond of her personal comfort to strike out on her own, with all the extra expense and responsibility that would entail. As much as Winnie loved her daughter, she wished she would get a place of her own. Her moodiness made life unbearable for them all at times. Since that dreadful business with Dougie she'd been more difficult than ever.

'I'll get out of your hair,' she said. 'Don't you worry about that. It might not be tomorrow, but I'll go, oh yes.'

Down went Winnie's knife and fork, and she gave an expressive sigh. 'Oh, do stop being so difficult, dear,' she said wearily. 'I've quite enough to worry about at the moment with your sister.'

There was a brief hiatus while Carol reviewed the situation. When she spoke again her manner had changed completely. She knew she could only push people so far, even her pliable parents.

'Don't worry about Gill, Mum,' she said, forcing herself to be pleasant. 'She'll be fine. She's still young; she'll soon meet someone else.'

Winnie gave her a sharp look. 'Oh my Lord, I should think finding another man is about the last thing on her mind at the moment,' she said.

'Eventually, I mean,' said Carol.

'Oh, yes, I suppose she will eventually,' Winnie agreed. 'They both will in time.'

'Definitely,' said Carol. 'It's only natural that they should do.'

Carol's parents would have been very shocked had they known how delighted she was about the break-up of her sister's marriage.

Carol hadn't had such good news in ages.

When the bell rang one Saturday evening in September Craig rushed to the front door because he knew it would be his father. The boy spent most Sundays with Arnie, who sometimes collected him after work on Saturday so that they could spend Saturday evening together too.

'Hello, Arnie,' said Gill, following her son to the door.

'Hi. How are you?'

'Fine thanks,' she said. 'You?'

'Mustn't grumble.'

She looked at Craig, whose face was wreathed in smiles. The way his whole being seemed to light up when he saw his father brought a lump to her throat. 'Have you got everything you need, Craig?' she asked.

'Yeah,' he said excitedly, clutching his overnight bag.

'Here, let me take that for you, son,' Arnie offered, reaching for the bag.

'It's okay, Dad,' he said with boyish eagerness to impress his father. 'I can manage.'

Arnie smiled knowingly, then looked at Gill. 'I'll have him back by about five thirty tomorrow, okay?' he said.

'That'll be fine,' she said amiably. 'No later than that, though. He has to be up early for school on Monday morning.'

'Sure.'

They fell silent. The atmosphere had become suddenly highly charged. She could feel the insistent pull of chemistry drawing them together and she sensed that he could feel it too.

The spell was broken by Craig. 'Are we going then, Dad?' he asked.

'Yep,' said Arnie, looking at him.

'Come on then,' he said eagerly.

'We'll be off then,' Arnie said to Gill.

'Okay.'

'Do you wanna come with us, Mum?' asked Craig as an innocent afterthought.

Gill felt his words like a blow. How could an eight-year-old be expected to understand the complicated nature of what went on between adults?

'I've things to do, love,' she said. 'You go off with Daddy and have a good time.'

'Okay.'

Sounding only mildly disappointed, he kissed his mother and trotted down the short path to wait for his father at his car.

'He's a bit too young to understand,' said Arnie sadly.

'Yeah. He seems to have accepted the fact that you don't live here any more,' she told him, 'but not the other things, like why you can't stay for supper and that sort of thing.'

'He'll get used to it eventually.'

'Course he will.'

192

'See you tomorrow, then.'

'Yeah.'

She closed the door and leant against it. She was trembling. It was six months since Arnie had left, and she was coping. Apart from whenever she saw him . . .

Her initial instinct after he'd gone had been to move away and start afresh somewhere else. But she had stayed because Craig was happy in Danny Gardens and had his friends here. And of course she had her teaching practice. Besides, she loved the house she and Arnie had chosen together, where they had been happy until their love had turned sour. The very walls were permeated with their life together – the fun as well as the fights – and she couldn't bear to lose that.

They were being very modern and civilised about their separation. The practicalities had been dealt with in a surprisingly amicable manner. He had insisted on continuing to pay the mortgage and the rates, so she had been equally as insistent about refusing maintenance payments from him because she thought that was only fair. She was determined to manage on the money she earned from teaching to keep herself and Craig.

For Craig's sake she gave Arnie unlimited access to their son on the understanding that their getting together didn't interfere with his schooling or any arrangements she had for him.

Now that the break had come the animosity had lessened, and they were getting on better than they had in ages. The worst had happened, so the situation was defused. Arnie had got a transfer to the Hammersmith shop and taken a flat nearby, so Gill was spared the fear of running into him every time she left the house.

Although the ending of her marriage was a lacerating heartache, it was also a relief to be free from the tension that had torn her apart day after day. Life was much quieter now, and more on an even keel. But it was also emptier. Whenever she saw Arnie she wanted him back with such ferocity that she could hardly keep her hands off him, even though she knew that a reconciliation would be a disaster for them all.

Now she was more or less self-supporting, money was an important factor in Gill's life again, and she had taken on more pupils to boost her income. She even did occasional playing jobs – accompanying a local soprano and playing for a dance class – for which she received modest fees. Peter Attwood had been helpful in this respect, and recommended her whenever anyone came into the shop looking for a good pianist.

The extra hours she spent teaching meant she had less time for her charitable work at St Theresa's, but still she was determined to continue. Cherry was her star pupil and was streets ahead of everyone else, including Gill's paying pupils. The girl's inception at the grammar school, with all its extra work and new interests, hadn't diminished her love of the piano. Gill had high hopes for her.

Gill wandered into the living room, weighed down with melancholy. Saturday nights were hard to take when Craig wasn't here. She went into the music room and started playing the first movement of Beethoven's *Moonlight* sonata, a piece she adored. Music was her personal bolt-hole, and she was always immediately soothed by it.

She was deeply immersed when the doorbell startled her.

'I've come to keep you company,' announced Carol, sweeping in clutching a bottle of wine. 'Mum told me that Craig was going to Arnie's so I guessed you'd be lonely.'

'Oh.'

Carol shot her a look. 'Well, don't look so pleased to see me,' she said sarcastically.

'Sorry, I wasn't expecting to see you, that's all . . .'

'I'll go if you like,' she said, offended.

'Don't be so sensitive.'

'I thought you'd be glad of the company.' Carol's eyes flashed with the beginnings of a tantrum, barely visible through the copious mascara which she wore to contrast with her fashionably pale make-up.

'And I am,' said Gill dutifully, though the last person in the world she wanted to see this evening was Carol, who could be exhausting if you were feeling a bit low.

'Good.' Carol handed over the wine and took off her coat to reveal a clingy white sweater and black tapered trousers. 'So, get the corkscrew out and we'll have a girls' night in.'

Gill opened the wine and the two women settled in the living room, chatting pleasantly about this and that.

'So, how was Arnie when he came to collect Craig?' Carol enquired casually.

'He seemed fine. Why?'

'No particular reason. I was just making conversation.'

'Oh.'

'Has he started seeing anyone else yet?' she asked.

'Not as far as I know.'

'And you would get to know, wouldn't you – if he did have a girlfriend?'

'Oh, yes. If he didn't mention it to me himself, someone else soon would. Mary or Phoebe would put me in the picture. They'd be sure to get to know if there was somebody, especially now that Phoebe works with Arnie.'

'Of course, his mother works at the Hammersmith branch of Bex Sports now, doesn't she?'

'That's right,' said Gill, 'and she thinks it's great.'

'Good for her.' Carol paused thoughtfully. 'So what does Arnie find to do in his spare time now he's on his own?'

'Apparently he does a lot of voluntary work for the supporters' club of Borough FC.'

'How very public-spirited of him!'

'Yes.'

'His having a new woman in his life is something you're going to have to face up to sooner or later, though, isn't it?' Carol's cheeks were beginning to flush from the effect of the alcohol.

'I suppose so.'

'I mean, he isn't likely to be on his own for ever,'

195

she persisted. 'Not a man like Arnie.'

'No,' said Gill. 'But what he does isn't my business any more.'

'You have to get on with your own life,' said Carol authoritatively.

'Yes, and I am doing.'

'I mean, you should find a new man.'

'That's the last thing I feel like doing at the moment,' Gill said emphatically.

'You used to tell me I had to go out and find someone else after Dougie dumped me.'

'Yes, but it's rather different in my case. I'm a married woman with a child.'

'Not married in the usual sense of the word, not any more,' Carol was keen to remind her.

'No, but I'm still the mother of a young child. My main priority is Craig. Not having a partner isn't important to me.'

'It is definitely over between you and Arnie, isn't it?'

'Yes, I've told you . . .'

'Well then, put your marriage behind you and find someone else.'

'I'm all right as I am, thank you.' Gill was beginning to feel edgy.

'All right, there's no need to snap.'

'I don't need you to tell me how to run my life, Carol.'

'You've done plenty of that to me.'

'You seemed to need it.'

'I was only trying to help.'

'I can do without it.'

'Okay, I'll shut up.'

'Good.'

Carol, in this mood, would inevitably put Gill's nerves on edge. Since Gill's marriage had broken up her sister had seen fit to appoint herself as her personal counsellor, her unsolicited advice never going beyond suggestions that Gill should find a replacement for Arnie. Having always needed reassurance in spades, Carol now seemed to have drawn strength from Gill's misfortune and had become annoyingly overbearing, while somehow not quite losing that air of vulnerability that made you afraid to upset her. Gill didn't know which was worse – Carol being desperately insecure and pathetic or Carol being infuriatingly strident.

'Are you absolutely sure it's over between you and Arnie?' Carol ventured again.

Gill threw a cushion at her.

'Just teasing,' said Carol, and poured them each another glass of wine.

One afternoon a few weeks later, Phoebe went into Len and Mary's office with a tray of tea and cream buns. Setting the tray down on the filing cabinet, she unloaded the contents on to the desks, though Len wasn't at his.

'It's my birthday,' she explained, 'so it's cream cakes all round.'

'That's very kind of you, Phoebe,' said Mary, smiling. She patted her middle and made a face. 'I shouldn't really indulge as I'm so overweight, but I'll start the diet tomorrow.'

'Plenty of time for that,' said Phoebe, laughing because Mary's diet was a standing joke. 'You wouldn't be Mary if you were skinny.'

'I'll never be thin because I'm not built that way,' she said. 'But I do need to shed some weight. I've let things get out of hand lately and it's making me feel tired and puffed out.'

Phoebe glanced across at Len's desk. 'I didn't realise Len wasn't here or I wouldn't have poured him a cuppa tea,' she said.

'He went over to the Fulham shop a few minutes ago,' said Mary.

'I was out at the baker's getting the cakes. Must have missed him.'

'Have you poured yourself some tea in the staff room?'

'Not yet.'

'Why not have the one you poured for Len and take your break in here with me?' offered Mary pleasantly. 'Have his bun and replace it later.'

'I'd like that,' said Phoebe in a friendly but polite manner. Even though she and Mary had become firm friends since she'd been working at the shop, Phoebe always respected the fact that Mary was her employer and never overstepped the fine line between friendliness and familiarity.

The two women were of a similar age, had the same sort of outlook on life, and had shared interests – not least the fact that they were the only females working for Bex Sports. They had both been very upset by the break-up of Gill and Arnie's marriage.

'Arnie's still like a fish out of water without Gill, somehow, despite his keeping a cheerful front here at the shop,' Mary remarked, finishing her cream bun and licking the cream off her fingers.

'Mm.' Phoebe nodded.

'So is Gill without him, come to that,' continued Mary. 'After all the misery they'd been going through together, you'd think it would be a relief to be apart. But they both seem lost.'

'Some couples can't be happy together or apart,' said Phoebe.

'That's true.'

'They were lovely together once, before the rot set in.' Phoebe became misty-eyed. 'Love's young dream, you might say – even though they were very different. Arnie was noisy and sociable, a bit of a tearaway when they first started going out. Gill was quieter, with a touch of class about her. But you could literally watch them come to life when they were together.'

'It's a pity it's ended so unhappily.'

'He's filling his life with work at the moment,' said Phoebe.

'So I've noticed,' said Mary. 'He's always here after everyone else has gone in the evening, checking stock, working out ideas for sales promotions and catching up on paperwork. We've never had such a diligent manager on our staff.'

'And when he isn't busy here he's working for the Supporters' Club,' said Phoebe. 'All that staying out and pubbing he did when he and Gill were together – which couldn't have helped matters – he doesn't bother with it now he's free to do so. He just works or stays at home, unless he's got Craig with him, of course.'

'He's using work as a crutch to get him through this bad time,' said Mary.

'Oh yes,' Phoebe agreed. 'He might think he's fooling us all into thinking he's happy, but anyone can see it's an act.'

'Gill's always just that bit too bright and cheerful for it to ring true too,' said Mary.

'I've noticed.'

'I suppose they'll each meet someone else eventually.'

'I hope they do, for their sakes,' said Phoebe. 'Even though it'll break my heart for them to be with other partners. I love Gill like a daughter, and that won't change when Arnie finds someone new.'

'There's no sense in either of them being lonely, though,' said Mary, sipping her tea. 'They've too many years ahead of them.'

'No sense in anyone being lonely if they don't have to be,' declared Phoebe. 'I'm an expert on loneliness after so many years on my own, and I don't recommend it.'

'I'm surprised you haven't married again, actually, a bright spark like you.' Mary looked at her friend thoughtfully. 'I can't believe you haven't had any offers.'

'Plenty when I was younger, but not necessarily of marriage.' Phoebe laughed, wiping her sticky fingers with a handkerchief.

'Oh, Phoebe, you are a case.'

'It's true,' she said lightly. 'The men I met weren't prepared to take on someone else's kids for life just because they wanted to get their mother into bed for the night.'

'Oh dear . . .'

'My boys always came first with me anyway,' said Phoebe. 'Blokes don't like that. They like to be number one.'

'What about later on, when the boys got older?' Mary asked.

'I got older too and the propositions got less,' said Phoebe.

'You're still a very attractive woman, though.'

Phoebe shrugged. 'I make the best of myself for my own satisfaction,' she said. 'But it would take a very special man to make me consider marriage after all this time. I'm set in my ways now, happy with my life the way it is. I've got my friend from the flat upstairs to go to bingo or the pictures with.'

'You're very sociable.'

'I've always enjoyed being with people. My husband was just the same. After he died I had to get out for the sake of my sanity. People thought I was terrible 'cause I didn't sit about moping. Even if I'd wanted to I couldn't afford to – I had to get earning. Best thing for us all that I did, an' all. I'd have gone crazy indoors all day. The kids would have suffered then.'

'You still have John at home now.'

'Yeah – but not for much longer, I shouldn't think. He'll be flying the nest soon, and when he's ready to go I won't shed any tears. It's the natural way of things, innit? As long as he comes to see me now and then, that's all I ask.'

Mary nodded.

'You and Len never had any kids then?'

'No. We wanted a family when we were young, but it didn't happen so we got used to the idea and drew closer together.'

'Sometimes it works the other way and drives couples apart.'

'I'm sure it does, but it hasn't been like that for us.'

'Len's a good 'un.'

'One of the best.'

Phoebe finished her tea. 'Well, I'd better get back into the shop or I'll have the manager after me,' she said. 'Just because he's my son doesn't mean I get any special privileges.'

'I should hope not,' said Mary, 'but I would say that, wouldn't I?'

Phoebe stood up and loaded the crockery on to the tray. 'See you later then.'

'I'll open the door for you.' Mary rose and headed for the door.

'Thanks, dear.'

Phoebe halted at the door with the tray. Mary hadn't opened it. Turning, Phoebe immediately saw that she wasn't able to.

'Mary . . . What's the matter, love? Oh my Lord!'

The tray crashed to the floor as Phoebe reached out for Mary, who was flushed, gasping for breath and swaying as though about to pass out.

By the time Phoebe had got her back to her chair, she seemed to be recovering. 'I'm so sorry,' she said in a whisper.

'Don't apologise . . .'

'I came over all hot and breathless,' she explained weakly, mopping her brow with a handkerchief. 'I'm all right now, though.'

'Are you sure?' To Phoebe, Mary looked very shaken. She was visibly trembling, the colour having drained from her face.

'Yes, really . . .'

'I'll ring the doctor.'

'No!' Mary was adamant. 'It was only a funny little turn . . . nothing to worry about.'

'I'll get Arnie to take you down to casualty in the car as Len isn't here,' Phoebe suggested.

'There's no need for that,' Mary insisted. 'I'm fine now.'

Phoebe was still doubtful. 'I think you should see a doctor just to be on the safe side.'

'No, really, there's no need to make a fuss,' she said. 'It was just a passing thing.'

'You've had this sort of thing before, haven't you?' said Phoebe.

'Yes, now and again this last few months,' admitted Mary. 'But it's nothing that the loss of a few pounds of flab won't cure, and it never lasts longer than a few minutes.'

'It isn't very nice for you, though, is it?' said Phoebe with concern.

'No, it isn't.'

'Have you seen a doctor about it?'

'Good Lord, no,' Mary said. 'I'm at a funny age . . . it's obviously got something to do with that. They say weird things happen to menopausal women, don't they?'

'It might be an idea to get it checked out, though,' advised Phoebe. 'It's probably nothing to worry about, but at least a check-up would put your mind at rest.'

'If the turns continue and begin to bother me, I'll go and see a doctor – but there's certainly no cause for that at the moment.'

'Shall I get on the phone to the Fulham shop to ask Len to come back?' Phoebe persisted, because Mary still didn't look at all well.

'Definitely not,' said Mary firmly. 'I don't want Len to know anything about this.'

'Surely he ought to—'

'No,' Mary insisted.

'Why?'

'I don't want him worried when it isn't necessary,' she said.

'He'd want to be told.'

'He'll only get into a panic when there's no need. He's a terrible fusspot when it comes to me.' She gave Phoebe a long, hard look. 'I mean it, Phoebe. I don't want Len to know anything about what happened today, and I shall be very cross indeed if you tell him. And that means not telling anyone in case they pass it on.'

'But—'

'Look . . .' Mary seemed suddenly stronger and more forceful than Pheobe had ever seen her. 'It's *my* health and *my* business. If and when I think Len should know, I shall tell him. Until then I must insist that you say nothing.'

'Okay, dear, don't upset yourself,' Phoebe agreed with reluctance. 'I'll clear up the mess on the floor.'

'Thank you.'

'No trouble at all.' Phoebe got down on her hands and knees to collect the broken pieces of china, her hands trembling. Mary had felt a lot worse than she'd admitted, if Phoebe was any judge, and she thought it was wrong for her to keep it from her husband.

Oh, well, it's none of my business, and I must respect her wishes, she thought, collecting as much of the smashed crockery as she could by hand and putting it on the tray before going to the staff room for the dustpan and brush to finish the job.

Despite Mary's casual attitude towards the incident, Phoebe felt thoroughly unnerved by it.

Chapter Twelve

A crowd of teenagers was clustered excitedly around the record counter in the music shop when Gill called there after her teaching session at St Theresa's one Saturday morning in November.

'Don't tell me,' she said, grinning at Peter, who had appeared from the office to serve her, leaving Wendy to deal with the customers in her own peer group. 'There's been a new Beatles release.'

'It's the latest Rolling Stones record that's causing all the excitement, actually,' Peter said.

' "Get Off Of My Cloud"?'

'That's the one,' he said. 'The kids are still going mad for it.'

'Beatlemania doesn't seem to have abated because of the Stones' rising popularity, though, does it?'

'No, not at all. I expect the Beatles will top the charts at Christmas.'

'I saw in the paper that they got the MBE,' remarked Gill.

'Yes, I saw that too.'

'There was practically mass hysteria among the fans outside Buckingham Palace when they drove through the gates in a Rolls-Royce to receive their gongs, apparently.'

'It was chaotic, from what I've heard,' Peter said. 'They had to draft in hundreds of extra police to control the excitement. Crowds of teenage girls, screaming, shouting, waving banners . . .'

'We used to drool over Elvis when I was a teenager,' said Gill.

'That can't be long ago.'

'Long enough,' she said with a grin. 'I'm twenty-six.'

'You poor old thing,' Peter said jokingly.

She laughed.

'Elvis is still regularly in the charts,' said Peter.

'So I gather.'

'Anyway, what can I do for you?'

'Do you have the music for the Grade Two piano exam . . . the London College Examining Board, please?' she asked. 'One of my December candidates has had his copy chewed to ribbons by his dog and I don't seem to have any spares.'

'Sure.'

Peter found the music she wanted and put it into a bag. 'So, how's life?' he enquired casually.

'Busy,' she said. 'I've more pupils than I can comfortably manage and I still have a long waiting list.'

'I meant, how's life as a single lady?' Peter had been given brief details of her separation when she'd asked him to recommend her for playing jobs.

'Not too bad . . . I'm surviving.'

'It gets easier with time.'

'Is that the voice of experience?' she enquired lightly.

'It is,' he confirmed. 'I've been divorced for a couple of years.'

'Oh, really?' she said, the knowledge making her feel less alone somehow.

'Yes, it's a miserable business,' Peter said, shaking his head sagely. 'No matter how bad things get when the marriage is in existence, it still hurts when it's over.'

'You don't have to tell me.' Gill took the bag and handed him the money. 'Do you have any children?'

'Two.'

'See them often?'

'About once a month.'

'My son sees his father most weekends.'

'That often?'

'Yes. I don't mind. In fact I encourage it,' she explained. 'Because Craig adores his dad and I don't want him to lose that bond.'

'Sounds to me as though you're being very fair about things.'

She nodded, taking her change and putting it into her purse. 'I find weekends difficult, though, with Craig being with his father on Sundays,' she said chattily.

'The weekends are difficult for most people who find themselves in that situation, I should imagine,' Peter said.

'This week it'll be even worse because my son is going to his father's tonight and staying over until tomorrow afternoon. There's something especially lonely, somehow, about being on your own on a Saturday evening.'

'You don't have to be alone tonight,' he said.

'I don't?'

'No. You could come out for a meal with me. I've nothing planned.'

'Oh, dear,' Gill said, embarrassed. 'I was just idly chatting. I wasn't angling for an invitation out.'

'I know you weren't,' he heartily assured her. 'But as we're both at a loose end, it makes sense to team up for a meal.'

'No, I couldn't, really,' she protested, feeling trapped into something she hadn't expected and wasn't sure she wanted. 'My sister will probably come over to my place anyway. She usually does if she knows I'm going to be on my own.'

'I was only suggesting we eat together to keep the loneliness at bay,' he said pointedly. 'I wasn't planning on anything more than that.'

'Now I really am embarrassed.'

'Don't be,' Peter said. 'It was only a spur-of-the-moment suggestion.' Unoffended, he was smiling at her, his eyes exuding warmth.

'It's just that I'm not ready for . . .'

'A new relationship.'

'Exactly.'

'I'm not sure I am either,' he said, 'so it would just be a meal – if you fancy it.'

'Okay,' she said, smiling at him. 'But only on the condition that we go dutch.'

'If that's what you want, that's how it'll be,' he said casually.

'I'll look forward to it then,' she said, realising how much she needed some fresh adult company.

One evening a few weeks later, Carol Miller was standing in the doorway of a shoe shop near Hammersmith Broadway with her eyes fixed on Bex Sports opposite. It was closed for the night, but she knew that Arnie was still inside, in the manager's office at the back of the shop, because she could see the light shining through the window. She had also taken the precaution of checking to make sure that his car was parked in a nearby side street.

She was not here by accident, nor as the result of a sudden whim. She had been planning this for months, and had done her homework beforehand. She had not deemed it wise to make a move too soon after Arnie's separation from Gill, in case it created bad feeling with her sister and their parents. But she had waited long enough; she daren't leave it any longer for fear he'd find someone else.

By artfully extracting information from Gill, and by making it her business to 'bump into' Arnie's mother in the street and interrogate her while supposedly having a neighbourly chat, she'd been able to keep up to date with his daily routine, which had allowed her to work out her strategy.

She knew that he never left the shop in the evening until long after everyone else, and more importantly she knew that he hadn't yet embarked upon another relationship with a woman.

It was a wet night with a penetrating chill, and she'd been standing here for nearly an hour. The cold and damp were seeping into her bones, something that wasn't helped by the fact that she wore her skirt mini length. Even though she was sheltered from the rain in the doorway it was cold and draughty, and every so often a blast of spray was blown into her face by the wind. Her feet, inside her long, black patent boots, were aching with the cold, her toes turning numb. She stamped her feet and pulled up the collar on her red wet-look raincoat.

She had lied to her mother. She'd told Winnie she wouldn't be home for tea because she was going to the cinema with a friend after work. She had actually come straight here so as not to miss him. That was one of the drawbacks of living at home: although it was cheap and convenient, with meals and laundry service included, it was also very restrictive because you were expected to account for your movements. This was annoying at the best of times and infuriating when you didn't want your parents to know what you were up to. Carol comforted herself with the thought that, if things went according to plan, she wouldn't be there for much longer.

But now things were happening across the street. The light in the office had gone out, which meant Arnie was on his way. Up went her umbrella and she sallied forth into the rain, crossing the road and positioning herself a short distance away from the entrance to the sports shop, ready to spring into action.

As Arnie emerged and turned back to lock the door, she marched in his direction as though she'd been walking for ages and was on her way somewhere, her eyes pointed towards the ground until she was parallel with him.

'Arnie,' she said, turning to look at him with feigned surprise. 'You're working late tonight.'

He peered at her in the pale glow from the street-light.

'Carol?'

'Yeah.'

'I thought I recognised your dulcet tones . . . What are you doin' around here?'

'I'm on my way to the bus stop to get the bus home,' she lied without compunction.

'Oh.'

'I went to a friend's place straight from work,' she said. 'We were supposed to be having something to eat there and going to the pictures together, but her boyfriend turned up so she went out with him instead.'

'And left you high and dry?'

'That's right.'

'Not nice.'

'Not nice at all.'

'Never mind,' he said with genuine sympathy – Arnie had always perceived Carol to be a sad sort of person who needed lots of encouragement. 'Better luck next time.'

'I hope so.' She gave a violent shiver, hugging herself. 'Cor, dear, it isn't half parky tonight.'

'Too cold to be hanging about at the bus stop.' He finished locking the door. 'Forget the bus. I'll run you home.'

'Oh, would you?' she said in a sweet, girlish voice. 'I'd be ever so grateful.'

'No trouble at all. It's the least I can do for my favourite sister-in-law.'

'I'm your *only* sister-in-law – and I'm not even that any more.'

'You are unless Gill and I get divorced,' he was quick to point out as they walked around the corner to the car together, the uneven plod of his limp and the sharp click of her stiletto heels resounding into the quiet of the side street. Thinking it would please her, Arnie added, 'You'll always be Gill's kid sister to me anyway.'

Not if I've got anything to do with it, Carol thought. She intended to alter his perception of her with all possible speed. But for now she just said, 'That's nice.'

'Well, there's no reason for the families not to stay friends just because Gill and I are no longer together, is there?' he remarked as they got into the car.

'None at all,' agreed Carol.

'So, what have you been doing with yourself lately?' he

enquired casually, keeping his eyes on the road ahead as the rain beat against the steamy windows, the wipers plodding to and fro.

'Nothing very exciting,' she said. 'The same old things . . .'

'Sounds to me as though there isn't a new man in your life yet.'

'There's been no one special since Dougie,' she told him.

'What's the matter with all the young blokes around here?' Arnie felt sorry for Carol, and was saying these things to be kind. 'They must want their brains tested.'

The compliment heartened her more then he could have realised. 'I've been out with a few, but nothing that lasted,' she said.

'You'll find the right one soon,' Arnie said reassuringly.

I found him a long time ago, but he's only just become available, she thought. She said, 'Yeah, course I will. And in the meantime I'm enjoying the freedom.'

'That's the spirit.'

'How about you? Are you enjoying being single again?'

'Not really.'

'Oh dear.' She sounded suitably sympathetic. 'Seems to me as though you're the one who needs to find someone.'

'No, not me.'

'Gill's seeing someone else . . .'

'What?' Arnie sounded devastated. 'Who is he?'

'The chap from the music shop,' Carol informed him with relish. 'She's been out with him quite a few times.'

'I didn't know that.'

'I'm not sure if it's serious between them . . .' Carol spoke with a falsely casual air. 'But I do know they've been out together quite regularly.'

There was a silence while Arnie digested this upsetting news.

'It's none of my business what Gill does any more,' he said at last.

'No.'

'I still can't get used to the idea that it isn't, though,' he added.

'I know the feeling,' she said chummily. 'I was just the same when I heard that Dougie had got engaged to someone else recently. I was hurt, even after all this time.'

'I'm sorry to hear that.'

'Don't be, I'm over it now,' she said. 'I think my pride was hurt more than anything.'

'That's only natural.'

Carol murmured in agreement. Then, choosing her moment, she said, 'Oh dear, I'm sinking with hunger.'

'Are you?'

'Yeah. I didn't get anything to eat at all in the end, and Mum won't have kept me anything 'cause I told her I was eating at my friend's . . .'

'Mm.' Arnie considered the matter for a few moments. 'I have to eat too, and I don't feel like cooking myself anything – so why don't we have a bite together somewhere?'

'You've no plans for this evening then?' she said, feeling triumphant.

'None at all.'

'Thanks very much, then,' she said, hardly able to believe how easy it had been. 'I'd like that.'

They went to a small place in Chelsea with pine walls, potted plants and scarlet tablecloths. The atmosphere was homely, the food delicious. Carol didn't often eat out, so it was a special treat for her. Arnie ordered steak, she had chilli con carne.

Hoping to please him, she got him talking about his charity work for Borough FC Supporters' Club. 'What do you do exactly?' she asked.

'Among other things, I organise the transport for the fans to go to the away matches,' he said, looking casually smart in a black polo-necked sweater over pale grey slacks. 'We've just managed to buy a coach for the disabled supporters, actually.'

'That must have cost a bomb.'

'It did.'

'How did you get enough money to pay for it?' she enquired with feigned interest, hoping to impress him.

'We raised it over a long period through various fund-raising social events, donations from businesses, collecting boxes on shop and pub counters and raffles,' he explained. 'If you want something bad enough, you get very persistent.'

Which is exactly what she intended to do.

'I admire you for giving so much of your time to charity work,' she said, though she would prefer he devoted his time to her.

'I'm not being holier than thou,' he said, forking a chip, 'I enjoy it.'

'It must be nice to do stuff for other people,' Carol said insincerely. 'I wonder if Gill gets a kick from teaching for free at St Theresa's.'

'I'm sure she does,' Arnie said, filled with regret for not taking more interest in Gill's work. He'd always been too full of himself to give her the support she'd deserved, he could see that now. Not a day had passed since they'd parted when he didn't remember something that made him sorry. 'She's a very charitable person.'

Carol instantly regretted bringing Gill into the conversation and would avoid it whenever possible in the future, because she couldn't bear the soft look that came into Arnie's eyes whenever her sister's name was mentioned.

She didn't see any reason to feel guilty about making a serious play for him. It wasn't as though she had ever tried to come between him and Gill when they were together, or tried to step into Gill's shoes while she was trying to adjust to the separation and still feeling wretched. She'd waited for a decent interval to elapse, giving Gill time to get him back if that was what she wanted. But no such moves had been made.

So she didn't have to feel bad.

Anyway, she had no intention of drawing back now,

whatever Gill felt about it. The girlish hero-worship Carol had once felt for Arnie had developed into an all-consuming passion. She wanted him with a compulsion that exceeded anything she'd felt for a man before. And she was going to have him, whatever the obstacles! It was as much as she could do to keep her hands off him now, but she was determined not to show it too soon.

Although she'd never admitted it to anyone, she knew that her tendency to make her feelings too obvious frightened men away. She wasn't going to risk having that happen with Arnie.

'From what I've heard Craig has inherited your sporting talents rather than Gill's musical ones,' she said, because she knew it would please him to talk about his son.

'Yeah, that does seem to be the case at the moment . . .'

Carol was fired with jealousy at the tenderness in his voice when he spoke of Craig. My God, she was up against strong opposition for his affections! She tried to get the conversation on to a more general plane by asking him if he'd seen the recently opened Post Office Tower, Britain's tallest building.

'I took Craig to see it the other weekend,' he informed her brightly. 'We went up in the lift to the public viewing gallery and had something to eat in the revolving restaurant. He thought it was great fun.'

Every road led back to Gill or Craig, she thought with annoyance, but smiled sweetly and said, 'Ah, bless him . . .'

While Arnie smoked a cigarette over coffee, Carol was working out how she could get him to agree to another meeting.

'I've really enjoyed myself this evening, Arnie,' she said, meeting his eyes. 'You've cheered me up no end.'

'Good.' He looked at her, seeing a young woman with nice eyes buried behind copious mascara. 'I've enjoyed it too.'

'Really?'

'Don't sound so surprised,' he said. 'Why wouldn't I enjoy having a meal out with an attractive young woman?'

She looked suitably coy. 'I do believe you're chatting me up, Arnie Briscoe,' she said.

'Leave it out, Carol,' he admonished firmly – because such a thing had never occurred to him, 'I wouldn't do a thing like that to my ex-wife's kid sister.'

'Hardly a kid, Arnie ... I'm twenty-three,' she pointed out.

'Yeah, I suppose you would be about that now,' he said casually. 'But it isn't a question of years. You'll always be Gill's little sister to me, and you're certainly not too old for me to tell you that you're wearing too much mascara.'

'Honestly,' she said, tutting.

'Are you tryin' to look like Dusty Springfield or somethin'?'

'Of course not. It's the fashion to look like this,' she said evenly. Although this light-hearted banter wasn't what she was after in the long term, at least his brotherly affection for her was something to build on.

'I've always put you right about things like that,' he said in a friendly manner. 'Remember when you were a teenager?'

'Will I ever forget?' she said, raising her eyes in mock disdain. 'It's a wonder I had the confidence to go out at all after you two had finished taking the mickey.'

'It was all very well intentioned. We had your interests at heart.' Arnie smiled, looking wistfully into the distance. 'Gill and I probably did give you a hard time, looking back on it. But only because we cared about you.'

'I'm sure.'

'We had some good times, didn't we? When I was one of the family.'

'Not half,' she agreed. 'I've missed your being around.'

'I've missed being around,' he told her. 'That's the sad thing when a marriage ends: other things you care about end too. People you counted as family aren't related any more.'

'It's a shame,' Carol said, seeing an opportunity to move things forward. 'But you and I could get together again sometime if you like.' She knew it would not occur to him to ask her out because he didn't think of her in those sorts of terms. She was going to have to break with tradition and take all the initiative if she wanted him – in the early stages anyway – because it was obvious he wasn't going to come to her of his own volition. 'I mean, we're both on our own, we might as well keep each other company.'

'Good idea.'

'When?'

'Oh, I dunno, sometime soon,' Arnie said vaguely, already thinking of other things.

'How about this time next week?' she persisted, trying not to sound too eager but anxious to pin him down. 'I could meet you at the shop after work if you like, about the same time as I did tonight. We could go for a meal, or just a drink if you'd rather . . . just for the sake of old times.'

Arnie looked at her. He'd always been fond of Carol in a brotherly sort of way. She'd always been a lonely soul, never seemed to have many friends or much luck with men. He remembered how worried they'd all been about her after Dougie had let her down so cruelly. Her family had thought she was heading for a breakdown then. But even as a youngster she'd been a loner. He recalled how she used to hang around with him and Gill when all they wanted was to be alone.

She'd changed a bit since then, though, he thought, becoming aware of the fact that she was an attractive woman with the sort of figure for which the mini skirt and tight sweaters had been invented. But for all that, Carol still seemed to need protecting. He recalled how protective Gill had been of her when she was younger.

Frankly, it didn't matter to Arnie one way or the other whether he spent an evening with her next week or not. The idea was not repugnant to him; neither was it important. But she seemed so lonely, he didn't want to hurt her feelings. It was almost as though in hurting her he would hurt Gill, who had always been so fond of her sister.

'Okay, Carol, let's make it the same time next week,' he heard himself say.

'Great, Arnie,' she said, reaching over and resting her hand on his on the table. 'I'll look forward to it.'

'You and Arnie!' Gill exclaimed in disbelief. It was a few weeks later, and Carol had called at the house unexpectedly. '*You* have been out with *Arnie*!'

'I've been out with him a few times, actually,' Carol blurted out.

'Oh, Carol . . .'

They were having coffee in the living room. Carol was cradling her mug in both hands and observing her sister with caution. 'There's no need to be quite so shocked,' she said, on the defensive as usual.

'Of course I am—'

'There's no reason why I shouldn't go out with him, is there?' Carol cut in sharply. 'He's free to go out with anyone he likes, the same as you are. Anyway, you're going out with Peter.'

'We're just friends.'

'And so are Arnie and I,' Carol said. 'For the moment anyway.'

Gill felt buffeted by this unexpected news, even though she knew she had no right to object. 'You're saying that you'll be more than just friends if you have your way, then?' she enquired.

'Yeah, sure. Why not?' Carol bit her lip. 'I've always liked Arnie . . . well, fancied him rotten, actually.'

'Does he know what you have in mind?'

'Of course not. I'm not that stupid,' she said. 'It'll take a bit of time for us to get to know each other properly.'

'You know what you want, I'll say that much for you,' said Gill.

'Look, Gill, it isn't as though I'm taking him away from

you or anything, is it?' said Carol crossly.

'Not much!'

'But it's over between you; you've said so many times. You've been separated for the best part of a year now. So why shouldn't Arnie and I get together? He's single and so am I. We've always got on well . . .'

'Everything you say is true,' said Gill. 'But it still hurts. This isn't about logic, Carol, it's about feelings.'

'Yeah, I suppose so.' Carol at least had the grace to look sheepish.

'Imagine how you would have felt if I'd started seeing Dougie after you split up with him.'

'That was different,' said Carol hotly. 'Dougie ditched me in the cruellest way possible. You and Arnie have split up by mutual agreement because it was over between you. Anyway, you've had plenty of time to change your mind and you've shown no interest in wanting him back.'

'Because it wouldn't work out, not because I don't still feel something for him.'

'You don't want him but you don't want anyone else to have him, is that it?' demanded Carol.

'That isn't how it is,' Gill denied. 'Of course he'll find someone new eventually. But my own sister . . .'

'Why shouldn't I be happy for a change?' she said. 'You've had your chance . . .' Her voice tailed off and there was an explosive silence as their eyes met. They both knew they were on the verge of a serious disagreement which could lead to a parting of the ways that neither of them wanted.

'Look, Gill,' Carol continued, feeling worse about this than she'd expected. 'I don't want to hurt you, but I really do like Arnie . . . Well, actually it's more than that. I'm in love with him.'

'Are you sure it isn't just love you want and Arnie just happens to be available to provide it if he's guided in the right direction?'

'That was a rotten thing to say.'

'Yes it was.' Gill had a sudden urge to grab Carol by the hair and shake her till she begged for mercy. 'I'm sorry. It isn't any of my business what Arnie does or who he sees.'

'No it isn't. I'm sorry if my seeing him upsets you,' said Carol. 'But I can't give him up now, Gill . . . I really can't.'

'I shall just have to learn to live with it then, won't I?'

Gill sat opposite Peter at a table in a small Italian restaurant in Fulham and poured her heart out to him over spaghetti bolognese.

'How could she do that? My own sister,' she said, gulping her Chianti in despair. 'Apart from the pain of seeing them together, can you imagine the hideous complications that will arise from this? My ex-husband and the father of my child would become my brother-in-law.'

'Hey, hang on, Gill. She's been out with him a few times, that's all,' Peter reminded her, twirling spaghetti around his fork. 'It probably won't go any further than that.'

'She seems very determined.'

'It takes two,' he said.

'Yes, there is that,' replied Gill, making a half-hearted effort to eat her meal. 'And I mustn't interfere.'

'No, you really mustn't do that,' he said emphatically.

'No?' she said, looking up quickly at his tone of voice.

'You're separated from Arnie,' he pointed out firmly. 'His love-life isn't your business any longer. Arnie and Carol are both single adults with minds of their own. They're entitled to give it a chance.'

She threw him a sharp look. 'And how would you feel if your ex-wife married your brother?'

'I don't have a brother, but I don't honestly think I would mind.'

'It's easy to say that when you know it can't happen.'

'I agree with you. It is easy to say it, but I do happen to believe it to be true,' he said. 'It's over between my wife and me. Whatever we once had is long gone, so it's immaterial to me who she is with now. She is getting married to someone I know, actually, and I don't mind a bit.'

'Oh. I'm sorry,' Gill said. 'You've never said much about your past.'

'Because it isn't important to me now,' he said. 'It's water under the bridge.'

'So is mine, I suppose.'

'Yes. But the difference between you and me is that you're still in love with your ex and I'm not in love with mine.'

'I didn't say I was still in love with Arnie,' she said.

'Why are you so upset about him seeing your sister then?'

She put her wine glass down slowly and leant her elbows on the table, resting her chin on her linked fingers. 'I do still feel something for Arnie, it's true,' she said.

'Tell me something I don't already know.'

'I must be completely bonkers after the life he led me. But I can't help it. He's just . . . always with me, somehow.'

'Is it worth giving your marriage another try, then?' Peter enquired. 'Before your sister gets too deeply involved with him?'

'Definitely not,' she said without hesitation. 'We were incompatible for years before we actually split up. I couldn't go through that again and I should think it's the last thing Arnie wants. All those terrible arguments and the bad atmosphere in the house . . . It was hell.'

'Sounds to me as though you'd come to the end of the line.'

'We had.'

'There you are, then . . .'

'But when you've been with someone a long time, you can't just feel nothing for them.'

'No, but you still have to move on, whatever you're feeling,' he said. 'It's no good hanging on to the past.'

Gill looked into his comforting grey eyes, the undulating candlelight gleaming on his face, which was too thin and angular to be handsome but was pleasant with smooth skin and a well-shaped mouth. Casually dressed as ever, Peter was wearing a black shirt and jeans, his long hair shining with cleanliness but chaotic in a way that suited his bohemian image.

They had been out together quite a few times now, and she looked on him as a true friend. Their most common interest was music. Peter was an accomplished guitarist and gave lessons after hours in the room at the back of the shop.

He had a very gentle nature and she could talk to him about anything. As there was no question of sex to complicate matters, he was very easy to be with. He'd seemed to accept what she'd said at the beginning – that she wasn't ready for a relationship – and was happy just to be her friend.

'By that you mean I should stand back from Arnie and Carol,' she said, 'and let it happen if it's going to.'

'It's the only thing you can do, isn't it?' he said in a definite tone. 'After all, you no longer have any claim on Arnie.'

'You certainly tell it like it is, don't you?' she said.

'For your own sake.'

'Really?'

'Yes. Because you don't only have to let go of the past for Arnie and Carol's sake,' he said. 'You have to do it for yourself too. It's over between you and Arnie, so stop hankering for him and let yourself move on.'

'Easier said than done.'

'You have to do it though, Gill,' he advised with sincerity. 'You can't spend the rest of your life clinging to an old love and getting all bitter and twisted if he and your sister make a go of it. You're still young, you have a lot of life ahead of you. Don't let it pass you by.'

She knew he was right. 'That was quite a speech.'

'I can manage to string a few words together when I put my mind to it,' he grinned.

'It's strange how I can take it from you,' she said. 'But I get angry if anyone else suggests the same thing.'

'Maybe that's because we're both in a similar situation,' he suggested.

She put her fork down and reached across the table for his hand. 'You've been a good friend to me,' she said, realising at that moment how much difference he had made to her life. 'It's so good having someone to talk to, someone to go out with.'

'It isn't all one-sided, you know,' he said. 'I enjoy it too.'

'Good.'

As she drew her hand away, he raised his glass to her. 'And long may it continue.'

'Yes.'

She lifted her glass and chinked it with his, their eyes meeting. She wasn't naive enough to think their friendship would continue in this undemanding and platonic way for ever. But for the moment it was just what she needed.

Carol wasn't finding it as easy to move her friendship with Arnie on to another stage as she'd hoped. He was friendly enough to her and seemed to enjoy being with her, but he was often vague and preoccupied and she had difficulty getting him to commit himself to another meeting.

'I'll see you soon,' he'd say, or, 'I'll give you a bell in a few days.'

She was far too desperate to worry about seeming too presumptuous, so when he didn't call her she telephoned him and suggested a meeting. Once reminded of her existence, he usually agreed to take her out for a meal or a drink.

Anxious to keep the conversation away from the family and Gill, Carol encouraged him to talk about his work. That was always a safe bet. She even made a token suggestion that she could help him with his charity work. He replied casually that he'd take her up on her offer one of these days.

But still there was no hint of romance. The most promising sign she'd had in that direction was a friendly kiss on the cheek when they parted. She suspected that anything else just hadn't occurred to him.

But she simply couldn't accept that he wouldn't fancy her once he stopped seeing her as Gill's sister.

So far she'd managed to keep the extent of her feelings from him, but how much longer she could keep it quiet she didn't know – because she wanted him with ever-increasing ferocity.

Drastic action was going to be called for if she didn't make progress soon. But timing was crucial. She'd know when the moment was right, and she'd move in with all guns blazing.

Arnie Briscoe would be hers, one way or another!

Chapter Thirteen

'Well, how do I look?' Mary asked, sweeping into the lounge of the Bexes' home in Putney with an uncharacteristic flourish and giving her husband a twirl, the blue taffeta folds of her evening dress rustling around her ankles.

'Beautiful . . . really beautiful.' Len was looking very smart himself, in a tuxedo with a crisp white shirt, his grey hair giving him a distinguished air.

'You don't look so bad yourself,' Mary commented, her face specially made up for the occasion, hair freshly done at the hairdresser's that afternoon.

It was the beginning of another year, and they were going to a hotel in the West End to a charity dinner in aid of an association for disabled sportsmen, of which Len was the president.

'It's worth making the effort for a special do like the one tonight,' he said.

'Not half,' she agreed. 'There'll be some smart frocks there tonight, I bet. If you can afford the price of a ticket, you can afford something a bit special to wear.'

'The tickets are a bit pricey, I know,' remarked Len. 'But people with dough to spend are only too happy to splash out to help a good cause if they know they're gonna have a good time in the process.'

'That's understandable.'

'Yeah.' He looked at his watch. 'Are you ready, love? The taxi will be here in a minute.'

'I'll be two minutes,' she said. 'I just have to pop upstairs to get my coat and handbag.'

223

In a spontaneous action, he swept her into his arms with a growling sound. 'You're very glamorous tonight,' he whispered into her hair. 'You'll upstage all the competition.'

'Leave it out, Len,' she laughed. 'I was never competitive in that way when I was young, let alone now.'

'You're not even fifty yet.'

'I'm not twenty either.' She drew away, smiling at him. 'And snogging is off the menu because it'll ruin my make-up and hair.'

She left him grinning and departed for the bedroom. This, their sanctuary, was lavishly appointed with all the trappings that years of hard work had enabled them to afford – endless fitted wardrobes, gilt-edged mirrors, deep-pile carpet . . . Slipping into her white fur evening jacket, Mary picked up her dainty sequinned bag from the dressing-table and checked its contents before heading for the door.

In the centre of the room she stopped, rooted to the spot as the symptoms that were becoming all too familiar engulfed her. Her body was on fire, and she couldn't breathe. It was as though a heavy weight had smashed into her chest in a painful blast.

Trying not to panic, she fought against the faintness but the room was spinning horribly. Drenched in perspiration and gasping for breath, she finally felt her legs buckle and she sank to the floor.

For how long she sat there on the carpet she didn't know, but eventually she became distantly aware of Len calling her from downstairs.

'Mary! What the devil are you doing up there?' he was shouting. 'The taxi's here and the meter's running.'

Mercifully the abnormal sensations began to subside, and with a supreme effort she managed to struggle to her feet. Relieved to find her strength returning, she retouched her make-up, tidied her hair and made her way downstairs, hoping she didn't look as shaky as she felt.

'Ah, there you are at last.' Len gave her a close look,

frowning. 'Are you all right, love? You've gone a bit pale.'

She hesitated, wondering if she ought to tell him about the funny turns she'd been having lately. But he was such a worrier when it came to her – which was understandable, since they only had each other. Anyway, these uncomfortable spells didn't last long; they were probably menopausal and would, therefore, stop troubling her in due course. She would seek medical advice if they got any worse, and talk to Len about it then. In the meantime, there was no point in bothering him if she didn't have to.

'I'm fine,' she assured him brightly. 'So let's go out and paint the town red.'

Arnie let himself into his flat, the echoing silence of its emptiness hitting him as soon as he set foot inside the door. At one time he'd had so much to come home to: a wife and son he adored, a comfortable house throbbing with family life – a piano playing in one room, the telly blaring in another, the smell of something cooking in the kitchen ... Now he returned from work to an empty flat and something on a tray in front of the television, if he hadn't stopped off for a pie and a pint in the pub on the way home.

His present abysmal circumstances were entirely of his own making; he fully accepted that. He'd been vain and selfish in the glory days, self-pitying and guilt-ridden later, all his resentment aimed at Gill. God, how he had made that woman suffer! He wondered if he was a wicked man. He'd been weak and self-obsessed, certainly. In retrospect, it was as though he hadn't been in control of his own actions for a while.

Knowing that he was to blame for the failure of his marriage didn't make the regrets any easier to bear. Fortunately, he had a job that interested him and took his mind off things during the day. He had Gill to thank for that – and he'd been arrogant enough to object to her approaching Len on his behalf. His behaviour didn't bear thinking about.

Now that he lived alone he put far more into his work than

was expected of him, just to help fill the lonely hours. But no matter how fulfilling the job, it couldn't possibly make up for the loss of the woman he loved.

Still, at least the flat is reasonably comfortable, he told himself, even if it did feel like a butcher's cold-room after being empty all day. He switched on the underfloor heating and wandered into the living room, turning on the television which was transmitting an episode of *Coronation Street*. This immediately made him think of Gill – it was one of her favourites.

His flat was in a modern block not far from the river at Hammersmith. It was adequately furnished but noticeably lacking in imagination. When he'd moved in he hadn't had the heart to do more than install the basics. It was a roof over his head rather than a home.

He sank into an armchair, keeping his coat on until the place warmed up, and stared blankly at the TV screen, wondering if there was anything edible in the kitchen. At best there would be the ingredients for cheese on toast.

Further investigation revealed some dodgy-smelling ham, a knob of cheese with a hairy green forest growing on it, and half a loaf of bread that was so hard you could break ice with it. Oh, well, it'll have to be fish and chips again tonight, he thought, cheering himself with the idea of stopping off at the pub on the way for a pint and a spot of company. He didn't go to pubs much these days, compared to the amount of time he'd spent in them in the dying days of his marriage.

His marriage . . . He must have been crazy to let something so precious slip through his fingers. Oh well. No point in fretting. It was too late to do anything about it now.

He was on his way to the front door when the telephone rang in the hall.

'Hi, Arnie, it's Carol.'

'Hi, Carol,' he said, glad to hear a friendly voice. 'How are you?'

'Fine.'

'Good.'

'I just wondered if you were doin' anything this evening,' she said.

'Nothing that you could call anything,' he told her. 'I'm just on my way out to the chippy to get my supper, as a matter of fact.'

'Oh.' There was a short silence. 'In that case why don't I come over to your place and bring fish and chips for us both, save you going out?' she suggested.

Although he was tempted to agree, his sense of decency forced him to say, 'It's a nice thought, Carol, but I don't wanna drag you over to Hammersmith on a cold night like this.'

'I can easily hop on to a bus,' she said, though she had already done so and was in the phone box at the end of his road.

'I wouldn't want to put you to all that trouble just for a fish and chip supper.'

'I'd like to,' she said. 'I've nothing else to do and it would be company for me.'

'You've not eaten either, then?'

'No. I didn't fancy what Mum had cooked so I left most of mine,' she said. 'Fish and chips would be just the job.'

'Well, if you're sure . . .'

'I am.'

'You got enough money?'

'Yeah.'

'I'll pay you back when you get here.'

'Okay. See you soon.'

As he replaced the receiver, Arnie felt considerably brighter. Having known Carol for such a long time he found her easy to be with; and at least the evening no longer loomed miserably ahead with only the television for company.

He said as much to Carol later, after they had washed the dishes and were relaxing with a cup of coffee. 'You've really cheered me up tonight,' he told her. 'I was properly down in the dumps before you phoned.'

'You should have contacted me if you fancied some company,' she said.

'I didn't think of it,' he said, a little too truthfully for Carol's liking.

'Out of sight, out of mind, eh?' she said, keeping her tone light.

'Sorry. I didn't mean it to sound like that.' He made a face.

' 'Sall right.'

'Anyway, you can't get on the blower to someone every time you're feeling a bit lonely, can you?'

'I'm not just someone, Arnie,' she said, looking at him with a serious expression. 'We go back a long way, you and me. You can turn to me for company any time you like.'

'Thanks. But a young, unattached woman like yourself should be out enjoying yourself,' he told her, 'not cheering up your miserable old sod of a brother-in-law.'

'You're not a miserable old sod,' she said firmly. 'And as I've told you before, you're not my brother-in-law now.'

'Legally I am.'

'It's just a technicality.'

'I suppose so,' he said, but he didn't sound convinced.

'I don't think of you as Gill's husband,' she told him, leaning back in the chair and looking at him through somnolent eyes, her heavy lids lowered slightly.

'No?'

'No. When I look at you I just see a very attractive man.'

Warning bells rang in his head, but Arnie wasn't in the mood to listen. He was drowning in self-loathing and regret for hurting Gill and wrecking their marriage. Flattery from an attractive female was just what he needed to help boost his confidence.

'It's nice of you to say so,' he said, meeting her eyes and feeling obliged to respond with a similar compliment. 'I must admit that I see Gill's sister when I look at you, but I also see a good-looking woman.'

'Thank you,' she said, smiling contentedly and snuggling

deeper into the chair, in a way that made Arnie uneasy. She was beginning to look so settled.

He looked meaningfully at his watch. 'Anyway, enough of all that. It's time I took you home,' he told her, suddenly aware that things could easily get out of control. 'We both have to be up early for work in the morning.'

'I don't have to go home,' she said. 'I'm quite willing to stay the night.'

'No, Carol!'

'But surely you don't want to go out in the cold to drive me home?'

'I don't mind,' he said, rising.

'I'd like to stay . . .'

'I'll get your coat.'

'Please Arnie,' she said, unashamedly coaxing him now. 'I'd really like to stay.'

'And I want you to go.'

'You don't mean that,' she said determinedly. 'You're just saying it because you think you ought to be a gentleman.'

In reply he marched into the hall and got her coat from the hook. 'Here, put this on,' he said, holding it out for her.

'Why can't I stay?'

'Because I can do without those sorts of complications,' he said firmly. 'Now put on your coat and let's be on our way . . . please!'

With great reluctance she did as he asked, and they drove through the cold winter streets in silence.

'I'm sorry to have upset you, Arnie,' she said as they turned into Maisie Road, afraid that she had ruined her chances altogether by being too eager.

'Don't apologise,' he said. 'It's my fault for being so naive. There's obviously been some sort of a misunderstanding.'

Carol was disappointed, but not deterred. 'Will I see you again?' she asked.

'Yeah, course you will, kid,' he said, making his tone casual.

'Don't call me kid.'

'I'll remember that in future.'

'So, when will I see you?'

'I'll give you a bell sometime.'

Which meant he had no intention of doing any such thing – but Carol wasn't prepared to give up. She'd grovel if she had to.

'Don't be cold towards me, please, Arnie,' she said, injecting a sob into her voice. 'I didn't mean any harm. I only wanted to be there for you 'cause I know you're lonely.'

He drew up outside her house and turned to her, his heart turning over to see how forlorn she looked sitting there with her hands in her lap, her head lowered.

'Hey, come on, there's nothing to cry about,' he said, slipping a friendly arm around her shoulders. 'It's no big deal.'

'You must know that I've always thought a lot of you,' she said, turning to him so that even in the dim glow of the street-lights he could see tears glistening in her eyes.

'And I like you too,' he said, choosing his words carefully.

'But you don't fancy me?'

'It isn't a question of that,' he assured her, curbing his impatience because of her sensitive nature. He knew he must be gentle with her.

'Why didn't you want me to stay then?' she sniffed.

'I've told you . . . because it'll complicate everything,' he said, moving away from her. 'I'd prefer things to stay as they are between us. I like it the way it is with us being mates.'

'Oh,' she said, making a show of her disappointment to try to win him over. 'God, I feel so humiliated.'

'There's no need.' He leaned towards her again in a gesture of kindness. 'This is me – Arnie, who you've known for ever. You don't have to feel that way because of me.'

'Don't I?' she mumbled, sounding pathetic but quietly working out her next move.

'Of course you don't. Because we're good friends, Carol. But let's just leave it at that, shall we?'

She had no intention whatsoever of settling for friendship, but she said in a compliant manner, 'Okay, if that's what you want . . .'

He took a handkerchief from his pocket and gently dabbed her eyes. 'That's better,' he said softly.

'Thanks.'

'Thanks for coming over tonight,' he said. 'I enjoyed your company.'

She reached for the door handle. 'I'll see you soon then, yeah?' she said hopefully.

'Yeah.'

It would be soon, too, because she was going to make an absolute point of it. She would do anything to get him, *anything* at all.

'Night, then.'

'Night, Carol.'

Driving back to Hammersmith, Arnie regretted the fact that things had got complicated with Carol. It would be all too easy to have a fling with her. He was lonely, and she was willing. But he would never forgive himself if he took advantage of Gill's sister, who had already been driven to the brink of a nervous breakdown because of a love affair. Hurting Carol would be like betraying Gill's trust, and he'd done quite enough of that already.

He would have to tread carefully with Carol in future, though. He didn't want to hurt her, but neither did he want to have an affair with her. The sensible thing would be not to see her at all. But he had a horrible suspicion that it wasn't going to be as simple as that.

Ah well, another day tomorrow, he thought, letting himself into his flat and feeling its stillness close around him for the second time that day. It was even more depressing this time, too, after the recent warmth of company.

Mary Bex called on Gill at home one morning unexpectedly.

'I was practically passing the end of your road on my way back from the accountant's office, so I thought I'd come and scrounge a cup of coffee.'

'I'm glad you did,' said Gill, filling the kettle and plugging it in while Mary sat down at the kitchen table. 'It's nice to see you, and it'll give me an excuse to take a break. I'm catching up on my paperwork . . . piles of the stuff.'

'Even piano teachers have to do that, then?' asked Mary.

'Of course,' said Gill, spooning coffee into the mugs. 'As well as keeping my books up to date for the Inland Revenue, there's all the administration for the exam entries and pupils who are entering for competitions to be dealt with too.'

'It's obvious that you would have office-work to do, the same as anyone else in business,' Mary said, 'but for some reason I never associate musicians with anything as mundane as paperwork.'

'If I only had a few pupils I might not have to bother, but as I run it as a business I have to keep things in order.'

'Mm.'

'I enjoy having a busy schedule, though – which is just as well as it pays our keep.'

'How's Craig?'

'Full of beans,' said Gill. 'And still football mad.'

'Yes, so Arnie was saying in the shop the other day. He's really tickled about it, isn't he?'

Gill nodded. 'I think he's hoping to relive his glory days through his son,' she said, putting a plate of biscuits and two mugs of coffee on the table before sitting down opposite her friend.

Something about her tone of voice made Mary say, 'You haven't changed your mind about Craig becoming a footballer, then?'

'Definitely not.'

'I can see you and Arnie fighting that one out,' said Mary.

'So what's new about us two fighting?' Gill grinned.

Mary laughed. She had made it plain at the time of the

separation that she wouldn't take sides, since she was a good friend of Gill's as well as a colleague of Arnie's. 'If there wasn't an issue, you two would find one to argue about.'

'We're getting on better now we're not together, though.'

'Really?'

'Yes.'

'But how are things developing with the man from the music shop?'

'They're not,' Gill said. 'Not in the way you mean, anyway.'

'No romance yet then?'

'Sorry to disappoint you, but we're just friends.'

'I'm your friend, but I don't take you out for candlelit meals of an evening,' Mary said with a wicked grin.

'Neither does he.' Gill thought about this. 'Well, there are candles on the tables at an Italian place we go to sometimes, but it's purely coincidental. Anyway, I always insist on paying my share.'

'So that there's no misunderstanding, eh?' said Mary.

'Something like that.' Gill paused. 'I've grown to like Peter a lot, though, and I enjoy his company. I'd miss him if he disappeared off the scene now. He's such a dear and very easy to talk to. He's certainly easier to be with than Arnie ever was, and we have more in common.'

'Music?'

'Mainly that,' she said, 'then of course there's the fact that we're both victims of a broken marriage.'

'You and Arnie have that in common too,' teased Mary.

'Oh, very droll.' Gill laughed.

'Well, I still think it's a heck of a shame about you two,' said Mary. 'You were so right for each other, somehow.'

'So much so that we couldn't say a civil word to each other when we were together.'

'I know.' Mary sighed.

They moved on to other things, touching briefly on the new roadside breathalyser test that was soon to be introduced for drivers.

'It isn't a bad thing,' said Mary. 'Though I doubt if Len will agree. He'll say it's an infringement of liberty.'

'That would probably be Arnie's response to it too,' said Gill.

'Typical male reaction,' Mary said. 'And only because they don't want to have to watch how much they have, when they pop into the pub for a "quick one" and want to drive home afterwards.' She paused. 'And talking of driving, it's time I was off.'

'Are you going back to the shop?' Gill asked at the front door.

'Yes. Better do a bit to earn my keep.' Mary looked at her watch. 'Gosh, is that the time? Len will be wondering where I've got to.'

'Shall I ring him to let him know you're on your way?'

'There's no need . . . it won't take me long to get there in the car.'

'Well, thanks for calling in,' said Gill, giving her friend a hug. 'It's always nice to see you.'

'You too. We'll have to go out for a meal together one of these nights,' Mary suggested casually. 'When Len's out on one of his men-only dos, we could have a girls' night out.'

'That would be smashing.'

'But in the meantime, it's back to the grind for us both . . .'

Gill stood at the front door waiting for Mary to walk through the doorway. But nothing happened. Gill turned to her, instantly realising that her friend was ill. Her face was feverishly bright and beaded with perspiration. Even as Gill watched, her skin became ashen.

'Mary? What's the matter?'

'I've come over a bit queer all of a sudden,' she said in a whisper, eyes rolling, body swaying.

'Come back inside and sit down,' Gill suggested, feeling some concern.

'It's nothing, just one of my funny turns . . . I do get them from time to time, but . . . Oh, I think I'm gonna pass out . . .'

Her body crumpled and she slumped against Gill, who eased her gently to the floor.

On her knees, Gill leant over her, speaking in a soothing voice. 'It's all right,' she said softly, smoothing her hand over Mary's damp brow. 'I'll get a doctor, you'll be fine.'

'There's no need. I'll be all right in a minute,' Mary said weakly.

'Okay. Whatever you want . . . but don't upset yourself.'

'Len . . .' Mary said feebly.

'I'll give him a ring.'

'Please get him,' she said, just before her body went limp and she closed her eyes.

Terrified but still managing to stay in control, Gill realised that this was more serious than just a fainting fit. With great relief, she found a pulse.

Mary's eyelids began to flicker and she opened her eyes. 'Len,' she said again.

'Don't worry,' said Gill, 'I'll ring him right away.'

'Thanks.' Mary's lids flickered then closed again as she sank into unconsciousness.

'Oh my God,' gasped Gill. She rushed to the telephone and rang for an ambulance, her heart beating so fast she thought it would explode.

Len and Arnie were talking business in the shop with the sales rep from a sports-shoe company when the telephone rang. As the manager of the shop, Arnie had authority to order stock from any of the reps without referring to Len or Mary. But if Len was around and not too busy when one of them called, he usually took part in the discussion, especially if it was a new company coming into the market and he wanted to know more about them.

'I'll answer it,' said Phoebe, who was at the counter but not actually serving anyone at that moment.

'Thanks, Mum,' said Arnie.

She went into Arnie's small glass-fronted office at the back of the shop to take the call. When she emerged a few minutes later, pale and trembling, she walked over to Len on legs of jelly.

'Can you tell whoever it is that I'll ring them back later, please, dear?' Len said. 'I'm tied up at the moment—'

'It was Gill.' Phoebe sounded dazed. 'She's at the hospital.'

'Gill's at the hospital?' Arnie gasped in an immediate panic. 'What's happened to her? Has she had an accident? Oh my God . . .'

Phoebe put a steadying hand on his arm. 'Calm down, now, son,' she said firmly. 'It isn't Gill.'

'It isn't . . .' Arnie's voice was suddenly light with relief. 'So, who . . . ?'

Phoebe looked gravely at Len. 'It's Mary,' she said. 'I'm afraid she's been taken ill.'

Len's face was brightly suffused for a moment, then became bloodless. Phoebe thought he was going to pass out cold. But he said in a breathless voice, 'Which hospital?'

'Hammersmith.'

Even as she said the word he was already hurrying to the shop door.

'You'd better go with him, Mum,' Arnie suggested wisely. 'He needs someone and I have to look after things here.'

Without even stopping to get her coat she tore after him, catching him up at his Jaguar, which was parked in his regular place in a side street. Len didn't argue about her going with him to the hospital, he just opened the passenger door for her to get into the car. He was about to drive away when Arnie came tearing towards them, carrying their coats.

'You'll freeze to death without these in this weather,' he said. 'We don't want you in hospital an' all.'

'Thanks, son,' Phoebe said, taking the coats from him. 'That was thoughtful of you.'

'I feel terrible about this, but I'll have to go in a minute,' Gill

236

said to Phoebe that afternoon. 'As much as I'd like to stay, I have to collect Craig from school.'

Phoebe nodded.

'I would ring my mum and ask her to collect him, but she's gone to Essex to see her sister for the day.'

'You go, love,' Phoebe urged her. 'I'll stay with Len.'

They were still at the hospital, in the waiting area outside the ward where Mary lay in a coma having suffered a massive heart attack. The doctors said her condition was critical. Len was with her now – Gill and Phoebe had left him to be alone with his wife. They were both in a state of shock.

'I feel awful about leaving while Mary's so ill,' Gill said.

'You have to look after your child,' Phoebe sensibly pointed out. 'Mary would hate to think you were neglecting your duties because of her. And I'll keep you informed about what's happening here. I'll get on the blower to you soon as there's any news.'

'Okay.' Gill paused and looked at the other woman with tears in her eyes. 'Oh, Phoebe, it's so terrible. Why Mary, of all people?'

'I dunno, love,' she said with a sad shake of the head. 'I really don't.'

'She was fine this morning,' Gill said. 'Then, bang, this happens, right out of the blue. No warning, nothing!'

'There, there,' said Phoebe, giving Gill a comforting hug. 'I'm not so sure that this was right out of the blue. I don't think she's been feeling herself for a long time, even though she wouldn't admit it.'

'Poor Mary.'

'Poor Len an' all,' said Phoebe worriedly. 'He's in a hell of a state.' She drew back. 'But off you go, love, or young Craig will be hanging about waiting for you at the school gate.'

Soon after Gill had left, Len emerged unsteadily from the ward with a nurse holding his arm. Phoebe could tell by the stricken look on his face that the worst had happened. The nurse took Phoebe to one side and confirmed this, asking if she was a member of Mr Bex's family. Len stood silently by, looking stunned and showing no curiosity as to what they were talking about. The poor man seemed to be in a world of his own.

'I'm a friend of the family,' Phoebe explained to the nurse.

'Mr Bex is in a bad way. We had to drag him away from his wife after she'd slipped away,' she explained sadly.

'How sad.'

'He's in shock.'

'The poor dear.'

'He says there are no children to be with him at this sad time.'

'No.'

The nurse looked worried. 'It isn't a good idea for him to be on his own at the moment,' she said.

'Don't worry, nurse, I'll look after him,' said Phoebe.

'Thank you,' said the nurse, with obvious relief. 'I'll go and see if I can get you both some tea.'

Phoebe turned to Len, saw the pain in his eyes. His face was almost the same colour as his hair, his eyes bloodshot and vacant. Her own aching grief for Mary had to take second place to her concern for him.

'Come on, Len,' she said softly, taking his arm. 'Let's go and find somewhere comfortable to sit while the nurse gets us some tea.'

Normally a man of robust self-confidence, always in control and at the centre of things, now he allowed her to lead him away like a mother leading her child.

Chapter Fourteen

The crowd that came to pay their last respects to Mary was a testimony to her popularity. Their numbers spread far and wide in the cemetery on that bitter cold February day, as a piercing wind howled through the gravestones beneath angry grey skies that threatened snow.

Standing near to the graveside, the ground hard and slippery underfoot, it occurred to Gill that she had never heard anyone say a bad word about Mary in all the time she'd known her. Quite an achievement for someone involved in business and likely, therefore, to make enemies.

Glancing across at Len, standing between Phoebe and Arnie, Gill couldn't get over how much he had changed in such a short time. Usually so vigorous and sure of himself, he looked now like an emaciated old man, faltering both in speech and movement. It was heartbreaking to see him like this.

Afterwards, when the mourners were gathered at Len's house in Putney, Gill, Phoebe and Arnie hosted the party, as Len was too frail and tearful to take charge of the occasion. Gill and Phoebe had prepared a light buffet, and Arnie was in charge of the drinks.

'God knows how he's going to manage without her,' Gill remarked to Arnie in a quiet moment when the guests were all attended to.

'I've been thinking about that too.'

'Len was always the one with all the front, but I got the idea that Mary was the source of his strength in her quiet, homely way.'

'I shouldn't be at all surprised,' Arnie said.

'He just seems to have fallen apart.'

'Yeah. Poor bloke.' Arnie sighed and shook his head. 'He doesn't even have any kids to turn to for comfort.'

'He doesn't seem to have any close relatives either.'

'No. I reckon he and Mary were so complete in themselves, they didn't need anyone else.' Arnie looked across the room at Len who was standing by the window with a glass of whisky in his hand, puffing on a cigarette. Phoebe was trying to coax him into taking a sandwich from the plate she was offering but he was shaking his head. He'd eaten practically nothing this past week.

'And I suppose they drifted away from relatives over the years because of that,' Gill said.

'Now, when he needs someone, there's no family to turn to.'

She nodded sadly. 'Your mother's been wonderful to him, though,' she said.

'Yeah,' he agreed. 'I don't know what he'd have done without her to be perfectly honest.'

'I don't either.'

He threw Gill a look. 'But how are you coping with it?' he asked. 'Her death must have come as a blow to you. I know what good friends you were.'

'I'm still numb,' she confessed. 'I don't think it's really sunk in yet.'

'It's shaken me up an' all.'

'Something like this certainly puts things into perspective, doesn't it?' she said. 'Makes you realise that life's too short to waste time worrying about trivialities.'

'I'll say.' Arnie sighed. 'We'll all still do it, though, won't we – when the shock of her death has worn off?'

'Very probably,' she agreed chattily. 'We'll soon forget how frighteningly aware we were made of our own mortality.'

'I've had no end of funny pains since it happened.'

'Me too,' she said, smiling. 'The most harmless of twinges

have been heart attacks in the making this past few days.'

He laughed. Drawn together by adversity, the atmosphere between them was warm. Neither Peter nor Carol was mentioned.

'So, what's happening in the office without Mary?' asked Gill.

'I've had to get a temp in, someone who can do a bit of everything,' he said. 'Mum's doing what she can to help but she isn't trained for office-work.'

'She's very quick on the uptake, though. She'd soon pick it up,' Gill said.

'Yes, she would – especially as there's hardly any typing to do.' Arnie paused. 'But we need someone who's familiar with the PAYE system because of the staff wages.'

'You'll get someone permanent to replace Mary once the dust settles, will you?'

'I suppose we'll have to, but that will be Len's decision. And he has no interest in the shops whatsoever at the moment. He's told me to do whatever I think best and not bother him about business.'

'So everything's been left to you?'

'That's right. And because the overall administration is done in the office above our shop, the responsibility for all the branches seems to have fallen into my lap,' he told her. 'Not that I mind. I'm only too happy to do what I can to help. But at the end of the day it is Len's business – and I don't want to do anything he might not approve of later, when he's feeling better.'

'It's a big responsibility.'

'Not half.'

'But now the funeral's over he'll gradually begin to take an interest again, I should think,' Gill said encouragingly. 'It might take a bit of time, though.'

'It isn't gonna happen overnight, that's for sure.' Arnie stared into space, an impressive figure in a dark suit and black tie. He looked exhausted though, tension pulling tight around his eyes. 'Poor old Len. He's been knocked sideways. I only wish there was something I could do to make him feel better.'

'All any of us can do is be there for him,' Gill said.

'Yeah.'

Suddenly the atmosphere between them became highly charged. Their eyes met and they both looked away quickly. Arnie glanced at his watch in hope of restoring normality. 'Time certainly goes on, doesn't it?' he said unnecessarily.

'It sure does.'

'Would you like me to collect Craig from school today?' he offered. 'If you want to hang on here for a while?'

'Thanks, but I've already made arrangements,' she said. 'My mum's collecting him today because I wasn't sure what time I would be back. I shall stay on here to help Phoebe clear up.'

'Are you teaching?'

'No, I cancelled everything for today,' she told him.

He fell silent. Gill's heart raced as she thought he was going to suggest that he come over to the house later on, so that they could be together at this sad time. She viewed the idea with a certain trepidation because, as much as she wanted to be with him, she knew it would be a bad idea. There was no point inflaming old passions just because they were both at a low ebb in the aftermath of Mary's death – it would be too painful later.

'It was probably the best idea,' Arnie said to stop the conversation from flagging. 'I shall have to go back to work soon, though. It isn't fair to leave the staff on their own for too long.'

For all her common sense, Gill ached with disappointment that he hadn't suggested they get together later. Today she needed him more than ever before. 'You're quite the dedicated businessman these days,' she said lightly.

'I have to be,' he said. 'If I don't apply myself to the job I won't last long as manager.'

'No.'

242

'But I like the work anyway, so it isn't a problem.'

'Good.'

Feeling dangerously emotional, Gill knew she must distance herself from him before instinct took over and she suggested something she would later regret. 'Well, I'd better take the sandwiches around again,' she said. 'Or we'll end up giving them to the birds.'

'See you, then.'

'Yes.'

For some reason the light tone of their conversation seemed to put a seal on the end of their marriage. It was as though they had now reached the stage where they could converse in the detached way of strangers at a party, and part with an equal lack of feeling.

The latter was just an illusion, though. There was no lack of feeling – not on Gill's part, anyway.

When she got to her mother's to collect Craig that evening, having helped Phoebe clear up at Len's place and left her to keep him company, Gill was imbued with sadness. For the first time since it had happened, the implications of Mary's death really came home to her. Now that the horror of her passing was over, Gill had to face the dull reality of her friend not being around any more. She missed her already.

'Are you staying to eat with us?' asked Winnie, who was seated at the table with Hal, Carol and Craig when Gill arrived. 'You'll have to wait for Craig to finish anyway.'

'Just a cup of tea for me, thanks, Mum.' Gill sat down and poured herself a cup from the large pot on the table. 'I've been eating bits and pieces all afternoon at Len's place.'

'How is the poor man?'

'In a bad way.'

'Shame,' said Hal.

'He might start to pick up now that the funeral is over,' said Winnie. 'Once he gets back to work.'

'That's what I'm hoping,' said Gill.

'Awful for him,' said Hal. 'Especially having no family.'

'Phoebe is being very good to him, though,' said Gill.

I'll bet she is, Winnie couldn't help thinking. If she gets her claws into him and all his money she'll be set up for life. But she kept her uncharitable thoughts to herself to avoid a storm of protest from Hal and Gill.

'Who's actually running the business with Mary gone and Len in a state of shock?' Hal asked, forking a piece of meat pie.

'Arnie's in charge at the moment,' said Gill. 'The whole thing seems to have fallen on to his shoulders.'

'It's a lot of responsibility for him,' remarked Hal.

'That's what I said.'

'He doesn't mind, does he?' said Winnie.

'Oh no, he doesn't mind in the least,' said Gill proudly. 'But it's a lot of extra work and worry, with Len being out of the picture altogether.'

'Mm,' said her father.

'He couldn't even stay long at the funeral because of the pressure of work,' Gill continued. 'He went back to the shop quite early on and God knows what time he'll get home tonight.'

'He'll be worn out,' said Winnie.

'He certainly will,' said Gill. 'And, of course, he's quite cut up about Mary's death too. They did work together, after all.'

'Poor old Arnie,' said Carol, joining in the conversation with feigned compassion. It was as much as she could do not to show her delight, because the opportunity she had been waiting for had just presented itself – and she was going after it with everything she'd got.

Gill had a long soak in the bath after she'd put Craig to bed that night. Her muscles ached with the tension of the last week. As she began to unwind she felt hot, salty tears running down her wet cheeks: tears for the loss of a true friend, a woman who had still had so much to give. She lay there for a long time letting the sadness come, her tears mingling with the steamy bath water.

She had just dried herself and slipped into her dressing gown when the front doorbell rang.

'I hope it isn't someone enquiring about piano lessons at this hour,' she muttered to herself as she hurried downstairs. She wasn't expecting anyone but Peter sometimes called round unexpectedly.

'Peter,' she said looking pleased. 'How nice to see you! Come on in.'

'I thought you might need cheering up after what must have been a lousy day,' he said, handing her a bottle of wine. He glanced at her apparel. 'I hope you weren't just going to bed, though.'

'No, not this early,' she explained. 'I've just got out of the bath.'

'So, how was the funeral?'

'I'm very glad it's over.'

'I can imagine.'

She handed the wine back to him. 'Thanks for this,' she said. 'You go and do the honours while I slip upstairs and get dressed. You know where everything is.'

'Will do.'

Upstairs she put on a pair of jeans and a sweater. On the way back down she popped into Craig's room and pulled the covers up over his shoulders.

'Who's downstairs?' he asked, stirring.

'Uncle Peter.'

'What's he come for?'

'To keep me company.'

'Oh.' He sounded satisfied. He'd met Peter several times and seemed to get along with him. His eyes closed. 'Night, Mum.'

'Night, love.'

Downstairs, Peter had poured the wine and put some crisps into a dish.

'Oh, Peter, this is the first time I've felt remotely human since before Mary died,' Gill said with a sigh of relief, sinking into an armchair by the fire opposite him. 'It was so thoughtful of you to come over.'

'I wanted to,' he said, looking at her over the rim of his wine glass. 'I want to be there for you whenever you need me.'

'Yes, I know,' she said softly, realising the extent of her affection for him. 'And I really appreciate it.'

'My pleasure.'

They chatted about things other than Mary's death; Gill had had enough morbidity for one day. Peter suggested that they take Cherry Betts to a concert sometime soon.

'What a lovely idea,' she said.

'I'll look out for something that won't be too heavy for her and get some tickets.'

'Thank you. She'll be thrilled,' Gill said, warming to him even more. 'We'll have to keep an eye out to see what's on.'

The evening passed quickly and all too soon Peter said he had to be going.

'Already?' she said, depressed at the thought of being alone. 'I could sit here talking to you for ever.'

'Me too,' he said, 'but I have to be up early for work tomorrow.'

She got his coat from the hall and held it out for him. He slipped into it and turned to her.

'Gill . . .' he began uncertainly. 'This probably isn't the time . . .'

'Probably not, but go on.'

'You must know how I feel about you,' he said hoarsely.

'I think I can guess,' she said with great tenderness.

Her need to be loved at that moment was overwhelming. The grief of losing a dear friend combined with the realisation that her marriage really was over culminated in a feeling of indescribable loneliness. She needed so much to be held, to be reminded that she was alive and not repulsive to the opposite sex.

She responded to his embrace instinctively. This was the first time she'd felt like a woman for a long time – far too long. Because of this she welcomed his arms around her and revelled in the throb of physical contact.

Vaguely aware of passing through an important turning point in her relationship with Peter that she had resisted for so long, she realised that somehow she didn't mind now.

Arnie was feeling like death when he finally got home from work on the night of Mary's funeral. He hadn't been as close to her as he was to Len, but he'd known her well enough to feel shock and sorrow at her passing. Mostly, though, his grief was for Len, who was a broken man.

That night Arnie's thoughts were also with Gill. He was aware of having let her down today in his attempt to behave honourably. Knowing she was feeling awful about her friend's death, he'd wanted to hold her in his arms and soothe away her pain. Instead he'd made small talk, because to follow his heart would be to hurt her even more in the long run. If he'd given in to his feelings he would have put them both on a roller-coaster back to hell.

Heartsick and tormented, he mooched into the kitchen and put the kettle on for coffee, then checked out the food situation. Baked beans on toast, he decided in the absence of a choice.

He'd just put some bread under the grill when the doorbell rang.

'Carol!'

'Hi, Arnie.'

'What are you doing here?'

'Don't go overboard with the welcome,' she said with mild sarcasm.

'Sorry.'

'And so you should be.'

'I wasn't expecting you,' he said, 'and I'm absolutely shattered.'

'Aren't you going to ask me in?'

He hesitated, chewing his lip anxiously. 'Actually, I'm not in the mood for company,' he said, knowing he was being bad-mannered but sensing danger in letting her over the threshold on this particular occasion. 'It's been one hell of a rotten day.'

'Yes, I know. That's why I'm here,' she explained.

'It's very nice of you to bother to come over, Carol,' he said patiently, 'but I'm really not feeling sociable. I'm gonna have something to eat and go straight to bed.'

'You shouldn't be on your own, not tonight,' she said.

'I think I ought to be the judge of that, don't you?'

'Look. There's no point in your trying to send me away,' she declared with an air of ruthless determination he hadn't seen in her before, 'because I simply won't go.'

'But—'

'You shut the door on me and I'll ring the doorbell again and again . . . I'll keep on doing it until you do let me in.'

'Why?'

'Because you need someone.'

'I don't, but come in anyway,' he said with an exasperated sigh, moving back so that she could step inside.

'Thank you.'

Taking off her coat, she hung it on the hook in the hall to reveal a tight black sweater worn with a mini skirt.

She sniffed. 'Something's burning,' she said.

'The toast,' he said, rushing to the kitchen to retrieve it.

She followed him into the kitchen and stood behind him while he scraped the blackened toast over the sink.

'I keep meaning to get a pop-up toaster,' he said in an effort to head off the situation he suspected was about to develop.

'Do you?'

'Yes. Burnt toast has become the bane of my life since I've been living on my own.'

'You need someone to look after you, that's your trouble.'

'No I don't,' he protested. 'I manage well enough.'

Having decided that subtlety was not an option she could afford to consider in this instance, she slipped her arms around him from behind and pressed her face against his back, breathing deeply, her eyes closing with pleasure. She could feel the throb of his heartbeat through his sweater. God, how she wanted him.

'Leave the toast,' she said.

'I have to eat.'

'I know that, but—'

'Please stop playing games, Carol,' Arnie cut in irritably, trying to extricate himself from her by pulling away.

'This is no game.'

'I'm hungry and I want to have my supper,' he said as an excuse.

'You need me more than you need food at this precise moment,' she said blatantly.

'So you know more about what I need than I do?' he said.

'No. You know it too,' she said. 'So forget about your supper and I'll get us both something to eat later on.'

'But, Carol . . .' he said, his tone still admonishing but slightly less firm now.

'Don't pretend you don't need someone tonight, Arnie,' she said.

'I'm not pretending anything—'

'I think you are.'

'What makes you think that?'

'Because it's obvious after the sort of day you've had.'

He didn't reply, but she could feel the resonance of his body as nature took over from his intellect.

'You're feeling rotten . . . you're as lonely as hell,' she continued.

As he turned slowly round to face her, the toast slipped from his trembling fingers into the washing-up bowl. 'Sure I'm lonely,' he said, struggling to stay in control.

'Well then . . .'

'But I'm not in the habit of using my friends just because I'm feeling a bit low,' he said. 'I'm not that degenerate.'

'Don't be so silly,' she said in a soothing whisper, stroking his face with her hands. 'That's what friends are for. That's what this friend is for anyway.'

'Carol ... stop it,' he said. 'This has gone quite far enough.'

'I want to be with you, Arnie, to make you feel better,' she said softly, urgently. 'I want to make love to you.'

'No—'

'There'll be no strings attached,' she lied, 'I promise you.'

'For God's sake, Carol, this is madness,' he muttered thickly.

'If you're thinking about Gill you can forget her, because she's got someone else.'

'That makes no difference ... This isn't right, not you and me,' he protested.

'It feels right enough to me,' she said in a strong voice tinged with jubilance. 'Very right indeed.'

And his biology couldn't argue with that. She felt warm and welcoming against him and it was so good and natural to have a woman close to him again after so long.

'Oh God,' he muttered.

The toast turned soggy in the bowl and the baked beans remained in the unopened can as he finally gave up the fight against Carol's relentless persistence.

Chapter Fifteen

'Oh, it's you,' said Len in a bellicose manner.

Arnie had called at his employer's house on a matter of business, having used his own lunch hour for the visit. 'Can I come in, mate?' he asked when it became clear that Len wasn't going to offer.

'Yeah, I s'pose you'd better,' was Len's gruff reply.

Arnie followed him into the lounge, the expensive furnishings barely noticeable beneath the muddle.

'Blimey!' Arnie exclaimed, almost choking on the smell of stale booze and cigarette smoke. Thick layers of dust covered everything, and were made more obvious by the shafts of sunlight beaming through the mucky windows. The room was littered with overflowing ashtrays, used teacups and crumpled newspapers.

'Is your cleaner on strike or something?'

'No.' Len's tone was contemptuous.

'But . . .' Arnie cast an indicative glance around the room.

'I've told her not to clean in here.' Len also looked grubby and unkempt. 'I don't want some strange woman coming in here and invading my privacy.'

The problem would be far more expediently solved if Len was out of the house during the day looking after his business instead of sitting about indoors feeling sorry for himself, Arnie thought, but he said, 'Oh, I see. It's a bit of tip though, innit, mate?'

Len shrugged as though he couldn't care less.

'Mary must be turning in her grave,' remarked Arnie.

The other man threw him a piercingly critical look, cheeks sunken in his lean face, eyes bloodshot and lacklustre. 'I've always thought that was a ridiculous saying,' he snapped. 'I mean, how the hell can someone disapprove of anything if they've passed on?'

'It's just a figure of speech,' said Arnie, trying to be tactful. 'To remind us of the sort of person they were.'

'I know exactly what it means, thank you very much,' Len barked. 'And I don't want to hear you saying it again.'

'Okay, boss.' Arnie sat down and opened his briefcase. 'No offence meant.'

'That's all right then,' Len growled.

'I've just come over with the wages cheque for you to sign and one or two queries I need to discuss with you.'

'Do you wanna drink?' offered Len.

'Yes, please. I'll have a small beer if you've got one,' said Arnie, taking the papers relating to the staff wages from his briefcase.

'I don't have any beer.' Len picked his way over to a drinks cabinet. 'Will whisky do?'

'Not for me, thanks,' said Arnie. 'I've a lot to do this afternoon and whisky will send me to sleep.' He looked at his watch. 'I don't really have time for a drink, anyway.' He got up and handed some papers to Len. 'So if you could just check the figures and sign the cheque . . .'

Len signed the cheque but didn't bother to check the figures on the wages sheet. He finished his drink, immediately poured another, and settled back in his armchair.

'Everyone at the firm is wondering when you'll be coming back to work,' said Arnie pointedly. 'It's four months since—'

'I know how long it's been, and I'll come back when I'm ready.'

'Fair enough.' Arnie put the papers back into the briefcase and took out a wholesaler's catalogue of sportsgear, which he handed to Len.

'What do you want me to do with this?' Len asked in a disgruntled manner.

'We've been offered a special deal on cricket gear by this firm,' Arnie explained. 'I thought you might like to have a look through it to see what they have to offer.'

'I'm not bothered.'

'Oh!' Arnie paused, silently counting to ten. 'Well, they're offering us such good rates, I was thinking of putting some stuff on sale at reduced prices.'

'This early in the season?' said Len scathingly. 'You must be joking!'

'It isn't early in terms of trade though, is it?' Arnie was worried by Len's reaction to his suggestion; to him it illustrated just how out of touch with the business he had become. 'Most of the clubs already have everything they need for this year.'

'Yeah, yeah,' said Len, losing interest. 'You do whatever you think best.'

'Okay.'

'So is that it, then?' Len asked, keen to be alone again with his grief.

'There's just one other thing I'd like to discuss with you,' Arnie ventured.

'What is it?' Len enquired with rising impatience.

'My mother has been helping out in the office, and she seems to be getting the hang of things really well under the guidance of the temp we're using from the agency. She even seems to have come to grips with the PAYE system, which means she could cope with the staff wages if necessary...'

'So?'

'I was wondering if it might be a good idea to move her into the office permanently when the temp has trained her up properly,' said Arnie. 'Mum's only a two-finger typist but there's hardly any typing to do anyway.'

'Who'll cover for your mother in the shop?' Len asked in a perfunctory manner.

'We'd have to get someone to replace her, of course. But I thought . . . rather than have a stranger working with you in the office when you come back to work, you might prefer someone you already know.'

Len couldn't even bear to think about the office without his darling Mary in it. 'If you think that's the best thing then go ahead and do it,' he said sharply. 'Don't bother me with every little detail.'

Hardly a little detail, Arnie thought. 'There's no need to bite my head off, mate. I'm doing my best.'

'Yeah, yeah, I know,' Len said, with a glimmer of remorse. 'You're managing okay, though, aren't you?'

'Yes, I'm managing.' Indeed, Arnie had amazed himself by coping with the responsibility for the entire Bex chain in Len's absence. A few years ago he wouldn't have believed himself capable.

Len looked at him through narrowed eyes, as though seeing him through mist. 'Well carry on doing it then,' he said miserably, 'and leave me alone.'

'Fair enough, boss.' Arnie gathered the rest of his papers and put them into the briefcase. 'I'd better be getting back to work. Don't come to the door, I'll see myself out.'

'Cheers,' said Len absently, sinking back into his own personal sorrow without noticing how worried Arnie had looked when he left.

'The man has become completely impossible,' Arnie complained to Gill one Sunday evening a few weeks later; he had just brought Craig back from a trip to Chessington Zoo. 'I've never known anyone change so much as Len has. He's like a stranger . . . and so damned aggressive.'

'That's what grief does to people,' Gill said with a sad shake of the head. 'His life, as it used to be, has been completely demolished, and he just can't cope with it.'

'I'm worried sick about him.'

Arnie had sat down at the kitchen table while they'd been

talking. Gill looked at him. 'Fancy a cup of tea?'

'Please,' he said in a preoccupied manner because he was still thinking about Len.

She put the kettle on and went to the larder for the tea-caddy. It constantly surprised her to find how well she and Arnie got along these days. She'd thought that now they were both seeing someone else there'd have been awkwardness. But it seemed to have eased the tension between them even more. It was strange!

'He's lost in a world of his own,' Arnie continued. 'He doesn't seem to give a damn about anyone or anything. And he's lost interest in his business altogether.'

'That isn't like Len.'

'It isn't,' he agreed. 'I'm beginning to think that Mary really was the driving force behind it all. As you said – she was quiet and homely, and he appeared to be the stronger of the two, but he must have been heavily reliant on her.'

Gill nodded. 'So, what does he do all day if he doesn't go to work?' she asked.

'Sits at home chain-smoking and boozing, from what I can gather.'

'While you're rushed off your feet running his business?'

'I honestly don't mind that,' said Arnie emphatically. 'I want to do whatever I can to help.' He shook his head gravely. 'But Len means a lot to me, and I don't know what's gonna become of him. I mean, he isn't going to come to terms with Mary's death and rebuild his life this way, is he? He'll just get more and more miserable and out of touch with things.'

'Mm.' Gill brought the teapot to the table. 'Len has always struck me as a man who needs to be at the centre of things, not stuck at home alone.'

'Exactly. And the only way he's ever going to get back on his feet again is to come back to work. But if I so much as hint at that he hits the roof.'

Gill pondered the problem as she poured tea. 'Well, Arnie,

I think you are just going to have to give Len a dose of his own medicine.'

'What do you mean?'

'Do you remember when you resigned from the job – when you found out I'd been to see Len – and he got tough with you?'

Arnie nodded.

'Well, it worked for you, didn't it?' Gill said. 'You went back to work.'

'Hmmm.' Arnie was thoughtful. 'You're forgetting one important detail, though . . .'

'I am?'

'Yeah – he's the boss,' he reminded her. 'If I start getting stroppy with him I could find myself out of work.'

'You do have a point,' she said, putting a mug of tea down in front of him and sitting down. 'But there are times in life when you have to take a personal risk for the benefit of someone else. I believe that this is one of those times.'

'And what do I do if he fires me?' Arnie asked with a wry grin.

'Get another job.'

'Just like that?'

'Yes. You're an experienced retail manager now,' she reminded him. 'You shouldn't have too much trouble finding something suitable.'

'I suppose not.'

'But I don't think it'll come to that, anyway.'

'I'll be round here with murder in mind if it does,' he joked. 'I like working for Len and I don't want to change my job.'

'I've got Craig to protect me,' she said with a giggle.

And suddenly they were both laughing at the sheer idiocy of the conversation, as they had done in their halcyon days. It felt so wonderfully exhilarating to have a rapport with Arnie again.

Wondering what was causing the hilarity, Craig appeared

from the other room. 'What are you two laughing at?' he asked with a half smile.

'Nothing that you would find funny, son,' said Arnie.

'Just your dad being daft,' Gill said, exchanging a glance with Arnie.

If only we could have got on like this when we were together, she thought wistfully.

Smoking a cigarette in his armchair, Len glowered at Arnie. He didn't appreciate having home truths frankly spelled out to him. 'You've got a nerve, coming round here telling me what I ought to be doing!' he roared. '*You* work for *me*, remember, not the other way around.'

Arnie could have pointed out to him that he was currently doing the job of a managing director on the salary of a branch manager, but he didn't want to kick a man when he was down. 'I'm well aware of that, Len,' he replied. 'But that doesn't mean I don't worry about what happens to you.'

'Staff don't worry about the boss . . . that isn't the way it works,' Len said. 'Anyway, I'm quite capable of looking after myself.'

'It doesn't look that way from where I'm sitting.' Arnie cast a disapproving eye over Len's scruffy appearance before letting it wander over the untidy room.

'Meaning?'

'You're a bloody mess,' Arnie declared, determined to stand his ground for Len's sake no matter how angry the man became. 'And you have been ever since Mary died. It's high time you pulled yourself together and came back to work.'

'Shut it!'

'Sorry if the truth hurts, mate,' Arnie replied, undaunted, 'but someone needs to give it to you straight now that Mary isn't here to do it.'

Seeing the other man wince, Arnie was filled with compassion. But if Len was to come through this trauma and take up his life again, certain things had to be said. Arnie

257

would be as brutal as he considered necessary.

'I've told you not to mention Mary's death,' Len said crossly.

'It happened, Len. Mary died several months ago and now life goes on, however much you want it to be otherwise. I realise that you're missing her something awful, but you have to get out there and face up to things without her now. Shutting yourself away from the world isn't going to solve anything.'

'I haven't shut myself away.'

'That's what it seems like to me.'

'I go out . . .'

'Yeah, to the pub and the off-licence to get your fags and booze,' Arnie said harshly. 'But I can count the times you've been into the office since Mary died on one hand. And on the odd occasion that you have shown your face you couldn't get away quick enough.' He paused. 'Don't get me wrong, boss, I'm quite happy to run things for you and to come out here to your house to get cheques signed and queries answered for as long as you want me to. But when it comes to the crunch, it's your business and not mine. You're the guvnor, and you need to be there in the thick of it, to keep abreast with what's going on.'

'I'm glad you've remembered that I'm the guvnor . . .' Len puffed at a cigarette. 'Because you're fired.'

'What!'

'You heard,' Len said, erupting into a fit of coughing.

'Isn't that a bit unfair?' suggested Arnie, brows raised.

Len ignored the question. 'I don't know what makes you think you have the right to come round here telling me how to run my life,' he said. 'But I'm not gonna put up with it, so I'm sacking you and putting an end to it. You're finished with this company as from this minute.'

Although Arnie had known he was putting his job at risk by speaking out, this was still a blow. He enjoyed working at Bex Sports, thought the world of Len, and didn't want to work anywhere else. No doubt if he apologised and grovelled a bit Len would eventually reconsider. But that would be tantamount to condoning his behaviour, and Arnie wasn't prepared to do that. He'd sooner look for another job.

'If that's how you feel, then fair enough.' Arnie decided not to press the fact that a week's notice on either side was clearly stated in the terms of his employment. If he had to leave, the sooner he went the better. 'I'll go back to the shop and clear my stuff out.'

'Yeah, you do that,' said Len.

The house felt achingly quiet after Arnie had left. Shaky from the reaction of the argument – because he was fond of Arnie and had thought of him as a mate until now – Len lit another cigarette and sunk back in his chair, deep in thought.

Arnie had got too big for his boots. Who did he think he was – coming round here throwing his weight about? He'd do well to remember that he'd been unemployed and wallowing in self-pity himself when Len had first met him. Len recalled a time when he'd had to be heavy with the truth to him. And here he was telling the guvnor what to do, the cheeky bugger.

Just because he'd done well in the job and become an asset to the firm, he'd got above himself. Well, Bex Sports was well rid of someone who thought they were God's gift just because they'd been running the show for a while.

Running the show! Arnie had been running the whole damned shooting match!

For the first time since Mary's death, the fog in Len's mind cleared sufficiently for him to realise the position Arnie had been in these last few months. He'd been in sole control of a high-turnover business, looking after the needs of all the other managers as well as running his own branch. The man must have been working all hours to keep on top of things . . . and all for no extra money!

A lesser man might have used the situation for his own ends – to go on the fiddle without the beady eye of the guvnor about – but all Arnie seemed to want was Len back at work.

Smarting with his conscience, Len cast a wary eye around the room, forcing himself to see the dust and smell the foul air. He got up and flung open all the windows, noticing the garden bathed in sunshine and wanting to cry because Mary wasn't here to share it with him.

Moving away from the window, he caught sight of himself in the mirror above the fireplace. Blimey, what a sight! Arnie was right – he was a mess.

He went into the hall to the telephone and phoned the office.

'Hello, Phoebe,' he said.

'Wotcha, Len,' she replied, sounding pleased to hear his voice. 'How are you?'

'Not so dusty.'

'I'm pleased to hear that.'

'Look ... er, Arnie is on his way back to the shop.' He cleared his throat. 'We've had a few cross words to tell you the truth. But can you tell him not to go anywhere until I get there?'

'You're coming into the office?' she said, sounding even more delighted.

'Yeah.'

'That *is* good news,' she enthused. 'Everyone here will be so pleased to see you.'

Moved by her warmth, tears burned beneath Len's eyelids. 'I'll be there soon,' he said, adding silently, just as soon as I've cleaned myself up.

'So he sacked you and reinstated you, all on the same day?' said Gill. It was the following evening, and Arnie had come to collect Craig to take him to see a midweek, out-of-season football match.

'All within a couple of hours, actually,' said Arnie.

'Even better.'

'And that isn't all ...'

'No?'

'He's made me a partner in the business.'

'Oh, Arnie, that's wonderful!' Gill gave him a beaming smile. 'Fancy it coming out of the blue like that.'

'Len said that my looking after things while he was away has made him realise how valuable I am to the firm,' he explained.

'That *really* is something,' she said. 'Congratulations!'

'Thanks.'

They had been chatting in the kitchen, but now they wandered into the living room where Carol was ensconced on the sofa looking through a women's magazine, having come to spend the evening with Gill.

'Arnie's been made a partner in Bex Sports, Carol.' She paused thoughtfully. 'But I expect you already know about it.'

'No, I didn't know,' she said, scowling.

'Oh,' said Gill, feeling suddenly awkward.

'It only happened yesterday,' Arnie said rather sheepishly, as though he needed to justify himself to Carol for not telling her first.

'Well, anyway, it's terrific news, isn't it?' said Gill.

'Yeah, great,' Carol said flatly.

'It's good about Len going back to work too,' said Gill, looking at Arnie.

'And all thanks to you,' said Arnie with a warm smile.

'Me?'

'It was you who suggested I take a hard line with him,' he said.

'So I did,' she said, adding jokingly, 'I'll have my fee in hard cash, please.'

They were both laughing when Craig entered the room dressed in a replica strip of Arnie's old football club.

'All set, son?' Arnie asked.

'Yes, Dad.'

'Right. Let's be on our way then or we'll miss the kick off.' He looked at Carol. 'See you soon. I'll give you a bell.'

'Okay,' said Carol moodily, turning her attention back to her magazine.

Gill went out to the car with Arnie and Craig. It was a fine summer's evening, the scent of garden flowers faintly perceptible above the urban dust and traffic fumes that drifted from the busy main roads and lingered in this quiet street of traditional houses, their tiny front gardens fringed in places with privet hedges.

'Have a good time then, fellas,' said Gill. 'And don't get too rowdy.'

'As if we would,' said Arnie with irony, ruffling Craig's hair affectionately and exchanging a conspiratorial look with him.

The boy grinned knowingly at his father who opened the car door for him.

'Just as well I'm not coming with you, for your sakes,' said Gill, remembering a time when the three of them had done things together as a family. 'I'd make you behave.'

Arnie gave her a slow grin, as though he was sharing her thoughts. 'See you later,' he said through the car window as he turned the key. 'Shan't be late back.'

'Okay.'

Gill stood at the gate waving until they had turned the corner out of sight. Overcome by a current of bitter-sweet emotion, she composed herself before going inside to face Carol.

Watching this happy family scene from the window, Carol was aflame with jealousy. Gill and Arnie shared something that she could never be a part of – their child. They were also getting to be very chummy lately, she'd noticed. Could it be that Arnie was still in love with Gill after all that had happened? The thought struck fear into her heart. The way Arnie looked at her sister often made Carol feel quite ill with worry.

Although Carol was seeing Arnie on a regular basis, he

was very casual about their meetings and the initiative was still almost entirely hers. He seemed to have taken her literally when she'd told him there would be no strings attached. She'd hoped to have extracted some sort of commitment from him by now. In fact, she had expected him to ask her to move in with him. She'd thought there would be talk of his getting a divorce from Gill so that he could marry her.

But even though she and Arnie got on well together and were now lovers, she was conscious of a definite holding back on his part. Although she didn't often allow herself to admit the depressing truth, she knew in her heart that he didn't feel the same about her as she felt about him. In fact, if she was brutally honest, she knew that their relationship would never have gone beyond friendship if she hadn't seduced him into it when he was at a low ebb.

Even now she always made the first move in that direction. But, determined as she was to have him, she didn't see these things as a deterrent, and was still convinced that he would grow to love her in time if she persisted.

Then he would be truly happy, because she loved him deeply and wanted nothing more than to devote her life to him. One thing she did know for certain, she wasn't going to give up. She would be his wife one day or die in the attempt.

Meanwhile, the frustration of not making headway as quickly as she'd hoped was beginning to take its toll on her.

So, if a nudge was what Arnie needed to guide him in the right direction, then that was what he would get. The sooner the better, too. As long as she chose her time carefully.

As it happened, the perfect moment for Carol to try to alter the course of her relationship with Arnie came the following Sunday afternoon when they were strolling through Hyde Park in the sunshine.

Carol had been delighted when he'd agreed to a trip up West with her, even though she knew he had only done so because Craig had gone out to a birthday party this

Sunday, leaving his father at a loose end.

'The way some blokes dress these days you'd think they were pansies,' Arnie remarked as they passed a long-haired hippie dressed in an Eastern-style kaftan and beads. He had his arm around an extremely attractive young woman with long blonde hair. 'But they don't seem to have any problem getting good-looking women, do they?'

'It's just the fashion for some men to dress like that,' said Carol, who was very up to date in the ubiquitous mini-dress, her shoulder-length hair worn loose. 'You should try it. After all, I wear all the latest gear.'

'Me, go about in a dress?' he said predictably. 'Not bloomin' likely.'

'They're not dresses,' she corrected. 'They're kaftans. They can be worn by women or men.'

'They look like frocks to me, and the blokes who wear 'em look like ponces,' Arnie said.

'You should be more trendy . . .'

'If that's being trendy I want no part of it,' he said, appalled at the idea. 'Anyway, I'm a bit past faddy dressing.'

'Rubbish. You're only twenty-eight,' she reminded him.

'I wouldn't wear that sort o' gear if I was seventeen.'

'You wore teddy boy clothes when you were a teenager, and that was even more in for a dig,' she said in teasing admonition. 'I remember Mum and Dad going on about it when you and Gill started going out together.'

'I'll have you know I was wearing an army uniform when I was eighteen, young lady,' he said lightly.

'Well, things have changed since then. National service has finished.'

'Just as well,' he laughed. 'It would kill the hippies.'

'There you go again, being old fashioned and talking like an old man,' she teased, enjoying the happy atmosphere between them. 'You're beginning to sound like my dad.'

'You don't have to wear dresses to be in fashion, you know,' he said playfully, twirling around to show off the slim-line trousers he wore with a striped shirt with a white collar. 'Some of the pop stars are dressing like this.'

'You'll do,' she said, linking arms with him and smiling up at him adoringly.

They walked on towards the Serpentine, which was crowded with boats and gleaming in the sunshine on this fine afternoon, gulls soaring and swooping across the lightly rippling waters. They couldn't find any unoccupied deck-chairs so they sat down on the grass under a tree, away from the main crowds gathered around the lake.

'It's almost like being at the seaside,' remarked Carol.

'Yeah, it's lovely,' he replied, leaning back on his hands with his legs stretched out in front of him. 'So, what do you fancy doing later on?'

She laughed saucily.

'Apart from that, you sexpot,' he grinned.

'What did you have in mind?'

'We could have tea somewhere and then see a film at the Marble Arch Odeon, if you like.'

At moments like this Carol felt as though Arnie was hers and she had the power to make him do anything she wanted. Nibbling the end of a blade of grass, she said, 'I honestly don't mind what we do. As long as I'm with you I'm happy.'

He looked away quickly and she thought she'd upset him by being too affectionate. But he turned back to her and smiled.

'I should hate to think I make you miserable,' he said.

'Far from it. Actually, Arnie . . .' she began, emboldened by the warmth of the atmosphere between them. 'I've been thinking lately that it might be a good idea if I were to move in with you.'

His mood took a dive. He'd been dreading something like this. Carol had been hounding him for months and he didn't know how to put an end to her unwanted attention. He'd been trying to find the courage to tell her he wanted to stop seeing her for ages. But somehow he never could. She had a way of evoking pity, and at the back of his mind lay the fear that she would become seriously depressed again if he told her it was over, as she had after Dougie had let her down.

Anyone else would have got the message long ago from the deliberate casualness of his behaviour. Every one of their meetings was at Carol's instigation; surely that must speak for itself. But the truth had obviously not dawned on the girl, who seemed so fixated with him that he was beginning to feel suffocated. These past few months he had begun to understand why Dougie hadn't been able to go through with the wedding, or break off their engagement any earlier than the actual day.

It wasn't that Arnie wasn't fond of Carol, because he was. And this made it even more difficult. The last thing in the world he wanted to do was hurt her. But he wasn't in love with her and never would be. He was angry with himself, for allowing her to manipulate him into this position.

He would have to nip this latest idea of hers in the bud, or heaven only knew where it would end.

'I don't think that's a good idea,' he forced himself to say, feeling like a brute as her soulful eyes rested on him.

'Why not?'

'For one thing, it would upset your family,' he said.

'It isn't unheard of for a couple to live together these days.'

'No—'

'Well then . . .'

'But your parents are old fashioned, and I am still married to Gill.'

'But it'll take ages for your divorce to come through,' she said, pouting. 'We can't wait until then to live together.'

'Divorce?' He sounded shocked.

'Surely you're going to start proceedings eventually,' she said.

'Gill and I have never discussed it,' he said.

'Oh.' A surge of anger scorched through her, similar to a feeling she had been prone to as a child, when she couldn't get her own way about something. Then she used to throw a tantrum and keep it going until she finally wore her mother down. But this needed more careful handling. She knew she risked losing him altogether if she got careless and showed her hand too clearly. She'd managed to become his lover by blatant means, but the long-term situation called for a more delicate touch.

'It's just one of those things we haven't got around to yet,' Arnie said, adding pointedly, 'As neither of us is planning to get married again it hasn't seemed important.'

'I see,' Carol said, biting back her fury and smiling sweetly at him. 'But even so, I still think it would be a good idea for me to move in with you. It would be much more convenient for us both.'

'Why don't we just leave things as they are for the moment and see how it goes?' he said. He was trying to be gentle.

With a supreme effort Carol managed to restrain herself from physically attacking him in her frustration. 'Okay, Arnie, if that's the way you want it, then that's fine with me,' she said with a calmness she didn't feel.

'Good.'

'I just thought it would have been easier for us both, and nice for you to have someone there when you get home from work to cook you a meal and so on,' she said in one last attempt to persuade him. 'But, as you say, it's probably best to leave it and see how things go.'

With the pressure off, Arnie felt more charitable towards her again. 'I'm sure that's the right thing,' he said, smiling at her.

Behind Carol's returned smile a plan was forming. If he wouldn't do what she wanted of his own volition, she would have to resort to devious means. There's more than one way to get a man to the altar!

'Shall we go and get some tea then?' she suggested, getting up and brushing grass from her dress.

'Yes, let's do that,' he said, and they strolled towards Marble Arch together.

Chapter Sixteen

While Carol and Arnie were going for tea, Gill, Peter and Cherry Betts were among the crowds pouring out of the Royal Festival Hall on the south bank of the Thames. There were hordes of people about on this lovely afternoon, ambling along in groups eating ice creams and chatting, watching the boats on the river, filling the paths and benches.

Having first got permission from the nuns, Gill and Peter had taken Cherry to a concert given by a youth orchestra featuring performances by young soloists. The highlight of the afternoon had been a piano recital by a woman of eighteen who obviously had a future as a concert pianist.

'So, what did you think of the concert, Cherry?' Gill asked as they strolled beside water splintered with sunlight, formations of swans riding its gentle waves with a proprietary air, oblivious to the attention of the camera-waving tourists.

'It was smashing, miss.' Cherry was now a developing twelve-year-old with the beginnings of a new shape filling out her summer dress. 'I wish I was as good at playing the piano as that gel who played on the stage.'

'One day you will be, if you keep at it,' said Gill.

'Do you really think so, miss?'

'I certainly do. As long as you continue to come for your lessons and practise regularly.'

'That gel goes to music college, though, don't she?' said Cherry enviously. 'It said so on the programme.'

'Yes, I read that too,' said Peter, exchanging a look with Gill.

'I suppose you've gotta go to college to study music proper if you wanna be a concert pianist,' said Cherry.

'It does help,' said Gill.

'I'd love to do that.'

'Then maybe you will when you're old enough,' said Peter.

'Nah, not me. It'll cost too much. The nuns won't be able to afford it.'

'There might be a way of getting over that,' Peter said.

'Really?' Cherry's face lit with hope.

'I'm not absolutely certain, but I've an idea there are sometimes grants and scholarships available for students who show real potential but don't have the means to go to college,' he explained.

'But you've a long time to go before you even need to think about anything like that,' said Gill cautiously. She didn't want to raise the girl's hopes only to have them dashed later on, since Cherry had no relatives to support her through any sort of further education. 'You concentrate on your school-work for the moment.'

'And the piano,' Cherry said quickly, as though needing reassurance.

'Of course,' Gill replied. 'That goes without saying.'

'I'll never give the piano up, no matter what job I do when I leave school,' Cherry said ardently. 'Even if I have to work in a factory all day to keep myself, I won't give up the piano. I'll save up and buy myself a second-hand one when I leave Terry's.'

'Good for you,' said Gill.

They stayed for a while by the river, eating ice creams and idly chatting, until Peter suggested they have tea out some-where.

'Ooh, smashing!' Cherry enthused.

They got into Peter's car and headed for a place he knew of in the King's Road, Chelsea.

'Cor, the King's Road!' said Cherry, whose knowledge of the world outside St Theresa's came mostly from hearsay.

'Isn't that where all the trendy people go?'

'It's supposed to be one of the places they gravitate towards, yes,' said Gill.

'Some of the older girls at school come here to get their clothes,' Cherry said excitedly as they passed Mary Quant's boutique and various other well known emporiums, all closed on this Sunday afternoon. 'I've heard 'em talking about it in the playground. My mates at Terry's'll be green with envy when I tell 'em I've actually *been* here.'

Peter parked the car and they went into a café with wooden tables and pine walls liberally sprinkled with contemporary art and hand-written poetry. They tucked into a pile of sandwiches, a huge plate of home-made cakes and a pot of tea. Most of the other people were arty types: long-haired men with beards, women in loose tops and tight trousers.

'How come you know this place?' Gill asked when the owner addressed Peter by his name.

'I used to play my guitar in here at one time,' he explained. 'They sometimes have live music in the evenings.'

'How fab!' said Cherry.

Looking at her glowing little face, the darting eyes devouring everything she saw with relish, Gill shared a smile with Peter. Giving Cherry a treat had brought its own rewards; the girl was living proof that giving can be better than receiving.

Later that evening, when Craig was safely tucked up in bed, Gill and Peter were relaxing downstairs with a glass of wine.

'Thanks for getting the tickets for the concert,' Gill said. 'It was thoughtful of you to organise an outing for Cherry.'

'My pleasure,' Peter said graciously. 'It was nice to meet her at last. I've heard so much about her.'

'I think she loved every moment.'

'Yes, she did seem to, didn't she?' he said. 'I enjoyed it too.'

'So did I,' Gill said. 'But then you and I usually manage to enjoy ourselves wherever we go, don't we?'

'We do.' He lapsed into a thoughtful silence. 'Actually, Gill, I think it's about time we had a talk, and now seems as good a time as any.'

'What about?'

'Us.'

'Oh dear,' she said, making a face. 'That has the ring of gravity about it. Am I about to get the elbow?'

'Quite the opposite.'

'Oh?'

'The fact is, I'd like to know where I stand . . . to know where our relationship is going,' he said solemnly. 'What is all of this leading to?'

'Well it can't go much further, since I'm still married to Arnie.'

'I want more, Gill,' Peter said, giving her a penetrating look. 'I want us to be together properly – to get married, when you are free to. Until then . . .' His voice tailed off.

'You want us to move in together?'

'Yes. Don't you think it would be a good idea?' he said. 'I mean, I spend so much time here anyway, it would be far more convenient for us both. And Craig and I get along well enough. I would suggest that you both move in with me, but I don't think you'd fancy living in a flat.'

'Oh, no. I don't want to move away from this house,' she said at once. 'I wouldn't want to uproot Craig. Anyway, my teaching practice is established here.'

'So, I'll move in with you then . . .'

She had known that it would only be a matter of time for this question to arise, but she had chosen to put it out of her mind. Now she could avoid it no longer. She drank a sip of wine to give her courage. 'Please don't take this the wrong way . . .' she began.

'But you'd rather I didn't move in with you,' he cut in sharply.

She sighed. 'I'm quite happy to carry on as we are,' she explained.

'Oh.' He sounded downhearted.

'Everything's fine as it is. Why complicate matters?'

'You don't want to make a commitment to me, do you?'

'Let's just say I don't feel ready to make *that* sort of commitment at the moment,' she told him.

'You might never . . . ?'

'You're right,' she agreed with candour. 'I might never feel ready. So if you'd rather stop seeing me, knowing that, I'll understand.' She looked at him over the rim of her wine glass. 'I wouldn't half miss you, though.'

'There's no question of my not seeing you,' he said.

'Oh, Peter, I am glad,' she said. 'I really value our time together.'

'I'm an incurable optimist,' he told her, smiling. But she knew he was bitterly disappointed by her answer.

'Actually, Peter,' she said with some hesitance, 'now that you've put things between us on to a more serious plane, even though we're going to carry on as we are for the moment . . . er, there's something about me I think you should know.'

'I don't like the sound of that,' he said with forced levity.

'I can't have any more children,' she said, the pain rising in her voice even after all this time. 'I have some permanent damage as a result of a miscarriage a few years ago.'

'Oh, that's a shame . . . I'm very sorry, for your sake,' he said with genuine compassion, sensing her regret. 'But it doesn't make any difference to the way I feel about you. I still want to share my life with you.'

'Don't you want a family?'

'It doesn't bother me unduly,' he said. 'It isn't as though I don't have children already from my first marriage.'

'There is that . . .'

'It obviously bothers you quite a lot, though,' he commented.

'I must admit I did want to have more children,' she confessed. 'I'd have loved to have a daughter, and I was devastated when I first knew I couldn't have any more. But

I've accepted it now, and most of the time I'm okay about it. Sometimes it hits me and I feel terrible. I'm still only twenty-seven . . . it's young to know your child-bearing days are over.'

He nodded.

'But I'm luckier than a lot of women because I have Craig.'

'Yes.'

They lapsed into a comfortable silence, both immersed in their own thoughts. That was the good thing about Peter's company, Gill thought, there were never any of those exhausting silences that happened with some people.

A dark shadow had fallen over her mood, though. In wanting more than she felt able to give, Peter had forced her to face up to her own feelings. She didn't want to make a life-long commitment to Peter, because she was still in love with Arnie. No matter how wrong he was for her, he still made every other man pale in comparison.

But she couldn't continue to live in the past for ever, clinging to something that could never be. And she didn't want to lose Peter. At some point in the future he was going to force the issue. Perhaps then she would find the courage to let go of the past and allow herself to move on to the next stage in her life.

Arnie poked his head into the office. 'Can you give us a hand in the shop, please, Mum?' he asked. 'The place is packed to the doors and I'm short-staffed.'

'Course I can, son,' Phoebe said good-naturedly, putting her pen down and getting up from her desk where she had been working on some figures. 'I'll be glad of a break from the paperwork.'

'Thank God for that,' Arnie said, and made a hasty exit.

'What it is to be needed, eh?' remarked Len, who was busy at his desk, studying the turnover for each of the shops as at Friday night's close of business, a regular Saturday-afternoon ritual.

'I thrive on it,' she told him. 'As much as I enjoy working

in the office, I like to get out there among the punters every so often.' She hurried across to the door. 'See you later.'

And she was gone like a whirlwind, leaving the office with a feeling of emptiness. Her boundless energy seemed to make any room she was in throb with vitality. Whereas Mary had been quiet and gentle of manner, Phoebe was like a gale-force wind in comparison. This was an observation rather than a criticism; Len liked Phoebe, and considered her to be valuable to the business, being popular with staff and customers alike. He could see from where the Briscoe brothers got their personality. Mother and sons had all proved to be an asset to him. Even young John, who had got off to such a bad start, had knuckled down once his problem had been solved, and was doing well at the Fulham branch. As for Phoebe – well, nothing was too much trouble for her.

Giving the matter some thought, Len supposed that this job was something of a promotion for her after working on the counter in Woolworth's. Here at Bex Sports she ran the office, helped out in the shop and made an intelligent contribution to the general running of the business. She also did all sorts of personal errands for Len, like taking his suits to the cleaners and doing his shopping. As he had to have someone other than Mary working in the office, he was glad it was Phoebe.

Half an hour or so later she came bursting back in. 'Cor blimey! It was like Wembley Stadium on cup final day out there for a while,' she told him. 'Talk about busy.'

'It's music to my ears,' he replied lightly, 'to know that punters are keen to offload their money in our direction.'

'Not half.' Phoebe sat back down and looked at her watch. 'Soon be time to knock off. I'll just have time to finish this.'

They were both silent for a while, each concentrating on the job in hand.

'Saturday night again, eh, Len?' Phoebe said after a while. She had got to the end of what she was doing and was tidying her desk. 'How the week flies past.'

'Yeah.'

'Are you going out anywhere tonight?' she enquired chattily.

'No.'

'Do you fancy coming down the Rose and Thistle with me?' she asked casually. 'They have live entertainment there on a Saturday night. Some good turns an' all.'

'No thanks,' he said. 'I'm not in the mood for pubbing.'

'Oh, go on,' she urged, 'be a devil. Let yourself go for a couple of hours.'

'No, honestly . . .'

'It'll do you good to get out, and you'd be doing me a favour 'cause I'd like to go and I can't very well go on my own.'

'What about that friend o' yours – the one you go to bingo with?'

'She's doing something else tonight.'

'Oh.'

'That only leaves my John, and I can't see him agreeing to go out with his mother on a Saturday night, can you?'

'Not really,' Len said. 'He'll be off to some disco or other, I expect.'

Phoebe's expression became serious. 'Thanks to you, Len, he's free to go out and enjoy himself,' she said. 'If he'd carried on hanging out with Harris and his mates he'd most probably be banged up by now.'

'Yeah, well, that's all in the past, isn't it?' said Len. 'I'm glad he's a bit more choosy about his friends now.'

'Me an' all.' Phoebe grinned. 'Kids, eh . . . who'd have 'em?'

'I wouldn't have minded . . .'

'It was a shame you didn't,' she said, keeping her tone light so as not to depress him. 'But it just wasn't to be.'

He tidied the papers in front of him with an air of finality.

'Well, Len, that's enough work for one week,' she said looking at her watch again. 'It's time we weren't here.'

'I'll be here for a while longer, just to go over things with Arnie when he's cashed up,' he said. 'But you get off home, ducks.'

'I will if you don't mind,' she said. 'I have to call in at the fish and chip shop on my way home. I don't cook on a Saturday night. It's one of my house rules.'

'I don't blame you.'

She took her coat from the stand and slipped into it. 'See you Monday then,' she said.

'Yeah.'

'Have a nice weekend.'

Len nodded, but he knew there wasn't much chance of that. Weekends for him were simply long expanses of loneliness that had to be endured.

'And you.'

'I will . . . Don't worry,' she said, 'I'll find someone to go down the Rose and Thistle with.'

As she reached the door a sudden impulse made him call her name. She turned to look at him and smiled.

'I was wondering . . .' he began hesitantly. 'Can I change my mind about coming with you?'

'Course you can,' she beamed.

'What time shall I pick you up then?'

'Oh, about eight o'clock will be fine,' she said delightedly.

There's nothing quite like a sentimental ballad to make the hairs on the back of your neck stand on end, Phoebe thought that evening, especially when you'd had a few gins and were in the mood to enjoy yourself. She and Len were sitting at a table in the crowded functions room of the Rose and Thistle with their eyes glued to the stage, where a broad-chested man with a black shirt open almost to the waist was belting out the Tom Jones hit 'The Green Green Grass of Home'.

'Good, wasn't he?' she said as the singer concluded the first half of the entertainment to loud clapping and whistling.

'Not half.'

'Some of these singers who work the pubs are every bit as good as those we see on the telly, I reckon.'

Len nodded. 'The comedian was pretty pathetic though, wasn't he?' he remarked, smiling and puffing heavily on his cigar.

'Oh, yeah, wasn't he awful?' Phoebe giggled at the memory. 'I felt quite sorry for him when all of his jokes died the death.'

'Poor bugger,' said Len, 'at least he was having a go.'

'They say comedy is the hardest thing of them all to do, don't they?'

'I have heard that.' He finished his drink and gave her an enquiring look. 'What are you having?'

'A gin and tonic, please.'

'Coming up, right away,' he said jovially, leaving the table and pushing his way through the crowds to the bar.

Phoebe looked around the large room, at the heavy red and gold wallpaper, the maroon curtains and the stage, on which stood the equipment of the three-piece band and a microphone in the centre. Small tables, squashed together to provide maximum seating, covered the whole area. Opposite the stage was a bar around which people were swarming to get their drinks before the second half of the show. The atmosphere was warm and friendly, a boisterous roar of conversation and laughter filling the air. Looking through a pall of cigarette smoke, Phoebe saw Len idly chatting to the man standing next to him as he waited to get served. She thought he was magnificent. A king among men, tall and distinguished with his mane of thick white hair and large features, which might be ugly to some but were attractive to her.

He was still slimmer than he'd been before he lost Mary, but now that the awful emaciated look had gone the weight-loss suited him, and his jacket sat well on his broad shoulders. Even from this distance she could recognise his charisma.

He was everything Phoebe had ever wanted in a man. The fact that he was comfortably off had nothing to do with it. He was strong, but not invulnerable – as his reaction to Mary's death had proved; he was kind-hearted without being weak; and when he was on form he had a terrific sense of humour, which made him an entertaining companion. He was also in very good physical shape for a man in his fifties.

She was well aware of the fact that women of a certain age weren't supposed to have sexual desires. They were encouraged to believe that the only sort of feelings they had to look forward to were hot flushes and the mild palpitations of a modest win at bingo. But Len had made her realise that there was more to maturity than that.

He wasn't interested in her as a woman, she knew that. He was far too busy worshipping Mary's memory to open his mind to the possibility of a new relationship with someone else. At the moment he just saw Phoebe as someone useful to have around in the office, someone who didn't mind helping out with personal errands too.

But as time passed, his grief would inevitably begin to lessen. And when that happened, Phoebe would be on hand to help him see her in a different light. And if that didn't happen, she would still be there for him simply because she wanted to be.

But now she was jolted out of her reverie by Len returning to the table with their drinks.

'I thought I'd never get served. It's like a ruddy battleground at the bar,' he said.

'I noticed.'

'They must be making a fortune.'

'A lot of the pubs around here have stopped having live entertainment and make do with the juke box,' she said. 'That's why people flock to this one on a Saturday night.'

'I see.'

'The landlord probably gets back what he pays the acts in extra business.'

'Trebles his money, I should think.'

'Could be.' She raised her glass. 'Thanks, Len . . . Cheers.'

'Cheers,' he said warmly. 'I haven't had a night out since before Mary died.' He made a face. 'And I'm ashamed to say I'm enjoying myself.'

'There's no need to be ashamed.'

'No?'

'Course not!' she exclaimed. 'It's been more than eight months. You're not expected to go about with a long face for ever. That's the last thing Mary would have wanted.'

'You're right.' Len paused, his eyes filling with tears. 'I'm so lost without her, Phoebe.'

'Now don't upset yourself,' she said, patting his hand companionably.

'I didn't know that such pain existed until she was taken from me,' he said.

She nodded sympathetically.

'I haven't wanted to go out anywhere – except perhaps to my local, but that was only to anaesthetise myself,' he said.

'Getting back to work must have helped, though,' she said.

'It's helped, yes, but it's still been an effort to talk to people outside of that,' he said. 'The last thing I want to do when I get home is go out socialising.'

Sipping her drink, Phoebe looked at him with tenderness in her eyes. 'It is hard when you lose your partner,' she said. 'But we all react differently and cope in our own way. After my husband died I felt the need to go out and be with people . . . to take my mind off the pain, I suppose. I was a lot younger too. But I didn't get much chance to get out of an evening with two young boys to look after. Whenever I did manage it, it made me feel human and part of the world again. You feel so cut off from other people, don't you? So isolated, somehow, because you're feeling so awful and they aren't. And no one can really help because it's all locked inside.'

'Yeah, that just about sums it up,' Len said.

'It does get easier eventually, though,' she told him. 'And I can say that with the benefit of experience.'

'I don't think I'll ever stop missing Mary,' he said sadly.

'I don't suppose you will either, but time does make a difference,' she said with conviction. 'It's nature's way.'

'I'm not sure I want to stop missing her,' he said.

'I remember feeling like that about my husband,' she said. 'But although it's a very gradual process you do get over it.'

'I'll never, *ever* get married again,' he stated categorically.

'It's still early days . . .'

'Yes, but I mean what I say.' He said it with such emphasis that she wondered if he was making his position clear should she be harbouring any romantic notions about him. 'Mary was the only woman I ever wanted to be married to, and I shan't be doing it again.' He gave her a questioning look. 'You never have?'

'No.'

'You've never felt the need to share your life with anyone?'

Not until I met you, she thought. But she said, 'I've often wished I had someone. But there was always the boys to consider . . .'

'Yes, of course. I bet you've been glad of them, though.'

'Not half,' she said. 'They were my life . . . They still are.'

'It must have been hard bringing them up on your own.'

'Yeah, but it was rewarding too,' she said. 'And now that they're grown up it means I never feel really alone.'

'Whereas I—'

'You've got lots of friends who care a lot about you,' Phoebe said quickly.

'I know, I'm lucky.'

'Luck doesn't come into it,' she said in a definite tone. 'You get back from people what you give to them.'

'You reckon?'

'Yes, I do. You look after your staff and treat them as people with a right to consideration and respect, unlike some of the employers I've worked for. There isn't a person on the staff in any of your shops who doesn't like and respect you.'

'Here, give over, Pheeb . . . You'll have me blushing in a minute,' he said lightly to cover his embarrassment.

The awkward moment soon passed, however, as the compère returned to the stage and called for silence so that the entertainment could continue.

The comedian came on for his second slot, and sadly showed no sign of improvement. He was followed by a hilariously incompetent magician and a female singer who did a reasonable impersonation of Dusty Springfield. Then came the finale: the black-shirted male singer with a heart-stopping version of 'Danny Boy'.

'Not a bad show, was it?' said Phoebe as they sat chatting and finishing their drinks.

'I thought it was excellent.'

'So, now that you've had a night out and managed to enjoy yourself, I hope you'll do it again,' she said casually.

'Well, actually, it's set me thinking,' he said warily.

'Oh?'

'Well, as you know I'm involved with various organisations for business and charitable reasons . . .' he said.

'Yes, I do know that.'

'Which means I'm expected to attend certain social functions.'

'Mm. I remember Mary talking about all the dinners she used to go to with you.'

'I haven't been to anything like that since she died,' he confessed. 'I've always managed to make up some excuse.'

'I'm sure the people concerned understand,' she said.

'I'm sure they do, but I ought to start supporting these things again.'

'Perhaps you'll feel more like it now you've taken that first step and been out for a social evening,' she said.

'Yes. The thing is . . .' He cleared his throat nervously. 'I really need a partner to go with, a lady to accompany me on these occasions . . .'

'I suppose you would do,' she said, wondering where all this was leading.

'And . . . actually, I wondered if you might be willing to

help me out. Purely as a friend, you understand. There would be no funny business, I promise you.'

Phoebe was more flattered than he could possibly have imagined. 'I'd love to do this for you, Len,' she said, her enthusiasm fading with a realistic thought. 'But . . . er, I can't.'

'Oh? Why not?'

'Because I don't have anything posh enough to wear to the sort of do you're talking about,' she said, looking down at her sequinned sweater which she wore with an ordinary black skirt. 'This is about the dressiest thing I've got.'

'That's no problem,' he said. 'I'll stand the cost of any clothes you need.'

'Really?'

'Well, I can hardly expect you to pay for them out of the wages I pay you, can I?'

'In that case I'd love to do it for you,' she said, smiling.

'Smashing,' he said. 'I'll find out when the next one is and you can get yourself kitted out ready.'

'I can't wait,' Phoebe said, hardly able to believe her luck. This was the most exciting thing that had happened to her in years.

Chapter Seventeen

Towards the end of the year an unexpected new dimension was added to Gill's work: an influx of adult pupils. It began with a genteel little man called Horace, who found himself with time on his hands after retiring.

'Every house in the street had a piano in the front room when I was a boy,' he explained mistily. 'I didn't have the patience to learn how to play then, and I didn't have the time when I grew up and had a living to earn. Now my time's my own, I fancy giving it a try.'

'Good for you.'

'My wife says she'll take lessons as well if I get on all right with it,' he said, adding jokily, 'We'll be able to play duets together.'

His wife became a pupil soon afterwards, and other retired people followed as word got around. Inspired by the amount of adult interest – and the fact that she could fit them in, because the majority could come in the daytime rather than after school hours when she was fully booked with children – Gill put a card in the music-shop window advertising the fact that people of all ages were welcome.

The response was good – and wasn't limited to the retired. An aspiring young pop-star with shoulder-length hair and an embroidered shirt billowing over his skin-tight jeans joined her band of learners. He was a guitarist in a rock band, and hoped that being able to play the piano would be an advantage to him in his career. He looked a bit wild and threatening, but was actually very charming. She liked him at once.

As well as receiving fulfilment from the extra work, the increase in pupils meant a boost to Gill's income. At last she could afford her own transport, and she bought a second-hand Triumph Herald early in 1967.

The time seemed to fly past, and Gill found it hard to believe that Craig would be ten years old that summer. It was a different world now to the one he had been born into. Who could have predicted then the extent of the social revolution just a decade later, the changes to people's attitudes towards class and sex?

Although the hippies and the flower-power cult movement were outside Gill's personal experience, she noticed an increase in the hippie style of dress on the streets. Some young people were turning their backs on conventional living altogether in favour of a less materialistic way of life.

But grim reality was piped into the homes of the majority as the horrors of the Vietnam War filled their television screens. The reports made Gill's blood run cold.

Things remained much the same between her and Peter, and she continued to have an amicable relationship with Arnie. He was still seeing Carol on a regular basis, but Gill perceived a definite reluctance on his part when he and Carol were together. It seemed incredible that Carol couldn't see it too. Gill guessed it was a case of there being none so blind as those who didn't want to see.

She feared it would all end in tears, but if she so much as hinted this to her sister it was seen as jealousy and she was aggressively reminded that it was none of her business. Sadly, Gill accepted the fact that the time had long passed when Carol would listen to the advice of her elder sister.

Their mother wasn't happy about Carol and Arnie's relationship either.

'It's all wrong, a woman and her sister's ex-husband,' she was often heard to say. 'There used to be a law against that kind of thing.'

Just lately, however, someone else had been setting the

tongues wagging in Maisie Road . . .

'That Phoebe Briscoe's doing all right for herself,' Winnie said to Gill, who had called round one afternoon when Hal and Carol were at work. 'The poor bloke won't stand a chance once she gets her claws into him.'

'That isn't how it is, Mum.' Gill had heard all about Phoebe's exciting new social life from the woman herself, whom she still saw regularly despite her separation from Arnie. 'Phoebe's only going out with him because he needs a partner at certain functions and he hasn't got a wife to go with him now.'

'Humph.'

'It's purely an arrangement of convenience.'

'And I'm Jean Shrimpton,' snorted Winnie.

'Mu-m.'

'Whatever the truth, she's having a high old time with him.'

'Good for her.'

'He's even buying her clothes to go in an' all,' said Winnie. 'And I know that's true 'cause Carol told me and she heard it from Arnie.'

'Yes, it is true,' Gill confirmed. 'And it's only right that he should pay for the clothes. Phoebe can't afford to buy the classy gear she needs to go in, not out of her salary. It's all part of the deal they have. Honestly, Mum, they're just friends and she's helping him out.'

'Helping herself, more like.'

'Personally, I think it's about time Phoebe had some pleasure,' Gill said. 'She hasn't had an easy life.'

'All right, I know I'm being bitchy,' Winnie admitted with a surge of conscience.

'Yes, you are.' Gill paused. 'I wouldn't mind someone buying me nice clothes and taking me to posh places, no strings attached. You must admit, it's very exciting for her.'

'Oh, it's exciting for her all right,' said Winnie. 'But that woman always seems to come up smelling of roses.'

'I don't know how you can say that,' said Gill with strong

disapproval. 'She lost her husband when she was still young and had two kids to bring up on her own. The poor woman had to work hard to put food on the table. Getting that job at Bex Sports was the first chance she'd ever had to show what she was really capable of, and she's practically running the business with Len now. If anyone deserves a bit of pleasure it's Phoebe.'

'Yes, yes, I know all that,' said Winnie. 'And what I meant by her always coming up smelling of roses is that, no matter how many knocks she takes, Phoebe Briscoe always picks herself up and carries on as though she owns Selfridge's.'

'That's what comes of being on her own for all those years,' said Gill. 'You have to be bold with no one to fight your battles for you – I can vouch for that.'

'Confidence is what she has more than her share of.' Winnie felt a stab of envy at the way Phoebe sailed merrily through life with all its hardships. 'Because she has so much of it, if she were to fall into a sewer she'd behave as though she smelled of Chanel when she came out.'

Gill smiled reflectively. 'Yes, I know what you mean,' she said. 'She's become an expert in putting on a brave face, I think.'

'She really has fallen on her feet this time, though,' said Winnie. 'If she manages to get Len Bex to the altar she'll want for nothing.'

'It isn't like that between them, though, Mum,' Gill told her again. 'Len doesn't want to get married again. He's made that very clear to Phoebe.'

'Time will tell . . .' said Winnie insistently. 'Time will tell.'

One bitterly cold February evening Arnie came out of the factory of a sportsgear manufacturer on the Fulham–Chelsea borders. He'd been there at the invitation of the management for a tour of their works, and had taken advantage of the occasion to negotiate a special price on boys' football strips on orders above a certain amount. He'd done good business, and was feeling pleased with himself.

The area was practically deserted after working hours along this industrial stretch of the river, and his footsteps echoed eerily as he walked towards his car, parked on derelict ground not far from the British Railways freight depot. The tall chimney stacks of Fulham electricity power station dominated the landscape above abundant dumps of wrecked cars, gas works, and large expanses of industrial wasteland, shadowy and sinister in the pale glow of the street lighting. The floodlights of Stamford Bridge Football Stadium were visible behind the looming gas-holders.

There had been a lot of talk in the local press about plans to smarten up this scruffy bank of the Thames, by replacing old-fashioned factories with modern office blocks and building stylish residential accommodation. Arnie didn't know if the plans would actually come to fruition, but he wouldn't be surprised, because the tide of gentrification had already begun in Fulham where it met the Chelsea borders.

But as the penetrating cold cut deep into his bones and a far more pressing personal matter came into his mind, Arnie couldn't bring himself to care one way or the other about it.

Carol! What am I going to do about her? he asked himself, shivering violently as he got into his car. There was only one decent thing to do, and he'd been trying to do it for months. He must come right out and tell her that he didn't want to continue with their relationship any longer. Things certainly couldn't go on as they were.

Her determination to take over his life was crushing him. If she wasn't waiting for him outside the shop when he finished work, she was at his flat when he got home, having persuaded him to give her a key. She insisted on cooking his meals and tidying the place, even though he begged her not to. When he'd got in the other night she was even doing his ironing, and had turned on the tears when he'd been none too pleased.

Once she'd been fun to be with and he'd enjoyed her

company. Now all he wanted to do was put distance between them. He'd hinted at how he felt a million times, but she simply didn't hear what he was trying to say. So he was going to have to spell it out for her loud and clear. His heart lurched at the thought, because she would be very hurt and he was still fond of her.

He leaned his arms on the steering wheel for a moment, his thoughts lingering on Gill's sister. She had seemed different lately, happier and annoyingly ebullient, as though something had happened to please her, though she hadn't mentioned anything in particular.

That would all change when he'd said what he had to say. But he must do it, the very next time he saw her, which would probably be tonight because she rarely left him in peace of an evening.

'It's very good of you to go to all this trouble for me, Carol,' he said when he got home to find the table laid for supper and Carol bustling around in a pinafore, having prepared them a meal of spaghetti bolognese. 'But I've told you before, I'd rather you didn't.'

'It's no trouble at all,' she said, beaming at him as she put the plates on the table. 'I enjoy doing it.' She patted the chair with cloying sweetness that made his skin crawl. 'So come and sit down before the food gets cold.'

'The thing is, Carol . . .' he began.

'The wine!' she said, ignoring him. 'I almost forgot.'

'Wine . . . on a Wednesday?'

'Yeah. I thought I'd treat us . . . It's in the kitchen,' she smiled. 'I'll leave you to do the honours.'

'Carol, I've something to tell you . . .'

'In a minute,' she said, sitting down at the table. 'Go and open the wine first.'

He did as she said, returning and pouring them both a glass. She looked flushed and happy and he felt like a heel. He didn't know how he was going to swallow so much as a morsel of food. But when he'd said his piece Carol wouldn't want anything to eat either. If he hesitated now he'd be lost, as had happened on every other occasion when he'd tried to tell her. She had the knack of stopping him in his tracks.

'The thing is, Carol . . .' he began again.

She raised her glass. 'I'm not actually going to drink any of this, you know,' she said mysteriously.

'No?'

She shook her head.

'Why go to the trouble of buying it then?' he asked.

'To keep you company in a celebration,' she said with a giggle.

He gave her a questioning look, a dull ache beginning to nag in the pit of his stomach as he realised he was being deliberately deterred from saying his piece – almost as though she knew what it was about. 'Celebration?' he said.

'I'm pregnant,' she announced excitedly. 'I found out for sure today. Isn't it *wonderful*? I'm going to have our baby!'

The words buffeted him. The thought of becoming a father again barely registered against the dramatic implications of this development.

'What . . .' he managed at last.

Her face crumpled into a pout. 'You don't sound very pleased,' she said.

'Don't I?' he muttered, hardly knowing what he was saying.

'No.'

'It's so . . . unexpected.'

'I don't see why it should be,' she said pointedly.

'You told me you were on the pill,' he said, remembering how keen she'd been to take care of that side of things, how she had insisted most adamantly that the contraceptive pill would be the safest method.

'And so I was, but I must have forgotten to take it on the odd occasion,' she lied. She'd come off the pill months ago, conception firmly in mind.

He was far too traumatised to pretend to be pleased,

because he knew there could be no escape from Carol now. He was completely trapped.

He rested his elbows on the table and put his head on his hands. 'Bloody hell, Carol,' he said involuntarily. 'What a mess!'

'Is that all you can say?' she said with a sob in her voice.

'I'm still trying to get used to the idea,' he replied dully.

'The least you can do is show a bit of enthusiasm.'

'I'm sorry, Carol. But I hadn't reckoned on anything like this . . . which is why I wanted to take precautions against it,' he said. 'I mean, ours isn't a having-a-family sort of relationship, is it?'

'It is now, mate,' she said, and the triumph in her voice told him the reason for her recent cheerful mood. She'd used the oldest trick in the book to get what she wanted.

'You planned this, didn't you?' he said, his eyes narrowed with suspicion. 'You stopped taking the pill on purpose.'

Huge tears began to roll down her cheeks, forming black rivers of mascara. 'I thought you'd be pleased,' she sobbed pathetically, 'and all you can do is accuse me of getting pregnant on purpose.'

She looked so vulnerable sitting there with her make-up smudged, shoulders drooping, Arnie didn't have the heart to continue with the accusation. 'It's come as a bit of a shock,' he told her. 'And it's certainly gonna complicate matters . . .'

'It'll bring things to a head, if that's what you mean.'

'Yeah.'

'You'll have to get a divorce from Gill now,' she said. 'So that you can marry me.'

'Mm. I suppose I will,' he said with a worried look.

'There's no "suppose" about it,' she said in a voice thick with tears but strong with determination. 'I'm not having my baby brought up as a bastard.'

'All right, Carol,' he sighed. 'You've made your point.'

'No one except the two families and our close friends need know we're not married, because we'll be living as man and wife when the baby is born,' she informed him in a manner that didn't invite argument. 'Then, as soon as your divorce comes through, we'll slip off quietly to the register office and make it legal.'

'You've got it all worked out.'

'You can't leave things to chance when there's a child involved.'

'No.'

Carol wiped her eyes with her handkerchief, leaving black smears on her cheeks. 'It's going to be wonderful, Arnie,' she said, brightening considerably. She knew there was no way out for a man like Arnie, whose conscience wouldn't allow him to leave her in the lurch. 'The three of us – you, me and our baby – will have a good life. We'll be a proper family.'

'Course we will.'

She fiddled with her handkerchief, affecting nervousness to evoke his pity. 'You won't leave me, will you?' she said, tear-rinsed eyes beseeching him. 'You will stand by me through this?'

What else could he do? He knew that she had set him up. But he wasn't going to make an issue about it. Carol was a very insecure and complicated person who found it difficult to sustain relationships with men. She had known he would never marry her of his own accord, and had been determined to get him by whatever means it took.

He couldn't help feeling angry and tricked. But he had done the deed – so now he must pay the price. Carol was carrying his child and was therefore his responsibility. There simply wasn't a choice.

For the first time he thought of the child as an actual human being and experienced a leap of pleasure. 'No, I won't leave you,' he said, standing up and opening his arms to her.

'Not ever?' she queried, wanting reassurance as usual.

'Not ever,' he repeated dutifully, slipping his arms around her and holding her gently against him. 'You can rely on me. I'll look after you and the baby. Everything will be all right.'

'Oh, Arnie,' she sighed, looking up at him lovingly.

'Can you do me one favour, though?'

'Depends what it is.'

'Will you let me tell Gill before you tell anyone else at all?' he requested. 'I'd rather she heard it from me.'

'Sure,' she agreed, for she now had nothing further to gain. 'If that's what you want.'

Gill stared at Arnie in a state of shock. He'd called at the house to see her during his lunch hour, and they were having a sandwich at her kitchen table.

'A divorce,' she said through dry lips, her heart pounding. 'You want a divorce . . .'

'Yes.' He had to force the words out. 'That's right.'

'Well, I suppose it is time we did something definite about our situation,' she said, though the idea depressed her more than she could possibly have imagined. 'We've been separated long enough now. It will tidy things up.'

'That isn't the reason,' he said, his voice ragged with emotion.

'No?'

He shook his head.

'What's happened?'

He took a deep breath.

'Carol's pregnant.'

'Oh!' His words felt like a fist in Gill's face. 'Oh, I see . . .'

'So I need to get divorce proceedings under way right now,' he explained, his heart breaking as he saw his own pain mirrored in Gill's eyes, 'so that I can marry Carol as soon as possible.'

'Yes, of course.'

'Obviously we won't make it in time for the baby's birth, but the sooner things get started the better for the child's sake.'

'Mm.'

'I'll pay all the legal fees. Carol being pregnant will be proof of adultery even though that isn't why the marriage broke up.' He spoke rapidly, as though he wanted to get the discussion over. 'The solicitors might find the information useful to speed things up.'

'Yes, they might,' Gill said dully, her voice barely audible.

'It's all just a question of getting it to go through as soon as possible because of the circumstances,' he said, scratching his head in agitation.

She nodded. 'When's the baby due?'

'July.'

'Oh, another July baby, the same as Craig,' she remarked, forcing a light note, though this only added to her pain somehow. 'There'll be exactly ten years between them.'

'I wonder how he'll feel about having a new half-sister or -brother.'

'I don't know,' she said. 'How about you? Are you pleased?'

'I'm thrilled about the baby...'

'And the rest?' she asked.

'I wasn't planning on getting married again,' he said.

'I thought not.'

'But now this has happened. So I'm going to do everything I possibly can to make a go of it,' he told her. 'I messed it up with you. Now I want to get it right with Carol – which is something I know will please you, given how protective you've always been of your sister.'

Protectiveness was the last thing she was feeling now. At that precise moment she wanted to slit Carol's throat. 'I suppose she will move into your flat,' she said.

'To begin with, yeah. But I suppose we'll have to start looking for a house with the idea of moving in before the baby's born,' he said thoughtfully. 'A fourth-floor flat won't be very convenient with a baby.'

'No.'

'Strange, isn't it?' Arnie said, looking at her in a curious way. 'How much different divorce seems to separation.'

'I'm still recovering from the shock of hearing you say it,

293

actually,' she said. 'Which is quite ridiculous since we've been apart for nearly two years and our marriage was in trouble for a long time before that. But I won't lie to you, Arnie: the thought of a divorce really hurts.'

'It hurts me too,' he confessed, looking at her with anguish in his eyes. 'It's so final.'

'Yes.'

'In my heart I'd always hoped we might give it another try sometime,' he told her. 'No chance of that now . . .'

'None at all.' She paused. 'What's really tearing me apart is that Carol is having your baby,' she said, her voice quivering slightly. 'I know I'm being selfish, but I do find that hard to take. I wanted another child – your child – so much.'

'Oh, Gill,' he said in a broken voice, coming towards her, 'I'm so sorry.'

'Arnie . . .'

And she was in his arms, feeling his lips on hers, firm and sweet and thrilling after such a long absence, their tears mingling. How could they have been so stupid as to let something as precious as this slip from their grasp?

'I love you, Gill.'

'Don't,' she said, drawing back. 'You mustn't say things like that.'

'I know I shouldn't, but it's true,' he said, his face wet with tears. 'I've never stopped loving you. Through all the bad times, all the grief and heartache I gave you, I always loved you . . . I always will.'

'I feel the same, but there's no future for us now.'

'No, there isn't,' he agreed, his voice becoming hard. 'I have to fully commit myself to Carol from now on.'

'We shall have to be very firm with ourselves about it,' she said miserably. 'No more lapses of control like this one.'

'No.'

'It's bizarre,' she said with a disbelieving shake of the head. 'I mean, we won't even be able to avoid seeing each other as we're still going to be related to each other.'

'When I screw things up, I really do it in grand style.'

'You certainly do.'

'I can't believe what a fool I've been,' he said. 'How can anyone be that stupid?'

'It wasn't all your fault, Arnie,' she said, looking into his eyes. 'I made mistakes too. I let resentment linger when I shouldn't have. I couldn't forgive you.'

'I shouldn't have done all that stuff in the first place.'

'It's all water under the bridge now,' she said, managing a brave smile. 'I think the only way we're going to cope with this new situation is to put our feelings for each other behind us.'

'We can't do that.'

'Not literally, no,' she said, 'but we can behave as though they don't exist. And we must. It's the only chance you and Carol have of happiness, and the best chance for any of us to move forward to the way our lives must be from now on.'

'It'll be difficult . . .'

'But we have to do it.'

'I know,' Arnie said with a deep sigh of resignation.

They embraced briefly and she showed him to the door, watching as he walked to his car. She'd be seeing him all the time. When he came to collect Craig, at family occasions . . . He would be her *brother-in-law*. Although she had known for a long time that a reconciliation wasn't possible, now that the last shred of hope had gone, the pain was unbearable.

That evening Gill telephoned her sister and asked her to meet her for lunch the next day.

'Congratulations, Carol,' she said when they met in a coffee bar near to where her sister worked. 'Arnie's told me your news.'

'Thanks, sis,' said Carol, far too immersed in her own success to worry about how Gill might be feeling. 'I can hardly believe it's happened at last. It's what I've always wanted.'

'Arnie, you mean?'

'Yeah. Marriage, babies – the whole thing. I won't have to slave my guts out at a desk any more. Arnie says I can give up work as soon as I like. With him being a partner in the business, we can afford for me not to have to go out to work.'

'You do love him, though, don't you?' said Gill, studying the hand-written menu.

'Course I do,' Carol said. 'What on earth made you ask that?'

'You seem to be more interested in marriage and babies than the man himself.'

The waitress came to take their order, which was chilli con carne for them both.

'Trust you to come out with a snide remark like that,' snapped Carol. 'Just because you're as jealous as hell . . .'

'I'm a human being, not some kind of a saint,' said Gill. 'Of course I'm jealous, because you're having his baby.'

'You and Peter might . . .'

'You know I can't have any more children,' Gill reminded her sharply.

At least Carol had the decency to look a little shamefaced. 'Sorry, sis,' she said, her manner becoming contrite. 'That slipped my mind for a moment. I really am sorry for you.'

'Don't make me feel worse by giving me your pity,' said Gill. 'That really would be twisting the knife.'

'I was only trying to be civil.'

The silence was fraught with tension.

'I was surprised to hear that you're pregnant, actually,' Gill said eventually.

'These things happen,' said Carol, adding meaningfully, 'as you very well know.'

'Yes, but there wasn't a contraceptive pill available when it happened to me,' said Gill. 'And you've made no secret of the fact that you're one of the pill's biggest fans.'

Carol grinned and shrugged her shoulders nonchalantly. 'I am, but I forgot to take it,' she said. 'So what?'

Gill threw her a shrewd look. 'You stopped taking it with the deliberate intention of trapping Arnie into marriage, didn't you?' she said.

'So what if I did?' There was no mistaking the smugness in Carol's tone.

'Carol, how could you?'

'Well . . . if I'd waited for Arnie to ask me to marry him I'd have been too old to have babies.' She gave her sister a warning look. 'And if you tell him I've admitted it, I shall deny it.'

'I shan't say a word,' Gill said. 'There would be no point.'

'Good.'

'You must have been desperate to get him to resort to something like that.'

'I was desperate,' admitted Carol. 'I love him so much, and I just couldn't get him to make a commitment to me.'

'But this way . . . ?'

'He's had his fun,' Carol cut in. 'Now he has to face up to his responsibilities.'

'It isn't much of a basis for marriage, though, is it?' said Gill.

'You're in no position to judge me, considering you were already in the club when you married him.'

'I didn't trick him into it, though.'

'You didn't manage to hang on to him either, did you?'

'True.'

'So stop criticising.'

'Believe it or not, I care about you both,' Gill said truthfully. 'I admit I wanted to scratch your eyes out when Arnie told me you were pregnant. But now that I've calmed down and accepted the fact that I can't have him, I want it to work out for the two of you.'

'And it will.'

'I hope so.'

'Why shouldn't it? I'm in love with Arnie and I'm planning on being a good wife to him. Okay, so he needed a shove in the right direction, and I gave him one. There's nothing too terrible about that. It happens to an awful lot of people and they go on to have happy marriages.'

The conversation was interrupted by the waitress with their meal.

'Look, Gill,' Carol said, twisting a huge wooden pepper-mill over her food, 'I've never had much luck with men. Now, at last, I have the chance to be happy, and I'm grabbing it with both hands. We shall all have to forget that you were once married to Arnie, or things could be very awkward.'

'Don't worry,' said Gill, 'Arnie and me are past history. I won't do anything to make things difficult for you.'

'Thanks, sis.'

'That's okay.'

'Do you think you and Peter will get married when the divorce comes through?'

'I don't know,' Gill said. 'I'm still uncertain about that.'

'Perhaps Arnie and I getting together properly might help you to make up your mind about him,' suggested Carol.

'Maybe.'

'I hope you get your life sorted out.'

'I will, don't worry . . . And I'm glad you're happy.' Gill reached across the table and touched her sister's hand. She was besieged by a mixture of emotions. She was sad to have lost Arnie for ever, and envious of her sister, who was starting a new life with him . . . but by some strange mechanism of thought – presumably born of blood ties and sisterly affection – she also found herself hoping ardently that Carol would find the contentment that had eluded her for so long.

This was a watershed in all their lives. Carol and Arnie were about to become a family. Gill had to look to the future now too, and decide what to do about Peter.

She was recalled to the present by Carol, who was saying, 'I'm going to tell Mum and Dad tonight. I don't know quite how they'll take it.'

Gill had a pretty good idea, but she kept her thoughts on the subject to herself.

'Getting one of my daughters into trouble was bad enough, Arnie Briscoe,' said Winnie the following day, after she'd marched into the shop and demanded to see him in private, 'but doing it to them both is a damned disgrace.'

'I know how you must be feeling—'

'No woman is safe with you,' she ranted.

He didn't reply.

'You ought to get treatment.'

'Oh, that's a bit strong!' he blurted out. 'Carol is a full-grown adult; no one forced her into anything.'

Quite the opposite, Arnie thought. If anyone was the victim in this affair it was him. It occurred to him how shocked Winnie would be if she knew of her younger daughter's deviousness and astonishing sexual prowess, and how she used it as a means of getting what she wanted.

'That doesn't alter the principle of the thing,' Winnie reproved.

Wanting to be courteous, Arnie waited in silence for her to continue.

'Surely you can see that getting both sisters pregnant is beyond the pale.'

He certainly could – and, yes, he was ashamed of himself, more for causing Gill such pain over the years than for getting Carol pregnant, since that was so obviously what the woman wanted. She was positively radiant.

Winnie's hair was almost white now. Her grey eyes burned with indignation as she glared at the man who had violated the daughter she saw as a wronged woman. But despite all her abrasiveness Arnie knew she was a good sort, and he had no intention of shattering her rosy maternal illusions by telling her the truth. Winnie was a devoted mother who was obeying her primal instinct to protect her young. The fact that both her daughters were grown women made no difference, apparently.

'Yeah, of course I can see that,' he said, 'I'm not a complete moron.'

'I'm glad to hear it!'

'I didn't want this to happen any more than you do, you know.'

'You should have had more sense.'

'I know that.'

'When it happened to Gill it was excusable because you were just a boy,' she continued, 'but you're going on for thirty now. It's high time you knew better.'

'You're right,' Arnie agreed wholeheartedly. 'You are absolutely right.'

'Really?' She seemed deflated by his ready agreement.

'You seem surprised to hear me agree with you,' he said.

'Yes. I was expecting to have a real barney with you.'

'How can I argue with you when everything you say is true?' he said. 'I know only too well that I'm old enough to know better. I know I've made a mess of Gill's life . . . and my own.'

'I'm glad to hear you admit it.'

'How can I deny it when it's true?'

'I felt I had to come and talk to you without Carol being around,' she said, feeling more inclined to explain since he was being so decent. 'Without any of them around.'

'I understand.'

'You've given Gill enough heartache over the years—'

'And you're here to tell me that if I do the same to your other daughter, you'll have my guts for garters.'

'Something along those lines, yeah,' she said. 'And I mean it.'

'You've nothing to worry about as far as Carol is concerned.'

'I hope not.'

Winnie was so genuine in her concern for her daughter, Arnie decided that she deserved the part of the truth that couldn't hurt her.

'I'd like to be really honest with you,' he said, looking her straight in the eyes.

'Go on.'

'I wasn't planning on sharing my life with Carol, and I wasn't pleased when she told me she was pregnant,' he said.

'I never saw the two of you making a go of it, I must admit,' she said.

'But I'm used to the idea now, and I intend to do everything I can to make sure that Carol and our child have a happy life. So you can rest easy in your bed at night.'

'You'd better mean it an' all, Arnie Briscoe,' she said, but all the threat had gone from her voice now, because she believed him.

'I do.'

'Carol isn't the easiest of people to get on with,' she said, thawing slightly now that he had reassured her of his intentions. 'As much as I love her, even I have to admit that.'

'We've spent enough time together for me to know that,' he said.

'She was always a difficult child, you know,' Winnie confessed.

'I can imagine.'

'She'd throw herself into the most awful tantrum if she couldn't get her own way over even the smallest thing.' She paused. 'I used to give in to her more than I should have, perhaps.'

He thought she was probably right, but felt it wise not to say so.

'You'll have to be firm with her.'

'Yes.'

'She's a strange girl,' Winnie continued.

'Always seems so insecure,' he said.

'God knows why, because she had a stable enough upbringing . . .'

'It's more to do with adult love, I think,' he said.

'Yes. She seems to need more love and attention than the rest of us.'

'Perhaps,' he said. He didn't add that he was only too painfully aware of Carol's constant need for love and reassurance, which was already exhausting him. 'But you can stop worrying about her from now on. Because I shall be a good husband to her, I promise you.'

'I believe you.'

'Now, how about a cup of coffee to warm you up before you go?' he suggested pleasantly.

'That's very nice of you,' Winnie said, thinking that perhaps she might enjoy having him back in the family again after all. And she knew for certain that her husband would.

'Two sugars, isn't it?'

'That's right,' she said, surprised and warmed by the fact that he had remembered.

Chapter Eighteen

It was the evening of Donna Briscoe's third birthday, a fine Sunday in the summer of 1970. There had been a kiddies' tea-party that afternoon at Carol and Arnie's Chiswick home, and the family members had stayed on afterwards. Taking advantage of the nice weather, they were in the garden.

Carol was making no secret of the fact that she couldn't wait to see the back of them. The last thing she wanted was the bother of entertaining visitors after coping with an invasion of hell-raising three-year-olds all afternoon. But Arnie had been keen to make a night of it and had, for once, put his foot down.

Because Arnie was such a considerate husband and Carol got her own way about almost everything, when he did make a stand she found it hard to take. Not being blessed with the patience to hide her feelings for the sake of others, her displeasure was being made obvious to their guests as she stamped thunderously about offering savoury nibbles and uttering the odd disinterested comment.

'Your sister's in a right old mood tonight,' remarked Peter quietly to Gill as they sat on the patio watching the dying sun slip behind the suburban rooftops in a glorious blaze of orange. 'She looks as though she could cheerfully murder the lot of us.'

'She didn't want to have an adult do after the kids' party,' whispered Gill, who was wearing a floral mini-dress, her dark hair shoulder-length and casual. 'She wanted us all to leave at the same time as the children so that she could relax and put her feet up.'

'Why are we here then?'

'Arnie insisted that the family stay on into the evening for a few drinks, apparently,' she said. 'He's a great one for family get-togethers.'

'The poor devil's probably glad of some company, the terrible life Carol gives him,' said Peter, who was casually dressed in jeans and a white open-necked shirt. 'I don't know how Arnie puts up with her, I really don't. The woman gets away with murder from what I've seen.'

Gill couldn't argue with that. Arnie's determination not to repeat past mistakes with this marriage had made him rather too eager to please, and Carol capitalised on this to the enth degree. She was sulky and demanding, and thought nothing of nagging him in public. Frankly, Gill thought he was a saint to stand for it. He certainly wouldn't have let her get away with that sort of behaviour when she'd been married to him. A contributory factor to his submissive behaviour, in her opinion, was the fact that he'd not been a good husband to her. With a weird kind of logic, he was trying to make up for that by being good to Carol. Whatever the reason, he certainly was an exemplary husband. But watching Arnie being so attentive to Carol had been harder to take than she could possibly have imagined – even though, perversely, she knew she would have quarrelled with him if he hadn't treated her sister right.

'Does she have to make it so obvious that she wants us all to leave?' Peter continued. 'I feel most uncomfortable.'

'I don't think she can help it.'

'Rubbish!'

'Carol never has been able to hide her feelings,' said Gill, instinctively defensive towards her sibling. 'If she's in a bad temper, the world knows about it.'

'She should make more of an effort, for all our sakes.'

'Yes, all right, Peter,' said Gill, sighing. 'Don't go on about it.' She paused, watching her sister storm towards the house carrying a tray of used crockery. 'I'd better go and give her a hand before she ruins the party completely by driving everybody out.'

'Don't do that.'

'Why not?'

'Because you do more than enough for your sister already,' he said, putting a restraining hand on her arm. 'You're always running around after her, helping her to look after Donna and baby-sitting for her. Arnie's done most of the entertaining here today, anyway. He seems to have done all the work.'

'But—'

'Let them get on with it,' he persisted. 'It's their party, not yours. You've been here all afternoon helping with the children . . . you've done more than your share. So why not just relax and enjoy yourself – as far as that's possible with old Sour-Chops about? You are supposed to be a guest, after all.'

He was right. She did do too much for her sister. But it was more for Donna than for Carol. Gill had been smitten with her niece from the moment she'd first set eyes on her, and welcomed the chance to look after her on the frequent occasions when Carol wanted to off-load her. Carol had a very low threshold to the demands of small children.

'I am family, though,' she said now, 'which isn't quite the same thing as being just a guest.'

'And don't I know it,' said Peter sharply. Gill had unintentionally hit a sore spot.

'Oh, Peter,' she said, looking into his troubled eyes with a sinking heart. 'You know I didn't mean anything by that. I meant that if you're family you always get roped in to help.'

'I do know what family is all about, you know,' he hissed. 'Just because you won't let me be a part of yours doesn't mean I don't know what being family feels like.'

'This isn't the time, Peter,' she said in gentle admonition.

'I know.' He sighed. 'Sorry.'

'We will talk about it, though,' she said, 'I promise.'

Peter had moved in with Gill soon after Carol had moved in with Arnie. Gill had known that she either had to commit herself to Peter or end their relationship altogether, and she couldn't face that. Gill and Peter were never going to have the love affair of the century, but they got on well enough. At least, they had done at first. But when Gill's divorce from Arnie had been made absolute and Arnie and Carol had quietly made their union legal, Peter had wanted to do the same with Gill. And she couldn't bring herself to agree.

What was the difference? she constantly asked herself. She shared her life with Peter anyway, so why not go ahead and get that vital piece of paper? But for all that it made sense she didn't want to do it, and this upset Peter who saw her reluctance as a personal slight.

But now someone was nudging her knee and she looked down to see a pretty little thing in a blue party frock, light brown curly hair tumbling over her forehead, cheeks flushed from running around.

'Donna, my special birthday girl . . .' Gill swept her adored niece up on to her lap and smothered her with kisses. 'You're up late tonight, precious.'

'Mummy says I can stay up late 'cause it's my birthday,' she said, yawning widely. 'No bed, no bed, no bed.'

'All right, sweetheart, don't panic.' Gill smiled. 'But you must go to bed without a fuss when Mummy says it's time.'

'I want you to put me to bed tonight, Auntie Gill.'

'All right, but only if Mummy says I can,' she said, ever careful not to undermine Carol's authority. Even though Carol was usually delighted to hand her exuberant daughter over to Gill if she happened to be around at Donna's bedtime, if you took anything for granted and Carol was in the mood to take umbrage she would fly into a rage. Carol had never been an easy person, but she'd been more difficult than ever since she'd been with Arnie.

'Will you read me a story at bedtime, Auntie Gill?'

'Yes, course I will, darling.'

But Donna's childish mind had already moved to other things.

'Craig. Where's Craig?' she asked.

'He's around somewhere, love.'

'We were playing at hidin' and I don't know where he's gone.'

At that moment Craig, now a lanky thirteen-year-old who got more like his father every day, sauntered into view.

'Ah, there you are,' he said, smiling affectionately at Donna, on whom he doted. Unusually for someone entering adolescence, with its tendency towards self-centredness, he had endless patience with his half-sister. 'You were supposed to come looking for me. I got fed up of waiting.'

'I don't think she's quite old enough to play hide and seek properly,' Gill said to her son. 'Ring a ring a roses is more up her street.'

This struck an instant chord with Donna. 'Me want roses, Auntie Gill, me want roses,' she chanted.

'Come on, then.' Gill set her down on the ground and took hold of her hand. 'Let's go on to the lawn.' She grinned at Peter. 'Come on. Come and join us.'

'No thanks,' he told her, miffed because he had lost her attention.

'See you in a minute then,' she said, turning a blind eye to his disapproval because she didn't want Donna's birthday to be spoiled by adult disagreements.

Dragging Craig on to the grass, the three of them joined hands, Donna squealing with delight at the traditional repetition of the nursery rhyme.

'Come and join in, you lazy lot,' Gill called to her parents and Phoebe and Len, who were sitting on the patio with John Briscoe.

'We'll leave that one to you,' said Winnie, smiling. 'We're all still recovering from this afternoon's shindig.'

Arnie, who appeared from the house with a tray of drinks,

handed them out and joined Gill and the others on the lawn.

'Okay then, Donna,' he said, smiling at his daughter and taking her hand and Craig's on the other side, 'let's show them how this should be done.'

Donna was in her element as the four of them moved round in a circle, laughing breathlessly when they got to the bit where they 'all fall down'.

'I'm too exhausted to get up,' Gill said to Arnie, who was sitting beside her on the grass. 'Your daughter has run the legs off me today.'

'You and me both,' he said, helping her up. 'She's tireless.'

In the kitchen, fixing herself yet another gin and tonic, Carol turned to the window just at the moment when Arnie was helping Gill to her feet, the two of them laughing with Craig and Donna.

Carol spent most of her life in a state of jealousy, forever tormenting herself with thoughts of Gill and Arnie having an affair. Now the green-eyed monster consumed her completely, rooting her to the spot, glass in hand, as this happy family scene tore at her heart. Arnie and Gill, happy together, laughing and talking, probably planning some assignation . . . Craig and Donna barely registered. The only thing Carol could see was her husband and her sister enjoying themselves together.

'I'll soon put a stop to that,' she muttered to herself.

Making short work of her drink, she marched purposefully out into the garden and on to the lawn.

'I know what you two are up to, so don't think you can pull the wool over my eyes,' she said with loud belligerence, bringing the hubbub of conversation to an abrupt halt. 'I know you're having an affair.'

'Carol!' gasped Arnie, his eyes glinting with anger. 'Don't be so ridiculous.'

'Don't try and fob me off,' she said, her voice rising, the guests on the patio listening in shocked silence. 'I'm not a fool; I know what's going on.'

'Nothing's going on,' said Gill.

'I won't have it. Do you understand me?' she rasped as though Gill hadn't spoken, her voice harsh and resonant in the evening air. 'I won't let you make a fool of me!'

Frightened by this sudden hostility, Donna started to cry. Before her despair had time to take root, Craig picked her up and carried her over to the swing, talking to her loudly enough to drown out the sound of her mother's voice.

'Calm down, Carol,' Arnie ordered in a low voice. 'You're upsetting Donna.'

'Don't patronise me!' she screamed. 'I'm not a child.'

'Stop behaving like one, then, and pull yourself together,' he said in a quiet but firm voice. 'You're upsetting Donna and embarrassing our guests.'

'That's all you care about – your daughter, your son and your bloody ex-wife!' she shrieked, completely out of control.

'Carol, that's enough,' said Gill, taking her by the arm.

'Don't touch me, you slut,' Carol said through gritted teeth, pushing Gill away. 'You've never been able to accept the fact that Arnie isn't yours any more. Well, it's time you did. You just keep your hands off him!'

Arnie exchanged a glance with Gill. This wasn't the first time they had had to suffer a scene like this one; Carol was prone to slanging matches, especially when she'd had a few drinks. But this was the first time she'd done it in public.

'Okay, Carol, that's it,' Arnie said, taking her arm in a firm grip. 'That's quite enough from you for one party.' And he propelled her, protesting loudly, into the house.

When Winnie went to go after them, Gill said, 'Leave them alone to sort it out, Mum. Carol doesn't know what she's saying. She's had too much to drink, that's all.'

Gill was feeling very shaky herself as she went over to the swing and began to push it for Donna.

'Higher, Auntie Gill,' shouted her niece. 'I want to go higher.'

'Okay, darling,' said Gill, glad that Carol's ranting didn't seem to have had any lasting effect on her daughter. The poor little thing must have got used to it.

'Carol wants her backside smacking,' Winnie said to Hal in a low voice so that she couldn't be overheard by the others. 'Carrying on like that in public ... I've never been so embarrassed.'

'God knows what happened to the manners we taught her,' said Hal.

'That's what comes of marrying a man who's already been married to your sister,' said Winnie sagely. 'It's bound to lead to trouble.'

'Fancy accusing Gill of something like that, though,' said Hal.

'And in front of Peter too,' Winnie said, glancing towards Peter who was talking to Phoebe and Len near the French doors.

'It is definitely all over between Gill and Arnie, isn't it?' said Hal.

'Course it is,' she said. 'Carol doesn't know when she's well off. Arnie's a husband in a million to her ... a damned sight better than he ever was to Gill.'

'That's true,' said Hal.

They stopped speaking abruptly as Gill came towards them, leaving Craig in charge of Donna on the swing.

'Don't worry about it, Mum,' Gill said. She knew her mother would be upset by what had happened. 'You know what Carol's like when she's in one of her moods. She'll have forgotten all about it tomorrow.'

'She might have, but I certainly won't,' snorted Winnie. 'Showing us all up like that ... It was a damned disgrace.'

'I don't know why people bother to get married. All they seem to do is fight with each other.' John Briscoe was sitting with his mother and Len Bex, Peter having wandered off to talk to Gill. 'It puts me right off, I can tell you.'

310

'It isn't like that for everyone,' Phoebe pointed out.

'Course it isn't,' agreed Len.

'Doesn't seem like a barrel-load of laughs between those two from what I've seen of it,' John persisted. 'Carol always seems to be having a go at Arnie about something.'

'Take no notice of that, son,' said Len, who had become like one of the Briscoe family over the last few years. 'While we're all sitting here worrying about them, those two will be all lovey-dovey. It's all part of the fun.'

'Fun? Shoving sharp needles up your nose would be more fun than that.' John was now twenty-four, enjoying a bachelor life in a modern flat in Hammersmith. He was smart and trendy, with long hair and a light jacket worn over slim-fitting trousers. 'Give me the single life any day, where you can come and go as you please with no one to answer to.'

'You'll change your mind when the right one comes along,' said Len.

John sipped at a glass of beer, looking at Len thoughtfully. 'You don't seem in any hurry to try it again, though, do you?' he said tactlessly. 'And you've been going out with Mum for yonks.'

'John!' Phoebe said, smarting with embarrassment.

'I'm only saying—'

'Well don't,' Phoebe rebuked.

'What's the fuss?' said John casually. 'It's no big deal, I was only making a comment.'

'I'd rather you didn't.'

'Let him speak,' said Len, putting a steadying hand on her arm. 'He has every right to be concerned about his mother.' He looked at John. 'Your mother and I are very good friends and we're happy to carry on as we are. It doesn't suit us to get married.' He turned to Phoebe. 'Ain't that right, Pheeb?'

Wrong, thought Phoebe, but she nodded and said, 'That's right.'

'Oh well, whatever lights your candle,' said John breezily.

For a while Phoebe had been Len's partner only every few

months at the social occasions he was obliged to attend. But they had got on so well together he'd begun to suggest other outings too, and they had gradually become established companions.

Being together all day at work brought them even closer. But Len still made it plain that he had no intention of remarrying or of them moving in together. It was all to do with his lingering devotion for Mary, Phoebe guessed. But although she wanted that final commitment from him, she knew she must either accept him on his own terms or end their relationship altogether. And as that was the last thing she wanted, she carried on regardless and enjoyed having him as a close friend with the occasional bit of something else to spice things up.

'There you are, what did I tell you?' Len said as Carol and Arnie reappeared together and mingled with their guests as though nothing untoward had happened. 'They've made it up. They're all over each other now.'

'Don't you believe it,' said Phoebe, noticing Carol's bloodshot eyes despite the extra make-up she'd piled on to hide the fact that she'd been crying. 'That's all show, put on for our benefit and instigated by Arnie.'

'Perhaps you're right,' said Len. 'The poor bloke must have wanted the floor to open up and swallow him.'

'He's got his hands full with Carol all right,' she said with motherly concern. 'Those two are not right for each other and they both know it.'

'Oh well, I'm gonna go and ask Arnie for another drink,' said John, getting up. 'Either of you want one?'

They both shook their heads.

'Gill has always been the only girl for Arnie, despite all their troubles,' Phoebe said to Len after John had wandered off.

'Do you think Carol knows that and that's why she's so jealous?'

'Probably. And if today's performance is anything to go by

she's getting paranoid about it,' declared Phoebe. 'I'm amazed Arnie puts up with her tantrums.'

'He does seem exceptionally patient, I must say,' said Len.

'Guilt,' declared Phoebe. 'He's letting her get away with murder to make up for the fact that he isn't in love with her. Arnie's trouble is, he doesn't know a good thing when he has it.'

'Gill?'

'The worst thing he ever did was letting her go,' Phoebe said, shaking her head sadly. 'And I bet he knows it now that it's too late.'

It is easy to see how the British got their reputation for stoicism, Gill thought, observing the way everyone carried on regardless in the aftermath of Carol's blistering performance. Carol and Arnie continued to host the party as though everything was normal, though not without the presence of simmering undertones.

Gill couldn't bring herself to be civil to her sister until she had received an apology. This came, albeit grudgingly, after Donna was in bed, having been bathed and read to by Gill. Apart from Peter, who was downstairs talking to Arnie, everyone else had gone, and the two women found themselves alone together on the landing on the way downstairs.

'Look, I'm sorry, okay?' Carol said in a perfunctory manner.

'And so you damned well ought to be,' rasped Gill, keeping her voice down so that she couldn't be heard in Donna's bedroom. 'You were right out of order.'

'Maybe I was, but I still say that you and Arnie fancy the pants off each other,' she said, her eyes narrow with accusation. 'And don't bother to deny it.'

Gill emitted a sigh. 'How many more times must I tell you? There is nothing going on between us,' she said. 'And there never will be.'

'There had better not be either,' Carol said vehemently.

313

'I'll kill the pair of you if I ever find out that there is.'

'Don't you ever give up, Carol?' Gill said in frustration. 'The only thing that is going on between Arnie and me is inside your head.'

'Oh, so I'm some sort of a loony now, am I?' she snarled.

'You will be if you don't calm down and stop imagining things.'

'Bloody cheek!' Carol exclaimed. 'How dare you suggest I'm not right in the head!'

'I'm just trying to get through to you . . .'

'Don't try and get out of it by making out I'm mental.'

'I've nothing to get out of,' said Gill, clinging to her rapidly diminishing patience. 'And I am sick to death of all these ridiculous accusations. The best thing I can do is stay away from you and Arnie altogether.'

Carol's attitude changed instantly – it wasn't in her interests for Gill not to be around when she needed her. 'You can't do that,' she said. 'It would break Donna's heart.'

'Yes, it would.' Gill's heart turned over at the thought of not seeing her niece on a regular basis. She knew Carol would miss her too, because she was useful to her as a companion as well as baby-sitter.

'So you can't stay away.'

'Mum will probably help out with Donna instead of me.'

'It wouldn't be the same,' said Carol, fear in her eyes because she was reliant on her sister in so many ways. 'Donna dotes on you. She loves coming over to your place.'

'I would never stop her from coming over, you know that, but I don't want to be in the firing line of your nasty accusations any more,' said Gill. 'So I think it'll be best if I collect and deliver Donna but don't stay around to listen to your rotten insults.'

'I won't do it again, Gill, I promise.' As well as Gill's usefulness to Carol, it had also occurred to her that she would incur Arnie's anger if she caused a family rift. 'Just don't give up on me, please.'

'Well . . .'

'Don't stay away from us . . .'

Gill sighed, knowing she couldn't refuse her. Carol was weak and selfish, but the sisterly bond remained as strong as ever. Gill was actually rather sorry for Carol. It must be dreadful to feel so insecure that you lashed out with accusations without the slightest justification.

'All right.'

'Oh, thanks, Gill.' Carol hugged her. 'You're a pal.'

'You don't seem to appreciate what a gem of a husband you have in Arnie,' Gill said in a warning tone.

'I do.'

'You don't seem to,' Gill repeated. 'And if you carry on as you have been you'll drive him away. Not in my direction, but he'll go – and no one will blame him.'

Carol gasped, clutching her throat in a theatrical over-reaction. 'Don't say that, Gill!' she said, her eyes half-closed as though the mere thought of losing Arnie caused her physical pain. 'I couldn't bear to lose him.'

'Stop behaving like a sulky teenager then, and work at hanging on to him. You're a wife and mother now. It's time you grew up.'

'I don't know what happens to me,' Carol said. 'I get so terrified of losing him that my thoughts run wild and I lose control. That's why I say these things.'

'Calm down and give him some space and there won't be any question of your losing him,' said Gill. 'Arnie's a good man – better than he's ever been now. He's improved a lot with maturity. You treat him right and he'll be with you for ever.'

'I'll try,' she said.

'I'm really sorry about what happened earlier, babe,' Carol said to Arnie later that same evening. Gill and Peter had just left, and Carol had gone into their living room to find Arnie watching the ten o'clock news.

' 'S all right,' Arnie mumbled. He was sitting in an arm-chair near the open window, his eyes glued to the TV. The news was dominated by the recently elected Conservative Prime Minister, Edward Heath, who had declared a state of emergency as the dockers staged their first national strike since 1926. Attractively appointed in the contemporary style and decorated in a variety of blue tones, the room was cool and comfortable. It was situated at the front of the house, overlooking a pleasant suburban street.

'I promise you it won't happen again,' Carol said ardently.

'Yeah, yeah, okay,' Arnie said, still looking at the screen as the sports news came on.

'You don't believe me, do you?' she persisted.

'Hang on a minute, Carol,' he said without looking at her. 'I want to see what the scores were at Wimbledon.'

Rage scorched through her because she couldn't get his immediate attention. How dare he ignore her! She had to restrain herself physically from rushing over to the television and turning it off, because she knew that would make things even worse. She sat down in an armchair opposite him and managed, with great difficulty, to stay silent until he'd heard what he wanted to.

'I don't know what gets into me,' she said the instant she saw the opportunity to capture his attention.

'Forget it,' said Arnie. He was so tired by now of her temper tantrums and endless chatter, he could hardly bear to look at her.

'I mean, it isn't as though anything would be going on between you.' She paused, then added, 'Is it?'

'Oh not again, Carol,' Arnie sighed, looking at her now even though he was exhausted by her insane jealousy. 'Please don't start on about that again.'

'I just want to make sure, then I'll never mention it again.'

'There is nothing going on, nor is there ever likely to be, between myself and Gill,' he said through clenched teeth. 'Now give us a break and let the subject drop.'

'Okay, Arnie,' she said meekly.

She knew she had pushed him as far as she dared – today. Oh God, if only the suspicions that plagued her during her every waking moment would go away and leave her in peace!

Gill was glad to get home that night. 'Phew! I don't want another evening like that for a long time,' she said to Peter after Craig had gone to bed and they were relaxing with some music on the record player.

'Me neither,' said Peter.

'Surely Carol doesn't really believe there's anything going on between Arnie and me, does she?' she remarked idly.

'I don't know if she does or not,' he said in an odd tone.

'Peter?' she said, looking at him sharply. 'What's the matter?'

'Nothing.'

'There is, I can tell.'

He sighed. 'Well, I can sympathise with Carol in a way,' he said.

'Surely you're not suggesting—'

'I'm not suggesting anything,' he cut in. 'But I am saying that there is *something* between you and Arnie . . .'

'I swear there's nothing going on.'

'You're not having an affair with him, I know that,' he went on. 'But there's still something going on between you, whether you intend it or not. It's like electricity in the air. I can feel it when you're together, and Carol obviously can too . . . That's why she gets these awful fits of jealousy.'

'I *was* married to the man,' said Gill, strongly defensive now. 'There's bound to be some sort of a bond; we have a son, for goodness' sake.'

'I'm not criticising you,' Peter pointed out. 'I'm just telling you the way it is between you and Arnie, how it must be for Carol.'

'It isn't intentional . . .'

'I know that.'

'Look, Peter,' Gill said, feeling a surge of tenderness for him; she thought she must inadvertently have hurt him. Perhaps it wasn't fair to him to leave things the way they were between them. 'I think it's time we talked . . . about us.'

'Oh?'

'About putting things on to a more permanent footing.'

'Getting married, you mean?'

'Yes.'

'This isn't the time,' he said quietly, surprising her with his lack of interest.

'You usually want to talk about it.'

'Yes, I do – but you're only suggesting it because you're feeling guilty about what I've just said.'

'Of course I'm feeling guilty. I don't want to hurt you . . .'

'Forget it.'

'I really think we should talk.'

'Not now, Gill,' he said wearily.

'But, Peter . . .'

'It's been a hell of an evening,' he said. 'So let's just leave it and relax.'

'Okay, if that's what you really want,' she agreed, but she felt very troubled. Peter seemed strange, different towards her suddenly. It was so unlike him to be off-hand about setting a date for their wedding. He'd been pestering her about it for months.

Something was wrong, she could feel it in the atmosphere. And she had a horrible suspicion that it was serious.

Chapter Nineteen

A few weeks later Gill went to see the mother superior in her office. She perched on a chair facing the nun, who was sitting behind her desk regarding her visitor quizzically. On the wall behind her a wooden crucifix hung next to some glass-fronted bookshelves, upon which stood a white plaster statuette of the Virgin Mary wearing a blue robe.

'So, how can I help you?' the nun asked in the soft, breathless way she had of speaking. 'You said on the telephone that it was a matter of some urgency.'

'Yes, it is rather urgent,' Gill confirmed.

The nun looked troubled. 'I do hope you're not having problems with any of our girls.'

'Nothing like that,' Gill quickly assured her. 'All the girls from here are a joy to teach. Cherry Betts in particular.'

'Ah, yes. What a difference music has made to that child's personality.' The mother superior gave a small smile. 'She used to be such a naughty girl, before she discovered her musical talent.'

'So I understand.' Gill paused. 'Actually, Cherry is the reason I've come to see you.'

'Oh?'

'Yes. She is exceptionally talented and has worked very hard at her music. She's passed all her exams with flying colours, as you know . . .'

'Indeed I do,' said the nun expectantly, wondering what Gill was leading up to. 'We're all very proud of her here at St Theresa's.'

'With the right training, I think she could have a career in music,' Gill continued.

'And . . . ?' The nun clasped her large hands together on the desk, waiting for Gill to come to the point.

'I've heard of a piano competition I think she should enter.'

'And you want my permission to put her name forward?' The mother superior looked puzzled. Cherry regularly competed in musical events, and permission was normally dealt with by Sister Maud. 'It goes without saying that you can go ahead and enter her. We always encourage our girls to compete. That sort of thing helps to build the character of a child.'

'This competition is rather different, though,' Gill started warily.

'Some kind of special event?' speculated the other woman.

'Very special indeed,' said Gill. 'So special, in fact, that the winner will be given the opportunity to study music at college as a full-time student, all expenses paid by the competition sponsors.'

'Oh, now wouldn't that be wonderful for Cherry?' said the nun, blue eyes sparkling for a moment before becoming serious. 'But nothing that good comes easily. She has to win the competition first.'

'Winning the competition is the least of our problems,' said Gill.

'Really?'

Gill nodded. 'The event is an international one. It's being staged in Boston . . . in America,' she explained. 'Cherry would have to find the money for her fare and enough to cover her expenses while she's in the States.'

'Oh, dear.' The nun brushed her brow with her hand worriedly. 'We help our girls as much as we can from our special fund, particularly if they have a genuine talent. But I don't think we could run to sending one of them to America. I wouldn't feel justified in spending so much money on one girl when we have so many to consider.'

'If she were to win the competition she would be able to study music at the famous Alder College in Boston.' Gill was desperate to emphasise the magnitude of the opportunity. 'It would be the chance of a lifetime for her.'

'I understand that, and we would be prepared to contribute to the cost – but we couldn't possibly manage it all.' She shook her head. 'And we couldn't allow her to go alone, so that would mean double the expense.'

'If we were somehow able to raise the money, would one of the nuns be able to go with her?' Gill asked. 'I'd go with her myself, but I have too many commitments here.'

'I'm sure we could spare one of the sisters to accompany her,' said the nun. 'That isn't a problem. Finding the money is.'

'Yes, I thought you might say something along these lines – which is why I haven't said anything to Cherry about it.' Gill paused. 'The trouble is, and the reason I said it was urgent . . . the entries have to be in quite soon in time for the closing date, though the competition isn't until December.'

The mother superior stroked her chin, staring meditatively into space. 'I would so much like her to have this opportunity,' she said sadly, 'but we just don't have that kind of money.'

'What if I were able to raise *some* of the money?' said Gill, desperate that Cherry shouldn't miss this opportunity.

'That would put a different light on the matter altogether. As I've said, we could make a contribution.'

'Good.'

'But if this was to be a serious possibility we'd need to work out the exact cost, so we'd know what sort of sum we're talking about.'

'I've already done that,' said Gill. What had been a vague idea was now becoming a definite challenge. 'Because I *will* come up with the cash we need.'

'You have that sort of money yourself?' queried the nun.

'Oh no,' Gill said with a wry grin. 'But Cherry is going to have her chance, even if I have to go out begging in the streets for the money.' She gave the nun a wicked smile. 'Fortunately that won't be necessary, because I have a much better idea . . .'

Gill was so excited about her plan that she couldn't wait until the evening to tell Peter about it. She stopped off at the music shop on the way home.

'He isn't here,' explained Wendy, sitting on a stool behind the record counter filing her nails.

'Will he be long?'

'Shouldn't think so,' she said casually, 'he's only gone to the bank.'

'I'll wait for him then.'

'Sure.'

Gill stood aside while Wendy went off to sell a woman a metronome and a man a music stand. The long-haired youth who had been drooling over an electric guitar departed, leaving the shop without customers.

'God, I hate weekdays when the shop's as quiet as this,' said Wendy, yawning.

'Some people would welcome the chance of not having much to do,' Gill remarked, just to be sociable.

'Not me. The time drags too much when the place is like a morgue,' Wendy said. 'Give me a busy Saturday when the place is packed out any time. The time just whizzes by then.'

'Yes, I suppose it would do,' said Gill, looking at her watch.

'He should be back any minute,' said Wendy.

'If he isn't back soon I'll leave it and see him tonight.'

'He'll have met someone in the street and got chatting, I expect.'

Gill nodded.

'The good thing about Peter is that he's very easygoing about things like that,' said Wendy. 'He lets me pop out to the shops during working hours and doesn't tell me off if I'm a few minutes late in the morning.'

'I can imagine him being easy to work with,' said Gill.

'I shan't half miss him.'

'Miss him?'

'Yeah. God knows what the new bloke will be like.'

'New bloke?'

'The new manager taking over from Peter,' Wendy explained.

'Someone else is taking over?'

'When Peter leaves, yeah.' Wendy was beginning to sound bored.

Gill was astounded. 'Peter's leaving the shop?'

'Yeah, that's right.' Wendy studied her nails before resuming work with the file. 'He's got himself a job up north somewhere.' She looked at Gill thoughtfully. 'But surely you know about it . . . I just assumed you'd be going with him.'

'I suppose he hasn't got around to telling me about it yet,' Gill said lamely.

'He's leaving it a bit late,' Wendy said. 'He finishes here a week Saturday.'

Gill was too stunned to speak.

'Ooh, blimey!' Wendy made a face. 'I hope I haven't dropped him in it.'

'Tell him I'll see him tonight,' said Gill, and she hurried from the shop.

Gill waited until Craig had gone out to football training that evening and she and Peter were sitting down in the living room before she confronted him with what she'd heard.

'Oh dear,' he said, looking shamefaced at her across the hearth. 'I'm sorry you had to hear about it from someone else. I was waiting for an opportunity to tell you.'

She couldn't believe it. All afternoon she'd been telling herself it must be a mistake, that Wendy had got hold of the wrong end of the stick. She'd barely been able to concentrate on her teaching for thinking about it.

'I take it by that that I'm not included in your plans,' she said, deeply hurt.

He scratched his head, then looked her straight in the eyes.

'No, I'm afraid not,' he said. 'I want to make a new start in the north.'

'The north,' Gill repeated dumbly.

'I've a cousin in Leeds. I'll doss down with him until I find a place of my own.'

'Oh, Peter . . .' Gill's voice was leaden with disappointment. 'I can't believe you'd be so devious. To do something like this without telling me . . . You and I have always been so honest with each other.'

'Yes, well, it hasn't been an easy decision to make,' he told her soberly. 'I wanted everything in place before I said anything to you . . . so that I wouldn't change my mind. I don't want to hurt you, but this is how it has to be.'

'But why?' she asked, her voice rising. 'Why are you doing this?'

'Because you and I don't have a future together,' he stated.

'But I told you we'd set a date to get married.'

He shook his head. 'Getting married isn't going to change anything,' he said. 'It's taken me long enough to realise it, but I've finally accepted it.'

'What are you talking about?' she asked, shaking her head in despair.

'I thought that us getting married was the answer, that it would bring us together, would make you love me.' He looked at her unwaveringly, his mouth set in a grim line. 'But I know now that it wouldn't make any difference.'

She combed her hair from her brow with her fingers, feeling distraught and let down. 'And may I ask what's brought you to this sudden conclusion?' she asked coldly.

'It isn't sudden, not really,' he said. 'I think I've always known it but wasn't man enough to face up to the root of the trouble – the reason why you aren't able to give me the sort of commitment that I want from you.'

'And the reason is . . . ?'

'You're still in love with Arnie,' he replied with a sigh of resignation. 'And that's something I can't compete with.'

Gill was assailed by a variety of emotions – guilt, sadness, anger at having been betrayed by Peter . . . She couldn't deny that he was right about her feelings for Arnie, but that didn't mean she couldn't care for him too. She had done her best to make him happy while they'd been together. Whatever her true feelings, she had shared her life with him. Surely she deserved better than to have him end their relationship without so much as a word to her about it. It was deeply wounding!

'As I've told you before, it's only natural that I should still feel something special for Arnie,' she said. 'I was married to the man for a long time; there's bound to be a bond between us. I've never denied that.'

'When you and I first started seeing each other it was quite soon after your separation from Arnie,' he said. 'I thought you'd get over him eventually. But now I don't believe anyone else stands a chance against him. It's no wonder Carol gets so worked up about it.'

'Ah, so that's at the bottom of all this,' she said with sudden realisation. 'My sister's performance at Donna's party.'

'That's what set me thinking seriously about it, yes,' he admitted. 'But it was there at the back of my mind anyway.'

'Why take notice of Carol when we all know she's paranoid about Arnie?'

'She has the whole thing out of proportion,' he admitted. 'But I see you and Arnie with the same eye as she does when you're together. I know what it feels like to be on the outside of something as rock solid as that.'

'But Arnie and I don't do anything out of place,' she said.

'You don't have to do anything for your feelings to be obvious,' he said. 'To me, anyway – and to Carol, apparently.'

'Oh?'

'Something happens to you when the two of you are together,' Peter said. 'You come to life in a way that you never do when you're with me.'

'Not intentionally.'

'Which makes it even worse from my point of view.

Because it's inside you and not within your control. There's nothing that you or I or anyone else can do about it. It's just there, like the air we breathe.'

'I care a lot about you, Peter,' Gill said, and it was the truth.

'But not in the way that I want.'

'It was enough once.'

'Yes. I thought I could cope with being just "good old Peter",' he said. 'But it isn't enough for me now, Gill, I want a woman who lights up for me like you do for Arnie.'

'I can't force something that isn't there,' she admitted. 'But I've been so happy with you. I don't want us to split up.'

'I'm sorry, Gill,' he said, 'but my mind is made up.'

'I'm sorry too. Really sorry. I'm going to miss you.'

He stood up purposefully. 'I think it'll probably be best if I move out of here right away,' he said. 'I can stay with a mate until I've worked out my notice at the music shop.'

'If that's what you want,' Gill said, because she could tell his decision was final.

'I'll go and pack my things then.'

'Okay.'

Sitting in the chair by the fire, listening to him moving about upstairs, Gill was smarting with rejection, desperately sad at the thought of not having him around. But she felt no impulse to fight for him, no urge to persuade him to change his mind. Because deep in her heart she knew that what he was doing was the right thing for them both.

Peter hadn't been the only one to delude himself while they had been together. She had done her share of that too, trying to convince herself that what she felt for him was sufficient to choose him as her partner for life, when it wasn't.

God, what a mess!

The following Sunday, when the family was gathered at her parents' house for lunch, Gill made her announcement.

'I've two things to tell you all,' she said. 'The first is that Peter and I have split up.'

Her mother gasped and her father stopped carving the joint, standing with the knife poised in mid-air while a shocked silence fell over the room.

'Don't worry, I'm all right,' she said, looking at her parents and then at Carol – but not allowing her eyes to linger on Arnie because Peter's comments had made her afraid even to cast a glance in his direction. 'It's all for the best. We were never really right for each other.'

'Perhaps you'll patch things up,' Winnie suggested hopefully.

'No, it isn't the sort of thing you can patch up,' explained Gill. 'We didn't have a quarrel as such. It was more a mutual facing up to things. Peter's going to live in Leeds.'

'Oh, I *am* sorry, love,' said her mother.

Knowing that the last thing Gill would want was pity, Arnie made a hasty intervention.

'So, what was the other thing you had to tell us?' he asked.

'That's much more cheerful,' she said, brightening. 'I'm going to put on a concert to raise money.' She explained why she needed to do this. 'And I'm going to need your help.'

'She's already got me down as general dogsbody,' said Craig.

'Me wannabe a dogbody,' chanted Donna, causing a roar of laughter.

'Who's going to be taking part in this concert?' Hal enquired with interest, slicing the beef while Winnie served them all with Yorkshire pudding.

'My pupils,' she said, 'with Cherry as top of the bill.'

'What a smashing idea!' said Arnie, no stranger to fund-raising. 'We'll do whatever we can to help.' He looked at Carol, careful as always to ensure she wasn't excluded. 'Won't we, love?'

'Yeah, course we will,' she said in a casual manner that belied the fact that she was in a state of high agitation. Her mind was still reeling with her sister's first piece of news. The fact that Gill had been in a settled relationship had been Carol's safeguard against Arnie's committing adultery. To her fevered imagination the presence of Peter in Gill's life was the only thing that prevented her and Arnie from having an affair. Carol didn't credit either of them with so much as a crumb of decency. Now that Gill had returned to the single state, she felt more seriously threatened than ever and would have to keep an even closer eye on them. But she daren't be too obvious about it. She didn't want to put them on their guard. 'Anything at all we can do to help,' she said evenly, 'just let us know.'

'You'll probably live to regret having said that.' Gill grinned. 'By the time I've got the show organised you'll all be worn out.'

The main hall at St Theresa's was transformed into a perfect auditorium for the November concert, the mother superior having been delighted to allow Gill the use of it for the evening. The stage from which morning assembly was normally taken was now colourfully banked by flowers and graced with a grand piano, the former donated by an acquaintance of Len's who owned a flower shop, the latter on loan from the music shop, courtesy of the new manager.

The show was drawing to a close and Gill was waiting at the side of the stage to deliver her speech of thanks, listening as Cherry finished a technically brilliant and moving performance of Mozart's Sonata in C.

Every seat was taken. Gill was touched by the practical help and support she had received in putting the concert on. Arnie had been an absolute godsend, turning his hand to anything from organising sponsorship to persuading the shopkeepers of West London to sell tickets. He had even set to and painted the walls of the hall in honour of the occasion, assisted by John and Craig. Phoebe, Winnie and Carol had worked together to provide the light refreshments that had been on sale in the interval, and Len and Hal had been selling programmes and raffle tickets at the door.

As the applause rose for Cherry, who stood up and bowed graciously to the audience, Gill prepared herself for a moment, then stepped on to the stage, elegantly attired for the occasion in a white satin evening blouse and a long black skirt.

'Thank you for coming to our concert tonight,' she said when the applause had finally died away and Cherry had left the stage. 'I'm thrilled to be able to tell you that, thanks to your support, we have reached our target.' She paused for a moment as the buzz of excitement grew. 'Which means that the star of our show, Cherry Betts, will be able to go to America to take part in the piano competition that could change her life.'

Cheers rose to the rafters and Gill beckoned to Cherry, who was sitting with the other young performers in the front row. The girl's eyes were brimming with tears as she came back on stage and stood beside Gill, who was herself feeling very emotional.

'I'd like to thank everybody who helped make our concert possible,' Gill managed, albeit with a wobble in her voice. 'Especially my family and friends who gave so generously of their time to make this evening an occasion to remember.'

Another burst of applause.

'And last, but by no means least, my final thanks go to our young performers who have given us such a treat this evening, and who I would like to welcome back on stage.'

And with her heart so full she thought it would burst, Gill watched her talented charges file back on to the stage to join her and Cherry, their faces flushed with pleasure. She was completely overwhelmed when Donna, looking adorable in a red velvet dress with a white lacy collar and accompanied by her mother, trailed on to the stage carrying a bouquet of flowers which she handed to her aunt. This was almost too much for Gill, who took her final bow through a blur of tears, after which Cherry went over to the piano to end the show with the national anthem.

The warmth of spirit in that hall on that cold November evening was something Gill knew she would never forget.

'What a night!' she said later, when family and friends had gathered at her house for an informal supper. 'I won't forget that in a hurry.'

'Neither will anyone else,' said Winnie, as everyone helped themselves to the buffet meal laid out on Gill's kitchen table. 'And it's all down to you, Gill. You put the whole thing together.'

'Hear, hear!' said her father.

'You were great,' said Winnie.

'Terrific,' added Carol.

'I couldn't have done it without your help, all of you,' Gill was quick to point out.

'We didn't have much choice with you bullying us into it,' joked Phoebe.

'The bouquet at the end was a lovely surprise.' Gill looked at her sister, who had just put the sleeping Donna into the spare bed. 'How on earth did you manage to keep Donna awake so late?'

'She had a long sleep this afternoon,' explained Carol. 'She's fast asleep now, though.'

'You can leave her here for the night if you like,' Gill suggested in her usual helpful manner. 'To save disturbing her when you go. I'll bring her home in the morning.'

'Thanks,' said Carol, taking Gill's accommodating nature for granted as usual.

'And thanks for the flowers,' said Gill warmly, though she couldn't help being puzzled by her sister's sudden burst of good nature.

'I'm glad you were pleased.' Carol had come up with the idea of organising a bouquet for her sister. For her it was a way of hiding her savage jealousy, which grew and festered with every passing day, filling her with hatred for her sister. Try as she might to put the torturous suspicions out of her mind, they just wouldn't go away. Gill and Arnie – Arnie and Gill . . . Thoughts of them together absorbed her so completely, she could hardly think of anything else. The run-up to the concert had been agonising, as Arnie had immersed himself in helping Gill with the organisation. Carol had only got involved herself in an effort to prevent them being alone together.

'Young Cherry was a smash hit,' said Phoebe, helping herself to a slice of pork pie and pickles. 'What a talent!'

'She certainly deserves a chance to show what she can do in America,' said Len, forking some ham on to his plate.

'I thought all the kids were good.' Arnie almost added something complimentary about Gill's part in their success, but thought better of it because of the effect such a remark would have on Carol. Even the most casual compliment would be seen by his wife as evidence of his love for Gill and further fuel for Carol's obsession.

'It says something for your teaching, Gill,' said Carol, forcing a smile to hide what she was really feeling.

'It's very satisfying, seeing the children perform so well,' Gill said.

'It's a good experience for them an' all,' said Winnie.

'Not to mention the proud parents,' chuckled Phoebe. 'Someone could have done a good trade in paper hankies tonight.'

'That's what Mum and Dad will be like when I play in my first cup final.' Craig looked at his mother and added saucily, 'You'll go all soppy then, won't you, Mum?'

'You know my feelings about that,' she said, smiling so as not to spoil the party but feeling a shadow dampen her mood.

'We'll all be in tears on that day,' said Hal happily.

'Not half,' agreed Arnie.

Although the mood was light and the remarks made in a jokey manner, the fact that Craig spoke with increasing frequency about a career in football was seriously beginning to worry Gill. When everyone began to drift into the other room with their supper, she took the opportunity of a few words with Arnie on the subject as he limped out of the kitchen behind Carol.

'I think Craig really believes he can become a professional footballer, you know,' she said, waylaying Arnie by the door.

'I'm sure he does, and I agree with him,' he said, moving back into the kitchen and perching on a stool by the worktop – he still needed to rest his leg at night if he'd had a busy day.

'You really think he's good enough, then?' Gill said, standing opposite him with a plate in her hand.

'No question about it,' he said. 'With the right training he could be a really good player.'

'I don't want this idea encouraged,' she said anxiously.

'Why not?'

'Because I think it would be better for him to concentrate on getting some qualifications so that he can get a steady job.'

'But if football is what he wants to do for a career—'

'He doesn't know what's best for him at the moment,' she said.

'I'm not so sure about that.'

'It's up to us as responsible parents to give him the right guidance,' she said emphatically. 'Being a footballer is every working-class boy's dream. But how many of them make it?'

'I did.'

'You were one of the few. And look what it did to you – it changed you and almost wrecked your life. I don't want that to happen to him.'

'It's a sin to waste talent, Gill,' Arnie pointed out gravely. 'You of all people should know that, given that you spend your life nurturing talent and have spent so much time and effort to give young Cherry Betts a chance.'

'That's a different thing altogether,' insisted Gill.

'Different subject, same principle,' Arnie said in a firm

tone. 'A life in music is not a secure one by any means. How many of the people who want a performing career actually make a full-time living at it?'

'Only a small percentage,' Gill was forced to admit, 'but that isn't the point. I don't think it would be right to encourage Craig to think of football as a career.'

'It's early days yet, anyway,' Arnie said in an effort to defuse the situation; Gill was getting heated, and this was neither the time nor the place for an argument. 'Let's just wait and see what happens when he gets a bit older, shall we?'

'Just as long as you know where I stand on this one,' she said ardently. 'I really feel strongly about it.'

'Okay. Point taken.'

'Good.'

'So, having established that you don't want another footballer in the family, let's go and join the others.'

'Yes, let's do that,' she said, smiling to indicate that there were no hard feelings.

At this moment, there was an unexpected interruption.

'Oh, *very cosy*,' Carol's voice was clipped with rage.

'Carol . . .' Arnie said in a warning tone.

'So, you don't even bother to be discreet about what you're up to now.'

Gill's tolerance on this subject was becoming threadbare. 'For heaven's sake—'

'It's a wonder I don't actually catch you at it—'

'We were only talking about Craig,' Gill cut in, her stomach knotting with tension.

'Oh yeah?' Carol sneered.

'Yes, we were.'

'Give it a rest, Carol,' said Arnie.

'Don't you speak to me like that, you two-timing git.'

Gill stepped forward and took her sister by both arms, staring into her face. 'Look . . . Arnie and I were doing no harm. We were simply having a conversation about our son, whose welfare is something we share whether you like it or not.'

'Talking about Craig, my foot,' Carol said, pulling away.

'You're being ridiculous.'

'And you're a slut.'

'Just listen to yourself, Carol—'

'Shut up!'

'You made a damned good job of ruining Donna's birthday celebrations, but you're not going to spoil the party here tonight.' Gill looked at her sister, forbidding her to argue. 'So either behave in a normal, civilised manner or go home. But don't subject us all to your idiotic notions yet again.'

'We'll both go,' said Arnie. 'That'll be the best thing for everyone.'

'Surely there's no need for that,' said Gill, disappointed to have the evening spoiled so unnecessarily.

'There's no point in us staying with Carol in this mood,' Arnie said, looking sharply at his wife, who seemed to have retreated into a sulky silence. 'I'll only be on edge, wondering what she's gonna come out with next.'

'Don't talk about me as though I'm not here,' Carol objected.

'Don't behave so disgracefully that we're driven to, then,' said Gill.

Arnie walked towards the door. 'Come on, Carol,' he said resignedly, 'I'll get our coats.'

As he left the room and Carol went to follow, Gill put a restraining hand on her sister's arm. 'You won't be happy until you've wrecked all our lives, will you?' she said, and without waiting for a reply she turned away and went to join the others in the living room, her light-hearted mood shattered.

Chapter Twenty

Although Arnie was an expert at putting on a front, he couldn't fool his mother.

'What's up, son?' she asked, one Saturday afternoon the following January. Arnie had come into the office with a query, and Phoebe was alone because Len was at one of the other branches.

'Nothin'.'

'Come on, Arnie, this is your mum you're talking to,' she said. 'I know there's something wrong, no matter how much you pretend otherwise.'

'Leave it, Mum.'

But Phoebe wasn't easily deterred when someone she cared about was unhappy. 'Carol's giving you a hard time again, isn't she?' she said, having witnessed his wife's neurotic behaviour on too many occasions.

The understatement of the decade, Arnie thought gloomily. Marriage to Carol had become so unbearable that he dreaded going home. Hardly a day passed when she didn't pick an argument with him about his supposed adultery with Gill.

Her neurosis ran to a pattern: she would assail him with accusations until he finally managed to convince her that her suspicions were groundless, when she would calm down; but a day or so later the whole process would begin again. He was reaching the end of his tether.

Normally he would not discuss the subject with anyone, out of loyalty to his wife, but the need to share his problem was suddenly overwhelming.

He sat down opposite his mother. 'She's driving me crazy.'

'Oh, son . . .'

'And the worst part is, I don't think she can help it.'

'That's awful.'

'I just don't know what to do about it, Mum,' he confessed. 'She's making her own life a misery as well as mine. And who knows what sort of effect all this is having on Donna?'

'Kids are very resilient, you know,' she said. She could see how distressed he was and was anxious to reassure him.

'But Carol is so wound up all the time. She's obsessed with her suspicions about me and Gill, and it's making her bad tempered with Donna.'

'I think Carol should see a doctor,' said Phoebe, 'to get something to calm her down.'

'I think so too, but if I suggest it to her she flies off the handle,' he said. 'And I can't force her to go.'

'Course you can't.'

'One mention of medical help and she says I'm trying to cover my own tracks by pretending that she's mental.'

'Oh dear.' Phoebe was worried sick.

'She's even accused me of wanting her to go on tranquillisers to dull her senses so that she won't notice what's going on.'

'Sounds to me as though she really does need help.' Phoebe tutted.

'I wouldn't mind if I was getting up to mischief,' he said. 'But I'm not, I swear it.'

'I believe you.'

'I'll admit I wouldn't have married Carol if I'd had any choice. But knowing I had to, I went into the marriage determined to make a go of it.' Arnie felt on the verge of tears finally, after keeping his feelings to himself for so long. 'And I'm still doing my damnedest. But Carol isn't making it easy.'

'She must be feeling very insecure about you,' said Phoebe.

'That's the problem,' he said, shaking his head in despair. 'But how can I convince her that she's got nothing to worry about when she just won't accept it?'

'I wish I knew the answers,' said Phoebe, leaning towards him with her forearms on the desk.

'I try to give her a good life,' Arnie said. 'She wants for nothing.'

'No one would argue with that.' Phoebe was thoughtful. 'Why don't you take her away for a weekend? Just the two of you. Go to a posh hotel somewhere and spoil her rotten,' she suggested. 'It'll do you both good to get away, and it's time you had a Saturday off from work.'

'At this time of the year?'

'Yeah, why not?' Phoebe said with rising enthusiasm. 'Somewhere in the country would be nice. It's a bit bleak for the seaside in winter.'

'What about Donna?'

'Gill would probably be willing to look after her for a weekend,' she said. 'I'd have her myself but I'm at the shop all day on a Saturday.'

'Mm.'

'And there's always Winnie if Gill can't do it for some reason,' said Phoebe, hoping to remove all the obstacles. 'But Gill is nuts about Donna so I can't see her refusing the chance of having her to herself for a weekend.'

'There is that,' Arnie said, smiling at the thought of his adored daughter.

'Donna is the daughter Gill will never have,' Phoebe remarked. 'And for all Carol's bad feeling about her sister, she always seems pleased enough to use her as a baby-sitter if she wants to go off somewhere.'

'It's a thought,' said Arnie. 'But I don't know if Carol will agree to it. She can be so damned awkward these days.'

'Get it all organised before you say anything to her, then give her a surprise,' Phoebe suggested. 'That way she'll be far too thrilled that you've gone to all that trouble on her behalf to make any objections.'

'You reckon?'

'I think it's worth a try.'

But he had his doubts about Carol's reaction to the idea. She could twist the most well-meant intention into a plan of evil intent. 'I'm not sure, Mum,' he sighed.

'The first thing you need to do is arrange for Gill to look after Donna.' Phoebe persisted in the thought that anything was worth doing if there was the slightest chance of it improving the appalling state of her son's marriage. 'Once that's settled you can go ahead and book a hotel – one of those places you see advertised in the paper with log fires and a cosy bar would be nice . . .' But Phoebe could see he still wasn't convinced. 'It's only a suggestion, son, but it's well worth considering.'

'Yeah, I'll give it some thought.'

It was on Arnie's mind for the rest of the afternoon. He was still mulling it over as he drove home through the darkened streets, a nocturnal frost already beginning to form on garden walls and rooftops, the street-lights blurred by a gathering mist.

As a partner in a thriving business he could afford to take his wife somewhere special. Surely even Carol's warped mind couldn't misconstrue his motives for a weekend away for the two of them.

Thinking ahead to the reality of two days alone with Carol, without Donna's entertaining company as a diversion, he wasn't sure if he could cope with it. Even apart from his wife's recent behaviour, they had little in common. But if it would help to make her feel more secure, it was worth making the effort. Yes, he would do it, and the sooner he got it arranged the better.

With his mother's advice in mind about his first move, he turned off the main Chiswick road and headed back to Fulham to ask Gill to look after Donna for a weekend.

Carol looked at the kitchen clock, her temper rising. Arnie was late home from work. Admittedly only by about fifteen minutes, but it was annoying just the same. On weekdays he could never be sure exactly what time he would be home because he often had things to do after the shop closed; but on Saturdays she insisted he be home by six o'clock. It was the weekend, for heaven's sake! The meal was ready and keeping warm in the oven; the least he could do was make sure she wasn't kept waiting.

Donna had gone to Winnie and Hal's for the afternoon and they hadn't brought her back yet, so Carol didn't even have her daughter to take her mind off Arnie's non-appearance. Fraught with tension, she stamped across to the living-room window and peered through the curtains into the street, the lights in the houses opposite obscured by the mist. No sign of Arnie. She marched angrily to the telephone in the hall and dialled the number of the shop. No reply! Becoming more furious with every second that passed, she dialled his mother's number.

'Hello, Phoebe, it's Carol. Is Arnie there?' she asked.

'Well, no,' said Phoebe, surprised at the question.

'Oh. He isn't home yet and I couldn't think where else he might be,' Carol explained. 'I've rung the shop and there's no reply.'

'There wouldn't be. He left at the same time as Len and me,' said Phoebe. 'You know Arnie, he never hangs about on a Saturday.'

'Did he say he was stopping off anywhere on the way home?'

'No.'

'Oh.'

'It's quite foggy,' Phoebe pointed out, 'so he wouldn't have been able to put his foot down like he usually does.'

'It doesn't look all that foggy outside to me,' said Carol.

'It's patchy,' said Phoebe, 'and very deceiving. He's probably having to drive at a crawl.'

'That must be what it is then,' said Carol, not believing it at all.

'He'll be in in a minute, love,' said Phoebe confidently. 'Don't worry.'

'Okay. See you.'

Replacing the receiver, Carol paced about the house, her temper getting more explosive by the second. 'Held up by the fog, my Aunt Fanny,' she muttered to herself, looking out of the window again. 'It's hardly more than a mist.'

Arnie wasn't yet even half an hour later than usual, but to Carol it was more than long enough. Her rage at being kept waiting turned to icy fear as a terrible suspicion came into her mind. The bugger had gone to Gill's. That's where he was – *with her!* The thought buffeted her, causing her to rush to the bathroom to be sick.

Emerging in a cold sweat and beyond reasonable thought, she tore to the telephone in the hall and feverishly began to dial Gill's number. But when she got to the last digit she stopped and slammed down the receiver. What would a telephone call achieve? Arnie wouldn't answer someone else's phone, and Gill was hardly likely to admit to Carol that he was there with her.

She ran a trembling hand over her clammy brow. She *had* to know for sure if he was there, and the only way to find out was to go to Gill's to see for herself. If she didn't know for certain it would torment her for days. If she was wrong – and please God that she was – she could rest easy.

Damp with nervous perspiration, her heart thundering in her ears, she threw on her coat and rushed from the house, the meal in the oven forgotten, as well as the imminent return of her daughter.

Phoebe was right, Carol thought in the car. The mist really was denser than it had seemed from the window, and the roads were icy. Normally Carol would have been too afraid to drive her car in these conditions, but her unstable frame of mind obliterated all fear and trepidation. All that mattered was knowing the truth, and she was aware of nothing but this as she roared towards Fulham.

As she drew up outside Gill's house her heart turned over. Arnie's car was parked outside! So now she really did know the truth. But she wished she didn't.

She put her head in her hands in despair.

'Blimey, is that the time?' Arnie looked at the clock on the mantelpiece in Gill's living room. 'Carol will murder me. She goes berserk if I'm late home from work on a Saturday. Six o'clock on the dot or I'm a dead man.'

'It isn't long past six,' said Gill. 'You've hardly been here any time at all.'

'I'll still be late, though.'

'In Carol's interests . . .' Gill reminded him.

'She doesn't know that,' he said. 'And it'll spoil the surprise if we tell her.'

'Perhaps you'd better ring her and tell her you're on your way, if she's that particular.'

'She's bound to ask where I'm calling from and I'll have to lie or give the game away,' he said. 'I don't wanna tell porkies.'

'It shows how little time you've been here,' she remarked, glancing at the biscuit-coloured suede coat he was wearing. 'You haven't even stayed long enough to take your coat off.'

'True.' He walked across the room to the door, Gill following him. 'Just long enough to get you to agree to have Donna for a weekend.'

'It'll be a pleasure,' said Gill. 'I shall look forward to it.'

'Thanks, Gill.'

She paused, remembering something. 'Oh, by the way, I had a letter from Cherry this morning.'

'Did you?' Arnie said with interest. 'How's she getting on?'

'She seems to be having a wonderful time,' she said. 'She's made friends at the music college and loves living in Boston.'

'All your efforts were worthwhile then,' he said.

'*Our* efforts . . . all of us.'

'Well, whatever,' he said lightly. 'But is she doing wild

341

teenage things now that she's out of sight of the nuns?'

'No chance,' Gill said with a wry grin. 'She's staying at a local convent. The nuns at St Theresa's arranged for her to have a room there. They're all of the same order, apparently.'

'No wild parties for Cherry then.'

'Not for the moment, anyway.'

They were startled by a continuous ringing at the doorbell.

'That'll be Craig back from football, I expect,' said Gill, crossing to the front door. 'He must have forgotten his key.'

'Good. It'll give me a chance to say hello to him,' said Arnie.

Gill opened the door. 'Carol, hi!' she said with surprise and instinctive trepidation. 'I wasn't expecting to see you tonight.'

'Obviously not,' rasped Carol, pushing past her sister into the hall where Arnie was standing, her eyes wild with jealousy. 'Now, what have the pair of you got to say for yourselves?'

'What are you doing here, Carol?' asked Arnie, his eyes dark with dread.

'You were late home,' she said. 'I guessed you'd be here.'

'You drove here on a foggy night like this just because I was a few minutes late?'

'No, I drove here because I suspected you'd be with *her* and I had to know for sure,' she corrected, her voice rising hysterically. 'And I certainly know the truth now, don't I?'

'Where's Donna?' Arnie asked.

She stared at him blankly, in such a state of confusion that she could hardly remember where her daughter was. 'With my parents,' she said at last.

'Thank God for that,' he said, his voice dropping with relief. 'For a minute I thought she was in the car . . . that you'd driven the car with her in it, while you're in this state, and in this weather.'

'You're not talking your way out of this one by making out that I'm in some sort of a state,' Carol said, looking from

Arnie to Gill with unveiled hatred. 'The cat really is out of the bag now.'

'Oh, don't be so bloody daft,' Arnie said with impatience. 'I called in to see Gill about—'

'About what, Arnie?' Carol said accusingly. 'Come on, let's see how creative you can be this time with your story.'

'Carol, please stop this,' Gill put in.

'Don't you talk to me, you cow.' Carol swung round on Gill and punched her hard in the face before clawing her cheek with her fingernails, drawing blood.

'Hey, now, calm down!' Arnie stepped forward and dragged her away from Gill. 'This has gone quite far enough, Carol.'

'What you two have been doing has gone too far for my liking,' Carol said, her face crumpling and voice breaking as she collapsed into tears. 'Well I've come to the end; I've had enough of it, do you understand? From now on you're welcome to each other.' Her voice was distorted with anguish. 'You've betrayed me and I want nothing more to do with either of you.'

'Carol, it isn't what you think,' said Arnie, recognising the depth of his wife's distress and softening towards her.

'Nothing's happened between us, I promise you,' said Gill, holding a handkerchief to her cheek to wipe away the blood. She was shocked by her sister's sudden display of raw despair. This had not been evident before. For the first time since all this began Gill perceived real pain, rather than just the tiresome ramblings of a neurotic woman seeking attention from her husband.

'Don't make things worse by insulting my intelligence,' Carol said, though the words were barely audible because she was sobbing so much. 'I'm not a fool.'

'What Gill says is true,' Arnie said emphatically, knowing now that he must tell the truth about why he was here. 'I only came here tonight to organise a surprise for you.'

'Oh, do me a favour,' Carol sobbed cynically. 'Which film did you pinch that from?'

'Please believe him,' Gill urged, her cheek smarting from the nail-wound and her head throbbing from the blow.

'Oh, shut up the pair of you!' Carol spat.

'You're torturing yourself for nothing, believe me,' said Gill.

'I won't believe anything you say ever again,' Carol said.

'Please, Carol . . .'

'I never want to see either of you again.'

Crying loudly, she ran out of the front door with Arnie in hot pursuit.

He caught up with her at her car and put a restraining hand on her arm. 'Carol, you're wrong—'

'Don't touch me!' she cut in, her voice deep and guttural. 'But . . .'

In reply she brought her foot up and kicked him sharply on the shin. As he recoiled in agony she gave him a violent shove which sent him crashing to the frosty ground.

While her sister was helping him to his feet, Carol got into the car and roared off into the mist.

'I'll go after her,' Arnie said, scrambling to his feet.

'Yes, I think you'd better,' Gill agreed, feeling shaken. 'God knows what she'll do if she's at home on her own.'

In a state of shock and bewilderment, Gill stood in the freezing street watching Arnie's car disappear around the corner.

With the combined effects of tears, the patchy fog and an icy windscreen, Carol's vision was seriously impaired as she headed for home, despite having got out of the car to scrape off ice that had quickly reformed. Peering ahead, her eyes narrowed in concentration, she drove towards the main road in a state of high anxiety.

Images of Gill and Arnie filled her mind, her venom towards them all-consuming. As for that story about him going to Gill's to arrange a surprise for her . . . Oh, really. Did they take her for a complete idiot?

If only it could be true, though. The thought was so pleasant, Carol lingered on the possibility of it being genuine. After all, it was still only early evening – an odd time of day for a romantic liaison, especially when he knew he had to get home to his wife.

Something else occurred to her too. Arnie had been wearing his outdoor coat, and had seemed about to leave. So he couldn't have been there long, because the shop didn't close until half past five, after which time he still had to cash up.

Don't be so naive, she told herself as she approached the main road – Arnie was there because he is in love with Gill and always will be.

The truth stayed in her mind with throbbing intensity. This was the first time she had accepted this as an actual fact rather than just a tormenting suspicion.

Whether or not they had actually been having an affair became irrelevant, as Carol finally accepted the painful fact that Arnie would never love her in the same way as he loved Gill, and there was nothing on God's earth she could do about it.

What a fool she had been to try. What a prize idiot she'd been to trap him into marriage in the first place. She'd been driving herself crazy with worry about them being together, when it would have made no difference to his feelings for Gill whether he was with her or not. Because he didn't just fancy Gill. He *loved* her. It was Gill he wanted to be with. Even though they hadn't been able to live together in harmony, they still wanted each other.

Tears rushed down her cheeks as the truth took root. But with this acceptance came a new feeling of peace, too, as she hit rock bottom, all hope of Arnie's love gone. She would be better off without him; she knew that now. But she didn't have the courage to try to manage on her own with a child to raise. God, what a mess she had created for herself – for all of them!

Engrossed in thought as she came to the junction with the main road, she gave a cursory glance to the right and saw only a bank of fog. In her preoccupied state she pulled out too swiftly...

Inside the car, the noise was deafening. The vehicle travelling from the right crashed into the side of hers with such force that both cars were shunted several yards from the point of impact.

The pain was so excruciating, Carol couldn't identify where she was hurting. She couldn't even cry out. Relief came only when she passed out, slumped over the steering wheel.

The noise of the impact of metal on metal had been muffled in the foggy night air. A line of cars soon began to form, stretching away from the crash site. Unaware of the cause, Arnie sat in the tailback, cursing the traffic.

Chapter Twenty-One

The medical team at Hammersmith hospital was doing everything they possibly could for Carol, but she had sustained serious injuries, and the family had been told to prepare themselves for the worst.

'This is all my fault,' Gill said to Arnie in the early hours of the next morning, when they emerged from the side-ward to allow Winnie and Hal a few moments alone with their daughter, even though she was still unconscious.

Phoebe was at Arnie's place looking after Donna. Craig had come to the hospital with Gill but had now gone off in search of coffee for them all, needing a break from the tension, she suspected.

'What on earth makes you think that?' Arnie asked, sinking wearily on to a seat in the corridor, grey with worry, his eyes red and shadowed.

'I should have been more patient with her, tried harder to convince her that she was wrong to doubt us,' she said, sitting beside him, her mind still racing though she was physically exhausted.

'If I'd managed to do that she wouldn't have gone rushing off in a rage – and in no fit state to be driving in such dangerous weather conditions.'

Arnie shook his head. 'You've nothing to reproach yourself for,' he said firmly.

'She shouldn't have been at the wheel of a car, and she *wouldn't* have been if it hadn't been for her suspicions about us.'

'I'm to blame for the accident, Gill, not you,' said Arnie.

'But you had no more chance of calming her down than I did.'

'I'm not talking about what happened last night,' he said grimly. 'The cause of the trouble goes back further than that.'

She waited for him to continue.

'I should never have got involved with Carol in the first place, when I knew that affection was the most I could ever feel for her,' he explained. 'I think she's always known in her heart that it was you I wanted and not her. That's the cause of the obsession that drove her to the brink of insanity, and caused her to go out in her car on such a terrible night. If she and I had never got together, she wouldn't be at death's door now.'

'Oh, Arnie, you mustn't think like that,' Gill said with feeling. 'Carol was determined to have you at any price . . . and you've given her so much. You've been a wonderful husband and a marvellous father to Donna. No man could have done more.'

'It wasn't enough to make up for the one thing I could never give her, though, was it?'

'You can't blame yourself for Carol's confused state of mind.'

'I can, because I caused it,' he said. 'I'm responsible for what happened to her last night, and nothing anyone says will make me believe otherwise.'

The conversation was interrupted by Gill's father, with the news that Carol had regained consciousness and was asking to see them.

Weak with nerves and hardly able to swallow because her throat was so dry and constricted, Gill followed Arnie to Carol's bed. She was barely recognisable. Her head was swathed in bandages, lips grotesquely cracked and swollen, cheeks grazed and blotched purple with bruising.

Winnie was sitting by the bed holding her daughter's hand. She got up and moved back so that Arnie could get near to his wife.

'Hi,' he said, gently taking her hand in both of his.

She opened her mouth as though to speak but was unable to. Visibly distressed by this, she shifted her head slightly, tears glistening.

'Don't try to talk, love,' Arnie said with infinite tenderness.

'Gill,' she managed to say after a great deal of effort.

'Gill's here.' He beckoned to Gill, who sat beside him, staying within her sister's range of vision which was limited because of her restricted head movement.

'You and Gill,' muttered Carol.

'Nothing's going on between us,' said Gill. 'I promise you.'

'I swear to you on my mother's life that I really did go to Gill's to ask her to help me in a surprise I'm planning for you,' Arnie said. 'She's agreed to look after Donna while I take you away for a weekend, just the two of us.' In a bizarre attempt to sound positive in a hopeless situation, he added, 'As soon as you get out of here we'll be off, just the two of us, for a weekend of self-indulgence.'

Carol managed a smile, more evident in her eyes than her mouth which was too sore to move more than a fraction. 'You and Gill,' she said again.

'There's nothing going on,' he told her again.

Clearly upset, she moved her head from side to side as far as she was able, to indicate that he had misunderstood her. 'I know now that I can never make you love me ... because you're still in love with Gill,' she managed with a great deal of effort, her voice scratchy and barely audible.

'Oh, Carol, please don't,' Arnie said, huge tears rolling down his cheeks. The fact that he wasn't in love with her didn't stop him aching with sorrow. There was more than one way to love someone.

'You don't understand. I want you to be together now,' Carol said in a whisper, her lips hardly moving. 'It's the way it should be. And Donna will be happy with the two of you. I trust you to take good care of her for me.'

My God, she knows she's going to die, thought Gill, her

blood running cold. She wants to bow out with good grace. She bit back the tears, hardly able to bear the pain. She couldn't move or speak, so she just sat there, frozen in the horror of the moment.

When she was able to function again a few moments later, Gill put her lips to Carol's brow just seconds before she slipped back into oblivion.

They were all with her when she died peacefully an hour or so later – all except Craig, who was overcome by youthful fear of death at such close range and retreated to the corridor.

Leaving the ward with the others in a stunned silence, Gill felt buffeted and broken inside. But she knew she must stay in control for the sake of her parents, whose suffering must surely be greater than her own; no parent expects to outlive their offspring. And, seeing Arnie so obviously tormented, she wondered how he was going to cope with the guilt of believing that he was responsible.

The shock-waves of Carol's death reverberated throughout the neighbourhood. She had only been twenty-nine years old.

The fact that it need never have happened made the pain even more intense for Gill. Carol hadn't been the most endearing person, especially lately, but she had been a part of Gill's life and her death left a void. She concentrated on comforting her parents to try to make herself feel better.

Surprisingly, her mother proved to be the soul of fortitude while her father shocked everyone by falling apart. The poor man was inconsolable. Even when the trauma of the funeral was over he couldn't contain his grief, and had to take time off work because of a tendency to weep on duty.

It was Arnie who worried Gill most of all, though. Deeply depressed, he seemed locked in a world of his own. Neither he nor Gill mentioned her sister's dying wish. Even apart from the fact that it didn't seem appropriate so soon after the death, Arnie's cool restraint towards her made it obvious that he wasn't interested in Gill other than as an aunt to his daughter, whom Gill looked after while he was at work, assisted by Winnie who helped out when she was teaching.

Gill was imbued with pity for Arnie. Carol's death alone was punishment enough, but to castigate himself for causing it must be living hell. She wanted desperately to help him, but he had created a barrier between them.

Despite her efforts to stifle a nagging feeling of resentment – that Arnie wasn't there for her when she needed him so badly – Gill couldn't help feeling let down. She didn't mention it to him until about two months after the funeral. The subject arose one day when he called at her house to collect Donna after work.

'I wanna stay here with Auntie Gill and Craig,' the little girl announced in recalcitrant mood, her saucer eyes resting on her father in a challenge.

'But you have to go home with Daddy now, sweetheart,' said Gill.

'Why?'

'Because it's where you live, darling, where all your things are . . . your toys and everything.'

'Don't wanna go,' Donna said, her mouth set determinedly. 'I like it here with you and Craig.'

'But Daddy will be lonely if he doesn't have his little girl at home with him,' said Gill persuasively.

'Won't.'

'He will,' said Gill.

'Don't care. I wanna stay here.'

'Put your coat on now, Donna,' Arnie intervened firmly, holding out the garment for her to put her arms in.

'No,' she said stubbornly.

'You'll do as you're told,' he said with noticeable impatience.

Giving him a reproving look, Gill said to Donna, 'Will you be a good girl and go into the living room with Craig for a few minutes – while Daddy and I have a little talk?'

The child scampered off and Gill led Arnie into the kitchen and closed the door behind them.

'There's no point in getting angry because your daughter wants to be with me instead of you,' she said, sitting down at the table and indicating for him to do the same.

'It's annoying when she won't do as she's told, that's all,' Arnie said.

'She's a little girl who's lost her mother and is with me all day while you're at work,' Gill said. 'It's natural she wants to stay because she feels secure here. And if you're no more cheerful at home than you are outside of it, then she's better off staying here.'

'I'm doing my best,' he said, staring at his clasped hands on the table.

'If losing your temper with her as soon as she shows the slightest resistance to what you want her to do is your best, then I don't think you're trying hard enough.'

'You're probably right,' Arnie said in a defeated way that twisted Gill's heart. 'I'm failing her like I did her mother.'

'You didn't fail Carol, and you're not failing Donna,' she told him. 'If you're failing anyone, it's me.'

He looked up sharply, his eyes resting on her questioningly.

'By pretending there's nothing between us,' she explained.

'Oh, that,' he said dully.

'Yes, *that*. It was painful enough staying apart when you were married to Carol. Don't let's punish ourselves by doing the same thing now that she isn't around,' she said. 'All right, so our marriage didn't work out. But neither did the divorce. It didn't kill what we had between us.'

'It was what we had that killed Carol . . .'

'It was her insane jealousy that killed her,' Gill said, having given the matter a great deal of thought over the last couple of months, and having come to the conclusion that neither of them was to blame for what Carol had brought on herself. 'She would have been paranoid about you even if there had never been anything between us. She was that sort of a person.

352

She needed so much love . . . too much. The man hasn't been born who could satisfy Carol.'

'I'm better off without a woman in my life anyway,' Arnie said grumpily. 'This way I can't ruin things for anyone else.'

'What about Carol's last wish?'

'She was seriously ill. She didn't know what she was saying.'

'I believe she did.'

'That's something we'll never know,' he said, shrugging his shoulders.

Gill studied her nails, wondering where to go next with this conversation. 'Has Carol's death changed your feelings towards me?' she asked.

'Having her death on my conscience dominates me to such an extent, I hardly know what I feel any more,' he confessed, his skin tinged with a terrible pallor even now. 'The guilt is already bad enough. It would be a thousand times worse if you and I were to get back together.'

'Carol's dead, Arnie,' she said. 'You can't hurt her now.'

'Guilt about Carol isn't the only thing I have to contend with.'

'You mean you're afraid to commit yourself to anyone again?'

'It scares the hell out of me,' he readily admitted. 'No relationship, no complications.'

'That's no way to live.'

'I'll only screw up like I did before and you'll get hurt,' he said. 'This way will be safer for us both.'

'You're going to spend the rest of your life running away, then?'

He looked at her broodingly. 'If you like,' he said. 'But I'd sooner do it than wreck your life.'

'And I have no say in the matter?'

'Look, Gill, there's a little girl in the other room who doesn't have a mother because of me,' he said, his voice quivering with emotion. 'My son was brought up without his father in the family home because I ruined our marriage. I'm a walking disaster and I've done enough damage. I don't want to do any more.'

'What about me?' she enquired. 'Don't my feelings count for anything?'

'They count for everything,' he said hoarsely. 'I want to be with you more than anything else in the world. To be a family with you and Donna and Craig is all I could ever want from life. But it would be the wrong thing to do.'

'I can see why you feel this way,' she said compassionately, 'but I don't think you're right.'

'It's time I stopped acting on instinct, doing what I want to do regardless of the consequences,' he told her gravely. 'It's time I did what I know is right.'

'Oh.' Gill couldn't help feeling dejected as it became more obvious that he was immovable on the subject.

'I'm sorry if I've been off-hand with you lately,' he said with genuine contrition.

'You're sorry, but you're still going to hurt me?' she said.

'I have to, Gill,' he said from the heart. 'I've needed you *so much*, and I knew you needed me – but I also knew that I would hurt you more in the long run if I didn't keep my distance.'

'None of us have been thinking straight after the shock of Carol's death,' she said. 'But I do know that you and I should be together, Arnie. It's what Carol wanted at the end.'

'It wouldn't work.'

Although she was deeply hurt and didn't agree with his logic, she knew it would be wrong to try to persuade him to act against his principles. This was something he obviously felt strongly about and must work out for himself. 'All right, Arnie, if that's the way you really want it, then that's how it will be,' she said, standing up with an air of finality and changing the subject. 'Now, about Donna – would it be a good idea to let her stay overnight here on the evenings that you're going to be late back from work? It's so late for her by the time you get her home and into bed.'

'I'd miss her.'

'You could always call in and see her on your way home if she's still awake,' Gill said. 'At least she wouldn't have to be dragged out in all weathers when she's tired.'

He still looked doubtful.

'It would probably be the best thing for her,' she pointed out.

'Yeah, I suppose so,' Arnie said with a sigh of resignation. 'Shall I let her stay tonight as she really wants to, or would that be giving in to her?'

'Let her stay,' Gill advised. 'By the time you get her home she'll be thoroughly overtired.'

'It's very good of you to look after her for me. I do appreciate it,' he said. 'It can't always be easy, what with teaching and everything.'

'My mum's a great help,' she said. 'And I enjoy having Donna. It's lovely having a little girl around the house.' She paused and gave him a small grin. 'I've managed to get her to do something I was never able to get Craig to do.'

'Really?'

'Yes. She's let me teach her a little tune on the piano,' she said. 'Only a very easy one, but it's a start.'

'Oh, you must be really chuffed,' Arnie said, brightening. 'Craig was always a non-starter in that direction.'

'He's never had any time for anything except football,' she said. 'But Donna really seems to like it. She's been pestering the life out of me to teach her some more.'

'That's Donna,' he laughed. 'She knows what she wants and goes all out to get it.'

Just like her mother, thought Gill. But she said, 'I'll say she does.'

'Thanks anyway, Gill, for looking after her,' he said.

'I'm glad to be in a position to do so,' she said. 'It's what Carol would have wanted.'

'Yes.'

There was an awkward silence as they both remembered Carol's last words.

'Let's go and tell Donna she can stay here tonight, then, shall we?' Gill said, stifling the need to cry at the sheer sadness of everything.

'Yeah, let's do that.'

They went into the other room, both feeling emotionally exhausted after such a highly charged interlude.

One day in April, when Winnie was shopping in Hammersmith, she was struck with a sudden unexpected longing for a chat with Phoebe Briscoe.

Not normally an impulsive woman, today she found herself inside the shop before she'd had time to think about it.

'I hope I'm not imposing,' she said, having been taken to the office where Phoebe and Len were working at their desks. 'But I just . . .' Her voice tailed off. She could hardly believe she had been so hasty in coming, and now she wasn't at all sure why she was here. 'Er . . . I felt like a chat, but it doesn't matter. I can see that you're busy. Silly of me to call to see you at work . . .'

'Don't be daft, love,' said Phoebe warmly. 'We're pleased to see you.'

She exchanged a glance with Len, who immediately caught on. 'Course we are,' he said, standing up. 'I've got something I need to do in the shop anyway . . .' He paused, looking at Winnie whom he had last seen at Carol's funeral. 'How are you now, ducks?'

'Oh, bearing up, you know,' she said, embarrassed to have burst in on them like this and painfully aware that Len was about to make himself scarce for her benefit. She couldn't imagine what had possessed her to come in off the street to talk to a woman she had never even liked.

'Cuppa tea?' Phoebe offered, smiling that warm smile of hers.

Winnie opened her mouth to reply and collapsed in tears

356

instead, sobbing loudly and uncontrollably.

Phoebe put her arms around her and held her. 'There, there. Let go and let it all out, love,' she soothed.

'Oh dear,' Winnie said when she was able to get a word out, mopping her face with her handkerchief and drawing back from Phoebe. 'I really don't know what's got into me today. This isn't like me at all. I'm ever so sorry.'

'Don't apologise,' said Phoebe. 'I expect you've been bottling up your feelings ever since Carol died. You had to let go sometime.'

'You're probably right,' Winnie agreed, blowing her nose. 'I got this sudden urge to talk to someone, and you must have come to mind because I was near the shop. Sorry to burden you . . .'

'You're not burdening me.' Phoebe was emphatic about this. 'I'm only too pleased to help. You should have come to see me before. We live in the same street; you only had to pop over . . .'

'I never thought . . .'

'It sometimes helps to talk to someone outside of your immediate family.'

'It just never entered my head,' Winnie said. 'I can't talk to Hal or Gill about how I *really* feel because I don't want to upset them any more than they are already.'

'You've been so busy being strong for everyone else, you've neglected your own feelings.'

'I suppose I must have,' she agreed. 'I've been worried sick about Hal. He's taken Carol's death so badly.'

'So I've heard.'

'Being the strong one has helped me to cope somehow.'

'But today you need someone to lean on,' said Phoebe.

'Yes, today I do,' she said.

'And the family isn't always the answer at a time like this, 'cause you're all hurting too much,' Phoebe said kindly. 'I mean, I was devastated by Carol's death, of course, but it isn't quite the same as losing my own child.' She shook her head.

357

'I can't even begin to imagine what it would be like to lose Arnie or John.'

'And I couldn't begin to describe it,' said Winnie. 'I don't think I'll ever get over it.'

'I don't suppose you will, dear,' said Phoebe thoughtfully. 'But the pain will lessen in time, I expect. It's nature's way, isn't it? And if it helps to talk about it, come and see me. You're welcome any time.'

'I've been feeling so queer, sort of tight inside,' said Winnie, 'and I couldn't seem to shed a tear.'

'Thank God you've managed it now,' said Phoebe, adding with a grin, 'That's what I do to people. One look at me and they burst into tears.'

'Oh, Phoebe,' said Winnie, laughing and crying simultaneously, 'you are a case.'

'At least I've brought a smile to your face,' she said. 'Now I'll pop out to the kitchen and make some tea.'

When she returned, Winnie said, 'I'll go as soon as I've had this. You'll be wanting to get on with your work . . .'

'Relax and have your tea,' said Phoebe. 'I'll catch up later.'

Glad of the drink to moisten her parched mouth, Winnie sipped thirstily.

'Arnie's taken Carol's death very hard,' remarked Phoebe. 'He's gone right into himself. He's like a different man now . . . so quiet and withdrawn.'

'Yet they weren't the happiest of couples, were they?' said Winnie.

'No.'

'It was always Arnie and Gill, even though they were divorced,' said Winnie. 'Carol just couldn't cope with that.'

'Actually, I thought Arnie and Gill would turn to each other for comfort, but they don't seem to have done it yet.'

'Perhaps they think it's too soon after her death to get back together,' suggested Winnie.

'I think it might be more than that,' said Phoebe, her brow creasing into a frown. 'He hasn't said much about it to me, but I get the impression that Arnie blames himself for Carol's death. I reckon that's what's keeping them apart.'

'That's terrible.' Winnie frowned. 'He shouldn't punish himself that way.'

'I agree with you, but we daren't interfere,' said Phoebe.

'No.'

'This is something he and Gill have to work out for themselves.'

'Yes,' agreed Winnie, pausing for a moment as she remembered her younger daughter's dying wish. 'I'm afraid you're right.'

She left the shop shortly afterwards feeling better than she had in ages, warmed by the knowledge that she could call on Phoebe at any time and receive a genuine welcome. After all these years, the woman she had always disapproved of had become her friend. It was a wonderful feeling.

One evening the following week, Phoebe and Len were drinking coffee at Phoebe's place, having been to the cinema to see *The French Connection*.

'I enjoyed the car chase,' said Phoebe. 'That was the best part of the film for me. How about you?'

'Er . . . yeah. It was quite entertaining,' Len said in a preoccupied manner.

'What's up?' Phoebe asked, noticing that he wasn't nearly as chatty as usual. 'You've been a bit quiet all evening. Things on your mind?'

'Mm.'

'Oh dear,' she said, immediately concerned. 'Well, you know what they say about a trouble shared . . .'

'It isn't really a trouble,' he said, stroking his chin ponderously. 'More a decision I am trying to come to.'

'Same thing applies,' she said, her blue eyes bright with friendliness, bleached hair dramatically corn-coloured in the electric light. 'But if you'd rather not talk about it . . .'

That's Phoebe, Len thought affectionately – ever respectful

of his privacy and careful not to intrude upon his space. In all the years they had been going out together, she had never once ventured beyond a certain point in her attitude towards him, because he had made it clear at the beginning that that was what he wanted.

But just lately Len had not been happy with the present arrangement. He had found himself wishing she was with him all the time, rather than just going out together and staying at each other's places occasionally. He often found he wanted to share a passing thought with her, or a joke. The other night he'd actually started to say something to her about something he was watching on the television, before realising that she wasn't there.

She'd become important to him so gradually that he hadn't noticed it happening. But she was an independent lady used to managing her own affairs, having brought up her sons single-handedly. Admittedly he had made the rules at the beginning, but she seemed quite content with the way things were. Maybe she wouldn't welcome a change.

'Oh, I want to talk about it all right,' he said now, looking worried.

'What's stopping you then?'

'I'm not quite sure what your reaction will be.'

'Oh Gawd, Len,' she said anxiously, 'I don't like the sound of that. I hope you're not gonna give me notice at the shop.'

'That's the last thing—'

'Thank God for that, 'cause I love my job.' She threw him a sharp look. 'But if it isn't that, what is it?'

He took a deep breath. 'I was wondering what you'd think about us . . . er, getting married,' he said.

'Well, it's taken you long enough to get round to asking me,' she said, grinning even though there were tears in her eyes.

'It has?'

'I'll say it has,' she said, her voice cracked with emotion. 'If you'd left it much longer I'd have been too old to get myself all glammed up for the wedding.'

'Not you, Phoebe. You'll never be too old to be the star of the show,' he said, adding hesitantly, 'But is that a yes?'

'You bet it's a yes,' she said, standing up with her arms open to him, her face wreathed in smiles. 'Come here, you daft bugger, and I'll show you just how much of a yes it is!'

Chapter Twenty-Two

'What's wrong, love?' Winnie enquired. Gill had called in to see her mother after shopping in North End Road market. Donna was at nursery school and Gill's father was out at work, so the two women were alone.

'Nothing.'

'Oh, come off it . . .'

'I've come to see how *you* are, not to burden you with *my* problems.'

'Don't worry about me,' said Winnie, 'I'm all right.'

'Yes, you're looking a lot better,' Gill remarked, noticing that her mother was much less emaciated than she'd been in the period immediately following Carol's death. There was colour in her cheeks again too. 'Being pally with Phoebe seems to agree with you.'

'It does.'

'What a pity she's moved to Len's place now that they're married. Just when you and she had made friends.'

'Still, she's only a bus-ride away,' Winnie said. 'And just knowing she's on the end of a telephone has made a lot of difference to me.'

'It's odd, the two of you becoming friends now that she's moved out of Maisie Road,' remarked Gill, 'after living in the same street for all those years and never much liking each other.'

'Yeah, it's funny how things work out,' agreed Winnie. 'I was a bit overawed by her until recently. She always seemed too full of herself for my liking. I was probably jealous of her if the truth is known, her being so sociable and popular, but I get on really well with her now that I've got to know her better.'

'I'm glad.'

'She's the first close woman friend I've had since before I was married,' Winnie went on. 'I was always too wrapped up with the family to bother about making friends. But it's nice having a female of my own age to talk to.'

'It must be.'

Outside it was cold and grey, with rolling clouds and rain in the air; inside they were cosily ensconced in armchairs either side of Winnie's living-room fire with coffee and biscuits.

'But don't change the subject,' said Winnie, fixing her daughter with a penetrating look. 'I asked you what was up.'

'What makes you so sure that anything's the matter?'

'I'm your mother,' she said, as though that was sufficient explanation.

'Oh, well, you'll get to know soon enough anyway, I suppose,' sighed Gill, cradling her coffee mug in her hands and regarding her mother thoughtfully. 'But don't say anything to Phoebe in case Arnie hasn't mentioned it to her yet . . .'

'About what?'

'He's moving away from London.'

'*Never in a million years!*' Winnie exclaimed, eyes wide with shock.

'It's surprising, I know, but it's true.'

'But Arnie would be like a fish out of water anywhere else.'

'That's what I think, but he seems determined to go,' said Gill. 'He wants to make a fresh start somewhere else with Donna.'

'Oh, that poor child,' Winnie said, shaking her head and tutting loudly. 'First she loses her mother, now she's going to lose you . . . and me, on a daily basis anyway.'

'I'm worried to death about her,' Gill confessed. 'Well, about them both really. I'm sure he's making a big mistake.'

'I'm certain of it.' Winnie sipped her coffee. 'Where's he going?'

'He doesn't know yet,' said Gill. 'He's still looking for a job in the trade journals. He doesn't seem to care where he goes, as long as it's away from London and all the bad memories. And, more importantly, away from me.'

'You?'

'That's right . . . He thinks his feelings for me caused Carol's death.'

'That's plain stupid.'

'He's got it into his head that it would be wrong for us to get back together, and it will be easier if he isn't around.'

'And you?'

'I've never stopped loving him.'

'I know that,' said Winnie, 'but will his going away make it easier for you?'

'I shouldn't think so. While he's around there's always a chance,' she said, 'once he's gone we'll drift even further apart.'

'Mm.'

'But my main concern in all this is Donna.'

'Poor little mite.'

'The trouble is, he really believes that his leaving London is the right thing for all of us,' Gill said, her dark eyes full of sorrow. 'He's making a sacrifice that he thinks will stop me being hurt, but he's hurting us all by doing it, not least himself.'

'There must be something you can do to make him change his mind.'

Gill gave a slow shake of the head, emitting a lengthy sigh. 'I've already tried,' she said. 'But there's nothing anyone can do. He's made up his mind and that's all there is to it.'

We'll see about that, thought Winnie. 'That man is his own worst enemy,' she said.

'You can say that again,' agreed Gill.

* * *

That same evening, Winnie took the tube to Chiswick Park station and walked to Arnie's house in the rain. Not wanting to worry Hal with the problem in the hope of solving it herself, she had told him she was popping over to Gill's for an hour or so. She didn't telephone Arnie to say she was coming in case he tried to put her off; and had guessed he would be at home because of Donna, who only stayed overnight at Gill's sometimes.

He seemed surprised to see her, but greeted her warmly. 'You're out of luck if you've come to see your granddaughter because she's fast asleep,' he told her, taking her raincoat and hanging it up in the cupboard.

'It's you I've come to see,' Winnie told him, sitting in an armchair in the living room. 'And I'll come straight to the point.'

'Cuppa tea?'

'In a minute, when we've had a talk.'

'Oh,' he said, sitting down opposite her.

She could see how tormented he was by the tension around his eyes and the grim set of his mouth.

'I've heard you're thinking of moving away,' she said.

'That's right.'

'You want your brains testing.'

'With respect, I think that's for me to decide,' he told her.

'If you were the only one affected, that would be quite true. But you're not, which is why I feel justified in interfering,' she said. 'You're going to hurt a lot of people by doing this, Arnie, particularly my daughter and my granddaughter. Donna needs people she loves around her at the moment. It would be cruel to take her away.'

'She's young enough to adjust, which is why I think I should do it now rather than later,' he said.

'Why do it at all?'

'I can't stay around here, Winnie,' he said forcefully. 'So the sooner we go the better – before Donna starts school,

365

when a disruption really would be upsetting for her.'

'And all this because you blame yourself for Carol's death?'

'Mainly, yes,' he said, too distressed to wonder how she knew.

'But you can't take a thing like that on your shoulders, son,' she said in a kindly tone.

Looking up sharply, Arnie said, 'I should have thought you would jump at the chance to blame me. You never wanted me as a son-in-law.'

'I admit that at one time I didn't think you were good enough for either of my daughters,' she said. 'You were a right tearaway when you were young and you've made plenty of mistakes over the years, including breaking Gill's heart . . .'

'Exactly.'

'But this last few years you've changed and I've seen you in a new light.'

His brows rose in surprise.

'You were a damned fine husband to Carol,' she continued. 'You did everything you possibly could to give her and Donna a good life.'

'It was my duty.'

'I saw the patient way you dealt with Carol's tantrums and her demanding nature,' Winnie continued. 'You never put a foot wrong when you had every provocation, especially as it was Gill you really wanted.'

'That obvious, eh?'

'To people who know you, yeah.'

'Unfortunately Carol knew it too – and that's why she died,' he said.

'That simply isn't true, Arnie,' Winnie said emphatically.

'She shouldn't have been out driving—'

'She was a full-grown adult with a mind of her own,' Winnie interrupted with feeling. 'You couldn't have stopped her going out in the fog that night any more than I could. You know as well as I do that Carol always did exactly what she wanted and no one on earth could make her do otherwise if she'd set her mind on a thing. As much as I loved my daughter, I wasn't blind to her faults. I brought her up, remember. I know just how difficult she could be.'

'Even so—'

'From what I can make out she was torturing herself unnecessarily about something that wasn't happening.'

'You're right about that.'

'So your conscience should be clear.'

'It isn't as simple as that.'

Winnie sighed. 'Don't break Gill's heart a second time, please, Arnie,' she entreated.

'That's what I'm trying to avoid.'

'You won't avoid it by going away,' she said. 'She wants you to be together. Don't let her down by turning your back on her. It's what Carol wanted at the end – the two of you together with the children.'

His brows rose questioningly.

'I was in the room . . . I heard her last words,' Winnie explained.

'She was very sick at the time.'

'She meant what she said, though. I'd stake my life on it.'

Arnie leant forward with his elbows on his knees, hands clasped. 'I can't explain how I feel,' he said. 'There's something deep inside of me that says it's wrong for Gill and me to be happy together. As you said, I've made enough mistakes. I don't want to make another. I have to do what I believe to be right.'

'You feel you have to be made to suffer for Carol's death?'

'Yes, I suppose that's about the size of it,' he said.

'And Gill and Donna and Craig have to be punished too?'

'Donna won't suffer, I'll make sure of that. And Craig's almost grown up now, he has a life of his own. Anyway, he's old enough to come and visit us on his own.'

'It won't be the same, though,' Winnie said. 'You've always lived near enough to have a close relationship with him. Don't throw it away.'

'Look, I know you mean well, Winnie, but I have to work this thing out for myself,' he said, standing up suddenly in an obvious state of anxiety. 'I'll make us some tea.'

'Not for me, thanks,' she said sadly, knowing there was nothing more she could say to persuade him. A change of heart had to come from within him. 'I'd better be getting off home. I've said my piece. That's all I came for.'

'I'll run you back,' he offered. 'It's a terrible night.'

'I'd rather make my own way, thanks,' she said. 'I need to be on my own for a while.'

'As you wish,' Arnie said, and showed her to the door, his limp noticeable as it always was at the end of the day.

Gales of laughter and the sound of a tinkling piano drifted from inside the house in Danny Gardens. Arnie rang the doorbell and waited on the doorstep in the smoky autumn dusk for someone to let him in to collect his daughter. He'd left the shop earlier than usual today, with the intention of spending more time with Donna before he put her to bed.

He wanted to get into the habit of doing this. When they moved away from London Donna would have someone other than Gill or Winnie looking after her while he was at work. Then it would be vital to spend as much time as he possibly could with his daughter.

His heart lurched at the thought of Donna in the care of a stranger. Soon she would be starting full-time school, but he still needed someone to collect her and look after her until he got home from work, and to be on hand in the holidays. A nanny cum housekeeper would be his best bet.

Winnie's visit last week had really set him thinking. Although he still couldn't agree with her about his staying in London, he had thought of little else but making sure Donna had a happy and secure future.

'Hi, Dad,' Craig said, opening the door and standing back for his father to enter, a smile lingering on his face as though he was still amused by some recent happening.

'Wotcha, son,' Arnie said. 'What's so funny?'

'Donna,' said Craig affectionately. 'You're just in time to hear her doing her stuff at the piano. Mum finished with her pupils early, so the two of them are having some fun.'

'I didn't think it sounded like an ordinary lesson,' remarked Arnie.

'Mum says Donna has a lot of potential, but I don't think she's gonna be entering any competitions just yet awhile.'

'She's much too little for anything like that,' said Arnie fondly.

'Yeah.' Craig glanced towards the closed door of the music room, from where the first few notes of 'Twinkle Twinkle Little Star' could be vaguely distinguished. 'You'd better go on in. I don't think Mum heard the doorbell.'

'She wasn't expecting me to be here this early,' he explained.

'I must get on, Dad.' Craig was already heading for the stairs. 'I have to get my gear ready for football training.'

'Okay, son.'

Arnie opened the music-room door and was instantly overwhelmed by an atmosphere of affection, so strong and sweet it brought a lump to his throat. Gill and Donna were seated side-by-side at the piano with their backs to the door, far too engrossed in what they were doing to have heard him come in.

He stood in the doorway, soothed and softened by the special essence of this room. It was not a tidy chamber by any means. Sheet music and primers were piled around the room in varying degrees of disorder; Gill's desk was littered with paperwork – she had always been a more dedicated musician than she was office worker.

Donna's small body was rigid with concentration as Gill showed her which notes to play. She hit a wrong key and giggles erupted before Gill gently corrected her, leaning over and kissing Donna's head in a natural action. More concentration, more laughter . . .

Arnie tried to curb the flow of tears. But he was so unbearably moved by their unity, the rightness of their being together, that he couldn't hold back. How could he have even thought of taking Donna away? She needed Gill and Craig. And Arnie needed them all. Carol had known and accepted this before she died.

Suddenly a future with Gill didn't seem wrong and selfish but the only right thing to do.

His thoughts were interrupted by Craig's exuberant tones booming from upstairs. 'Mu-m! Where are my football shorts?' he called urgently. 'They were in my sports bag and they've disappeared.'

Gill turned around to shout back to him and saw Arnie standing in the doorway. 'Arnie! I didn't realise you were here,' she said in surprise.

'Daddy!' Donna whooped, slipping off her chair and tearing towards him, throwing her arms around his legs and clutching him.

'Hello sweetheart,' he said thickly, sweeping her into his arms and kissing her.

'I'm playing toons,' she said proudly.

'I've been listening,' he said. 'You're doing very well.'

Donna peered into his face. 'Why are your eyes watering, Daddy?' she asked.

'Because I'm happy,' he said.

Craig's voice bellowed down the stairs again. 'Mu-m . . .'

'They're washed and ironed and in the airing cupboard!' she shouted.

'Oh!' he called back. 'I didn't realise they were dirty.'

'Dirty!' she screeched in amusement. 'I've seen less mud on the Thames riverbed at low tide.'

'They weren't that bad . . .'

'Give me strength,' said Gill, tutting affectionately. 'That boy wouldn't notice mud if I filled his bed with it.'

Donna struggled out of her father's arms and bounded up the stairs to Craig.

'Gill,' Arnie said, moving into the room and looking at her solemnly.

'What is it, Arnie?' she asked, frowning. 'You look worried.'

'Can you ever forgive me?'

Her heart fluttered, but she was afraid to raise her hopes. 'It depends which particular sin you are referring to,' she said, teasing him.

'For everything I've done to hurt you over the years, and especially for not being there for you since Carol died,' he said.

'Oh, Arnie,' she breathed.

'I've been confused and I'm so very sorry for everything,' he said softly. 'Please let me put things right.'

'I might consider it,' she said, slipping her arms around him. 'But only if you're very good and you stop all this talk about moving away.'

'I don't know how I could have even considered it,' he said, kissing her. 'This is where I'm meant to be, with you and the children.'

One spring afternoon the following year, Gill and Arnie and their family and friends were gathered in a stand at Wembley Stadium to watch Craig play football in the National Schoolboys' Cup Final. Pale sunshine slanted across the green and hallowed Wembley turf. The stands were resonant with the exuberance of youth, the adult contingent mostly made up of relatives of the players and PE teachers. The atmosphere was warm and vibrant, the excitement rising as the game drew towards the end of the first half.

'Come on you whites!' yelled Arnie, cheering on his son's team.

'Come on whites,' echoed Donna who was sitting on her father's shoulders.

'Get in there, Craig!' shouted Arnie. 'Go on, shoot, boy! Go on . . . *Yes!* Nice one!'

'Well done, Craig!' Gill shouted proudly, jumping up and down and squealing with excitement as her son scored a goal, then throwing her arms around Arnie in jubilation.

Sitting on Gill's other side were Hal and Winnie, next to Phoebe and Len.

'Makes you wanna weep with pride for our grandson, doesn't it, Win?' said Phoebe, shouting to make herself heard above the roar of the crowd.

'Not half!'

'Things worked out all right in the end for our two eldest,' said Phoebe.

'Yeah,' said Winnie, adding sadly, 'I'm still grieving for Carol, but at least Gill seems settled at last.'

Phoebe nodded. 'She and Arnie seem to be getting it right the second time around,' she said.

'They've had time to grow up since they got married the first time,' said Winnie.

'True.'

'Looks like you'll be having another wedding in the family before long,' said Winnie, peering beyond her friend to where John Briscoe was sitting with his arm around a pretty young woman with long blonde hair. 'He's had that same girlfriend for ages, hasn't he?'

'Yeah, they have been knocking about together for quite a while. I hope he settles down with her,' said Phoebe.

'She seems nice.'

'She's a lovely girl, and they get on well together. Of course it doesn't necessarily follow that they'll get married. People don't always bother these days.'

'It's all changed since we were young.'

'A different world.'

'You've never regretted marrying for the second time, have you, Phoebe?'

'I'll say I haven't,' she said. 'I've never been happier than I am with Len.'

A roar from the crowd drowned their chatter as a goal was

almost scored. They turned their attention back to the game, comfortable with each other and glad to be friends.

At half-time the others went to stretch their legs, while Gill and Arnie stayed in their seats drinking Coca-Cola and chatting. Donna went in search of ice cream with her two adoring grannies.

'Craig is so much like you were when you were young, on the football pitch, Arnie,' she said. 'It's almost uncanny.'

'Is he?'

'I'll say he is,' she said. 'It really takes me back.'

'Seeing him out there takes me back to my playing days an' all,' he said. 'He's achieved something I never managed and he's only fifteen.'

'What's that?'

'He's playing on Wembley turf,' he told her wistfully.

'Yes, of course,' she said, recalling a time when Arnie couldn't have spoken about the tragic end to his career without bitterness. 'It was tough luck your coming out of football the year before Borough FC got into the cup final.'

'Yeah, it was. Still, it's just the luck of the draw, innit?'

Gill remembered how traumatised he'd been at the time. How long ago those dark days seemed now. And how good it was that he was now able to embrace the game again, albeit only as a spectator and ardent fan of his son.

'Maybe you'll achieve your cup final dream vicariously through Craig,' she said, with a smile in her voice that made him turn to her in surprise.

Craig had recently received an offer from Arnie's old football club to join them as an apprentice player when he left school. Their scouts had seen him play on several occasions and were eager to sign him up with the idea of developing his talent for a future as a professional player. Very few boys were offered such an opportunity, and he'd been thrilled.

His joy had been marred, however, by Gill's insistence that

he should have a steady job. He'd been bitterly disappointed by her reaction. They all knew how much he wanted to accept the offer, but he said he would turn it down if it was going to upset his mother.

'You mean . . . ?' Arnie said now.

'I've been giving it a lot of thought,' she said ponderously.

'And . . . ?'

'And after seeing him play today, I've realised that I don't have the right to stand in his way,' she said.

'Oh, Gill, I'm really chuffed – and so will Craig be.'

'He's more than just good – he's brilliant. And a special talent like that must be developed,' she said. 'As Cherry was born to play the piano, so Craig was born to play football.'

'You've no need to worry about Craig,' said Arnie, 'he won't ruin his chances like I did, he's far too sensible.'

'I know now that he stands more chance of ruining his life in a steady job,' she said. 'Because his heart wouldn't be in it. He'd always be thinking of what he'd missed because of me.'

'I can't disagree with you about that,' Arnie said. 'My career as a footballer may have been short, but I wouldn't have missed it for anything.'

'As soon as the match is over I'm going to give him my blessing to go ahead and accept their offer,' she said.

'You'll make him the happiest lad on the planet,' he said, smiling at her and thanking God for this second chance with her.

'The teams are coming out for the second half,' Gill said, looking towards the pitch to see the youngsters resuming their positions.

The others returned to their seats, and Donna decided to sit on Winnie's lap as the second half got under way. Gill had only a distant view of her son from where they were in the stands, but she could see that he was in his element. Her heart swelled with pride as she watched him go into action, the personification of his father at a younger age.

As she was rummaging in her handbag for a handkerchief

to dry her tears, Arnie took her hand. Together they watched their son capture the heart of the crowd, a golden future ahead of him.

Always There

To Fred and the family, with love

Chapter One

Undesirables were no rarity on the streets of Notting Hill Gate after dark in 1954, and Daisy Rivers ran into a crowd of them one night as she walked home from the station.

A gang of Teddy boys, gathered outside a late-night café, were amusing themselves by hurling abuse across the street to a group of West Indian youths, whose wide-brimmed fedoras were visible in the neon glare of the street lighting, as characteristic of them as the DA haircuts were of the Teds. The balmy summer night was fraught with obscenities.

'Excuse me, please,' requested Daisy, a petite woman of twenty-five, unfashionably dressed in a cotton dress that was thin and faded from the wear of many summers. 'Can I get by?'

The Teds, who were blocking the pavement and some of the road, ignored her.

'Excuse me,' she repeated more assertively, 'can I get through here . . . *please*?'

Heads turned towards her but none of the gang moved; they just eyed her with a kind of lazy disdain. The Teds around here had a proprietorial attitude towards the streets, almost to the point where the other residents felt they should ask their permission to use them. It was impossible for Daisy not to feel intimidated by these lads, whose drainpipe trousers, crepe-soled shoes and drape jackets were synonymous for many people with the coshes, razors and flick knives some of them were known to carry beneath their Edwardian finery, and which gave the entire youth cult a bad name. Not every boy who belonged to this minority group was a thug – some just liked the clothes – but rebellion against authority and antisocial behaviour were common among the big gangs.

Daisy daren't allow herself to be too unnerved by these or any other dodgy characters because her evening job as a waitress at a Bayswater hotel meant she had no choice but to be out at night on her own. She needed the money to support her two little daughters.

'So, you wanna get by, do yer . . .? Well, we're not sure about that, are we, lads?' one of the youths finally responded in a slow, mocking voice. He had a heavily greased quiff and a frightening earnestness about him.

In the luminous glow from the streetlamps Daisy could see the malevolence in his eyes; could feel it emanating from him, a tangible thing. The implied violence in his manner stirred a feeling of panic within her which wasn't entirely related to this situation, and her nerves jangled even more. Desperate to get home, she tried to break through the wall of aggression by pushing past into the road, only to have a youth with protruding teeth and elongated sideburns place himself deliberately in her way. He was wearing the uniform of his kind – a long jacket, plain white shirt with a bootlace tie, a silver chain jangling on his wrist.

It had been a long day and Daisy was tired. 'Oh, for goodness' sake, can't you stop behaving like morons just for long enough to let me get by?' she snapped.

'Ooh, hark at her,' sneered someone.

'Dunno who she thinks she is,' said another.

'Look,' she began through gritted teeth, 'you lot might have nothing better to do than roam the streets making a nuisance of yourselves but I've been working and I want to get home.'

'Don't waste your time on 'er,' one of the others suggested. 'Let 'er pass.'

Daisy had neither the time nor the money to look glamorous, as such, but she was easy on the eye with her big tawny eyes, dainty features and luxuriant light brown hair that fell loosely around her face when it wasn't tucked into her waitress's cap. Her looks didn't go unnoticed by the Teds.

'Fancy her, do yer?' taunted his mate, sizing Daisy up.

'I wouldn't say no,' came the boastful reply. 'She's not smart or nothin'. But she's not bad-looking, and older women are more experienced.' He paused, grinning. 'If you know what I mean.'

'Get out of my way,' demanded Daisy, trying to push past.

'Don't waste your energy trying to stop 'er,' said one of the gang. 'She ain't worth botherin' with. We've more important things to do.'

'Like stirring up trouble with the boys across the street, I suppose,' blurted out the indomitable Daisy.

'So what if we are? They shouldn't be here, stealing our homes and our jobs. They ought to go back to the jungle,' was the youth's ignorant reply.

'That's just the sort of stupid comment I'd expect from a bunch of goons like you,' Daisy said bravely. But she was frighteningly aware that the Teds weren't the only promoters of racial tension around here, which was growing along with the increasing number of immigrants. The Government didn't seem to do much to ease the inevitable culture clash, and the housing shortage didn't help.

'Nigger lover,' the ignorant one accused.

'Black man's trollop,' said another.

'Don't you dare talk to me like that,' Daisy objected.

'Why are you sticking up for 'em if you're not going with 'em?' the first one wanted to know.

'Because of something you wouldn't understand,' was her answer. 'It's called decency.'

One of their number stepped forward and stood so close to her she wanted to retch from a pungent mixture of nicotine breath and Brylcreem. 'We've had enough of you. We don't want black sympathisers polluting the air near us, so sling your hook before we catch something off you,' he said to a roar of support from the rest, and they all moved back to let her through, pushing and jeering.

Angry, but realising that further argument would serve no useful purpose and probably fire them up even more on the subject, she went on her way, eventually turning into Portobello Road. This narrow, winding thoroughfare – which was flanked by terraces of small shops and drew crowds to its famous market by day – seemed dismal and sinister at this hour, the heady sounds of jazz music and drunken laughter drifting from the basement windows of a drinking club. There were still some people about, despite the late hour: men talking and shouting outside a pub, some of them staggering; a noisy crowd coming out of a grill-room restaurant; a gathering of youths leaning against a wall and wolf-whistling at some girls, who shrieked expletives in return. It was no wonder this area had a bad reputation, Daisy thought, even more so since the Christie murders at Rillington Place had given it worldwide notoriety.

Turning into a side street, she headed past bomb sites, tumbledown crescents and cavities where the bulldozers had been. Despite the much-needed slum clearance programme in the area, more slums had been created than cleared as the bomb-damaged properties deteriorated further and the housing shortage continued despite some of the slum-dwellers being rehoused in the new towns and suburbs.

This was a contrasting corner of London where occasional gentrified areas thrived alongside poor but cosy

4

neighbourhoods, the latter mostly tenanted by members of the indigenous population, where a sense of community and true neighbourliness still existed. Different again were the large, multi-tenanted houses that were filled with outsiders like Daisy, who lived there because they had nowhere else to go and the accommodation was cheap.

Benly Square came into this category. Huge terraced houses, split into bedsits and flatlets, stood around a small area of balding grassland scattered with broken milk bottles and household litter. Despite the general air of degradation, Daisy felt a warm feeling inside as she hurried up the crumbling steps of number twenty to the dilapidated front door with peeling paint and a rusty knocker.

This neighbourhood was a residential sewer and her tiny part of this house just a couple of shabby furnished rooms in the attic. But they were her home, hers and her daughters'. Rented accommodation was extremely scarce in central London, and unfurnished rooms almost nonexistent so she was grateful to have a roof over her head. Anyway, living in an area like this did have its advantages: there was a kind of freedom here because no one asked you who you were or where you came from or where your children's father was. She could hardly bear to imagine the persecution she would have had to endure in a respectable leafy suburb.

Refusing to dwell on the fact that the new landlord was making the future at the house uncertain for all of his statutory tenants lately, she put her key in the lock, heaving a sigh of relief to be indoors. She made her way up the stairs, careful not to trip on the craters in the lino.

'I'll make us some cocoa, shall I, dear?' offered Nora Dove, Daisy's friend, neighbour and baby-sitter, a middle-aged spinster who lived in the attic rooms across the landing. She was a tall, angular woman with strong arms, large hands and feet and a little round face that seemed out of proportion with the rest of her. Her poker-straight ginger hair was heavily peppered with grey and clipped to the side with kirby grips. Intelligent, vivid blue eyes beamed out from a sea of freckles, sometimes from behind the spectacles that she strung around her neck because she was always losing them.

'Yes, please,' approved Daisy, emerging from the adjoining bedroom where she'd been checking on her sleeping daughters. She and Nora usually had a companionable bedtime drink together when Daisy got home from work. It was almost a ritual.

'You look dead on your feet,' remarked the older woman, sniffing the milk bottle before pouring some of its contents into a saucepan and putting it on the gas to heat. She and Daisy were quite at home in each other's places and never stood on ceremony.

'We were busy at the hotel tonight so I do feel a bit whacked. But I shall sleep the sleep of the shattered and be fine in the morning,' she said, making light of her tiredness. 'You know me, I'm as strong as a horse.'

Nora nodded but they both knew that wasn't quite true. Daisy's strict upbringing in a Catholic orphanage had given her immense strength of character but her physical health wasn't so robust. Although she didn't make much of it, she was quite delicate and suffered dreadfully from bronchitis in the winter.

'Any problems with the girls while I was out?' Daisy enquired, taking a packet of digestive biscuits out of the cupboard and arranging some on a plate carefully. Poor living conditions hadn't robbed her of the will to maintain certain standards.

'None at all, dear. They're never any trouble to me, as you know.' Nora's beautiful diction was incongruous with her humble surroundings but natural to her, and her deep husky

6

voice somehow reflected her warm personality even though it made her sound like a chain smoker. 'They love that Enid Blyton book I got from the library to read to them.'

'I guessed they would,' smiled Daisy.

'They were really tired tonight, though,' Nora went on. 'Neither of them could keep their eyes open beyond the first few pages.'

'That'll be the effect of the warm weather and the fresh air, I expect,' Daisy suggested. 'I took them to Avondale Park this afternoon as a change from playing in the street. At least it's grass under their feet. They certainly got rid of some of their excess energy.'

'They told me all about it,' said Nora, smiling at the memory. 'They had a whale of a time.'

'I try to take them to the park as often as I can in the summer.' The tiny backyard was full of potholes and smelly dustbins so she couldn't let her children play there. 'They're happy enough playing in the street with their skipping ropes and whips and tops but I don't want them to become complete street urchins like some of the poor little devils who play barefoot out there while their mums are in the pub. Once they start school it won't matter so much because they'll be out during the day.'

'Life will be easier for you altogether when they start school,' her friend suggested.

'Yeah, it will but I'm not wishing the time onwards because I enjoy having them at home so much.'

'Enjoy it while you can, dear, they'll grow up fast enough,' nodded Nora. 'Anyway, I'll take them over the park on Sunday for a breather while you're doing your lunchtime shift at the hotel, if the weather's fine.'

Daisy's heart warmed at Nora's endless supply of kindness, all the more genuine because she refused to take payment for looking after Shirley and Belinda, who were just coming up to five and four respectively. Because Daisy couldn't bear the idea of having them minded by a stranger, she worked weekday evenings, when Nora was around to look after them, and the lunchtime shift on Sundays because Nora was at home then too.

'That'll please them,' said Daisy, as the two women settled down with their cocoa in matching ancient and torn brown leatherette armchairs by the open sash window through which a light breeze was wafting, bringing with it foul fumes from the gasworks. 'What would we do without you?'

'You'd manage,' said Nora, settling back. 'But you won't have to because I'll be here for you for as long as you need me.'

While they were talking Daisy glanced idly round the room. Even the most ardently self-deluded couldn't call it smart. But with a little ingenuity and minimum expense, Daisy had managed to create an air of cosiness, despite the landlord's ugly furnishings and the smell of damp that lingered even in summer. New curtains with a bright contemporary pattern added colour to the room and a few cheap ornaments and vases gave it a homely touch. She had even, with the previous landlord's permission, repapered the walls during the six years she'd been here, and bought a second-hand wireless set, which sat on top of the sideboard, from the market.

The kitchen corner was small and basic, with a cooker, a table and a free-standing food cupboard. The cold water sink, which she shared with Nora, was on the landing. There was a leaky, smelly communal bathroom and lavatory for all the tenants on the ground floor.

'You're so good to us,' said Daisy.

'No more than you are to me,' Nora was quick to point out. 'What sort of a life would it be if we didn't help each other?'

'You always seem to be the one doing the helping, though,'

observed Daisy, who was deeply indebted to this dear person, 'looking after the girls while I go out to work at night and giving me so much back-up support with them. I only wish there was more I could do for you.'

'You let me be part of your life and I don't need anything more,' Nora assured her. 'Besides, you've got the kiddies to bring up on your own, and I've only got myself to look out for. It's good for me to have someone else to think about. Anyway, I like to think I'm one of the family.'

'And you are.'

Daisy and Nora had become friends almost as soon as Daisy had moved in here. They were mutually supportive but the only practical way Daisy knew of to repay Nora, since she wouldn't take money, was to invite her to share meals with her and the girls on a regular basis and bring her a bottle of stout from the off-licence every so often.

'That means a lot to me,' said Nora.

Of a different generation, they were none the less two of a kind: both outcasts from society's norm, Daisy because she was an unmarried mother, Nora because she was a spinster. Nora, well-spoken and with such lovely manners, was an educated woman from a good family. Daisy had been told her friend's story and found it heartbreaking . . .

Having been an exceptionally bright pupil at school, Nora had gone on to train as a teacher. But while on the training course she'd fallen in love with a fellow student, a young man of a frail constitution. When she'd got pregnant, her outraged parents had banished her from the family in disgust but her lover had stood by her and promised to marry her. But the consumption that had taken so many lives back in the nineteen twenties had already got a hold on him and he'd become sick and died before the two had had a chance to marry.

The shock of his death had resulted in a miscarriage, the

strain and grief eventually culminating in a nervous break-down. Although she'd recovered, her loss of confidence was such that she didn't feel able to do anything other than menial kitchen work, which was why she now worked in a factory canteen instead of a library or a school, and lived in a shabby tenement house instead of a home of her own.

She found great pleasure in books, though. Daisy thought Nora must be one of the library's most regular borrowers, which accounted for her huge store of general knowledge. She was also an avid reader of newspapers so was always well informed about what was going on in the world. She was wise, sensitive and funny – some might say a little eccentric with her idealistic views – but Daisy admired her intelligence; it gave her such dignity.

Sadly, Nora was entirely alone in the world for there had never been a reconciliation with her family, or another man in her life. Once she'd reached an age to be labelled a spinster, men steered clear. Since Daisy had no family either, and had been motherless since she was five, they found strength and encouragement in each other. Nora was the most loving surrogate grannie her daughters could have wished for and the closest friend Daisy had ever had.

Now Daisy told Nora about the Teddy boys she had encountered on the way home.

'Young buggers. They're attention-seeking, that's all,' announced Nora. 'There was an article in the paper the other day about these Teddy boy gangs we've been seeing on the streets just lately. They're just working-class boys looking for some sort of an identity by wearing outrageous clothes and behaving badly.'

'Some of them can get quite violent, though,' declared Daisy, 'pursuing vandalism in the streets and dance halls. They smashed up a café the other week, according to the local paper.'

'Their violence is usually directed at other gangs, though, I think,' Nora pointed out in an effort to reassure Daisy. 'They might give you a lot of cheek but I don't think they'd actually harm you physically.'

'They were spoiling for a fight with the West Indian lads tonight,' Daisy told her.

'Because they're a rival group and the Teds see them as a threat,' surmised Nora. 'I don't think people like us are in any danger from them.'

'I don't either, but it doesn't feel like that when you come up against a crowd of them,' Daisy told her. 'I tried not to show it but they scared the pants off me.'

'Who wouldn't be scared?' Nora sympathised. 'Anyway, it's not nice for you to be out on the streets at that time of night on your own.'

'I don't have any choice, unless I put the girls into a nursery and go to work during the day,' Daisy reminded her. 'Working evenings suits me for the moment.'

Nora loved Daisy as her own, and her heart ached to see her struggling to raise her daughters with no contribution from their father, Nat Barker, who scrounged off her and used her. He hadn't actually deserted her when she fell pregnant but he hadn't helped her either. In Nora's opinion he was a thoroughly bad lot who didn't give a damn about Daisy or his beautiful daughters and didn't deserve her loyalty.

'Yes, I realise that, dear. So you'll just have to try not to let all this talk of Teddy boy violence in the papers frighten you on the way home. After all, we haven't yet reached a stage where a woman isn't safe to walk the streets at night, not even around here.'

Daisy cradled her cocoa mug in her hands, hesitant about her next words because she knew Nora didn't approve of the subject of her enquiry. 'Did anyone call while I was out?' she asked.

11

The other woman knew exactly who she meant but just said, 'No, dear. Nobody called.'

'Oh.' Her obvious disappointment twisted Nora's heart. 'I just thought Nat might have popped in to see the girls, if he happened to be passing. He knows I'd be at work so he wouldn't have called to see me.' She paused. 'Still, I suppose he guessed that the girls would be in bed.'

Nora believed that the main reason Nat Barker was likely to call on Daisy was to get his thieving hands on her pay packet. Either that or something of a carnal nature. It certainly wouldn't be out of genuine concern for her. Nora had been there to pick up the pieces on too many occasions to think well of him. He'd let Daisy down, broken promises and even stolen money from her purse. Her loveless childhood had made her strong and independent but it had also made her hungry for love, and she was a naturally warm and giving woman with a weak spot when it came to Nat.

'You're better off when he stays away,' she blurted out.

'Nat's all right,' defended Daisy, who had a tigerish need to stand by her man.

'He breaks your heart on a regular basis,' Nora couldn't help pointing out, though she did try not to make her feelings known too often because Daisy was so defensive of him. 'You should value yourself more than to let him go on doing it.'

'I never was attracted to gentlemanly types.' Daisy kept her tone light to avoid a serious argument. 'Anyway, he's the father of my kids, and we are sort of engaged. I know I don't have a ring but we do have an understanding.'

'If he had any sense of responsibility, you wouldn't have to go out waiting on tables at night to feed the girls because he'd be doing what he should and looking after you all,' was Nora's impulsive response.

In common with many women, marriage was the ultimate to Daisy. She didn't want a career or a good job or

12

independence, just marriage to Nat and a family life for her children. 'He'll make an honest woman of me one of these days, you'll see,' she said.

The older woman frowned. Nat had been promising to do that ever since Nora had known Daisy. 'You're worth better than him,' she burst out. 'The best thing you can do is get rid of him.'

'If only it was that simple,' sighed Daisy, and the troubled expression in her eyes pierced Nora's heart. 'You're an intelligent woman, Nora. You were in love once. You must know that we don't have a choice in these things, and you can't stop loving someone just because they don't treat you right. Maybe it's the bad boy in him that attracts me to him – women have fallen for rogues since time began. I don't know why, but I do know that I can't change the way I feel about him.'

Nora regretted having let her affection for Daisy cause her to speak from the heart. It was bad enough falling for someone like Nat. Daisy didn't need to have it rubbed in. 'I shouldn't have spoken out like that. You've enough problems. You don't need me going on at you.'

'That's all right,' said Daisy with a shrug. 'I know it's because you care about me.'

Nora nodded.

'In romantic stories the orphan girl usually claws her way out of poverty and finds herself a rich husband and lives happily ever after,' Daisy went on. 'Unfortunately, it doesn't work like that in real life. I didn't plan to get involved with someone like Nat, a ducker and diver who's never had a proper job in his life and who ignores me and the girls for weeks at a time. But I have done, and that's all there is to it.' She paused, thinking back to the time when Nat had asked her to marry him and how wonderful and romantic that had been. After he'd persuaded her to sleep with him, however,

13

he'd said the wedding would have to wait until he had enough money to give her the sort of wedding she deserved; then the delay had been because he didn't have a decent home to offer her. By the time she'd realised he was just making excuses she'd been too hopelessly besotted to end the relationship, and also pregnant with Shirley as a result of Daisy's idealistic Catholic views on contraception that she'd been later forced to revise for practical reasons after Belinda's birth. 'I have to go on believing that he'll marry me one day because I so much want us to be together.'

Lowering her eyes, Nora tightened her jaw with the effort of holding back. She'd already said too much on the subject. It was obvious to her that Nat Barker had no intention of marrying Daisy and she believed that the young woman knew that in her heart too. Nora had seen her reviled and abused because of her status as an unmarried mother; she'd even been refused help with the pain during labour when she was having the girls because she wasn't married. Nat could have spared her all that but he'd chosen not to because he was too damned selfish.

Nora's dearest wish was to see Daisy married to a decent man who would treat her with the love and respect she deserved. But what chance did a single woman with two kids and a ruined reputation have of finding someone like that?

'I can't pretend to like Nat or think he's right for you, dear,' she said kindly. 'But if he really is the one you want, I hope it works out for you, and I'll try not to go on at you about him.'

'Thanks, Nora.'

'And on a lighter note,' said Nora, hoping to defuse the tension with a swift change of subject, 'are you coming down the Porto tomorrow?'

'You bet,' replied Daisy. They always went to Portobello market together on a Saturday afternoon.

14

Nora had a sudden idea to remove any lingering awkwardness between them. 'How about us having a ceremonial tearing up of ration books as we won't be needing them any more after today?' she suggested.

'What a smashing idea.'

Daisy went to the sideboard drawer to get hers while Nora popped across the landing for her own. Together they ripped the ration books into little pieces and threw them in the air to celebrate the end of all rationing after fourteen years, with meat the last thing to go. As the books turned to confetti, Daisy began to laugh, filling the room with the infectious giggle that was so much a part of her. They had come to the end of a punishing era and it felt so good they both went into paroxysms of laughter at the sheer joy of it.

The streetlights shining through the attic window was sufficient for Daisy to see to get undressed without switching on the bedroom light and possibly disturbing the girls. Slipping her nightdress over her head, she looked at them in the double bed they shared, two heads close together, brown hair spread over the pillow. They were very much alike to look at and had their mother's colouring as well as her eyes. Studying them now in repose, Daisy found their innocence and childish beauty bringing tears to her eyes. Her relationship with her children was the most important and sustaining thing in her life.

Daisy had had a sister once a long time ago; the age difference between them had been about the same as it was between her own daughters. Before the orphanage, they'd shared a bed too, just like Shirley and Belinda did now. She remembered less about her sister than the indescribable pain of losing her when she'd been taken away for adoption. Daisy had cried herself to sleep every night for ages after that. She still couldn't think of it without wanting to weep.

It was as though her sister had never existed after that. Daisy had been told by the nuns that she'd gone away to a new life, and was ordered to forget her. She'd done her best because the nuns were strict disciplinarians and she'd been terrified to defy them, even in thought. Looking back at her childhood from the perspective of a parent, she could see that some of the nuns' treatment of the children had been harsh to the point of cruelty, and their methods were not what she'd use on any child of hers. But although she'd never felt loved, and had truly hated some of the nuns at the time, she'd always felt secure in their care. As an adult, considering her upbringing she'd come to the conclusion that the nuns must have believed their rigid regime to be in the children's best interests. The kids had certainly known what to expect – even if it was a good hiding.

There had been happiness of a kind at the home too, a camaraderie with the other children which meant she'd never felt alone. She'd been bereft of this security and companionship when she left there at fifteen to make her own way in the world.

At some point she must have been told that her father had abandoned her and her sister because that's what she'd grown up to believe. You learned not to ask questions when you lived in an orphanage in the nineteen thirties and forties because it wasn't considered right to give a child personal information.

She'd often wondered what sort of a life her sister was having and longed to see her again. But since Daisy had left St Clare's she'd been too busy surviving from day to day to do anything about finding her. She'd had a variety of jobs: she'd worked in a factory, been a café counterhand, and had got into hotel waitressing after the girls were born.

The very last thing she'd planned was to bring up two children outside of marriage. But having got pregnant, her

16

strict Catholic upbringing had ruled out an illegal abortion and she hadn't been able to bring herself to put her babies up for adoption, or to do what her father had done to her and her sister, just abandon them. She was very glad she hadn't been driven by desperation to take any of these steps because the girls were her *raison d'être*. Her religious faith had been a great strength and comfort to her through it all, in spite of the guilt that came with it.

Gently she covered them up, placed a kiss on each brow and got into the single bed beside them, saying a silent prayer for all the people she cared about, including one of the gentler nuns at St Clare's with whom Daisy had stayed in touch by letter.

In reflective mood as she closed her eyes, she found herself troubled again by the same uneasy feeling she'd had earlier that had been triggered off by the Teddy boys' threatening attitude. Her eyes snapped open as she tried to banish tormenting thoughts. When she was feeling calmer, she turned over on to her side and curled up into her favourite sleeping position.

She was just dozing off when she was woken with a start by a loud din from downstairs: jazz music filling the house and booming voices, shrill laughter, drunken singing. The unmistakable sound of a riotous party.

'Oh, no, not again,' she groaned, because this sort of thing was getting to be a regular occurrence since the musicians had moved into the basement. Nobody minded a party but these shindigs didn't start until decent people had gone to bed and went on until all hours. It was generally believed among the statutory tenants here that the rowdy parties were being encouraged by the landlord as part of his plot to harass and drive them out so that he could relet the rooms at higher rents.

Judging by the fact that all complaints had fallen on deaf ears, the speculation would seem to be correct. Rent restrictions meant nothing to the unscrupulous man who had recently taken over the house. He knew his tenants weren't likely to report him because they were of the disadvantaged classes who felt powerless against the likes of him and his strong-arm tactics.

Rumour had it that he wanted to emulate other landlords in the area by removing white tenants so that he could exploit West Indian immigrants by charging them per head rather than for the room with as many as six to a room. The newcomers were particularly vulnerable because many property owners refused to rent to them. Some of the tenants here believed that the landlord also wanted to relet some of the rooms to prostitutes on a daily basis.

'Mummy,' murmured Shirley sleepily, 'what's happening? What's that noise?'

'It's all right, darling,' soothed Daisy, gently brushing the child's hair from her brow with her hand. 'It's only someone having a party. Go back to sleep, love, or you'll wake Belinda.'

In the attic, the noise from below wasn't as distressing as it would be for the tenants on the lower floors, and the children usually managed to sleep through most of it, albeit restlessly. Waiting until Shirley had gone back to sleep, Daisy went across the landing and tapped on Nora's door. She could hear people downstairs shouting at the basement tenants for the noise to stop and banging on the door of the offenders.

'Just popped across to see if you're OK with all the racket going on downstairs,' she said when Nora opened the door.

'I'm all right, dear,' Nora assured her. 'It's just a question of sticking our fingers in our ears and trying to sleep through it. As we know from past experience, if we try to make them stop they'll do it all the more. The tenants who are down there objecting ought to realise that by now.'

Daisy nodded in agreement. Previous confrontations with

the basement tenants had resulted only in foul language and even louder music. 'I think I'd better pay our landlord a visit in the morning,' she decided. 'Something's got to be done about this. Can the girls come in with you while I'm out?'

'Course they can.' Nora looked worried. 'But you be careful. He's a nasty piece of work and can be dangerous to those who cross him, so I've heard. He isn't much of a muscleman himself but the blokes who work for him are real heavyweights.'

'Mm, I know,' said Daisy. 'But I can't just sit back and take it.'

'I'll come with you?' offered Nora.

'No. I'd rather you stayed here to look after the girls, if you don't mind.'

'Right you are, dear,' Nora agreed. 'Good luck. And mind how you go.'

'Don't worry about me,' said Daisy, moving back to her own door. 'I'll see you in the morning.'

Roland Ellwood lived in a ground-floor flat in a tenement house he owned a few minutes' walk from Benly Square. He didn't try to hide away from his tenants so Daisy didn't anticipate trouble in getting to see him. For the moment it suited him to be seen to be a caring landlord who was accessible to anyone with a problem, something she guessed would change as soon as he got rich enough to conceal himself in a mansion somewhere away from the area.

'So . . . what can I do for you?' he asked, showing her into a sitting room-cum-office where easy chairs were intermingled with a desk and a filing cabinet.

'It's about the people in the basement flat at number twenty Benly Square and the noise they make at nights with their parties,' she explained.

A small dapper man of about forty-five with heavily

greased grey hair worn flat to his head and thin features, Ellwood was well turned out in a suit, but flashy with a bow tie and purple waistcoat. He leaned back in his chair, smoking a cigar and looking bored with Daisy's comments.

'People are entitled to let their hair down now and again, you know,' he pointed out.

'Of course they are. And nobody minds it now and again but this is a lot more often than that,' she told him. 'It's two or three times a week and it goes on for most of the night. The tenants on the lower floors are being driven mad.' She paused, giving him a knowing look. 'But you already know that, don't you?'

'It has been mentioned to me, yes,' he confirmed, his manner studiously congenial.

'Well, I'm mentioning it again.'

'With the idea that I'll have a few words with the offenders, I assume?'

'As long as you don't tell them to carry on with the good work,' she blurted out.

His dark, deep-set eyes hardened. 'What exactly are you implying?' he asked.

'I think you know.'

'Do I?' His gaze didn't falter.

'You're trying to drive us statutory tenants out so that you can let the flats at a higher rent and make a fortune,' she informed him briskly. 'Well, you won't get away with it as far as I'm concerned because I have a proper rent agreement from the previous owner and I'm staying put. So please get the noise at nights stopped. I've got two little girls and they need their sleep.'

Ellwood puffed on his cigar and exhaled a cloud of smoke. 'I'm not trying to drive you out but neither am I forcing you to stay,' he said after some consideration. 'Maybe you'd be happier living somewhere quieter.'

'And play right into your hands?' she replied, puffing her lips out in disgust. 'Not likely.'

His manner changed completely, the urbane attitude replaced by brutal honesty. 'You'd do well to realise, you stupid woman, that all my money is tied up in the houses I own and I've every right to get as much as I can in rent. I'm the one who has to pay for all the repairs and maintenance.'

'Repairs! Maintenance!' Daisy exploded. 'When do you ever do either? You've done nothing since you bought the house. The banisters are broken, the paint's peeling and the bathroom basin started leaking soon after you took over, and you've done nothing about any of it.'

'If you're so dissatisfied I'm sure you'd be better suited living somewhere else,' he suggested again.

'Oh, no. As I've just told you, you won't get rid of me that easily,' she made it clear. 'I'm not going anywhere.'

'In that case you'll have to put up with any . . .' he paused; she waited, 'with any little inconveniences that might arise, won't you?'

She knew he was threatening her. 'I'm not going to just sit back and take it, if that's what you think,' she declared.

Ellwood gave her a contemptuous look and dropped all pretence of civility. 'You're taking up space in my house that I could fill more profitably and, yes, I do want you out,' he informed her gruffly. 'People are crying out for accommodation in this area and I don't have any petty restrictions in my properties. I'm not prejudiced like some landlords around here. You won't see a "No Blacks, No Irish, No Dogs" sign on any of my houses.'

'I should think not,' said the outraged Daisy.

'There are plenty who aren't so easy-going as I am.' He paused, fixing her with a vicious look. 'I must be broad-minded. I even let unmarried mothers in,' he said pointedly.

She should have been immune to this sort of insult but it

still hurt. She was suddenly painfully aware of what she had known all along: that he had all the power in this argument and she had none. But she wouldn't give in. 'You're all heart. You'll have me in tears in a minute,' she said sarcastically.

'The fact of the matter is, I want you and the rest of the statutory tenants out of my house,' he continued. 'And you'll go, I can promise you that. As you've told me, I can't throw you out because of your agreement but you'll go of your own accord, I can guarantee it. It might take a bit of time but you'll leave and be glad to.'

Put like that, it was frightening. 'This is harassment,' she retaliated. 'I've a good mind to report you.'

'Who to?' he challenged, his thin lips curling into a triumphant smile. 'The authorities won't be interested because this is private rented accommodation, not council housing. With the housing shortage in this area being so serious, I'm sure they've got better things to do with their time than bother about some moaning mother of two who got herself knocked up.' He paused for a moment, looking at her with malice. 'And not just once either, but twice, and probably doesn't even know who the father of her kids is.'

'That isn't true.' Daisy was shaking with rage now.

'There are no witnesses to this conversation so it would just be your word against mine, if you were foolish enough to go to the authorities,' Ellwood went on as though she hadn't spoken. 'And no one is going to take any notice of you. No one cares about scum like you and your kind – no-hopers who don't have two ha'pennies to rub together and no place in decent society.'

It was as much as Daisy could do to keep her hands off him but she managed to restrain herself, only because she didn't want to give him even more of an upper hand. 'You really are an evil little man,' she told him.

'If you say so,' he said indifferently. 'Though I see myself more as a good businessman. So why don't you go and get the local paper and see if you can find yourself somewhere else to live because you don't have a future in any of my houses.'

'You won't force me out.'

'Just watch me.' He drew on his cigar. 'In the meantime, I'd like you to leave. I'm a very busy man.' His tone was vicious. 'So get out.'

'I'll be glad to,' she said. 'Just being in the same room as you makes me want to throw up.'

And with that she hurried from the house. For all her ostensible courage, her legs felt like jelly and the stress had made her feel sick. Nora was right: he was a dangerous man. She wouldn't be beaten by him but his threats were scary, mostly because she had the girls to think of.

Unfortunately, she couldn't afford to pay more rent than she paid now, even if she could manage to find somewhere else to live, which was doubtful. But Roland Ellwood obviously intended to make life wretched for her and the others if they stayed on. Terrorising tenants was his speciality, so she'd heard. What made it even harder to take was knowing that some of what he said was true. People like her and Nora and the other tenants just didn't have a voice against someone like him.

All she could do was deal with whatever came as best as she could and not be driven out, she told herself, as she hurried through the grimy, run-down streets. There was always the faint hope that Nat would come to the rescue by keeping his long-term promise to marry her. But it was such a remote possibility, the thought didn't linger.

Shirley and Belinda were very taken with some glass beads on a stall in the Portobello market that afternoon. Amber and emerald winked in the sunlight among strings of simulated pearls and flashy cameo brooches.

'Ten bob,' announced the female stallholder, a bottle blonde with a shelf-like bosom and a multitude of chins.

'You do mean for two necklaces, don't you?' queried Daisy meaningfully.

'Don't try and rob me,' objected the woman. 'These are quality gear, the genuine article. Ten bob each.'

'Oh, do me a favour,' bartered Daisy. 'They're too expensive at half that price.'

'Daylight robbery,' put in Nora.

'OK, two for ten bob, one each for the little girls and that's my last offer,' said the woman.

'Five bob each for junk like that?' was Daisy's sparky response. 'A shilling is the most I'd pay.'

'Four bob each,' the woman offered.

'Three,' countered Daisy.

'Now you're just taking the mick.'

The stallholder was obviously not prepared to haggle further so Daisy and the others moved on. Her daughters looked somewhat downcast but not for long because they weren't used to expensive treats. Anyway, they still had the highlight of the week to look forward to – a visit to the sweet shop where they could choose what they wanted. The narrow street was heaving with noisy humanity and fringed by stalls displaying everything from cucumbers to Chippendale chairs.

Saturday was the big day here, especially recently since the antique trade had begun to arrive and the market was expanded by a few antique and junk stalls. Daisy and co. wandered from stall to stall, seeing silver trays and meat platters, antique clocks and Victorian china. Even rusty old lamps found a buyer here.

Being out among the crowds, with good-humoured bargaining all around her, cheered Daisy up after the traumatic meeting with Roland Ellwood. Nora had been a tower of strength too. Nothing was ever quite so bad when she'd talked to her about it.

Having rummaged through the entire stock at a second-hand clothes stall, they wandered on to the food barrows where Daisy bought fresh fruit and vegetables, giving the girls an apple each to eat right away.

'Wotcha, Daisy,' said a deep male voice, a hand simultaneously clamped on her shoulder. 'I guessed I'd find you around here somewhere.'

'Nat,' said Daisy, smiling at a stockily built man in a navy-blue pinstripe suit and a garish, multicoloured tie. Every inch a spiv, he had rich dark eyes, a dazzling smile and black hair with long sideburns. He wasn't handsome as such – his features were too uneven for that – but his rough charm was magnetic. 'We haven't seen you for ages.'

'Sorry about that, love, but I've been busy,' he said, spreading his hands apologetically.

'Doing what?' she enquired lightly.

With a nonchalant shrug, he cocked his head and told her uninformatively, 'Oh, a bit o' this, a bit o' that. You know me, I've always got something on the go.'

He dealt in anything with a potential market and carried out his business anywhere he could find customers: in pubs and clubs, even from a suitcase in the street.

'Surely you could have found the time to call round to see us?' she said in a tone of mild admonition.

'Don't give me a hard time,' he said with boyish persuasion.

'Well, you could have made an effort.'

'You know I'd have been round if I'd had the time,' he went on. 'Anyway, there's no point in my coming round in the evening, is there, as you're out working?'

'You could have popped in to see the girls.'

'OK, I should have but I didn't and I'm wrong and I'm sorry,' he reeled off. 'But don't have a go at me.'

Shirley had cuddled closer to her mother, Belinda was clutching Nora's hand. They were shy of their father, who rarely took any notice of them. When he came to the flat it was usually after they were in bed. Daisy drew comfort from the fact that he hadn't deserted her when she fell pregnant like many men would in that situation. But she wished most ardently that he would take more of a fatherly role, and constantly strived to encourage some sort of a rapport between him and his daughters, for their sake.

'Hey, you two,' she said, smiling down at them reassuringly, 'aren't you going to say hello to your dad?'

''Ello,' they chorused obediently, unusually subdued.

'Wotcha, girls,' Nat said awkwardly. He wasn't at ease with children; never knew what to say to them so said the first thing that came into his mind. 'How's school?'

'We don't go to school yet,' informed Shirley, staring at him accusingly. 'We can't start until we're five.'

'Whoops. Sorry.' He grinned, unbothered by the mistake. 'Trust me to get it wrong.'

Nora made a timely intervention. 'Come on, girls,' she said kindly. 'Let's walk on to the sweet shop while your mum and dad have a chat, and you can start choosing what you want. I know how long it takes you to make up your mind sometimes.'

'I'll meet you there in about ten minutes,' said Daisy, and they trotted off holding Nora's hand, two endearing little figures in summer frocks, each with light brown hair tied with a bow of blue ribbon on the side.

'I'll see to it that she doesn't keep you waiting, Nora,' Nat called after them.

'Sweet, aren't they?' she said to him, yearning for some sign of affection for them from him.

But all he said was, 'Yeah, they're nice kids, a real credit to you, Daisy.'

'Thanks.'

'So, how's it going?' he asked.

'I've had better days,' she told him.

'Why, what's happened?'

'I had a run-in with the landlord this morning.' She went on to tell him more about it.

'Blimey, that's a bit rough,' said Nat, who had furnished rooms in Paddington which he never offered to share with Daisy or invited her to visit. He said the place was barely big enough for one and was far too small to accommodate visitors.

'You can say that again.'

'There's a lot of that sort of thing going on around here.'

'Of course, if we were to get married,' Daisy began in a persuasive tone, 'that would solve my problem.'

She knew she was being pushy but Nat was the sort of man who needed a shove to get him to make any sort of a commitment beyond the next half-hour. He wasn't the marrying kind but she had an unwavering belief that she was the only woman in his life and if he married anyone it would be her; she also believed that if she waited long enough it would happen.

In Daisy's opinion love wasn't about owning someone and she would never try to do that. But at the same time she had been involved with him since she was nineteen and felt she knew him well enough to exert a little gentle pressure from time to time.

'All in good time, babe,' he said predictably, putting his head to one side and tapping it. 'I've got it in mind. It's all up here.'

'Fibber,' she joshed, keeping the mood light because if she came on too strong he'd just find an excuse to leave.

'Don't be like that,' he coaxed, putting his hand on her arm. 'You know you're the only woman for me, and that I'll marry you, eventually.'

'I hope you manage it before the girls make grandparents of us,' she quipped.

'Oh, Daisy, you are a case,' he laughed.

'And you're a dead loss as a boyfriend.'

'You don't mean that.'

'I do,' she said, but there was a smile in her voice. 'I don't know what I see in you.'

'It must be my good looks.' He was teasing her.

'It certainly isn't your modesty.'

'Being humble never got anyone anywhere.'

'You might be right at that,' she agreed, becoming deadly serious as she remembered the meeting with the landlord.

Seeing the change in Daisy's expression and suspecting that things might begin to get heavy, Nat effected a swift change of subject. 'You and me ought to have a night out together soon, when you get an evening off. What do you say?'

She threw him a shrewd look. 'You wouldn't be trying to change the subject so that I won't mention the M word again, would you?' she suggested.

'As if I would . . .'

'You do it all the time.'

He made a face. 'You know how allergic I am to it.'

'Oh, Nat,' she rebuked.

'I thought you'd like a night out.'

'I would.'

'Well then, let's go out and enjoy ourselves,' he grinned. 'Plenty of time to talk marriage, later on.'

She should have been angry but suddenly it didn't matter because he gave her one of his most melting smiles and took her in his arms. All she could think of was how good it felt to be close to him; even after all this time the magic was still there. As they stood there hugging each other with the crowds milling about all around them, she remembered why she had fallen in love with him all those years ago when they'd met in a café in Paddington where she'd been working. They'd had such fun in those early days. He could be loving and tender now too, when he was in the mood.

Nora only saw Nat's worst side, the side of him that caused him to let Daisy down and refuse to give her the respectability of marriage. She didn't see the tenderness he showed to her when they were on their own, or experience the sweet intensity of feeling that filled her whenever he was near. Daisy realised that a lot of women wouldn't put up with his offhand ways. The truth was she would sooner have him this way than not at all.

When, in the next instant, he tried to cadge money from her, she despaired of him. Her common sense told her she would be better off without him. But there was no logic to her feelings and she knew with absolute certainty that she could never give him up.

Chapter Two

Later that same day June Masters was dressed in a sun top and shorts, and sprawled out in a deck chair on the top-floor balcony of the Cliff Head Hotel on the outskirts of Torquay. The view of the bay was stunning from here. Elegant white hotels sat high above thickly wooded slopes that swept down to golden sands, the entire scene washed with early evening sunlight that turned the sea turquoise. The beaches and promenade were beginning to empty as holidaymakers headed back to hotels and guesthouses for their evening meals.

Glancing at her watch, June finished her tea and hurried inside to the flat, which was cool and luxuriously appointed, as might be expected of the private accommodation of the proprietors' son and his wife.

'Ah, there you are. I was just about to give you a call,' said her husband, Alan, appearing from the bedroom, fastening a black bow tie around the neck of a starched white shirt. 'Thought you might have forgotten the time.'

'No. I was just enjoying a few extra minutes in the sunshine. It's lovely out there,' she told him, taking her teacup to the kitchen, then joining him in the bedroom. 'But I'll start getting ready to go on duty now.'

Because they worked such late hours in the hotel, they needed to rest for an hour or two in the afternoons. He usually went to bed; she just sat on the balcony if the weather was nice, or relaxed in an armchair inside if it wasn't.

'Did you get some sleep?' she enquired.

'Yeah, I managed an hour and feel all the better for it,' he replied, slipping into a black tuxedo. 'I'll be glad later on as we're in for a busy night. There's nothing worse than feeling shattered on duty. I don't know how you keep going without a nap.'

'Plenty of staying power, I suppose,' she suggested. 'I never feel tired enough to sleep during the day.'

'You should come to bed with me,' he suggested waggishly. 'You'd sleep then . . . eventually.'

'Animal,' she accused jokingly.

'I try,' he laughed.

She smiled, slipping out of her clothes and into a housecoat ready for a bath. 'So . . . you reckon we're going to have a busy night, then?'

'Very,' he nodded, brushing his hair in front of the wardrobe mirror. 'Saturday nights in high season are hectic enough anyway, but it'll be especially mad tonight as we have a couple of parties of nonresidents booked into the restaurant as well. We're stretching our numbers to the limit.'

'But we'd be worried if we weren't rushed off our feet at the height of the season,' she commented.

'Exactly,' he agreed. 'It isn't good business practice to turn people away if we can possibly accommodate them.'

Alan was front-of-house manager in his parents' hotel and also a partner in the business. June worked in reception but would turn her hand to anything. Having worked here for nine years, she'd learned to be versatile.

But now Alan turned to her, looking magnificent, his brown curly hair brushed back from a tanned countenance blessed with shandy-coloured eyes and fine-cut features. At twenty-eight he was gorgeous and she was proud to be married to him, even after seven years together.

'I'll head off downstairs then.' His voice was deep and rich, a boarding school education having eliminated any tendency towards a Devonshire accent. 'I'll see you down there when you're ready.'

'You don't need to go on duty yet,' she pointed out, purely with his interests at heart. 'You could stay up here for another half-hour at least.'

'I'd sooner go down,' was his predictable response. 'You know me, I'm never happier than when I'm in the thick of it down in the hotel.'

'I just thought you could relax for a while longer, love, as it's going to be a long night.'

'As I'm ready I might as well go.'

She shrugged. 'If it's what you want,' she said amiably.

Alan had been brought up at the hotel and, apart from a spell in the army, had worked here since he left school. He was totally absorbed in the affairs of the Cliff Head, and dedicated to his job. Although it carried some weight in theory, he was very much subject to his parents, especially when it came to decisions. They lived off-site now but were still active in the running of the hotel, albeit that they worked fewer hours than they had in their younger days. They had a variety of duties behind the scenes, and June couldn't imagine them ever letting go of the reins, especially Alan's mother.

'See you later then,' he said, kissing her lightly on the cheek and striding purposefully from the room.

June had a quick bath and got dressed in a crisp white blouse and black skirt deemed suitable by Alan's mother for the receptionist of this prestigious hotel, which was traditional and run on formal lines.

Applying her make-up at the dressing-table mirror, June saw an attractive face with fine bone structure, striking dark eyes and glossy black hair worn in a sleek shoulder-length

33

bob, which was looked after regularly by one of the town's leading hairdressers.

She was well aware of the fact that she was extremely fortunate. At twenty-six she had more than most women could reasonably hope for: a husband she adored, a comfortable home, nice clothes and no shortage of money. People probably said she'd done very well for herself, and they would be right.

Following a miserable childhood she'd left home in a London suburb at fifteen, found cheap lodgings and worked in a factory until the war ended two years later. One day she'd spotted an advertisement in the *Evening News* which had changed her life. It was for a kitchen worker at a Torquay hotel. Attracted by the thought of living on the coast and the fact that accommodation was provided, she'd applied.

Determined to make something of herself, she'd worked hard in the kitchens here, while at the same time finding out everything she could about hotel administration so that when a vacancy for a receptionist had arisen, she'd got the job, assisted by the refined demeanour she'd had drummed into her as a child. Two years after her arrival here, when she was nineteen, she'd married the boss's son.

But now this woman of beauty and good fortune was suddenly overcome by the despair she'd been stifling all afternoon. She wept uncontrollably, rivers of mascara streaking her cheeks, make-up turning to blotches. She put her head on her hands on the dressing table and sobbed with the misery of knowing that she wasn't worthy of her husband's love.

Managing eventually to pull herself together, she washed her face and reapplied her make-up, combed her hair, straightened her clothes and left the flat, heading for the ground floor in the rattly old-fashioned lift.

To the casual observer she was a sophisticated and

composed woman in control of her life. Because she was so skilled in projecting this image, nobody would suspect the depth of her emotional problems.

'If you'd just like to sign the register, I'll have someone take your luggage up to your room for you,' June said to a couple of late arrivals, handing them the key to their room across the reception desk. 'You're on the third floor but the lift is just down the passage on the left.' She paused, smiling from one to the other. 'May I take this opportunity to welcome you to the Cliff Head Hotel. All of us here wish you a very happy holiday and hope you'll enjoy your stay with us.'

'I'm sure we will,' said the man, glancing around. 'It seems very nice.'

'We think so,' said June truthfully.

Purpose-built as a hotel in the early part of the century, but tastefully modernised internally, the hotel was white-rendered, had balconies to all the front rooms and was set in extensive grounds. Here in the foyer, the walls were wood-panelled and a wide staircase rose to the gallery in a wealth of polished mahogany. On the ground floor there were various public rooms including a bar and restaurant that were open to nonresidents.

With expert timing, Alan appeared with the teenage boy they employed as a porter and general runaround. Alan introduced himself to the new arrivals and the boy led them to the lift, carrying their luggage.

'Are we expecting any more new arrivals tonight?' Alan enquired.

'No, they're the last,' June told him, glancing at the reservations book. 'A few are expected tomorrow but apart from them the guests for this week are all present and correct, and every room booked.'

'That's the way we like it, eh?' he smiled.

'It certainly is.'

It was turned ten o'clock and people were milling about in the foyer, some going out for after-dinner strolls, others asking at the desk for their keys so that they could turn in for the night. People tended to speak in hushed tones because this was a select hotel catering for a refined clientele. A mausoleum, June had been known to call it when she and Alan were alone. They both thought it needed an injection of new life and had discussed the possibility of making the place more child-friendly and attractive to families. They'd even talked about introducing some sort of evening entertainment such as weekly dances and cabaret nights. One of the lounges could easily be adapted to accommodate such functions.

But Alan's parents were fiercely opposed to any such changes, which they believed would lower the tone of the hotel. Apart from a period during the war, when it was requisitioned by the Government as a convalescent home for wounded soldiers, the hotel had been run on the same traditional lines for two generations. People came here for peace and tranquillity, was the Masters' argument. With characteristic hauteur they claimed that there were places like Butlins for people who needed entertainment and didn't mind dance music blaring out at all hours, or children shouting and screaming about the place.

June had no say in such matters, and it annoyed her that Alan had so little power. She wished he would be more assertive towards his parents, and told him so from time to time. But his easy-going nature and love of the hotel made him malleable.

Now a youngish man, with blond hair and blue eyes, and wearing a tuxedo, came up to the reception desk – Jack Saunders, the restaurant manager. 'Could you order a taxi, please, June?'

'Sure. Who's it for?'

'A Mr and Mrs Taylor from one of the nonresident parties.'

'Is the party breaking up already?' She was surprised. 'They looked in fine form and set to stay until we chuck them out when I passed the restaurant a little while ago.'

'The others in the party probably are,' he told her. 'But Mrs Taylor isn't feeling well so they're leaving early.'

'Oh dear,' she frowned. 'Nothing she's eaten, I hope.'

'In our restaurant, *never*,' Jack grinned. 'I suspect the answer lies in a few too many gins.'

June and Alan both chuckled. The same age as Alan, Jack was a pal of his, and June liked him too. Born and raised in London's East End, Jack had gone to Australia with his family in the post-war emigration craze. The rest of the family had settled there but Jack hadn't been happy so had come back to England after a couple of years. He'd gained hotel experience as a waiter, then head waiter in one of the big London hotels before coming to the Cliff Head three years ago.

'I'll do it right away,' said June, picking up the phone.

'Fancy a drink after work, you two?' Jack suggested. His voice was deep and husky with an attractive hint of his East End roots.

'Love to,' smiled June. They usually needed to wind down when they came off duty after a busy night or it was difficult to sleep.

'Suits me,' added Alan.

'I'll need to relax a bit after the night I'm having,' said Jack. 'What with Chef going into a mood and throwing his weight about, and a table for six being double-booked, I'll be glad when this shift is over.'

'Double-booked?' queried June in concern, putting the phone down for a moment.

'That's right,' he confirmed. 'Table number twenty. We had to set up another table sharpish since we couldn't turn the

37

customers away as they'd made a booking, even though we were fully stretched. It's crowded in the restaurant, to say the very least.'

'Whoever took the first booking must have forgotten to write it down,' she said.

He shrugged. 'Exactly.'

A look passed between June and Jack. The culprit was probably Alan's mother, Irene, who liked to be seen front of house and sometimes covered in reception when June wasn't on duty if there was no other member of staff available. In her work behind the scenes Irene was reasonably competent, but efficiency took second place to vanity when she was out front. June's guess was that she'd been busy trying to impress someone in the foyer when the restaurant booking had come in, so had failed to enter it.

Jack was also thinking this but was far too diplomatic to say anything to Alan – partly because he was merely an employee, but also because Alan was fond of his mother, who would rather die than admit to any sort of error.

'Not guilty.' June met her husband's questioning look. 'You know me better than that.'

'It must have been one of the staff then,' tutted Alan, becoming noticeably tense. 'People really should be more careful about that sort of thing.'

'No real harm done,' intervened Jack speedily. 'We soon got the problem sorted, and if Chef can't cope with a few extra covers at short notice he doesn't deserve to be in the job.'

'True,' agreed June.

Spotting the arrival of Irene and Gerald Masters, Jack prepared to make a hasty retreat, arranging to see Alan and June in the bar after work.

Alan greeted his parents in a jovial manner. 'Can't you two keep away from the place?' He was teasing them because

38

they weren't on duty at night, on grounds of seniority. 'Talk about gluttons for punishment.'

'We're not here to work,' explained Gerald, who was quintessentially English, in a blazer and flannels and smoking a pipe. 'We've just called in for a nightcap.'

'Looking for some company, eh?' suggested Alan. His father was the gregarious type and liked to sit in the bar of an evening, chatting to the guests.

Alan's parents had used to live in the flat that June and Alan now occupied. These days Gerald and Irene had a house within walking distance and most nights they turned up here, probably because they'd always been too wrapped up in the hotel to have much of a social life outside of it, June guessed. She got on better with Gerald than his wife, but couldn't claim to be fond of either. He wasn't openly hostile towards her but neither did he go out of his way to make her feel like one of the family. He went along with the views of his wife because it was easier, she suspected, and Irene never left June in any doubt as to how disappointed she was in her son's choice of wife.

'That's right, son,' confirmed Gerald. 'It doesn't do any harm to be sociable to the guests . . . it creates goodwill.'

'I can't argue with that,' agreed Alan.

'Is everything all right here?' enquired Irene, a short, plump woman with cold grey eyes and honey-rinsed grey hair which was tightly permed and immaculate. She was wearing a royal-blue crêpe-de-Chine cocktail dress with sequins around the neckline.

'Everything's fine,' her son assured her, 'apart from someone double-booking a table in the restaurant.'

Irene's brow furrowed. 'You ought to watch that, June,' she said, with her usual propensity to blame her daughter-in-law.

'It wasn't me,' denied June.

'You're our head receptionist,' Irene reminded her coolly.

'Bookings are your responsibility.'

'Not when I'm off duty.'

'You're not being fair, Mother,' Alan was swift to defend. 'If June says it wasn't her, then it wasn't. And she can't be held responsible for what other people do when she isn't on duty.'

'No, no, of course she can't,' conceded Irene quickly; she normally kept her hostility towards June out of her son's hearing and had slipped up on this occasion. 'It must have been one of the staff filling in on the desk. You need to deal with that, Alan. That sort of inefficiency is bad for business.'

'I'll look into it,' he told her.

Alan could hardly be unaware of the fact that his wife and mother didn't get on, given the tension that was always present between them. But he didn't know the extent of Irene's enmity towards June because she was so sly about it. June was only human and had mentioned some of what went on to Alan. But she wasn't heartless enough to shatter all his illusions about his mother by telling him everything.

'You've been on the desk a few times during the week, haven't you, Irene?' June didn't see why the older woman should get off scot-free when she was so eager to pass the buck.

Irene was full of affront. 'I hope you're not implying that I'm at fault,' she objected. 'I'm hardly likely to make such a careless mistake after all my experience in the hotel trade.'

'Anyone can make a mistake,' June pointed out. 'We're all only human.'

'I could run the reception desk in my sleep,' was her sharp answer to that.

A sudden flurry of guests needing attention ended any further discussion, and Irene and Gerald headed for the bar. People were checking breakfast times and ordering

40

newspapers and early morning tea, asking for keys and making general enquiries.

Although June managed to conceal it, she was inwardly quivering. Irene usually managed to unnerve her, even after all these years. Her contempt was an ever-present force even when she was pretending to be friendly for Alan's benefit. From the instant he had shown a serious interest in June, Irene had systematically tried to break them up. It would have suited her if Alan had married Paula Bright, the daughter of one of the Masters' few friends, a couple who were Torquay hoteliers.

June had hoped that Irene's hate campaign would lessen once their marriage was an established fact. But, if anything, it had become more intense. When Alan was out of earshot, she didn't try to hide her venom and had told June often and in a variety of ways how she wasn't good enough for Alan. June sometimes wondered how much more she could take, especially as she had reason to agree with her mother-in-law.

'Jack's a really good bloke, don't you think?' remarked Alan later that same night when he and June were getting ready for bed, having spent an enjoyable hour in the company of the restaurant manager.

'Yeah, he is good company,' she agreed. 'I enjoy his down-to-earth sense of humour.'

Alan tutted in an affectionate manner as he unbuttoned his shirt. 'Him and that damned motorbike of his,' he said, smiling. 'Talk about besotted.'

She laughed. 'I don't think any woman will ever come close to that thing in his priorities.'

Jack Saunders was a motorbike fanatic and devoted to the Harley-Davidson he'd bought second-hand and done up. It looked like new but he was always tinkering with it.

41

'It would have to be someone really special, that's for sure,' Alan agreed.

'He doesn't have any trouble getting women, though, does he?' June mentioned casually.

'He's a good-looking bloke, that's why,' said Alan. 'He's had a few girlfriends since he's been here.'

'Mm. There was that woman from Exeter he was going out with,' she remembered. 'I thought that might come to something but it went the same way as all the others.'

'I suppose he just hasn't met anyone he wants to settle down with yet,' observed Alan. 'He's happy as he is. What with the motorbike and his old cottage miles from anywhere, he's a one-off.'

'A good restaurant manager, though,' she pointed out. 'That's the main thing as far as we're concerned.'

'He's very good,' he agreed. 'He has a way with the guests, and he knows how to get the best out of the staff.' He paused thoughtfully, taking off his shirt. 'Yet I took a chance in giving him the job because he hadn't managed a restaurant, as such, before he came to work for us. It's just as well I interviewed him. I don't think Mum or Dad would have taken him on.'

'Which just goes to show what good judgement you have,' June praised him.

'A lucky guess more like it. I just knew he was right for the job, somehow.'

'You spotted something special in him,' she insisted, sitting on the edge of the bed in her slip to take off her stockings, 'which makes you a brilliant judge of character in my book.'

'Nice of you to say so.'

June was sitting with her back to Alan and she felt the bed shake as he got into it. She tensed as the moment she was dreading drew near. But for the time being he seemed content to chat about the hotel. 'It was a good night, wasn't it?' he said.

'It was busy, certainly,' she replied.

'Busy and good are the same thing to me,' he responded with enthusiasm. 'There's nothing like the feeling I get when we've got a full house. Even apart from the business side of it, it gives me a real buzz. When Mum and Dad retire and I'm running the place, I'll have this hotel humming with life. There'll be a feeling here . . . an atmosphere so cheerful and warm, people won't be able to wait to come back.'

'Why wait until they retire before doing it?'

'You know why, June,' he reminded her. 'They want things to stay as they are.'

'So . . . persuade them otherwise,' she challenged.

He paused before answering. 'My time will come,' he said in a tone of resignation.

Because she didn't want to pressurise him into something he didn't feel right about, she just said encouragingly, 'Yeah, course it will.'

She had often wondered if they should break away from his parents' business altogether, partly because she feared that Irene would eventually come between them, but mainly because she believed Alan needed to succeed at something in his own right, away from their control, to find true fulfilment. But she couldn't seriously expect him to leave this place. It was in his blood, was his birthright, and would be his eventually.

'Anyway,' he said, yawning and sliding his hand over her back, 'that's enough shop talk. Come to bed before I get too tired to make love to you.'

'I won't be a minute.' Maybe if he fell asleep she wouldn't have to tell him.

But no such luck. He sat up, caressing her shoulders. She moved away quickly and stood up, facing him.

'What's the matter?' He frowned at her.

'I can't.'

'Why not?'

She bit her lip, hating to utter the words she knew would distress him. 'I ... I got my period this afternoon,' she explained through dry lips.

'Oh, oh, I see.' He rolled over and lay on his back, unable to hide his disappointment.

'I'm sorry there's not going to be a baby, Alan,' she told him miserably, slipping into her nightdress.

'Yeah, so am I.' He paused and she could feel tension draw tight between them as he struggled to compose himself. 'But we mustn't lose heart. It'll happen one day.'

'I hope so,' she said with feeling. 'I really do.'

He lay still, staring at the ceiling for a while, then turned his head towards her. 'Look, June, I know how upset you must be feeling but you mustn't let it get to you,' he said.

'How can I not? I feel terrible, not only for myself but for you. I know how much you want kids.'

'We both do, don't we? But there's plenty of time.' She knew he was forcing himself to stay positive with great difficulty. 'We're still quite young. Maybe next month your period will oblige us and stay away.'

They'd been saying that for seven years and still a pregnancy eluded them. 'We'll just have to keep hoping,' she said.

'We will indeed.' He patted the bed beside him. 'Come on,' he urged her. 'I think we both need a cuddle.'

She slipped in beside him, only partly reassured to have him close to her. 'I feel as though I'm failing you, Alan,' she confessed.

'Don't be daft, of course you're not. It takes two to make a baby, remember.' He slipped his arm around her and she snuggled against him.

'I suppose so.'

'But for both our sakes, perhaps it's time we thought about getting some medical advice, as nothing seems to be happening in that direction,' he suggested. 'I was reading something about it the other day. Apparently, quite often just a minor adjustment is needed.'

June froze and he felt her trembling.

'Hey, why so tense?'

'It must be the thought of an operation,' she fibbed.

'Surgery probably won't even be necessary,' he was quick to reassure her. 'There might not be anything wrong at all. But if we see a doctor, at least we'll have more of an idea of what we're up against.'

'It's probably just a question of time,' she suggested, as though she really believed it. 'Unexplained infertility, they call it.'

'Exactly,' he agreed. 'But it won't do any harm to get some professional advice, will it?'

'It might be worth looking into . . . at some point,' she hedged.

'I think we should do it sooner rather than later. I know we're still young but we have been trying for quite a long time.'

'I'll think about it.'

'Promise?'

'I promise.'

'Good,' he said sleepily.

How hurt he would be to know what a fraud she was, she thought. She had no intention of going to see any doctor *ever* about her inability to conceive because she knew exactly why it wasn't happening. But she couldn't tell him the reason. God, what a mess this was.

'Oh well, tomorrow's another day,' he yawned, kissing the top of her head. 'Good night, darling.'

'Good night, Alan.'

Just as she had settled to go to sleep the memory came, bringing her to with a start. She was trembling, her heart palpitating horribly. It always seemed to resurface when she was worried or upset about something and was always so vivid she could almost taste the fear as though it had happened yesterday instead of twenty years ago at least. Why it continued to bother her, she didn't know. But every so often back it came, unfaded by the passing of time.

Far too tense now to sleep, she slipped out of bed and went to the kitchen to make some tea, which she took into the living room, still feeling shaky. Her memory of her early childhood was somewhat sketchy, probably because she'd been told to forget everything before adoption. She knew she'd been six when she was adopted and that she hadn't been at the orphanage very long. She knew that her birth mother was dead and that she and her sister had been abandoned by their father. The rest was a mystery. She'd learned never to ask questions of her new parents, especially about her original background.

As always the flashback evoked memories of her sister, a small child with pigtails and a giggle, as far as she could remember. The pain of their parting had been awful. She'd never forget it. She'd often thought about her and wondered how life had treated her, particularly as she'd grown into adulthood. She'd wanted to see her again but, having been brought up to believe that she must leave her alone to get on with her own life, she'd never made a move in that direction.

Drinking her tea, she came back to the present and her current problems, of which there seemed no way out. She couldn't give Alan the child he wanted, and didn't know for how much longer she could go on fooling him into believing that she could. If her reproductive apparatus was in good working order, it would have happened by now.

She finished her tea and went back to bed, careful not to disturb Alan. Listening to his even breathing beside her, she was imbued with love for him. There had been tension between them lately because she couldn't get pregnant. How long would it be before it destroyed their marriage altogether?

One afternoon a few weeks later, June found herself alone in the office with her mother-in-law, having gone there to collect some of the forms she used to make up the guests' bills. The office was behind the reception area and it was here that all the major hotel administration happened: the ordering of food and drink, the organisation of staff and wages, everything apart from the receptionist's work, which included hotel and restaurant bookings, making up guests' bills, answering the telephone and dealing with all enquiries.

It was a quiet time between lunch and tea. The guests were either out or resting. Gerald and Alan were taking a break and the secretary had gone to the kitchen to get some tea.

'Oh, hello, Irene,' said June. 'I didn't realise you were still here. I thought you'd have gone home by now.'

'I bet you did,' snapped Irene, who was seated at a desk, holding her spectacles between thumb and forefinger and idly swinging them to and fro. 'You wouldn't have come in if you'd known I was in here on my own.'

'Too true, I wouldn't.' June and Irene didn't pretend to like each other when they were alone. 'I'm not a masochist.'

'Sorry to disappoint you.'

June said nothing; just went to the store cupboard and took out a batch of the forms she needed. 'I'll take plenty of these,' she told her. 'I'm right out of them.'

'Fine.'

June walked to the door.

'While we're on our own,' began Irene, making June's

heart sink because those words always heralded criticism of some sort, 'I'd like a word.'

June turned to face her, clutching the pile of forms. 'What about?'

'I'd like to know how much longer I'm going to have to wait for a grandchild.'

It wasn't the first time Irene had asked such an impertinent question but the subject was so raw and at the forefront of June's mind at the moment, it had more of an impact than usual. She turned scarlet, the forms slipping from her grasp and falling with a thud into an untidy heap on the floor. 'I think that's a personal matter between Alan and myself, don't you?' she replied, unable to conceal the quiver in her voice.

'Alan is our only child,' the other woman pointed out, her grey eyes resting coldly on June. 'Naturally Gerald and I are keen to have a grandchild. We want the family line to continue and not end with Alan. Surely you can understand that.'

'Of course.'

'As you know, this hotel has been in Gerald's family for a long time and we want to know that it will pass on through the generations after our time and Alan's,' she went on as though June had said nothing. 'And that can't happen if there are no succeeding generations, can it?'

'Obviously not.'

'Anyway, it's the natural thing to want grandchildren, and I don't want to be deprived of them or be too old to enjoy them if they do come along.'

'There's plenty of time,' June said steadily. 'Alan and I are both still in our twenties, and you're not exactly in your dotage.'

'Even so, you've been married long enough.' She was like a dog with a bone.

June felt her temper rising at this blatant intrusion of

privacy. 'It's a personal matter,' she told her again. 'I can understand your wanting a grandchild but that doesn't give you the right to pry into our private life. Alan's a grown man now. He doesn't have to account to you and neither do I.'

'Maybe not. But Alan makes no secret of the fact that he wants a child,' Irene reminded her. 'You can't deny that.'

'I wouldn't dream of denying it,' June protested. 'All I can say is, that when we have any news on that subject, you and Gerald will be the first to know.'

'You've no reason to put it off,' the other woman persisted, as though trying to drive June into a corner. 'I mean, it isn't as though there's any shortage of money. You do well out of this business and could afford to move out of the flat and into accommodation more suited to a family.'

June went down on her haunches to gather the forms that were all over the floor. 'Drop the subject, for goodness' sake,' she said, standing up. 'It's none of your business.'

'I think it is,' the other woman disagreed. 'Alan is my son and when he isn't happy, I don't like it.'

Smarting from the impact of her words, June asked, 'What makes you think he isn't happy?'

'It's obvious. How can he be happy when he hasn't got the child he wants so badly?' she declared. 'He can't be properly fulfilled without that.'

June was so shocked to have her own fears spelled out so clearly, her head spun and she felt sick. She offloaded the forms on to the secretary's desk and held the edge for a moment to steady herself. But she was determined not to give Irene the satisfaction of knowing how rattled she was. 'He's contented enough as things are, with just the two of us,' she told her mother-in-law.

'He might pretend to be—'

'He isn't just pretending.'

'You don't believe that any more than I do.'

June was forced to stare at the floor so that Irene couldn't see the pain in her eyes.

'Is there a problem?' asked Irene, her eyes narrowing on June in a questioning manner. 'Is that it? Is all not well in that department?'

Choking back the tears, June was unable to answer and Irene took this to be a confirmation. 'Have you taken medical advice?' she enquired.

'No,' June managed to utter.

'Why not?'

'Because I've been hoping it would happen and there would be no need,' she said, and it wasn't a lie. 'Not that it's anything to do with you.'

'You can't leave something as important as that to chance,' Irene nagged.

'Give it a rest, Irene, please.'

'That's typical of you to let something as vital as that go on unchecked.'

June brushed a tired hand across her brow. 'How do you know what is typical of me?' she asked. 'You've never taken the trouble to get to know me.'

'You and I are poles apart so I couldn't see the point.'

'Do you hate me so much, you find it impossible to leave me alone?' June wanted to know.

'I don't hate you,' Irene corrected, 'I just don't think you're the right woman for my son.'

'I'd never have guessed,' June said with bitter irony. 'But apart from the fact that I'm not Paula Bright, what else have you got against me? I'm a good wife to him. I love him. He's my life and I'd do anything for him.'

'You hold him back,' Irene stated categorically. 'You always have done in other ways and now you're doing it in the worst way possible – by depriving him of a child.'

'I've never held Alan back,' June disagreed. 'If I've held

anyone back, it's you and Gerald by getting in the way of your plans for him and Paula Bright, which would have made things nice and cosy, all good friends together.'

'And what's wrong with that?' Irene wanted to know. 'At least he'd have been with someone of his own type.'

'Instead of a jumped-up kitchen hand?'

'You said it,' returned Irene. 'If the cap fits . . .'

'You really are vicious.'

'I've never pretended to be a saint.'

'Except in front of Alan.'

Irene gave her a sharp look. 'Look, I'm just a mother who wants the best for her son. I've never made any secret of the fact that I wanted him to marry Paula,' she responded. 'Those two would have been perfect for each other.'

'Alan obviously didn't think so or he'd have married her.'

'And he would have done if you hadn't got your claws into him.'

'That just isn't true. I worked and lived at this hotel for a long time before I married him, remember?' June pointed out. 'And I know that nothing was ever going to happen between him and Paula Bright. Not on his part, anyway. He never felt anything of a romantic nature for her.'

'Only because you stood in the way of it,' Irene persisted. 'Once you'd set your sights on him no one else stood a chance. You were absolutely determined to have him from the minute you set foot inside this hotel.'

June couldn't deny that she'd been smitten with him the moment she'd set eyes on him. She'd been seventeen, he nineteen, a soldier home on leave. The war was over but he'd still had some service left to do. She had wanted him desperately but she certainly hadn't entered into a callous campaign to get him in the way that Irene was suggesting. It had been a mutual thing. 'I fell for him at the start, I won't deny that,' she admitted. 'The feeling was reciprocated or

51

we'd never have got together. Alan's very much his own man.' She paused before adding pointedly, 'Except, of course, in his dealings with you and Gerald.'

Irene chose to ignore this last remark. 'All men are susceptible to a flirtatious woman,' she declared, 'and Alan is no exception.'

'We fell in love. It wouldn't have gone beyond a flirtation if we hadn't.'

'Yes, well, that's all water under the bridge,' Irene said impatiently. 'As you did get your hooks into him, the least you can do is give him a child.' She hesitated for a moment, looking at June. 'If you have a medical problem, you must get it seen to without delay. You owe him that much.'

All the fight went out of June, just drained away with the awful truth of Irene's words. 'I'm fully aware of what I owe your son and I have his best interests at heart always, you have my word on that,' she said dully. 'I don't need you to tell me what I have to do.' She was ashen-faced and longing to get away from this woman's cruel tongue. 'Anyway, it's time I took a break from duty until this evening so I'll get some cover in reception and go upstairs to the flat for a couple of hours.'

And with that she left the office.

Alan was sitting in a deck chair on the balcony reading the *Hoteliers' Chronicle* when June got back to the flat.

'Not doing any serious sleeping this afternoon, then?' she said with false levity.

'I will have a snooze in a minute,' he told her. 'I was just glancing through this to keep up to date with what's going on in the trade.'

'We might as well make the most of the nice weather,' she remarked, sitting in the chair beside him and glancing out across the sunlit bay. 'It'll be winter soon enough.'

'You look as though you could do with some sun,' he mentioned, giving her a close look.

'Do I?'

'I'll say you do. You're very pale.' He looked concerned. 'You feeling all right?'

'I'm fine,' she assured him quickly, avoiding his eyes. 'I'll make a cup of tea and join you out here.'

'No tea for me, thanks. I'm going for a kip.' He put the magazine on the table and got up. 'See you later.'

'OK.'

She didn't bother to make tea for herself but sat alone on the balcony, browsing absently through the *Chronicle*. But thoughts of the encounter with Irene lingered, making concentration impossible. The advertisements were about all she could take in so she put the magazine down on the small table beside her and gave her thoughts full rein.

Alan was a good and loving husband. Irene was right when she said June owed it to him to give him the child he wanted. She had been nothing when she'd met him, just a seventeen-year-old kitchen worker who'd run away from home at fifteen. As his wife she'd enjoyed status and a good standard of living. All she'd had to give him in return was her love and loyalty. She didn't have Paula Bright's family background or connections in the hotel trade. And now it seemed she didn't even have the capacity to fulfil that most basic of all human needs.

Even worse was the fact that she couldn't be honest with him about it. Although he was supportive and reassuring to her, the lack of a baby was beginning to put a strain on their relationship. She could feel tension simmering below the surface with ever increasing frequency. That would get worse as it became obvious that a pregnancy wasn't going to happen. Alan was much too good-natured to admit it, but a barren wife would become a burden to him eventually.

She couldn't allow that to happen. She loved him too much. So she must leave. Disappear from his life and give him the freedom to make a new start with someone who could make his life complete. She must do it in such a way that he wouldn't be able to talk her out of it. Irene's lethal tongue had accelerated this decision but it wasn't the cause. Sooner or later, June knew, she would have realised that this was the only solution.

Remembering something that had only half registered a few minutes ago, she reached across to the table and picked up the *Chronicle*, searching for an advertisement that had caught her eye and now seemed vital.

'Receptionist/bookings clerk wanted for busy London hotel. Marble Arch area. Experience essential – accommodation available if required.'

There was a telephone number and a box number.

Hesitating for only a moment, she went inside and found a pencil with which she ringed the advert. Then she took the magazine and went to the telephone in the hall, closing the door carefully behind her.

Early the next morning while the hotel was still silent she slipped out of bed, packed a small bag, put an envelope containing a short letter on the kitchen table, planted a kiss on her sleeping husband's brow, took one last long look at him and stepped quietly from the room.

She left the Cliff Head and headed for the station to get an early train. There was hardly anyone about to see this sad figure walking through the streets carrying a holdall, tears streaming down her cheeks.

Later that morning, Alan stood with his finger on the doorbell of his parents' house near the seafront. When his mother came to the door, he stormed inside, waving a letter at her.

'What have you said to her?' he demanded. 'What have you done?'

'What have I said and done to whom, dear?' She was genuinely puzzled.

'To June, of course,' he blasted. 'She's gone. Left me. Just like that.'

Irene's eyes widened with surprise. 'Oh,' was all she could manage. She was careful to conceal her delight. 'How dreadful for you.'

'That must be the biggest understatement in the history of the world.' He was distraught. 'She wouldn't have just gone unless something had really upset her. So, Mother, I'll ask you again, what have you said to her?'

'Your wife's departure has nothing to do with me,' insisted Irene, secretly wondering if her conversation with June yesterday had had anything to do with it. 'Does she mention me in that letter you're flapping about?'

'No.'

'Why blame me then?'

'Because it's obvious that you don't like her.'

'I never have liked her but it doesn't follow that she left because of me,' she pointed out.

'What else could it be?'

'I've no idea,' she told him. 'What reason does she give in the letter?'

'She doesn't give one,' he explained distractedly. 'She just says she can't stay and it's better for us both if she goes, and I have to trust that she's made the right decision. No forwarding address or clue as to where she's going – nothing.'

'You're better off without her,' his mother couldn't help blurting out. 'I've always thought you were too good for her.'

They were ill-chosen words which served only to fuel his anger even more. 'You've never given her a chance or made any effort to like her,' he accused. 'I bet you've said things to her that I don't know about. It's sure to be something you've said that's finally driven her away. June wouldn't just go off and hurt me like this for no reason.'

Gerald appeared from another room and wanted to know what all the noise was about.

'His wife's gone,' Irene informed him. 'Walked out on him, just like that.'

'No!' gasped Gerald.

'Yes,' Irene confirmed triumphantly.

'I'm not letting her go,' mumbled Alan, holding his head in despair.

'She's already gone, son,' his father said gently.

'I'll find her,' Alan told them. 'I'm not leaving it at this. She loves me, I know that.'

'She's got a funny way of showing it,' was his mother's cynical reaction.

'Has she got another man, do you think?' suggested Gerald tactlessly.

'Definitely not,' was Alan's categorical reply. 'I would have known if anything like that had been going on. Anyway, she never goes anywhere to meet anyone. She could hardly have an affair when she's always at the hotel with me.'

'The best thing you can do is forget all about her, son,' his father advised.

'No!' roared Alan.

'You'll be a fool if you don't,' Gerald went on. 'Anyone who's capable of doing something like that isn't worth bothering with.'

'Your father's right.' Irene was in her element.

'She was never really one of us, anyway,' Gerald opined.

'Of course she was one of us,' Alan disagreed, his voice rising. 'She's my wife, which automatically makes her one of us, despite the fact that you two didn't accept her.'

'Yes, of course it does, dear,' conceded Irene, changing

56

tack for fear of losing too much favour with her son. 'Your father and I are just upset on your behalf.'

'I've got to get her back but I don't know where to start looking.' He combed his hair back with his fingers in agitation. 'She could have gone anywhere.'

'Her mother's perhaps?' suggested Irene.

'She definitely wouldn't have gone there.' That much he did know. 'They don't get on. She hasn't lived at home since she was fifteen.'

'She'll have to let her mother know where she is at some point, though, won't she?' Irene pointed out, deeming it beneficial to her own relationship with her son to seem to be helpful and reassuring and not too damning about June at this point. 'She's still her daughter even if they hate the sight of each other. You can get her new address from her.'

'I can't because I don't have an address or phone number for her mother,' he muttered absently. 'All I know about her is that she lives in London somewhere. June has never said much about her family.'

'Oh, well,' sighed Irene. 'Perhaps June will get in touch with you to let you know where she is, eventually. As you said, she wouldn't just walk out for no reason at all. Perhaps it's just a temporary thing. She might have got into a mood about something and wants some extra attention.'

He shook his head. 'That's the last thing June would ever do. She isn't the type to seek attention.' He was adamant. 'No, she means it. She won't come back of her own accord, which is why I have to find her.'

'I don't see how you can, son, as you've got nothing to go on,' said his mother.

'Me neither,' added his father.

'Did she say anything at all or give any indication to either of you that she wasn't happy lately?' enquired Alan, looking from one of them to the other.

Irene wondered if it would be a good or bad move to mention the childlessness. She decided it wouldn't do any harm to remind him of his wife's flaws. 'I think perhaps she might have been fretting because a baby is a long time in coming,' she told him.

Alan scratched his head, pondering. 'Mm, there is that,' he said. 'I told her not to worry about it.'

'I said much the same thing,' lied Irene. 'These things happen in their own good time, that's what I told her.'

'She wouldn't have walked out on me just because of that, though, surely,' he said, becoming more frantic with every passing moment. 'There must be more to it than that. I have to find her; find out what all this is about.'

'Calm down,' advised his mother.

'How can I when I feel so powerless?' he snapped. 'How could she do this to me? How could she?'

'Come and sit down and have a cup of tea, dear,' suggested his mother. 'Have you had breakfast?'

'Breakfast!' he exploded. 'My world's just fallen apart and you ask me if I've had breakfast?'

'You must eat, son,' said Gerald.

'Of course you must.' Irene put her hand on Alan's arm. 'Just some tea and toast then.'

'No. I don't want any bloody toast, Mother, thank you very much,' he shouted at her. 'And will you please stop treating me like a five-year-old child?'

'Just trying to help.'

He sighed. 'I know you are and I'm sorry. I must go. There's no point in my staying here upsetting you.'

'I'd better come with you,' she said.

'Whatever for?' he thundered, misunderstanding her motive.

'To replace June in reception, of course,' she explained. 'Someone will have to do it until we get a new receptionist.'

'Oh, yes, of course,' he muttered. 'But that's the least of my worries at this precise moment. The way I feel, the hotel can grind to a halt for all I care.'

'That's an extremely selfish and irresponsible attitude,' admonished his father.

'I know it is,' Alan agreed, 'but I think I can be forgiven for a little selfishness when my wife's just left me. I'm hardly likely to be full of the joys of spring, am I?'

'No. But business must go on, whatever your personal problems,' preached his father.

'Yeah, yeah,' sighed Alan. 'I know all about that so you can spare me the lecture.'

But Gerald wasn't that easily silenced when it came to the subject of his hotel. 'The guests have paid good money to be well looked after and it's our job to see that they are, no matter what's going on in our personal lives,' he went on. 'They come to us to have a good holiday and if they don't have it, it must be through no fault of ours. A reputation can take years to build but it can be ruined much quicker.'

'Don't worry, I won't drive them all away with my bad temper. I'm too well trained for that,' Alan told him. 'To the guests, I'll be my charming self, as usual.'

'You can take the morning off if you don't feel up to it,' offered his father. 'Your mother and I will stand in for you.'

'No, no,' said Alan. 'As you say, the show must go on and I intend to see that it does.'

'That's the spirit,' approved Gerald.

'I'll be over in a few minutes,' Irene told him. 'I'll just wash the dishes and make myself look decent.'

'I'll come with her,' said Gerald.

Alan softened towards them. They meant well and it wasn't their fault that he hadn't been able to hang on to his wife. 'Thanks for the support,' he said.

'The least we can do,' said his mother.

Alan left and walked back to the Cliff Head. He couldn't ever remember feeling this desolate. There had been bad times when he'd been in action during the war, but at least he'd been able to fight back then. How could he fight back now when he didn't know what he was up against? Even worse was the thought that if he did find her, June might not want to come back. How could he reverse the process if she'd fallen out of love with him?

No, he couldn't accept that that's what had happened. He and June had had their ups and downs and things had been a bit strained between them lately because she couldn't get pregnant. But they still loved each other, despite everything. He was convinced of that. Why then had she left him?

His head was throbbing with tension as he made his way up the wide stone steps and into the hotel foyer.

Chapter Three

During a prolonged spell of wet weather in August that confined two lively little girls to two small rooms for longer than their ability to amuse themselves, Daisy saved the sanity of them all by teaching them how to play snap.

Being about right for their age group, the game quickly became a favourite, producing fun and sibling rivalry in equal measures. Shrieks of excitement and laughter were punctuated with howls of disagreement after simultaneous cries of 'snap'. They kept themselves amused for ages and Daisy congratulated herself on finding such a gem.

One rainy Saturday evening, when Daisy had a rare night off from waitressing, the girls persuaded her and Nora to join them in a game, and a companionable atmosphere settled over Daisy's flat as the four of them entered into this childish activity with gusto. To make her night off into a special occasion for them all, Daisy had bought crisps, pop, and a bottle of stout for Nora.

'Snap!' yelled Shirley, eyes gleaming victoriously.

'It was me, I said it first,' disputed Belinda heatedly.

'You did *not*, I did,' argued her sister.

'Liar,' came the vehement accusation.

'You're the liar,' Shirley returned hotly. 'Tell her, Mum. Go on, tell her.'

'That's quite enough squabbling, both of you,' admonished their mother. 'So pack it in.'

'It's her fault.' Belinda was very put out, her lips turned down at the corners and trembling slightly. 'She's cheating.'

'No she is *not*,' intervened the fair-minded Daisy. 'Shirley called snap first so don't spoil the game by being a bad sport.'

'She's the bad sport,' huffed Belinda, glaring at her sister. 'It's not fair.'

'Shirley was first to say it,' Daisy told her youngest daughter again and with emphasis.

'Your mother's right,' came back-up support from Nora.

'I said it first.' Belinda was really digging her heels in on this one.

But her mother could be equally as determined. 'I was listening carefully and I heard you both,' she said firmly to Belinda. 'She beat you to it by a fraction of a second but she *was* first. You'll probably do it next time, love.'

'I did it this time,' the child insisted, eyes brimming with angry tears at this conspiracy against her.

'Right, that's it.' Daisy decided it was time to get tough. 'You, Belinda, are behaving like a spoiled little brat and you'll go to bed if you don't give up . . . and you can stop smirking, Shirley, or you'll go with her. If the two of you can't play together without practically coming to blows, I shall confiscate the cards so that you can't play at all. I've never heard such a carry-on. You don't usually behave like this, do they, Nora?'

'Not normally, no,' supported the other woman, switching her gaze to the girls and adding, 'but you're like a couple of spiteful cats tonight.'

Belinda pouted a bit but finally decided to swallow her pride and they continued the game with noisy hilarity. Amid the gales of laughter there was an assertive knock at the door.

'You play my cards for me, Nora,' requested Daisy, smiling

as she went to answer it. 'I won't be a minute.'

Opening the door to find herself confronted by two men she hadn't seen before, Daisy felt a chill settle over her at the air of menace about them. Tall and muscular, they both had their hair slicked back with grease and were wearing open-necked shirts with the sleeves rolled up to reveal big, solid arms. Each man was holding an Alsatian dog on a leash, one of which strained towards Daisy, barking and baring its teeth.

Its keeper pulled at the lead. 'Heel, boy,' he ordered gruffly, and the animal quietened down, though a growl continued to rumble in the back of its throat.

'Yes?' she said enquiringly, struggling to quell her rising panic.

'Rent,' was the brief reply.

'Oh? But it isn't due until Monday,' she explained. 'Someone usually comes to collect it on a Monday morning.'

'The boss wants it today,' she was informed by the man who seemed to be the spokesman.

As it happened she did have the rent money put aside so early payment wasn't a problem. But she was curious as to the reason for this premature demand. 'Does this mean you'll always be collecting on Saturdays in future?' she asked.

The man shrugged indifferently. 'Dunno,' he told her. 'We're just carrying out orders.'

She went inside to get the money from one of a series of empty jam jars in which she kept the cash for various bills, and handed it over with the rent book in which he entered the amount.

Giving her the book back, he spoke to her in a gruff monotone. 'We've got a message for you from the boss.'

'Oh?'

'Mr Ellwood said to tell you that he hopes your kids ain't afraid of dogs,' he informed her, looking towards the animals. 'He said to tell you that these two can get very vicious.'

'He ought to be ashamed of himself, threatening the safety of little children,' declared an outraged Nora, who had come up behind Daisy, leaving the girls sitting at the table waiting for the game to continue.

'Nothing to do with us, missus.' The second man spoke at last. 'We're just messengers.'

'You ought to be ashamed of yourselves too, working for a man like Ellwood,' Nora continued, 'someone who goes about threatening decent people with dangerous dogs.'

The man just shrugged.

While Nora went to her rooms to get her rent money, muttering furiously under her breath, Daisy stepped outside and pulled the door to behind her so that the children were out of earshot. 'You tell Mr Ellwood that if those dogs go anywhere near my children, I'll have him done for threatening behaviour.' The protective instinct towards her children was so strong as to make her fearless, despite her obvious vulnerability. 'I'll have the law on to him so fast he'll wonder what's hit him.'

The thug's manner was completely insouciant. 'We'll tell him,' he said lazily, and they turned and went towards Nora's front door, collected her rent, then made their way downstairs.

'That Ellwood is really stepping up his campaign to get us out, isn't he?' observed Nora, as the men's footsteps receded down the stairs. 'He's putting pressure on from all sides now.'

'Yeah, it's a real worry.'

Over the past month or so, since Daisy's confrontation with the landlord, the annoyance factor in the house had worsened. There were more frequent and louder all-night parties in the basement, radiograms playing at all hours and drunken brawls. Several of the other statutory tenants had left.

'Are we still agreed that we won't be moved, though?' asked Nora.

'I'm not prepared to be driven out of my home by a thug like Ellwood, are you?'

'Not likely,' Nora confirmed. 'The way I see it, it's a war of attrition. He'll try to wear us down and frighten us, but he wouldn't dare to cause us or the kids actual physical harm because then we really would have grounds to involve the law and he wouldn't want the police sniffing around.' She shook her head, puffing out her lips to emphasise the point. 'Oh, no. He's far too dodgy to let that happen.'

'Exactly,' agreed Daisy. 'So we have to stand firm and make sure that we keep that in mind when he makes things difficult for us. We mustn't be panicked into leaving and making ourselves homeless. It's a question of keeping our nerve no matter what he comes up with to scare us.'

'And in the meantime, we have a game of snap awaiting our attention.'

Daisy grinned. 'That's right. It'll take more than a couple of heavies and their snarling mutts to spoil our evening, eh, Nora?'

'Not half,' was her hearty agreement, and they went back inside together.

Within minutes the game was back underway, a warm, enveloping buzz of conversation and laughter filling the room as though they hadn't had visitors with a sinister message. Even the sound of the rain beating against the creaky old windows was barely noticeable alongside the merry din. But Daisy was far more worried than she was letting on. She could be brave when facing thugs, and positive in front of Nora and the children, but what chance did she and Nora really stand against someone like Roland Ellwood, who had money behind him and an army of strong men on his payroll? For how much longer could the women hold out against him if he was determined to get them out of here? And what lengths was he prepared to go to, to destat his property?

Although she hated to admit it, the prospect of homelessness was beginning to loom with sickening intensity. If that were to happen and the authorities got to know about it, they would try to take the girls away from her.

She was recalled to the present by Belinda telling her it was her turn. 'If you don't pay attention, Mum, you'll have to stop playing because we don't want daydreamers in our game,' she said in an amusing parody of her mother.

'Don't push your luck, my girl.' But Daisy was smiling as she put her card down and shouted, 'Snap.'

Imbued by a strong feeling of wellbeing generated by the company, she felt cheered by a surge of new resolve. She had a huge incentive to fight back against the landlord: two little girls who were reliant on her to put a roof over their heads, and a neighbour she'd grown to love as a mother. They might all be society's cast-offs but they were a unit in themselves, a caring little sisterhood making the best of life at the bottom of the pile. This attic was cold, damp and hopelessly inadequate but it was their home and she was damned if she'd let a skunk like Roland Ellwood drive them out because of greed. If they ever did move from here it would be from choice and because they had somewhere better to go, she was determined about that.

It was raining heavily in Torquay that Saturday night, too.

'Bloody weather,' Alan complained to Jack Saunders, with whom he was having a drink at the bar after work. 'It's more like November than August.'

'That's the British summer for you,' said Jack. 'Unreliable to say the least.'

'You must have been mad to leave all that lovely Australian sunshine behind to come back to our miserable weather,' commented Alan, who had been in the blackest of moods since June's departure a week ago.

'There's more to a place than good weather, mate,' he pointed out. 'It's a completely different way of life out there.'

'That's why people go abroad to live, surely.'

'And why some of them come back,' was Jack's answer to that. 'You've got to actually experience a country to know if you're going to take to it. Australia's a beautiful place with wonderful scenery and bags of opportunity – I can't speak highly enough of the country – but it just wasn't for me. It wasn't easy leaving my folks out there, but the longing to come home was just too strong in the end.'

'I suppose there was no point in your staying if you felt like that.' Alan sipped his beer, gloomily looking at the rain running down the windows. 'The way I feel at the moment I'd go there tomorrow if I could.'

'It isn't just the weather that's making you feel like that, though, is it?'

'No, of course not,' he confirmed. 'But the weather doesn't help when you're feeling down – not when you're running a seaside hotel, anyway.'

'Our line of business does make us more susceptible to the rain, I must admit,' agreed Jack.

'It isn't much fun for the guests when the weather does the dirty on them,' Alan went on. 'All year they look forward to a holiday by the sea and the last thing they want is to spend the whole time sitting about the hotel lounge playing cards and waiting for the rain to stop.'

'Still, at least we've had a television installed for them,' Jack reminded him. 'That helps to keep them entertained.'

Alan nodded. 'Mm. There is that. But people don't go on holiday to watch the telly. It's the kids I feel sorry for. I know we don't have many children staying at the Cliff Head but you see them trailing around the town with their mums and dads, hoping it will stop raining. All they want is for the sun to come out so they can go on the beach with their buckets and spades.'

'They're better off at home when it's like this.'

'They are,' agreed Alan. 'If I had my way I'd turn this place into a family hotel with an indoor pool and entertainment laid on for the bad weather.' He sighed resignedly. 'Still, I'm not likely to get my way about that, so there's no point my going on about it.'

'I gather from your mood that there's still no news of June, then,' Jack surmised.

'Not a word, mate,' Alan told him. 'What the hell possessed her to go off like that?'

'Don't ask me,' said Jack. 'I'm just a single bloke, and the last person to know what goes on in a woman's mind.'

Alan cast a studious eye over his handsome pal. 'You must know a thing or two about them, though,' he suggested. 'I mean, you're not exactly a novice in that direction, are you?'

'There have been women in my life, naturally,' Jack confirmed. 'I'm a normal, healthy twenty-eight-year-old.'

'But you haven't got married . . .'

'I've come close to it,' he confessed. 'But never actually did the deed.'

'Wouldn't you like someone to share your life with?' asked Alan, who'd loathed the single life this past week.

'Wouldn't we all? But not just anyone to save me from being alone,' he explained. 'I'm still soft enough to believe that there's someone specially for me out there somewhere. And if I meet her – wonderful. But until that happens my bachelor life suits me down to the ground. I've got my motorbike, my cottage and my freedom – that'll do me.'

'You can't seriously compare those things to a woman in your life?' said Alan.

'I'm not that weird,' Jack protested, 'but I'd never get married just because it's the thing to do. Anyway, I've got a bit set in my ways now. I come and go as I please. It would take someone really special to make me want to change my way of life.'

'Don't you get lonely living at the cottage on your own?' Alan asked. 'With it being a bit off the beaten track.'

Jack had an old stone cottage on the seashore at Gullscombe Bay, a small village a few miles outside Torquay. It was a beautiful spot but very remote, with a long sandy beach, rugged red cliffs and large expanses of open grassland.

'No, not at all,' he said without hesitation. 'I'm here at the hotel surrounded by people most of the time, anyway. And when I'm off duty I've got a friendly local pub where I can go at any time and find someone I know to talk to.' He shrugged. 'If I feel in need of something a bit more sophisticated, I just get on the bike and come in to town. It only takes about ten minutes. And Exeter's no distance on the bike if I fancy something livelier.'

'Sounds as though you've got yourself sorted.'

'I've no complaints.'

'Was it just the price that made you buy a place in such an out-of-the-way spot?' Alan enquired chattily.

'The fact that it was dirt cheap was the deciding factor, yeah,' he confirmed. 'But I've got to love it there and I wouldn't want to live anywhere else, especially now that I've renovated the cottage and got it how I want it. The location's great for me. I enjoy all that open space and rolling surf on my doorstep.' He grinned, raising his brows. 'And I don't live like a recluse. I do have the occasional female visitor.'

'Footloose and fancy-free, eh?' Alan was staring moodily into his beer glass.

'Exactly.'

'Technically that's what I am now, I suppose, now that my wife's left me,' Alan pondered. 'But I don't feel free. I just feel lonely and miserable.'

'Yeah, well, you're bound to feel like that at this early

stage. Anyone would.' Jack was thoughtful. 'I still can't help thinking that there's more to June going off than you know about.'

'Another man is odds-on favourite among the staff, I bet,' assumed Alan. 'The gossips must be having a field day. It's wives who usually get deserted, not the other way round. She's made a right fool of me.'

'I expect there is gossip, but not in front of me,' Jack was quick to assure him. 'They wouldn't dare because they know we're friendly, and I would give them a mouthful. June was devoted to you, anyone could see that. And she certainly isn't the type to play around. You'd have spotted the signs if anything like that had been going on.'

'Yeah, I think so too – and being made a fool of is the least of my worries, to be honest.' He paused, looking at Jack in a questioning manner. 'You knew her quite well. Had she seemed to be worried or unhappy to you just lately?'

'No,' was Jack's considered reply. 'She didn't get on with your folks, that's common knowledge. But I don't think she'd have left over that at this stage because it's been going on for so long. You never know what someone's feeling inside, of course, but I got the impression she was used to the way things were between them and her, and didn't let it get her down.'

'It always seemed like that. And my mother swears blind she hadn't said anything to upset her.' Alan raised his eyes, tutting. 'God, I feel so powerless. If only I knew where she was.'

'You can't force her to come back, though.'

'No. But if I knew where she was, at least I could try to find out what it's all about.'

'Maybe she just needs some time on her own,' suggested Jack.

'Mm.' Alan pondered the idea. 'I've been assuming that she

left on the spur of the moment, but when you think about it, she must have had somewhere to go. She wouldn't just walk out of here with nowhere to stay, would she? So she must have planned it.'

'Not necessarily,' Jack disagreed. 'If she'd gone to a relative she'd have felt she could just turn up without warning.'

'As far as I know she doesn't have any relatives apart from her mother,' Alan said. 'And she'd sooner sleep on a park bench than go to her.'

'Really?'

Alan nodded. 'That's the impression she gave me, anyway, though she never said what the trouble was. She never talked about her parents and I didn't press her to do so as it was obvious she didn't want to. I've never even met them. They didn't come to the wedding and she didn't want me to go with her to her father's funeral.'

Suddenly this seemed hugely significant to Alan. Surely it was unusual for a wife not to talk to her husband about her family background. Glancing back on their life together, in the light of what had now happened, he could see that there had always been an air of mystery about June.

'I can't imagine June doing anything underhand,' said Jack, 'so I don't think she would have planned it in advance.'

'No, I suppose not,' agreed Alan. 'But where the hell is she?'

'Search me, mate,' was all Jack could say. 'All you can do is hope for a lead.'

'One of those isn't going to drop into my lap, is it?'

'Something will turn up, eventually,' Jack suggested hopefully. 'And in the meantime, you'll just have to try and stop tearing your hair out and carry on as best as you can without her. You know where I am if you need a mate.'

'Thanks, Jack.'

It was well after hours. The bar was closed, the customers all departed and the bar staff gone off duty. Alan went behind the counter and got them each another drink – just a small glass of beer for Jack as he had to go home on the motorbike.

'Did you see that article in the *Hoteliers' Chronicle* about private bathrooms?' Jack asked, deliberately changing the subject to take Alan's mind off things.

'No, I only flicked through this month's issue,' Alan told him. 'Why? Is it interesting?'

'It's worth a look,' replied Jack. 'They reckon that en suite bathrooms will eventually become standard in all decent class hotels, rather than just a luxury that people pay extra for.'

'They must be talking a long time into the future then,' frowned Alan.

'They're not expecting it to happen tomorrow or next week,' Jack agreed. 'But whoever wrote the article seems to think that private facilities are going to be more in demand in the not-too-distant future. Some of the new hotels being built will have them to every room as a matter of course.'

'Seems a bit far-fetched to me,' said Alan.

'That's what I thought.'

'If it does happen, though, it'll create pressure for the rest of us to do the same or lose out to the opposition,' Alan observed darkly. 'And something like that is right out of our league here at the Cliff Head. It would cost an absolute fortune to get all our rooms upgraded.'

'Mm.'

'So whatever the trend is we'll have to manage with the few rooms with private bathrooms we already have,' Alan went on. 'It isn't as though we don't have hot and cold running water in every room.'

'They're taking the view that hotel proprietors will make the changes gradually over a long period, a room at a time,' Jack explained. 'Anyway, the article's worth a few minutes of your time. It might take your mind off your problems.'

'I'll have a look if the *Chronicle* hasn't been chucked out by mistake in all the upheaval of June going. I've been that distracted this week.'

'I've still got my copy if you can't find yours.' Jack finished his beer. 'Anyway, I must be off. If I have any more to drink I won't be in a fit state to go at all.'

'I'm a bad influence on you, keeping you out so late,' Alan apologised. 'I dread going to bed, that's why. Too many thoughts and too much emptiness upstairs in the flat.' He finished his drink and slipped off the bar stool with a purposeful air. 'But it has to be done and I must be man enough to do it. I mustn't keep you from your bed just because I don't want to face mine.'

'See you tomorrow.'

'Sure.'

Jack departed and Alan went behind the bar and rinsed their glasses. Then he turned off the lights and made his lonely way up to the flat in the lift.

The place felt like a morgue without her, Alan thought, as he stood in the living room staring out of the rain-soaked windows across the bay, the lights of Torquay hazed by the wet.

Still unable to face the prospect of the empty bed, he turned away from the window and rummaged through the untidy heap of newspapers and magazines on the coffee table until he found the *Hoteliers' Chronicle*. Settling into an armchair, he flicked through the pages until he found the article Jack had mentioned, which he read with interest.

The journalist predicted that hotels would thrive in the current affluent climate, which was expected to last for a while yet. People had more money to spend on leisure, which meant more of them could afford to go away on holiday, which in turn meant hoteliers would increase their profits, which would pay for them to improve their accommodation. The bit about the large increase in people taking their holidays abroad was rather worrying but the rest was fairly positive.

Alan leaned back in the chair, feeling slightly more relaxed for the diversion. He turned the pages in search of something to hold his attention until he was sleepy enough to face the lonely bedroom. Something caught his eye in the advertisement section. It wasn't the advertisement, as such, that interested him but the fact that it had a pencil ring around it. June was the only other person who would have looked at this copy of the *Chronicle* so she must have circled it. Why had she been interested in an advert?

When he read the advertisement – particularly the bit about accommodation being available – he understood why, and his heart leaped with new hope of finding her. There was no address and the name of the hotel wasn't given, but there was a phone number. It was a bit of a long shot but this just might be the lead he thought would never come. With optimism boosted considerably, he hurried to the telephone in the hall and asked the operator for a long-distance call to London.

'Central Hotel,' said a male voice he presumed to be that of the night porter.

'Sorry to bother you so late,' said Alan, pulses racing at this unexpected clue.

'No trouble at all, sir,' said the voice. 'That's what I'm here for.'

'The thing is,' began Alan, 'I have to meet someone at your hotel tomorrow and I'm not sure of your exact location. Can you help me with this, please?'

'Certainly, sir,' replied the man, and proceeded to give Alan the full address and directions to get there.

'Why did you do it, June?' Alan felt sad and puzzled rather than angry now that he'd actually found her. 'In heaven's name, why did you walk out on me?'

It was the evening of the next day and they were sitting drinking coffee in June's tiny room at the back of the hotel on the top floor. She'd moved in right away, having been given the job at the interview. She'd been very shaken on duty earlier when Alan had walked into reception with an overnight bag and booked a room for the night. When he'd explained how he'd tracked her down she'd cursed her carelessness. After she'd dealt with his booking, as though he was just any other guest, he'd asked for the chance to speak to her. She'd met him in the foyer when she came off duty and brought him up here because it was private.

'As I said in my letter, it's for the best.' She hadn't expected to have to confront him personally at this stage and was somewhat lost for words, as the truth wasn't an option. 'Believe me when I tell you that you're better off without me.'

'What's that supposed to mean?' he demanded, temper rising again. 'You're talking in riddles.'

'It hasn't been working for a while between us,' she stated categorically.

'That just isn't true.'

'You won't deny there's been tension between us lately,' she said.

'A little maybe, over this baby business,' he was forced to admit. 'But no marriage is a bed of roses all the time, and we shouldn't expect ours to be.'

'I realise that but—'

'Stop fobbing me off with excuses and tell me what's going on, June.' He was becoming aggressive now. 'I want to know why you walked out and I'm not leaving here until you tell me.'

She couldn't tell him the real reason without hurting him even more so she said rather feebly, 'I've never really fitted in at the Cliff Head.'

'You've always fitted in as far as I'm concerned. Surely that's what matters,' he was quick to point out. 'OK, so you never hit it off with my parents, but it's me you're married to, me you shared your life with, not them.' He fixed her with a stare. 'Anyway, if they were getting you down, you should have told me and I've have done something about it.' He paused again, squinting at her in a questioning manner. 'I don't believe that's why you left. We've been married for seven years and you've taken all that stuff with my parents in your stride. So let's have the real reason you walked out.'

His eyes were so full of hurt, she longed to hold him in her arms and soothe it away. But to do so would give him false hope because there was no possibility of her going back to him. She hadn't left on a whim. The decision to go had been a sudden one but she'd always known deep in her heart that she should never have married him.

Because she couldn't be honest with him, she just said, 'It wasn't any one thing—'

'It's got something to do with your not getting pregnant, hasn't it?' he guessed.

She reeled from his words but managed to answer in an even tone. 'No,' she lied to avoid any possibility of persuasion or suggestion of medical advice.

'I want a child. I'd be lying if I said otherwise,' he admitted. 'But if it isn't meant to be, I'll have to cope with that and so will you. But we will face it together. There's no point in your running away from it, June.'

'I'm sorry, Alan, but I'm not coming back.' She knew she must be strong, for his sake. 'I know it was a terrible thing for me to walk out without any warning. But I knew you'd try and stop me if I told you, and I really did have to go.'

He ran a critical eye around the room, which was sparsely furnished and so small as to be more of a cupboard than a room. There were no facilities beyond a bed, a wardrobe and the chairs they were sitting on. She had to go down the corridor to the bathroom, staff kitchen and sitting room.

'Look what you've come down to,' he told her. 'This is little more than a rabbit hutch.' He went to the window and stared out at the dreary view of the windows of buildings opposite and a yard far below. 'You must really be desperate to get away from me to have given up a comfortable home with a seaview for a miserable little gaff like this.' He turned to look into her face. 'We had a good life, didn't we? What more did you want from me?'

'Nothing at all, Alan,' she assured him. 'My leaving had nothing to do with any fault in you, or the way we lived.'

'All right, so we had to work bloody hard in the season,' he went on, as though trying to make sense of it. 'But things are not so bad in the winter. I was even going to suggest that we think about going abroad for a holiday this winter. Somewhere warm. I thought you'd like that.'

'I would, of course—' she began.

'Our future is assured, June,' he continued as though she hadn't spoken, too distressed for rational conversation. 'The Cliff Head will be ours one day.'

'Yours,' she corrected.

'Same thing. What's mine is yours.'

'It's irrelevant anyway because I'm not coming back.'

'I can't understand it.' He looked bewildered. 'Instead of staying to work with me and reap the rewards of our hard work, you choose to turn your back on it all, for this.'

'It's a job and a roof over my head,' she pointed out dully. 'It'll do for now.'

'But you don't need to make do in a place like this.' He

spread his hands expressively. 'Your home is with me at the Cliff Head.'

'Not any more, Alan,' she said sadly.

He was silent for a while. Then: 'In all the years we've been together, I've never thought of you as a selfish person.' His voice was distorted with anguish and frustration. 'But that's the only conclusion I can come to now. You're being downright selfish, June. Have you any idea what you're doing to me?'

'Of course I have.' She was struggling not to break down.

'So why put me through it, then?'

'It's something I have to do, Alan.' She was very subdued. 'I really am very sorry.'

'You're *sorry*? You walk out on me after seven years and all you can say is sorry?'

She bit her lip. 'It's awful, I know.'

'That's an understatement, if ever I heard one.' Really distressed now, he paced around the small room, head down, hands in pockets. 'OK, you say you weren't discontented with the way we lived. You say it isn't my parents who have driven you out and it isn't our apparent lack of ability to procreate. So the only explanation left is that you don't love me any more.'

'Leave it, Alan—'

'So tell me, when exactly did you fall out of love with me?'

She winced. Nothing could be further from the truth, but if his believing that would help him to accept the fact that she wasn't going back to Devon with him and that he must make a life without her, she would go along with it. 'It was a gradual thing,' she lied, staring at the floor.

'So . . . you don't even fancy me now, then?'

She forced herself to look up and face the torture in his eyes. 'I'm so sorry,' she said.

'Did I suddenly become repulsive to you? Did you have to

shut your eyes and think of other things or pretend that I was someone else?' He wasn't going to let this go. 'Is that how it was?'

'Alan, stop it.'

'I want to know.'

'I don't know exactly,' she said through dry lips. 'I didn't keep a record of my emotions.'

He grabbed her by the arms. 'Of course you don't know because it isn't true.' He was shouting now. 'I refuse to believe that you don't love me or fancy me. I just won't have it.'

'Go home, Alan,' she urged him, exhausted by the trauma. 'It's busy at this time of the year at the Cliff Head. You'll have made things very awkward for the others by rushing off and leaving them to it.'

'They'll just have to manage without me,' he said. 'This is more important.'

'Nothing you say will make me change my mind.' She was adamant. 'So there's no point in continuing with this conversation. All you're doing is upsetting us both.'

'Oh, so it's all my fault, is it?'

'Of course not.'

He moved forward and took her face in his hands, forcing her to look at him. 'Look me in the eyes and tell me you don't love me. Go on, say it.'

She tried to avoid his probing gaze but failed completely. The depth and richness of his eyes drew her to him, making tears swell beneath her lids.

'Go on,' he ordered. 'Let me hear you say it.'

'All right.' She took a deep breath and forced the words out. 'I don't love you, Alan. And I'm not coming back to Devon with you – *not ever.*'

He stared at her in silence, then: 'I still don't believe that you don't love me,' he challenged her.

'You might not want to believe it, Alan,' she told him. 'But it's true.'

He looked so utterly stricken, for a moment she thought she was going to weaken and pour her heart out to him. She had to restrain herself physically from abandoning this whole thing and taking him in her arms. But she was saved from temptation when he flew into a sudden rage, fuelled by his powerlessness over the situation.

'You selfish cow,' he said with vehemence. 'My mother was right all the time. You're not worth bothering about.'

'I wondered how long it would be before she came into it,' June blurted out.

'Any woman who can do what you've done to me can't be worth bothering with,' he ground out. 'I don't need my mother to tell me that.'

'You're right. I'm not going to argue with you about it,' she told him wearily. 'So go home to Torquay and forget about me. You can divorce me if you wish. I won't put up any opposition.'

'You speak about divorce as though it's of no more importance than what's on at the cinema,' he exploded.

'I didn't mean to give that impression.'

'I don't believe I'm hearing any of this.' He shook his head. 'I really thought I knew you. I thought we were soul mates.'

'We were for a while,' she said. 'Everything has its time, and the time for us has gone.'

'I thought you women were red hot about remembering your marriage vows but you seem to have forgotten yours completely,' he said bitterly. 'Marriage doesn't have its time. It's a forever thing . . . in good times and bad.'

'Things aren't always that neat and tidy.'

'Apparently not. After all we've been to each other, I thought I knew you,' he said through tight lips, as though she hadn't spoken. 'But you're like a stranger now.'

'No one ever really knows anyone else, Alan,' June pointed out. 'We're all on our own when it comes down to it.'

'I can do without the psychology, thank you very much.' His voice was tight with controlled rage. 'I'm just an ordinary bloke who thought he had a decent marriage. I don't need a lecture on the deeper side of human nature.'

'This isn't getting us anywhere so I think you'd better leave.' She stood up. 'If I were you, I'd get some sleep and take an early train back to Torquay in the morning.'

'I will, don't worry.' His attitude was harsh now, with a new edge of determination as he accepted the fact that she wasn't going to change her mind. 'But I can tell you one thing: you'll be sorry you did this, *very sorry*.'

He couldn't know how bitterly she regretted it already. 'Perhaps,' she sighed.

'No perhaps about it.' He was hitting out and saying things he didn't mean in the heat of the moment. 'Even if you don't miss me personally, when the novelty of freedom wears off and you're stuck in this miserable hole with no home comforts, you'll realise what you've turned your back on.'

She nodded.

'You could have had it all, June – a good life with a secure future – and you've just thrown it all away.'

'Which proves how serious I am about not coming back.' Her mouth was so parched she could hardly speak. 'No one chooses to live in accommodation like this.'

'If I'd treated you badly, what you've done would be justifiable.' It was as though he was thinking aloud. 'But I've never been unfaithful, never laid a finger on you.'

'I've told you that none of this is your fault.'

'Right, that's enough begging and pleading,' he said, his tone ice-hard. 'You've just blown your last chance with me. I wouldn't have you back now if you got down on your knees and begged me.'

She didn't say anything.

'So don't come crawling back when you've had enough of being on your own because my door will be closed to you,' he roared. 'Understand?'

Still she didn't put up a fight or try to explain the real reason for her behaviour. There was no point as she had no defence she could tell him about. There hadn't been a word of truth in what she'd said. Her brutal callousness was the best thing for him in the long term and she must stand by her decision. 'I understand,' she said in a subdued tone.

'What shall I do with your stuff?' he asked bitterly. 'You only took the basic essentials.'

'Perhaps you could give it to a charity, or if that's too much bother just throw it out,' she suggested sadly.

He gave her a long hard look, the fury in his eyes softening momentarily into a look of pleading. She almost weakened but managed to stand firm.

Without another word, he marched to the door and opened it, turning towards her. 'I hope you rot in hell,' he said, and left, slamming the door behind him.

She couldn't move; just stood where she was, frozen to the spot. She had experienced terrible things in her life, things most people couldn't even imagine: indescribable pain and humiliation almost beyond human endurance. But she couldn't remember ever feeling this desolate before.

Forcing her limbs to work, she walked slowly over to the bed in the corner and lay face down, burying her head in the pillow, unable even to relieve herself in tears. She thought this must surely be her darkest moment.

Chapter Four

It was a big day in the Rivers household because Shirley was starting school. Despite her mother's most ardent reassurance, the little girl was beset with doubts about the 'new adventure' on account of something she'd heard from an authority on the subject, a seasoned schoolgirl of several months' standing whom she played with in the street.

'She said the teachers are all horrid old witches who shout at you and make you stand in the corner if you do anything wrong,' she said while Daisy was brushing her daughter's hair and putting an Alice band on it.

'The teachers aren't all horrid old witches at all,' Daisy assured her. 'They're good people who'll teach you to do lots of new things.'

'They're horrid.' Shirley was convinced. 'Jane said if you're really bad you get the cane, though I think that mostly happens to the boys.'

'Whoever's been filling your head with these stories obviously doesn't behave herself.' Daisy chose her words carefully, wanting to be honest without frightening her. 'If you're naughty, of course the teacher will get cross with you, the same as I do. But I'm sure you won't give her any cause. And as for getting the cane, well, that's very unlikely.'

'I wish I didn't have to go, Mum.'

'I know, love. But once you get there with all the other children, you'll be fine, I promise,' Daisy told her, swallowing a lump in her throat. 'I'll be at the school gate waiting for you when you come out and you'll be dying to tell me about all the new things you've been doing.'

A cheery rat-a-tat at the door announced the arrival of Nora, who had called in on her way to work to wish Shirley luck. 'My word, someone looks smart this morning,' she complimented, admiring Shirley's navy-blue gymslip and white blouse, both bought second-hand and made to look new by Daisy.

Shirley managed a stiff little smile but her lips were dry and her eyes like saucers in a face that was pale with nervous apprehension. 'Thank you,' she said politely.

'She's got navy-blue knickers on,' divulged Belinda, triumphant to be the bearer of such privileged information.

'She would do now that she's going to school,' was Nora's reaction. 'All schoolgirls wear those.'

'I want a pair, Mum.' Belinda didn't like to be left out.

'When you go to school you'll have them whether you like it or not,' she was told by her mother. 'This time next year you'll both be wearing navy-blue drawers.'

'A year's a long time, isn't it?' said the wistful Belinda.

'It'll come round before you know it . . . much too quickly for me,' remarked Daisy, managing to sound chirpy though there was a certain poignancy in the air, today being the end of an era as well as a new beginning. 'You're both growing up so fast I'm losing my babies.'

'Well, I'm off to work then,' announced Nora. 'See you later. Have a good day, Sherl. Ta-ta all.'

'Ta-ta,' they chorused.

Daisy and Belinda walked to the school with Shirley, who carried a navy-blue shoe bag containing a pair of plimsolls, as instructed on the school list Daisy had received in advance. It

84

was a crisp autumn morning with the promise of sunshine, though a smoky mist currently shrouded the dusty streets. There was a steady procession of children trekking towards the school, the new ones staying close to their mothers, the old hands making their own way, scuffing and pushing and showing off.

As it was Shirley's first day, Daisy was allowed inside the school to deliver her into the care of the reception teacher, a painful business for both mother and daughter. After a last brave hug, Daisy left feeling heartless. Knowing that to send a child forth was just one of life's brutal necessities didn't make her feel any the less emotional about it. Daisy hoped most fervently that the day would be kind to her first-born.

'Well, Belinda love, it's just you and me today,' she remarked, as they headed home hand in hand. When there was no reply she looked down to see that the small child was crying silently. 'Aah, what's the matter?'

'I want Shirley,' she sobbed, huge tears meandering down her cheeks.

'She's only gone to school, darling,' Daisy pointed out. 'She'll be back this afternoon.'

But the child wasn't soothed. 'I want Shirley, I want my sister,' she wailed.

The look of sheer misery on her face triggered off a memory with such painful clarity that Daisy felt winded by it. More than twenty years ago she'd said the same thing about her own sister and received a good hiding for daring to mention her. 'She'll be home before you know it,' she said kindly, wiping her daughter's eyes with a rag hanky and giving her a cuddle. 'It'll soon be time for us to come back to the school to meet her.'

Belinda seemed pacified with this and Daisy thanked God she could give her that reassurance. She herself hadn't been blessed in that way. In retrospect she could see that she'd never felt complete after losing her sister, and resolved there and then that her own daughters wouldn't be put through the misery of being parted, not while she had breath in her body. Perhaps in these enlightened times more thought was given to the agony of splitting up siblings. But no one had considered it important back in the 1930s. Feed them, keep them clean and teach them right from wrong, that had been the maxim for children in care. Their emotional wellbeing hadn't entered into the equation.

'How long till she comes home?' enquired Belinda, her voice still wobbling slightly.

'A few hours, that's all,' replied Daisy. 'She's gone to school – not emigrated.'

'Hours means ages,' she sighed.

'How about us doing something nice to make it go quicker for you?' suggested Daisy in a positive manner. 'We could go to the swings later on and have a sticky bun in a café afterwards. Would you like that?'

'Ooh, yes, please, Mum.'

The bond between siblings was a curious one, thought Daisy, because within minutes of Shirley being home from school she and Belinda would probably be scrapping like street dogs. Yet, such was the complexity of human nature, they hated to be apart. She wondered how she would have got on with her sister in adulthood had they stayed together. Would they have remained close or drifted apart? That was something she would never know.

Just when Daisy had given Nat up as a complete dead loss, he would do something to redeem himself.

This happened one evening in November. After not show-ing his face for a couple of weeks, he turned up at Daisy's place on her Saturday night off, gave her some money towards the bills, brought sweets for the girls and offered to take Daisy to the pictures. Nora was enlisted as baby-sitter, and the couple went to see *Young at Heart* with Doris Day and Frank Sinatra. All of this and chocolates too, a half-pound box no less, and he also took her for a couple of drinks at the pub afterwards.

She guessed he'd done some lucrative business deal but she knew better than to quiz him about it, and just accepted the treat graciously.

'This is lovely,' she said, sipping a gin and orange at a table in the crowded pub. 'Us having a night out together. We should do it more often.'

Reluctant as ever to commit himself to anything beyond the current moment, Nat said, 'Yeah, it would be nice but it isn't that easy, is it? Because of the girls.'

'Nora is always willing to sit with them if we want to go out on my night off,' Daisy pointed out, her joy at this rare attention from him giving her an added radiance, eyes shining, cheeks glowing prettily against her bright red coat. 'We could take the girls out sometimes too. During the day on a Saturday, for instance . . . to the park or the river.'

'Mm.'

'Don't overdo the enthusiasm.'

'You know me,' he reminded her. 'I'm not at my best with kids. I never know what to say to them.'

'These aren't just any kids, they're your daughters,' Daisy was quick to point out. 'You'd know what to say to them if you would only take the trouble to spend time with them and get to know them. They're growing faster than weeds. Surely you don't want to turn around one day to find that they're adults and you're a stranger to them.'

'Of course I don't.' He wasn't really bothered and didn't want to talk about his responsibilities when he'd gone out to enjoy himself for the evening. 'I suppose I've just never got round to spending time with them.'

'You are their father, Nat,' she said. 'You really should make the effort.'

'Yeah, yeah. Don't spoil a good night out by giving me a load of grief,' he protested. 'I'll try to be better in the future.'

'I've heard that before.'

'I mean it this time.'

'I wish I could believe that.'

He reached for her hand across the table. 'I know I'm a bit unreliable sometimes but you mean the world to me,' he said, his mood becoming tender.

'You don't love me enough to marry me, though.' She had seized the opportunity to make a point but was doing so in an affectionate manner.

'I will, one day.'

'I've waited so long, I'm beginning to lose hope.'

'It'll happen, Daisy,' he said softly, 'I promise.'

In this mood he was irresistible, and the common sense she usually had in such abundance just vanished. She could have wept with love for him. 'I believe you, thousands wouldn't,' she said lightly.

They had another drink, then walked home hand in hand. It felt utterly perfect and Daisy was content. At the bottom of the attic stairs, he commented on the fact that the whole area was in darkness as it had been the last time he was here. 'It's about time this light was fixed, isn't it?' he observed. 'Some-one could fall and hurt themselves.'

'You don't have to tell me how dangerous it is,' she said. 'We have to use candles to go up and down stairs at night, and to use the sink on the landing. It's a damned nuisance, especially when one of the kids wants to go to the bathroom in the night.'

'I take it it doesn't just need a new bulb then?'

'If it was as simple as that we'd have seen to it by now,' she pointed out. 'It's a job for an electrician and the landlord's responsibility. He's supposed to be dealing with it but we're not holding our breath.'

'He can't be bothered, I suppose.'

'There's more to it than that,' she informed him. 'It's all part of his plan to get us out of here. When something needs fixing in the house, he leaves it in the hope that the inconvenience will drive us out. Some of the other long-term tenants have left. But Nora and I won't budge.'

'Wouldn't it be easier to just leave?' he suggested.

'Where would I find a place at a price I can afford?' she asked, reminded again of his lack of interest in her problems.

'It would be difficult, I suppose . . .'

'Anyway, it's downright wicked what Ellwood is doing – trying to drive decent people out of their homes,' Daisy continued. 'And you never know what stunt he's going to pull next. What with getting people to keep us awake at night with loud music and parties, employing gangster types to collect the rent in a menacing manner, and withdrawing any sort of maintenance, I don't know where it will all end.'

There was a silence, then he said worriedly, 'You know that I'm not in a position to offer you and the girls a home with me at the moment, don't you, Daisy? I would if I could but I just don't have the room.'

She was used to the fact that he shirked involvement. But for some reason it touched a raw nerve and something rose in her, something so strong it pushed aside her devotion to him so that she was able to take a clear, realistic look at the situation. Not only did he refuse to offer her and the girls a home or financial support, he didn't give them any practical help either. He never offered to speak to the landlord on her behalf, or to have a few words with the offending neighbours in the hope of making them more considerate. His children could fall down the stairs and break their necks without a light to see by and his only contribution was a feeble remark

89

about the light needing fixing. Where were his paternal instincts? Where was his sense of duty towards her? Absolutely nonexistent.

Tears swelled beneath her lids and she admonished herself for being so soft. After all, it was a long time since she'd been under any illusions about Nat. If he'd had a responsible bone in his body she'd have spotted it by now. She'd always accepted him as he was, with all his faults. But tonight, for some reason, his attitude stuck in her craw.

'I'd have to be really thick not to realise that, Nat,' she snapped. 'So you can stop panicking. The last thing I would ever do is ask you for help.'

She couldn't see his face in the dark but guessed his expression would be one of relief. He didn't even bother to make a token protest and they made their way up the darkened stairs slowly and carefully, in silence.

Because Nat had no sense of diplomacy, he made the reason for the evening's generosity glaringly obvious as soon as Nora had gone and he and Daisy were alone. He slipped his arms around her as she waited for the kettle to boil for coffee.

'Don't, Nat,' she said, pushing him away.

'Why not?'

'Because I don't want you to.'

'The girls are asleep and the bedroom door's closed,' he pointed out, insistently putting his arms around her again. 'So we've got this room to ourselves.'

'No.' Her tone was more assertive.

'Oh, I get it. It's the time of the month.'

'No, it isn't that.'

'What then?'

'I just don't want to,' she informed him briskly, pouring water on to the bottled coffee essence in the cups.

Nat wasn't easily deterred when it came to pleasures of the

flesh. He grabbed her by the arms roughly and pulled her round to face him. 'Come on, Daisy. Don't mess me about,' he said in a threatening manner.

She was sickened by him; even more by herself for allowing him to use her and take her for granted for so long. She'd cheapened herself because of her feelings for him and she felt dirty and stupid suddenly. 'I'm not messing you about,' she told him. 'I'm just being truthful. I don't want to do it and that's that.'

'There's a name for women who lead men on,' he declared.

'I haven't led you on.'

'Oh, not much,' he said vehemently. 'You were all over me when we were out, while I was spending money on you. Now you don't want to know.'

She was deeply hurt but her spirit remained intact. 'It was a trip to the local cinema, for heaven's sake, not a weekend at the Ritz,' she reminded him. 'And now I'm expected to show you how grateful I am.'

'There's no need to make it sound as though I'm committing some sort of a crime in expecting it,' he admonished sulkily. 'That's how these things work. I haven't noticed you putting up any objections before.'

'Maybe I'm beginning to wake up and see things in a different light,' she told him. 'After all this time I can see that the only thing that stops my relationship with you being prostitution is the fact that I do it for nothing.'

'There's no need to be vulgar, Daisy,' he rebuked primly. 'It doesn't suit you.'

'The truth can be crude.'

'Well, that's gratitude for you.' He was outraged. 'I took you out, gave you a good time, I even bought you chocolates—'

'And a couple of drinks at the pub and my cinema ticket. And you gave me money towards the bills.' She was furious now. 'As I'm not prepared to pay you in kind perhaps you'd like me to give you the money back. I'll have to repay what you've already spent on a weekly basis.' She paused for a moment, then added with emphasis, 'Unlike you, I don't have any spare cash to hand.'

'You can mock,' he chided her. 'But it all added up to quite a bit in the end.'

She marched across to the sideboard and took her purse out of her handbag. Dragging out the ten-shilling note he'd given her, she thrust it towards him. 'Here, have it back,' she demanded.

'Don't be like that.'

'You might as well take it 'cause you'll get no other form of payment from me.' She waved the note at him. 'Go on, take it. You know you want to.'

Surely even Nat wouldn't sink that low, she thought, but he said, 'All right, I will,' and snatched the money from her.

'You disgust me.' Her voice was dull with disappointment now. 'Get out.'

He walked to the door, paused for a moment, then turned and came back to her. Handing the money to her, he said in a conciliatory manner, 'Daisy, love, this is silly and beginning to get out of hand. Don't let's part on bad terms.'

'Just go.'

'You and me have been together a long time and we've always managed to patch things up before.'

'Only because I'm soft.' She didn't take the money.

'That's one of the things I love most about you,' he told her, his manner blatantly persuasive now. 'The fact that you're so warm and loving.'

'I'm also a fool,' she said coldly.

His limited patience soon ran out. 'Oh, I'm not staying here with you in this mood. I came here for pleasure not punishment,' he said irritably, walking to the door, stuffing

92

the money into his pocket. 'I'll see you around.'

The door closed behind him and Daisy heard him cursing as he fumbled his way down the stairs in the dark. She felt battered and broken inside. How can he still have such power to hurt me? she wondered, sitting in the chair with a cup of coffee. After all these years and my knowing him for what he is?

With the same certainty that she knew he would be back, she knew she would forgive him. It was no life, being in a perpetual sulk with someone you cared about. At times she wished she'd never set eyes on him but mostly she didn't regret falling in love with him. How could she when he had given her the girls who were so obviously meant to be? Anyway, it wasn't as if he was wicked. He was just extremely immature and selfish. You had to make the most of what life sent you and Nat was part of her package.

As basic and poky as it was, the 'miserable little gaff' that Alan had been so derisive about did actually begin to feel like home to June that autumn. It was a far cry from the comfortable accommodation she'd been used to, but it was surprising how quickly she adapted to it. There was a certain comfort in being one of a number in the staff quarters, all people who for one reason or another had nowhere else to live.

There were foreign waiters, and waitresses and chamber maids from all over the UK. As they shared a sitting room and kitchen, naturally camaraderie evolved. There was always company on hand if June wanted it. Obviously she couldn't stay here for ever but it suited her in the short term.

She didn't hear from Alan again, but adjusting to life without him didn't seem any easier for that. Her salvation was the job, which was far more demanding than her position at the Cliff Head had been. The atmosphere here was totally different: much busier and less personal. The well-to-do guests in this central London hotel wanted efficiency and privacy rather than personal conversation. The phone rang constantly and there were always people milling about in the foyer, many of them from abroad.

The human touch was something she missed but she enjoyed the challenge of the work, which was never less than absorbing. No matter how desperate she was feeling about the state of her personal life, while she was actually on duty, she was forced to put it to the back of her mind.

At night it tormented her, though. On her own in her lonely room she longed for Alan and wondered how he was.

Day followed day, though, and life went on. Somehow June was managing without him, albeit that she seemed merely to be skimming over the surface of everyday life.

One afternoon in early November two policemen walked into the hotel reception while she was on duty and said they were looking for Mrs June Masters.

Instantly alarmed at the thought that something must have happened to Alan, June's hand flew to her throat. 'I'm June Masters,' she said with a pounding heart. 'Has something happened to my husband?'

'Not as far as we know,' replied one of the officers, adding quickly, 'But we would like a word. Can someone take over from you here for a few minutes?'

Before June had a chance to arrange cover on the desk, the front-of-house manager bustled on to the scene and whisked her and her visitors out of sight into a small office behind reception. Policemen at the hotel were not good for business.

'So, what's all this about?' she asked through dry lips as soon as they were alone.

'You are the daughter of Margaret Grey?' The policeman needed it confirmed.

'That's right,' she said with a nod. 'Is my mother ill?'

'She's had an accident, I'm afraid,' he explained in an even

94

tone. 'She was knocked down by a car in Hounslow High Street earlier this afternoon.'

'Is she . . . is she badly hurt?'

The man hesitated, his mouth tightening slightly. 'I'm sorry to have to tell you that she died in the ambulance on the way to the hospital,' he informed her gravely.

'Oh . . .'

'The person your mother was with at the time of the accident told us she had a daughter and we tracked you down through an address book in her handbag,' he explained.

'I see.'

'I'm afraid we'll have to ask you, as her next of kin, to make a formal identification,' one of the officers told her. 'But there's no hurry. You've time for a cup of tea to steady your nerves first.'

'I'm all right,' she said, though she was breathless with shock. 'I'll just go and tell my boss what's happened, then I'll come with you.'

'If you're sure you're feeling up to it . . .?' he said kindly.

'I'm sure.'

June thought the policemen might be shocked to know that her prevailing emotion was one of relief that nothing bad had happened to Alan.

The death of her adopted mother barely touched her at the time. There had been no love lost between them anyway, but the all-consuming pain of missing Alan meant that everything else paled into insignificance. June even arranged the funeral and endured it without much emotion.

It was only when she was at the house in Hounslow where she'd grown up, sorting through her mother's things and getting the property she'd inherited, as next of kin, ready for sale that memories of the past began to flood in. Sitting at the bureau in the living room one morning, going through some family papers, she discovered a photograph of herself with her adopted parents that caused tears to flow. Not with sadness because they were both now dead but because of the agony of her life with them.

In the photograph, the three of them were in the garden of this house, standing under the lilac tree, June between the two grown-ups. Anyone else would see a picture of family contentment. But the mere sight of her father sent shivers up her spine. She still couldn't bear to look at him, and he'd been dead for four years.

Both parents had died relatively young – in their fifties – thus disproving the theory that only the good did that. It would have been hypocritical of her to pretend grief at the passing of either. It was hard to grieve for anyone you'd feared and hated. Adulthood and distance hadn't warmed her to them on her rare duty visits.

She tore the photograph up and let it flutter into the wastepaper bin. There were others that received the same treatment. She didn't want anything left to remind her of them. There were various family documents: her father's army discharge papers, her parents' marriage certificate.

Coming across a large fat brown envelope, June opened it curiously, her heart turning somersaults as she realised it was the official correspondence between her parents and the adoption authorities.

It was a weird feeling to see details of yourself in black and white; strange and rather frightening to be confronted with your background after a lifetime of ignorance. Her hand trembled as she fingered a letter, words and sentences leaping out at her.

Regarding your application to adopt legally June Rivers, currently in care at St Clare's Home for Destitute Children in Hammersmith, we feel it necessary to point out that the case of the Rivers sisters is a particularly tragic one. June may be mentally disturbed after such a sudden loss of parents and family life. It is deemed to be in the children's interest for them to remain unaware of the shocking circumstances that resulted in their being taken into the care of the authorities.

We also believe it important to June's future stability for her to be encouraged to forget her previous background, including her sister, as this may impede her progress in adapting to a new and stable family life again.

As June read other correspondence and newspaper cuttings which gave her the basic details of what the 'shocking circumstances' actually were, she shook violently from head to toe, bile rising in her throat and sending her scurrying to the bathroom. Now at last she knew why she and her sister had been abandoned, but the reason was so dreadful she wished she'd never found out. She could understand the authorities' logic in not telling two little girls about their original background. Knowing something that horrifying at such a young age could have damaged them for life.

But June did know now. And she couldn't erase the knowledge or leave it at that. She had to learn the full story. Washing her hands and face, she went back to the living room. Jotting down a few dates, she got her coat and hurried to the nearest library.

Finding 1934 in the book of old copies of a national newspaper in the reference section of the library, June began to turn the pages. The story of her early background unfolded. It was like reading cheap horror fiction but it had all actually happened. When she saw the name Morris Dodd in print, she knew with sickening certainty why she'd been haunted by the memory of him for all these years. Her heart pounded at the huge significance it now had.

There was one thing she now had to do urgently. She had to find her sister, Daisy. This filled her with excitement, then despair at the impossibility of the task. Twenty years was a long time – she could be anywhere. She might not even have survived the war. St Clare's was June's only lead. It was a long shot after all these years but they just might have some idea of where she was.

'Please, God, let her still be alive,' she prayed silently as she left the library and headed for the tube station, en route for Hammersmith.

Later that same day June walked through the squalid backstreets of Notting Hill, past windows boarded up, stucco rotting on the front of terraces, fumes from the local factories mingling with the stench from wasteland used as an open rubbish dump.

It was a cold and misty November day but small children played in the street despite the weather, women stood at front doors gossiping, a crowd of young West Indian men stood on the corner engaged in conversation.

Although June's circumstances had taken a dive when she'd left Alan, the area in which she now lived was, none the less, a world apart from this, yet less than two miles away. She couldn't help but be shocked by the deprivation of the neighbourhood and was ashamed of her disgust.

She found the address in Benly Square the nuns had given her and knocked on the front door, which swung open at her touch because the lock was broken. Finding herself in a hallway that was foul with the smell of damp and stale cooking, she didn't know what to do next. The address just said number twenty Benly Square; there was nothing about a flat number.

A woman came out of one of the rooms and walked towards the front door dressed in a brown mac and carrying a shopping bag. Her eyes rose at the sight of June's smart grey suit and high-heeled court shoes.

'You looking for someone?' she asked without much interest.

June nodded. 'Daisy,' she said. 'Daisy Rivers she was. She might not be using that name now.'

'Up in the attic,' the woman informed her, and left the house.

June made her way up the creaking stairs, becoming increasingly horrified at the conditions. At the top of the attic stairs, she was greeted by a middle-aged woman with wild ginger hair and enquiring blue eyes. 'Can I help you?' she asked in a cultured voice that didn't match the ambience.

'I'm looking for Daisy,' June explained.

'She's gone to meet her little girl from school,' Nora explained pleasantly. 'She's taken her other daughter with her so there's no one in her flat at the moment.'

'Do you think she'll be long?'

'She should be back at any minute.'

'Thank you.'

'You're welcome to come and have a cup of tea in my place while you're waiting,' Nora offered, curious as to who June was but courteous enough not to enquire. 'Daisy and I are very good friends.' She gave her a wide grin. 'Well, we're more like family, really. I know she'd want me to make you welcome.'

'It's very kind of you to offer but I think I'll wait outside as she'll only be a minute,' June said, first because she was feeling emotional about the imminent reunion and needed to be on her own, and secondly because the oppressive atmosphere inside this building was making her nauseous and she was desperate for some fresh air.

'As you wish, dear,' said Nora.

'See you later then,' said June, and made her way down the broken stairs.

Relieved to be outside, despite the cold grimy atmosphere, she took a deep breath to prepare herself for the meeting. Suddenly the sound of laughter filled the air, and looking down the street she saw a small woman in a red coat – with several inches of grey skirt showing beneath it – coming towards her holding the hands of two little girls, one of them dressed in a navy-blue school raincoat. They stopped for a moment, listening to the girl in the raincoat, then there were gales of laughter.

Obviously it wasn't possible to recognise the adult from the child she remembered but she knew instinctively that the woman was Daisy, and the thing that struck June was the closeness of the trio, obviously happy to be together. On jelly legs, her heart thudding madly, June walked towards them.

Shirley was regaling her mother and sister with the story of one boy, Paul, in her class who had taken his pet mouse to school in his pocket and how it had escaped and everyone had screamed and stood on their desks, even the teacher. Daisy and Belinda had thought this hilarious.

'What happened to the mouse?'

'Paul found it and the caretaker looked after it until it was time to go home and Paul took it with him,' Shirley explained. 'Miss was very cross with him for bringing it to school and scaring everybody.'

'I expect she was,' said Daisy, imagining the teacher's embarrassment if Shirley's version of her behaviour hadn't been exaggerated.

'What's for tea, Mum?' asked Belinda.

'Fish paste sandwiches and toasted buns.'

'Toasted buns, yippee,' cried Shirley.

Immersed in her children, Daisy hadn't paid any attention to someone approaching but looked up now to see an extremely smart woman in a fitted suit and high-heeled shoes. She's out of place around here, Daisy thought, and hoped she hadn't come from the landlord with some message of doom.

'Daisy?'

'That's me,' she replied, noticing how strikingly attractive the woman was, with fine features and sleek, dark hair. 'What can I do for you?'

The woman seemed upset about something, too upset to answer; there were tears running down her cheeks.

'Shirley, love, give the lady your hanky,' said Daisy, because Shirley was the only one who had a proper handkerchief for school; the others had rag ones.

Shirley handed her the handkerchief, which seemed to make her cry even more.

'Oh, my Lord, you are in a state,' was Daisy's kind response; she was too concerned about the woman to ask how she knew her name. 'Can I help in any way?'

June stared at her.

'Whatever it is that's troubling you, you'll feel better for a cup of tea and a sit-down,' said Daisy warmly. 'You don't want to be out on the street when you're so upset, love. We only live a few doors down. So come in and have a cup of tea with us.'

'Oh, Daisy, don't you see,' said the woman, 'I'm not crying because I'm sad.'

'I dread to think what you'd be like if you were then,' quipped Daisy. 'The whole of London would be under water.'

'Daisy,' the other woman began in muffled tones, 'do you remember that you once had a sister?'

'Course I remember,' Daisy told her. 'I'm not likely to forget a thing like that.'

The woman stared at her meaningfully.

Daisy gulped, her eyes narrowing on her in a questioning manner. 'You?' she gasped.

'That's right. I'm June,' she informed her thickly. 'I'm your sister.'

'You never are,' said Daisy, staring at her in disbelief, trying to recognise something about her and remembering only that the child in her memory had had dark hair.

'I am.'

'But how—'

'I'll tell you everything all in good time,' said June. 'But for now, let me give you a hug.'

Now Daisy was weeping unashamedly. After all these years she'd come face to face with her own flesh and blood. The little girls looked on in bewilderment as the two women clutched each other, wailing loudly.

'Are we going in for tea soon?' asked Shirley at last, bringing an air of normality to the proceedings. 'It's cold out here and I'm starving.'

'Yes, love, we're going indoors for tea now.' She looked at June. 'You will join us, won't you?'

'Love to.' The terrible miasma inside the house was forgotten in the joy of the moment.

'This is your Auntie June, girls,' said Daisy, sniffing into the handkerchief.

'What, a *real* auntie?' queried Shirley. 'Not a pretend one like Nora is our pretend grannie?'

'No, this is your real auntie,' Daisy confirmed.

'Cor,' approved Shirley.

'Smashing,' added Belinda.

It was strange, thought June, an hour or so later, how the pungent hallway and landings of the dilapidated building ceased to exist once you were inside Daisy's flat, the gas fire spreading a glow over the shabby room, the curtains drawn against the murky weather outside and the crumbling window sills.

Nora went to the bakers to get more buns, which were toasted with a fork on the gas fire, and they all sat around the table having tea and talking, the sweet scent of cinnamon from the buns filling the air.

Daisy had insisted that Nora stay. 'She's like a mum to me,' she'd explained to June, 'and I wouldn't want her to miss out on a special occasion like this.'

'Of course not,' June had approved.

The two sisters had exchanged basics about themselves, their jobs, their personal circumstances. June knew Daisy was an unmarried mum. June mentioned that she'd recently separated from her husband and touched on her life as a hotelier's wife but offered no details about the cause of the separation. They both agreed how fortunate it was that Daisy had kept in touch with St Clare's, who'd been able to direct June straight to her. They both had so much to say, though Daisy did mention that she had to keep her eye on the time because she was on duty this evening. June said she was having a couple of days off to sort out her late mother's affairs.

'But tell me, June,' said Daisy, when everyone had finished eating, 'why come looking for me now, after all this time?'

'I've always wanted to, of course—'

'I know that,' cut in Daisy, because they had already discussed how their upbringing had deterred them from looking for each other, 'but what actually drove you to do something about it at this particular time?'

June bit her lip, looking uncomfortable. 'It's a bit delicate, actually,' she told her.

'Come on, girls,' said Nora, taking the hint. 'Let's go and have a game of snap in my place while your mother and her sister have a chat.'

They went without argument because snap was still a big favourite with them.

'So, what is it you have to tell me that isn't suitable for little ears?' asked Daisy.

June moistened her lips. 'I've had to go through my adopted mother's papers following her death,' she explained, 'and I've found out how we came to be in St Clare's.'

'We already know,' Daisy pointed out. 'Our mother died and our father abandoned us.'

'Yes. Basically that's true,' June confirmed, 'but there was much more to it than that.'

Daisy waited for her to go on.

After taking a deep breath to try to calm herself, June asked, 'Do you remember a man called Morris Dodd?'

'Mr Dodd,' she responded, looking startled. 'Yeah, I remember him all right.'

'You remember that night he threatened us, don't you?' June guessed. 'I can tell from the look on your face.'

'It's haunted me on and off all through my life,' Daisy confided, eyes glazed as she recalled the incident. 'You and I were in bed when we heard shouting downstairs.'

'And we crept halfway down, scared to go further because we were supposed to be asleep and would have got told off if Mum had found out.'

'Mr Dodd was in the hall on his way to the front door,' Daisy continued.

'And he grabbed us and shook us and told us to go back to bed and if we ever told anyone he'd been at our house that night, he'd come after us and do something so terrible we'd wish we were dead.'

'I was so scared I nearly wet myself,' remembered Daisy. 'I still go cold when I think about it.'

'Me too,' said June. 'I can still see those eyes, glaring at us, his face close to mine. Ugh.'

'The memory of it has kept me awake many a night and I don't know what it means,' confessed Daisy.

'Neither did I until today,' June told her. 'Now I know why he was so rough with us that night.'

'And?'

She took another deep breath before uttering her next words. 'Our mother didn't die of natural causes,' she said through dry lips. 'She was murdered.'

Daisy turned pale; she was too shocked to speak.

'It gets worse,' June warned her. 'Our father was convicted of the murder. That's why we were abandoned.'

'Our father a murderer?' Daisy couldn't believe it.

'He was found guilty, yes.'

'Was he . . . was he hanged?'

'No, it wasn't considered to be premeditated so the sentence was commuted to life imprisonment,' she explained. 'You'll have to come with me to the library to read the newspaper reports of the trial to get the full story. But I don't think our father did it. Morris Dodd was our mother's lover, apparently, and I think he killed her.'

'Why do you think that?'

'Because our father claimed throughout the trial that he was innocent and Dodd killed her. Dodd denied being at our house on the night of the murder, which I reckon is the same night he scared the living daylights out of us, as we ended up in St Clare's soon after,' said June. 'That's why he was so keen to keep us quiet.'

'Ooh, June, I think you're right.'

'According to the reports, no one saw him arrive or leave the house and his wife claimed that he was with her on the night of the murder,' June went on to say. 'But we both know that he was there at the house, don't we?'

'Yeah.'

'And we are the only people alive, apart from our father

and the Dodds, who know that he was lying,' June continued. 'I don't know if our father is still alive. But I do know that you and I are the only people who can clear his name.'

'Oh, June,' gasped Daisy.

'Big responsibility, isn't it?'

'Huge,' agreed her sister.

Chapter Five

'Mother murdered while babes sleep' was just one of the gruesome headlines that confronted the sisters at Kensington reference library the next day when they scoured the old newspapers for reports of the trial in 1934 of Lionel Rivers for the murder of his wife, Rose.

'It simply beggars belief that such a thing could have happened in the house while we were actually in it without us knowing about it,' Daisy said to June as they comforted themselves with a steaming espresso in one of the new-style coffee bars that had opened recently in Kensington High Street. As today was Saturday, Daisy had been able to leave the girls with Nora in whom she'd confided. 'Our mother strangled to death, our father sent to prison and we knew nothing about any of it until now. It's incredible.'

'Spooky,' was June's opinion. 'I can understand why we weren't told, though, can't you?'

Daisy sipped her coffee, pondering on this for a moment. 'Having to cope with the ghastly truth at that age wouldn't exactly have helped us through life.'

'Quite. I suppose we were considered too young to be questioned by the police about whether we saw or heard anything too,' suggested June, 'especially as we were assumed to have slept through the whole thing.'

'We must have been whisked away into care as soon as the

police came on the scene, to protect us from the horror of it all,' Daisy surmised.

'I expect that's the sort of thing that would happen in a case like that but I don't remember anything about that part of it.'

'Me neither.'

'Do you think we were from a Catholic family, as we were sent to St Clare's?' wondered June.

'That doesn't necessarily follow,' Daisy replied. 'It could just have been that they happened to have room for us there. There were lots of children in care then. Homes got overcrowded.'

'Mm, there is that.'

A thoughtful silence descended.

'Just think of the difference it would have made to our father's case if we'd told someone we'd seen Morris Dodd at the house that night,' mused Daisy.

'I've been agonising over that too.' June shook her head, sighing. 'But we weren't to know that, as we had no idea what had happened.'

'We probably wouldn't have realised the significance if we had known, being so little. We'd have been too terrified to open our mouths, anyway, after that roughing up from Mr Dodd,' was Daisy's opinion. 'At that age you just do what you're told.'

'Especially in those days,' added June. 'Children were very much seen and not heard then.'

'Still are in a lot of families,' Daisy mentioned chattily. 'But not in mine. My daughters have plenty to say for themselves and I wouldn't have it any other way. I'd hate them to have a childhood as strict and loveless as mine was.'

'They're lovely kids,' June smiled. 'You're very lucky to have them.'

Lucky wasn't a word much used to describe Daisy, whose circumstances meant she was either perceived as a cheap little tart or a husbandless no-hoper burdened by a couple of bastards. 'Yes, I am,' she agreed wholeheartedly, 'and every day I thank God for them. They're everything to me.'

'And you are to them,' June told her. 'It shines bright from all of you. Nora as well.'

Daisy smiled, and June couldn't remember having met anyone who exuded such warmth before. So, which of the two of them had fared better from life, she found herself wondering: a child 'favoured' by adoption, who'd grown up in a comfortable home to have good manners and refined speech, and now had a broken marriage, an inability to have children and no real friends because her childhood had robbed her of the capacity for friendship? Or Daisy, an orphanage girl struggling to raise two children on her own in poor accommodation and living from hand to mouth, but having the unqualified love of her daughters, the affection of a close woman friend and a generous heart towards everyone? The question answered itself.

'Yeah, we're a close little band, and Nora's like one of the family.' Daisy sensed a profound sadness in June that her general air of confidence couldn't hide. Presumably her broken marriage was the cause. It must be heartbreaking to have had something as precious as that and lost it, she thought, her mind drifting to her own long-standing desire for marriage to Nat, with whom she'd made her peace last week as predicted. 'She's the nearest thing I have to a mum – one that I can remember, anyway. My memories of our real mother are quite vague.'

'Mine too. Which is only natural as we lost her so young,' said June.

'And when you think about it, she must have been a bit preoccupied at the end of her life too, as she was having an affair with Morris Dodd,' Daisy pointed out, her thoughts returning to the findings in the library. 'I wonder what she did with us while she was with him.'

'Perhaps we were at school or something,' suggested June. 'It said in the paper that Morris Dodd was some sort of a sales rep. Those people can be flexible during the working day as they're out and about, so he could have seen her then, while our father was out at work.'

'The mind boggles,' said Daisy. 'An adulterous mother doesn't exactly match the cosy maternal figure I imagined her to be all these years.'

June gave an understanding nod. 'Morris Dodd was a family friend, apparently, which is how she knew him and why we remembered him being familiar to us.'

'So, let's run through it,' began Daisy, wanting to summarise the whole dreadful business. 'According to our father's evidence, Mother ended the affair but Morris Dodd is the sort of man who likes to get his own way so he went round to the house with the idea of persuading her to reconsider her decision.'

'He just burst in there apparently, and the whole thing got out of hand,' June continued. 'He confronted her in front of Dad and when she wouldn't agree to leave him, Dodd lost his temper and started knocking her about, which accounts for the shouting we heard from upstairs. Dad tried to fight him off and was knocked unconscious. When he came to, Dodd had gone and Mother was dead, strangled. Dodd must have been running from the scene of the crime when he saw us.'

'It sends shivers right through me,' said Daisy, sucking in her breath and wriggling her shoulders, 'to think what was going on downstairs while we were in bed.'

'It must have been all over by the time we crept down the stairs, though,' June speculated.

'Though Dodd tells a different story.'

June nodded. 'He denied being at the house at all that night and his alibi is watertight because his wife swore

110

under oath that he was at home with her,' she went on. 'Because no one could prove otherwise, his version of events was believed and it was assumed that Dad was lying to save his own skin.'

'Of course, we can't be absolutely certain that the night Morris Dodd terrorised us was the night of the murder because we were just children and it was a long time ago.' June wanted to be realistic.

'I'm sure in my own mind, though,' Daisy responded thoughtfully. 'I remember that nothing was ever the same again after that.'

'No it wasn't.' June paused, sipping her coffee. 'Not that anyone in authority will believe us. Two women suddenly claiming to remember something they saw over twenty years ago when they were children won't carry any weight at all. We won't stand a chance of getting the case reopened on that alone.'

'There is one other person besides us and our father who knows that Dodd was lying in court.'

'His wife.'

'Exactly.'

'She's not likely to admit to perjury, though, is she?' June pointed out.

'Not without a very strong incentive,' Daisy was forced to agree. 'But she's the only person who can back up our story so we have to try to find her and see if she can't somehow be persuaded to co-operate. Don't ask me how because I haven't a clue at this stage. But I do know we must at least try to clear our father's name, however hopeless it seems.'

'You won't get any objections from me,' June assured her. 'But before we do anything about that side of it there's something more important we must do.'

'Find out if our father is still alive and, if so, where he is, then arrange to pay him a visit,' guessed Daisy.

111

'You've got it,' confirmed June. 'I've no idea how to set about it, though. Have you?'

'Not really. But I should think the police station would be a good starting point,' suggested Daisy. 'They'll know what the procedure is for finding out which prison someone is in.'

Because both sisters had jobs and Daisy also had the children to consider, they couldn't just drop everything and devote all their time to their father's plight, as much as they both wanted to. But they both gave the matter a great deal of thought and did what they could within the parameters of their other commitments.

June had access to the telephone books at work and planned to make a list of all the Dodds in the London area. As personal calls from work were prohibited she intended to use a call box to contact them.

Her first task, however, was a visit to the police station where she was informed that information about relatives in custody could be obtained from the Home Office, who would issue a visiting order only if the prisoner agreed to it. They gave her the address and she got a detailed letter in the post immediately.

Meanwhile, Daisy was keeping busy. In the hope of moving things forward with regard to finding the Dodds, she approached the Salvation Army, having heard that they offered a service for tracing missing people. But the job was too big for them because she had no information beyond what she'd read in the paper: that the Dodds had once lived in Wembley, where the crime had taken place. The Salvation Army officer suggested that she contact them again if she could get more details for them to work with. It was a huge disappointment.

The keenly awaited news from the Home Office was better. After opening the envelope with a great deal of trepidation,

June learned that Lionel Rivers was indeed still alive and had agreed to see his daughters.

So it was that one bitterly cold afternoon in December, June and Daisy travelled together to Wormwood Scrubs.

Daisy's desire to see her father was strong, but she felt somewhat tremulous and her stomach churned horribly on the bus to the prison.

'Weird, isn't it,' she remarked to June, to take her mind off the imminent meeting which could turn out to be an ordeal, 'us being together like this? It seems unreal.'

'It is peculiar,' agreed her sister. 'The last thing I expected to be doing was going to see a father I've not seen for over twenty years – in prison.'

'I meant more in terms of us getting back together after all these years,' Daisy amended.

'Oh, I see. Yes, it does seem too good to be true.'

'You haven't said much about your childhood,' commented Daisy.

'Haven't I?' June was deliberately vague.

'I imagine from the way you've turned out, being so smart and well spoken and everything, that it was a damned sight better than mine.'

'I doubt it,' she surprised Daisy by saying.

'Oh? But you were one of the chosen few who got out of St Clare's and into a proper home,' Daisy reminded her.

'There's more to a happy life than a comfortable house, Daisy,' June pointed out.

'I realise that but—'

'Let's not talk about me,' she cut in quickly. 'Tell me about yourself.'

'There's nothing much to say really,' Daisy told her. 'I stayed at St Clare's until I was fifteen.'

'It must have been hard, having to stay there for such a

113

long time,' sympathised June. 'I remember what tartars some of the nuns were.'

'They were strict, yeah. But they had to be with all those kids to look after,' said Daisy. 'Without discipline we'd have run wild. I've a lot to thank them for. They gave me a decent upbringing and I'm grateful for that.'

'Did you stay with Catholicism after you left there?' June enquired with interest.

She nodded. 'Did you?'

'No. My adopted parents had once been practising Catholics, which was why they went to St Clare's looking for a child to adopt, but they lapsed and I didn't take it up.'

'My faith is important to me. I really need it,' Daisy went on. 'I don't know how I'd have managed without it through the bad times. When all else failed, I still had that.'

'It must be nice to have something like that to turn to.'

'It is a comfort.' Again Daisy perceived deep unhappiness in her sister but didn't pry as June had made it obvious that she'd said as much as she was going to about her past life. It was still early days in their new relationship. Daisy hoped that at some point in the future June might trust her enough to confide.

'Can you remember what our father looked like?' asked June chattily.

'I've been thinking, and all I can remember about him is that he was a big man with dark hair.'

'I remember him being big too,' said June, 'He had a loud voice and a booming laugh too.'

'Oh, yeah,' smiled Daisy. 'Now you come to mention it, I remember that too.'

Far from being large and dark, Lionel Rivers was short and stockily built, with a bald head and wispy white tufts at the side of his heavily lined countenance. He didn't have a loud voice either but was quietly spoken with sad brown eyes and a look of defeat about him. He didn't look as though he'd laughed in years, in a booming way or otherwise – which was hardly surprising considering what he'd been through, Daisy thought. He couldn't be more than about fifty but he looked like an old man.

Dressed in prison uniform of a drab grey woollen jacket and trousers with a whitish flannel shirt, he observed them with an air of bewilderment across a table in the visitors' room. 'I couldn't believe it when they told me my daughters wanted to see me,' he said, his voice shaking with emotion. 'I'm sorry to have to admit this but you're so different to how I remember you, I'm not sure which is which.'

'I'm Daisy.'

'And I'm June.'

The silence was piercing; there was so much to say but no one knew where to start. He stared from one to the other, as though searching their faces for some sign of recognition.

'It doesn't half feel queer to be looking at the two of you as women,' he said at last. 'You've always been nippers in my memory, you see.' He shook his head slowly. 'Too many years have passed since I saw you.' He sounded so sad, Daisy thought he was about to burst into tears, which made her wonder if this visit was such a good idea after all.

'I've got two little girls of my own now,' Daisy told him, struggling with her own turmoil.

'Grandchildren.' His face worked.

'That's right.'

He didn't say anything; was obviously trying to compose himself. 'That's lovely,' he uttered eventually. 'I've often thought about the two of you, wondered how you were getting on. But I never thought I'd see either of you again.'

'If we'd known what had happened, we'd have been here long before this,' Daisy was keen for him to know.

'How did you find out where I was?' he asked. 'You were supposed never to know.'

'It's a long story,' June told him. 'Too long to go into in one visiting session. The important thing is, we know why you're here and why we were taken into care.'

His eyes widened. 'Oh, I see.' He swallowed hard. 'At the time you thought I'd abandoned you, didn't you?' he muttered thickly. 'Just dumped you because I didn't want to keep you?'

They both nodded.

'It broke my heart, having you think that I would do a thing like that. But it was considered best for you to grow up believing that, rather than know the truth. There were no relatives willing to take you in, you see,' he explained. 'And I was ordered not to try and contact you or to find out where you were.' He emitted a dry, humourless laugh. 'I'd have had a job, being locked up in here.'

'We've worked all of that out for ourselves,' Daisy said gently.

'You must have been very hurt at the time, though.'

'I was,' said June.

Daisy nodded, biting back the tears. 'But that's all in the past,' she said in a positive tone. 'Now we're in the picture. We've read the reports of the murder trial in the old newspapers in the library.'

'You bothered to do that?' He sounded astonished, his face lighting up.

'It was the only way we could find out more about it,' explained June.

Lionel put his hand to his head. 'You poor things.' He looked distressed. 'It must have been a shock to read such things about your parents.'

'It was,' they confessed in unison.

'For what it's worth, I didn't kill your mother,' he said, his

116

tired brown eyes brimming with tears.

'We know that.' June was unsure how to address him. 'Lionel' didn't seem appropriate and 'Dad' was still a label she associated with a man she'd hated.

'We know it was Morris Dodd,' added Daisy.

His eyes bulged. 'How could you possibly know that?'

Between them they told him.

'Well, stone me,' was his amazed reaction.

'We want to try to clear your name and get you out of here,' Daisy informed him.

His face worked with emotion, muscles tightening, mouth twitching slightly. 'It's very kind of you to want to do that for me, but, being realistic, you'll be wasting your time after all these years.' He shook his head sagely. 'We'll never get the case reopened now. You can only get an appeal if there's new evidence. They won't consider your childhood memories to be evidence.' He cleared his throat. 'They'll say you just imagined it unless you have proof to back it up.' He rummaged in his pocket, produced a rag handkerchief and blew his nose. 'Anyway, you've got your own lives to lead. Don't waste your time on my account.'

'June and I have discussed it at length and we know they won't take our word for it,' Daisy made clear. 'We also realise that Dodd won't admit the truth. But we're thinking in terms of trying to get the truth out of his wife, somehow. We know for a fact that she lied under oath.'

'She'd never admit it,' he stated categorically.

'We think it's unlikely too, but we want to try and find the Dodds anyway,' June was firm on this point, 'see if we can't persuade her to do the right thing.'

'Look, I'm really touched that you want to do this for me but there's no need,' he tried to convince them. 'You know that I didn't murder your mother and that I didn't just abandon you because I didn't want you, and that's enough for

117

me.' He shrugged. 'I've been here so long I'm resigned to prison life. It's all I know after all this time.'

'But you're locked up for something you didn't do,' emphasised Daisy. 'Justice must be done.'

'Fine words, love, but I don't want you getting mixed up with the likes of Morris Dodd,' he told them. 'Your mother lost her life because of his vile temper so I think you should steer well clear of him. I've found you again after all these years and that's all that matters to me.'

The two women exchanged glances. This was what the justice system had done to him. It had beaten the spirit out of him and killed his appetite for normal life.

'You can't just give in,' Daisy admonished.

'It took a while but I eventually accepted my fate because I had no choice,' he explained. 'I couldn't fight back because I had no ammunition with which to do so. No one was interested in the truth. To you that might seem pathetic – to me it's plain common sense.'

'But you've got us on your side now,' Daisy encouraged.

'You can't possibly know what that means to me.' His voice was muffled by stifled tears. 'But I don't want you getting into trouble on my behalf. Come and see me every now and again when you can manage it. That'll do for me.'

'We'll be the judge of that.' Daisy fell silent, a question burning inside her. 'Do you mind if I ask you something, though it might be painful for you?'

'Fire away,' he urged her. 'I'm long past secrets.'

She chewed her bottom lip; this was a delicate matter. 'Why did our mother have an affair?' she blurted out, adding quickly, 'Sorry, I realise the subject might hurt.'

'It does, of course, though time in here has toughened me up,' he told her. 'I must stress that your mother wasn't in the habit of taking lovers. She was the last person on earth you'd expect to get involved in that sort of thing. She'd always been a good wife and mother, the homely type.'

'Having an affair with a married man isn't a very homely thing to do,' June couldn't help mentioning. 'Especially when you've a couple of young kids to look after.'

'I can't argue with you about that,' Lionel agreed dully.

'Why do you think she did it?' wondered June. 'If she cared so much about her family?'

'Morris Dodd was a charmer in those days and he turned her head,' he told them. 'I was a gardener working for the parks department of the council, always in overalls; he was a rep for a firm of stationers, earning good money; he had nice clothes and plenty of chat. He had a reputation with women – knew how to make them feel good. I got to know him in our local pub and he and his wife became family friends – well, more just acquaintances really. They weren't our usual type but he was good company in small doses. From the way he used to talk to the men in the pub I knew he didn't have much in the way of morals but that was his business. I never dreamed he would go after my wife.'

'How did you find out about the affair?' asked Daisy.

'Your mother told me,' he explained. 'Said she'd come to her senses and couldn't carry on deceiving me any longer. She said she had ended the affair with him and begged me to forgive her and give her another chance. I don't think she ever loved him. She was infatuated for a while, that's all. Anyway, I agreed to try and forgive her, for the sake of the family. And because I still loved her, despite what she'd done.' He sighed. 'What happened after that is history, as they say.'

June cleared her throat; Daisy blew her nose. They were both struggling not to break down.

Lionel stared mistily into space. 'Life was so good before she got involved with that bugger. Everything changed so suddenly I was in a state of shock for months.' He gave them a wry look. 'Now I can hardly believe I ever had any other life but this.'

'It's so sad,' murmured June almost to herself.

'Don't feel sorry for me,' he was quick to protest. 'I'm all right, honestly. I'm in good health and that's worth a lot. You mustn't worry about me.'

'Easier said than done.' Daisy paused thoughtfully. 'Do you have any idea how we might find the Dodds?'

'I've told you I don't want you getting involved with them,' he reminded her. 'He's a nasty piece of work.'

'There are two of us so we'll be quite safe,' Daisy assured him. 'If he bumped us off he'd be signing his own death warrant. He wouldn't get away with it a second time.'

'The fact of the matter is, we've decided to try to find Mr and Mrs Dodd with or without your co-operation,' June added in a tone that didn't invite argument. 'So if you've any ideas, you'll save us time by sharing them with us.'

'All right,' Lionel conceded with an eloquent sigh. 'They used to live near us in Wembley, but it's most unlikely that they'd still be there now. They wouldn't have stayed there after all the scandal, not with his affair being splashed all over the papers in connection with the murder. His wife wouldn't have stood for that.'

'No, probably not,' agreed June.

'They could be anywhere now,' he went on. 'They could have moved away from London altogether.'

'But if we had their last address it would be a start,' Daisy pointed out. 'I doubt if they'll be there now but someone in the neighbourhood might have stayed in touch with them or have some sort of a clue as to where they went. So can you remember the address?'

'That's one I'll never forget,' he told them. 'It's number three Laverstock Avenue, Wembley.'

Daisy repeated it. 'That's an easy one to remember,' she remarked.

'You be careful.'

'Don't worry,' she told him kindly. 'We won't put ourselves at risk.'

'I'll make sure of that,' June further assured him.

'I'll have to take your word on that.' He looked from one to the other. 'Anyway, that's enough about the Dodds. I want to know all about you. You've grown up into such fine women, just like your mother.'

They both shot him a look.

'She *was* basically a good woman, no matter what you may be thinking about her,' he told them. 'She was human, she made a mistake.'

Daisy couldn't help thinking about the high cost of that mistake, to them all.

'Yes, well, I think we'll have to leave the catching up until next time,' mentioned June, glancing towards the warder, who was looking at his watch. 'It's time we were going.'

'You'll be coming again then?' Lionel suggested hopefully.

'Try keeping us away,' said Daisy.

'Thank you.' His humility tore at their hearts.

As they watched him being led away, they held their tears in check. Once outside the prison, they broke down and sobbed in each other's arms.

The warders on duty near Lionel's cell heard the sound of muffled weeping despite his attempts to conceal it for fear of seeming weak. Prison life had hardened him. There had been so much pain he'd grown several skins. Over the years he'd lost all purpose in life; had just let day follow day in a state of indifference. Not feeble, just resigned. But seeing his daughters again had inspired him with new life and purpose; had given him a reason to live.

121

Naturally in the past there had been times when he'd imagined what it would be like to walk along the street again, a free man, despite the stoicism he'd needed to carry him through. He was a realist, however, and knew that freedom wasn't something he was likely to taste again, despite his daughters' best endeavours. But even if he ended his days in custody he would die a happy man having seen them again and knowing that they knew the truth about him. His tears were a glorious outpouring of joy.

'Well, I think the whole thing is downright ridiculous,' disapproved Nat one evening a week or two later. 'I don't think you should waste another minute looking for these Dodd characters. You'll never find them after all this time, not in a million years.'

It was Daisy's night off so she and June had taken the opportunity to go to Laverstock Avenue, where they had drawn a complete blank.

'Be fair, Nat,' she said in a tone of mild admonition. 'The Wembley address was just a starting point. We didn't really expect to find them there. That would have been too easy.'

'But you've just said that you knocked on every door in the streets around there and no one knew where they'd gone to. So use your loaf and give up before you waste any more time on a wild-goose chase.' Because Nat was the man in her life Daisy had confided in him about the extraordinary revelations regarding her background. 'And even if you were to find them, what good would it do? I mean, this Dodd bloke isn't likely to confess to a murder, is he?'

'We're prepared for that,' Daisy told him.

'What's the point of chasing after him then?' Nat wanted to know, his voice rising.

'Don't shout, you'll wake the children,' Daisy rebuked. 'And to answer your question, the point of chasing the Dodds is because our father is in prison for something he didn't do. He's our *father, our own flesh and blood*. We can't just let him rot in prison when he's innocent without lifting a finger to help him. We have to take some sort of action.'

'I don't see why,' scoffed Nat. 'So what if he is your own flesh and blood? You haven't seen him for over twenty years. He can't possibly mean anything to you. The man's a stranger.'

'Of course he is, and he will be until we get to know him,' admitted Daisy. 'But he's been wrongfully imprisoned and we are the only people apart from him and the Dodds who know that. How can we live with ourselves if we don't do something for him? I admit it's going to be like looking for a needle in a haystack, but I'm not prepared to give up.'

'Personally,' intervened Nora, 'I think it's one of the saddest stories I've ever heard, even apart from the fact that he's the girls' father. That poor man locked up for all those years for something he didn't do – it's only natural they would want to do something to help him, even if it's only to tell that Morris Dodd that they're on to him, that he hasn't quite got away with it after all.'

Nat gave her a withering look. He thought Nora was an interfering old bag. She had far too much to say on the subject of his treatment of Daisy, and ought to learn to mind her own business. 'They were little kids when the murder happened, for God's sake,' he pointed out scathingly. 'Daisy was five years old. How can she possibly remember something that happened as far back as that?'

'I can remember my first day at school,' claimed Nora.

'Rubbish,' dismissed Nat.

'I know what I remember,' retorted Nora.

'No one can remember that far back,' argued Nat. 'Daisy probably imagined seeing the geezer at the house that night.'

'You're wrong about that,' June was quick to amend,

'because I saw him too and we can't both have imagined it. And before you say that I put ideas into her head, I didn't. She remembered it without any help from me.'

This sister of Daisy's had a bit too much to say for herself as well, Nat thought gloomily. This wasn't the first time she'd tried to put him in his place. Left alone, Daisy was as sweet as a nut. He could twist her around his little finger. But having the influence of opinionated types like Nora and June around made things more difficult for him.

'All right, so you both think you remember it, but I still think you're on a hiding to nothing in trying to clear your father's name,' he persisted.

'We know it won't be easy,' admitted Daisy. 'But we're going to give it our best shot.'

'Why are you so dead set against it anyway?' Nora wanted to know. 'It isn't as if she's asking you to help. I can't see why it matters to you one way or the other.'

'It matters to me, *my dear*,' he said with seething impatience and strong emphasis to indicate the opposite to endearment, 'because I care what happens to Daisy and I don't want her getting mixed up in something that's out of her league.'

'Cut out the squabbling, for goodness' sake,' rebuked Daisy, 'and let's see if we can't come up with something constructive between us.'

'As I've already said, I'll look in the phone book at work,' said June, 'and phone any Dodds in the London area from a call box. They have all the phone books in the library for a more thorough search, though as we haven't a clue which area they're in, that could take for ever.'

'The same thing applies to the electoral roll at the library and town hall,' Nora put in thoughtfully. 'As you don't know where they're living you'd need two lifetimes to get through the job.'

Daisy thought about this. 'I don't think they would have moved away from London, you know,' she observed. 'A different neighbourhood – yeah, definitely. But they're Londoners and the place would be in their bones, especially as they could escape from the scandal just by moving across town. A few miles up the road and you're a stranger in this city of ours. You don't need to move away from the capital to make a new start.'

'I still don't think the electoral register would be a good idea, though,' said Nora after more consideration. 'London's a densely populated place. Without knowing the actual borough, it just wouldn't be viable.'

Daisy and June nodded in agreement.

'You wouldn't believe it could be this difficult to find someone, would you?' mentioned Daisy.

'If it were easy, people wouldn't manage to stay missing and detective agencies wouldn't thrive,' Nora pointed out.

'True. Anyway, June's idea of going through the phone books is a good one,' said Daisy.

'We're frantically busy at work in the run-up to Christmas but I'm not going to let that stop me,' said June determinedly.

'I've got to work more shifts because of all the Christmas functions too,' Daisy informed them. 'I'm glad of the additional hours because of the extra dosh, but I'm going to find the time to go back to Wembley in daytime and ask around in the local shops. Someone might know something.'

'Good thinking,' approved June.

'I should forget about it altogether if I were you,' muttered Nat sulkily.

'I'm not going to do that, Nat,' asserted Daisy. 'So you may as well stop being such a doom merchant.'

'Suit yourself,' was his sharp retort. 'Frankly, I'm bored stiff with the whole flaming subject.' He threw a glare in June's direction, then looked back at Daisy. 'You've thought about nothing else but your father since your sister turned up.'

'Nat,' rebuked Daisy, flushing with embarrassment. 'Don't be so rude.'

'I'm only saying what's true,' he insisted. 'And as you obviously prefer your sister's company to mine, I might as well go down the pub.'

'Don't be like that.' Daisy looked worried now; she was only prepared to go so far in defiance of him.

'Don't leave on my account,' June told him frostily. 'It's time I was off anyway.'

'Me too,' said Nora.

And they both made hasty departures, leaving Daisy and Nat to sort out their differences in private.

'I wish you would try to be a bit nicer to my sister.' Daisy and Nat were sitting on the sofa.

'She's a stuck-up cow with her la-di-la voice and her posh clothes,' was his opinion.

'I think she speaks lovely. I could listen to her talk for hours,' Daisy said. 'Anyway, she has to be well presented in her job at a West End hotel.'

'She isn't my sort of person at all.'

'Maybe not, but she is my sister and therefore part of me,' Daisy reminded him. 'And as you're part of my life too, it would make things easier for me if you could make some sort of an effort to get along with her.'

'You haven't been the same person since she arrived on the scene,' he complained. 'You've changed.'

'Have I . . . really?'

'That's what I said.'

'It isn't intentional but I suppose June coming back into my life is bound to have an effect,' she reasoned. 'I've never had anyone of my own before.'

'You've got me.'

Even Daisy, with her huge capacity for self-delusion where Nat was concerned, could see what a gross distortion of the facts that was. She hadn't 'got him', as he put it. She never had. He appeared without prior notice at odd times and was never there when she needed him. She'd never met any of his relatives because he didn't go in for all that 'family stuff'. But there was no point in her complaining about it because he would never change. She either gave him up or accepted him as he was.

'My relationship with June is very important to me,' she said, 'but it hasn't affected my feelings for you.'

'Ooh, not much,' he disagreed. 'It's June this, June that, my father this, my father that.'

'Surely you're not jealous.'

'Do me a favour . . .'

'Be pleased for me then.'

'I am, of course,' he said rather unconvincingly. 'It's just that with your sister and Nora being around so much I never get a chance to be on my own with you.'

Privacy had never been readily available to them, given the size of the flat and the fact that the girls were always around. 'Yeah, I can see your point about that,' Daisy agreed. 'But as I never know when you're going to turn up I can't keep people away on the off chance that you'll pay me a visit, can I?'

'I suppose not.' There were no promises of reliability in the future. That wasn't his way.

'You can't complain if other people are here then, can you?' she said.

'Oh, stop yapping, woman,' he said, putting his arm around her, 'and give us a kiss.'

This wasn't a problem for her because she was still attracted to him, however deeply in the doghouse he was. But something was missing lately; she was becoming increasingly conscious of a change in her attitude towards him, a need to draw back. Maybe having relatives thrust upon her suddenly had altered her. But it wasn't just that. June and her father had given Daisy's life a new meaning certainly, but subtle changes in her feelings towards Nat had begun before they'd appeared. She was irritated with him more often now, less willing to be a doormat.

But then he whispered the magic words into her ear, 'I love you, Daisy,' and she could forget all her complicated emotions and succumb to the sheer pleasure of him.

'And I love you too,' she sighed.

June sat on the tube back to Marble Arch thinking about Nat and his appalling behaviour towards Daisy, and pondering on the power of human emotions that allowed people to make such fools of themselves. An intelligent and spirited woman like Daisy would never put up with that sort of treatment were she not besotted.

Having seen the way Nat behaved towards her sister had made June reappraise Alan's virtues. He'd been no saint but he'd always treated her with respect and listened to her opinions. Whereas Nat behaved as though Daisy was some half-wit who existed purely for his convenience.

His abysmal manners obviously embarrassed her and you could tell she was hurt by his lack of interest in the girls. But still the relationship continued. Complicated things, love affairs. However crazy or unbalanced they might seem to those on the outside, only the participants knew about the indefinable ingredient that held it together.

There was one thing that June did know for sure, though. However much she might feel compelled to voice her opinion of Nat to Daisy, to do so would almost certainly damage her new adult relationship with Daisy, who would take the side of the man she loved against a sister she hardly knew. So June would hold her tongue rather than jeopardise something of such value to her, especially while it was still embryonic and delicate.

Her thoughts drifted back to Alan. She was still thinking about him as she emerged into the street, the Christmas lights shining brightly along Oxford Street, a cheering spectacle of colour and festivity which eliminated the winter gloom and made her want to cry with the pain of missing Alan. Her first Christmas without him was going to be hardly bearable, she thought, heading off down a side street to the Central Hotel in the cold December night.

Chapter Six

The next morning while June was on duty, a tall, thin man of about fifty emerged scowling from the lift, marched across to the reception desk and fixed her with a stony stare. 'I want to see the manager,' he demanded, obviously simmering with umbrage.

To save the unnecessary use of management time, receptionists here were encouraged to deal with complaints in the first instance, referring them to a higher level only if their own efforts at conciliation failed.

'Certainly, sir,' she said with immaculate manners. 'Is there a problem?'

'Ooh, not so you'd notice,' was his ironic reply.

'Perhaps you'd like to tell me about it.'

'I'm suffering from exhaustion with every possibility of pneumonia developing,' he explained through clenched teeth, pale face set in a grim expression; his short brown hair was worn in a traditional style with a side parting and greased flat to his head, making him look even sterner. 'And the appalling standards in this hotel are to blame.' His eyes rolled heavenwards in tandem with a supercilious sigh. 'Quite frankly I'd be better off sleeping in a shop doorway, and since you charge the earth for a room here, that's nothing short of a disgrace.'

'I'm so sorry to hear you're not enjoying your stay with

us,' June said in the courteous, noncommittal tone she was trained to adopt in such a situation. 'Would you like to tell me what in particular hasn't pleased you?'

'Nothing has pleased me,' he informed her brusquely. 'This place is a joke.'

Needing to get to the crux of the matter, she asked, 'Is there something wrong with your room, sir?'

'You'd be nearer the mark to ask if there's anything right with it,' he barked at her. 'I was kept awake all night by the noise. I haven't had a wink of sleep.'

'Ah, I see.' She gave a sympathetic tut. 'People come up to town for Christmas functions at this time of the year and book in here overnight. I'm afraid the festive spirit makes some of our guests a little boisterous when they come back to the hotel.'

'It wasn't the other guests who disturbed me.'

'Really?'

'No. It was the traffic.' He became incandescent with rage as he thought back on it. 'Roaring past my window all night long. I've never heard such a racket.'

'The traffic noise can be disturbing if you're not used to it,' June agreed in an understanding manner. 'Unfortunately – with the best will in the world – we can't do anything about that as the hotel is situated in London's West End. Traffic noise is par for the course around here.'

'All night?'

'It does ease off in the small hours, naturally, but it doesn't usually stop altogether.'

'Nobody told me that when I booked.'

'They must have assumed you would guess,' she suggested politely, 'this being the capital city.'

His eyes bulged at this implied criticism and June had to think fast to head off an explosion. 'What's your room number, sir?' she enquired.

132

'Ninety-two.'

She gave him a knowing nod. 'Now I understand. That room is on the corner of the hotel directly above the traffic lights,' she explained. 'Vehicles stop outside with their engines throbbing, then roar away when the lights change. I know what it's like because I live here at the hotel and my room is on the same corner but much higher up. The noise used to be a problem for me when I first moved in. But it doesn't bother me now that I'm used to it.'

'I'm booked in here for three more nights and I can assure you that I have no intention of getting used to it,' the man made clear with seething irritation.

'Of course not, and we wouldn't expect you to.' June was a very fair-minded woman and could usually see the customer's point of view. But she knew instinctively that this man was the type to find fault with the service at Buckingham Palace were he ever invited as a guest. She took a deep breath, keeping a grip on her professionalism. 'Would you like me to see if we have a vacant room in another part of the hotel, further away from that junction?'

'There's no point,' he snapped. 'Because the noise isn't the only thing that's wrong.'

Here comes the cause of his possible pneumonia, she thought, but said, 'Could you tell me what else is troubling you, sir, so that we can put it right? Our guests' comfort is everything to us here at the Central Hotel. If you're not happy, we're concerned.'

'My room is freezing,' he informed her. 'I've been chilled to the bone all night.'

This puzzled her because the heating in this hotel was excellent and she hadn't been notified of any problem in the boiler room. 'Oh? Is the radiator not working?'

'I wouldn't be complaining if it was, would I?' was his abrupt reply. 'It's stone-cold.'

'That's strange.' At this crucial moment in customer relations, the telephone rang. 'Please excuse me for a moment,' she said.

He frowned in reply.

'Central Hotel. Good morning,' she said in her best business voice. 'Can I help you?'

The operator's voice crackled down the line informing her of a long-distance call from Torquay. With heart pounding, June told her to put it through.

'Hello, June.'

'Alan.' She quivered from top to toe. 'How are you?'

'I'm all right. Yourself?'

'I'm fine.'

'I'll come straight to the point as I'm calling long distance,' he began.

'Look, Alan, I can't talk—'

'The fact is, June,' he went on as though her interruption hadn't registered, 'I'm calling you on impulse because I still miss you and I just can't bear the thought of Christmas without you.'

'Oh,' was the best she could manage. With the furious guest focusing her with a disapproving stare, this wasn't the time for a personal conversation.

'So, I was wondering if you might consider coming down to Torquay for the holiday,' Alan continued. 'So that we can talk things over.'

'No, Alan, that isn't a good idea.' It was a wonder to June that she didn't wither and turn to dust under the lethal glare of the disgruntled guest. It was her job to pacify him and the need to do so grew more urgent by the second. If he reported her to the management for taking a personal call when she was supposed to be giving him her undivided attention, she could lose her job, which would render her homeless as well as unemployed. 'I really can't talk now, I'm sorry,' she said *sotto voce*.

'Oh. Oh, I see.' He sounded hurt; obviously thought she was just putting him off. Although Alan was familiar with how things were on the working side of a hotel reception desk, the Cliff Head reception was a playground compared to this one, and he couldn't possibly imagine how ill-timed his call was.

'I'm on duty, Alan.' She spoke in a whisper. It wasn't possible for her to explain to him that she had every hotelier's nightmare giving her the look of death, without the man hearing her. 'It's difficult right now.'

'Oh, don't worry about me,' said the man with seething sarcasm. 'I'm only a paying guest. I should hate to interfere with your private life.'

She put her hand over the mouthpiece and looked at him anxiously. 'Sorry about this, sir. I'll be with you in a second,' she assured him.

'Don't bother to find me another room,' he roared, almost beside himself with rage now. 'I'll check out of this dump and find somewhere else to stay as the receptionist here is too busy with a personal call to attend to me. I want my money back for last night, though. I'm not paying for a room in which it's impossible to sleep.' He puffed out his lips. 'Not likely.'

A demand for a refund as well as a customer complaint about the conduct of the duty receptionist would almost certainly result in dismissal. 'I have to go now, Alan,' June said quickly, and replaced the receiver without waiting for his reaction.

She was trembling from the effect of contact with Alan as she turned her attention back to the man, though she concealed it well. 'I really am very sorry about that, sir,' she apologised again.

He gave her a curt nod.

Being accustomed to dealing with the public at large, June

was a consummate professional and could turn on the charm when necessary. She gave him one of her most melting smiles and behaved as though his threats to leave hadn't happened. 'Now, about the radiator in your room. It's cold, you say?'

'That's right.'

'And it's definitely turned on?'

He gave her a pitying look. 'Of course it is,' he said in a superior manner.

'That's really odd,' she said in a confiding manner, 'because the heating seems to be working well enough in the rest of the hotel.' She paused, choosing her words carefully. 'I wonder if perhaps the previous occupant of your room preferred a cool temperature and turned the radiator off.'

'How could they have done when the heating is controlled from a central point by your people?' he blasted.

'You're quite right, of course,' she conceded gracefully. 'The heating is controlled from a central point by us. But each radiator is also self-regulating and can be individually operated as long as the system is turned on, which it is in the winter.'

'Oh.'

At least he had the grace to look sheepish so she decided to help him out. 'Some of the older central heating systems don't have that individual facility,' she pointed out, 'but ours has been recently modernised.'

'I know how central heating works.' He obviously hadn't realised but would sooner die than lose face by admitting it. 'Obviously I checked to see if the radiator was turned on. And I can assure you that it was, and it was cold.'

'Yes, I understand,' she said, managing to sound convincing. 'I'll have one of our maintenance men go up to take a look.'

'Thank you.' He was noticeably more subdued.

A swift look at the hotel booking plan revealed a room

vacant in a different part of the hotel. 'As luck would have it, we've had a cancellation so I can have you moved to a quieter room if you wish, though we can't erase the noise of the traffic altogether any more than any other hotel in central London can.'

He appeared to be pondering the question.

Winning him over had become a challenge to June now. 'Or, if you'd rather, I'll ring through for the manager to come and see you if you still wish to make a formal complaint and continue with your plans to check out.' She gave him a look of concern. 'But to make sure you're not left without a bed for the night, I can ring a few hotels to find out if they have any vacancies. Most London hotels are fully booked in the run-up to Christmas with so many people coming up to town for shopping.'

The extent of her helpfulness took the sting out of his argument. Much to her relief her ploy worked. 'No, no,' he said. 'If you get me moved to a different room for tonight, I'll give it a try.' He gave her a stern look. 'But if I have so much as a hint of cause for complaint, you'll be hearing from me again.'

I bet we will, she thought, but said sweetly, 'I'll have someone move your things.'

Clearly impressed by the lengths she was prepared to go to in his interests, he became much more amenable. 'That's very nice of you,' he said. 'Thank you.'

'A pleasure,' she assured him. 'No trouble at all.' She smiled at him and decided she might as well grovel some more in the interests of customer relations. 'Might I suggest that while we're organising your move, you make yourself comfortable in the lounge and I'll have some coffee and biscuits brought to you.'

'That would be lovely.' He was smiling now and looked almost human. There was even some colour in his cheeks.

'I'll arrange everything and coffee will be along in a minute,' she said.

He nodded, then walked away towards the lounge with an air of triumph, obviously congratulating himself on winning all this attention.

But as far as June was concerned, she was the victor in this battle. Sighing with relief, she rang through to the kitchen to order his coffee.

As soon as she came off duty June went to the telephone box around the corner armed with coins, and put in a long-distance call to Torquay. Christmas with Alan was out of the question but she didn't want him to think she'd snubbed him. The mere thought of hurting him in that way upset her.

'Cliff Head Hotel, can I help you?'

Much to her annoyance June realised the voice belonged to her mother-in-law.

'Hello, Irene,' she said nervously. 'This is June.'

There was a brief silence while she digested the information. 'My God, you've got a nerve, ringing up here after what you've done to my son,' was her acerbic reaction.

'Is Alan there, please?' June wasn't prepared to waste time in conversation with Irene, since the call was costing a fortune and the money running out fast.

'No, he isn't.'

'Could you put me through to the flat then, please?'

'He isn't there either.'

'Oh. So he isn't in the hotel at all?'

'That's right. He's out on business.'

'Do you know when he'll be back?'

'No.'

'Look, I really need to speak to him urgently,' June continued, daunted but not deterred by the resistance Irene was giving her. 'He rang me earlier and I couldn't speak to him because I was on duty. It's a very busy hotel where I work and I need to explain that to him.'

'You can't if he isn't here, can you?' said the other woman unhelpfully.

'Will you tell him I called then, please?' June requested.

'Yes, I'll do that.'

'Can you explain to him why I wasn't able to speak to him?' June asked, feeling desperate now. 'I was dealing with a difficult customer when his call came through and I couldn't pay attention to him. You know how it is in a hotel reception.'

'I'll tell him.'

'Thank you . . .' The pips interrupted the conversation and the line went dead.

Her first instinct was to call again later and try to speak to Alan personally, but a call box wasn't really suitable for something of such a sensitive nature with the money running out with the speed of light. The message she'd left for him would be enough to convince him she hadn't just been putting him off.

Just as Irene was replacing the receiver after the call from June, Alan walked into reception from the restaurant where he'd been discussing something with Jack about the large private function they had booked for this evening. Despite what she'd said to June, his mother had been fully aware of his whereabouts.

Passing the desk on his way to the office, he noticed that she looked cross. 'What's up, Mother?' he asked. 'You're looking a bit rattled.'

'I'm all right,' she said innocently.

'You could turn milk sour all the way to Exeter with that face,' he teased her. 'Has someone on the phone upset you?'

'No,' she denied swiftly. 'It was someone making a

restaurant booking for next week. Just a routine call.'

He gave her a shrewd look. 'You've definitely got the look of battle about you, as though you've just been putting someone in their place.' He wasn't as cheerful as he sounded after the disappointing call he'd made to June earlier, and was just putting on a front. 'Are you sure you haven't just had a complaint?'

'What, against the Cliff Head Hotel?' She made a joke of it. 'Never let it be said.'

'Spoken like a true professional,' he approved, moving away. 'If you need me I'll be in the office.'

'All right, son.'

She had no intention of telling him about June's call. It would only unsettle him. He needed to get that dreadful woman out of his system so that he could get on with his life. And the sooner he forgot about her the better.

'I've rung all the Dodds I could find in the phone book but none of them has a Morris in the family, not even a distant relative,' June informed her sister.

'And I've had no luck in the shops around Wembley,' said Daisy, looking disappointed. 'Still, we didn't expect it to be easy, did we? We'll just have to keep trying.'

It was Sunday morning at Daisy's place. She and the girls hadn't long been back from Mass and she was peeling a pile of sprouts to go with the piece of scrag end of lamb she was cooking for lunch with roast potatoes. Shirley and Belinda were in Nora's flat, making paper chains with her.

'It's all we can do,' June agreed. 'But I thought I'd better pop over and let you know how I'd got on, even though it's a negative result.'

'I appreciate that,' Daisy said. 'It's a pity we don't have a phone we can use to save you coming over every time there's a message.'

140

'It's no trouble,' June assured her. 'It's only three stops on the tube.'

'Would you like to join us for lunch?' invited Daisy impulsively. 'I can easily do a few more spuds. Nora will be coming in. We always have Sunday lunch together if I'm not out working. Otherwise she gives the girls theirs.'

'I'd love to but I'm on duty at half-past twelve,' June told her.

'Another time then perhaps,' suggested Daisy.

'Thanks. I'd like that.' June paused thoughtfully. 'How come you're not working today?'

'I am. We're having a very early lunch and I'm going in to work as soon as I've eaten mine,' she explained. 'At the hotel where I work they don't start serving lunches until half-past twelve and I don't think they're likely to complain if I'm a bit late getting in today as I've agreed to stay on to serve afternoon teas and dinner tonight. As I'll be out all day until after the girls go to bed, I want to have lunch with them before I go.'

June nodded.

'I try to spend as much time as I possibly can with them, especially at this time of the year. But it's never enough.'

'Are you working over Christmas?' June enquired.

'No fear,' Daisy said. 'You?'

'No.'

'Are you doing anything exciting on Christmas Day?' Daisy asked casually.

'I've nothing planned,' June informed her gloomily. 'I suppose there might be a few of us in the staff quarters with nothing on, so maybe we'll get together for Christmas dinner. No one's said anything about it, though.'

Seeing the sadness in her sister's eyes, Daisy realised that Christmas would be difficult for her, having recently parted from her husband. She cast her eye around the room. 'This isn't exactly the Ritz,' she pointed out unnecessarily, 'but we usually manage to enjoy ourselves in our own simple way at Christmas. You're very welcome to join us.'

June was more touched than Daisy could possibly know. 'I'd really love that, Daisy, but—'

'Don't feel you have to say yes,' she cut in defensively. 'I realise it isn't what you're used to.'

'I live in a basic little room in staff accommodation, for heaven's sake,' her sister reminded her, tutting to emphasise the point.

'Now you do, yes, but you have been used to better things,' Daisy went on.

'Yes, I have,' June wasn't ashamed to admit. 'But that isn't the reason I hesitated before accepting your invitation. I didn't say yes because I don't want to spoil Christmas for Nat. I'm not exactly his favourite person, am I?'

'Nat won't be here,' Daisy was quick to inform her. 'We never see him over Christmas. He goes to relatives in the East End somewhere. Some sort of a family commitment, apparently. I don't know the details.'

'And you and the girls don't go with him, not even for part of the time?' June was incredulous at this further evidence of the man's cavalier attitude.

'Nat isn't the type to take his girlfriend home to meet the family,' Daisy explained. 'That isn't his style.'

A stab of rage towards Nat whipped through June. Surely Daisy and the girls should have first call on his time at Christmas. But if her sister was upset she wasn't showing it. Probably so used to his shabby treatment as to have become immune, June guessed. 'In that case I'd love to join you,' she smiled. 'But only on the condition that I pay my share.'

'You won't get any argument from me about that,' Daisy told her with a wry grin. 'Christmas is an expensive business when you've got two kids with high expectations in the Santa department.'

'That's settled then.'

'Lovely.'

Warmth towards Daisy swept over June, making her eyes feel hot and moist. 'I haven't been looking forward to Christmas one little bit this year, but you've just taken the dread out of it for me,' she said with feeling. 'And I thank you for that with all my heart.'

Daisy smiled, her cheeks flushed with pleasure. But she wasn't given to extravagant displays of sentimentality so she just said, 'We'll be delighted to have you. The more the merrier.'

Lionel Rivers lay on his bunk reading the letter for the umpteenth time, staring at the words and drinking in the joy of them. A letter in itself was a huge event for him. One like this was enough to make him shout with the pleasure of it.

It was from a friend of his daughters', someone called Nora Dove. She hoped he didn't mind her writing to him but Daisy and June had told her his story and she was so moved by it she wanted to write to offer her support and friendship. She went on to explain that she was of his generation rather than his daughters' and thought he might appreciate having someone of his own age to communicate with. She was keen to make the point that he mustn't feel under any obligation to correspond with her if he'd rather not.

She mentioned his daughters' determination to try to clear his name, adding that it might take a long time. He must take comfort in the fact that they would do everything in their power to see that justice was done. They were fine young women and he could be proud to be their father.

The letter was warm and chatty, and contained several amusing anecdotes about his granddaughters, and how they and Daisy meant so much to Nora. The letter didn't spare him the grim realities of life outside altogether. She mentioned a ruthless landlord and the possibility of herself and Daisy losing their home.

'You reading that letter again?' asked Lionel's cell mate from the bunk below.'

'That's right.'

'Blimey, you must know it off by heart now,' the other man joshed. 'I haven't had a word out of you for hours and it'll be lights out soon.'

'Mm.'

'It must be from a woman to keep you that interested,' the other man went on to say.

'It's from a friend and the fact that she happens to be a woman is irrelevant,' explained Lionel. His words had a strange ring to them because it had been so long since he'd called anyone a friend. He couldn't wait to reply to her.

'There's no need to look quite so fed up, Alan,' admonished Paula Bright, a smart woman in her late twenties with short fashionably cut red hair and sparkling blue eyes. 'I realise that our parents' Christmas get-together isn't the most exciting event on your social calendar but it isn't that bad.'

'Sorry,' he apologised. 'Am I being very rude?'

'I wouldn't go so far as to say that,' she said. 'But you're not exactly lively company.'

'It's nothing personal,' he smiled, making an effort. 'I'm just not feeling very sociable this evening. But that's no excuse for bad manners.'

'Don't worry about it.' She seemed very relaxed on the subject. 'I realise that you only came to this little soirée because your parents would have given you a whole lot of grief if you hadn't.'

He gave her a knowing look. 'You too?' he said.

'Surely you don't think I enjoyed being thrown together with you at every possible opportunity when we were growing up in the hope that someday the two of us would make a go of it, do you?' she asked candidly.

'I'd never really thought about it from your point of view,' he was forced to admit.

'Too busy trying to protect yourself, I expect,' she chuckled.

'Something like that.'

'In actual fact I was about as interested in you romantically as you were in me,' she informed him. 'It was a relief to me when you got married.' She raised her eyes, tutting. 'Of course, now that you've split up with your wife, the folks will probably start to get ideas again. But you can relax in the knowledge that they're wasting their time as far as I'm concerned.'

'Oh.'

She cupped her hand behind her ear as though listening to something in the distance. 'Is that the shattering of an ego I can hear?' she chuckled.

'Just a little bruised perhaps,' he smiled, finding her candour rather entertaining.

'You men want it both ways,' she opined. 'You can't bear the idea of a woman not being interested in you even if that woman is the last person on earth you want to be with.'

'I don't think that's a gender thing,' he said. 'It's just a quirk of human nature.'

She shrugged. 'Maybe,' she conceded.

'I'm glad we've got things clear between us at last, anyway.'

'Me too.'

It was the evening of the day before Christmas Eve and he and Paula were sitting chatting at a table in the Cliff Head bar. She had come over with her parents for a seasonal drink with the Masters and other friends of her and Alan's parents.

The older generation were standing in a group talking nearby. Alan and Paula had drifted into conversation as a matter of course.

'I should have thought that being sociable was second nature to you, as a hotelier, whether you're in the mood or not,' she remarked, sipping her gin and tonic, blue eyes peering at him over the rim of the glass. 'It's all in a day's work to us.'

'That's true . . . up to a point.'

'But the sparkling conversation doesn't happen instinctively for a friend of the family who isn't going to pay the going rate for a room?' she suggested with a knowing twinkle in her eye. 'Am I right?'

'It isn't a conscious thing on my part but there might be something in what you say,' he returned, Paula's light-hearted manner cheering him up. 'As you say, being sociable is an automatic thing in our business.'

'Dare I ask what's made you so gloomy?' she enquired casually.

The breakdown of his marriage was the answer to that but he wasn't going to bare his soul to Paula about the fact that his wife couldn't even spare the time to talk to him on the phone or return his call. After the painful rejection she'd given him at the hotel in London, it had taken a lot of courage to call her and suggest they spend Christmas together. And she wouldn't even consider it; just put the phone down on him. Ever since then he'd been struggling to accept the truth – that it was over between them and there was no point in his trying to get her back.

He thought back to happier times. They had both been so full of hope and harmony when they'd got married. And the sad thing was he'd never noticed it slip away; still couldn't fully accept that it had. But for some reason best known to herself, June didn't want him in her life. She seemed so cold and distant now. Not the woman he had fallen in love with at all.

But now Paula was saying, 'Talk to yourself, why don't you, Paula? It seems as though that's the only way you're going to get any answers.'

'Sorry.' Alan gave her a wry grin. 'I was miles away.'

'Problems of a personal nature rather than business, I suspect,' she speculated.

He gave her his full attention. 'You're very astute.'

'Difficult guests and hotel disasters don't carry the same look of pain somehow,' she said lightly. 'I know about these things; I'm in the same line of business, remember.'

'Yes, of course.'

Her expression became more serious. 'I was sorry to hear that you and your wife had parted,' she told him. 'Even though it's probably turned our folks into dedicated match-makers again, now that you're back in circulation. You and your wife seemed good together whenever I saw you. From what I knew of June, she seemed nice.'

'I always thought so.'

'You're speaking in the past tense, I notice,' Paula pointed out. 'And that seems a bit harsh. Just because it didn't work out for the two of you, that doesn't mean she's a lesser person than you thought she was.'

'I know that,' he corrected. 'I meant more that I feel I couldn't have ever really known her. I mean, before this happened I would have staked my life on her loyalty, on her staying with me until we were a couple of old codgers. But to just walk out like that with no warning . . .' He sighed, shaking his head. 'It still shocks me to think about it.'

'She must have had a very good reason,' was Paula's opinion. 'Or thought she had.'

Deciding he'd already said too much, he called a halt.

Despite what she'd done, it seemed disloyal to June to discuss their problems with a relative stranger.

'Yeah, I expect you're right.' He looked at her and saw shining blue eyes, a flawless skin suffused with cleverly applied make-up. A fitted black suit sat well on her trim figure. She wasn't a stunning beauty but she was attractive and sexy. 'But that's quite enough about me. Let's talk about you now. Is there anyone serious in your life?'

'I'm not about to get married, if that's what you mean,' she told him.

'I'm surprised you're not married already.'

'Most people are,' she told him. 'A man can stay single beyond the age of about twenty-five and everyone assumes he's enjoying life as a bachelor too much to want to settle down. A woman does it and they think there must be something wrong with her because she can't get a man. It never occurs to anyone that she might actually enjoy the single life.'

'I thought most women wanted to get married,' Alan said. 'Thought it was the natural thing, all part of the nesting instinct.'

'It is,' she agreed. 'Finding a husband and settling down to have babies is the life plan of the average 1950s woman. I suppose that was all I wanted too up until I was about twenty. But when it didn't happen, I got to thinking that being single wasn't so bad after all, especially as I got more involved in the management of the hotel. I'd like to meet Mr Right, of course, but if it isn't meant to be I can live with it. I realise that I'm some sort of a freak because I didn't rush up the aisle at the first opportunity.'

'I'm sure there was no lack of offers.'

'I've had a few.'

'You just didn't fancy them?'

'I've had my moments,' she said with a wicked grin. 'But

that doesn't mean I was ready to give up my independence and settle down just because it's the done thing. I haven't yet met anyone I'd want to give up my single status for, even if that does mean people will soon start calling me an old maid. Anyway, apart from anything else, I have to make sure it's me they want and not the hotel. Like you, Alan, I'm an only child. My parents' hotel is worth a lot of money and will be mine one day. That factor alone makes me attractive in some men's eyes.'

'You're attractive anyway,' he told her, and meant it. 'Regardless of your material assets.'

'Thank you.' She smiled, seeming pleased.

'It was never that I didn't find you attractive.' It suddenly seemed important that she knew that. 'It was just the minute I clapped eyes on June there was no one else for me.'

'Explanations aren't necessary,' Paula assured him breezily. 'As I've said, it was a mutual thing.'

'You're doing terrible things to my ego again,' he teased her.

She laughed. 'Your sense of humour didn't die altogether when June left then,' she remarked.

'Apparently not, I'm surprised to discover.'

'I suppose one of the reasons our folks were so keen for us to get together was because we each had our own assets,' she said thoughtfully. 'So they could be sure that if it did happen it wouldn't be for material gain on either side.'

'Mm.' Alan's thoughts turned to less personal matters. 'But tell me, do you still close your hotel over Christmas?'

'That's right.'

'Same here. But I'd like to throw open the doors and make a big thing of it. Do a special Christmas programme.'

'Would you get any takers, though,' she wondered, 'Christmas being a home and family time?'

'I think we might. A lot of people would probably welcome

the chance to escape from all the domestic slavery that goes on at Christmas.'

'Why don't you give it a try then?'

'Mum and Dad won't hear of it,' he explained. 'They want things to stay exactly as they have always been at the Cliff Head.' He paused, looking at her. 'I expect you have the same trouble with your folks, don't you?'

'Not at all,' she surprised him by saying. 'My parents are leaving things to me increasingly. They're content to take a back seat and let me shoulder the responsibility, glad to have some time to themselves.'

'So, you have a real say in what goes on, then?' he said thoughtfully.

'More than that, I practically run the place nowadays – with a good team of staff, of course,' she replied.

'I didn't realise your parents had retired.'

'They haven't – officially. They're still working but they've handed a lot of the responsibility over to me. They trust me to keep the place flourishing and they seem to like my new ideas. They've worked hard all their lives. Now they're only too pleased to take things a bit easier.'

'Lucky you.'

'I've no complaints.'

'I'd like to turn this place into a family hotel,' Alan said, looking around the room at the dark furnishings and décor, a few tasteful Christmas decorations dotted about, a sprig of holly here, a touch of tinsel there. 'I think we should be more child-friendly and liven the place up with entertainment and so on – something for the whole family to enjoy on holiday.'

She made a face. 'I can't see Irene and Gerald going for that one. The Cliff Head has always been a quiet, select hotel.'

'I wasn't thinking of turning it into a glorified holiday camp,' was his answer to that. 'I just want to give it some new life. It's too staid, too old-fashioned.'

'With all due respect to your parents, I agree with you. A few changes can only be a good thing,' Paula enthused. 'All of us in the hotel trade are going to have to look to our laurels over the next few years.'

'Because of the competition from holiday camps, you mean?'

'Yes, holiday camps are a worry.'

'But Butlins wouldn't appeal to the sort of people who like a hotel holiday,' Alan pointed out.

'I wouldn't bank on that,' Paula warned. 'People can easily get converted. They try a holiday camp once to see what it's like and want to go back the next year. Anyway, I think we have a much more powerful opponent looming.'

'Oh?'

'Holidays abroad.'

'Surely not.' He was sceptical. 'Only a tiny proportion of the population can afford to go abroad.'

'At the moment, yes,' she agreed. 'But foreign package holidays are getting more popular all the time. People aren't afraid of a foreign holiday if everything is organised for them and they have the security of the tour company behind them.'

'But package holidays abroad are still very much in their infancy,' he debated. 'They are only within the reach of a fraction of the market.'

'At the moment you're absolutely right,' Paula nodded. 'But they'll be a force to be reckoned with in the future if things go on as they are and the economy continues to improve. You must have read all the talk about it in the trade press.'

'I have, but I didn't think there was an immediate threat.'

'There isn't but, at the same time, we can't just sit back and expect things to stay the same for ever.' She was very confident. 'We're living in an age of prosperity and we have to bear in mind the fact that foreign holidays will get cheaper as the demand for them grows.'

'There is that.'

'Ask yourself, Alan, if you had a choice between a holiday in Spain with guaranteed sunshine, cheap drinks and entertainment laid on, or a fortnight in Torquay in a hotel with no entertainment and the possibility of tramping about the town all day in the rain, which would you choose?'

'Mm, I see your point,' he was forced to concede. 'So are you planning on doing anything about it at your place?'

'We certainly are,' she informed him brightly. 'For starters we're going to be installing an indoor swimming pool.'

'Wow!'

'That will be only our first move,' Paula explained. 'We are intending to make other improvements too, gradually. We're planning on having a games room and dancing in the dining room a couple of times a week.'

'You've really done your thinking,' he approved.

'You have to think ahead if you're to survive in business these days.' She looked at him thoughtfully. 'Is that the sort of thing you'd like to do in your dream hotel?'

'That would be a part of it,' he replied. 'And those sorts of improvements would have to be made, of course. But my dream is more to create a feeling, an atmosphere.'

'The facilities would have to come first, though.'

'Of course. But then I'd want to build something over and above that. Something that can be created only by a human touch. A welcome so warm people would want to book ahead for the following year.'

'Well, you've certainly got the enthusiasm,' she told him. 'And that's the sort of attitude that breeds success. I think you should persuade your parents to let you go ahead with it. You seem to know exactly what you want, so talk to them about it again, sell them the idea.'

How many times had June told him the same thing? How many times had he tried to get his parents to listen to his ideas? Paula was a similar age to him and she was practically running the Brights' family-owned hotel. Discontent flashed through him. It really was time he was given some credibility around here. He would talk to them, make a stand. Be determined.

'You're absolutely right,' he said, her optimism filling him with fresh hope. 'I'll raise the subject again as soon as I see the opportunity.'

'Good for you,' she said. 'I wish you luck.'

'Thanks.'

This was the first time he'd had a proper conversation with her and he was beginning to enjoy himself. At least it had taken his mind off his problems. Now that he knew her better, he liked Paula and was enjoying her company. They had plenty in common and she talked a lot of sense.

'You must let me know the outcome,' she suggested casually. 'I'd be interested to hear how you get on.'

'Yeah, I'll do that.' He gave her an uncertain smile. 'Perhaps we could meet up for a drink sometime – just for a chat.'

'I'd like that.'

'I'll give you a ring to get something arranged then, sometime in the new year,' he told her.

'I'll look forward to it.'

'In the meantime, can I get you a drink?'

'That would be lovely,' she smiled. 'I'd like a gin and tonic, please.'

'A pleasure.'

As he walked towards the bar, he was aware of approving

glances being cast in his direction from his parents. With June out of the way, their hopes for Paula and himself had been given a new lease of life. Fortunately, now that he and Paula understood each other, there wasn't a problem.

Chapter Seven

'It's your go, Auntie June.' Shirley passed her aunt the little plastic cup containing the dice; they were playing a game of snakes and ladders.

There were shrieks of triumphant laughter from her opponents when she landed on a snake and had to move her counter down the board. 'Oh, not again,' she wailed, entering into the spirit of rivalry with a good heart. 'I think you lot have fixed the dice to go against me.'

'Now, now,' joshed Nora. 'Don't let's have any bad sportsmanship.'

'Bad sports aren't allowed in our house, Mum says, even if they are grown-ups,' Belinda told her solemnly. 'So you'd better watch out, Auntie.'

'Ooh, hark who's talking,' retaliated June, winking at the others. 'Who was it who got a fit of the sulks when she didn't win at ludo earlier on?'

'Now then, kiddies, and that includes you, June,' began Daisy, who was so glad she'd invited her sister; she was such good fun, and wonderful with the children, 'can we have a bit less mucking about and more concentration, please? There's a serious game in progress here.'

'Yes, ma'am,' said June, making the children laugh with her mock salute.

It was the evening of Christmas Day and they'd decided on

a board game in the hope of quietening the mood before the girls' bedtime, after the excitement of the day. But June could see no sign of a slow-down; they were still as lively as a couple of puppies.

Her gaze wandered idly around the room, which was suggestive of a grotto with its dazzling festive décor. A Christmas tree glowed in the window, the ceiling was a mass of home-made paper chains and lanterns, while a plethora of cardboard Santas, snowmen and reindeers beamed from various points.

Garish and tasteless was how Alan's parents would describe it, she thought wryly. And yes, perhaps it was a bit excessive. It was also a triumph of the human spirit, in June's opinion. Scraping the money together from her meagre resources, Daisy had transformed this tatty room in a seedy tenement house into a seasonal wonder for two little girls. No child could have had a Christmas richer in goodwill. And by working all hours Daisy had ensured they didn't go short of presents either.

Never mind the fetid hallway and dangerously dark landing and stairs – inside this room the heart and spirit were so uplifted, it was all that seemed to matter.

Alan hadn't been far from June's thoughts all day and the festive season emphasised the sadness of her fractured life. But being here with this little family had eased her path through what could otherwise have been an unbearable time. In concentrating on making the occasion a happy one for the children, she'd cast out her own problems; had even managed to experience moments of genuine pleasure since she arrived last night, having come on the tube before public transport had stopped for the holiday. Nora had put her up on a camp bed in her flat as Daisy was pushed for space.

The girls had been beside themselves this morning, feverishly unwrapping parcels, then rummaging in their stockings to find an apple and orange, little packages of sweets, a comb, new hair ribbons and a few cheap sundries. The only expensive items were the roller skates that Daisy had been saving for all year. These had already made their debut on the street, the aspiring skaters clinging for dear life to walls, lamp-posts and each other. June had given them satin pyjama cases, on which their names were embroidered, complete with new pyjamas. She'd given Daisy a talcum and soap set, and a book of Betjeman poems for Nora because she knew he was a favourite of hers. She herself had received apple blossom bath cubes from Daisy and a letter-writing set from Nora.

But now the game was coming to an end and the children's reserves of energy were finally running out. Bedtime didn't bring forth its usual crop of protests tonight, though, because of the lure of the new pyjamas.

'They're absolutely whacked,' said Daisy when the three women were settled with glasses of port from the bottle June had brought with her, Daisy and Nora on the sofa, June in the armchair. 'It's been quite a day for them.'

'For me too,' added June. 'It's lovely having children around at Christmas; makes such a difference.'

Daisy gave her a questioning grin. 'You managed to survive their high spirits without losing your sanity then,' she remarked light-heartedly. 'Their boisterousness can be a bit much if you're not used to it.'

'It didn't worry me.' It was true to say that the girls' exuberance didn't bother June but she didn't feel entirely at ease with them either. Suddenly finding herself with two lively nieces was something of a challenge to someone with no experience of children, and she wasn't yet confident in her new role. Some aunts would probably consider their function to be that of an authority figure, an issuer of discipline and back-up support to the children's mother. But June, in the ardent pursuit of their love and friendship, saw herself more as a purveyor of fun and pleasure. She had to admit, though, that the playful persona she thought would appeal to their age group and win her popularity had proved difficult to sustain over a long period.

'They've worn me out today, I know that much,' Nora confessed wearily. 'I'll be asleep as soon as my head touches the pillow tonight.'

'Me too,' said Daisy, covering a yawn with her hand. 'The little perishers had us up so early this morning, it's no wonder we're exhausted.'

'Anyway.' June raised her glass. 'How about a toast? To absent friends.'

'Absent friends,' they chanted.

'Wouldn't it be great if Dad was able to spend Christmas with us next year?' said June.

'Mm,' agreed Daisy. 'I think having us visit him just before the holiday will have helped him through Christmas this year. From what he's said, visitors have been nonexistent until now, except perhaps for official prison visitors.'

'His friends have probably shunned him, thinking he was a murderer,' suggested June.

'Yeah. He's got himself a pen pal now, though, hasn't he, Nora?' smiled Daisy, turning towards her friend. 'He was tickled pink with your letter.'

'It was kind of you, Nora,' approved June.

'I probably got as much pleasure from writing it as he did receiving it.' She was quite frank about it. 'I've always enjoyed letter-writing so I was glad of an excuse to put pen to paper.'

'It was appreciated, anyway,' said June. 'And while we're on the subject of appreciation, I want to thank you both for helping me through my first Christmas without Alan. You've made me feel so welcome here, it's made all the difference.' She lifted her glass. 'To many more Christmases together.'

'I'll drink to that,' cheered Daisy, swigging her port, cheeks suffused from the alcohol and the heat from the gas fire. 'Though God knows where we'll be next year.'

Nora nodded sagely. 'Don't let's think about that, dear, not on Christmas Day,' she said.

June had gathered from what had been said that they were having trouble with their landlord but she didn't know how serious the situation actually was. 'Are things bad enough for you to move out, then?' she enquired.

Daisy sighed. 'It's getting to be that way. It depends how much more we can take of our landlord's devious tactics.'

'Didn't you say something about being determined to stand firm against him?' June queried.

'That's the plan, but we have to be realistic about it. It's all very well standing up for your rights, and we'll do that for as long as we can, but I have the kids to think of,' Daisy pointed out. 'If things get any worse we might be forced to leave here but don't ask me where we'll go because I haven't got a clue, with the housing shortage being so bad in London.'

'A hundred thousand houses were destroyed completely in London during the war, and another million were war-damaged,' Nora explained. 'That's why people like Roland Ellwood are so powerful.'

'But the war has been over for nearly ten years,' June objected. 'Surely new houses have been built.'

'Plenty of them – out in the suburbs and new towns,' Daisy told her. 'But around here the crisis is as bad as ever.'

'What about council housing?' asked June.

'Don't make me laugh,' was Daisy's quick reply. 'I've been on the waiting list for years.'

'This borough has the lowest level of council housing in London,' added the knowledgeable Nora.

'I see . . .' said June.

Daisy went on to tell her sister about the way some landlords were exploiting the West Indian immigrants by charging per head. 'Six to a room and sleeping in shifts. The property owners are making a fortune and the immigrants are so grateful to have a roof over their heads they pay up and think the landlords are wonderful.'

'There must be someone you can complain to about the situation,' was June's outraged reaction.

Daisy shook her head. 'There isn't, believe me. We've been down that road and it leads nowhere. The authorities have got so many homeless people to deal with, they just haven't the time to bother about the conditions people *with* homes are living under. Anyway, this place is better than some of the others. You should see the squalor some people have to live in around here – rat-infested places with no facilities and barely any sanitation.'

'Having no light on the stairs and landing is bad enough, though,' said June. 'Especially with two children needing to go up and down after dark.'

'Ellwood's probably hoping one of us will fall down the stairs and hurt ourselves; not seriously – just enough to unnerve us into moving out,' Daisy suggested. 'He's got a mind like a cash register. All he can see is the money he could make from the rooms if we weren't here.'

'I didn't realise that things were so bad,' June confessed.

'I don't suppose people outside the area do realise what it's like. Why should they?' Daisy shrugged. 'You've got to live here to know what's going on.' She gave June a shrewd look. 'And of course you were sheltered from inner city problems when you were living in Torquay.'

'You're not kidding,' she swiftly agreed. 'I'm beginning to understand just how easy I had it down in Devon.'

'If we had anywhere else to go we'd have been out of here long ago,' Daisy went on to say. 'Wouldn't we, Nora?'

'Not half.'

'Enough about that,' Daisy said hastily. 'It's Christmas night and not a time to be moaning and groaning. So let's talk about something else.'

But June had lapsed into thought, plans of her own coming into focus suddenly and forming an idea that would benefit them all. 'I've just realised that I can help,' she said after a while, her voice rising with excitement.

They both gave her a questioning look.

'Don't say you're thinking of trying to fix us up in the staff accommodation at the hotel where you work,' grinned Daisy, making a joke of it to lift the gloom that had crept into the atmosphere. 'Somehow I don't think the management would be too keen on that idea.'

'Don't be daft. I'm going to be moving out of staff accommodation myself soon anyway,' June explained with growing enthusiasm. 'And when I do, I can solve your problem too, make things better for us all.'

'How?' Daisy wanted to know.

'Well, my mother's little house in Hounslow came to me automatically when she died and I put it up for sale straight away because I didn't want to live in it. I've found a buyer and am just waiting for the sale to be finalised. With the money I get for it I'm going to buy somewhere else.'

'And invite us over to give us a break from this dump?' surmised Daisy.

'No. I was thinking more in terms of you all moving in with me.' Seeing the question in Nora's eyes, she added quickly, 'You too, Nora.'

'Ooh, I like the sound of that,' beamed the older woman. 'What a smashing idea.'

But Daisy reacted differently and her fierce opposition was completely unexpected to both June and Nora. Her eyes blazed, her lips tightened and an angry flush stained her

161

cheeks. 'I might not have much but I'm not a charity case yet,' she said coldly.

An abrasive silence fell over the room.

'No one is suggesting that you are,' June said at last. 'And I'm not offering charity.'

'Sounds remarkably like it to me,' snapped Daisy.

'You must have misunderstood me, then,' June was quick to point out. 'Because with the best will in the world, I'm not in a position to offer charity to anyone. I don't have any money.'

'Oh, not much,' uttered Daisy with uncharacteristic scorn. 'You've enough to buy a house and you say you've no dough. You're living in a different world.'

'Look – the only reason I can buy a house is because my adopted parents' place came to me as their next of kin,' she explained. 'I'm not saying that I'm not lucky to have it because I know that I am – *very lucky*. But it's a one-off and certainly doesn't mean I have money, as such. By the time I've paid for somewhere to live I'll be skint again, and I'll find it difficult to afford the costs of running a house on my own because I'm not on a high salary. I work in a West End hotel, yes, but I am only a receptionist. I probably don't earn much more than either of you.'

'You don't know what hardship is,' accused Daisy with unusual hostility. 'You've had it good for most of your life. Adopted by people who were well off enough to own a house, got yourself a rich husband with a part-share in some posh hotel.'

June wasn't prepared to supply her with details about her past so she just said, 'But I left all that behind me and I'm in the same boat as you are now, except that I don't have any children to support. I'm a single woman looking out for myself, just like you are. We're two of a kind.'

'Don't make me laugh,' came Daisy's cynical response.

'You'll never be the same kind as me, not with the start in life that you've had.'

'Look, Daisy, I can't help the way it worked out for us when we were children,' June reminded her. 'I didn't have any say in what happened any more than you did, and you know that in your heart.' She moved on swiftly, rather than dwell on those unhappy times. 'Anyway, when I suggested that you all move in with me, I was thinking in terms of us sharing the house, rather than my just letting you some rooms.'

'Sounds good to me,' approved Nora.

'We'd still be your lodgers.' Daisy looked extremely doubtful.

'Technically, I suppose you would be my lodgers. But what I have in mind would be more of a house-sharing arrangement, all of us on an equal footing,' June told her. 'I thought we could live like a family and split all the costs three ways: coal, gas and electric, the rates, all the running costs of the house plus any decorating and maintenance bills. It would be a joint enterprise. We'd each do our share of the chores.'

'What about rent?' asked Daisy.

'I haven't got round to thinking about that yet. But obviously if I can pay for the house outright from the sale of the other one, and you're paying your share of everything else I won't need to charge rent—' she began.

'Forget it,' cut in Daisy rudely.

'Daisy,' rebuked Nora, frowning at her.

But Daisy was at the mercy of new emotions which she could neither understand nor control, and she was deaf to Nora's protests. Her voice was shaking as she spoke. 'I'm prepared to accept any sort of a hand-out for the sake of my kids, and I'll grovel with the best of 'em for their benefit. But I won't take charity from my sister.' She shook her head in despair. 'I just can't do it.'

'It isn't charity, I've told you,' insisted June, distressed by this turn of events. 'You'd be the ones being charitable because you'd be doing me a favour if you move in with me. I don't want to live in a house on my own.'

'Oh, for goodness' sake,' Daisy sneered. 'Do you think I'm thick or something? You must do if you reckon I'd swallow that load of old rubbish.'

'If it would make you feel better, pay me some rent then.' June was at a loss to know what to say.

'Now you really are being patronising,' retorted Daisy through tight lips.

June was perplexed. What had seemed like a fantastic idea just a few minutes ago had turned into an explosive situation she couldn't handle. Whatever she said would be misunderstood by Daisy in this mood. 'I'm sorry you feel like that about it. I really didn't mean to upset you.'

'For heaven's sake, Daisy,' said Nora in a firm tone, 'June isn't trying to belittle you in any way. She's come up with a scheme to help us all, herself included.'

'Nora's right.' June was glad of the support. 'The idea popped into my mind just now and seemed like a practical solution for us all. You have problems with your landlord and I can't afford to rattle around in a house in my own. So the sensible thing is for us all to move in together. Even apart from the financial side, I don't fancy the idea of living by myself. It isn't as though I've got any friends in London. Sharing might be fun and it would give you and me a chance to get to know each other again after all these years.' She gave Daisy a look of defiance. 'And yes, I did think it would make things better for you. There wouldn't be any point in my asking you to move in with me otherwise, would there?'

Daisy shrugged, feigning indifference.

'You can't deny that it will be easier for you than staying on here, worried to death the whole time about what the landlord will do next,' June continued.

'Course it will be better,' confirmed Nora. 'And if you weren't so stubborn, you'd see that, Daisy.'

'I don't know yet what sort of a place I can get with the money from the sale,' June continued. 'I didn't get a fortune for my mother's house because it's out of town and anything in central London will be a lot more expensive so it won't be anything too grand. If you did decide to come in on it with me, we might have to settle for something that needs doing up to get enough room for us all at the price I can afford. But you'd certainly have more space and freedom than you have here, especially if I can get something with a little garden for the girls to play in.'

'I'm not so dim that I can't tell whether someone's being big-hearted or big-headed, you know,' expressed Daisy.

June felt as though she'd been physically slapped. 'I didn't mean to be either of those things,' she tried to make her sister understand. 'It was a spur-of-the-moment idea which would benefit me as much as you.'

Daisy pondered on this. 'Mm, maybe it would but I can't do it,' she told her.

Nora couldn't believe she was hearing this. Daisy must be having some sort of a brainstorm to behave in this way because she was usually so sensitive to other people's feelings and completely unashamed of her impecunious state. It was obvious how hurt poor June was and it was unlike Daisy to be cruel to anyone. The two of them were so different, Nora observed, Daisy so open-hearted and straightforward, June more secretive and withdrawn but equally as vulnerable, somehow. They needed each other and it tore at Nora's heart to see their new-found relationship foundering before it had got past the first post. Deciding, however, that this was a family matter and it was time she made a diplomatic exit, she said, 'Well, I'll leave you two to fight it out.'

'Don't go,' urged Daisy, feeling guilty for spoiling the evening for them all.

'It's time I was in bed anyway,' said Nora, affecting a yawn as she stood up. 'It's been a long day.'

'I'll come with you.' June got up and looked down at Daisy, who was sitting on the sofa looking forlorn. 'Thanks for a lovely day. It's been really great.' She paused, fiddling with her fingernails nervously. 'Look, forget the idea of us all moving in together. I should never have suggested it. The last thing I wanted to do was upset you, especially at Christmas.'

'Don't worry about it.' Daisy was very subdued.

Tension drew tight in the air. Nora could almost taste the bitterness between the sisters. Although she wanted to put her arms around them both and guide them out of this impasse, she knew she mustn't interfere. This was something they had to work out for themselves. 'G'night, love,' she said to Daisy. 'See you in the morning.'

''Night, Daisy,' added June.

''Night, both.'

As the door closed behind them, Daisy sat motionless on the sofa, feeling terrible. Looking around her, she noticed how the Christmas decorations had an irrelevant look about them now somehow. The happy day had ended on a sour note. She tried to comfort herself with the thought that it hadn't been spoiled for the children. But it didn't help.

Lying in the bed next to her sleeping daughters, listening to the now familiar sound of music and laughter from a party in the lower regions of the house, Daisy felt physically ill with remorse as she replayed the altercation in her mind and recalled how hateful she had been to June.

What made it even worse was the fact that she could see how stupid she'd been to react so negatively to the idea of them all moving in together when it was the perfect solution.

Why was it so easy for her to give yet so hard for her to take? If anyone knew about Christian charity, Daisy did, after the upbringing she'd had. She knew all about kindness and generosity, and give and take. It wasn't as though she hadn't been on the receiving end of kindness before. She'd had it in abundance from Nora. So why did it stick in her throat when it came from June?

Sibling rivalry and pride, she was ashamed to admit. But looking at the matter logically, June really did stand to gain as much as Daisy and the others from such an arrangement. It hadn't been an act of charity but an opportunity for them all. Company for June and the chance of a decent home for her and the girls and Nora. God knows, they needed it. And what had she done? Thrown it back in her sister's face, and deprived her children of a better standard of living because she was too proud to accept something in the spirit with which it was given.

She was furious with herself, and sad. Nat came into her mind for some reason and she felt a pang. Trust him not to be around when she needed him. June was right when she said they were both in the same boat. Neither had a man to love and comfort her. Nat loved her in his way – if she didn't believe that she'd have given up on him long ago – but, although it hurt to admit it, he was only a part-time lover.

But she and June did have each other. Fate had brought them together again and their relationship could become special, given time. Why throw the chance of that away just because of sisterly competition?

Weary of tossing and turning, she got up and went in the other room and curled up in the armchair with her dressing gown over her, waiting for the agonising night to end so that she could put things right.

The girls slept in the next morning after the late night. As

167

soon as Daisy heard signs of life from across the landing, she went and tapped on Nora's door.

June opened the door in her dressing gown, looking tired and pale and extremely wary of her sister.

'You don't look as though you've had any more sleep than I have,' Daisy observed.

'I've had better nights,' was June's cool response.

Daisy bit her lip; she was full of contrition. 'Look, I'm really sorry about last night,' she said. 'I said some horrid things.'

'You're entitled to your opinion,' June told her frostily. 'I told you to forget it.'

'I know you did but I don't want to forget it.' She made a face. 'Help me out here, June. I'm trying to put things right.'

'Why the change of heart?'

'I was stupid. I don't know what got into me.' She looked at her persuasively. 'I'm sorry. And I'd really like us all to move in together. It's a brilliant idea.'

June was so thrilled she didn't bear a grudge. 'If you're sure, then that's what we'll do,' she smiled.

'As long as you let me pay my way,' Daisy made it clear in a warning tone.

'I won't have any choice about that.' June's tone was just as firm. 'As I've already said, I can't afford to keep you and the kids as well as myself. I'm only a hotel receptionist.'

'I'll have to make sure you're not out of pocket then, won't I?' said Daisy, satisfied now on this point.

'We'll work out the details when we've found somewhere. I haven't even started looking for a place yet.' She paused. 'Perhaps we could do that together, all of us.'

'That would be smashing,' enthused Daisy.

With the release of tension, they both got a fit of the giggles, hugging each other and hovering between laughter and tears.

'What's going on out here?' came Nora's throaty tones as she scuttled on to the scene in her dressing gown and slippers. 'What's all the noise about?'

Daisy grabbed hold of her and swung her round. 'We're getting out of here,' she said excitedly, linking arms with her and dancing round, lifting her knees in the air. 'We're all going to be living together . . . so what do you think of that?'

'Thank God you've come to your senses,' was Nora's enthusiastic reaction. 'It's the best bit of news I've heard in a very long time.'

In the same way as June found salvation over Christmas in Daisy and the girls and Nora, Alan found comfort in Jack Saunders' company and large quantities of alcohol drunk together in a matey fashion on Christmas Eve after work. On Christmas Day he went to his parents' house where everything was pin neat and traditional, with turkey and stuffing and perfect mince pies.

The business being a family one, shop talk was never taboo, even at Christmas. So as they lingered at the table over lunch, Alan decided to take the opportunity to raise the subject that had been on his mind ever since he'd discussed it with Paula.

'I really believe it's time for some changes at the Cliff Head,' he said in conclusion, having outlined his ideas.

'But you already know what we think about turning our hotel into a bear garden,' said Gerald.

'Bear garden, my foot. It would be a bit livelier, that's all,' corrected Alan, managing to stay calm. 'There would be no lowering of standards.'

'It's Christmas,' interrupted Irene, staidly clad in a navy-blue twinset, her hair welded into place with setting lotion. 'Not a time to talk business.'

'It's the very best time to do it,' Alan disagreed. 'We can

169

talk without being interrupted.'

'We've been through all this before, son,' pointed out his father smugly, cheeks flushed from his pre-prandial tipple. 'And your mother and I have agreed that it wouldn't be wise to introduce the changes you're proposing to the Cliff Head.'

'Why doesn't that surprise me?' Alan said cuttingly.

'Don't be facetious, dear,' requested his mother primly.

Alan looked from one to the other. 'I know you don't, personally, want to consider my ideas but give me one good solid reason why some changes wouldn't be wise from a business point of view.'

'You know why.' His father was impatient now. 'Because we are a refined hotel catering for people who want peace and quiet. We'd lose all our customers if we changed our policy.'

'We'd gain more than we'd lose.' Alan was adamant about this. 'There's a gap in the market for a family hotel. There aren't enough of them around.'

'Maybe not,' said his mother, helping herself to more Christmas pudding. 'But we are not going to add to their numbers.'

'Hear! Hear!' Gerald supported.

'So, you won't even think about it then?' said Alan, looking from one to the other.

'We already have done and the answer is no,' confirmed his father dismissively. 'So let's forget it and talk about our plans for the coming season.'

'I thought I was supposed to be a partner in the business,' Alan reminded them.

'And you are, dear,' his mother assured him. 'That isn't in question.'

'I'm questioning it.' He was really fired up now. 'I might as well be a chamber maid for all the say I get in the running of the hotel. My ideas are never even given any consideration, just dismissed out of hand.'

'That isn't fair,' his father argued. 'It's just this one thing we can't agree on.'

'No, Dad, it's everything.'

'Rubbish!'

Alan thought his father probably believed his own words so it was useless to argue the toss over that one. But he wasn't ready to give up on the main point. 'Why exactly are you so much against the ideas I've just outlined anyway?' he asked, getting heated. 'I know you're keen on all things traditional but there must be more to it than that.'

'It's Christmas, Alan,' his mother reminded him again. 'I don't want any arguments.'

'I have no intention of having an argument,' he assured her. 'I just want a straight answer to my question.'

'All right, I'll give it to you straight,' said his father, leaning back slightly in his chair and regarding his son with an air of complacency. 'Even apart from believing that a family hotel isn't right for the Cliff Head, I don't actually *want* to run the sort of place you have in mind. I would hate it.'

'Me too,' added Irene.

'But you're a sociable sort of a chap,' Alan pointed out, looking at his father. 'I should have thought you'd enjoy working in a livelier environment.'

'I might be sociable but I'm very selective about the company I keep and I'm quite happy with the way things are,' he stated. 'I don't want our refined cocktail bar to become like the public bar of some backstreet pub.'

Alan gave a dry laugh. 'You'd vet the guests before you took their booking if you could afford to turn people away, wouldn't you?' he said bitterly.

'I certainly would.' Gerald wasn't ashamed of his snobbery. 'I don't want riffraff in my hotel, neither do I want snotty-nosed kids making a racket about the place.'

'You're quite right, dear,' agreed Irene.

171

'It may be a very good idea in principle and right for other hoteliers, but it would never work for us,' boomed Gerald. 'So accept it once and for all, boy, and let's hear no more about it.'

In a defining moment Alan finally did exactly that: he faced up to the truth. Not only would they never agree to make the changes he wanted, it would be a disaster if they did. Anything outside of the hushed atmosphere they were used to would be anathema to them so their presence would not be conducive to the atmosphere Alan had in mind.

He'd clung to the idea because he was a man with a dream, but it was *his* dream not theirs. If he wanted a different kind of hotel he would have to do it without them. And as that was completely out of the question, he had no choice but to put it out of his mind and satisfy himself with the Cliff Head as it was, and likely to stay – in his parents' lifetime, anyway. There was certainly no point in trying to persuade them into changes that were wrong for them.

'Yes, Dad,' he said with a sigh of resignation. 'I'll do that.'

'Thank God we've got through to you at last about this,' said his father.

His mother looked relieved. 'Mince pies anyone?' she offered, smiling.

The two men answered rather absently in the affirmative and she scuttled off to the kitchen to get them. 'While we're on the subject of business,' Gerald began, 'there's a hotel and catering exhibition at Earls Court in March. I've had some literature in about it. Wondered if you fancied going.'

'I suppose it might be quite interesting.' Alan was too disappointed about the other thing to show much enthusiasm.

'It'll be worth a visit, certainly. It's always a good idea to keep up to date with what's going on in the trade.' He gave his son a wry grin. 'As long as you don't come back with more ideas for this wretched family-style hotel you're so keen on.'

Alan ignored his attempt at humour. 'Aren't you going then?' he asked.

'No. I don't fancy the London crowds,' his father explained. 'I thought you might like to go instead. Stay overnight. Give yourself a break. There won't be a problem with your getting away at that time of the year.'

'I'll think about it.'

Suddenly Alan felt about six years old. Then it had been sweets and toys, now it was a trip to London to keep his parents in his favour. Did they really not know how transparent these attempts to placate him were?

Something significant happened to him at that moment. He realised with blinding clarity what he'd known for years and not allowed himself to fully admit: he needed to find his own way, to fail or succeed for himself, away from his parents. But he was trapped. Even apart from the hideous personal complications of breaking away, he had very little in the way of material assets outside the Cliff Head.

'Here we are,' said Irene, bustling back into the room with a plate of mince pies. 'Nice and warm, straight from the oven. When we've had these we'll go in the other room and listen to the Queen's speech.'

'Lovely, dear,' enthused Gerald, helping himself to one and munching into it.

'Come on, Alan, tuck in,' urged his mother.

'I don't think I can manage one after all,' said Alan, feeling suffocated.

'Don't be silly, dear,' she admonished as though Alan was an infant. 'Of course you can manage one.'

He was so angry he wanted to slap her. 'I think I'm old enough to judge my own appetite, thank you, Mother,' he snapped.

She shot him a look. 'Don't you dare raise your voice to me,' she warned. 'A lot of hard work has gone into making

173

Christmas a happy time for us all.'

Her rebuke produced the desired effect and filled him with compunction. 'Sorry,' he said, taking a mince pie and forcing himself to eat it, just to keep the peace. But he longed for some breathing space from a relationship that was becoming unbearably claustrophobic.

'You're getting to be good at this, aren't you?' Jack Saunders complimented Alan when the latter beat him at a game of darts in the Gullscombe Arms on the evening of Boxing Day. 'You'd better watch yourself, mate. They'll try to rope you into the darts team if you carry on like this.'

'Fancy another game?' suggested Alan.

'You can't get enough of it now,' grinned Jack. 'But let's take a break and have another game later; leave the board free for someone else to have a go.' He paused, looking at him. 'It's my shout, as you won, so what's it to be?'

'A pint, please.'

'Coming up.'

The Gullscombe Arms was an old-world tavern in the picturesque village of Gullscombe Bay. The pub was at the centre of village life and was warm and cosy, with oak beams, fishing nets on the walls and log fires. It was Jack's local and he knew everyone by name. It wasn't too crowded tonight as some of the locals were at Boxing Day parties so the two men were able to find a table near the fire where logs were crackling.

'My folks would have a fit if they knew that I was drinking pints and getting to be red hot at the dart board,' Alan remarked, taking the top off his pint. 'Gin and tonics at the golf club are more the sort of thing they have in mind for me. And for you too, if it comes down to it, you being their restaurant manager.'

'Yeah, well, I think it's my right to do what I feel

comfortable with when I'm off duty, as long as it doesn't hurt anyone and is legal,' observed Jack. 'Same applies to you, in my opinion. If you enjoy a pint and a game of darts, you're perfectly entitled to have one, regardless of the social implications.'

'You're right, of course.' He made a face. 'But I must admit I find it easier not to mention these things to the folks. It causes too much trouble. They're good people and have done their best for me but our ideas and opinions don't often seem to coincide these days.'

'You'd be a bit odd if they did,' was Jack's opinion. 'Every generation has its own ideas. Anyway, we're all individuals – freethinkers, thank God.' He cast his eye around the pub. 'There's nothing nicer to me than a game of darts and a sociable pint in a pub where everyone knows my name. And if anyone objects to that, that's their problem.'

'It's different for you,' Alan pointed out. 'You're a free agent with no one to answer to.'

'So are you now that you've split up with June.'

Alan's features tightened at the mention of it but he just said, 'I do have my parents to answer to, you know.'

'Only to a certain extent,' Jack told him. 'You're a grown man, a responsible adult.'

'Because I work with them I'm still under their control,' Alan explained.

'Then you shouldn't be, not at your age,' Jack disapproved.

'It's just the way things are.'

'You can't spend your whole life doing what they want, if it isn't what you want,' Jack went on. 'I'd still be in Australia if I'd done that.'

'It took courage to come back.'

'Don't talk daft,' laughed the modest Jack. 'Where's the bottle in getting on a ship and coming home?'

'You cut your family ties and came back on your own, to

start again from scratch with no back-up,' Alan reminded him. 'That seems quite a brave thing to me.'

'My mother would probably call it selfish, going off and leaving the family like that.' He smiled with fond memories. 'Mum's a good sort, though. She wished me well and said I must do what I felt was right for me. It was traumatic for us all. I mean, Australia is the other side of the world, not near enough to go for a holiday – not unless you've got plenty of dough, anyway. But I was convinced that I had to make the move back to England while I was still young. I didn't want to go against my instincts and stay there just because it was easier, then be full of regrets on my sixty-fifth birthday because I'd been trapped by family ties.'

'I'm up to my neck in family ties at the moment.' Alan went on to tell his friend about his ideas and the frustrations he was having at the Cliff Head.

'Strike out on your own, mate,' was Jack's immediate reaction, 'if you're feeling that fed up.'

'Easier said than done,' Alan pointed out. 'Even apart from the emotional element – and make no mistake about it, my parents would be devastated if I left the partnership – what would I do if I did leave? Get a job as a hotel manager working for someone else? I don't think so.'

'You want a family hotel, so go out there and get one,' Jack suggested.

'What with? I've got a bit saved but not enough to buy a hotel, nowhere near.'

'You could raise the dough if you sold your share in the business,' advised Jack.

'If I ever were to leave, I'd give them my share, not sell it,' Alan said. 'But I couldn't walk out on them. It would break my mother's heart.'

'She's probably tougher than you think.'

'Even so . . .'

176

'Parents want the best for their offspring; it goes with the job, apparently, or that's how it's supposed to work. So once they got used to the idea, they'd want you to do what you know is right for you.' Knowing Alan's parents, and judging them to be extremely self-centred, Jack had grave doubts about this but kept them to himself because Alan needed encouragement to break away and live his own life. 'I'm sure they wouldn't want to hold you back once they realised how much you want to do it.'

'But how would they manage without me?'

'By employing somebody to do the job that you do, of course,' Jack replied. 'No one's indispensable.'

'I couldn't do it to them,' Alan insisted. 'They'd be absolutely devastated.'

Jack shrugged. 'So what are you going to do then? Wait until they retire or die, then do what you want with the Cliff Head? And in the meantime get increasingly frustrated and miserable? You'll grow into a crusty old sod if you don't get your life sorted out.'

'I don't have a choice.'

'You're an unattached man, Alan,' Jack reminded him firmly. 'Of course you have a choice.'

'You make it seem so simple.'

'I'm not saying it will be easy but it certainly isn't impossible, and if you stay as you are, you'll never know if you could have made it on your own. This idea of yours isn't going to go away. You're stuck with it. And taking over the Cliff Head when your folks retire won't be the same thing as making a success of something in your own right, not the same thing at all.'

'I can't just disregard obligations.'

'Look, it's natural to grow up and make your own way in the world – we all do it,' Jack reminded Alan. 'You went into the family business instead. I'm not saying there's anything wrong with that. It works very well for some people, but obviously not you, or we wouldn't be having this conversation. So, take the plunge and do something about it.'

'Everything you say is true but I couldn't desert Mum and Dad,' Alan said. 'It would be too cruel.'

Jack tutted. For years he'd watched Alan be browbeaten by the people he was so loyal to, and thought he deserved better. 'Your parents aren't disabled or even very old,' he said gently. 'They'll be fine.'

'It was different for you when you made the break,' said Alan. 'You weren't locked into a family business.'

'I was part of a family, though,' Jack was keen to point out. 'Even now, I still miss them all – Mum and Dad, my sister and brother. How do you think it feels, knowing that they're so far away and I probably won't ever see them again?'

'I didn't realise,' Alan confessed. 'You always seem so cheerful and in control.'

'That sort of thing stays inside. I made my choice and I have to get on with things. No point in going about with a long face and making other people miserable. I like my life here and you can't have everything, can you? Not many people get that.'

'Exactly,' agreed Alan. 'And I have so much more than most. A partnership in a thriving business and financial security if I stay with it.'

'None of it's worth a light if you're permanently frustrated, though, is it?'

'I'm not so sure.'

'If you don't break away and become your own man, you'll never have peace of mind,' Jack lectured.

Alan shrugged. 'Maybe not. But it's just something I'll have to live with.'

'It's your choice, but I reckon you'll live to regret it.'

'All right, Jack, you've made your point,' said Alan firmly.

'Now let's change the subject before we come to blows over it.'

'Suits me,' agreed Jack with a shrug.

'How do you fancy coming with me to London in March?' asked Alan. 'All expenses paid by the Cliff Head.'

Jack's eyes lit with interest. 'I wouldn't say no. Why, what's on?'

Alan told him about the exhibition. 'I'd be glad of the company,' he explained. 'And it'll be of interest to us both as it's our line of business. I'll arrange for you to have the time off. They can manage without you in the restaurant for a couple of days.'

'I'm game,' enthused Jack.

'Good. I'll book us some accommodation when things open up again after the holiday. In the meantime, let's have another drink. A pint for you?'

Jack nodded. 'I'll come to the bar with you,' he grinned. 'The new barmaid's quite tasty.'

Standing at the bar counter waiting to be served while Jack chatted to the barmaid, Alan reflected on the conversation they had just had. Jack talked a lot of sense and made a change of course seem so straightforward, whereas to Alan it was impossible.

June came into his mind and he knew instinctively that she would agree with Jack. He also knew that he could never make that break. The emotional ties were just too strong.

Chapter Eight

'Did you have a good Christmas, Nat?' Daisy enquired sociably.

'Yeah. It was all right,' he told her with an air of disinterest. 'How about you?'

'I had a lovely time.' Enthusiasm radiated from her. 'It was really smashing this year. One of the best Christmases I've ever had, I think.'

'Why?' His dark eyes rested on her with lurking disapproval as he took a slow, contemplative drag on his cigarette. The knowledge that Daisy was capable of having a good time without him was unsettling because it challenged his power over her. 'What did you do that made it better than usual?'

'Nothing different. Just stayed at home and did all the normal festive things with the girls and Nora,' she told him. 'But June was with us and that made it sort of special, somehow. She's ever such good company and the kids have taken to her in a big way. Having a real auntie is still a novelty to them, and she seems very fond of them.'

It was evening, a couple of days after Christmas. The girls were in bed, and Daisy and Nat were ensconced on the sofa. Daisy was enjoying the fact that she didn't have to go back to work until tomorrow night.

He laughed drily. 'Must have been a barrel-load of laughs

with that stuck-up cow under your feet all over the holiday,' he said sarcastically.

'I wish you wouldn't say such horrible things about her,' she frowned. 'You know how it upsets me. June's great. You haven't given her a chance.'

'Why should I make an effort with someone who thinks she's a cut above the rest of us?'

'She doesn't think that,' defended Daisy heatedly. 'Just because she's got a touch of class you've branded her a snob and she isn't like that at all. Far from it.'

'You're so taken with the idea of having a posh sister, you can't see what she's really like,' he said calumniously.

'That just isn't true,' she denied, her voice rising. 'You know very well that I'm the last person on earth to be impressed by someone because they're posh.' She was reminded of the altercation she'd had with June on Christmas night, which proved her point.

Even Nat could see that his accusation didn't carry any weight. 'Yeah, I s'pose so,' he muttered grudgingly.

'Anyway, I'm not going to argue with you over it.' A gleam came into her eyes and she smiled. 'Because I've got something far more exciting to tell you.'

He exhaled a cloud of smoke, looking at her thoughtfully. 'You're like a dog with two tails tonight.'

'And with very good reason.' She told him she would soon be having a change of address and gave him the details. 'Isn't it wonderful?' she enthused. 'At last I can get the girls out of this stinking hovel, get us all away from the landlord and his vile threats.'

'Where exactly will you be moving to?' Nat showed not a grain of enthusiasm.

'Not sure yet,' she told him excitedly. 'It depends where we find a house that's big enough for us all and within June's price range. We won't be moving far, though, because we all need to stay within easy reach of our jobs.'

'What's all this "we" business?' he queried disagreeably. 'It'll be your sister's house. You won't get a say in its location, or anything else for that matter.'

'We will,' she corrected. 'She wants it to be a joint venture and we're all going to have a say in everything. She's quite definite about that.'

'Use the brains you were born with, Daisy,' he warned nastily. 'You and Nora will just be lodgers.'

'No we won't.'

'Of course you will,' he insisted. 'You'll be subject to all sorts of petty rules and regulations like they are in boarding houses where the landlady lives in the house.'

'It won't be like that at all because we're going to live together as a family, on equal terms.'

'Equal terms, my arse.'

'Don't be so cynical.'

'Surely you don't really believe you're going to be equal with June?'

'Yes, I do, as it happens.'

'It'll be her house, for God's sake,' he blasted. 'Of course she's going to rule the roost.'

'The house will be hers, and she'll have the responsibility for it, obviously. But it won't be like you're suggesting.'

'Give me strength,' he sighed emphatically. 'I really don't think you should do this. It'll be a disaster.'

Naturally she was disappointed by his reaction. 'I don't know why you're getting so het up about it,' she said.

'Because you're being so blind,' he ranted on. 'Three women and two kids sharing the same house – you'll be at each other's throats in no time. And then where will you be? You'll have burned your boats with this place.'

'I certainly won't lose any sleep over that.'

'At least here you have a degree of privacy,' Nat pointed

out. 'You've got your own cooking facilities and that. All right, so the landlord is a bit of a bugger but at least he doesn't live in the house, checking up on everything you do.'

'And neither will June.' Daisy was beginning to get exasperated now. 'The three of us have discussed it thoroughly and agreed that if this thing is to work we must respect each other's privacy. The girls will probably have to share a bedroom as they do now. But we're hoping that the rest of us will have our own rooms where we can go when we want to be on our own.'

'You'll have to share the kitchen and bathroom, though . . .'

'And the living room, and sitting room if there is one,' she added with an air of defiance.

'You're asking for trouble if you go ahead with this move.' He shook his head. 'I'm telling you.'

'Why do you want to spoil it for me?' Daisy asked. 'This chance means a lot to me.'

'I'm just trying to save you from yourself,' he insisted. 'It's no good shutting your eyes to the actual reality of something like this.'

'My eyes are wide open,' she assured him. 'And I know it's going to be good.'

'Oh, well, it's your funeral,' he said in a doom-laden voice.

'Yes, it is.' She stood firm.

'Anyway, I thought you were planning to stay on here to prove that the landlord can't drive you out.'

'We're not being driven out,' she reminded him. 'We're moving out of our own accord to somewhere better, so it's not my loss.'

'Even so . . .'

'I'd be mad to turn this opportunity down,' she said with a sigh of irritation. 'It'll be so much better for the girls, especially if we can get a place with a little garden.'

184

'That sister of yours will have a field day, lording it over you and Nora.'

'There won't be anything like that.' Having cleared the air about this on Christmas night, she could be confident. 'I've told you, we're going to live as a family.'

'Family be buggered,' Nat scorned. 'It'll be one big battle-ground once the novelty wears off.'

She was hurt by his attitude but determined not to let him bully her into changing her mind. 'Whatever happens it's got to be better than this,' she said, waving her hand towards the room. 'And let's face it, Nat, I'm not going to get the chance of family life with the father of my children, am I? So I might as well go for the next best thing.'

'How many more times must I tell you, we'll get married eventually.' He was impatient now. 'We're all right as we are for the moment.'

'Of course we're not all right,' she disagreed. 'The situation is ridiculous.'

'Don't start—'

'I'm not starting anything; just defending myself against your unreasonable disapproval of my plans to move in with June,' she declared. 'I don't ask much from life – you know that. As long as my girls are happy, then so am I. But I'm only human and I want a decent life for them, for all of us.' She paused. 'Nothing too flash. Just somewhere reasonable to live without the constant threat of eviction.'

'I'll give you that.'

'If I wait for you to face up to your responsibilities, I'll be an old woman.'

'You're nagging again.'

'Do the right thing and I won't have to.'

'Yeah, yeah, I will.'

'And while I'm waiting for you to grow up, it's up to me to look out for myself and get the best I can for our daughters.'

'You won't find the best with your sister,' was his gruff prediction. 'I can promise you that.'

'I can't see why you're so much against it because it won't affect you, except, of course, that you'll see more of June.' She paused, her eyes narrowing in thought. 'That's it, isn't it? You'll feel uncomfortable visiting me in her house.'

'I'm not scared of her,' he objected heatedly. 'I won't like that aspect of it because I can't stand the woman, but that isn't why I think it's wrong for you. I think you're doing the wrong thing because it'll be like living in lodgings and too restricting.'

'And I'm not restricted now?'

Nat glanced around the room. 'Not as much as you will be playing happy families with your sister. Anyway, living with relatives never works out, it's a well-known fact; there are always petty squabbles.'

'Having relatives to squabble with is a first for me so I'll have to learn as I go along,' she told him. 'I'm looking forward to it, whatever you say.'

'I'm only thinking of you, Daisy.' Not true. His comments were entirely selfish. He could hardly bear to imagine what it would be like when he went to see Daisy with that high-and-mighty sister of hers hovering in the background just waiting to find fault. It was bad enough having Nora bend his ear at the slightest opportunity. With two of them on his back about the way he treated Daisy, it was going to be hellish, especially as the house would be June's. 'As I've told you before, that sister of yours has changed you. She's a bad influence, first of all filling your head with rubbish about trying to clear your ol' man's name – now this.'

'Clearing my father's name is *not* rubbish,' Daisy was quick to amend. 'We're serious about it.'

'You've got your head in the clouds if you think you can beat the system and get him out of prison.'

'I don't agree with you.' She wouldn't be put off. 'If we get new evidence, we can appeal and he'll be released once the truth comes out. He needs help, and June and I are all he's got. If we can find Morris Dodd and his wife we'll—'

'You're as powerless as your ol' man is, can't you see that?' he interrupted rudely. 'You don't stand a cat's chance in hell of finding them.'

Daisy couldn't deny that there was some truth in what he said. 'I know it seems hopeless but we're not going to give up,' she said. 'So you might as well face up to it and stop being such a doom merchant.'

He shrugged, stubbing out his cigarette in a saucer. 'All right, have it your own way,' he told her.

Daisy was still worried to death about her father and wouldn't rest until justice was done. But things had come to a halt for the moment. How did you find someone after more than twenty years when you had no idea where to start looking? Even a seasoned detective would be at a loss with nothing to go on at all. There was a way, she was convinced of that; something they'd yet to think of. 'I admit we're at a dead end at the moment,' she confessed. 'But we'll think of a way, given time. And it'll be easier once June and I are living in the same house because we'll have more of a chance to discuss it, to pool our ideas and work out what to do next.'

'I still say that sister of yours is bad news.' Nat just wouldn't give up. 'She unsettles you, gets you fired up about things.'

'I do have a mind of my own,' Daisy reminded him.

'I know you do. But she's the type who can manipulate anyone,' he stated categorically. 'You hardly know her, even though she's your sister.'

'That's one thing you are right about,' she conceded. 'And what better way to rectify that than to share a house with her. There'll be times when we don't see eye to eye, of course.

But I'm optimistic, and if it doesn't work out . . . well, I'll just have to cross that bridge when I come to it.' She took his arm impulsively, her mood softening as she looked into his eyes. 'Be pleased for me, eh? It would mean so much to me.'

Noticing how pretty she looked, her eyes sparkling with enthusiasm, her luxuriant hair shining in the light, his heart melted. He wasn't a romantic man and never thought in terms of 'love' as such, but he did feel something for her and still fancied her, even after all these years.

'OK, babe,' he said with a sigh of resignation. 'If it's what you really want I'll try not to spoil it for you.'

'Thanks, Nat.'

'And while we've got a bit of privacy we might as well make the most of it,' he suggested. 'There'll be precious little of it when you move house.'

'There will if I have my own bedroom,' Daisy pointed out with a giggle. 'We can shut ourselves away in there.'

'Not if the Gestapo have anything to do with it,' he said with a wry look. 'I'll be lucky if I'm allowed inside the house at all, let alone into your bedroom, with that pair of prison warders living there with you.'

'Whereas if we were to get married, we could move into a place of our own and have as much privacy as we want.' Her tone was light. She wasn't being serious; not this time.

'Yeah, yeah, I know,' he murmured into her hair. 'We're a pair, you and me. You know we'll do that, all in good time.' He paused, turning her face to his. 'Don't you?'

And because Daisy wanted to believe him she said, 'Yeah, course I do.'

The area north of Holland Park Avenue up as far as the Harrow Road – which was regarded loosely these days as Notting Hill but more usually known to its residents as North Kensington – was still riddled with building sites in the winter of 1955, as the slum clearance programme continued. Plans for major improvements and a massive road-widening scheme at Notting Hill Gate were heavily rumoured.

But at the moment, in stark contrast to its affluent neighbour Holland Park, the Notting Hill area in the majority was poor, overcrowded and grimy, with pockets of bohemia adding life and colour in some parts. Even before the Caribbeans had arrived there had been a multi-ethnic mix of Eastern European, Russian-Polish Jewish, Cypriots and so on. But the area was becoming increasingly cosmopolitan as ever larger numbers of West Indians continued to move in. Integration into the white community was still very poor.

House buying was a completely new experience for Daisy and she was surprised at the difficulty in finding somewhere suitable. There were properties for sale, of course, but many were big, brooding terraces, more suitable as letting houses than for single-family occupancy. Either that or they were in a state of neglect and needing major structural work, so couldn't be considered.

As conditions continued to deteriorate for Daisy and co. at Benly Square – a leaking sink on the landing, a faulty lavatory cistern and broken bathroom window now adding to the other miseries they had to endure – they were increasingly anxious to find a place with all possible speed.

Then one cold Sunday morning in January, with watery sunlight beaming through the clouds intermittently, they discovered number seventeen Larby Gardens, a terraced house on the hinterland of Notting Hill in the direction of Shepherd's Bush.

'So, what do you think?' asked June as they studied the house from the outside.

'Needs a lick of paint,' observed Daisy in a gross under-statement because the paint had peeled down to the bare wood in places around the windows.

'A good few gallons, I'd say,' added Nora.

'It's structurally sound, according to the agent,' June told them, 'though I'd have to get a survey done, of course.'

'Looks a bit run down,' Daisy felt obliged to point out, still rather in awe of this entire venture.

'Anything we can afford with enough bedrooms for us all isn't going to be in top-class condition,' June told them. 'We'll have to allow enough cash for furniture and decorating, remember. This is central London. It might be a run-down neighbourhood but it's still close to the West End, walking distance of Marble Arch in comfortable shoes. We can't afford to be too choosy, not unless we move further out, which none of us wants because of our work.'

'It's your money that's being spent, June,' Daisy reminded her. 'It has to be your decision.'

'Exactly,' agreed Nora.

'You know that isn't the way I want it to be.' June was adamant. 'We agreed that the choice of house would be something we were all happy with. And I really do want your honest opinion.'

Daisy looked down the street, which was a cul-de-sac full of ragged children playing and women gossiping on their doorsteps. It wasn't salubrious by any means but some of the homes showed signs of pride unknown in Benly Square. A few of the houses here even looked as though they'd been recently painted and had net curtains several shades lighter than the decaying grey lace that hung in the windows around there. Larby Gardens was only about ten minutes' walk from where they lived now, and undeniably shabby, but there was a friendly feel about it somehow, a sense of hope and possibility. 'I think it's got definite potential,' she stated.

'I like it around here,' said Shirley, looking enviously at a group of scruffy children playing marbles in the gutter nearby.

'So do I,' put in Belinda.

'We'd better go and see what it's like inside, then, hadn't we?' smiled June, the agent having given them the key as the property was empty.

Watched by a crowd of curious children who had no inhibitions about asking if Daisy's girls would be joining them as playmates, June unlocked the front door and they all trooped into a dusty hallway.

'Very promising,' was Daisy's instinctive verdict as they clattered through the empty rooms, their footsteps echoing on the bare floorboards, the air thick and musty from being closed up. 'It needs plenty of work but I think we could make this into a home. There's a nice feel about it somehow.'

'Not a bad size either,' added Nora.

As was so often the case with old terraced houses, this one was bigger than it appeared from the outside. There were four rooms upstairs and a hideous bathroom with a stained bath, and a sink that was coming away from the wall. Downstairs there were two reception rooms and an old-fashioned kitchen with a small lobby that led into the back garden. Through the window they could see that the latter was pocket-sized, and beyond the high wall at the bottom, a factory chimney towered over everything. But the house did have a garden. As tiny and overgrown as it was, it was somewhere for the children to play outside in safety.

'Cor, a garden,' shrieked Shirley in delight, as June opened the back door. 'Ooh, can we live here, please? Please, Auntie June, please say that we can.'

The three women exchanged glances.

'You two go outside and have a look while we talk about it,' she requested of them.

The little girls bounded through the door; they were well wrapped up in red coats with red and white pixie hoods that matched their gloves, and which Nora had knitted for them.

191

'So, what's it to be?' asked June, looking at Daisy and Nora. 'Do I go ahead and make an offer?'

Daisy cast her eye around the ancient, browning wallpaper, a flash of sunlight through the window emphasising the stains, the cracked square sink and worn-out wooden draining board. 'I feel as though I want to open all the windows and let some fresh air in,' she said excitedly. 'And tear all that awful wallpaper off and paint the walls in lovely light colours.' She paused, looking at her sister. 'But yes, I think it's right for us.'

'Hear, hear,' added Nora.

'Well, I hope you two are handy with wallpaper scrapers and paintbrushes,' grinned June, 'because you'll need to be if we take this place on. It would cost a fortune to have a professional in to do all the decorating.'

'I'm game,' smiled Daisy.

'Me too,' said Nora.

'Looks like we've found our new address then, doesn't it?' said June, looking pleased.

Daisy giggled. 'Larby Gardens, here we come,' she said, making a pattern with her finger on the dusty window.

'Cor, am I glad to take the weight off my feet,' said Jack when he and Alan finally managed to find a table to sit down to lunch on pie and chips in the cafeteria at Earls Court. 'It's a smashing exhibition but more exhausting than a week's work.'

'It's all the pushing and shoving to get through the crowds,' Alan commented, glancing around. The place was heaving; the queue at the self-service counter was snaking around the cafeteria and people were milling about with trays, trying to find somewhere to sit with their food.

'I'm enjoying it, though,' Jack remarked, shaking the ketchup bottle. 'It's really interesting.'

'It is,' nodded Alan, sprinkling salt on his chips. 'But I

think we've seen enough now, having been here all day yesterday as well as this morning.'

'Which leaves us with the rest of the afternoon free,' Jack pointed out, 'as we're not going back until tomorrow.'

'That's right.'

Pouring a dollop of ketchup on to the side of his plate, Jack said conversationally, 'I think the thing that's impressed me most here is the hotel kitchen equipment.'

'Mm.'

'Mind you, it needs to be special at the price they're asking,' he chatted on. 'The trouble with exhibitions is that they make you want everything on show.' He concentrated on his food for a few moments. 'Still, I suppose that's the whole point.'

Alan nodded but he wasn't really listening. He was tormented by the fact that he was in London and so was June. He wanted to see her *so* much. The change of address card she'd sent him recently was in his wallet and filling him with temptation. But it would be pointless to visit her. Why should he chase after a woman who didn't want him?

'What about that cocktail bar they had on display?' Jack continued to enthuse. 'Wasn't that something? Too much of a contemporary look for the Cliff Head, of course, but very smart with all that mirror glass and Formica . . . Alan, are you listening to me?'

His friend started slightly. 'No, I wasn't. Sorry.'

'At least you're honest,' was Jack's breezy reply. 'So what's making you so preoccupied?' He squinted at Alan knowingly. 'As if I didn't know.'

'It's being in the same town as her,' he admitted with a wry look. 'Naturally, she's on my mind. She is my wife, after all.'

'We're free this afternoon if you want to pay her a visit,' suggested Jack, who still thought Alan and June were made for each other.

'She'll probably be out at work.'

Jack shrugged. 'If she is, we'll go and see her there. You know where she works, don't you?'

'Yeah, but it might make it awkward for her,' said Alan, whose common sense was fighting with his desire to see her. 'Anyway, what would be the point? She's made it clear that it's over between us.'

'No harm in calling in for old times' sake, is there?' said Jack. 'As we're in London with time to spare, I'll go with you to make it seem more casual.'

'No. I'd better stay away.'

'It's up to you,' Jack told him with a sage look. 'But I think you'll regret it if you go back without even seeing her.'

Was it worth giving it one more try? Alan wondered. In his heart he knew he'd never forgive himself if he went back to Devon without making a final attempt. But this was her last chance. If she turned him down again this time, he would *never, ever* approach her again. And that was definite.

'You're right,' he said, his voice rising excitedly. 'I'll get a London A to Z and work out exactly where she lives when we've finished here.'

Daisy was listening to *Woman's Hour* as she worked with the scraper on the living-room walls. I'll have bigger muscles than Tarzan's by the time we've got rid of this horrible wallpaper, she thought, standing halfway up the ladder, rubbing her aching arm. But it'll be worth it in the end.

It was a March afternoon and a blustery wind whistled through the house, rattling the windows and seeming to send the dark clouds scuttling across the metal-grey skies. Daisy was alone in the house. June was out at work, Shirley was at school. It was Nora's day off and she'd taken Belinda to the park so that Daisy could get on with the decorating. Daisy had teased her; said she herself had drawn the short straw.

There had been plenty of laughter since they'd moved in here together.

Having given the walls a thorough soaking, Daisy got busy with the scraper, tearing off a sizeable strip and being rewarded with a moment of satisfaction. It was more than a month since they'd moved in and, by pulling together, had made good progress with the decorating, spurred on by a mutual desire to get the place into some sort of shape. There was still chaos on a grand scale in this room, though, with tattered curtains inherited from the previous owners, a carpet of newspaper on the bare boards, partly stripped walls and only deck chairs to sit on. When the work was finished, June was going to buy furniture and they were all very excited about that.

While she worked, Daisy listened with interest to a debate on the programme. Two women were getting quite heated about women's role in contemporary Britain. One of the debaters was a feminist whose views seemed extremely daring in that they challenged the accepted view that a woman's place was indisputably at home. The feminist speaker believed passionately that women were conditioned to enjoy a form of dedicated slavery, and that they shouldn't be made to feel guilty if they didn't enjoy being tied to the house, looking after children all day. If a woman preferred to go out to work, it didn't mean that she was flawed as a mother or loved her children less. Her opposer was rattled by this and quoted from a recent bestselling book by some doctor, who was also an expert in child care, and stated in print that the mothers of young children were not free to earn.

'Some of us don't have any choice, mate,' Daisy muttered under her breath. 'And you can't make me feel any more guilty than I already do for going out to work and leaving my girls.' As usual unmarried mothers weren't mentioned in the discussion. Daisy had accepted long ago that women in her position didn't exist except to be quoted as a bad example. She was enjoying the discussion, though. It was rather refreshing to hear a different point of view.

Pushing her hair back from her brow, she looked at the clock on the mantelpiece and wondered if she could afford the time to stop for a tea break. In the end she decided to carry on working because Nora and Belinda would be back at any minute and it would soon be time to break off to collect Shirley from school anyway. Most of the local children walked to school together but Daisy wasn't ready to let her go on her own just yet.

No sooner had she denied herself a rest than there was a knock at the front door so she had to stop work anyway. Opening the door she found herself confronted by two smartly dressed men in suits and dark overcoats. Immediately her guard was up. A well-dressed man around here was either a rent man, an insurance man or a doctor; definitely officialdom of some sort.

'Yes?' she said nervously, unable to see beyond the smart clothes and their implication.

'Is June Masters in, please?' asked one of them, a young-ish, good-looking man with brown curly hair and a worried expression in his eyes.

Daisy looked at him warily and didn't reply. Good suits spelled trouble.

'Well?' he continued, looking questioningly at Daisy. 'Is she here or not?'

'Who wants to know?'

'I asked the question first.'

Years of being in thrall to rent collectors had made her ultra-sensitive about them. 'If you've come for the rent, you've come to the wrong house, mate,' she blurted out. 'We don't pay rent here. My sister owns this house.'

His face worked with astonishment and he looked very tense. 'Really?' he said.

Daisy was still afraid to admit to anything. She stared at him, pulling the door to in front of her as though to stop them entering.

'We're not gangsters about to force our way in, you know,' she was informed by the other man. 'So you're quite safe.'

'Perhaps I'd better explain,' said the first man. 'June sent me a card with her new address on it. We're in London on business and decided to call on the off chance that she might be in.'

The tone of the conversation now indicated that they weren't officials of any sort so Daisy relaxed a little. 'You know my sister well then?' she said enquiringly.

'I ought to,' he said with a half-smile. 'I'm her husband.'

'Oh, oh, I see.' He was the last person she expected it to be because he lived so far away.

He thrust his hand forward. 'Alan's the name,' he announced in a friendly manner.

'I'm Daisy,' she said, shaking his hand.

'Pleased to meet you.'

He being a relation altered things considerably. Her instinct was to invite them in and make them welcome. But would June want her estranged husband in her home? Daisy didn't know how civilised the break-up had been. If it had been a bitter parting, June wasn't going to thank Daisy for making him welcome here. 'As you've probably gathered, she's not at home at the moment,' she informed them. 'She's out at work.'

'What time are you expecting her back?'

'About five thirty.'

Alan looked at his watch. 'We'll come back later then, shall we?' he said.

'I suppose that would be best.' Daisy felt awkward. It seemed so rude not to ask them in.

'We're in London for a hotelier's exhibition,' he chose to explain. 'But we're going back to Devon first thing in the morning. It would be nice to see June before we go back, just to say hello. It didn't seem right to be so near and not call in.'

It went against the grain with Daisy to turn someone away without so much as a cup of tea on a winter's afternoon. But her name would be mud with June if she didn't want him encouraged to stay around. On the other hand, her sister had sent him her new address so she must have wanted him to know where she was, and he was going to come back later, anyway.

She was still debating the issue when Alan's companion made a timely intervention. 'We could murder a cuppa tea,' he said, winking at her. 'There's a bitter wind blowing out here and walking around the exhibition has done terrible things to our feet.'

Alan tutted and looked at him with mock disapproval, then turned back to Daisy. 'This is a friend of mine, Jack Saunders,' he informed her. 'He's a bit of a big mouth, I'm afraid.'

'So I gather.'

'We could freeze to death while you two stand there beating about the bush,' said Jack, and Daisy noticed his strong London accent. 'The two of you are sort of related and the two of us are dying for a cup of tea and a sit-down. Makes sense to put the two things together.'

Focusing her gaze on him, Daisy saw a pair of laughing blue eyes beaming at her from a fine countenance topped by short blond hair being blown flat to his head by the wind. Smiling almost despite herself, she succumbed to impulse, opened the door and invited them inside.

'Excuse the state of the place,' she said, leading them into the living room, waving her hand towards the patchy walls and indicating that they make themselves comfortable in the deck chairs that were near the fire, which she stirred into life with the poker. 'As you can see, we're in the middle of doing it up.'

They nodded politely. Daisy took their coats and hung them up in the hall on the hooks that had been left by the previous occupants.

'I didn't know that June had a sister,' Alan informed her when she came back into the room.

She explained briefly about their recent reunion. 'It's a long story,' she concluded. 'I'm sure June will give you all the details.'

He nodded. 'Is it just the two of you living here?' he enquired with interest.

Daisy explained the setup.

'Cosy,' remarked Alan.

'It is, very,' said Daisy, saddened by the bitter edge to his tone; the sorrow that was very often visible in June's eyes she could now see reflected in his.

She went to the kitchen to make tea and when she came back into the room with a tray of tea and biscuits, Jack did most of the talking. Alan just added the odd polite comment. Daisy felt sorry for him. He seemed preoccupied and had a bewildered look about him; had obviously known nothing about how June had become a home owner.

'Terrible job, that, isn't it,' remarked Jack, looking at the walls, 'stripping off wallpaper?'

'Sounds as though you're speaking from experience,' Daisy replied, sitting in another deck chair with a cup of tea and a biscuit.

'From more experience than I care to think about,' he said lightly. 'I bought an old cottage and spent what seemed like the whole of the first year getting all the old wallpaper off.'

'I hope it was worth it and you've got it as you want it now,' she said chattily.

'More or less,' he replied. 'There's always something else

you want to do, though. By the time you get to the end of it, the beginning needs doing again.'

'Don't say that.' She made a face. 'We've only just started on this place and I feel as though I've had enough already.'

'I know the feeling.'

'We all have jobs so can only work on it at odd times,' she told him.

'I did mine that way too.'

'I shouldn't be taking this break now, to tell you the truth,' she confided. 'I wouldn't have stopped work if you hadn't arrived.'

'I bet you're glad we turned up then,' he joked.

'Ooh, yeah,' she admitted with a grin. 'Any excuse to put that damned stripper down.' She sipped her tea. 'I would have to be stopping soon anyway, though, because it's nearly time I went to collect my daughter from school.'

'You have a daughter?' he said with the note of surprise the absence of a wedding ring evoked in people.

'I have two daughters.' The sound of voices at the back door indicated the arrival of Nora and Belinda. 'One of them has just come in now.'

Belinda, a dainty, talkative child with her mother's smiling eyes, came into the room like a great bolt of energy and immediately launched into an enthusiastic account of the trip to the park and how she'd been on the swings and they'd seen some flowers which Nora had said were crocuses. Daisy gave her a hug and listened with interest, making introductions and explaining that the men were waiting for Auntie June.

They all had more tea and Daisy said she had to go and collect Shirley from school. The men talked about leaving and coming back later, whereupon Nora took it upon herself to say that they were very welcome to stay, rather than roam the streets in the cold, until June got home.

Jack astonished them all by saying, 'It's nice of you to

offer but if we stay we make ourselves useful, right? So have you got another one of those wallpaper strippers?'

When Daisy left, both men had their jackets off and sleeves rolled up and were working with the strippers on the walls. When she got back from school with Shirley, the wall she'd been working on was bare of wallpaper and they were making inroads into another, ably assisted by Belinda, who was collecting the strippings into a bucket and keeping up a constant flow of chatter. Daisy was infused with the warmth of the atmosphere as soon as she entered the room.

'Wow. You haven't half shifted.' She was impressed.

'We don't hang about,' grinned Jack. 'Anyway, there are two of us at it.'

'You must be supermen to have done all that in such a short time,' she teased them lightly.

'I'm the superman,' claimed Jack, making the little girls laugh by pulling a face at Alan, 'because I've had plenty of practice. Whereas my mate here doesn't have to do his own dirty work so is a bit of an amateur.'

Alan took it all in good part, even though he still seemed worried, obviously anxious about the meeting with June. 'Honestly, you'd think he had a degree in interior decorating to hear him talk,' was his jokey response. 'Just because he bought a ruin of a cottage and made it habitable.'

'What's a cottage?' Shirley wanted to know.

'A small house, love,' her mother explained.

'Like the ones in storybooks that are always in the country?' she said. 'Is yours in the country?'

'Mine's even better than that,' Jack told her. 'It's by the seaside.'

'Seaside, like Southend?' said Belinda.

'That's right,' said Jack.

'Do you make sandcastles?' she wanted to know.

'I'm a bit old to want to do that sort of thing myself,' he

told her. 'But it's a good sandy beach and children do make them there.'

'Ooh . . .' Belinda was breathless with awe.

'Sounds lovely, and I bet you've made your cottage a lot more than just habitable,' said Daisy, because Jack Saunders had the air of someone who would make a thoroughly good job of anything he took on.

'I suppose I might manage to admit to it being comfortable,' amended Alan, teasing his pal.

'You're just jealous,' joshed Jack.

'Jealous because I don't live miles from anywhere?' he returned. 'Don't kid yourself.'

'Anyway, do we have another volunteer?' asked Jack, smiling at Shirley.

'I don't mind,' said Shirley, giving him a shy look. 'But only if you'll tell us more about your cottage at the seaside.'

'It's a deal,' he agreed. 'You help your sister pick up the paper and I'll keep talking.'

'OK. I'll just go and get changed,' she said, immediately at ease with him.

'You've both done wonders in this room,' praised Nora, who had fallen under the spell of these two amiable young men.

'You certainly have,' grinned Daisy. 'You can keep it up for as long as you like.'

'Are you going to get another paint stripper and give a hand?' asked Jack.

'Afraid not,' she told him. 'I have to get ready for work in a minute.'

'Work?' he said with interest.

She told him what she did and explained that she was given a free meal at the hotel when she was on duty so wouldn't be staying for supper with the others.

'I hope you two boys will stay for a bite to eat with us,

202

though,' Nora said. 'It's nothing special but there's plenty if you'd like to join us.'

'Please stay,' chorused the little girls.

'You'll have to ask the boss about that,' Jack told her, grinning towards Alan.

'Do stay,' Shirley urged Alan, adding as an extra incentive, 'we'll show you our bedroom, if you like.'

'It's been done up and it's very pretty,' Belinda put in. 'Mummy and Auntie June and Nora painted it and put wallpaper up for us. It's got toys on it.'

'In that case, how can we say no?' said Alan.

'Hurray!' shrieked the girls, who, like their mother, were very sociable.

'You seem to have made a hit,' remarked Daisy, looking from one of the men to the other.

'If only it was that easy with bigger girls,' was Jack's light-hearted response.

'I can't believe that you'd have any trouble,' said Daisy.

'He doesn't,' Alan informed her. 'So don't listen to him. He's just trying it on.'

Daisy was amused by their banter. They were all laughing when June walked in, smiling, her face instinctively lighting up when she saw Alan, then becoming grim when the reality of the situation registered fully.

'What are you doing here?' she demanded coldly.

The laughter ended abruptly and tension crackled in the air as the couple stared at each other in stony silence.

Chapter Nine

Daisy's journey to and from work took a bit longer from Larby Gardens because she had further to walk from the station. But the extra travelling time was the last thing on her mind that night on her way home on the tube. She was lost in thought, reliving that terrible moment when June had walked in and sent the atmosphere in the house plummeting to freezing point.

Even the children had been subdued, though not for long, thanks to Jack's entertaining company. After June and Alan had made a silent departure to her room, leaving a resounding hush behind them, Jack had carried on stripping the wallpaper, chatting to the girls as though nothing untoward was happening.

Heaven knows what had happened since then. Daisy had gone to work soon after, leaving the girls in Nora's care, assisted by Jack, who was regaling them with tales of life at the seaside.

Running over June's arrival again, Daisy recalled her initial joy at seeing Alan. She'd simply lit up at the sight of him. Daisy wondered what the problem could possibly be because the couple obviously adored each other. Whatever it was it must be serious because June didn't seem like the sort of person to walk out on someone on a whim.

Her thoughts turned to Jack with whom Daisy had struck

an instant rapport. He'd made a big impression on her with his casual charm and sense of humour. His blond good looks hadn't gone unnoticed either. Oh well, they'll both be gone when I get home, she thought. June would surely have sorted things out one way or the other by now.

She was jolted out of her thoughts when someone approached her in the station foyer. 'Hello, Daisy,' he greeted her.

'Jack?' She smiled broadly, pleased but astonished to see him. 'What are you doing here?'

'That's the second time today I've heard that question,' he said with a wry grin. 'Fortunately, this time it wasn't said with quite the same venom.'

She made a face. 'Wasn't it awful?' she said, tutting. 'June was really fierce, wasn't she?'

'Enough to frighten the pants off Alan.'

'What happened after I left?' she asked, pulling her coat collar up against the strong wind as they made their way out of the station into the street.

'They stayed upstairs until supper.'

'And then . . .?'

'They came down and we all ate a meal together.'

'In agonising silence, I suppose.'

'They weren't exactly laughing and joking but they did make an effort at polite conversation so it wasn't too bad,' he told her. 'And the rest of us did enough talking to cover the tension. The kids kept things moving along. With them around there weren't any awkward silences.'

Daisy smiled affectionately at the thought of them. 'Just as well they aren't any good at keeping quiet, in this particular instance then,' she remarked.

'Absolutely.'

'So, what's happening with June and Alan?' she asked.

'They went back upstairs to June's room after the meal and

were still there when I came out,' he told her. 'I called up the stairs to them to tell them where I was going and Alan shouted down in reply. So they haven't murdered each other. That's all I know.'

'What are you doing here anyway?' she asked again. 'I thought you'd be back at your hotel by now, going to bed at a decent hour as you're going back to Devon in the morning.'

'That was the original intention. But I couldn't very well drag Alan away while he was in the middle of an emotional crisis, could I? And poor Nora looked so whacked, I told her to go to bed and not worry about staying up to entertain me,' he explained. 'I thought I might as well come and walk you home, to save sitting around at your place on my own. Nora gave me all the gen so that I knew where to meet you.'

'It's very kind of you,' Daisy said as they left the station lights behind and began to stride out against the wind, passing a staggering drunk, a tramp in a shop doorway and a crowd of Teddy boys hanging around on a street corner.

'It wasn't kindness that inspired me to come,' he confessed.

'No? What then?'

'I enjoyed your company so much earlier, I wanted some more of it.'

'At least you're honest,' she approved. 'And I'm flattered.'

They walked on in comfortable silence for a while, then: 'I shouldn't really say this but I'm going to stick my neck out and say it anyway,' he began hesitantly. 'Is it a good idea for you to be out on the streets on your own at this time of night with so many dodgy characters about?'

'No choice, I'm afraid,' she informed him chirpily. 'Anyway, I'm used to it so it doesn't worry me.'

'Wouldn't a daytime job be better for you?'

Daisy explained her situation and her reasons for working unsociable hours.

'Where's the kids' father?' Jack asked.

'He's around and we're still together,' she said, adding in the defensive way that had become almost second nature to her, 'We'll be getting married, eventually.'

'Doesn't he worry about you being out on your own at night in such a dangerous part of London?' he queried. 'I know I would if you were my girlfriend.'

'I don't think Nat ever gives it a thought, to be perfectly honest,' she replied. 'We're Londoners; urban life is what we know. Anyway, it isn't as dangerous as it might seem to an outsider. It can't be because I always get home safe and sound.'

'I'm not a complete outsider, you know,' he pointed out. 'I haven't always lived out in the sticks in deepest Devon. I'm originally from Hackney.'

Which explained the accent, she noted, but said, 'You've lived away for quite a while, though, haven't you? So you've probably got a bit out of touch with the way things are here.'

'Are you suggesting that I've become a bit of a yokel?' he grinned, teasing her.

'I wasn't, actually.' She paused, giggling. 'But I think you might look rather fetching in a smock.'

'Cheeky,' he admonished good-humouredly. 'We don't all have straw in our hair down there, you know.'

'And it isn't all pimps and prostitutes up here,' she countered quickly.

'I suppose I asked for that,' he laughed. 'But seriously, though, you must admit that this part of London does have a reputation for being a bit rough.'

'Things go on around here, so I've heard. But they don't affect me or my children,' Daisy said. 'I just get on with my life and let other people get on with theirs. Being out on my own at night isn't a problem.'

'As you say, I'm probably out of touch with how things are here now that I'm a country boy,' he conceded.

She nodded. 'You really like it down there then?'

'Love it.'

'Is it living by the sea that appeals to you in particular?'

'I enjoy having the ocean on my doorstep, yeah, sure. But I like the general feeling of space I get from living on the seashore,' Jack explained. 'I spent some time in Australia. I think that gave me a taste for the outdoors.'

'You wouldn't come back to London to live then?'

'It would have to be something really special to make me do that,' he told her. 'My folks are all settled in Australia so I don't have any family ties here now. I'm still a London boy at heart and I don't suppose I'll ever lose that. But I've got used to the slower pace of life down there. Clean air, not so much traffic. And the countryside is beautiful.'

'It sounds wonderful.'

'It is,' he confirmed. 'And my cottage is in a fantastic location.' He paused, turning to her with a wry look. 'Sorry, I'm probably being boring. I'm afraid I get a bit carried away with enthusiasm for the place.'

'You're not being at all boring.' She couldn't believe he would ever be that. 'But I must admit, I can't imagine you living miles from anywhere. You're far too sociable.'

'I'm no hermit, believe me,' he quickly put her right. 'I'm out at work a lot of the time and it's only ten minutes into town on my motorbike.'

'A motorbike eh?'

'My pride and joy.'

'What is it with men and motorbikes?'

'The speed, the freedom . . .'

'The wind in your hair?'

'Yeah, that too,' he laughed.

'You're building up a picture of a fabulous way of life.'

'It'll do for me.'

They moved on to other things. She told him about her job

and asked about his. He told her a bit about the Cliff Head and his position there.

'And you are best mates with Alan, despite the fact that his parents own the hotel?' she remarked. 'Some people might be put off by that.'

'The fact that he's the boss doesn't interfere with our friendship at all,' Jack told her. 'He doesn't pull rank on me when we're off duty or ram his position down my throat, that's why. We wouldn't be mates at all if he did and he knows it. We hit it off from the start. We're the same age and have similar views about things. It was only natural we should get pally.'

'You seem to know June quite well too.'

'Not as well as I know him but I was friendly with them as a couple before she did her disappearing act,' he explained. 'He turned to me then. The poor bloke was beside himself.'

'What happened to split them up?'

'No idea. And from what he's said, I don't think Alan knows either. She just went, out of the blue, leaving him completely shattered.' He paused thoughtfully. 'But you're her sister – hasn't she talked to you about it?'

'Hardly at all. She said that her husband was the son of a hotelier in Torquay and she left him but she's never said why, and she makes it clear she doesn't want to talk about it.'

'It's all very odd.'

'Mm.'

'Naturally there's been gossip,' he mentioned. 'Some people think his parents drove her out. But I think there's more to it than that. She's too strong-minded to be driven out of anywhere, and she's certainly a match for them.'

'She didn't get on with them, then?'

'They didn't get on with her, to be more precise, especially his mother. She gave June a really hard time. I've watched her in action. I've seen her put June through it over the years.'

'Didn't Alan stick up for her?'

'He did if he caught his mother at it,' he told her. 'But she was as nice as pie to June when he was around. Far too clever to let him get wind of what was really happening. June must have told him about it, I suppose, but maybe she didn't tell him just how bad it was. June's always struck me as a caring sort of a woman, despite what she's done to Alan. Maybe she didn't want to come between mother and son.'

'You could be right.'

'Anyway, I still don't think that was why she left,' Jack went on to say. 'But I'm convinced she must have had a very good reason to walk out like that. I worked with them for a long time. I've seen how they were together. She always seemed loyal and absolutely devoted to him. But you're her sister, you know what she's like.'

'I don't actually.' Daisy briefly explained the unusual situation with June and herself. 'I'm still getting to know her. She seems very deep; keeps things close to her chest.'

'Mm, you're probably right. Anyway, I hope they can patch their marriage up,' he said. 'They were a great team and Alan hasn't been the same man since she went.'

'Perhaps they're getting back together as we speak,' she suggested.

'If talking has anything to do with it, they will be,' he grinned. 'They've been at it long enough. He'll have to call it a day soon so that we can go back to the hotel to bed.'

'You're not staying at the hotel where June works, I take it, or she wouldn't have been so surprised to see you.'

'Alan didn't want to crowd her,' explained Jack. 'We only came to the house on the spur of the moment.'

'He seems very genuine to me.'

'He is.'

They'd reached the house and he stopped outside and turned to her, the wind blowing his hair about. 'In case Alan's

211

ready to leave and drags me off in a hurry and I don't get a chance to mention it,' he began, smiling uncertainly, 'I just want to say how much I've enjoyed meeting you.'

'The same goes for me too.' She shivered against the wind that was whipping around the buildings and sweeping litter along the pavement. 'It's been lovely.'

'And those daughters of yours are a couple of smashers,' he continued.

'Thank you.' She smiled broadly. Compliments about her children always pleased her.

'I wish you all the best for the future.'

'The same to you,' Daisy responded, noticing that his mood had become formal but oddly intimate somehow. 'When London seems especially hectic and the tube impossibly crowded, I'll think of you with envy in your cottage by the sea.'

'Anyway,' he said with a note of finality, thrusting his hand towards her. 'It's been a pleasure.'

'Likewise,' she said, shaking a hand that felt firm and strong.

'Come on then, let's go and see if those two have made any progress towards a reunion,' he said, and they walked up to the front door together.

'If you didn't want me to find you, why send me your change of address?' Alan wanted to know.

'How many more times must I tell you,' replied June impatiently. 'It was in case of an emergency. I just didn't feel able to move house without letting you know my address.'

'If you really wanted it to be over between us, you would have moved without giving me a second thought.'

'I was just being responsible. You could have had an accident or been seriously ill and needed to contact me,' she went on to explain. 'Or you could have wanted to file for divorce. There are any number of reasons why you needed to know where I was. It just didn't seem right not to tell you.'

'You didn't find it necessary when you left,' he reminded her. 'I had to use my own methods to track you down and only did so then because of luck.'

She lowered her eyes in shame. 'I know. That was really bad of me,' she admitted. 'I would have let you know eventually. You beat me to it, that's all.'

'Let's put all that behind us and you come home, June,' he begged for the umpteenth time.

'Alan, we've been going over this for hours and I've told you I'm not coming back,' she insisted. 'I can't. My life is here in London now.'

'The reason we've been going over it for hours is because we both want the same thing – to be back together. But you won't admit it for some reason best known to yourself.'

They were in her bedroom, not yet refurbished, the walls suffused with wallpaper darkened with age, the floorboards bare. He was sitting in a wicker chair near the sash window. They'd been talking for a long time but not only about their marriage. There had been a mutual exchange of news. She'd told him about the bizarre circumstances that had led to the reunion with Daisy, and their hopes to clear their father's name. She'd explained how she came to buy this house. He'd given her an update about things at the Cliff Head.

'Apart from anything else,' she said now, 'I need to be in London with Daisy to do what we can for our father.'

'So stay here for a while longer, and then come back,' Alan suggested. 'If I knew you were coming back eventually, I could live with that.'

'I'm not coming back, Alan,' she repeated. 'Not ever. So you must try to accept it.' She had to force the words out. 'When I made the decision to leave you, it was for good.'

His expression was grim. He stared at her, then looked

down at his hands as though pondering. When he spoke again, his tone was sad but positive. 'OK, I'll do what you want and go away and get on with my life without you. I won't come after you again. But don't expect me to believe that it's what you really want because I know that it isn't.' He raised his eyes to meet hers and added vehemently, 'I'll never believe that. Not ever.'

'That's up to you.'

The silence was painfully tense until Alan changed the subject completely. 'About this business of your father – I admire you for being willing to have a go and I don't want to put you off, but I think you should prepare yourself for disappointment. It all seems a bit pie-in-the-sky to me.'

'It is, extremely,' June agreed. 'We've got nothing to go on at all. But because Daisy and I know that he's innocent we have the motivation to keep trying. It could take years to find these people, and we might never do it but we can't give up. Can you understand that?'

'Yes, I think so. Just be careful.'

She nodded. His mood was now one of dull resignation and she guessed that he had, at last, accepted their separation as permanent. He was finished with shouting and pleading. He was going to make the best of his life without her. It broke her heart.

Noises from downstairs drifted up.

'Sounds as though the others are back,' Alan said, standing up with a purposeful air and a heartbreaking show of dignity. 'So I'd better be on my way.'

'Yes.'

'It isn't fair to keep Jack hanging about any longer,' he said lamely, in an effort to delay the inevitable.

'No it isn't.' She swallowed hard. 'Could you make my apologies to him for me, please?' Dangerously close to tears, she could barely trust herself to speak. 'I'd rather not go down and see him off. I'm sure he won't mind.'

'Of course he won't,' he said coolly, and left the room quietly while June remained where she was, sitting stiffly on the edge of the bed.

'No luck with June then?' observed Jack as he and Alan headed for the station.

'Does it look like it?'

'All right, no need to bite my head off, mate,' Jack retaliated. 'Just making conversation.'

'Save your breath,' was Alan's sharp response. 'I'm not in the mood for a chat.'

'Suits me fine,' said Jack, who knew Alan far too well to be offended.

'Good.'

Jack was concerned about his friend, of course, and hated to see him miserable. But thoughts of someone else were filling his mind as they walked through the dingy streets of Notting Hill, occasionally splashed with neon and the sound of jazz music drifting from some basement.

Daisy had made a huge impression on him and his heart lifted at the memory of her: her beaming smile, the things she'd said, the way she was with her children. She wasn't smart or glamorous but she was so richly endowed with warmth and vitality, a natural beauty radiated from her. Her sex appeal was magnetic, all the more so because it was completely uncontrived.

He longed to see her again but knew such feelings were pointless. Apart from the obvious geographical problem, she was still involved with the children's father, and therefore not available. She was as good as married, and married women were off limits as far as he was concerned. It was a pity, though, because he'd really taken a shine to her.

He was recalled to the present by Alan. 'Sorry I've been

such a pain, snapping your head off and keeping you waiting all that time at June's place.'

'No problem,' Jack was able to assure him honestly. If Alan hadn't decided to call on June, Jack would never have met Daisy. He'd probably never see her again but he felt richer for having briefly made her acquaintance.

Daisy was having much the same thoughts about him as she heated milk for cocoa in the kitchen. Meeting Jack had been a real tonic. He'd made her feel light-hearted and vibrant, somehow. It was a pity she wouldn't be seeing him again because he was such a smashing bloke. Ah well, ships that pass in the night, she thought wistfully. She'd not thought it possible to be so profoundly affected by a complete stranger. She barely knew him but he'd felt special to her. Her feelings for him weren't entirely platonic either, she admitted, grinning to herself. She'd been involved with Nat for so long she'd forgotten how exhilarating it was to fancy someone new.

Her mind drifted on to the other events of the evening and she was sad as she remembered Alan coming downstairs looking gloomy but proud, and leaving the house with Jack so quietly. He and June had obviously not managed to work things out.

The house felt achingly silent now. Usually at this time when she got back from work, she, June and Nora would have a cup of cocoa together and a chat before they went to bed. Nora had obviously been exhausted by the tension of it all but was probably lying awake worrying about it. June definitely wouldn't be asleep after such a trauma.

Suddenly decisive, Daisy heated more milk and made three mugs of cocoa, put them on a tray and carried it upstairs. Pausing outside June's room, she could just hear the low sound of stifled sobbing. June was obviously struggling very hard not to be heard. They had a strict house rule here: the privacy of someone's bedroom was sacrosanct. This was where you went when you wanted to be left alone and everyone respected that. If Daisy went in, she would be intruding. But her heart ached for her sister and she wanted to help. Surely it was permissible to bend the rules under the circumstances.

Holding the tray with one hand with her arm supporting it, she tapped tentatively on the door.

No reply.

She knocked again. 'I've brought you some cocoa, June,' she called.

All was silent.

'Can I come in?'

As the request was ignored and the crying continued, Daisy dispensed with house rules altogether and followed her instincts, turning the door handle and looking cautiously into the room. Her sister was lying face down on the bed, her body heaving.

'Oh, June, love.' Putting the tray on the dressing table, Daisy went over to the bed and sat down, putting a comforting arm around her sister's shoulders. 'You and Alan weren't able to sort things out then?'

'No, and we never will. We can't ever get back together, and I've told him that,' she spluttered. 'He shouldn't have come here. All he's done is upset us both.'

'Perhaps you shouldn't have let him know where you are if you feel that strongly about it,' was Daisy's cautious suggestion.

June turned over and sat up, mopping her face with a handkerchief. 'I couldn't just cut myself off from him altogether. It wouldn't have been fair,' she said, her voice muffled with tears. 'He needed to know my address, even if only because he wants to start divorce proceedings.'

'There is that, I suppose,' Daisy agreed.

'Sorry you've all been made to feel awkward in the house,' she apologised, sniffing into her hanky. 'And about my imitation of Niagara Falls.'

'Don't be silly,' Daisy assured her. 'I was out at work so I wasn't affected. And everyone's entitled to a good old weep now and again. I'm your sister. I want to be here for you.'

'And I'm your friend and the same goes for me,' added Nora, entering the room. 'The last thing I want to do is intrude but I heard you crying and I heard Daisy come in.' She paused, looking at June. 'I want to help, June.' She picked up the tray and offered the cocoa mugs to them.

June seemed to recover and managed a watery smile after moistening her mouth with the hot, sweet liquid. 'That means a lot to me,' she told them, her eyes glistening with fresh tears. 'I've never had any real friends before.'

'I am surprised,' expressed Daisy. 'You being so confident and everything.'

'That doesn't necessarily bring friends.' She didn't enlighten them as to the reason for her friendless state. She hated to talk about it, and, besides, she didn't want to burden them with her past. 'None that I was close to, anyway. I suppose Alan was the best friend I ever had. And even then there was always . . .' her voice tailed off.

'Always what?' urged Daisy.

'Nothing.'

'As Alan obviously means so much to you, and vice versa, is there no chance of your getting back together?' asked Daisy with feeling. 'It seems such a terrible waste. Anyone can see the two of you still love each other.'

'Love isn't always enough,' said June thickly.

'Surely it's the main ingredient, though,' suggested Daisy hopefully. 'If you've got that, the rest can be sorted out. Or am I just being naïve?'

'You are rather,' muttered June.

'You might feel better if you talk about it, dear,' suggested Nora kindly. 'A trouble shared and all that. It goes without saying that nothing you say will go any further.'

'There's nothing to say, honestly,' she insisted, composing herself suddenly, as though fearing they might persuade her to say something she would later regret. 'It's over between Alan and me, and that's that.'

Daisy knew that June's demons, whatever they were, had not been exorcised by her leaving Alan. She was still a very tormented woman. 'Well, you obviously know your own mind. And being completely selfish, we'd have missed you like mad if you'd gone back to Devon,' she said in an effort to lift the atmosphere as June obviously didn't want to confide.

'By the way,' began June, taking this opportunity to make something clear, 'if anything ever happened and I did have to sell up and go away for any reason at all, I would make sure you weren't left without a home.' She paused and added most emphatically, 'You have my word on that.'

'That's nice of you,' said Daisy.

'Yes,' added Nora.

'So, having cleared that up, let's talk about something more cheerful,' June suggested, trying without success to convince them that she was feeling better.

'One good thing has come out of today,' Daisy grinned, determined to cheer them all up.

They both looked at her enquiringly.

'All the old wallpaper has been stripped off in the living room, thanks to our visitors.'

'It is true what they say about an ill wind then,' said Nora with a chuckle.

Even June attempted a smile at Daisy's down-to-earth way of getting things back to normal.

★ ★ ★

219

As the air warmed and softened to spring and then summer, the occupants of number seventeen Larby Gardens lived in harmony together. Rooms turned from dingy and old-fashioned to fresh and contemporary as the decorating progressed. Furniture was bought, carpets laid and homeliness added with pictures, ornaments and lamps.

June paid for all of this from the money she'd put by from the sale of her mother's house, but everything else was shared: the chores, the bills, the decisions. Meals were eaten together whenever possible against a clamour of conversation, with the children making their contributions. Late-night cocoa continued to be a regular habit. Naturally there were differences of opinion but generally speaking they got on well.

But the long-term co-existence of human beings was rarely that simple, and Daisy's first falling-out with her sister was over Nat, and was very painful for them both.

'I don't know why you put up with it,' June blurted out one night when he'd not been near for a fortnight, then turned up just before bedtime, expecting Daisy to make supper for him, and had gone off in a huff when she'd refused. 'It's disgusting the way he treats you. Ignoring your existence for weeks on end, then turning up just when he feels like it. He's got a flaming cheek.'

Daisy wasn't easily offended and could take any amount of criticism about herself, but when it came to Nat, her defence mechanism went into top gear. 'My relationship with Nat is my business,' she told June sharply.

Having managed to restrain herself from saying too much about Nat's offhand behaviour towards her sister for all these months, now that she had spoken out, June couldn't stop.

'I'm only thinking of you,' she went on. 'That man has no right to treat you the way he does. You shouldn't stand for it.'

'It's got nothing to do with you.'

'It's pathetic, the way you let him get away with it,' June ranted on with her sister's interests at heart. 'You're not soft or stupid, so why keep him in your life when he obviously doesn't have a serious thought in his head as regards his intentions towards you? Why don't you just tell him to get lost?'

Daisy was furious. 'I don't have to explain myself to you,' she retaliated, her cheeks almost matching her red dressing gown. 'I don't tell you how to run your life so don't try and tell me how to run mine.'

'Girls, girls,' intervened Nora worriedly. They were in the living room, ready to go to bed, and until a few moments ago the atmosphere between them had been as jovial as ever. 'Calm down, both of you, before you say something you'll really regret.'

'You agree with me, surely?' said June, turning to Nora for support. 'You must be able to see how that dreadful man is using her.'

Indeed she could and had said so many times. But now wasn't the time to take sides. 'My opinion doesn't come into it.' She was treading warily. 'As Daisy says, it's her business. Only she knows how she feels about Nat. I think the two of you should agree to differ on this one.'

But June was too fired up in her sister's defence to stop now. 'You're an attractive and intelligent woman, Daisy. You can do a lot better than Nat Barker,' she went on. 'You're much too good for him.'

'Like you're too good for Alan. Is that what you do, June – judge people; give them points out of ten for good behaviour and character?' retorted Daisy, who wasn't normally sarcastic or cynical; this issue was beyond the intellect and was rooted entirely in the emotions. Words were flowing out of her mouth, almost as though someone else was saying them. 'Is

221

that why you left him, because he didn't measure up to your high standards?'

'My marriage to Alan has nothing to do with this,' she declared hotly.

'Oh, no, when it comes to your private life, you don't want it mentioned, do you? You clam up completely and no one's allowed to say a word. Yet you think you have the right to lecture me.' Daisy glared at her across the hearth. 'You are in no position to comment on my relationship with Nat since you couldn't even keep your own marriage together.'

'That has nothing to do with this issue,' June insisted. 'I can't stand by and see Nat treat you so badly.'

'How dare you preach to me?' said Daisy through clenched teeth. 'Nat is the man I chose, the man I fell in love with. Whether I stay with him or not is my decision, *not yours*. It's nothing to do with you so keep your big nose out of my business.'

'You must be able to see—'

'I do have eyes in my head and a brain,' Daisy roared. 'Of course I can see that he isn't perfect, and that he pushes his luck with me something rotten. What do you think I am? Some sort of halfwit?'

'Haven't I just said the opposite to that?' June replied angrily. 'It's because I know that you're an intelligent woman and worth better, I think you should get rid of him.'

'And as I've just said, what I choose to do about Nat is my business and nobody else's, certainly not yours,' Daisy told her. 'People are people, a mixture of everything, and we all have some good and bad in us. Not only the decent, well-behaved ones are lovable, you know.'

'Now you're suggesting that *I'm* a halfwit.'

'If the cap fits . . .'

June didn't reply to this, just looked at Daisy in outrage, cheeks scarlet in her otherwise pale countenance.

'To hear you talk anyone would think you were an expert on men,' Daisy ranted.

'I've never claimed that.'

'You couldn't very well, could you? Because you wouldn't have a leg to stand on.' Daisy was out of control, driven on by her protective instincts towards Nat and her right to live her life in the way she chose. 'And even if you did have a more impressive track record in that direction, you'd still have no right to tell me what to do. I know you own this house and I'm just a lodger but that doesn't mean you can interfere in my life.'

June was further enraged by this suggestion. 'This has nothing to do with the house,' she denied hotly. 'I've told you that I never think of you and Nora as lodgers. This is a personal thing.'

Daisy stood up, her voice shaking with emotion. 'Be that as it may, Nat is the man I love and the father of my children, so I would thank you to respect that fact in future. Whatever he does, however badly he behaves, it has *nothing whatsoever* to do with you. Is that clear? It's my life, so just leave me alone to get on with it in the way that I choose.'

And with that she rushed from the room.

Ashen-faced and shaky, June looked at Nora contritely. 'I don't know what came over me,' she said, biting her lip. 'It all just came pouring out.'

'Nat has the same effect on me and I've had plenty of words with Daisy about him in the past,' Nora told her. 'But I try to keep shtoom now because she's very sensitive about it and won't hear a word against him.' She sighed. 'And what she says is quite true, of course. It isn't any of our business. Daisy's no fool. She knows in her heart that Nat is no good for her but she loves him. And us being critical doesn't help because she knows she can never give him up. He can twist her around his little finger.'

'It makes me so mad.'

'Me too, but it'll never change. It's been going on too long. So we might as well accept it and keep our opinions to ourselves.'

June looked worried. 'I don't know what to do, Nora,' she confessed, raking her hair with her fingers anxiously and biting her lip. 'The last thing I want is to be at war with Daisy.'

'Give her a few minutes to calm down, then go up and see her,' suggested Nora.

'Yes, I think I shall have to,' agreed June. 'Because I can't leave it like this.'

Daisy was sitting up in bed looking at a magazine when June made a cautious entry, having tapped on the door first.

'If you've come to say more horrible things about Nat, then you're wasting your time because I don't want to hear them so I won't listen,' she said, holding the magazine open and keeping her eyes fixed on it.

'I've come to apologise actually,' June said sheepishly.

'Oh.' Now Daisy put the magazine down and looked at her sister, waiting for her to go on.

'I shouldn't have said those things,' June admitted ruefully. 'I really am very sorry.'

'You're right, you shouldn't have said all that stuff,' Daisy responded coolly.

'You said some pretty rotten things to me too, you know,' June pointed out.

'Only after serious provocation.'

'I suppose you're right.'

'You shouldn't have got me fired up like that,' Daisy told her, her tone becoming warmer. 'You can't expect to say things like that to someone about their man and not expect them to retaliate.'

224

'In future then the least said the soonest mended when it comes to Nat,' suggested June.

'I think we need more than just that to keep the peace between us on the subject,' Daisy informed her.

'Meaning . . .?'

'Whether you like it or not, Nat is the man in my life,' she began, 'and he comes to this house as a guest of mine.'

June waited.

'So I'd appreciate it if you could treat him with courtesy, in the same way as I do when your friends come to the house,' Daisy requested.

'I'm always polite to him.'

Daisy gave a dry laugh. 'In an arctic sort of way,' she pointed out. 'You could make him feel welcome when he's here, rather than painfully uncomfortable.'

'Point taken.'

'Good.'

'I'm sorry about just now, Daisy, I really am,' said June, keen to make amends. 'I went too far.'

'Yes, you did, and I hope you truly realise that.'

'I do.' June paused. 'And I really don't think of you and Nora as lodgers. I think of us all as friends sharing a house.'

Daisy was ashamed now. 'Yeah, I know you do,' she sighed. 'I was angry . . . I said things I didn't mean.'

'We both did.'

'Except for the things you said about Nat.' Daisy gave her sister a questioning look. 'You did mean those, didn't you?'

'I'm sorry, Daisy.' June made a face. 'There's no point in my lying about it. But I will make an effort to make him feel more welcome here.'

'Thanks. Live and let live, eh?'

June nodded. 'Friends again?' she asked hopefully.

'Yeah, course we are,' said Daisy, sitting up and giving her sister a hug. 'It'll take more than a man to split us up.'

But June sensed that this was a fragile peace that needed looking after. She knew she must tread carefully on the subject of Nat or risk losing Daisy.

And Daisy knew that Nat would remain a sore point between them even if he wasn't mentioned. The fact that June was absolutely right in everything she said about him didn't make any difference. He was Daisy's man and she would defend him against anyone.

Chapter Ten

On duty one evening in late July, Daisy served roast beef to the wrong table, knocked a jug of water over on another and got more coffee in the saucers than the cups when pouring. When she compounded the whole shoddy performance by dropping a pile of dirty plates on to the hotel kitchen floor, sending broken china and food leftovers flying everywhere, the head waiter suggested, quite forcibly, that she go home as she obviously wasn't fit for work.

'Anyone can see that you're ill.' He was a small immaculate man of Italian extraction, with dark hair greased close to his head and a neat moustache. He'd lived in London for most of his life and spoke perfect English.

'I'm all right, honestly, and I'm sorry I've been so careless.' She was afraid for her job. 'I'll be more careful from now on so it won't happen again.'

'It certainly won't happen again tonight because you're going off duty right now,' he announced, far more concerned about the smooth running of the hotel restaurant than a sick member of staff. A complaint about the service would mean a reprimand for him from the manager. 'You shouldn't have come in to work if you weren't feeling well.'

'I didn't want to let you down,' she said weakly. 'Anyway, I need the money.'

'You're not doing yourself or us any favours by being

here,' he insisted in a firm but not wholly unkind manner. 'It's no wonder you dropped the plates – you're shivering too much to hang on to anything.'

'I can't afford to take time off work. You know I have two kids to feed,' she reminded him.

'You'll just have to manage with sick pay from the State because you're certainly no good to us around here,' he insisted. 'You should be at home in bed.'

'I'll be all right, really—'

'Go home before you pass out, girl.' He was ordering her to go now.

Although she protested some more, Daisy knew he was right because she did feel terrible. In the staff room, changing out of her black and white uniform, her teeth were chattering and she was covered in goose pimples but her skin was hot and painful. Every bit of her hurt, and when she took off her black cap, with its starched white trim, it felt as though she was making a flesh wound on her scalp. She hadn't felt well for the last couple of days, ever since she'd got drenched in a heavy summer shower while out shopping at Portobello market and her clothes had dried on her. She seemed to be more susceptible to chills than most people; she always had been and put it down to her weak chest.

But now she headed for the tube and home, feeling worse by the second.

'Into bed with you,' Nora said when Daisy stumbled into the house, feeling faint.

'We'll bring you up a hot drink and some aspirin in a minute,' said June.

'The girls—' Daisy began.

'The girls are fast asleep,' Nora assured her. 'So go to bed before we have to pick you up off the floor.'

'Come on,' urged June, taking her sister's arm gently. 'Let me help you into bed.'

'There's no need for all this fuss,' she insisted. 'I'll be fine after a good night's sleep.'

But sleep wasn't for Daisy that night. As her condition worsened, she thrashed about in the sheets, shivering but soaked in sweat, her chest hurting, head aching, breathing painful. Nora and June were so alarmed the next morning, neither of them went to work. June rushed out to the phone box and called the doctor, who diagnosed pneumonia.

At the sight of an ambulance, a crowd gathered to watch the barely conscious Daisy being carried out of the house on a stretcher. June went with her in the ambulance and Nora stayed with the girls, who were pale with fright and staying very close to her. She put a comforting arm firmly round each one.

'I don't want Mummy to go away,' said Shirley tearfully, as the ambulance doors were closed.

'Nor do I,' added Belinda shakily, huge tears rolling down her cheeks.

'You want her to get better, though, don't you?'

They nodded.

'That's why she has to go to the hospital for a little while,' Nora explained. 'So that the doctors can make her better. I know that you two are going to be very brave.'

'I don't like it when Mummy's ill,' said Shirley. 'It makes me feel funny inside.'

'It makes me scared,' Belinda whispered.

'There, there, you two. She'll be back home before you know it,' said Nora, saying a silent prayer and trying not to show the little girls how worried she was.

Over the next day or so, Daisy wasn't aware of very much at all. Drifting in and out of consciousness, she realised in a vague sort of way that she was in hospital but was too ill to take notice or ask questions. But when the drugs started to work and her confusion began to clear a little, the first thing she said was, 'My children – where are they?'

'Your daughters are at home with your sister,' the nurse assured her calmly.

'But she has to go to work.'

'She's taken compassionate leave to look after them, apparently,' explained the nurse, a middle-aged woman of large proportions, with a nice smile and a kindly manner.

'My eldest is on school holidays,' muttered Daisy worriedly. 'The two of them together are quite a handful. My sister isn't used to coping with them on her own.'

'I'm sure she'll manage.' The nurse was very soothing. 'They're only children, not wild animals. And your friend helps out when she gets home from work, I believe.' At Daisy's querying look, she went on, 'We had a chat when they came to see you and they told me all about it. You were asleep. They asked me to give you their love when you were awake and taking notice.'

Daisy tried to sit up but fell back weakly against the pillows. 'I'm needed at home,' she said anxiously. 'I've got to get out of here.'

'You'll go when the doctor says you're ready.' The nurse was kind but firm. 'And that won't be for a while yet. You'll soon know how weak you are if you try to get out of that bed, my dear. So stop fretting.'

And Daisy felt too frail to argue.

'Will you eat your lunch, please, girls?' requested June of her nieces as they all sat at the kitchen table.

'No.' The gleam of rebellion was strong in Shirley's eyes.

'We don't like sausages,' added Belinda.

'Yes, you do,' June disagreed patiently. 'They're one of your favourites.'

'We only like them when Mummy's here,' said Shirley in truculent mood.

230

'We don't like *your* sausages,' added Belinda, fixing June with a hostile stare. 'We only like Mummy's; we're not eating your mouldy old sausages.'

'We want our mum,' announced Shirley, her little mouth set determinedly. 'We don't like you.'

'We hate you,' supported Belinda.

'You're horrible,' Shirley declared.

'Yeah,' was Belinda's contribution.

June guessed that part of the reason for their appalling behaviour was that they were missing their mother and taking it out on her. But she sensed also that they were testing her – and winning hands down at the moment, she was forced to admit. They were at an age of physical perfection, smooth-skinned and unblemished. She ached with love for them. They were so alike to look at, with the same shiny brown hair and their mother's beautiful tawny eyes, though theirs were currently simmering with resentment.

Although she was ostensibly calm, June was actually in despair, her nerves shattered by the monsters her nieces had become since she'd been in charge. It seemed feeble for a grown woman to have to admit but, without actual maternal experience, she felt vulnerable to the point of being almost afraid of these small children. Ridiculous, she knew, but she just didn't have Daisy's natural armoury which would enable her to be in a position of control with the girls. This whole miserable experience was particularly upsetting because until June had become a temporary substitute for Daisy, she'd prided herself on the rapport she was beginning to have with them. Maybe she'd never felt completely at ease but after her initial confusion as to her function, she'd settled into the role of indulgent aunt, giving them presents, attention and fun, and it had seemed to work very well.

Until these past few days, when they'd given her hell, arguing the toss about every single thing, from the food she gave them to having a bath and what clothes they would wear. At first she'd treated them with the gentle touch, sensitive to the fact that they were missing their mother. When they'd responded to this with mutiny, she'd tried being firm, but their enmity had continued. Yet Nora had no trouble with them at all. June couldn't bear to imagine what a battle there would be at bedtime if Nora wasn't at home then to give her some support.

She and Nora had agreed that June should be the one to take time off work to look after them as she was allowed some compassionate leave with pay – only for a limited period but long enough for Daisy to get back on her feet, she hoped. The important thing was that Daisy was over the worst and expecting to be discharged from hospital in a few days.

June was disappointed in herself for failing so miserably as Daisy's stand-in. She wanted so much to make the children feel secure and loved in her care. Not having any children of her own, from the minute she'd first set eyes on them she'd wanted to play a special part in their lives. It was Daisy's job to administer discipline, her own to supply pleasure. And what was her peculiar reward? Anarchy.

Working at the hotel was a holiday compared to looking after two stroppy kids. She'd sooner be dealing with tedious, unreasonable hotel guests than these two little horrors. They knew they had the upper hand and she didn't seem able to turn things around.

'OK, so you don't like me,' she said now in response to their hurtful utterings. 'Well, I don't like you very much at the moment either. But we're stuck with each other until your mother is better so let's try and get along, shall we?'

They stared at her in stony silence.

'All right, I'll do a deal with you.' Daisy would be appalled at such blatant bribery but she wasn't here, and June was desperate. 'You eat your lunch and I'll buy you some sweets when we go out to the shops. How about that?' She gave them a smile, forcing her tone to be softly persuasive, despite her sorely tried patience. 'And we could take a picnic to the park later on too, if you're good girls and eat your lunch. Would you like that?'

Shirley gave June a defiant look and pushed her plate away so violently it shot across the table. She then got up and ran towards the kitchen door. Belinda followed.

At that moment something snapped inside June. After days of torture from these horrors, she had finally had enough. Acting on instinct, she fled to the door and stood in front of it facing them, barring their way. 'Oh, no,' she told them with an air of grim command. 'You're not going anywhere. You're going to sit back at the table.' She paused, staring at them. '*Now.*'

Pale with shock at the dramatic change in their pushover aunt's manner, they did as she said without a word of argument, their sullenness now tinged with awe.

'Right,' June began, looking down at them from a standing position with her arms folded. She wasn't shouting; her manner of quiet assertiveness was far more effective. 'I've had it up to here with you two these past few days. You've been rude, disobedient and downright horrid and I'm not going to put up with any more of it, do you understand?'

Four tawny eyes rested on her; two little pink mouths began to tremble.

'I've taken the trouble to cook sausages and beans for your lunch because I know that you like them,' she went on. 'I could have given you something you don't like, like mince or liver. But, fool that I am, I made your favourite, which you now choose to say you don't like. All right, if you don't want what I've given you, don't eat it but you'll get nothing else. When you're hungry enough you'll eat what I put in front of you even if it's just a bit of dry bread; that's how nature works, you see. Meanwhile, there'll be no sweets, no park, no treats at all until you have both said sorry to me for your disgusting behaviour and promised to stop all this silly nonsense.'

They said nothing. Just sat close together, holding hands, staring at her, their eyes like great brown saucers against their sudden pallor.

'You might as well do as I ask because I'm going to make you sit there until you're ready to apologise to me for being nasty little brats your mother would be ashamed of,' she told them. 'I know that you're upset because your mum isn't around and you want to make me suffer for it.' She drew in her breath and turned up the volume. 'I've made allowances for all of that but now I have had enough.'

They sat there without moving. Neither said a word. The appearance of tears in their eyes twisted June's heart and she wanted to hug them better. But that must wait until later. All would be lost if she showed signs of weakening now. She could see that she'd been wrong to think she could be just their pal, someone who could be relied on for fun and pleasure. They were small children who looked to adults for authority. She could be their friend, yes, but they needed to know who was boss. Discipline gave them guidelines and made them feel secure, however bitter the pill was to swallow. Better she destroy any bond she might have with them and start again from scratch by taking a hard line than let them run rings around her. If she gave in now, they would lose all respect for her.

'So, what's it to be?'

Silence.

'I've got all the time in the world,' she told them, looking at her watch. 'I've taken days off work to look after you so I can wait here all afternoon if necessary.'

She wasn't as confident as she sounded. She was a novice

234

when it came to child psychology. Heaven only knew what her next move would be if this didn't work. With her heart in her mouth, she sat down at the table and waited.

Shirley was the first to crumble. The trembling lip began to wobble and she bowed her head and wept silently, followed soon after by her sister, who wailed loudly.

'You won't get round me that way,' said June, suspecting that they would because her heart was breaking for them. 'You can cry all you like but you're not leaving here until I've heard you both say sorry.'

She was surprised to observe that even at this tender age, pride was a problem. 'Sorry,' mumbled Shirley at last, head down, words barely audible.

'What was that, Shirley?' asked June. 'I didn't hear what you said.'

'Sorry.' Slowly she looked up at June, who watched all the defiance slip away, leaving the child looking forlorn but relieved. June had to bite back her own tears. 'I'm sorry I've been naughty, Auntie June. I'll be good now, I promise.'

'I'm sorry too, Auntie June,' echoed Belinda.

'That's better.' Swallowing hard, June opened her arms to them. 'Come here, come on, both of you,' she said thickly.

They both climbed on to her lap and cuddled into her, their lithe little bodies trembling. She held them close for a long time, knowing instinctively that the three of them had passed some sort of a watershed.

'Can we have our sausages and beans now please, Auntie June?' requested Shirley.

'Course you can, darling,' she said to them. 'But they'll be cold by now. I'll warm them up for you.'

'Thank you, Auntie June,' said Belinda.

'It's a pleasure.' Such was the strength of her love for her nieces at that particular moment, she knew she would brave fire and flood for them if ever it was necessary. These past few days had taught her that motherhood was not always a picnic but it had not lessened her longing for children of her own.

That evening they all went to the hospital to see Daisy. A maximum of two visitors at the bedside was the usual rule but the understanding sister turned a blind eye so that they could have a few minutes all together.

'How are you feeling, dear?' asked Nora.

'Fine,' said Daisy, who still looked ghastly. She was paper-white and skinny, with dark circles under her eyes and a general look of frailty about her.

'When are you coming home, Mum?' Belinda was eager to know.

'Very soon, I hope,' sighed Daisy wistfully. 'I miss you all so much. They're ever so good to me in here and everything, but I'm fed up with being stuck in hospital. I'll recover quicker at home.'

'It isn't wise to rush things, though,' warned Nora. 'You'll end up back in here if you do that.'

'We have to be realistic, Nora,' was Daisy's answer to that. 'I've got the girls to think about. June can't have time off work to look after them for too long.'

'But I can do it for a bit longer,' June assured her.

'And if she can't, I will,' Nora offered. 'We'll manage between us somehow. The important thing is for you to get well.'

'Even when you do come home, you'll have to take it easy for a while, I should think,' suggested June. 'You're not going to be able to get back to normal right away.'

'Don't you start,' Daisy responded in jovial admonition. 'I've had enough of that from the doctors. They've really been giving me earache about how I mustn't overdo things when they discharge me from here. I know they mean well

236

but they don't have a clue about what life is like for someone like me – well, they wouldn't, would they, being professionals with healthy salaries and sick pay when they're ill?' She paused and brushed a tired hand across her brow. 'All I hear from them is, "You need to go away on holiday and get some sea air and plenty of rest and good food to build yourself up." I mean, I ask you. How can I do any of those things? I need to get back to work as soon as possible and start earning again.'

'You won't be able to go back to work for a while, surely?' June was worried by her attitude.

'Let's just say that I won't be sitting about the house for any longer than I absolutely have to. But let's wait and see how I feel.' Daisy smiled at them all. 'That's quite enough about me. How are you all getting on?'

'We're missing you like mad, of course, and we can't wait for you to come home,' Nora told her. 'But everything's under control at the house and running smoothly.'

Daisy looked at her daughters, who were sitting either side of the bed, each holding one of her hands. She then fixed her gaze on June. 'How have they been behaving?' she asked lightly. 'Not giving you any trouble, I hope?'

A look passed between June and the children. She perceived a moment of apprehension as they wondered if she was going to spill the beans.

'No trouble at all,' she said to Daisy, then looked towards the children. 'We're getting along just fine, aren't we, girls?'

'Yes, Auntie June,' they chorused, looking relieved and beaming broadly at June and then their mother.

June smiled too. She wasn't naïve enough to expect it to be all plain sailing between herself and her nieces because human relations were never that easy, but she did feel a definite bond with them now. Something had happened this afternoon that would live on into the future; she could sense it and it warmed her heart.

But now another visitor arrived for Daisy and her face lit up with joy.

'Nat,' she said, beaming at him. 'How lovely to see you. It's good of you to come.'

Seeing this as their cue to make a diplomatic exit, June and Nora said their goodbyes and left with the children.

Daisy was shocked at the extent of her weakness when she got home from the hospital. Being in such a feeble state made her angry with herself. She'd expected to be back at work in a few days but she hardly had the strength to get out of bed, let alone go to work. It was as much as she could do to look after the girls and she didn't feel as though she was doing that properly.

Feeling this fragile wasn't like Daisy at all. She was a fighter; she had inner strengths and, no stranger to bad health, she usually managed to carry on however ill she felt. If she did have to take to her bed, it was never for long.

But this was different. It wasn't the illness itself but the aftermath, and she didn't seem to get any stronger despite all the beef tea and egg custards she was consuming to build herself up. Being at the mercy of extreme physical limitations made her low in spirits too. She just didn't seem able to cope with anything. Everything was too much effort; even taking care of her beloved daughters seemed beyond her. She was literally dragging herself around, even though she insisted that June go back to work.

'I don't think I'd better leave you. You're in no fit state to cope on your own just yet,' was June's reaction to that.

'For goodness' sake, June,' Daisy responded sharply, 'you've been absolutely brilliant and I'm really grateful to you for looking after the girls for me, but I'm back home now and I'm not an invalid.'

'But—'

'Look, June, the best thing for me is to get back into the swing of things.' She was trying to convince herself as much as June. 'I'll never get my strength back by taking it easy. The sooner we return to normal around here the better for us all. I want to go to work again in a day or two.'

But after almost passing out on Saturday when they were all out shopping in Portobello market, Daisy knew she must accept that recovery was going to take longer than she'd expected, and be patient.

'I know you like to be some sort of a superwoman but even you can't beat nature, Daisy,' said Nora that night after the girls had gone to bed. 'You simply have to let it take its course.'

'I know. But it's dragging on and I feel such a burden to the rest of you,' confided Daisy, tears running down her cheeks and making her feel worse because crying seemed like weakness.

'You're not being, so you can put that out of your mind,' June assured her.

'You've both been wonderful,' Daisy told them. 'But I'm not pulling my weight around here.'

'You've not heard us complaining, have you?' June was keen to point out. 'You've been ill and you need time to recover. So stop being so impatient.'

However, Daisy wouldn't be fully assured. 'I appreciate your support. But not only do I need to get back to work of an evening, I need to be more energetic during the day too. It's the school holidays. Belinda starts school in September and I want to take the girls out and about a bit before then.' She looked at Nora. 'We always go to Southend for the day around this time.'

'And we will do when you're feeling up to it.'

'It's no fun for them having me sitting about with hardly the strength to tie their hair ribbons for them, is it?' Daisy went on. 'I feel like a complete dead loss.'

'Oh, for goodness' sake,' rebuked Nora, 'you've only been home from hospital a few days. Nature will take longer to heal you if you fight it and go against how you feel.' She sighed, giving a worried tut. 'I know it isn't possible to have one, but the doctors were right when they said you need a holiday. It wouldn't do the girls any harm either, after all the disruption they've had. You and the girls need to get right away from here for a couple of weeks.'

'There are lots of things the girls and I need, Nora,' Daisy told her. 'But we're not going to get them so there's no point in thinking about them, is there?'

'I suppose not,' agreed Nora.

June had gone quiet, mulling something over. The next morning when she went out to get a Sunday paper, she then went to a telephone box and made a long-distance call.

Alan and Jack were having a drink together at the Cliff Head bar that Sunday night after work. The bar was closed and they had the place to themselves. They chatted about business for a while, moving on to some basic male observations about Marilyn Monroe, whose new film, *The Seven Year Itch*, had just come out. They enjoyed a spot of light-hearted crudity on the subject of sex, like most men when they were in all-male company.

'Talking of women,' said Alan, becoming more serious, 'I had a phone call from June this morning.'

'That sounds promising,' responded Jack.

'No. My relationship with her is well and truly over,' Alan said with a wry look. 'Her call had nothing to do with her and me.'

'What did she want then?'

'A favour,' he explained. 'She wants me to try and find some holiday accommodation for her sister, Daisy, and the little girls, for a couple of weeks.'

'Really?'

'Mm. Daisy's been ill, apparently.'

'Oh dear.' Jack was immediately concerned. 'Nothing serious, I hope.'

'Serious enough to put her in hospital. She's had pneumonia.'

Jack frowned. 'God, poor Daisy. How is she now?'

'She's at home, but very weak and run-down, apparently,' Alan informed him. 'So June's trying to arrange a holiday for her and the girls, to try to get her back on her feet.'

'We're fully booked here at this time of the year, I suppose,' Jack surmised.

Alan nodded. 'June said the Cliff Head wouldn't be suitable for them anyway,' he said. 'It's too quiet, too expensive and too restricting for the children. I agree with her about that. I mean, we don't actually ban children but we don't make them particularly welcome either.'

'What sort of place is Daisy looking for?' Jack enquired, his interest growing.

'Daisy isn't looking for anything,' Alan explained. 'In fact, she knows nothing about it yet. June wants to get everything arranged before she tells her so that she'll feel she can't refuse, if it's all booked up. Daisy can't afford a holiday so June is footing the bill. But Daisy is funny about that sort of thing, apparently. She's very proud and won't accept charity.'

'What a kind thing for June to do,' commented Jack.

'I thought so too.'

'Any luck with the accommodation?'

'None at all, so far. I've been on the phone to quite a few places, but it being the height of the season, all the hotels are booked up, which is why June's turned to me. She wants to get something organised double sharp because she and Nora are afraid that Daisy will go back to work before she's properly recovered and suffer a relapse. I've still got a few more places I can try. June's going to ring me tomorrow to find out if I've had any luck.'

'You need look no further,' announced Jack with a broad smile. 'Daisy and the girls can stay at my cottage.'

Alan gave him a questioning look.

'They'll all have to share my spare room and I'll have to get a couple of camp beds for the girls,' Jack went on enthusiastically, 'but I'd love to have them.'

Stroking his chin thoughtfully, Alan said, 'It's very good of you to offer, mate, but I'm not sure if that's the sort of thing June has in mind. I think she was thinking more in terms of a B. and B. on the seafront.'

'My place is on the seafront.'

'Here in Torquay, close to all the amenities, I mean,' Alan clarified. 'June wants me to keep an eye on them and make sure they're all right while they're here, with Daisy having been so ill. June can't go away with them because she can't get the time off work.'

'I'll look after them if they stay with me,' offered Jack. 'And you won't get a healthier place than Gullscombe Bay.'

'You seem very keen,' was Alan's shrewd observation.

Actually Jack couldn't believe his luck in being given a chance to see Daisy again, and he wasn't going to let the opportunity pass him by. 'Just trying to help, mate.'

'That's why you look as though you've just come into money, is it?' his friend joshed.

'All right, I admit it. I did take a fancy to Daisy when we were in London,' Jack confessed. 'But there would be no funny business if she stayed with me, I can promise you that. I genuinely want to help and I can't think of a better place to convalesce than Gullscombe Bay. Ideal for the kids too, with the safe beach being so close to the cottage.'

'But you'd be at work a lot of the time and they'd be stuck out there on their own, miles from everything,' Alan objected.

'Daisy is a town girl; she might feel too isolated.'

'Obviously I'd have to have some time off to look after them and entertain them,' Jack pointed out with a grin. 'But I've got some holidays owing to me.'

'At the height of our busy season, you must be joking.' Alan didn't look pleased.

'I've got a good deputy,' Jack reminded him. 'And I wouldn't take all that much time off – just a few evenings, and the odd day or two. I'm at home for part of the day anyway so they wouldn't be too lonely.'

'I'm relieved to hear you're not planning on deserting us for the whole two weeks,' said Alan ruefully. 'But I'm beginning to wish I'd never mentioned it.'

'I don't believe that,' challenged Jack. 'You'd do anything to please June.'

'Once that might have been true, but not now,' Alan said. 'But I'll pass on your invitation to her when she rings me tomorrow, see what she thinks about it.'

'I'll look forward to hearing her reaction,' beamed Jack.

A few days later, over breakfast, Daisy read a letter that had come for her in the post. She smiled, then frowned, then glared at her sister and said, 'You've been meddling, haven't you?'

'Meddling?'

'Don't try and tell me that this letter from Jack Saunders, inviting me and the kids for a holiday at his cottage, isn't your doing because I won't believe you.'

'I had nothing to do with that,' June denied truthfully.

'How did Jack know that I'd been ill then, if you didn't tell him?' Daisy wanted to know.

June bit her lip and held up her hands in a gesture of surrender. 'All right, I admit it. I got on the phone to Alan and asked him to find some accommodation for you. And before you go up in the air about it, I didn't tell you because I knew you would squash the whole idea even though it will be so good for you,' she explained. 'Anyway, Jack got to hear about it and offered for you to stay at his cottage. I really didn't have anything to do with that part of it. But knowing what your reaction would be to anyone doing anything for you at all, I asked Alan to ask Jack to write to you and invite you properly. Apparently he's dead keen for you and the girls to go. He's crazy about where he lives and wants to show it off.'

'You had no right to do this, June,' rebuked Daisy.

'She was only thinking of you, love,' intervened Nora, while the two little girls ate their cornflakes, listening.

'What am I, some hard-up half-wit who isn't capable of organising her own life, or something?' erupted Daisy, tears swelling beneath her lids. She was touched by June's attempts to help and that made her feel worse because she didn't have the means to accept and she felt so damned helpless. This weakness was making her spiteful to people who didn't deserve it and she hated herself but couldn't stop. 'I've had pneumonia, I haven't lost the use of my brain.'

'Look, I think you need a holiday, so I tried to organise one for you and I can pay the costs out of the money I had left over between selling my mother's house and buying this one,' June spelled out for her. 'I acted on impulse and Alan seemed the obvious person to approach as he's in a position to find out about seaside accommodation. Is that such a crime?'

At the word 'seaside' the children's interest was aroused.

'The seaside,' said Shirley excitedly. 'Are we going to Southend for the day?'

'The seaside, goodee,' enthused Belinda. 'Can we have a bucket and spade?'

Seeing those young eyes shining with hope, Daisy was filled with shame. She was spoiling everything for them as well as June because of her stupid pride. What right did she have to deprive them of a holiday, and June the pleasure of giving? June wanted to help her because she was her sister. If the situation was reversed she would want to do the same thing for her.

She remembered how upset she'd been initially when June had offered them a home. She'd grown closer to her since then; knew her well enough to recognise this for what it was – a kind gesture with no ulterior motive.

'Better than a day at Southend,' Daisy informed them with a tearful smile. 'Much, much better. Two whole weeks at the seaside in Devon thanks to your lovely Auntie June.'

Forgetting the table manners Daisy had been at pains to teach them since they were old enough to understand such things, they slipped off their chairs and tore around the kitchen, then up and down the hall, shrieking with delight. 'We're going to the seaside, the seaside, the seaside!'

'Sorry about just now, June,' said Daisy. 'I was an idiot. I think I must be touchy because I'm feeling so low physically. I didn't mean to be horrible.' She put her hand on her sister's arm. 'It's ever so good of you to do this for us and I really do appreciate it.'

'It's a pleasure,' beamed June, getting up and hugging her.

'Why are Mummy and Auntie June crying, Nora?' asked Shirley, looking worried.

'Because they're happy,' Nora explained.

'That's all right then,' said Shirley, looking happy too.

Predictably, the one person who wasn't happy about the forthcoming holiday was Nat.

'You're going to Devon to stay with some bloke,' he disapproved sternly, that same evening. 'Daisy, how could you?'

They were on the sofa in the living room; smart and comfy

now, it had been refurbished with bright contemporary wallpaper and a red carpet. The girls were in bed. June was washing her hair and Nora was in her room writing a letter.

'It isn't how you're making it sound,' she told him, having already given him full details of the holiday and how it had come about. 'Jack's offered to put the girls and me up, that's all. It's perfectly innocent.'

'You might be gullible enough to believe that, but I'm certainly not,' he barked.

'So, without knowing anything about him, you've got him down as a rapist, have you?'

'I didn't say that.'

'You're questioning my morals then?'

'No. I'm just saying that he's a man and he'll make the most of having you in the house.'

'And you think I'm daft enough to fall into his arms?'

'No. I'm just pointing out what could happen.'

'That is sick,' objected Daisy. 'You shouldn't judge other people by your own standards.'

'You're trying to tell me that you're going to be sharing a house with an unattached man for two weeks and nothing like that will happen?' he said cynically.

'Yes, I am telling you exactly that,' she said with emphasis. 'What do you take me for? A tramp? Such a thing hadn't even occurred to me.'

'Then it should have,' he warned her. 'You know nothing about the man. You don't know what he's capable of.'

'He seemed thoroughly decent to me on the one occasion that I met him.' She didn't add that she'd liked Jack a lot and knew somehow that he was to be trusted, because Nat would deliberately misunderstand her feelings. 'Anyway, June knows him quite well and she wouldn't have me stay with someone who isn't trustworthy. He'll be out at work a lot of the time anyway, apparently, and he's giving us the complete run of his house while he's out. Frankly, I think it's very kind of him.'

'Huh.'

'You're jealous, aren't you?' Daisy accused. 'That's what this is all about.'

'Well, how would you feel if I told you I was going away for a fortnight with a woman?' Nat challenged her.

'I wouldn't like it at all,' she admitted. 'But I'm not going away with a man. I'm simply using his house.' She sighed. 'Look, I've been ill and I've been advised to take a holiday by the doctors. Thanks to my sister's generosity and the kindness of one of her husband's friends, the girls and I can have one.'

'I don't think you should go.'

'Don't you want me to get better?'

'You'll get better if you stay here, eventually,' he said. 'Nature will take its course wherever you are.'

Daisy was very tired suddenly. 'You're probably right and the last thing I want to do is upset you, Nat,' she told him wearily. 'But I've been given this opportunity and I feel I must take it.'

'Even though I don't want you to.'

'If you won't change your mind, yes. I'm feeling so rotten I have to do something about it. Let's face it, I'm not much use to anyone as I am now, especially our little girls, the poor lambs. First I give them a scare when I'm carted off to hospital, then I'm like a wet weekend when I come home. I owe it to them to try and speed up my recovery. I've been so bad-tempered with them lately. Anyway, even apart from all of that, a holiday at the seaside will be really smashing for them. Surely you want something nice for your daughters.'

As mean and self-centred as Nat was, he wasn't entirely without feelings, and the sight of Daisy looking so pale and pinched touched something inside him. 'Yeah, course I do,' he said with a change of attitude.

'Really?'

'Yeah. You go and enjoy yourself.'

'Thanks, Nat,' she beamed.

He reached into his pocket and took out some notes. 'Here's some spending money for you, an' all,' he said, handing her a few pound notes. 'And I want you to come back with some colour in your cheeks, do you understand?'

'Oh, Nat, are you sure about this?' she queried, looking at the money.

Giving her one of his most dazzling smiles, he said, 'Go on. Take it before I change my mind.'

'You're all right, Nat Barker, do you know that?' she told him, slipping her arms around him.

'Glad you think so,' he muttered, looking bewildered. He was astonished by his own impulsive generosity, and was wondering what had come over him.

'You never cease to surprise me,' she told him. 'It's no wonder I still love you, even after all these years.'

'I make it my policy not to be too predictable,' he said, back on form with the chat. 'You might start to take me for granted if I did that.'

'Never.'

'And I intend to make sure it stays that way.'

'If this is how you're going to do it, you won't hear me complaining.'

Daisy had decided to go to Devon whatever Nat thought about it because she knew it was the right thing for everyone at the house. But having his blessing meant that she could go away with an easy mind and enter into the spirit of the holiday with the same enthusiasm as her excited daughters.

Chapter Eleven

The road from Torquay to Gullscombe Bay wound through lush green countryside, the soft undulating hills a patchwork of thickly wooded slopes and rich expanses of grassland. There were picturesque villages with cob-walled, thatched cottages, and stone-built bridges over clear streams. When the road became coastal – high above sea level – tantalising glimpses of the sea could be caught through the trees. Daisy had never seen anything like it before, and the girls were breathless with awe, shrieking with delight at every new view of the ocean.

'I thought they couldn't get any more excited than they were when June and Nora saw us off on the train,' Daisy confided to Jack, who had met them at Torquay station and was driving them to his cottage in a black Ford Anglia, she in the front with him, the girls in the back, 'but I was wrong because they've reached such a pitch now, I think they might explode.'

'There's nothing quite like the enthusiasm of childhood, is there?' he smiled.

'I'm not so sure about that because I'm nearly as bad as they are,' she admitted. 'None of us has been further than Southend until now, so this is all quite stunning for us.'

'You wait till you see Gullscombe Bay,' he said, sounding as thrilled to be showing them the area as they were to see it.

'We'll be there in a minute. It seems to be taking for ever because I'm used to whizzing to and fro on my motorbike.'

Daisy turned to observe his clean-cut profile, a summer tan making him look even more wholesome than she remembered, especially with the white sports shirt he was wearing with lightweight fawn slacks. 'You have a car as well as a motorbike then?'

'No. This little motor belongs to a pal of mine. He's given me the use of it while you're here,' Jack explained, deeming it wise to alter the facts slightly so as not to mention that he had actually hired the car from a friend who had a car-hire firm, and paid the going rate for it because he wanted Daisy and the girls to travel in comfort while they were on holiday. He'd been warned by Alan, who'd been briefed by June, to be extremely cautious about anything with so much as a hint of charity.

'That's very nice of him but won't he be needing it himself?' she enquired.

'No. He has another vehicle he can use.' At least that was no lie.

'Two cars. Wow.' She was impressed. 'I can see that the scenery around here isn't the only thing that's different from what I'm used to. I don't know anyone with one car, let alone two.'

Jack didn't reply to that; just concentrated on the road. 'We're about to turn into Gullscombe Bay now.' His voice rose with enthusiasm. 'It's just round the bend.'

They turned a corner and began to descend a steep hill. Daisy gasped at the sight ahead of them. Golden sands fringed the sea round a bay flanked by red cliffs, the turquoise ocean shimmering in the afternoon sun and dotted with little white sailing boats. At the foot of the hill there were huge expanses of meadow edged with sand dunes leading to the beach. A little further on they came to Gullscombe Bay village, a pretty gathering of whitewashed thatched houses with a pub, a general store with a Post Office sign, and a church, all set around a village green.

Driving down a narrow track towards the seashore, Jack turned off the road and pulled up outside a cottage, the like of which Daisy had seen before only in picture books.

'Well, what do you think?' asked Jack proudly as she and the girls got out of the car and stared at the little whitewashed house with a blue door, a thatched roof and 'Seagull Cottage' written in bold letters on a sign on the front wall above a dazzling abundance of hollyhocks and wallflowers.

'It's beautiful, *really beautiful*,' breathed Daisy, turning to her wide-eyed daughters. 'Isn't it, girls?'

They nodded vigorously.

'Before we go inside, I want to show you what it's like out the back.' He looked at Daisy excitedly and grinned at the girls. 'Come on, follow your Uncle Jack.'

He led them through a blue wooded door at the side of the property into a garden with rolling lawns, bordered by trees and shrubs between which the sea could be seen. Going out of a gate at the bottom, they came to wide steps sloping down gently to a sandy beach, the cries of the gulls rising above the whisper of the sea at low tide.

'Cor,' gasped Shirley.

'The sea is in the back garden,' said Belinda in wonder.

'Not quite,' said Jack proudly. 'But almost.'

'So what do you think of that, eh, girls?' asked Daisy. 'Are we lucky to be here, or what?'

'Ooh, yeah,' enthused Shirley.

'Very lucky,' added her sister.

'It's safe for bathing,' Jack told Daisy. 'There aren't any strong currents in the shallow waters so you can let them paddle without any worries.'

Belinda was jumping up and down now with excitement.

251

'Can we go in the water? Can we, please, Mum? Can we?'

'When we've got our stuff out of the car and got changed, we'll go and dip our toes in,' promised Daisy.

'I expect you'd like something to eat too,' suggested Jack. 'I don't suppose you've had any lunch.'

'We haven't but I'm not expecting you to feed us,' Daisy was quick to point out. She thought he was doing quite enough by letting them stay and she wasn't prepared to impose further on his good nature. 'I saw a shop in the village. I can pop over there and get us something.'

'Don't be so silly.' He was outraged at the suggestion. 'I've got plenty of food in.'

Realising that to insist would be bad manners, she said graciously, 'Thank you. You're very kind.'

Inside the cottage there were wooden beams against buttercup-yellow walls in a living room with soft squashy sofas and French doors leading to the garden. Up a rickety wooden staircase, Jack showed them into a pretty room with low ceilings, a sea view and three beds, two of which were camp beds.

'I'm sorry you have to share,' he apologised, guessing it would embarrass Daisy if he were to give her his room and sleep on the sofa himself, as willing as he was to do this. 'I only have the one spare bedroom.'

'Don't apologise, for goodness' sake,' Daisy urged him. 'We're very grateful to be able to stay here. You've done us proud and I really do appreciate it.'

'It gives me a chance to show off my cottage,' he said lightly, and stepped towards the door. 'I'll leave you to sort yourselves out then. The bathroom is just along the landing and when you come downstairs I'll show you where everything else is.'

She smiled in thanks and told him they'd join him down there in a few minutes.

There were only two room downstairs – the kitchen and the living room – but both were of a reasonable size. The kitchen was quarry-tiled and oak-beamed, with a long farmhouse-style table. Jack made a pot of tea for Daisy and gave the girls a real treat: chilled lemonade with ice cubes from his fridge.

'I have to go to work now,' he explained to Daisy, 'but there's plenty of food so help yourselves to anything you fancy. There's fresh bread in the bread bin – and stuff to go with it in the fridge – ham, cheese, corned beef pie and so on. The larder's quite well stocked as well.'

'Sounds as though you've been having a busy time at the shops,' she said.

'Well, you do when you've got guests coming to stay, don't you?'

Having guests to stay didn't feature in Daisy's life but she just said, 'Yeah, I suppose so.' She hadn't expected this sort of hospitality and found herself in an awkward position. She didn't want to offend Jack but neither did she want to sponge on him. 'Look, Jack. It's very kind of you to put us up, but as I said just now, I don't expect you to feed us as well. So, let me give you some money.'

'Right. Since you've brought the subject up, we might as well get it sorted out here and now so that we both know where we are,' he said, his expression becoming grave. 'And this is how it will work. I want you to treat this place as your home for the next two weeks. That means having anything you want to eat and drink. But you are my guests so I want no talk of money.'

She bit her lip. 'Well, if you're sure . . .'

'I am, so let's hear no more about it,' he told her firmly. 'I won't be here all of the time because of work commitments but I've arranged to take some time off later on, to show you around the area.' He paused, spreading his hands, his blue eyes resting on Daisy. 'Please, please, make yourselves at home.' He winked at her. 'If you look in the ice-making compartment of the fridge you'll find something the kids might enjoy later on. I've arranged to get off early tonight so I'll be back about eight and I'll bring something from the hotel kitchen for our evening meal. OK?'

Without causing offence there wasn't much else Daisy could say except, 'Thank you so much.'

'Thanks aren't necessary because it's my pleasure.' He paused thoughtfully. 'My work number is on the pad by the telephone on the living-room windowsill. Any problem, or anything you want to know, give me a call.'

'Will do,' she said, and he left by the kitchen door.

Pressured by the girls for an immediate investigation of the ice box, they found a block of strawberry and vanilla ice cream which Shirley and Belinda were told they couldn't have until after they'd eaten some lunch. Daisy was just setting out some crusty bread and butter with fresh cheese and thick slices of ham and luscious tomatoes when Jack came back and popped his head around the door. 'I forgot to tell you that there are some deck chairs in the shed.' He grinned at the girls. 'There's a couple of buckets and spades in there too.'

The girls beamed. 'Bucket and spades . . . for us?' said Shirley. One treat after another – she could hardly believe it.

'Well, I didn't buy them for your mother,' he grinned. 'I think the deck chair is more up her alley.'

Daisy laughed, realising it was the first time she'd done so properly since her illness. 'Oh, Jack, this is so kind of you.' She turned to the girls. 'What do you say to Uncle Jack?'

'Thank you very much, Uncle Jack,' they chorused with delight.

'You're welcome,' he said, and left.

A few minutes later they heard his motorbike roar away. Daisy had to admit to being glad of this time to themselves to get used to the place. Although she felt very much at ease with Jack, he was little more than a stranger and she might have felt a bit awkward with him hovering over them so soon after their arrival.

What a kind and generous man he was. And with such a lovely home. His standard of living and the fact that he had modern refinements only dreamed of by Daisy – such as a fridge, a telephone, and a small television set in the corner of the living room – reminded her that he was in a management position and was therefore in a different league to her as a waitress. He was a smashing bloke, though, with no airs and graces.

Roaring through the lanes on his Harley-Davidson, the high speed causing an invigorating rush of cold air on his face around his goggles, Jack was thinking of Daisy and hoping he'd done the right thing in leaving her and the girls on their own so soon after they'd arrived.

Some people might think it was rather a rude thing to do but he'd given the matter some thought and decided to make himself scarce with the idea that she might feel more relaxed with the run of the place to herself, initially. He'd thought it best not to take the whole night off work too, to give them a chance to get settled in. Daisy needed to rest and enjoy the sea air for a few days, with just her children as much as possible. He smiled fondly, thinking of her tinkly laugh and the way she moved, quickly but with grace. Completely without the trappings of glamour that made most women look attractive, she had her own brand of natural beauty with her pert little face and slender body.

He smiled at the thought of the girls. Buying the buckets and spades had probably given him more pleasure than they'd had from receiving them. It was really important to him that they all had a good holiday. The weather had given them a warm welcome anyway, and he just couldn't wait to get back from work tonight to see them all again.

'I need more water for the moat,' announced Shirley, about to trail down to the sea with her bucket for the umpteenth time.

'Don't go out too far,' warned Daisy. 'You can't swim, remember. So stay at the edge.'

'Can me and Sherl learn to swim in the sea, Mum?' Belinda requested.

Her mother pondered the question. 'It might not be a bad idea to give it a try while we're here,' she said, settled in a deck chair on the sand, watching her daughters play. Both girls were proudly sporting bright yellow swimsuits that Nora had bought them as holiday treats. Daisy was less daring in a rather shapeless cotton dress she'd bought years ago in Portobello market. 'The school will be taking you to the swimming baths for lessons when you're a bit older but the sooner you can swim the better so I'll give it some thought.'

'I love it here, Mum,' enthused Belinda, looking around at the golden sand that was only lightly sprinkled with people, the bay being uncommercialised and off the beaten track.

'So do I,' added Shirley. 'I want to stay here for ever.'

Those were Daisy's sentiments exactly. She'd felt she belonged here from the minute they'd arrived. Realistically, it was too soon to feel any significant change in her health but she fancied that the air agreed with her. Being in such a weak state, she had been exhausted by the journey but after just one afternoon in the fresh air she felt stronger and more energetic. The girls' pasty London complexions were already beginning to glow with colour too.

'It's certainly a lovely place,' she agreed with her daughters.

Thank you so much, June and Jack, for giving us all this, she said silently, raising her face to the sun, its warmth softened by a light summer breeze. She couldn't remember feeling this relaxed in a very long time.

Observing his visitor across the table, Lionel Rivers thought she had one of the friendliest faces he'd ever seen, with her sparkling blue eyes and warm, engaging smile. Initially she'd seemed rather odd to look at: bright, disorderly hair, tall gangling frame and freckled face that was so much smaller than the rest of her. But the instant she smiled, he stopped noticing anything else.

'I'm glad you agreed to let them issue me with a visiting order,' Nora explained in her deep husky voice. 'I didn't want you to be without visitors as the girls couldn't make it this time.'

'I've been looking forward to meeting you at last,' he said, and she saw genuine pleasure in his warm brown eyes. 'Though I feel as if I know you already because of your letters.'

'I feel like that about you too.'

He frowned. 'I hope there's nothing wrong with the girls to keep them away.'

'Quite the reverse,' she was pleased to be able to assure him. 'Daisy's away on holiday in Devon and June's tied up at work so we decided between us that it would be a good idea for me to meet my pen pal on my day off.'

'I really am very grateful to you for coming.' He cast a disapproving eye around the room. 'But I don't like the idea of you, or the girls, having to come to such an awful place.'

'It doesn't worry me, dear,' Nora said, dismissing the subject by moving on, bringing him up to date with news of his daughters and telling him how Daisy's holiday had come about.

'I didn't even know she'd been ill,' Lionel said with concern.

257

'It happened only recently, and they'd have mentioned it next time they came to visit you, I expect,' she told him. 'Don't worry about Daisy. She'll be all right. She's tough. She's had to be, the amount of illness she's had in her life.'

'Really?'

She told him about Daisy's poor health. 'She's got stamina, though, that one. Never gives in. I've known her go to work when she's been half dead with bronchitis before now. She struggled on at work this time until they sent her home. She takes her responsibilities towards the girls very seriously.'

'Doesn't their father help her at all with their upkeep?' he wondered.

'No. Not on a regular basis,' Nora explained. 'He slips her a few bob now and again but that's about all.'

'Sounds as though you don't like him.'

'I don't. Because of the way he treats Daisy,' she admitted. 'The man's a complete dead loss. She knows he is too, in her heart, though she'd never admit it or give him up.' She shrugged, sighing. 'That's love for you.'

'It's weird to find out all these things about your own daughter at such a late stage,' Lionel told her.

'I'm sure it must be.'

'Finding them again is a dream come true, though.' He knew that Nora was fully in the picture about his family history. 'I thought I'd lost them for ever all those years ago. It was the worst moment of my life when I was told they were being taken into care. It was all so sudden. One minute I had a wife and family, the next I had no one. The girls were whisked out of the house sharpish, as soon as the police came. I wasn't even allowed to say goodbye to them before they carted me off to the nick.'

'It seems cruel but I suppose the authorities were acting in the children's best interests,' she said, her eyes moist with tears as she stared at this sad-eyed man whose face was lined beyond his years and who had a gentleness about him despite his tough appearance. The Rivers' story was one of the most poignant she'd ever heard. 'They would have needed to get the children away from the murder scene, and putting them into care was the only option they had with your wife dead, you in prison and no relatives willing to take them on.'

'They had no choice, I know that.' His eyes became glazed as he looked back. 'Losing my wife and being banged up for a murder I didn't do was bad enough, but losing my girls was the hardest blow of all. I thought they would think I'd abandoned them, which they did, of course.'

'It's all clear now as far as that's concerned, though,' Nora pointed out cheerfully.

'Yeah, thank God. Knowing that they don't think I stopped loving them has made me a happy man, and I'm so lucky to have them back in my life, even if that means only a brief visit now and then.'

'They're pleased to have found you too, and each other.' They'd been speaking in low voices but Nora lowered hers even more now against the prying ears of the warders. 'And although there's no movement at the moment, they are both still determined to clear your name and get you out of here.'

'It's good of them to want to do all that for me, but I'm not holding my breath.'

'That's very wise,' she said, nodding sagely. 'It was a long time ago and the people concerned could be anywhere by now. They might even be dead.'

'Which is what I told them,' he made clear. 'Anyway, I'm so used to prison life I'd probably be like a fish out of water if I ever did get out of here.'

'You'd be bound to feel strange at first, of course,' she told him. 'But now that you've got some family to help you, you'd soon adjust. You've got your daughters and granddaughters out there to welcome you.' She paused and gave him a shy grin. 'And me, of course. I'm part of the furniture.'

He smiled at her. 'Your letters mean a lot to me,' he said. 'They keep me going.'

'Good'. Nora paused thoughtfully, leaning towards him in a confidential manner. 'Look, even though it wouldn't be wise to bank on anything, you mustn't stop hoping. Just because nothing's happening at the moment, that doesn't mean it's been forgotten. The girls won't rest until they've found the Dodds. Daisy reckons they need just one break that'll set the whole thing in motion, and she's convinced that they'll get it sooner or later. That's Daisy for you – she always looks on the bright side and that's what you must do.'

Lionel nodded. 'You're sort of a mum to my daughters, then?' he assumed.

'Not to both of them. June and I are just friends because I haven't know her for so long. But I am like a mum to Daisy. She seems to want that. Daisy's strong but June has a tougher edge somehow. She isn't as open as Daisy so you can't get close to her.'

They were interrupted by the warder telling them that time was up.

'Thanks ever so much for coming,' Lionel said.

'It was a pleasure,' Nora smiled. 'I'll come again sometime if you'd like me to.'

'Yes, please.'

'I'll sort something out with the girls then, as you're only allowed a certain number of visits,' she told him.

He nodded in approval.

It was heartbreaking to see him being taken away, battered by the way life had treated him but retaining a proud stance, shoulders squared, chin up. She could see a lot of his younger daughter in him.

Nora's empathy for Lionel was strong because she'd had her share of loneliness; she knew what it was like to feel like an outsider. Until Daisy had come into her life she'd felt isolated from people because she was a spinster. It was the recognition of how true friendship had changed her life for the better that had inspired her to write to Lionel. She hoped she could give to him some of what his daughter had given her.

'Morning, madear,' the proprietor of the Gullscombe Bay village shop greeted Daisy in her rich Devonian accent. 'Another lovely day. You've certainly brought some good weather with you.'

'We seem to have – so far, anyway, Mrs Graham,' agreed Daisy. 'Let's hope it lasts.'

A plump-faced woman of middle years, with rosy cheeks and a fresh complexion, the shopkeeper turned her attention to Shirley and Belinda, to whom she'd taken a liking this past week. 'And how are my little maids today?' she asked.

'Very well, thank you, Mrs Graham,' they chanted politely, making their mother swell with pride at their lovely manners.

'That's good.' She turned to Daisy. 'Your usual this morning, madear?'

'Please.'

The other woman took a cottage loaf out of a basket, wrapped it in tissue paper and put it on the counter with a pint of milk. 'Anything else?'

'I think I'll take some apples and bananas too, please,' Daisy requested.

'Pick out what you want then, madear,' Mrs Graham instructed, 'and I'll weigh them up.'

While Daisy helped herself from the wooden trays and handed the fruit to the shopkeeper, Belinda asked in a proud tone, 'Do you know what I can do, Mrs Graham?'

'No, what's that, pet?' the woman smiled.

'I can swim.'

'Can you really?' Mrs Graham was most impressed. 'That's very good indeed.'

'She can't do it on her own yet.' Her sister's competitive streak went into top gear. 'She can only do it with the water wings on, same as me.'

'It's still swimming,' insisted Belinda.

'Not proper swimming until we can do it on our own,' argued Shirley. 'Uncle Jack says.'

Daisy gave Mrs Graham a wry grin. 'There's no shortage of sibling rivalry between these two.'

'No harm in a spot of healthy competition,' the shopkeeper pointed out.

'Jack's been helping me to teach them to swim,' Daisy told her. 'It would be good if they could do it before we go back. Once they've learned they've got it for ever.'

'If anyone can teach them, Jack will. He's got the patience of a saint, that man,' enthused Mrs Graham. 'You won't hear a bad word about him in this village.'

'Everyone seems to like him.'

'That's because he does so much for the people around here,' she confided. 'In the winter he clears the snow for the old folk; he even gets the coal in for them. And that's just two examples of the sort of man he is. Nothing's too much trouble.'

Jack was a local hero in these parts, Daisy had already gathered that. Gullscombe Bay was a small community, barely touched by tourism. There were no hotels or boarding houses. A few of the residents offered bed and breakfast in the summer but that was about it. Because Daisy and the girls were guests of the village hero, who had made it generally known that she was here to convalesce, they were being given the red-carpet treatment by the locals, many of whom had stories of courage and kindness to tell about Jack. Everything from rescuing a drowning man to lobbying the council to get more streetlights put up in the village.

'I've noticed that,' she agreed. 'It's very good of him to let us stay with him.'

'You're enjoying your holiday then.' It was a statement rather than a question since it would never occur to this local woman that any visitor to the area could do anything but enjoy themselves.

'I'll say we are,' enthused Daisy. 'We love it here. We won't want to go back when the time comes. Still, I won't think about that yet, as we've still got a week left.'

'Let's hope the weather stays fine.'

Daisy nodded, handing the woman some money. Daisy hadn't the means of knowing for sure but she believed that rain, shine, hail or storm, she would enjoy being in Gullscombe Bay.

'You're certainly looking a lot better than when you arrived,' observed the shopkeeper, handing Daisy her change. 'You looked quite poorly then.'

'I'm feeling heaps better now,' Daisy was pleased to be able to report.

After some more idle chat, she and the girls left the shop and walked across the village green and down the lane to the cottage. One of the highlights of the day for Daisy was walking to the shop every morning with the girls to get fresh bread and milk. She loved the smell of the sea in the morning air, the friendliness of the people she met and the fresh taste of the food when they got back to the cottage. The walk before breakfast gave them an appetite and they'd got into the habit of having just-baked bread and butter with fresh fruit or jam instead of the porridge and cornflakes they had in the mornings at home.

At the beginning Jack had offered quite insistently to do the morning trip to the shop but when Daisy explained how much she enjoyed it, he let her carry on while he had an extra half-hour in bed. There was a very relaxed atmosphere between them. Not once had he made her feel like a lodger in his house. Quite the opposite; he made her feel as though he was honoured to have her and the girls in the house.

So far, with such good weather, they'd been able to have breakfast in the garden looking out over the sea. It was the most wonderful start to the day. She could understand why Jack had settled here. It was the sort of place you never wanted to leave.

It was mid-afternoon and the residents of Seagull Cottage were all in the shallow waters of the sea. Even Daisy was wearing a swimsuit now, a flowery little one-piece she'd bought in Torquay when Jack had taken them in the car the other day for a look round. Because holidays away had been unknown to her until now, she hadn't owned such a thing before.

'Come on then, Shirley,' Jack instructed. 'Let's have some action here. Swim from your mum to me.'

The little girl looked doubtful. 'Not without the water wings,' she told him.

'You can do it on your own, I promise you,' he encouraged. 'That's why we took them off, so that you can try.'

'I'm scared to do it without them.'

'You've nothing to be scared of because you're ready to do it on your own now,' he promised her. 'Honestly, I wouldn't suggest you do it if I wasn't sure that you can. But I'm here to catch you if you can't manage.'

'Go on, love,' urged Daisy. 'Give it a try.'

Shirley tried and floundered, waving her arms in a panic.

'It's all right, I've got you,' said Jack, holding her firm until she was steady on her feet. Keen for her not to be put off by the failure, he suggested she should try again right away.

'Push yourself off from the bottom, come on, swim from Mummy to me.'

It worked. It was only a matter of a few yards but she did actually move through the water without artificial aid. By the end of the session she was swimming on her own and loving it, her sister almost ready to dispense with the water wings too.

Afterwards they got dried and had tea and scones in the garden. When they'd finished eating, the children went off to play on the sand where the adults could keep an eye on them.

'They can never have enough of the beach,' observed Daisy. 'Whenever it's time to go, it's too soon for them. I'm sure if we stayed till midnight I'd still have a battle to get them to come home.'

'That's all most kids want on holiday,' Jack remarked, 'sea, sand and sunshine.'

'They've never had it before,' she said. 'They are two happy little girls, thanks to you.'

'I do have an ulterior motive.'

She squinted at him, shielding her eyes from the sun with her hand. 'Yeah? What's that then?'

'I get to show off my little corner of the world,' he laughed.

'And understandably so,' she smiled. 'Gullscombe Bay has three more devoted fans now.'

'Good. Oh, and by the way,' he said, and Daisy sensed a sudden uneasiness in his manner, 'I'm not working tonight. I've got a night off.'

'Lovely,' she beamed. 'I'll cook for us.' She felt awkward suddenly and bit her lip. 'Sorry, I'm being presumptuous. You're probably going out – on a hot date or something.'

He looked at her, his heart melting at her smile and her shining eyes, her skin now suffused with a light tan, her brown hair bleached by the sun and blowing off her face in the light warm breeze. She'd even lost that raw skinniness she'd had when she first arrived. He'd made a point of studying her reaction to the news that he was going to be at home this evening, ever careful not to encroach upon her privacy. All week he'd given her the run of the cottage so she would feel completely at home without him around.

Now, halfway through the holiday, the time was right for him to get to know her better; before it was too late. He had nothing specific in mind for Daisy. He wasn't planning on making a move on her or anything because he knew she was involved with someone else. He just wanted to be with her because he was so smitten. There was no future in it but he couldn't help the way he felt.

'No hot date,' he informed her. 'Just a quiet night in . . . something good to eat and a bottle of wine, perhaps.'

'Wine, at home?' She looked surprised. 'I thought people only had wine at wedding receptions, or when they're staying at a posh hotel like the one where I work.' She gave him one of her delicious grins. 'But I'm forgetting, you being a restaurant manager you'd have more sophisticated tastes than me.'

'Don't be daft,' he said in a tone of light admonition. 'I just thought it would be a nice idea to make the meal a bit special, you being on holiday.'

'It's a lovely idea.'

'So if you tell me what you fancy to eat I'll pop into town on the bike and do some shopping.'

'You choose the food and I'll cook it,' she said, smiling into his eyes. 'Deal?'

'Deal,' he replied with a tender look.

That same evening June answered a knock at the door to find Nat Barker standing on the step. Naturally she was puzzled.

'Daisy's still away on holiday,' she reminded him.

'I know that,' he told her. 'I was just wondering if you'd heard from her.'

'No, not yet,' she replied. 'I expect we'll get a postcard in due course. I take it you haven't heard either.'

He shook his head, then enquired, 'Well, aren't you going to ask me in?'

She spread her hands, looking at him. 'Daisy isn't here so what would be the point?'

'So that we don't have to talk in full view of the neighbours is as good a reason as any,' he suggested. 'And also because I'm as good as your brother-in-law. I think that in itself warrants a cup of tea, don't you?'

'No,' was her frank reply. 'And you're about as likely to be my brother-in-law as the Duke of Edinburgh is.'

'Ooh,' he said, shaking his head disapprovingly and sucking in his breath, 'Daisy won't be pleased to hear that you kept me waiting on the doorstep, not pleased at all.'

He was right about that. June had promised Daisy that she'd be more sociable to Nat and she must keep that promise even though Daisy wasn't here. 'Come on in then,' she said with reluctance, ushering him into the living room.

'The sergeant major not about tonight then?' he said when she brought him a cup of tea a few minutes later.

'If you mean Nora, she's gone to her poetry group,' June informed him coolly. 'And I'd rather you didn't call her names, if you don't mind. The least she deserves is respect from you, considering she's been helping Daisy to raise your daughters for years with no assistance from you whatever.'

Nat shrugged indifferently. 'Poetry group, eh?' he said with a mocking grin.

'That's right,' she confirmed briskly. 'Nora likes that sort of thing. She's a very erudite woman.'

'That sounds like some sort of glue.'

'It means knowledgeable.'

'Yeah, well, books and stuff suit her,' he commented cynically. 'Both are as boring as hell.'

June didn't reply. She perched on the edge of an armchair opposite him, feeling intensely irritated and wondering again what Daisy saw in him. She supposed he was good-looking in a greasy sort of way but he had no dress sense whatever and, to her eyes, looked ridiculous with his quiffed hair, gaudy tie and royal-blue suit with a long jacket. It would be rude of her to leave him here on his own and she didn't want to give him any opportunity to make trouble between her and Daisy. But she didn't feel comfortable in the same room with him.

'Each to their own,' she said, keeping her temper, 'and Nora is very clever and well read.'

'She's a sad old bag.'

'Right, that's it.' This was justifiable grounds for eviction. 'I won't have my friends insulted in my own house. So get out. Go on, push off.'

'I haven't finished my tea yet.'

'Too bad. I want you out of here right now.'

'Look, I'm sorry,' he apologised, sounding unexpectedly contrite. 'I overstepped the mark.'

'It's no more than I've come to expect from you,' June said, 'as normal decent behaviour seems to be beyond you.'

'That's a bit strong,' he objected. 'Anyone would think I was some sort of ruffian to hear you talk.'

'I wonder why that is,' was her ironic retort.

Nat looked at her with a gleam in his eye. He hated the sight of the snooty cow and the way she looked down on him. He'd come here on impulse, as he'd been passing the end of the street, with no ulterior motive other than idling away a few minutes on his way to the pub. But with Daisy out of the way, he could see the perfect opportunity to bring her superior sister down a peg or two.

'Look, I know there's no love lost between us,' he said in a tone of fake conciliation, 'but can't we bury the hatchet for Daisy's sake? I know she would like us to get on better.'

June gave him a shrewd look. She didn't trust him an inch but if they could come to some understanding whereby they got along better, even if only in front of Daisy, it would make life easier for them all. If he was prepared to make an effort then so was she. 'OK. If you really mean it, I'm prepared to give it a try,' she told him.

'Good, I'm glad that's settled.' He looked at her innocently but was actually planning his next move. 'It's next Saturday Daisy gets back, isn't it?'

'That's right,' she confirmed. 'She's halfway through the holiday now. I hope she's enjoying herself. She's had a rough time and deserves a break.'

'Yeah, I hope she has a good time, an' all.' He fixed her with his dark, somnolent eyes. 'I know you don't think much of me but I do care about her, you know.'

'Don't make me laugh,' she said. 'You don't give a toss about her. There's only one person you care about and that's yourself.'

'Here, that's not very nice.' He looked peeved. 'I thought we'd agreed to call a truce.'

'Yes, we did,' she admitted, 'but if we're going to stay at peace we'd better steer clear of the subject of your feelings for Daisy.' She stood up. 'Anyway, I don't want to seem rude but I do have things to do.'

He drained his teacup and stood up.

She turned to lead him to the front door when she felt his arms slip around her from behind.

'What the hell do you think you're doing?' she gasped, turning to him and wrenching away.

'Come on, June, you know you want to,' he taunted.

'You must be off your head—'

'You don't like me but you do fancy me,' he interrupted. 'And don't deny it because I won't believe you.'

'You must be joking.'

'You women are all the same,' he persisted. 'You can't resist a bad boy.'

'Ugh!' She stared at him in disgust. 'I'd sooner be savaged by a mad Alsatian.'

'Don't give me that,' he persisted suggestively, coming towards her again. 'Why fight it when you know you won't win? What harm is there, eh? Daisy will never know.'

June whacked her hand across his face so hard it stung her. Caught unawares, he reeled back. 'You spiteful cow,' he muttered.

'Now get out,' she said, marching towards the door and opening it. 'Go on, get out – *now*.'

His eyes were simmering with rage. Such was his vanity, he'd planned only to get her interested, then make a fool of her by turning her down. The way she'd turned the tables on him was the ultimate humiliation. 'I'll get you for this,' he threatened. 'I can promise you that.'

'Just go,' she said, putting her hands on his chest and pushing him through the doorway.

'You'll pay for this, you bitch,' was his parting shot, and the haunting image she saw as she shut the door on him was his venomous eyes glaring at her.

Behind the closed door June was trembling, his threats making her shiver. How could someone as genuinely good-hearted as Daisy have got mixed up with such a brute? she wondered. Daisy really ought to have her eyes opened about the sort of man he was. But June knew that she could never hurt her sister by telling her what her beloved Nat had just done.

Chapter Twelve

'Thanks for helping us out with the wine, Paula. You're a pal.'
Alan was talking to his friend in the Cliff Head reception,
having just removed a dozen bottles of white wine from the
boot of her car. 'We've usually got plenty in stock but our
suppliers let us down at the last minute.' He tutted, giving her
a wry grin. 'And, of course, Sod's law being as it is, everyone
wants white wine tonight.'

'Isn't it always the way?'

'Yeah. Still, thanks to you we can stay in favour with the
customers.' He put the cardboard box containing the wine
down on the counter and looked at her, raising his eyes in a
gesture of self-deprecation. 'A decent-class hotel without any
white wine, I ask you.'

'These things happen in the most well-run establishments,'
she reminded him. 'And I'm sure you'd help us out in similar
circumstances.'

'Course we would.' He paused, looking at her. 'You should
have let me come to get it, though, to save you driving over.'

'I was glad of the break,' she admitted. 'It's always so
hectic on a Saturday night at our place.'

'Same here.' He glanced towards the wine. 'So, how much
do we owe you?'

'I don't know off the top of my head,' she said casually.
'I'll find out the trade price and let you know.'

'OK.' Saturday night was in full swing at the Cliff Head and Alan needed to get back to work but he didn't want to be rude. 'Can I get you a drink?' he offered. 'It's the least I can do after you've gone to such trouble on our behalf.'

'Thanks, Alan, but no. I've had a breather but I mustn't stop to socialise.' She threw him a knowing look. 'And neither, I suspect, must you.'

'I am a bit pushed,' he was forced to admit. 'Jack's got the night off.'

Her brows rose. 'The restaurant manager off duty on a Saturday night at the height of the season?'

Alan made a face. 'I'm a soft touch to have agreed to it, I know, but he's got people staying with him,' he explained. 'My wife's sister and her two children, as a matter of fact.' He leaned towards her, becoming confidential. 'I think he's fallen for my sister-in-law, actually. I haven't been able to get a sensible word out of him since she's been here. It's Daisy this, Daisy that . . .'

'He must be smitten to ask for a Saturday night off at this time of the year.'

Alan nodded. 'I didn't make an issue of it, though, because he's such an asset to this place and he never pushes his luck about time off as a rule.'

Unexpectedly, he found himself noticing how attractive Paula looked in a pale blue summer suit with a pencil skirt and high-heeled court shoes. Since they'd cleared the air last Christmas, their friendship had blossomed and they met up for a meal or a drink on a regular basis. They had all the right ingredients for a friendship, being in the same line of business, having parents who were friends, and sharing a similar sense of humour.

But meeting her clear blue eyes now and feeling the stirrings of a physical response, he wondered if, perhaps, there could be something more for them. He and June were

272

no longer at daggers drawn but she'd made it clear there was no future for them together. So maybe there could be one for him with Paula. Unlike Jack, Alan didn't enjoy the single life.

'How about dinner one evening soon?' he suggested. 'Once Jack's visitors have gone back to London and his mind is on the job again, I'll be able to get away, especially on a weekday evening.'

'That would be lovely, Alan,' she accepted graciously. 'I'd really like that.'

'I'll give you a ring soon to get something arranged then.'

'Sure.'

At that moment his mother sailed on to the scene from the direction of the restaurant. 'Alan, I've had to send— Oh, hello, Paula.' She looked from one to the other, beaming as she misread the situation. 'How nice to see you, dear. I didn't realise you were here.'

'I'm just on my way out,' Paula told her, making as though to leave. 'Nice to see you again, Mrs Masters. You're looking well. See you soon, Alan.'

'I'll ring you,' he said, smiling after her as she swung across the foyer in her high-heeled shoes.

His mother was looking very pleased with herself. 'You two seem to be getting along very well lately,' she observed.

'She came with the wine we needed, that's all,' Alan explained. 'It wasn't a social visit.'

'That doesn't alter the fact that the two of you seem to get on well now,' she persisted.

He shrugged and changed the subject. 'You wanted me for something?'

'Yes, so I did. I came to tell you that Chef isn't feeling well so I've sent him home. The sous-chef will have to take over.'

'Wonderful,' Alan said with irony. 'That's all we need.' He sighed. 'Oh, well, it's all in a night's work, I suppose.'

★ ★ ★

Daisy was feeling extremely happy and relaxed. The children were asleep in bed and she and Jack were having coffee in the living room at the cottage after dining on steak and salad, followed by chocolate eclairs, and all washed down with a bottle of wine.

Daisy had never talked to a man so much in her life – certainly not to Nat. There was something about Jack that made her want to confide. She was so much at ease she even told him about her background and her plans to get her father's name cleared. She told him everything.

Unlike Nát, Jack didn't react by immediately pouring scorn on the idea. But he was a little circumspect. 'Whilst I can understand your wanting to find this Morris Dodd and his wife, I think you should treat the whole thing with caution,' he told her. 'I mean, even if you do find him, he isn't going to put his hands up to the murder, is he? And he'll see you and your sister as a threat, turning up out of the blue after all these years. He could get nasty.'

'We've already thought of that and we'll be careful, of course,' she assured him. 'But it's his wife we're planning on dealing with, rather than him.'

'She isn't likely to admit to anything either.'

'Maybe not, but she holds the key to our father's freedom and the restoration of his good name,' Daisy pointed out. 'So I believe there must be some way to get her to admit that she lied under oath, and give us the evidence we need to get Dad's case reopened.'

Jack leaned back with his arms folded, considering the matter. 'The last thing I want to do is put you off because I can tell how much this means to you,' he began, 'but facts have to be faced. She's already committed perjury; she isn't going to change her story after all this time, is she? She'll be too scared of the consequences.'

'I know all that, Jack. But I'm still convinced that if we can only find the Dodds, we'll somehow be able to see that justice is done.' She shrugged, making a face. 'I admit we've come to a dead end at the moment but we're not going to give up because we *know* that the pair of them lied in court. That's got to give us a strong case for an appeal.'

'If you can get them to admit it, yes it will,' he said. 'And I agree with you that she's more likely to be persuaded to open up than he is. He was unfaithful to her, after all.'

'Exactly,' agreed Daisy. 'Look at this whole thing from Mrs Dodd's point of view: because of the murder the world knew that her husband had been cheating on her. That must have been extremely humiliating. Being betrayed by your husband is painful enough, I should imagine. Having everyone know about it must have been excruciating.'

'No doubt about that.'

'Even though she lied for him, she must have felt resentful towards him. Any woman would,' Daisy went on. 'And the fact that she knew he wasn't at home with her at the time of the murder, as they both claimed, must have made her wonder if he did actually do it, whatever lies he told her about that. Over the years she might have become bitter about it and be ready to shop him – with a little encouragement.'

'Not at the expense of her own liberty.' Jack didn't want Daisy to fool herself about this.

'I know it's a long shot.'

'They might not even still be together,' he pointed out.

'We've thought of that too, and I know that when you consider all the drawbacks, our chances of success don't look good.' She pondered for a moment. 'But all I can say is, I've got a feeling about this whole thing.' Her voice rose with ardour. 'If it takes the rest of my life I'll see my father's name cleared.' She paused, guessing his thoughts. 'Even if it is posthumously.'

There was obviously no point in trying to talk her out of it so he wanted to be helpful. 'You say you've come to a dead end in your search for them?'

'Yeah,' she sighed. 'If we had any idea of the area to look it would help, but we haven't a flaming clue.' She told him what they'd done so far.

'Quite a task.'

'You can say that again. The trouble is, neither June nor I have much spare time. We both have demanding jobs and I've got the girls to consider. But, as I said, we'll get it sorted out. I don't know when but we'll do it.'

Infected by her optimism, Jack believed her suddenly. She was the sort of person who would do anything she set her mind to. 'Yes, I think you will too,' he said.

'Oh.' She sounded surprised because of the odds stacked against a successful outcome. 'It's encouraging to know that someone's got faith in me.'

She was wearing a white sleeveless top with a round neck and a full floral skirt, her hair shining in the light. She looked so pretty, he couldn't help telling her so.

'Thank you.' She smiled, blushing. 'Flattery will get you everywhere.' The way he looked at her made her feel different – sort of beautiful and special. Warmth flowed between them like a living thing. She couldn't remember feeling this good in a very long time, if ever. But compunction hovered, nudging her into making sure that Nat didn't get forgotten. 'I'm not used to it because Nat isn't the complimentary type.'

'And talking of Nat,' he said, as though acknowledging the other man's place in her life, 'what does he think about these plans you have to help your father?'

'He doesn't approve.'

'Worried it might be risky for you, I suppose.'

'No, it isn't that,' she corrected with characteristic honesty. 'He just thinks it's a stupid idea that won't get a result.'

'You won't get any help from him then?'

Daisy puffed out her lips, shaking her head. 'Opposition is all I'll get from him,' she said with emphasis. 'Apart from anything else, he can't stand the sight of my sister so is against anything I do with her.'

'Tell me . . . are you actually engaged to him?' came Jack's tentative enquiry.

'Yeah, I suppose you could say that's what we are. I always think of us in that way.'

'You don't wear a ring, though.'

In the early days a ring had been promised but never materialised. But she just said, 'No. But we are seriously committed to each other.'

Jack nodded without comment.

'Poor old Nat is always in the doghouse with June and Nora over something or other,' she found herself saying without any prior intention. 'Neither of them likes him. They don't think he treats me right.'

'Really?' Jack said in a querying tone. 'And do they have a fair point?'

'He's not perfect, I'm the first to admit that,' she told him. 'He tends to be a bit too casual about things. But that's just his way. We can't all be steady and reliable, can we? It'd be a boring old world if we were.'

This Nat character sounded like a right cretin and obviously didn't value the prize he had in Daisy, thought Jack, finding himself angry about it. If the man had any sense or serious intentions he'd have married her years ago. But he spared her feelings and said, 'It certainly would.'

'Have you ever been married?' she asked conversationally.

'No.'

'Would you like to be?'

'Not especially, no. I'm quite happy as I am,' he informed her. 'I suppose I've got a bit selfish and set in my ways. You get used to pleasing yourself when you're on your own.'

'Yeah, I suppose you would.'

'Anyway,' he began, changing the subject, 'you're enjoying your stay in Gullscombe Bay?'

'I'll say. It's beautiful here. No wonder you made it your home. It's enough to tempt anyone. The idea of going back to Notting Hill isn't in the least appealing, I can tell you. The way I feel at the moment, I could happily stay away indefinitely.'

'Really?' He couldn't hide his enthusiasm.

'Yeah, really,' she confirmed with a wistful look. 'But I have to go back, of course.'

'Why?'

She threw him a puzzled look. 'I should have thought that was obvious,' she told him. 'My life is in London.'

'It doesn't have to be.'

'No, it doesn't have to be. But it is. I'm a Londoner, Jack.'

'So am I.'

'But it's where I belong. Everything I know is there,' she pointed out. 'Being here has made me understand why people move away from the city to places like this and I feel I'd like to do the same. But that's just the holiday atmosphere getting to me. Being realistic, it's just a holiday place, somewhere I'd love to come again for a visit. But not a place I could live in.'

'I've made it my home,' he reminded her.

'It's different for you,' she objected. 'You're a single man with only yourself to consider. Even apart from the fact that I couldn't leave Nat, I have the girls to support so I have to have steady work. And London is where the work is.'

He could hardly bear the thought of her leaving and wanted to beg her to stay. But he had no right. Her life was in London and she obviously thought the world of this Nat person. 'Yeah, of course it is,' he said in an understanding manner. 'It's just that . . . well, you seem to have taken the place so much to your heart and it obviously agrees with you. I

278

suppose my enthusiasm for the area got a bit out of hand.'

'That's understandable.'

'It's true about the place being good for you, though,' he added. 'You're hardly recognisable from the pale, sickly woman I met off the train a week ago.'

'I feel different too.'

'You're very beautiful, Daisy,' he blurted out.

'Here, leave off,' she said, embarrassed to find herself on the receiving end of his admiration for the second time. 'I think you've had one too many to drink.'

'I haven't—'

'Well, I think I have,' she cut in quickly because she was enjoying the attention rather too much and needed to come down to earth. 'I think it's time I went to bed.' She gave him a wry grin. 'After we've done the dishes, naturally.'

'I'll see to that,' he offered. 'You cooked the meal so it's only fair that I do the washing up.'

'Are you sure?'

'Quite sure,' he confirmed. 'You go to bed.'

She stood up. 'I'll have to take you up on that,' she said, stifling a yawn, 'before I get too sleepy to get up the stairs. All this fresh air knocks me out. I'll see you in the morning.'

'Yeah.'

'Thanks for a lovely evening.'

'Thank *you*, Daisy.'

''Night, Jack.'

''Night, Daisy.'

Daisy slipped into bed, her head swimming with happy memories of today and excited thoughts of tomorrow. That was how it was since she'd been in Gullscombe Bay. Each new day was a fresh treat to be anticipated with pleasure. This must be why people are so keen to go away on holiday, she thought, because it's just one long round of fun and recreation. How could you not be happy in surroundings like these, going to sleep every night to the soothing sound of the sea and waking up to it every morning?

Who was she kidding? It wasn't just the environment that was making her feel so happy and alive. It was going to sleep at night knowing that she would see *him* the next morning. She wanted to go on doing it, to go on being with him and feeling like this. Refusing to spoil the moment by dwelling on the sobering thought that it would end all too soon, she lay back on the pillow and drifted into a peaceful sleep.

Downstairs Jack was humming softly to himself as he washed the dishes and put them to drain on the draining board. It was so good having Daisy here, he was literally dreading her departure. As he'd said to her, living alone had made him selfish and set in his ways. But he didn't feel selfish when he was with her. He wanted to put himself out for her benefit; enjoyed her appreciation of every little thing. Having the kids around was great fun too, their youthful exuberance filling the house with noise and laughter. Their energy and nonstop chatter was positively uplifting to him. Selfish he might be but he couldn't do enough for this little family. The trouble was, he wanted to go on doing it, and this time next week they'd be back in London.

The trio had breathed new life into him, and the cottage was never going to be the same after they'd gone. The thought of their departure was so depressing he blotted it out of his mind and looked forward to tomorrow and waking up knowing that Daisy and the girls were in the house.

The next morning the unthinkable happened. They awoke to find rain trickling down the windows and forming puddles in the garden. Jack insisted on going to the shop, which opened for a few hours on a Sunday morning, to get the milk and bread to save Daisy a drenching as she had recently been ill.

Breakfast was eaten indoors, but by the time they'd finished and done the dishes, the rain had stopped. It was still overcast, though, so Jack suggested a walk along the beach. He had to go to work a bit later on but had time to spare for a stroll.

So, with sweaters over their summer clothes, they set off around the bay, the girls stopping every so often to collect shells in their buckets, Daisy observing the patches of woodland that fringed the shore. Having spent most of the time on the beach up until now, they hadn't walked as far as this before so this bit of the landscape was new to her.

'Well, has the place lost some of its magic now that you've seen it in the rain?' asked Jack.

'Not on your life,' she assured him. 'The rain has freshened everything up and made it even better.'

'You won't say that if it rains every day for the rest of your holiday,' he grinned.

'You can bet I won't,' she admitted with a smile. 'But I'm sure I'll still love the place whatever the weather.'

'Let's hope the sun comes out so you're not put to the test,' he remarked casually.

They ambled on in comfortable silence. The girls were dragging behind, poking about in the rock pools.

'Wow! What a lovely house,' enthused Daisy as a large stone-faced property came into view through the trees. 'It's huge. Is it a private house or some sort of an institution?'

'It's a private house,' Jack informed her. 'I believe they call it a gentleman's residence. It's known as Gullscombe Manor.'

'It's beautiful,' she breathed, noticing a turreted roof and a veranda facing the sea.

'It used to be,' he corrected as they stared at the property, the rear of which was facing them. 'But it's been empty for ages and just left to rot.'

'Who owns it?'

'A wealthy businessman; retired now, though, and getting on a bit in years,' he told her. 'He's got pots of money.'

'You'd need it to maintain a place like that,' was Daisy's opinion.

'You're right there.'

'So what happened to the owner?'

'No one knows for sure. Rumour has it that he's gone to live with his married daughter in Exeter.'

'What, just moved out and left the place?'

Jack nodded. 'They say he went a bit soft in the head after his wife died,' he explained. 'They'd lived there all their married life and he just couldn't cope with being there after she'd gone. It's all a bit sad really.'

'Mm. But surely one of his family could make sure the place was looked after,' Daisy suggested. 'Either that or sell it rather than leave it to deteriorate.'

'You'd think so, wouldn't you?' he agreed. 'Maybe he can't bring himself to take the final step of selling it. And perhaps his daughter doesn't fancy living in such a remote spot.'

'It's probably something like that,' remarked Daisy. 'But it's a terrible shame for it to be so neglected.' She paused, squinting at the house. 'What's it like at the front?'

'We'll go and have a look if you like,' he said. 'There's no one around to object.'

Having called to the girls, and helped them on with their shoes, they climbed up a sloping path through the trees into the gardens, which were extensive and very overgrown. Making their way through the long wet grass to the front, they came to a gravel forecourt at the end of a driveway leading to the road.

The house entrance was imposing, with wide stone steps leading up to double doors on which the varnish was dull and faded. Daisy peered through one of the dirty windows to see a large room with dust sheets covering the furniture.

'I bet the spiders are having a whale of a time in there with all those cobwebs,' she said, shivering at the thought. 'It's creepy, as though it's got caught in a time warp, as though life suddenly stopped in there.'

'That is what happened when his wife died,' Jack told her. 'He just upped and left.'

'What will happen to it ultimately, I wonder?'

'I suppose eventually it'll be sold,' he suggested. 'Or the owner's daughter and her husband will take it over.'

'It certainly needs urgent attention, so let's hope something happens sooner rather than later,' she commented. 'Before it gets any worse.'

'Mm.' Noticing that the skies were darkening, Jack said, 'Anyway, I think it's about to chuck it down with rain so we'd better find some shelter.'

He was right. The heavens opened and they made a dash for the only protection they could find, the veranda at the back of the house. It was an attractive structure with mosaic tiles underfoot and intricate laced metalwork arched between the supporting pillars. There were glass doors leading into the house through which they could see a spacious room in which dust covers were a dominant presence.

'This is handy for us, and very pretty too,' observed Daisy as the downpour drenched the gardens and bounced on to some decrepit wooden garden furniture. She turned and peered through the glass doors. 'They must have really lived in style. The rooms are enormous.'

'You wouldn't buy a place like this unless you could afford to live in style, would you?' he mentioned.

'No, not unless you bought it for commercial use,' she remarked casually, 'to change into a nursing home or something.'

Jack nodded, looking at his watch.

'Oh dear. Are you going to be late for work?' Daisy looked worried.

'Not yet. But I do need to keep an eye on the time,' he told her. 'Alan's being very good about my having time off, but I don't want to upset him, especially as I want some time off next week.'

'Don't get into trouble at work on our account,' she advised him. 'You don't have to stay home from work because of us. The girls and I will be fine on our own.'

'I know that but I want to spend time with you,' he said, taking her hand and squeezing it in a sudden impulse. 'I enjoy your company.'

'The feeling's mutual,' she blurted out, instinctively moving closer to him. 'I just don't want you to put yourself out any more than you already have.'

The atmosphere changed from warm and friendly to vibrantly intimate but was shattered almost instantly by the two girls running out into the rain in sheer devilment.

'Come back in here, you two,' called Daisy. 'Your clothes will get soaked.'

Shirley raised her face to the rain. 'It feels lovely, Mum,' she called, lifting her arms. 'It's washing my face and making the garden smell nice.'

Belinda copied her sister, tilting her head back to let the rain soak her face and hair. 'It doesn't feel cold, does it, Sherl?'

'No. It feels smashing.'

Daisy could understand them being inspired to do this because she too was tempted to run out into the rain. She felt so alive she wanted to touch the elements. But the sensible, maternal side of her nature prevailed. 'I'm sure it's really good fun but come into the shelter just the same,' she said with as much authority as she could muster in her carefree mood. 'We're going in a minute, as soon as the rain eases off a bit.'

They did as she said, and stood dripping on the veranda, giggling at the sheer boldness of getting soaked through with their clothes on.

Jack smiled. 'What it's like to be a kid, eh?' he said. 'They make you remember, bring it all back.'

'Those two aren't concerned with practicalities like drying wet clothes or catching cold,' Daisy said. 'Kids just follow their instincts. And boring old Mum had to go and spoil it all by being sensible.' She sighed. 'Still, childhood is short enough. I want them to enjoy it to the full.'

The rain stopped quite suddenly and they headed back towards the cottage, the girls running on ahead, eager now to get changed into dry clothes.

'Oh, by the way,' Jack said as they walked along the beach and the cottage came into view, 'I've been thinking about your search for the Dodds and I've got a suggestion.'

'Oh, yeah?'

'You've been thinking in terms of finding a way of finding them, which, as you've indicated, is an impossible task when you've no idea at all where they might be, and both you and June have other commitments. Right?'

'Yes, that's right,' she confirmed. 'We can't afford a private detective.'

'Maybe you should change your strategy altogether and have them come to you,' he told her intriguingly.

'How on earth would we do that?'

'This is how . . .' he began.

The following week passed all too quickly. After the rain on Sunday, the sun reappeared on Monday, and Daisy and the girls returned to their glorious outdoor routine. They were joined by Jack whenever he could get away from the hotel and Daisy was aware of a tacit closeness growing between them.

He arranged to have the whole day off on Friday as it was their last day. In the morning he drove Daisy and the girls into Torquay to buy gifts to take home. They didn't have much money but, because Jack had refused to take anything for their food, they were able to afford a few modest presents.

The many gift shops were filled with novelty items and they had fun choosing what to buy. Daisy bought a jewellery box made of seashells for June to put on her dressing table, and a china cat with ginger fur and luminous green eyes for Nora because she was very fond of cats. For Nat she purchased a cigarette case.

Shirley bought her aunt and surrogate grannie each a comb in a leather case with 'Torquay' boldly displayed in gold letters. Belinda treated them each to a large, Cellophane-wrapped pink seashell filled with sweets that looked like pebbles.

They all had a good laugh in one of the shops at a hideous duck ornament that looked as though it had been thrown together. It had a bright yellow beak that was crooked and shaped in such a way as to give the impression that the bird was laughing.

'Honestly, some of the stuff they expect you to part with your money for,' disapproved Daisy, but she couldn't help but smile at the grinning artefact.

'You don't like it then?' said Jack.

'Of course I don't. How could anyone like such a shoddy piece of workmanship? Whoever made it must have been drunk when they put it together. The whole thing's lopsided.'

'This probably makes me the king of bad taste but it actually appeals to me,' he confessed, picking it up and examining it more closely. 'I like it.'

'You can't possibly like it,' said Daisy in disbelief. 'You're teasing us.'

'No. I'm not, honest. I really think he's great,' he told the amazed Daisy with a devilish grin. 'And at least you wouldn't be miserable with it in the house because it makes you laugh just to look at it.'

'You laugh with the sheer awfulness of it,' was Daisy's opinion.

'I gather you're not going to take it back to London as a souvenir of Torquay then?'

'Not on your life,' she replied without hesitation.

Because they were catching an early train back to London the next morning, Daisy needed to have all but the last-minute packing done before they went to bed that night. This created an air of gloom because it reminded them that their departure was imminent and meant they had to come off the beach earlier than usual.

Still at least Jack wasn't working, and as it was their last night he and Daisy agreed that the girls could stay up to eat with them. So while Daisy bathed the girls and did the bulk of the packing, Jack went to get fish and chips for them all from a shopping parade further up the coast that was just a few minutes away on his motorbike.

When he got back Daisy had laid the table and the girls were in a silly mood, giggling and spluttering behind their hands.

'Have you two got ants in your pants again?' he asked, making them laugh all the more.

When they all sat down at the table and he saw a package wrapped in fancy paper by the side of his plate, he began to understand.

'I've had the devil's own job keeping them quiet about it all afternoon,' Daisy explained.

'What's this?'

'Just a little something to say thank you for giving us such a wonderful holiday,' she told him.

He looked at her sternly and then the girls. 'You shouldn't have,' he said, looking delighted despite his protests. 'There's really no need. I've loved having you.'

'Open it then,' urged Shirley.

'Go on,' added Belinda, jumping up and down in her seat.

The removal of the wrapping revealed a book on the history of motorcycles. Jack was so touched by their thoughtfulness, he couldn't speak for a moment.

'Don't you like it?' Shirley looked anxious.

'I love it.' He got up and gave them each a hug. 'I really love it. It's so kind of you.'

'We think you deserve it for putting up with us for two weeks, don't we, girls?' said Daisy.

The girls nodded, still seeming a bit odd, he thought. There was still plenty of giggling going on.

'We did our secret shopping when you'd had enough of trailing around the shops and went for coffee and left us to it,' Daisy explained.

'I knew I shouldn't have let you loose on Torquay town on your own,' he joshed. 'But thank you all very much for the book. I shall treasure it, always.'

'Um, that isn't quite all,' said Daisy, looking at Shirley, who left the room and returned with another package.

'This is an extra thing that Mum thought you might like,' she said, handing it to him.

Curiously he tore off the wrapping paper. A roar of laughter went up as he held up the laughing duck ornament.

'Something to remember us by,' Daisy grinned. 'You might have awful taste in ornaments but you're a wonderful host.'

Now there were tears clearly visible in his eyes and they were not entirely from laughing.

'Thank you.' His gaze focused on Daisy and they both knew that this was her gift to him and it was an adult thing. Then he looked at the children and added, 'I shall put him on the kitchen windowsill to cheer me up when I'm washing the dishes. I shall think of you all every time I look at him.'

Even the girls picked up on the emotion in the air and were subdued.

'Come on then, everyone,' urged Daisy in a rousing tone to get things back to normal. 'Eat your fish and chips before they get cold.'

'The holiday's gone so quick, I can hardly believe it's over,' said Daisy to Jack later that evening after the children had gone to bed. 'This time tomorrow the girls will be in their own beds at home.'

He nodded gloomily. 'And you?' he said in a querying tone. 'Will you be seeing Nat?'

'Depends if he remembers we're coming home and comes round,' she told him.

'Will you go to his place if he doesn't turn up?'

'No.' She wasn't in the mood to go into much detail about the peculiar nature of her relationship with Nat, especially as she knew Jack would disapprove. 'I'm tied because of the girls so he always comes to me. It's a habit we've slipped into over the years.'

'I see.'

They were in the living room, having a last cup of coffee together, she on the sofa, he in an armchair. They'd been sitting here talking since the girls went to bed, the tension becoming unbearable for Daisy as the evening drew to a close.

'Well, I suppose I'd better be making my way towards bed as we've got to be up early in the morning,' she said, finishing her coffee and standing up.

He got up too, his blue eyes fiercely bright. 'I don't want you to go, Daisy,' he said quickly.

'I can't stay up all night,' she said.

'That isn't what I mean . . .'

She met his eyes. 'I know,' she said softly, 'and I don't want to leave tomorrow either.'

'Marry me, Daisy,' he blurted out.

'What!'

'I love you and I want to marry you.'

She stared at him, his words echoing in the silence. He was as shocked as she was by his proposal.

'Don't be daft, Jack,' she said at last. She was thrilled by what he'd said but it was too sudden, too impossible to be taken seriously. 'Don't mess about.'

He shook his head, as though in disbelief at this unexpected turn of events. 'I had no intention of proposing to you. It just sort of came out. But I'm serious,' he said, his eyes never leaving her face. 'I've fallen in love with you. And I think . . . well, I hope that you feel the same about me.'

She bit her lip, absently combing her hair back from her brow with her fingers. 'Maybe I do feel something but it'll be just a holiday thing.' She was afraid of the strength of her feelings. Here with Jack everything seemed possible but, as the mother of two children, she had to keep her feet planted firmly on the ground. 'All this sunshine and fresh air has gone to my head.'

'It's more than that and we both know it,' he contradicted ardently. 'Don't go back to London. Stay here with me.'

Overwhelmed, she tried to keep things light to hide how deeply she felt for him. 'If I were to stay here, the novelty would soon wear off for you, believe me, under the strain of everyday life and having two noisy kids under your feet.'

'Why not stay and give me the chance to prove you wrong?' he suggested.

She shook her head. 'I can't, Jack. It's all happened too fast. I can't be irresponsible, not with two kids relying on me.'

'Look, this might sound a bit sloppy but I felt something special for you when we first met back in the spring,' he confessed. 'I know we haven't known each other long but these past two weeks have been the most wonderful time of my life. And I know you well enough to know that I love you and I want to be with you . . . and the girls – for the rest of my life.'

Suddenly Daisy didn't want to protest. She didn't want to be sensible and think about the impossibility of a future for her and Jack. She didn't want to consider tomorrow and the parting she knew must come. No one had ever looked at her in the way Jack was looking at her now, as though she was the most important person on earth. All she could think of was what she could see in Jack's eyes, and knew she would never see again after tonight. The only thing that seemed to matter was her feelings for him at this moment.

'Come here,' she said, reaching out for him.

'No, Jack, no,' Daisy said, pulling away from him and dragging her blouse into place. 'I can't do this.'

'All right, don't panic,' he told her, drawing back quickly, his voice quivering slightly. 'I'm not going to force you into anything.'

'I shouldn't have led you on. I'm sorry,' she said, her hands trembling as she sat at the far end of the sofa, doing up her blouse. 'I got carried away.'

'Things got a bit out of hand, that's all,' he assured her. 'It wasn't your fault.'

'I hope you don't think I make a habit of leading men on.'

'Of course not. Why would I think that?'

'It's all right, it's just me being ultra-sensitive,' she told him with a wry look. 'Being an unmarried mum brands you in the eyes of most people.'

'Not in mine,' he said. 'Things moved faster than we intended but it was only natural. We're a pair, you and me. We have a wonderful future ahead of us, you, me and the girls.'

Reality hit home like a physical blow. What was she doing allowing things to go this far? Had she lost her mind? 'No, Jack. Now is all there is,' she stated solemnly. 'I have to go home tomorrow.'

'Surely you're not going back to London as though nothing's changed.' He was distraught.

'Nothing's changed as far as my life there is concerned.' She was ignoring her heart and speaking from her mind because she knew she must be sensible. 'This . . . us, is lovely but it isn't the stuff of real life.'

'What we have is about as real as it gets,' he argued.

'I know it feels like that now but . . .' The sound of a child's voice calling to her from upstairs brought her even more firmly down to earth. When she came back downstairs, having given Shirley a drink of water, settled her and been reminded of her serious responsibilities, she was even more convinced that she must control these bewildering new feelings. 'There can't be a future for us and I shouldn't have let you think otherwise.'

Jack got up and paced around the room. 'You and I are right together,' he declared, standing still and looking down at her sitting stiffly on the sofa. 'Surely that's the most important thing.'

'In a sentimental love story it would be, but this isn't fiction and I'm not some teenager with no responsibilities. I have to go home tomorrow and get on with my life.'

'So, I mean nothing to you?'

'You know that isn't true. You mean the world to me,' she was quick to assure him. 'But nothing can come of it.'

'You're saying it's over between us then?'

'Oh, Jack, what is there to be over?' she said, spreading her hands in a gesture of helplessness. 'We've had two weeks together, that's all.'

'Don't trivialise something that means a lot to me,' he admonished sharply.

'It means a lot to me too,' Daisy made clear, 'but I'm a realist and I know that holiday romances rarely last.'

'This isn't just a holiday romance,' he insisted. 'We were drawn to each other when we met last spring. Now that we know each other better it's developed into something special. You must admit that's true.'

'I don't deny feeling something special for you, but I have commitments.'

'Nat, I suppose.'

'That's right,' she said, but there were many more confusing elements to it than that.

'You're not married to him,' he reminded her. 'You're not even officially engaged.'

'No, but he is the father of my children.'

'Are you in love with him?' he blurted out.

Once she would have said yes without hesitation. But she'd been disillusioned with Nat and much less besotted even before she'd met Jack, who was a better man than Nat would ever be. She still cared for Nat, despite all his faults, but she wasn't in love with him. Not now. But to marry her daughters' father was her long-held dream. There was a completeness in it somehow and she didn't feel able to let it go.

'I still feel something for him, yes.'

'That doesn't sound like a proclamation of love to me,' Jack said, his anger rising. 'It sounds more as though he's a habit you're afraid to break.'

'Don't get cross, please, Jack.' Daisy's eyes were full of regret. 'What you and I have shared this past two weeks has been wonderful, like nothing I have experienced before. And I'll never forget it. But that doesn't mean it will last.'

'I don't agree.' He was adamant. 'We have all the right ingredients to make it work.'

'There are too many complications . . .'

'Nothing that can't be resolved,' he told her. 'You'd be happy living here. I know it's right for you. The girls would love it and there's a school the other side of the village. It's a good place to bring children up. And think how healthy you've felt since you've been here. The air agrees with you. You've said so yourself.'

Daisy knew he was right and she wanted to stay more than anything. But her down-to-earth nature just wouldn't allow her to cut the ties with her other life. She'd never had any real stability and was afraid to leave her home and her job for a man she hardly knew and a relationship that could fizzle out under the strain of everyday life. Thinking she was in love with Jack wasn't enough to build a whole new life. She was a realist, used to hardship and disappointment. She couldn't believe that her life would change.

'And what would I do for money?' She was so accustomed to supporting herself and the girls, she couldn't imagine anything else. 'Move in here and sponge off you?'

'How can you sponge off me if you're my wife?' he wanted to know. 'I want to marry you, to look after you and support you . . . and the girls. So you wouldn't have to go out to work.'

'Oh . . .' She'd never imagined a man would ever be this caring to her. 'You're such a good man, Jack.'

'Of course, if you wanted to go out to work, I wouldn't try and stop you,' he added quickly. 'An experienced waitress is always in demand in Torquay. But you wouldn't have to work. The choice would be yours.'

'It's mostly seasonal work around here, I should imagine,'

she commented. 'Anyway, as I'm not staying, that's neither here nor there.'

'Why do you have to go back to Nat?' He was fighting for her now so the truth must be told. 'If he was going to marry you he'd have done it years ago.'

'That is one way of looking at it.'

'Why keep fooling yourself then?'

She sighed. 'I suppose it's because Nat and I go back a long way and he's the girls' father,' she tried to explain, thinking it through as she spoke because she was still very confused.

'I can see that his being the girls' dad would create a bond between you and I would never want to come between a man and his children. But if he made you happy, this thing that's grown between us this past fortnight wouldn't be there, and we wouldn't be having this conversation.'

In a moment of clarity, she realised that happiness wasn't something she'd ever expected to have with Nat. It was the familiar pattern of her life that was drawing her back – a case of the devil she knew, perhaps. 'You can't just snatch what seems good in the moment and hope for the best for the future, not when you've got two kids.'

'You're entitled to grab the chance of happiness, though.'

'That isn't my way, Jack.'

He wasn't ready to give up. 'Would it make any difference if I was prepared to move to London to be with you?'

'No. London isn't the issue,' she told him. 'Anyway, you'd hate living there.'

'Yes, but I'd do it if it meant having you,' he stated gravely. 'That's how much you mean to me.'

Daisy was shocked by the depth of his feelings for her. No one had ever felt that much for her before and it was a huge responsibility. Marriage and a proper family life was all she'd ever wanted. Now she was being offered it and she wasn't in a position to take it. She wanted to seize the moment and accept Jack's proposal. He'd shown her what it felt like to be truly loved by a man. But she still felt bound to the father of her children.

'Jack, you're a great bloke and you'll always be very special to me but I'm going to stay with my old life,' she said. 'It's what I know; what I'm used to.'

Something about her tone must have finally convinced him that she wasn't going to change her mind because his manner became one of cool resignation. 'It's your decision, of course. But I think it's the wrong one.'

'I'm sorry.'

'Don't be,' he said coldly. 'I don't have the right to make you do anything you don't want to do.'

'Jack—'

'I have no claim on you.'

'No, but—'

'It's a simple misunderstanding.' His manner was piercingly abrupt and she knew how much she had hurt him. 'I really believed that you and I had something.'

'And we do,' she told him with emphasis. 'But it can't be permanent.'

'It could be if you wanted it,' he declared briskly. 'But you don't, so let's forget it.'

'Don't be like that, Jack, please.' She felt awful.

'Would you like a drink of something before you go to bed?' he offered, ever the gentleman.

'No, thanks,' Daisy said. 'But I would like you to stop behaving like the perfect host.'

It was as though he'd shut himself off from her. 'I'll go on up to bed if you don't want anything,' he said in a formal tone. 'See you in the morning.'

'Yeah,' she said dismally to his retreating back.

She stayed where she was for a while, too distressed to

move. Eventually she made her way slowly up the stairs. Pausing outside his room, she reached for the door handle and almost touched it. But common sense finally prevailed and she moved on to the room she shared with her daughters and closed the door quietly behind her. She suspected that she'd just made the biggest mistake of her life but felt forced by circumstances to stand by her decision.

Chapter Thirteen

Daisy and the girls were out shopping with June and Nora in Portobello market. Weaving their way through the Saturday morning crowds, they purchased the weekend supply of fruit and vegetables, fresh flowers to brighten up the house, some fish and eggs, a joint of meat for Sunday dinner and a variety of other eatables.

They lingered at an antique stall where an oddly dressed man in a jauntily angled straw hat and a long black tailcoat was in the middle of an entertaining spiel on a rare item, a fine china cricket cage, which he claimed had been especially made for a rich oriental gentleman over two hundred years ago. According to the flamboyant trader's story, the man's servants would have collected the insects and put them into the cage where they would chirrup musically for the entertainment of their owner.

The crowd were taking a lively interest in what he was saying until the price of the unusual artefact was mentioned.

'Five quid for that piece o' junk? Don't make me laugh,' said someone.

'You'd have to pay me to take that lump o' rubbish off your hands,' added another.

'You want your head tested, mate, if you think anyone'll pay two bob for that, let alone five nicker,' came another disparaging utterance.

'Not very nice for the poor little crickets, being caged in,' was a typically soft-hearted reaction from Nora as the crowd began to disperse. 'Downright cruel, I reckon.'

'Have we finished then?' asked Daisy, as they were all weighed down with shopping bags.

Nora examined the list. 'Yes, that's about it for today,' she confirmed.

'I must just pop down to Notting Hill Gate to get my skirt from the dry-cleaner's,' June told them. 'I need it for work on Monday. You can start walking home if you like. I'll catch you up.'

'No. Let's all take a wander down there and have a cuppa coffee and a bun in the ABC,' suggested Daisy.

As the idea was greeted with approval, they left the market crowds behind and walked to the bustling shopping parade at Notting Hill Gate. While June went to Sketchleys, the others had a look round Woolworth's. Moving on past the Gaumont Cinema on their way to the teashop, Daisy noticed a sign in the window of an antique dealer's which read, 'STREET WIDENING MEANS WE MUST MOVE – STOCK CLEARANCE SALE.'

There were similar announcements in several of the shops around here.

'We won't recognise the old place when they've finished knocking it about, will we?' remarked Daisy.

'I hope we still can.' Nora looked concerned. 'It could do with smartening up but I hope they don't change it beyond recognition when they do finally do it.'

' "When" being the operative word,' expressed Daisy, because the Notting Hill Gate road widening and redevelopment scheme had been on the cards for years. 'The council have been talking about it for long enough.'

'Have they really?' enquired June, who had met them outside Woolworth's.

'The idea goes back to the last century,' informed the knowledgeable Nora, who was a member of a local history society and took a keen interest in local affairs. 'But it wasn't finally approved until the nineteen thirties, then it had to be postponed because of the outbreak of war. The latest news I've heard is that it's definitely scheduled to go ahead in the next year or two.'

'I'll believe that when I see it,' was Daisy's opinion.

'I think most people feel like that about it,' said Nora.

They reached the ABC – proudly declaring itself to be 'London's Popular Caterers' on the awning outside – and settled down at a table in the cafeteria with their elevenses.

'Just think, Daisy, a little over a week ago you were living it up by the seaside,' mentioned June conversationally, spreading a small pat of butter on her currant bun and trying, unsuccessfully, to make it reach the edges.

'I wouldn't call what we did "living it up" exactly,' said Daisy, sipping her coffee. 'It was all simple pleasure. But, yes, we were enjoying ourselves, weren't we, girls?'

'Cor, yeah,' enthused Shirley.

'I wish we were still there,' sighed Belinda.

'Are you telling us that you'd rather be at the seaside with Mummy than here at home with your Auntie June and me?' teased Nora.

'I'd rather we were all at Gullscombe Bay seaside than here,' the child clarified. 'You and Auntie June too.'

'So would I,' said her sister.

'Maybe the three of you can go again next year as you liked it so much,' suggested June, winking at the girls, then looking meaningfully at Daisy.

'We'll see.' Daisy was noncommittal but she knew she wouldn't go again. It would be far too complicated.

June gave her a close look. 'You did enjoy yourself, didn't you, Daisy?'

'Yeah, of course I did. Why?'

'Because the girls haven't stopped talking about it since they got back,' June pointed out. 'But you've been noticeably quiet.'

'I've told you, I had a wonderful time.'

'You certainly look better for it, anyway,' approved Nora.

'Positively blooming,' agreed June. 'Back at work and ready to take the world on.'

'That's right,' confirmed Daisy.

'Why so quiet then?' persisted June.

'Probably an anticlimax,' suggested Nora.

'You got on all right with Jack, didn't you?' June was being persistent because she wanted to make sure there had been no problems with the holiday she'd arranged for her sister. 'And everything was all right with the accommodation?'

'Everything was perfect at the cottage, and Jack and I got on like a house on fire.' Daisy hadn't been able to stop thinking about him all week, his wide smile, his warm eyes. Anticlimax wasn't the word for how she'd felt this past week. Hell would be nearer to it, without Jack around. Knowing she'd made the right decision – or rather the only possible decision – didn't help much either.

Nat had picked up on her mood this past week. He'd accused her of being preoccupied and not paying enough attention to him, which he thought was a bit much as he'd agreed to her going away and had even shelled out some spending money. He hadn't seemed particularly pleased with the cigarette case she'd brought back for him either; he preferred to use fags straight from the packet, apparently. She'd been irritated by his ingratitude; had found herself comparing him to Jack. That was unfair and pointless, and would have to stop.

But now she found herself wondering what Jack would be doing at this moment. She looked at the big clock on the wall.

It was eleven o'clock. He wouldn't have gone to work yet so he might have gone for a swim or be tinkering with that motorbike of his. Whatever he was doing, she wished she was still there with him.

June recalled her to the present, waving her hand in front of Daisy's eyes. 'Penny for them,' she said.

'I was just wondering,' she fibbed – because what had happened between her and Jack was too precious and delicate to talk about at the moment, and the subject she was about to raise needed discussion anyway – 'if you've thought any more about that idea I mentioned to you about finding the Dodds? The one that Jack came up with?'

'Yes, I've thought about it.' June pondered for a moment. 'And although it's a bit of a long shot, I think we should do it. I don't know why we didn't think of it before.'

'Me neither.' Daisy turned to Nora. 'What do you think?'

'It's worth a try.'

'Good,' said Daisy. 'Let's have a proper discussion about it tonight when I get back from work.'

The two other women nodded in agreement.

'In the meantime, let's finish here and get the shopping home,' Daisy suggested. 'I'm on duty at four o'clock this afternoon to serve the teas so it would be useful to me if we could have our lunch a bit early, if that's all right with you.'

'Sure,' agreed June.

'Suits me,' added Nora.

They left the café soon after, chatting in a friendly manner. But Daisy wasn't paying attention to what was being said; her thoughts were lingering on a certain cottage by the sea.

Jack was thinking about Daisy at that time too. He was washing his hands at the kitchen sink after messing about with his motorbike when he noticed the laughing duck grinning at him from the windowsill.

He dried his hands and picked it up, remembering the moment he'd received it and feeling again the joy that had filled the house at that time. It brought Daisy so close to him he could hear her laugh, smell her hair, feel her skin. He put the ornament back on the windowsill, smiling despite the mood of melancholy that had settled over him since Daisy and the girls had left. He couldn't have Daisy and that broke his heart. But they'd had two wonderful weeks together and if that was all there was, it was better than nothing.

Grinning to himself as he recalled Daisy's disgust at his taste in ornaments, he made a cup of coffee and took it into the garden to read the newspaper in the sunshine until it was time to get ready for work.

One autumn morning in the back garden of a small house in a quiet Ruislip street, a thin, grey-haired woman wearing a floral apron over a dowdy grey jumper and skirt, was pegging the last of her washing on the line. She was hoping that her next-door neighbour – who was also in her garden doing the same thing – wouldn't try to engage her in conversation over the fence. It was a Monday morning so washing was flapping in the wind in rear gardens the length of the street.

Her hopes were dashed when the neighbour said, 'Good morning.'

'G'morning,' responded Eileen Dodd coolly.

'Looks like it's gonna be a good drying day,' commented the neighbour in a friendly manner.

'Mm.'

'And thank God for that too,' the woman went on. 'Nothing worse than a wet Monday, is there? Wet washing all over the place, making everything steamy and damp. It always gives me the right hump.'

'Yeah.' Eileen kept her eyes down; she never looked at anyone when she spoke to them.

'There won't be many more nice days now that the summer is over,' the neighbour went on.

'I suppose not.' Eileen was moving towards the kitchen door as she spoke, in her eagerness to avoid any further dialogue. 'Ta-ta for now.'

'Ta-ta dear,' said the neighbour. 'See you again.'

Indoors Eileen made a sandwich with cold meat from yesterday's joint for her lunch, poured herself a cup of tea and went into the living room to eat it, her hand trembling slightly from the fright she had just had at being forced into conversation. That was what she had come down to: she was so introverted that just a few words with a next-door neighbour left her nerves in tatters. Any sort of social intercourse was difficult for Eileen, who was in her fifties and hadn't a friend in the world. It was just her and her husband, Morris, against the rest of the world.

Though that wasn't strictly true, she thought, slowly eating her sandwich. Morris wasn't with her against the world. He had a life of his own outside the house. As a representative for a fancy goods company, he met lots of people in the course of his work; he enjoyed a drink and a chat at the local, too. A gregarious man like Morris was never short of company.

Eileen hadn't always been a recluse. Years ago she'd had a normal life in Wembley with a happy marriage – or so she'd thought – and a social life.

Her life had changed so suddenly it was hardly believable in retrospect. One minute they'd been living an ordinary life in a quiet suburban street, the next they were the talk of the neighbourhood, her husband implicated in a murder case and his betrayal of his wife made public property by the newspapers. Immediately after the trial, they'd fled to an area where they weren't known. Morris would have been quite happy to stay put but she hadn't been able to cope with the shame, the gossip, the humiliation.

She'd known nothing of her husband's adultery with Rose Rivers until after the murder. The devastation she'd felt then still sent shock waves through her whenever it came into her mind. Rose had been a neighbour and friend. Suddenly she was Morris's dead lover. The whole terrible business had torn the heart out of Eileen; she'd never got over it.

The scandal of being associated with a murder investigation had never appeared to worry Morris. He'd even seemed to enjoy the notoriety. 'I've done nothing to be ashamed of, Eileen, except for being unfaithful to you, and that's nothing to do with anyone else,' he would say to her as she became increasingly reclusive. 'Lionel Rivers killed his wife, not me, and he's doing time for it. So there's no need for either of us to hide away. Nobody around here knows about our past, anyway.'

It was as though he actually believed that neither of them had done anything wrong in lying under oath. He'd made a great performance of regret over the death of his lover and remorse at his adultery when giving evidence at Lionel Rivers' trial. After that he just carried on with his life as though nothing much had happened, as though having his wife commit perjury for him was no more than her duty.

At the time, he'd told her it would make things easier if she said he was at home with her when the murder had taken place. She was to tell the court that he'd come home early from the pub because he'd not been feeling well and had got home just after nine, having left the pub just before nine, as verified by the barman. He'd told her that he'd walked the streets for hours, after leaving the pub, working out how he was going to end his affair with Rose Rivers. But he couldn't prove where he'd been at that time and people might get the wrong idea. He was at pains to convince her that the only reason he'd asked her to say he'd been home at the earlier time instead of much later on, after she'd gone to bed, was not because he'd done the murder. Oh, no. It was just to prevent the police putting two and two together and making five.

In retrospect, she could see that she'd been extremely gullible to have believed him, and she didn't think she ever had, not in her heart. But telling herself what he said was true had been more acceptable than the alternative. It was hardly bearable for a woman to suspect that she was married to a murderer. As well as the horror, fear and revulsion, there were practical considerations. She was reliant on him to provide for her. If he'd gone to prison, her life would have been ruined as well as his because she would have had no means of support. Only the poorest or most exceptional married women had gone out to work back in those days before the war.

So she'd complied with his wishes, telling herself she was merely preventing complications and not protecting a murderer. Once the lies had been uttered in court, there had been no going back. She'd never forget the sheer terror of knowing that she had committed a criminal offence. She'd tried to blot out her crime and get on with life in an area where no one knew them. But compunction and fear had plagued her constantly, making her bitter and depressed. The Dodds' home had become a battleground for its occupants.

Then one night during an argument, Morris had confessed to the murder in a fit of temper. He'd even boasted about it. Even though he'd let it slip in a moment of reckless rage, he'd not been too concerned because he'd known his secret was safe with her. As he'd taken great pains to point out, she had too much to lose to open her mouth. If she went to the police she'd go down with a prison sentence for perjury.

So she'd remained silent, the past standing between them, a chilling and tangible presence. They coexisted with cold indifference and occasional violent arguments. She'd grown to hate him more with every passing day, loathing him for his arrogance, his unfaithfulness, his cruelty and cowardice in letting someone else pay the price for his crime. They slept in separate bedrooms and any sort of physical contact between them was carefully avoided apart from when he lost his temper and knocked her about. She guessed he made other arrangements in the sexual department. That didn't bother her. After the terrible things he'd done, continued adultery was nothing.

The only thing that kept them together was mutual fear. She was afraid of life without him as breadwinner; he feared she might put them both in jail if he wasn't on hand to remind her of the serious consequences for herself should she get tempted to unburden her guilty conscience.

Self-loathing for her weakness had made her withdraw into herself. Even when she was forced to work during the war, she'd not mixed with her workmates at the factory. The people around here knew nothing of her past but she still felt set apart from them, whilst at the same time longing for friendship. Her only outings were to the local shops, an occasional visit to the doctor and dentist and a rare trip to a hairdresser's for a perm. If she happened to meet a neighbour she couldn't avoid while she was out, she greeted them briefly then escaped into the security of her home. Fortunately, in this quiet suburban neighbourhood, people tended to keep to themselves anyway. The loneliness was terrible, though. It nagged away at her like a physical pain day after day.

But now she finished her lunch and picked up the newspaper, which they had delivered every day because Morris liked to read it in the evening. She always looked through it; it helped pass the time in her isolation.

Some film star called James Dean had been killed in a car crash at the age of just twenty-four, she noted. She'd read about him in the paper but not seen any of his films because she never went to the cinema. There was also an article about the new television programme called *Double Your Money* with Hughie Green. That was something she did have experience of, because Morris had done so well with sales recently, he'd bought a television set for the opening of commercial television, a week or so ago.

She flicked through the rest of the paper absently, thinking she must get on and wash the dishes, then give the kitchen a thoroughly good clean prior to the washing being dry enough to iron. Very much a slave to routine, she hated to deviate from her daily pattern. She was about to put the paper down on the coffee table ready for Morris to look at tonight, when something towards the back, in the personal column, leaped out at her. She blinked, thinking she must have imagined it. She stared hard at the print again, finding it difficult to focus because her hands were shaking so much.

'Would Eileen Dodd, last heard of at number three Laverstock Avenue, Wembley, in the 1930s please get in touch with Box No. 3350.'

Her initial reaction was a feeling of hope for escape from the prison she was in. One of her old friends from Wembley must want to get in touch with her for a reunion. It must be that. Who else would be trying to contact her? Warmth spread through her. How good it felt to have someone seeking her company, someone she'd have something in common with because she'd known them when her life had been normal. She'd had some good friends in Wembley at one time. But she hadn't been able to face them after what had happened so had cut herself off from them. When she and Morris had left the area they hadn't said goodbye to anyone or left a forwarding address.

But now someone was looking for her. On the heels of joy came disappointment. She couldn't respond to this. Anyone

309

she knew from Wembley would know about her past. They didn't know the whole truth, of course, but they knew about Morris's public betrayal of her. She would be a laughing stock all over again and she simply couldn't face it.

But she looked longingly at the advertisement. Here was a chance to have company after all these years in the wilderness. To visit friends for tea, to go shopping with someone, all the ordinary everyday things other women took for granted. She stared at the words through a blur of tears as she accepted that she couldn't reply to it.

As a precaution, she carefully tore the advertisement out of the paper. If Morris spotted it he would force her to reply to it to see if there was anything of a financial nature in it for them, as was often the case when someone was being traced in this way. He would humiliate her all over again. She then screwed the piece of paper up and stuffed it in her apron pocket, collected her cup and plate and went to the kitchen to wash them.

'It doesn't look as though our plan is going to bear fruit, does it?' said Daisy gloomily, over a cup of bedtime cocoa one night in mid-October.

'It doesn't seem too hopeful,' agreed her sister, who was sitting on the sofa in her dressing gown with her legs curled under her. 'It's been two weeks since the advertisement went into the paper. If she was going to take the bait she'd have done so by now.'

'Not necessarily,' disagreed Nora. 'She could be busy and still trying to find the time to get down to writing a letter. For all we know she might be out at work all day.'

'That's true,' said Daisy. 'We have no idea what her circumstances are. Or even if she's alive.'

'Maybe she smelled a rat,' suggested June. 'Or her husband saw the advertisement and he did. It could be that they're staying well clear, to be on the safe side.'

'I honestly don't think it's that,' was Daisy's opinion. 'As we agreed when we decided to give this a try, they wouldn't connect a notice in the personal column of a national newspaper with the murder. They'd think in terms of the police if anything had arisen about that. Anyway, it's such a long while ago she wouldn't expect anything to happen about it after all this time.'

'She'll think it's a friend or relative she's lost touch with, as we planned,' said Nora. 'That's the sort of thing personal columns are made up of. Unless, of course, they think someone's left them some money.'

'In which case they definitely would have got in touch,' reasoned Daisy.

'Maybe she just didn't see it,' was another idea of Nora's. 'It could be that she doesn't read that particular paper. I think if she did see it, she couldn't help but be intrigued. I mean, you would be, wouldn't you? That's just natural human curiosity.'

'Perhaps the second entry will bring us a result,' suggested Daisy hopefully. 'We got cheap rates for having it in twice so it isn't as if it cost us all that much more.'

'If it doesn't work we could think in terms of trying another one of the nationals,' said June.

There was a murmur of agreement from the others.

'It's going in on Friday this time instead of Monday,' mused Nora. 'Being a different day of the week might help. Some people have days when they don't have time to look at the paper and other days when they do.'

'Fingers crossed for Friday then,' said June.

'And in the meantime,' yawned Daisy, finishing her cocoa and standing up, 'my bed is calling.'

The others were of similar opinions so they took their cups into the kitchen, turned off the lights and went upstairs to bed.

★ ★ ★

June couldn't sleep but it wasn't thoughts of finding the Dodds that were keeping her awake. It was Alan. Every time she closed her eyes she could see his face, his warm eyes, his tender smile. The images just wouldn't go away. She wondered if she would ever stop missing him. Even now, more than a year since she'd left, she still wasn't over him.

Inevitably he would find someone else. Indeed, that was why she'd left, so that he could have a chance of a normal family life with a 'proper' woman. Maybe he was already seeing someone. She wouldn't blame him. The thought hurt even though she knew she was being unreasonable. Weary of tossing and turning, she got out of bed and made her way quietly downstairs, careful not to disturb anyone. She was in the kitchen waiting for the kettle to boil when her sister appeared.

'Another one who's tired of counting sheep, eh?' June surmised.

'That's right.'

'What's keeping you from your beauty sleep then?'

'Nothing in particular,' fibbed Daisy, because if she were to tell June the truth – that she'd been kept awake tonight and many other nights since her holiday by thoughts of Jack, whose marriage proposal she had turned down because she'd been afraid to let go of the past and move into a new, unfamiliar world – June would erupt into a fury of disapproval. Daisy had enough trouble coping with the decision herself; the last thing she needed was an argument about it. 'How about you?'

'I don't know what it is,' lied June, because she was dangerously close to confiding in her sister about the series of events that had led to her decision to leave Alan. She wanted to tell her everything she'd kept locked inside her for so many years. But to share the hideous secrets of her past in a weak moment would make her feel vulnerable and she knew she would regret it.

'Tea is supposed to keep you awake,' mentioned Daisy. 'But I'm going to have one anyway.'

'I'll risk it too,' said June.

They drank their tea at the kitchen table in a comfortable silence, each lost on her own thoughts. Then they made their way back upstairs to bed.

Alan was awake too that night, thinking first about June, then wondering what to do about Paula, whom he'd been seeing with increasing regularity since the late summer.

He cast his mind back to the previous evening. He and Paula had been out to a restaurant and he'd driven her home afterwards to the smart block of flats overlooking the sea where she lived. They'd sat in his car talking about business, as they so often did, and discussing the pros and cons of living on the job, which she preferred not to do. Although the conversation hadn't been of an intimate nature, he'd felt a change in the air and sensed that they'd been just a hair's breadth away from becoming lovers.

She'd invited him in for coffee. He'd wanted to accept but had politely declined because he'd known what would happen if he had, and wasn't sure if he wanted all the emotional upheaval that a change from friends to lovers would entail. He wasn't in love with Paula but he liked and respected her far too much to have an affair with her without commitment.

They were both on their own. He was lonely and so, he suspected, was she. His wife didn't want him. From the signals Paula was giving out lately she obviously wouldn't be adverse to a change in their relationship. So why not?

Looking at the question logically, he could see that Paula was the way forward for him. They would be good for each other. June wasn't going to change her mind, and he couldn't avoid a serious attachment for the rest of his life just because his marriage had failed.

One thing he did know for sure: he and Paula could no longer be just friends. It wouldn't work that way now that another element had made itself known. He sighed, sensing a certain inevitability about the situation.

'Oh no, not again,' complained Morris Dodd, staring through a large hole in the newspaper he was reading. 'I wish you wouldn't keep tearing great lumps out of the paper before I've had a chance to look at it, Eileen.'

'I didn't think it would matter as there was nothing of interest on the other side,' she told him. 'It was only an advert for cough mixture. I did check.'

'That isn't the point,' he grumbled. 'It makes the paper in such a mess and you know how I hate that.'

'Sorry.'

'It isn't as if it's the first time you've done it lately,' he went on irritably.

'I've said I'm sorry.'

'What was so important you had to tear it out, anyway?' he demanded.

'A recipe,' she lied.

'Oh really. Surely you could have left the paper intact until after I'd read it,' he admonished sternly. 'You could have torn your bloody stupid recipe out any time.'

'I can't see that it matters as there was nothing you'd want to see on the other side.'

'Well, it does matter to me,' he growled. 'You can do what you like with the bloody paper when I've looked at it but until then show a bit of respect, will you? As I pay the newsagent's bill I think I'm entitled to that much.'

'All right, there's no need to go on about it.'

He scowled at her, grunted and went back to the paper

while Eileen stared absently at the wooden box in the corner. There was a serious play on the television and Morris didn't enjoy drama, apart from *Dixon of Dock Green*. Although the television set was still something of a novelty, Morris was selective in his viewing. He didn't like anything more demanding than sport, light comedy and variety shows.

Something seemed to have attracted his attention now, though, and he put the paper on his lap and stared at the screen. Eileen found herself observing him and thinking that he could still be considered an attractive man even though he was now in his fifties, and despite the fact that his dark hair was thinning and his figure gargantuan from his greedy appetite for food. He'd never been good-looking in the traditional sense – his dark eyes were too small, his nose too long. It was his personality that attracted women. He had a magnetism about him that was still very much in evidence, she guessed, even though it did nothing for her.

Eileen was having trouble concentrating on the television screen tonight, on account of what had really been on the bit she'd torn out of Morris's newspaper. Whoever it was who was looking for her must be serious about finding her to have put the notice in the paper again. Advertising in a national newspaper wasn't cheap. As well as being intriguing it was also rather worrying because if they put it in again and she missed it for some reason, Morris would spot it and take the matter out of her hands. The thought made her stomach churn.

But now he was bored with both the paper and the television apparently. 'I'm going out, down the pub,' he announced, getting up purposefully.

There was nothing new in that. It was Friday night and he always went out on Fridays. Whether he really went to the pub or had something of a more intimate nature lined up, she neither knew nor cared.

'All right,' she said indifferently.

'Don't wait up.'

'I won't.'

After the front door had closed behind him, she stayed where she was for a while, lost in thought. Eventually, she got up, went over to the sideboard and picked up her handbag. Hesitating for only a moment, she opened it and took out the crumpled piece of newspaper she'd removed earlier today and looked at it for a long time. Then, with her heart palpitating fit to burst, she took a writing pad out of the drawer, sat down at the table and began to write a letter, her hand trembling with a mixture of nervous apprehension and excitement.

Chapter Fourteen

Answering a knock at the front door one morning a week or so later, Eileen was confronted by two young women smiling at her on the doorstep.

'Yes?' she greeted in a cool, questioning manner.

'Good morning,' smiled the smarter of the two, who was tall, dark and slim, and carrying a small, brown attaché case.

'What do you want?' tutted Eileen, who wasn't about to indulge in doorstep small talk.

'We represent the Smithsons Vacuum Cleaner Company and we're in this area to tell people about the launch of our revolutionary new machine—'

'No thank you,' Eileen interrupted sharply. 'I already have a very good vacuum cleaner and I don't want another one.'

'But ours is no ordinary cleaner—'

'I never buy anything at the door.'

'And we don't sell at the door,' said the other woman, who was a tiny little thing, a bit on the shabby side, with big eyes and a shock of brown wind-blown hair.

'Why are you here then?'

The little woman moved closer to the door, which Eileen was about to close. 'Just for an informal chat.' She spread her hands. 'As you can see we have no cleaner with us to sell to you.'

'I don't care what sales pitch you're using,' the astute

Eileen made clear. 'I said no and I mean it.'

'Would we be right in thinking that the man of the house isn't home at this time of the day?' the dark woman enquired.

'Of course he isn't at home,' was Eileen's sharp retort. 'He's out earning his living, like any other responsible man.'

'That's why we call on people during the day, initially. We like to speak to the lady of the house about our product,' said the little woman, her manner becoming chummy. 'As women, we all know that men haven't a clue about how housework is done so we prefer to speak to the people who actually do the job. A sensible idea, don't you think, Mrs, er . . .'

'Dodd,' she said without thinking. 'And yes, it is a good idea but I'm still not going to buy a cleaner.'

'Look, I'll be straight with you.' The small woman moved her head forward and spoke to Eileen in a confiding manner. 'My colleague and I have to do a certain amount of preliminary presentations in the course of a working day, or we're in deep trouble back at the office. So . . .' she paused, smiling persuasively, 'I wonder if you could do us a favour and give us a few minutes of your time just so that we can put you down on our list of definite visits and stay sweet with the management.'

Eileen gave them full marks for persistence. She'd been married to a salesman for long enough to know that without tenacity you got nowhere in the job. Morris didn't sell door to door but the same principle applied to any form of selling. 'I'm too busy,' she said firmly. 'I'm sorry.'

'Ten minutes maximum,' the dark-haired woman requested insistently. 'Just let us come in to show you a few brochures, tell you how this new concept in cleaners works. Just so that we can put you down on our activity report for today.'

'And talk me into buying one of your cleaners at the same time,' was Eileen's cynical response.

'No, not at all,' denied the little one, who had a very pretty

318

smile Eileen couldn't help noticing. 'Honestly, that isn't what we have in mind.'

'My husband has all the spending power in this house anyway, so you'd be on to a loser.'

'The men usually do,' the small woman agreed in an understanding manner. 'They earn the money so they say how it's going to be spent – that's the way it seems to work in most of the homes that we visit, anyway. So our policy is to tell the lady of the house about the cleaner and if they like what we have to say and are interested in seeing the cleaner, we come back in the evening when the husband is at home to do a demonstration for them both. In your case, of course, that won't happen because you've told us that you definitely don't want to buy one, and we respect that. So we'll just run through some brochures with you, fill in our time sheet and be on our way.'

'There wouldn't be any point in your coming back at another time with the cleaner because my husband won't buy from anyone selling door to door, anyway,' Eileen stated.

'That's perfectly understandable,' said the dark woman in a matey tone. 'Some of the door-to-door salespeople around give the rest of us a bad name by talking people into buying all sorts of rubbish. But we're not like that. Oh no. And in your case, all we want is your co-operation in keeping the boss off our backs. Just the chance to go through our brochures with you. You've nothing to lose except ten minutes of your time.'

Eileen looked from one to the other; she was beginning to weaken under the influence of their friendly enthusiasm. It was a refreshing change to have females selling at the door. Most of those working on the knocker were men who wouldn't take no for an answer until she slammed the door in their faces.

These two were persistent but nice with it, somehow. She

thought of the lonely day ahead of her with not a soul to talk to. What harm could there be in letting them in for a few minutes to show her some brochures and tell her about their product? At least it would be human contact, and she'd made it clear that she wasn't going to buy from them.

'Ten minutes then,' she said, opening the door wider to let them in. 'When your time's up, you're out. Understand?'

'We understand,' said the small woman.

'Come on then, let's have a look at your brochures,' requested Eileen when she'd shown the two sales reps into the living room and offered them a seat.

The dark women opened her attaché case to reveal that it was empty. 'We don't have any brochures,' she said, turning the case upside down and shaking it to illustrate her point, her attitude now deadly serious.

'No brochures?' Eileen looked puzzled and somewhat annoyed. 'Why bother to talk me into letting you in then? How can you sell your cleaner without the product itself, or any sales literature?'

'We're not here to sell you a vacuum cleaner, Mrs Dodd,' said the little one.

'No?' Eileen was baffled. 'Then why—'

'We're here about this,' the dark woman told her, handing Eileen a newspaper cutting.

Eileen stared at it for a moment. 'You?' she said, looking from one to the other. 'You put that in the paper?'

'That's right,' the little one confirmed.

She gave them both a studious look, searching for some sort of recognition. 'I don't know you, so what was the advertisement all about?'

'We needed to find you urgently,' explained the dark-haired one. 'And now we have, thanks to your putting your address on your letter.'

320

'So it was all a trick to get into my house.' Eileen looked frightened now.

'Afraid so,' confirmed Daisy. Had they just knocked at her door and told her who they were, it would have been immediately slammed in their faces, which was why the rather elaborate subterfuge had been necessary.

'Who are you?' she demanded, her grey eyes darting from one to the other. 'What do you want with me?'

'I'm Daisy Rivers and this is my sister, June.'

Eileen's eyes popped. Her face flushed momentarily, then became bloodless. She sat down heavily on the sofa as though her legs had buckled beneath her. 'Rose Rivers's daughters,' she gasped, her hand flying to her head. 'I would never have known you.'

'Well, you wouldn't do, would you?' June pointed out. 'Being that we were just little kids when you last saw us.'

'What,' Eileen began in a dry anxious voice, 'do you want with me after all this time?'

'Justice,' announced Daisy.

'Justice?' Eileen echoed fearfully, her eyes clouded with worry.

'That's right,' confirmed June. 'Our father has been in prison for over twenty years for the murder of our mother because you lied under oath to give your husband an alibi. And we intend to see to it that you put things right.'

The older woman sprang to her feet. She was visibly trembling. 'Get out,' she ordered in a quivering voice. 'Get out of my house this minute, before I call the police.'

Daisy gave her a hard look. 'We're not going anywhere until you've heard what we have to say,' she told her in a commanding tone. 'So sit down.'

'How dare you tell me what to do in my own house?'

'Sit down,' repeated Daisy.

'I could have you done for slander, saying I lied under

321

'oath,' protested Eileen weakly.

'You won't, though, will you? Because you know what we're saying is true.'

'I didn't do it,' Eileen insisted, sinking down on the sofa. 'I don't know what's made you think I did.'

'We don't just *think* you lied,' June amended evenly, 'we *know* you did.'

'Don't be ridiculous, you can't do.'

'We know that you were lying about your husband being at home with you at the time of our mother's murder because he was at the house where we lived,' Daisy informed her. 'And we know that because we saw him there.'

'Rubbish.'

'He saw us too,' June enlightened her. 'He threatened us with terrible things if we told anyone we'd seen him.'

From the look of sheer horror on Eileen's face it was obvious that Morris had told her nothing of his encounter with them that terrible night.

'He didn't tell you anything about that, did he?' surmised June.

'There was nothing to tell me,' she bluffed. 'Because he wasn't at that house that night. As I told the court at the trial, he was at home with me.'

'Look,' began Daisy, stepping forward and looking down at her, 'all three of us know that isn't true so let's stop messing about.'

'Get out,' ordered Eileen again.

'It was your husband who murdered our mother and you damned well know it,' persisted Daisy. 'And it's time that terrible wrong was put right.'

'You've been imagining things,' claimed Eileen. 'You were just children back then. You couldn't possibly remember something that happened then, not after all this time.'

'We couldn't forget a thing like that,' June told her. 'Your husband put the fear of God into us in his anxiety to make sure we didn't spill the beans about his being there. We were too young to be questioned anyway so he was safe. As children we were powerless and no threat to him even though he was worried enough to terrorise us into keeping quiet. He made one fatal mistake, though. He didn't take into account the fact that one day we would grow up to be adults, and we would remember, and understand.'

'Childhood fantasies, nothing more,' Eileen taunted, becoming braver as she considered the flimsiness of their evidence. 'No one would believe a story like that.'

'Why did you commit perjury for such a man?' Daisy wanted to know. 'A man who had been unfaithful to you and humiliated you publicly, a man who killed his lover in a fit of rage. Was it because you were afraid of what he'd do to you if they didn't send him down for murder, was that it?'

'Or were you afraid of losing your breadwinner and your comfortable life?' added June.

The older woman didn't reply; she just sat there staring at her hands.

'If you were to make a confession to the police about what you've done and make it clear that your husband put pressure on you to lie for him, the courts might be lenient with you,' suggested Daisy hopefully.

Eileen clasped her head as though in pain. 'Stop it, stop saying these terrible things,' came her anguished cry. 'You tricked your way into my home and now you're behaving in a threatening manner. I could have the law on you.'

'You won't, though.' Daisy was confident about that. 'Because you wouldn't want to draw attention to yourself. You had enough of that in the past, when you lived in Wembley.'

'You've got nothing on me and my husband,' Eileen insisted, composing herself, 'so get out of my house.'

'We'll go,' complied Daisy. 'But just one thought before we leave, Mrs Dodd. For all these years you've thought you'd got away with what you've done, believing it was just a matter between you and your conscience, that no one else knew. But you won't be able to rest easy any longer because you know that we know the truth, and one way or another we'll see that justice is done. You could make things easier for yourself by telling the police the truth because it's going to come out anyway, I promise you.'

'You're talking rubbish,' Eileen blustered. 'No one would take you seriously if you were to come out with your outlandish story.' She narrowed her eyes on Daisy. 'And you know that. Otherwise you'd have gone to the police already.'

She was right, of course, but Daisy wasn't going to admit it. 'What does it feel like to live with a murderer, knowing that you helped to put an innocent man behind bars, and robbed two little girls of their father?' she asked.

'I don't know what that feels like because I haven't experienced it.' Eileen was adamant. 'And if you stay here all day you won't get me to say different, so you might as well sling your hook.'

'We're going,' Daisy told her, moving towards the living-room door. 'But you haven't seen the last of us or heard the last of this matter, believe me.'

'We'll be back,' added June.

And they walked to the front door and let themselves out, leaving Eileen sitting on the sofa.

'You're bound to be disappointed that nothing more constructive came out of it,' said Nora that evening when, over cocoa, the three of them were doing a post-mortem on the incident. 'But we all knew she wouldn't admit to anything right away, didn't we? It was unrealistic to think that she would. It'll take time.'

'I suppose so, but it's such an anticlimax,' complained Daisy. 'I thought we were home and dry when we found out where the Dodds lived. But we're no further forward. Unless she admits she was lying we don't have a case. We got her rattled and we can do so again and again, but we can't make her confess.'

'What should our next move be, do you think?' wondered June.

'I honestly don't know,' confessed Daisy. 'It needs more thought. The one thing we mustn't do is give up now we've come this far.' She looked at June. 'Do you agree?'

'Absolutely.'

Daisy burst out laughing as she remembered something. 'I wonder what our chances are as vacuum cleaner sales reps,' she giggled.

'As you managed to get through the door without so much as a brochure between you, or a cleaner to demonstrate, you must have had some sort of a flair,' smiled Nora.

'We were pretty convincing,' boasted Daisy.

'All that stuff you gave her about us being in trouble at the office if she didn't let us in to do a presentation was nothing short of genius,' grinned June. 'I almost believed it myself.'

'I had to think on my feet when she seemed determined not to let us in.'

'It was brilliant,' complimented June.

Daisy's mood became grim again. 'Seriously, though, we have to think of a way to finish the job we've started. Now that we've come this close and found Eileen Dodd, there must be a way to get her to admit the truth.'

The other two women nodded in agreement but none of them knew the answer.

Nat came to the house late one night a few days later. He said he just happened to be passing and had called in to see Daisy.

'She isn't home from work yet,' June told him at the door.

'I'll come in and wait then,' he took it on himself to announce. 'She shouldn't be long.'

'Why don't you go and meet her?' suggested June, who didn't feel comfortable with him in the house after that disgusting incident in the summer when Daisy had been away on holiday. It hadn't been mentioned but she could tell by the way he looked at her sometimes that he hadn't forgiven her for rejecting him. 'She can't be further than the end of the street and she'll be thrilled to have you walk the rest of the way home with her.'

'Nah. It isn't worth it,' he said. 'She'll be here in a minute.'

Not wishing to be found quarrelling with him by her sister, June invited him in with reluctance, offered him a seat in the living room, and made herself scarce in the kitchen so that she didn't have to be alone with him. Nora was upstairs getting ready for bed and would probably come down in her dressing gown for a cup of cocoa later when Daisy got in.

June used the time to wash some cups from earlier and tidy the kitchen. She was drying her hands at the sink when the door opened and Nat swaggered in with a purposeful air.

'You after a cup of tea?' she asked. 'I thought you'd wait and have one with Daisy.'

'I don't want a cuppa tea.'

As his manner suggested that he'd come into the kitchen for some definite purpose, she said, 'What do you want then?'

'Isn't it obvious?'

'Not to me, no.'

'Surely you didn't think I'd forgotten what happened between us in the summer.'

'Nothing happened.'

'Exactly,' he said, coming towards her with a horrible smile on his face. 'And I aim to change that.'

'Daisy will be in any minute, so don't try anything.' She tried to sound firm but her voice was shaking.

'I'm not worried about Daisy.'

There was something very stage-managed about the way he was behaving that June found disconcerting.

'You touch me and I'll scream for Nora,' she warned. 'I mean it, so don't come any closer.'

But he moved so swiftly she didn't have a chance to do anything as he pushed her backwards against the sink, pressing his body against hers and clamping his hand over her mouth. Her heart sank as she distantly heard the sound of the front door opening and closing and Daisy's cheerful voice calling out, 'Hello, you lot, I'm home.'

June struggled but the element of surprise and his physical strength meant she didn't stand a chance. He dragged her arms around his neck and put his face to hers for a few horrible seconds, the smell of his sweat and stale cigarette smoke making her nauseous. She heard the kitchen door open and almost immediately he sprang away from her.

'Daisy,' he said, as though shocked to see her. 'Thank God you're back. She's been coming on to me for months . . . just wouldn't take no for an answer. Perhaps she'll stop now you've caught her at it.'

'Don't listen to him,' said June, observing with dismay the horror in her sister's eyes. 'He's lying because he wants to come between you and me. He knew you'd be home from work at any minute and he set this whole thing up.'

June reeled at the disgust exuding from Daisy as she looked from one to the other, then back at June, her eyes narrowed. 'Don't try and make any more of a fool of me than you already have,' she said to her sister icily.

'Daisy, no, it isn't what you think.'

'You're nothing but a tart, a filthy, rotten tart. I don't know why I ever trusted you.'

'It was him, please believe me . . .' June could feel her truthful words distorted to sound like lies by the damning appearance of the situation. 'He tried it on with me while you were away in Devon and he's done this to get back at me for turning him down then. He isn't interested in me. He just wants to hurt me by turning you against me.'

'I know now why you've never had a good word to say for him,' Daisy went on through gritted teeth. 'You wanted him for yourself so you tried to turn me against him and break us up, you scheming cow.'

'That just isn't true.' June's voice was ragged with emotion. 'Can't you see what he's up to?'

'I can see what's been going on under my nose. That was made very clear to me as soon as I opened this door.' She turned to Nat, who was looking triumphant. 'And as for you, I don't suppose you put up much of a fight against her. So get out of my sight. I never want to see you again.'

'What on earth's going on here?' asked Nora, appearing in her red dressing gown. 'You'll wake the children up in a minute with all this shouting.'

'Did you know about it?' asked Daisy.

'Know about what?'

'That these two have been at it like rabbits every time my back is turned,' she explained.

'Daisy, what are you saying?' was Nora's shocked response.

'You obviously didn't know. Well, they've been having an affair behind my back.'

'No!' gasped Nora.

'Yes. It's true, and I've just caught them at it.' She looked from Nat to June, her eyes full of hurt. 'You're welcome to each other and I want nothing more to do with either of you,' she said, and fled from the room.

★　★　★

Daisy sat on the edge of her bed, staring dismally at the floor. A grinding pain in the pit of her stomach was dragging her down, and she wasn't sure which hurt the most, Nat's betrayal or June's. She decided it was definitely the latter. She remembered that she herself has almost succumbed to temptation with Jack in the summer and knew how easily these things could happen. Nat had been unable to resist June's advances in the same way as Daisy had almost yielded to her passion for Jack.

Nobody was immune to this sort of thing. What cut so deep with Daisy was June's deceit in pretending to disapprove of Nat and trying to turn Daisy against him when all the time she fancied the pants off him herself.

There was a tap on the bedroom door.

'Go away.'

June came in anyway and stood tentatively just beside the closed door. 'I swear to God, Daisy, that it wasn't the way it seemed down there tonight,' she told her.

Her sister shrugged.

'Nat doesn't want me any more than I want him,' June went on to say, keeping her voice low because the girls were asleep in the next room. 'He hates the sight of me and I wouldn't have him if he came with the crown jewels as part of the package.'

'That's why you had your arms wrapped around him, is it?' said Daisy, looking up. 'God knows what I'd have seen if I'd been a few minutes later.'

'It was all a put-up job, can't you see that?' June tried to convince her. 'This is his revenge on me for turning him down in the summer, and he only came on to me then to try and make a fool of me.'

'Don't make things worse by telling me a pack of lies.'

'I am not lying,' June told her. 'He knew exactly what time you'd be in from work tonight, and that you'd go straight to the kitchen if there was no one in the living room. You can't deny that's true. He came in and grabbed hold of me just seconds before you walked in so that you would see what he wanted you to see. He's trying to break us up, Daisy.'

'I know he isn't perfect but he isn't devious enough to come up with such a plan.'

'He is, Daisy, believe me.'

Daisy didn't respond; she sat staring at her feet, leaning forward slightly, her hands resting on her knees. 'I was so happy when you came back into my life, June,' she said sadly. 'After all those years, it was a dream come true for us to be together. The only thing that spoiled it was your disapproval of Nat, and you and I agreed to differ about that.' She looked up, her huge eyes heavy with disappointment. 'I'm not glamorous or sophisticated like you. There's only ever been one man in my life.' She paused, forced by her honest nature to correct this. 'Well, two actually. I got pretty close to Jack Saunders back in the summer.'

'Oh, really?' gasped June.

'You might find this hard to believe, but Jack asked me to marry him,' Daisy continued.

'Why on earth would I find that hard to believe?' June asked in astonishment.

'Because I'm not beautiful or refined.'

'Don't put yourself down,' admonished June angrily. 'You're very beautiful in a way that doesn't need make-up or smart clothes, as I do, and your manners are fine. This is what Nat's done to you. He's destroyed your sense of self-worth.'

'Maybe he has, I don't know. Anyway, that isn't the issue,' she went on. 'I was very tempted by Jack's offer, I admit. He's a really gorgeous bloke and I think the world of him. But in the end I chose the father of my children, the man I've been with for so long and who I believe does actually love me, despite what you think of him. And you have to wreck that for me.'

'Daisy, about tonight—'

'I feel sick to my stomach,' Daisy went on as though June hadn't spoken. 'To think that my sister, my own flesh and blood, could try to steal him from me.'

'I didn't—'

'Just leave it, will you?' Daisy cut in, putting her hands to her head wearily. 'I don't want to talk about it any more except to say that me and the girls will be moving out of here as soon as I can find somewhere else.'

'Oh, Daisy, no, you can't . . .'

'Surely you can see that I can't stay here now,' Daisy told her. 'I don't want to share a roof with someone I can't trust.'

'You've got it all wrong.'

'Can you go now, please?' Daisy requested. 'Tell Nora I won't be down for cocoa tonight.'

Knowing it was useless to argue, a very dejected June left the room.

'You can cut the atmosphere in our place with a knife, the way those daughters of yours are carrying on, and I'm stuck in the middle of it,' Nora told Lionel, a week or so later. 'I think I'd be more comfortable sharing a cell with you than I am at home at the moment.'

He grinned. He enjoyed Nora's company and had grown to look forward to her visits. 'I very much doubt that. But what's the trouble at your place, then?'

She gave him a brief outline of what had happened. 'They're only speaking to each other when it can't be avoided and being polite in front of the children. It's breaking my heart to see them destroying something that means so much to them both. Finding each other after all those years apart was a gift. And now they're like two cats, wanting to scratch

331

each other's eyes out the whole time.' She shook her head worriedly. 'Daisy's even looking for somewhere else to live.'

'Oh dear.' Lionel could see how concerned she was. 'Which one of them do you think is to blame?'

'Certainly not June. Daisy's being stubborn but it isn't really her fault either. Nat's the culprit here,' she had no hesitation in telling him. 'He obviously set the whole thing up, as June said, to break the sisters up. He's jealous of Daisy's relationship with June. June wouldn't be interested in him if he was the last man on earth. Neither she nor I can stand the sight of him. But Daisy can't see that. She's got a blind spot where he's concerned.'

'Have you tried talking to her?'

'I certainly have,' she told him. 'And she just accuses me of taking June's side because she knows I don't like Nat either. He's just using her and she can't see it – doesn't want to see it. I tell you, Lionel, it's given me no end of grief over the years, watching the way that man treats your daughter.'

'Daisy always strikes me as such a sensible sort of a girl too, not the type to be easily taken in,' he mentioned.

'Her feelings for Nat cut across her intellect, I think,' Nora explained. 'In every other area of her life she's full of common sense and she certainly doesn't let people trample on her. She's tough and independent, and has her eyes wide open about everything except this awful man she's got herself involved with.'

'I only wish I was in a position to do something to help.' He stroked his chin, looking worried. 'But I'm helpless being stuck in here . . .'

'You wouldn't be able to help even if you weren't stuck in here,' she pointed out. 'No one can help them on this one. The girls have to sort it out for themselves. And unless Daisy faces up to what Nat is really like, I can't see it having a happy conclusion. And as she hasn't been able to see the truth about him after all these years, it isn't very likely to happen now.'

'What a shame.'

'It's an absolute tragedy.' Seeing how concerned he was she wondered if she'd done the right thing in telling him. 'Maybe I shouldn't have burdened you with it.'

'Don't be daft. I want news of my family, the bad as well as the good,' he assured her. 'I want to feel involved, even though I can't actually be there to help.'

Nora looked at him and saw hardship written all over that lined and craggy countenance. She so much wanted him to enjoy the pleasures of freedom again, to go out for a walk and feel the sun on his face. How good it would be if the girls were able to make this possible for him. They'd asked Nora not to tell him that they'd located the Dodds, partly because they didn't want to raise his hopes too high at this stage and also because he'd been so wary of them getting involved with Morris Dodd, it might worry him.

Anyway, with the girls being at loggerheads, Nora didn't know what would happen about their plans to help their father, except that they would continue, somehow, bad friends or not.

'You want to know about your family – I'll tell you what your granddaughters have been up to, then, shall I?' she suggested to cheer him up.

'Yes, please,' he said eagerly.

Ever since her falling out with June, Daisy had been studiously polite to her and very careful not to be rude to her in front of the children. So she was shocked to hear what Shirley had to say one morning at breakfast.

'Why are you and Auntie June always cross with each other now, Mummy?' she asked.

'What makes you think we're cross with each other?'

'You look cross and you don't seem to like each other much now,' she replied.

'We like each other,' said Daisy, exchanging a glance with her sister. 'Don't we, June?'

'Yes. Course we do.'

'Why are you being so horrid to one another then?' the child wanted to know.

'None of your business,' Daisy told her quickly. 'Now finish your breakfast, both of you. It's nearly time to go to school.'

'You're not supposed to be mean to people.' Shirley was determined to have her say. 'That's what you always tell me and Belinda when we have an argument. And that's what the nuns tell us at Sunday school.'

'Yeah, they do,' was Belinda's predictable contribution.

'Stop yapping, for goodness' sake, and finish your toast,' said Daisy, because she didn't want to have a lengthy discourse with a couple of children about something they weren't old enough to understand.

Daisy hated what was happening between her and June. It was tearing her apart. The barrier between them was more unbearable with every passing day. She wasn't an unforgiving woman; she wanted to put the whole thing behind them and carry on as before. But every time she thought of June and Nat together, anger flared towards June for destroying her trust. This battle was about Daisy and June rather than Daisy and Nat.

She'd valued the warmth of the burgeoning friendship with her sister and had looked forward to becoming closer in the future. All that had been swept away by June's betrayal. The last thing Daisy wanted was to move out of here, to drag the girls away from a home where they were happy to some awful little bedsit somewhere. But after what had happened, and the bitter resentment it had caused, she didn't think it would be fair to any of them to stay on. Every time she looked at June, she became angry and spiteful, and she didn't want to be like that.

Things had been going so well, too. Why had June had to destroy what they had? Was June to blame, though? she found herself wondering. Was it possible she could be telling the truth, after all? No, it couldn't be. Daisy had seen her and Nat together. You didn't have your arms wrapped around a man's neck if you were trying to fight him off. Anyway, Nat might be a bit of a bugger – and Daisy wasn't naïve enough to believe that he never flirted with other women – but he wasn't so lacking in principles that he'd go after her sister.

What about that story June had come out with about him setting the whole thing up with the deliberate intention of coming between the sisters to get back at June? No. It was too far-fetched to be true. Only a fool would believe such a story. Her racing thoughts stilled for a moment. Maybe that could work both ways; only a fool would make up such a story. And June certainly wasn't one of those.

Nat hadn't been near since the incident two weeks ago. Daisy knew him too well to think that he'd taken her literally when she'd told him she never wanted to see him again. He'd turn up eventually, like the proverbial bad penny. He'd be waiting for her to cool down before he dared to show his face.

She decided suddenly that she wasn't prepared to wait for him, with resentment and suspicion eating away at her day after day. If he wouldn't come to her, she'd go to him and have this thing out once and for all. And the sooner the better.

Turning her mind to more immediate matters, she checked that the children had had enough to eat and got them ready for school, feeling slightly better for having made the decision to take some positive action.

Chapter Fifteen

Eileen was stirring gravy in a saucepan on the stove for the evening meal when there was a knock at the front door. She muttered a mild expletive because the liquid was at the crucial thickening stage and would go lumpy if left unstirred. Hearing Morris answer the door, however, she relaxed.

'The window cleaner wants paying,' he informed her, coming into the kitchen.

'Oh,' she said in surprise, continuing to stir. 'I didn't even realise he'd been.'

'He did the windows this morning, apparently,' he said, sounding bored. 'You must have been out shopping or something.'

She tutted. 'If I leave this now, to come to see to him, it'll be ruined.'

In a tone of mild irritation, Morris said, 'All right, tell me where the money is and I'll deal with it.' Domestic expenses such as window cleaning came out of Eileen's housekeeping money.

'You'll have to get it out of my purse,' she told him absently, her concentration focused on the contents of the saucepan. 'It's in my handbag on the sideboard, I think.'

'Right.' He headed off in search of the handbag.

She heard him talking to the window cleaner briefly before he shut the front door. A few minutes later, he marched into the kitchen seething with aggression, and waved a screwed-up scrap of newspaper under her nose.

'Perhaps you'd like to explain this,' he demanded, scowling at her. 'It fell out of your bag when I got your purse out.'

She was so startled, she dropped the wooden spoon on the floor and splashed gravy all over the cooker top, splattering her hand and staining the front of her apron. 'Junk has a habit of building up in my bag,' she said, blowing on her scalded hand and managing to recover sufficiently to look unconcerned about his discovery. 'Stick it in the bin for me, would you?'

'This isn't just a bit of handbag junk,' he stated, his eyes narrowed on her accusingly. 'It's a newspaper cutting with your name on it.'

'Is it?' She turned the gas off under the saucepan and bent down to pick the spoon up off the floor, trying to gather her wits and find a way out of this.

'You know perfectly well it is,' he snapped.

Morris was no fool and she'd been stupid to deny it. But she'd been caught unawares and panicked because she was terrified he would find out that the Rivers sisters had tracked them down because she'd responded to their advert and put her address on the letter. 'All right, so I know what it is,' she confessed. 'That isn't a crime, is it?'

'Who's looking for you?' He gave her a hard look. 'Have you been left some money or something?'

'Don't be ridiculous,' she protested. 'Who do I know with anything to leave?'

It was such a valid point he couldn't argue with it. 'What is it all about then and why did you say nothing to me about it?' he wanted to know.

'I don't know what it's all about because I didn't reply to it,' she continued to lie. 'And I didn't tell you because it didn't seem worth mentioning.'

He narrowed his eyes on her suspiciously. 'Your name in the paper, not worth mentioning? Don't take me for a mug, Eileen. You know damned well who's looking for you.'

'Why would I lie about it?'

'I don't know, but I intend to find out.'

'There's nothing to find out.'

'You're up to something, and I'll find out what it is one way or another,' he warned her. 'So you might as well make things easy for yourself and tell me.'

'I don't know who put that advertisement in the paper but it's obviously someone from the old days, wanting a get-together or something,' she tried to fob him off, a strong sense of self-preservation forcing the lies out of her. 'And because I don't want to see anyone from the past, I didn't bother to follow it up.'

'Why keep the advert hidden in your handbag, then?' Morris demanded.

'It wasn't hidden. It just happened to be in there.' She cursed herself for forgetting the advertisement was in her bag and telling Morris to look in there. If he discovered the truth he'd lose his temper and that meant bruises aplenty for her. 'I wouldn't have told you to go to my bag if I was hiding anything in there, would I?'

There was a brief hiatus while he pondered on this. 'I suppose not.' He was still doubtful, though. 'But you bothered to tear it out of the paper so you must have considered it important.'

'I was curious, naturally. Anyone would be, seeing their name in the newspaper.'

She didn't manage to convince him. 'You're keeping something from me,' he growled, gripping her arms so hard she cried out in pain. 'And I won't give up until you tell me what it is.'

'Morris, please . . . you're hurting me.'

'I think you did answer that advert.' He put his face close to hers. 'So tell me who's looking for you. Tell me, woman, before I break both your arms.'

'I don't know.'

Stars exploded in her head as he punched her face; she cowered back from him.

'There's plenty more where that came from if you don't tell me the truth,' he warned her.

'Don't hit me any more, please,' she begged.

'I'll stop when you tell me the truth.'

He hit her again, then took hold of her arms and held them so tight she could feel them bruising. 'There's nothing to tell.' Her voice was little more than a gasp.

'Do yourself a favour and tell me what's been going on,' he demanded, 'or I'll beat it out of you.'

Despite her dread of the brutality she knew from past experience he was capable of, she had a sudden unexpected surge of spirit, the misery of more than twenty years culminating in a blaze of fury. She knew she had no choice but to tell him the truth but she decided not to do so meekly, since he would punish her anyway. 'All right, I'll tell you,' she said, her voice rising with new courage. 'But you'll wish I hadn't.'

'Get on with it.'

'It was June and Daisy Rivers – the daughters of your dead lover,' she announced, her tone heavy with malice now. He'd been smug for too long. She wanted to see him suffer, and enjoyed seeing him struck with horror, eyes wide, mouth dropping open.

'Those little brats,' he gasped at last, letting go of Eileen in the shock of the moment. 'How did they find us?'

She told him. 'And they're not little brats now, Morris. Far from it,' she informed him with relish. 'They're women now. Intelligent women too.'

'What did they want with you?'

'Justice for their father.'

'What!'

'They know you killed their mother,' she told him with a note of triumph in her voice, the danger this posed to herself cast to one side in the pleasure of seeing the arrogant swine knocked off his perch. 'They saw you at the Rivers's house on the night of the murder so they know that we both lied under oath. They know, Morris.' Her voice rose, becoming shrill and hysterical as she recognised the gravity of the situation for them both. 'They know the truth.'

He couldn't hide his fear. 'They're bluffing,' he said. 'They must be.'

'You didn't tell me that someone besides Rose and Lionel Rivers knew you were at the house that night, did you?' she blurted out. 'You said no one could ever find out.'

'I didn't count a couple of little kids,' he was quick to point out. 'And I still don't. They can't possibly remember seeing me there after all this time.'

'They do.'

'Even if they do, who would believe them?' he scorned. 'Not a bloody soul, that's who. So I hope you haven't been opening your big mouth and admitting anything.'

'I'm not a complete idiot.'

'You were fool enough to put our address on your letter, though, weren't you?' he taunted.

'How was I to know they were behind the advert?'

'You should have been more careful.'

'I realise that now.'

'You've got as much to lose as I have in all this, remember,' he reminded her. 'If I go down, so do you.'

'As if I could ever forget.'

'And if it does happen it'll be because of your stupidity.'

Stress always inflamed Morris's temper. Rose Rivers had lost her life because of it and Eileen had sustained her share of injuries over the years. Now she took the full brunt as he looked at her with contempt, then pushed her hard against the wall and aimed one punishing blow after another at her face, her chest, her stomach.

'How dare you keep secrets from me?' he said, hitting her again and again. 'If those two come here again, I want to know about it. Understand? They can't prove anything so don't give them what they need by opening your mouth.'

She tried to get away but he dragged her back and hit her again in the stomach. 'I won't say anything, I promise,' she gasped at last, her hands raised to protect her head. 'But please stop hitting me . . . please.'

'You lied to your husband and that's wrong,' Another blow to the face.

'I'm sorry, I'm sorry . . .'

'You will be when I've finished with you.'

The violence continued until his anger finally abated and she was slumped on the floor, leaning against the wall, head down and sobbing quietly.

'You can stop snivelling and get my dinner,' he told her, walking to the door and turning, showing not a hint of remorse. 'I've been out working all day and I need a good meal when I get home. I don't expect to be kept waiting, either.'

The door closed after him. Slowly Eileen got up, her body racked with pain. She rinsed her face under the tap, wincing with the pain of a swollen eye and lip. The ruined gravy was poured down the sink and she got out the Bisto to make some more. She found herself with the chilling thought that one of these days her husband was going to go too far and she'd end up like Rose Rivers. In her dejected state, she didn't really care.

That same evening Daisy got the tube to Paddington and

walked briskly along the main road towards Nat's place. It was typical November weather, bitterly cold, with a greyish mist shrouding everything. She was shivering despite the thick sweater she was wearing under her coat.

She couldn't afford to take the night off work but had decided that this was important enough to lose money for. Having made the decision to take action this morning, she wanted to get on with it, and there was no point in trying to find Nat at home during the day. Nora minded the children in the evenings anyway so that wasn't a problem.

The streets seemed even scruffier and more sinister around here than the ones Daisy was used to. Marauding yobs were out in force, looking for trouble, drunks staggered out of pubs, young couples were locked in clinches in shop doorways, and there were overflowing rubbish bins everywhere. Daisy had only ever been to Nat's place once or twice and that was years ago, but she was able to find the dilapidated flatlet house.

The front door wasn't locked so she went in and knocked on the door of the ground-floor flat where he lived. A blonde of about thirty opened the door with a small child clutching at her skirt.

'Yeah?' she said.

Daisy frowned, wondering who the woman was. 'Is Nat in, please?' she asked.

'Nat?'

'That's right. Is he at home at the moment?'

'Never 'eard of anyone called Nat.'

Wondering if she'd come to the wrong house, Daisy looked around her and was sure she hadn't. She looked back at the woman whose dark roots matched her black sweater and tight skirt. 'Nat Barker,' she said hopefully.

'Oh, Mr Barker, I know 'im,' the woman told her. 'He lived here before we moved in six months ago.'

'He's moved out?' Daisy couldn't believe he would change his address without telling her.

'Well, he certainly ain't dossing down here with us, dear,' the blonde said. 'We've hardly got enough room for ourselves, let alone having a lodger about the place.'

Daisy's throat was so constricted she could hardly swallow. 'Do you happen to know where he moved to?' she managed to utter at last.

'Over Queens Park way somewhere, as far as I remember. Dunno exactly where, though.'

'He didn't leave a forwarding address then?' muttered the shocked Daisy.

'No, nothing like that.' The woman thought for a moment. 'You could ask him in there,' she suggested, pointing at the door of the flat opposite. 'I think they were quite matey so he might have an address.'

Numb with shock, Daisy walked to the other flat and knocked on the door.

Afterwards Daisy couldn't remember getting to Queens Park that night. She was weak from the shock, and bitterly hurt to think that Nat would have done something as major as moving house without telling her, the woman in his life for more than seven years.

Admittedly she wasn't in the habit of visiting him, but she needed to know where he was in case of an emergency. He was the father of her children, for goodness' sake.

She'd forgiven him most things over the years but he'd have to have a damned good explanation for this, she thought, as she came out of the station and walked down a street of towering Victorian terraced houses converted into flats. The house she was looking for was smarter than Nat's previous address, she noticed with surprise. She pushed the front door open and knocked on the first door she came to because the neighbour from Nat's old address had only given her the house number.

A heavily pregnant young woman wearing a red maternity smock answered the door.

'Sorry to bother you but can you tell me which flat Nat Barker lives in, please?' enquired Daisy politely. 'I've been given this address but not the actual flat number.'

The woman, who had long black hair and dark eyes, fixed her with a steady gaze. 'What do you want him for?' she asked in a chilly manner.

Daisy bristled. She was having a terrible night. She'd just discovered that her long-standing boyfriend had moved house without telling her and now some stranger had the cheek to pry into her personal affairs. 'I think that's my business, don't you?' was her brisk reply. 'So can you please tell me where I can find him?'

There was silence for a moment as the woman considered the matter. 'Nat,' she shouted into the flat, 'come here. There's someone to see you.'

To Daisy's utter astonishment he appeared.

'Daisy . . .' He was clearly as shocked to see her as she was to see him. 'What are you doing here?'

'I might ask you the same thing,' came her sharp reply. 'How could you do such a thing – change your address without telling me?'

'I can explain—'

'Why should he tell you where he lives?' demanded the other woman, throwing Daisy a glare.

'You'd better ask him that,' she suggested.

'Who is she, Nat?' asked the woman, turning to him. 'And why should you explain anything to her?'

'Never mind who I am,' snapped Daisy, resenting the stranger's proprietary attitude towards Nat. 'Who are you? That's what I'd like to know.'

'That's easily sorted,' she replied, exuding confidence and pausing briefly before continuing as though to create the maximum effect. 'I'm Nat's wife.'

The hallway spun around her. Daisy gripped the stair banisters to steady herself, cold sweat suffusing her skin, her legs buckling.

'You can't be,' she muttered.

'I can and I am.'

'You're lying.'

'With him standing next to me?' she said in a mocking tone. 'Don't be such a silly cow.'

Daisy stared at her, still unable to take it in but knowing with sickening certainty that it was true.

'I don't understand,' she said numbly.

'Nothing complicated about it,' the woman went on breezily. 'He's my husband. We've been married for six months and have a baby due in a few weeks' time.'

'A baby.'

The woman patted her bump with both hands, looking at Daisy with a half-smile. 'Well, this ain't the result of too many doughnuts, mate,' she said.

'Oh, Nat,' gasped Daisy, looking at him with disbelief. 'How could you?'

And she turned and rushed out of the house.

'I couldn't just let you go like that, not after all the years we've been together,' said Nat, having chased after Daisy and persuaded her to go into the nearest pub with him so that he could explain.

'Won't you be in trouble with your . . . with your . . .' she could hardly bear to utter the title she had believed would belong to her one day, 'with your wife for chasing after me? You'll certainly have some explaining to do.'

'I can handle Marge, don't worry.'

Daisy emitted a humourless laugh. Her pain and humiliation went too deep for tears. 'All these years I thought that the only reason you wouldn't marry me was because you didn't want to marry anyone,' she said bitterly. 'And then you go and marry someone else. How's that for a punch in the throat?'

'I didn't want to get married and I didn't intend to marry Marge,' he informed her.

'But you went ahead and did it, just the same.'

'When she got pregnant I didn't have any choice in the matter,' he told her.

'I got pregnant, twice,' she reminded him. 'But you didn't feel obliged to do the decent thing by me, did you? And that hurts, Nat, that really hurts.'

'Marge has a very persistent father,' he explained.

'So if I'd had a dad to twist your arm, you'd have married me then, is that what you're saying?' she suggested.

'Not exactly, no.'

'Why did it work for her then?'

'Marge's dad is a powerful man around here,' he said. 'He owns several other houses besides the one we live in.'

'Ah, so that's it.' She gave him a knowing look. 'She has something I could never give you – money.'

'It isn't like that,' he denied somewhat unconvincingly.

'What then?'

'Her ol' man put on the pressure for me to marry her and he's the sort of bloke you don't defy if you value your health. He employs morons to deal with people who don't do what he wants. And they don't go in for small injuries, I can tell you.'

Daisy didn't believe a word of it. He'd married Marge because he saw something in it for himself. He was just using her as he'd used Daisy for so long. But at least Marge got to raise her child within the security of marriage. 'How blind can you get?' she said dully. 'All these years I thought I was

347

the woman in your life when I was actually just your bit on the side.'

'No, Daisy, you were never that.' He looked suitably outraged at the suggestion.

'You must have been deceiving me for months,' she went on, her eyes narrowing in thought. 'No wonder you stayed away for weeks at a time. You had other fish to fry. God knows how many women there have been over the years, and I was too dim to suspect anything.' She paused, pondering, then added almost to herself, 'I suppose I knew in my heart there must be others but I didn't want to believe it so I deceived myself into thinking that I was the only one.'

He looked sheepish and didn't deny it.

'I don't suppose you ever loved me,' she went on. 'I was a fool to think you did.'

'I did love you, Daisy,' he claimed. 'I still do.'

'Don't make things worse by piling on the lies.' Her voice was hard. 'You've been found out so there's no point.'

He shrugged. 'I'm a bloke and we . . . well, these things just sort of happen,' he said lamely. 'It's different for men than it is for women. It's the way we're made.'

'Don't tar the whole of your gender with the same brush as yourself,' she admonished.

'You and me go back a long way, Daisy, and you are the only woman I've ever really loved.'

'How come you're married to Marge then?'

'I made a mistake and the choice was taken out of my hands, I told you.'

She took a large swallow of her gin and orange, looking at him. 'I don't think you're capable of loving anyone but yourself,' she told him. 'I don't suppose you even love your wife, the poor cow.'

He didn't say anything, just swigged his beer. 'You've every right to be upset,' he said after a while.

'You're not kidding.' She gave him a questioning look. 'One thing that does puzzle me: why bother to go on seeing me when you didn't want me?'

'I did want you.'

'But you had a wife, and a child on the way, a nice home and a rich father-in-law,' she pointed out. 'Why not be straight with me and tell me it was over?'

'I couldn't bring myself to end it, I suppose,' he told her. 'So I carried on seeing you.'

'In other words, you wanted to have your cake and eat it.'

'A woman would see it that way, I suppose.'

'Anyone with a scrap of decency in them would see it that way,' she amended.

With her perception altered by events, she saw him with a new and truthful eye. He was a flashily dressed man with greasy sideburns and a paunch around his middle, a chancer who cared for no one but himself. He wasn't even much to look at, if the truth be told. 'The reason I came looking for you tonight was because I was going to ask you to be honest with me about what happened between you and June,' she explained. 'Now that I know the sort of deception you are capable of, I don't suppose I need to.'

'I wanted to bring her down off her high horse,' he blurted out in a rare burst of honesty. 'I don't like her attitude. She thinks she's God's gift.'

'She's been telling the truth all along, hasn't she?'

He hesitated for only a second before nodding his head. Lying was like breathing to Nat, but even he could see that there was no point in continuing with the pretence now. 'I didn't fancy her,' he was keen to assure Daisy. 'The idea was to get her interested and then laugh in her face. I wanted to make her feel put down in the same way she always makes me feel, turning her nose up, the superior bitch. But she didn't want to know, turned me down flat. So I decided to get even with her by making trouble for her with you. That's why I set that scam up the other night.'

'Surely you've got better things to do with your time, now that you're a married man,' Daisy disapproved.

'My life and my feelings for you haven't ended just because I've married Marge, you know,' he informed her. 'I still have a life outside the home.'

'I bet you do,' she said harshly. 'If you hadn't been rumbled you'd have carried on seeing me, wouldn't you?'

He met her eyes. 'If I could have got away with it, yeah, I expect I would,' he admitted without shame.

'It's about time you grew up, Nat Barker,' she told him. 'My daughters have got more sense than you.'

'Our daughters,' he corrected.

'*My* daughters,' she countered, her voice rising. 'You've never wanted to be bothered with them, never been anything of a father to them.'

'Only because I'm no good with kids, you know that's the reason,' he defended.

'I know that you've never made any effort with them,' she said.

'Don't go on about it.'

'I'm not going to go on at you about anything ever again,' she made clear. 'I just hope you make a better job of fatherhood with your new baby than you ever did with Shirley and Belinda. Your poor wife doesn't know what she's letting herself in for with you. I wish her the best of luck.'

'Daisy, please, don't be so hard,' he urged her. 'It just isn't like you to be so nasty.'

'No, it isn't. And I should have been harder and nastier a long time ago as far as you were concerned. My biggest regret is that I didn't allow myself to see through you before,' she said, finishing her drink and standing up to go. 'You're a cheat and a liar and I never want to see you again.'

She left the pub with him in hot pursuit.

'Daisy, we can't part bad friends like this,' he said, taking her arm.

She pulled away from him and stared into his face. 'Don't you ever touch me again,' she ordered, her voice distorted with rage. 'Not ever!'

'But—'

'If you ever come near me or my girls again,' she said through gritted teeth, 'I'll go to the law and have a court order taken out against you.'

'Now you're just being bloody ridiculous,' he objected, moving back.

'You've got a wife at home waiting for you,' she reminded him tartly. 'So go to her and leave us alone. You're not fit to breathe the same air as my daughters or my sister or my dear friend Nora. So go away, you pathetic little man.'

'Don't worry,' he countered. 'I wouldn't want to come near you or your bastard brats again anyway.'

That was too much for even Daisy's patience. She clenched her fist and drove it hard into his face. 'That's for calling my daughters names,' she informed him, and walked away, leaving him looking after her with his handkerchief held to his bleeding nose.

When the parish priest went into the church to lock up he saw a woman sitting in the pew with her head bowed. He caught her eye and gave her a tentative smile.

'Are you waiting to lock up, Father?' she asked. It wasn't her local church so this priest was a stranger.

'When you're ready,' he said. 'No hurry.'

'I'll just be a few more minutes.'

'Take as long as you like.' He looked at her kindly. 'Is there anything I can do to help? I'm a good listener.'

'Thanks, Father. But not this time.'

He nodded and walked away, disappearing through the door to the vestry.

Daisy had never been able to define what the inside of a church meant to her. But she did know that part of it was a sense of belonging that dated back to the orphanage chapel. It was something familiar, something she'd grown up with. The atmosphere had comforted her as a child and still did today. She breathed in the lingering smell of incense and candlewax around her, finding it soothing.

She'd come in here on impulse tonight, passing the church on her way to the station after leaving Nat. Every nerve in her body had been stretched to the limit; she'd been full of disgust for him and humiliation for the years of self-delusion, believing that she and Nat had a future together.

But now, sitting here in tune with her spiritual self, she felt calmer and more able to clarify her thoughts. She'd been young and hungry for love when she'd fallen for Nat, dazzled by his confidence and colourful looks. She could see now that she'd clung on to what she'd thought they had, blinding herself to the truth even though the magic of that young love had gone long ago. She'd not allowed herself to move on from those immature feelings.

Looking back over the peculiar nature of their relationship and the fact that she had been excluded from so much of his life, it should have been obvious to her that there was more to him than she knew about. She could only assume that she hadn't wanted to face up to that so had told herself that it wasn't Nat's way to be bound by the normal rules of court-ship because he was unconventional, a free spirit. He'd let her down so many times, she should have been tough in the face of this ultimate humiliation. But she wasn't and the pain was profound.

Somewhere at the back of her mind, though, she recognised something else which she couldn't quite identify but could feel growing. It was a lightness of heart that felt remarkably like relief and something beyond that too – a kind of strength. Only now could she fully accept that loving Nat, or thinking she loved him, had been a burden; it had held her back, stunted her emotional growth. It had made her lose a good man she could have had a future with, and caused a serious rift between herself and her sister.

She would never deny that there had been good times with Nat, and he had given her her greatest gift: her lovely daughters. But he had been a negative influence in her life for a long time. Now it was over. It was the end of an era. She had to get on with her life without him. And there was one thing she must do before anything else. Maybe it was too late to put things right with Jack. But not with June.

As she got up to leave, the priest appeared and came over to her.

'Feeling better?' he asked.

'Much better, thank you,' she was able to say truthfully. 'Good night, Father.'

'Good night.'

Facing the altar, she genuflected, then turned and walked to the back of the church, her footsteps echoing on the stone floor in the silent building. She pushed open the heavy door and walked out into the cold night air.

June and Nora were in the living room having their cocoa when Daisy finally got home. She came straight to the point.

'I've been a complete idiot,' she told them, sitting down and looking from one to the other. 'Can you ever forgive me?'

'I'll go and get you some cocoa,' offered Nora, with the idea of making a diplomatic exit.

'No, don't go, Nora,' Daisy requested. 'I want you to stay and hear what I have to say.'

Nora sat back down and listened while Daisy told them

about the events of the evening.

'Daisy, love, I'm so sorry,' said Nora, removing her spectacles and rubbing the lens with the corner of her cardigan. 'I know I've sometimes upset you by speaking my mind about Nat but I wouldn't have had this happen to you for the world.'

'Nor me,' added June.

'I know you wouldn't and it's all right,' Daisy assured them. 'I feel OK about it now.'

'Are you sure?' asked Nora.

'Yeah. I'm very hurt, of course. It was one hell of a shock and I was shattered. But I think I needed something like this to make me face up to what I've known deep down all along and what the two of you have tried to make me see: that Nat doesn't live by the same rules as the rest of us.' Even now she couldn't bring herself to be unnecessarily hateful about him. 'I feel better now that it's finally over. It was never a proper relationship, even though I tried to tell myself it was.'

The two women looked at her in silence, a palpable sense of relief settling over the room.

'I'll go and get you that cup of cocoa now,' said Nora.

'Thanks, Nora.' Daisy managed a smile. 'And thanks, both of you, for not saying I told you so.'

Nora chortled. 'It's more than we dare do,' she told her. 'We're used to keeping quiet when it comes to Nat.'

'Not any more,' Daisy told them. 'That's all over and done with. From now on the shortcomings of Nat Barker are not unmentionable in this house.'

'Thank God for that,' said Nora, and disappeared into the kitchen to make Daisy some cocoa.

Hyped up by what had happened, Daisy didn't feel ready to go to bed when she'd finished her cocoa. June was upset on Daisy's behalf and feeling wakeful also, so they stayed up talking after Nora had gone to bed. Sitting either side of the dying embers of the fire, Daisy talked about Nat.

'I was young when I met him,' she said, in a reminiscent mood. 'Young and lonely and desperate for love, I suppose. I was very well looked after at St Clare's but there wasn't much love about.' She paused. 'So I fell for Nat in a big way.'

June gave her an understanding nod.

'Leaving the orphanage was worse than being there. Much worse. OK, so there are no home comforts in an institution but there was security and constant companionship. Coming into the outside world after all those years was a real shock to the system, I can tell you. I've never felt so alone as I did then.' Her eyes were glazed as she thought back on it. 'I had absolutely no one.'

'Didn't they do any sort of follow-up, to make sure you were all right?' enquired June.

'Oh, yeah, they did that. An aftercare officer used to visit me now and again to make sure I was surviving,' she explained. 'But they couldn't cure the grinding loneliness. Although I never felt loved at St Clare's, I never felt lonely either. But when I left there I felt as though I'd lost everything because my security had gone. I was fifteen and on my own in the world, or that's what it felt like. I missed St Clare's dreadfully.' She looked at her sister. 'You weren't there for long enough to remember much about it, I suppose.'

'No. But I know all about feeling alone and unloved.'

June had indicated before that her childhood had somehow been lacking. But as she'd made it obvious that she didn't want to talk about it, Daisy didn't like to press her. 'Really?' she said.

Meeting her sister's sympathetic eyes, June felt comforted. She'd never told anyone the truth about her childhood, not even Alan. She couldn't bear to talk about it because to do so evoked the painful memories she'd spent the whole of her adult life trying to blot out. But now she sensed that the time had come to bring it all out into the open. Suddenly she knew that she needed to face the memories if she was ever to erase her fear of them. 'Contrary to what you might expect, my life was hell after I left St Clare's.'

'Why?'

'Downright wicked are the only words I can think of to describe the people who adopted me.'

'No!' Daisy was shocked. 'How can that be? I mean, surely if they wanted a child desperately enough to adopt one, they would love and cherish it.'

'Oh, they claimed to love me,' June said, bitterness creeping into her tone. 'When they were beating me, they told me it was for my own good, that it would make me into a better person, and I would thank them for it one day.'

'They beat you?'

'On a regular basis.' She looked grim. 'But the beatings I could take.'

'There were worse things?'

June cleared her throat, finding it difficult to say the words after keeping it all locked away for so long. 'Mental torture, and lots of it, though I didn't know that was what it was called at the time, of course,' she explained. 'They constantly told me that I was a useless human being and they wished they'd never taken me on. They used to lock me in my bedroom for hours on end, whole weekends sometimes, as a punishment for something as small as being a few minutes late back from school because I'd been chatting to the other kids on the way home. They got even stricter about that as I grew older.'

'That's terrible.'

'It was, I can tell you. I wasn't allowed to have any friends at all outside of school hours.' June gave Daisy a wry look. 'I don't suppose they'd have allowed me to go to school if it hadn't been against the law to keep me home.'

'Why didn't they want you to mix?'

'They didn't want me corrupted by the other kids, was what they said. I believed them; kids believe anything adults tell them, don't they? Later I realised it was because they saw outside influences as a threat to their control over me.'

'I can't understand why they went to the trouble of adopting a child, as they obviously weren't suited to parenthood.'

'That's often puzzled me too,' said June thoughtfully. 'I can only think it must have been because they wanted someone to control, to manipulate. They probably even convinced themselves they were doing the best thing for me. They must have convinced the authorities that they were good people. I imagine that couples wanting to adopt were vetted, even in those days when there were so many children in care.'

'You must have been relieved when you were old enough to leave home.'

'Phew, I'll say I was. I left when I was fifteen,' she explained. 'Like you I was alone and in lodgings at that tender age.'

'What happened? Did you reach a point at home when you'd had enough so you just walked out?' Daisy enquired.

'No.' June turned very pale and Daisy could see that she was trembling. 'No, it wasn't like that. Something happened that made it impossible for me to stay there.'

'Oh . . .' Daisy didn't want to pry but she sensed that June needed to talk about whatever it was that still troubled her so deeply. She waited, hoping her sister would feel able to confide.

June stared at her shaking hands. 'I've never told a soul. I don't know if I can,' she began, looking up and biting her lip. 'It's just too awful to put into words. You'll be very shocked, Daisy.'

'Don't tell me if you'd rather not,' said her sister kindly.

'But it might help. And don't worry about shocking me. After tonight, I can face anything.'

There was a silence. June pushed her fingers distractedly through her hair. 'My adoptive father used to . . . to get fresh with me.' She paused, unable to continue. 'And then one time he raped me,' she finally managed to get out in a rush. 'And I got pregnant as a result.'

Daisy couldn't pretend not to be appalled. 'Oh, June, that's awful!' she gasped.

'That isn't all,' she went on, her skin paper-white but suffused with red blotches on her cheeks and neck. 'They made me have an abortion.'

The gasp emitted by Daisy filled the silent room.

'That's the bit I knew would upset you, you being a Catholic.' June was very distressed.

'I can't help it.'

'I had no choice in the matter,' June went on. 'I didn't know what was going to happen when they took me to this woman's house. Not until she took me into a room and locked the door. By that time it was too late. I struggled but there were three strong adults against a fifteen-year-old girl. My parents held me down. Even though I didn't want to carry a baby of that monster's, I didn't want to do that, believe me.'

'You don't have to justify yourself to me,' Daisy assured her. 'I'm not going to judge you.'

'I had a miscarriage that night but I was very ill for days afterwards, terrible pains, floodings, a fever,' she continued. 'I thought I was going to die. I think they did too but they daren't call a doctor because questions would have been asked.'

'They ought to have been reported for breaking the law,' said the outraged Daisy. 'Was there nobody you could turn to?'

'Nobody at all because they'd never allowed me to have

friends,' she explained. 'I wouldn't have said anything any-way because the shame was too great.'

'I can imagine.'

'Anyway, as soon as I was well enough after the abortion, I left,' she went on. 'I wasn't safe at home with him around. My mother wanted me out of the way by that time, too. She couldn't face up to what he was like and blamed me for the whole thing; she said I'd encouraged him. It was probably the only way she could bring herself to stay with him.'

'That's quite a story,' said Daisy.

'It's the reason why I left Alan,' June told her.

'Really?' Daisy was puzzled. 'Was it still haunting you and coming between you then?'

'It has always haunted me and always will do. But I was able to cope with it until Alan and I started to try for a baby and I couldn't get pregnant,' she explained. 'Obviously because of the damage caused by the abortion.'

'You don't know that for sure.'

'I can be pretty certain, though. I mean, what else could be stopping me from conceiving?'

'Any number of things.'

'With the abortion damage being the most likely.' June was in little doubt. 'Anyway, when Alan started talking about seeking medical advice, I knew it was time for me to leave. I couldn't risk having my past come out.'

'Surely, whatever the doctors discovered would have been confidential between you and them, wouldn't it?' suggested Daisy. 'I don't think it would be ethical for a doctor to discuss a patient's details with anyone else, even a husband.'

'But I would have had to lie to Alan about it,' she pointed out. 'And I didn't want to do that. I lied to him about my reasons for leaving him but I had to do that so that he would get on with his life without me.'

'So he still doesn't know why you left?'

'Of course not. I could hardly tell him a thing like that, could I? It's better this way. With me out of the picture he can find a woman who can give him the child he wants. He deserves that. He's a really decent bloke. What right do I have to stop him having kids?'

'Sounds as though you still love him.'

'Desperately,' June admitted. 'I walked out on him because I love him and want the best for him.'

'Sounds like cock-eyed logic to me,' Daisy disapproved. 'You could at least have given him the chance of an opinion on the matter.'

'I know what I did was right for him.'

'I suppose that's the important thing,' sighed Daisy. 'When it comes down to it, you have to trust your own judgement about something as personal as that.'

'Mm.' June threw her a look. 'So what do you think of your smart sophisticated sister now you know the truth about her?'

'I think it's sad,' was Daisy's honest reply. 'Sad that you've had such a rotten life. And kids growing up in an orphanage are always thought of as the hard-done-by ones.'

'I'm glad I've told you.'

'I'm glad it's helped.'

Something happened to June at that moment, and she broke down, the stifled pain of the past finally culminating in a great outpouring of grief.

Daisy went over to her and held her while she sobbed. 'You're not on your own any more,' she said, stroking her hair. 'And neither am I. We've got each other now. We were given a gift when fate brought us together again. We nearly lost that when we fell out over Nat. We mustn't let anything come between us ever again.'

'Definitely not,' agreed June, in a muffled tone, but feeling better for having let go. 'Nothing will part us now.'

'And now that we're friends again, we have a job to finish,' Daisy reminded her.

June nodded, blowing her nose and composing herself. 'We need to work out our next move,' she said shakily. 'Not that we have many options.'

'I was wondering,' began Daisy, 'if perhaps we should give some more thought to the one lead we do have.'

'Go straight to the organ grinder, you mean?' suggested June, catching on.

'Exactly,' Daisy confirmed. 'It might be a bit risky but there will be two of us. And I really do think it's our only hope.'

'What exactly do you have in mind?'

'This is my plan . . .' began Daisy.

'Good evening, Mrs Dodd,' said Daisy, when Eileen answered the door.

She gasped and shrank back. 'Oh, no. Not you two again,' she complained. 'I thought I'd made it clear that I don't want to see you around here again.'

'You made it very clear,' confirmed June.

'Why are you here then?'

'We've come to see your husband,' explained Daisy. 'Is he at home this evening?'

Eileen looked guarded and very frightened. 'No, he isn't,' she said, and went to close the door.

'I don't believe you,' said Daisy, stepping forward and pushing her foot against it.

'Clear off.'

'We're going to pester the life out of you until we do see him, so you might as well get it over with,' Daisy told her.

'What do you want with him?' Eileen's wary eyes rested on them suspiciously. 'I made our position very clear the last time you were here.'

'Let us in and you can listen to what we have to say,' Daisy said in reply.

A booming voice came from inside the house: 'Who is it, Eileen?'

'Just a couple of Jehovah's Witnesses,' she lied.

'Tell them to bugger off,' Morris bellowed back at her. 'I'm waiting for my pudding.'

Daisy moved forward and shouted into the house, 'It isn't Jehovah's Witnesses, Mr Dodd. It's Daisy and June Rivers and we're not going to go away until we've seen you so you might as well let us in.'

In an instant he was at the door, his beady little eyes darting from one to the other in search of recognition, not quite able to hide his fear. 'My wife's already told you that you're not welcome here, so clear off.'

Daisy found it an eerie experience to see him again after all these years. He'd been a shadowy image in her mind, except for those evil eyes, which had remained vivid. She couldn't stop imagining what his plump, stubby hands had done to their mother. Anger imbued her, which she knew she must control or ruin their plan. 'You'll regret it if you don't listen to what we have to say,' she told him.

'You've got nothing on me,' he responded with an air of indifference that didn't quite come off.

'We wouldn't be here if we hadn't,' Daisy pointed out.

'Shush, all of you,' Eileen urged them, looking into the street and peering both ways. 'There's no need to let the whole neighbourhood know our business.'

'The whole world will know your business if you don't let us in,' said June.

'You'd better do what they say, Morris,' Eileen advised him nervously.

'Oh, all right,' he tutted, moving aside to let them in and leading them into the living room where he stood with his

362

back to the fire. 'I won't offer you a seat because you won't be stopping. Just say what you have to say and get out.'

The sisters stood just inside the door 'How does it feel to see us again after all these years, Mr Dodd?' Daisy asked.

'It doesn't feel like anything in particular,' he replied with nonchalance that didn't ring true. 'You were nothing to me then and you're nothing now. Just the kids of a neighbour where we once lived, that's all.'

'Looking at you is like looking at the devil himself,' Daisy told him.

'For me too,' added June.

'My sister and I are the only people living who saw you at the house that night,' Daisy reminded him. 'Apart from our father, of course. And he's out of the picture for the moment.'

'Just temporarily,' June put in.

'I dunno what you're going on about,' Morris blustered. 'As I said just now, you've got nothing on me.'

'That's where you're wrong,' said Daisy, hoping to goad him into losing his temper which, from what they'd heard, shouldn't be too difficult.

'Very wrong,' June backed her up.

'We have something very incriminating,' Daisy went on. 'We have our own personal experience and the police will be interested to hear what we have to say about having seen you at our house on the night of our mother's murder.'

'You didn't see me there,' he denied. 'And if you think you did you're barmy.'

'We intend to leave no stone unturned to clear our father's name,' threatened Daisy. 'So be warned.'

'I knew there would be trouble.' Eileen was deathly white, her voice shaking. 'You shouldn't have done it, Morris.'

'Shut up, you stupid cow,' he bellowed at her. 'Keep your big mouth shut.'

'That's what you said to us that night,' Daisy reminded him.

'Rubbish!' he exclaimed. 'You were just a couple of snotty-nosed kids. You couldn't possibly remember anything as far back as that. This is just something you've dreamed up.'

'We wouldn't make a thing like that up.'

'There was only us and you in that hallway that night,' June reminded him. 'How could we know about it if we weren't actually there – that's the line the police will take.'

Daisy pointed to her head. 'It's all up here,' she informed him. 'And we intend to use it.'

'You know as well as I do that no one will believe such a story,' he challenged.

They did know that, which was why they needed Eileen to back them up and that was what they hoped to achieve with this visit. 'They'll have to look into what we have to say, whether they believe us or not,' Daisy bluffed. 'Especially as there are two of us.'

He narrowed his eyes on her. 'If you're so sure, why are you here bothering us?' he enquired. 'Why don't you just have done with it and go to the police?'

'It's only recently been possible but that's another story,' said June. 'We're here now because we wanted to see you, to see if you can look us in the eye after what you've done.'

'I've done nothing to be ashamed of.'

'I can believe that too, because you're the sort of man who wouldn't be ashamed of committing murder and letting someone else take the blame.' Daisy's tone was hard. 'We'll see you punished for it. No matter how long it takes, you'll pay for what you've done.'

'Do something, Morris,' cried Eileen in a panic. 'Do something or we'll both go down.'

His wife's fear seemed to enrage him and he replied with

364

his fist, hard across her mouth, which immediately spurted with blood. 'I've told you to shut your big gob. Now perhaps you'll do what you're told,' he roared.

'Are you going to let him get away with that, Eileen?' challenged Daisy.

'He's murdered one woman,' put in June. 'You might be the next. He's certainly capable of it.'

'Stop them, Morris,' wailed Eileen, holding a handkerchief to her bleeding lip.

In reply he struck her across the face so hard she fell to the floor. He then lunged towards her with the idea of aiming more blows. But Daisy intervened.

'That's enough of that,' she said, dragging him away with June's help.

He swung round, his fists flying. 'Get out of my house, the pair of you,' he ordered, his voice shaking with rage. 'Your mother was scum anyway, leading me on, then turning cold. She deserved everything she got.'

'You admit you killed her then?' said Daisy.

'Yeah, I admit it.' He was shouting now, his face red with fury and his eyes wild; he'd obviously lost control as the sisters had hoped he would. 'And bloody good riddance to her too. She should never have played us off one against the other.'

Daisy was about to strike him but was pre-empted by him aiming a blow to her face that made her see stars.

'You animal.' She tried to push him away but he was too strong for her, especially as she was still dazed from the blow. 'Get off of me.'

'Leave her alone,' shouted June, trying to drag him off her sister and failing against his strength.

Suddenly help came from an unexpected source.

'Haven't you done enough damage to these women, you evil bugger?' said Eileen, struggling up from the floor and grabbing him by his other arm so that, between them, she and

June were able to hold him back from Daisy. 'You robbed them of their parents when they were just little kids, and now you're trying to beat them up.'

'Shut up, Eileen.'

'No, I won't shut up,' she said, her voice distorted as she started to sob.

'You bloody well will.'

'You've ruined the childhood of these two women, and you've wrecked my life too,' she told him. 'But you've made my life a misery for long enough, I tell you. I'd sooner be in a prison cell than have to live another day with you.'

'Eileen,' he said in a warning tone, struggling to get free but failing because there were three women holding him now. 'What are you talking about?'

'I'm going to tell the police what you made me do, and get the case reopened so you will have to pay for your crime,' she said, her voice strong suddenly, despite the fact that she was crying.

'Don't make me laugh,' he scorned 'You won't have the bottle.'

'I will, you know. I'm going to tell the truth – that I lied under oath because you told me you hadn't done the murder,' she went on as though he hadn't spoken. 'I would never have lied if I'd known the truth. By the time I found out what you'd done I was caught in a trap that you'd put me in. Well, no more. Enough's enough.'

'You wouldn't dare.'

'Watch me.'

'You'll go down with me,' he warned.

'So what? I'm living in a prison now,' she told him. 'A real one can't be worse than the hell of a life I live with you.'

He made one last bid to get away and broke free, but Eileen landed him a blow to the face so hard he was stunned into immobility.

'Come on, girls,' she said to the astonished sisters. 'Let's go to the police station.'

While Morris was still gathering his wits from the shock of his wife's unprecedented violence, the three women fled from the house into the bitter night. They stopped only long enough for Daisy to grab a coat from the hallstand for Eileen.

Chapter Sixteen

Jack strode out along the beach, the cold January wind stinging his face, the tangy salt air filling his lungs and clearing his head. It was late Sunday morning and he didn't have to go on duty until this evening as they didn't open the restaurant for lunches in the winter. After a good hard walk, he'd have a sociable hour in the Gullscombe Arms, then go back to the cottage for a bite to eat followed by a leisurely browse through the Sunday papers by the fire until it was time to go to work. Smashing!

The sea breeze felt more like a gale this morning, the sky a great rolling dome of grey, the ocean rough and dark. The surf was so thunderous, each breaking wave seemed to shake the ground beneath his feet. Definitely not the sort of weather to attract the average person to the beach, but Jack had a curious fondness for it on wild winter days when the life force was so breathtakingly tangible. He found it invigorating and uplifting, especially as he was dressed for the elements, the hood of his duffel coat pulled right up over his ears.

There was hardly anyone about – just a man throwing sticks for a dog in the curve of the bay and a group of youngsters exploring the rock pools around the bottom of the cliffs, their high, youthful voices carried on the wind. Rock pools were like a magnet to kids, he thought, reminded of last summer and how Shirley and Belinda had loved poking about in them, looking for shells.

Of course, everything had been drenched in sunshine then: his life as well as the landscape, for that brief interlude when Daisy and her daughters had been a part of it. That was almost half a year ago, and nothing had been the same for him since. He didn't sit about feeling sorry for himself; that wasn't his way. He worked hard, went for long walks, tinkered with his motorbike and was his usual sociable self to anyone he encountered. He even dated women occasionally. But the dull ache of missing Daisy didn't go away.

He walked on with his head bent against the wind, passing Gullscombe Manor, more visible now than in summer because the trees were bare. Every time he passed this spot he thought of Daisy and how they'd sheltered from the rain on the veranda. He'd felt so close to her then; had really believed they had something worth nurturing.

But now, something attached to a post outside the house caught his eye and he halted in his step, peering at it. It looked like an estate agent's FOR SALE board but he couldn't see the details from this distance. Inspired by mild curiosity to take a closer look, he made his way up the sloping path through the trees.

It was an estate agent's board but with an auction notice pasted across it. He'd heard through the village grapevine that the owner had recently died. His descendants obviously wanted to dispose of the place as quickly as possible and it would go for a song at auction. There couldn't be much demand for a ruin like that, no matter how beautiful it had once been, because it would need such a huge injection of cash to return it to its former glory. So somebody would get a bargain.

A memory popped into his mind of a casual comment Daisy had made when they'd been here together, about the potential of the place for use as something other than a private house. He stood still, mulling a sudden idea over, then walked purposefully across the garden and down the slope to the beach. His step gathered momentum to such an extent that he was practically running back to the cottage in a fever of rising excitement. Stopping for only long enough to collect his crash helmet and goggles, he jumped on his motorbike and roared away towards town.

Alan and Jack were having a drink in a Torquay pub an hour or so later, Jack having turned up at Alan's flat in ebullient mood, saying he needed to speak to him urgently and in private away from the Cliff Head. When Alan heard what he had to say, his reaction was one of astonishment.

'You're saying that you want the two of us to go into partnership to buy Gullscombe Manor and turn it into a hotel that we will run together?' He was excited by the prospect, even though he wasn't in a position to consider such a proposition.

'That's exactly what I'm saying.' Jack was full of it. 'A great idea, isn't it?'

'But it's a wreck of a place,' Alan pointed out.

'Which is why it will go dirt cheap at auction.'

'It would need to go for practically nothing since it'll cost a fortune to restore,' was Alan's shrewd response. 'Even more to convert into a hotel.'

'If we got it at a low enough price, we should be able to manage it.' Jack's fervour was intense. 'Surely you can see how perfect the place would be as a hotel. The building and grounds, the location, everything.'

'Yeah, I can see the potential.' Alan would be a fool to deny it. 'I can also visualise the terrific amount of work it would take to renovate it and turn it into a hotel. And building work costs money, lots of it.'

'Just think, though, Alan, we could make it into a family hotel, the sort of place you've always dreamed of having,' Jack effused, his faith in the project causing him to ignore the obstacles Alan was putting in the way. 'It's the perfect setting, in extensive grounds with direct access to a safe beach. What could be better?'

'It's a good position but—'

'I know we could make a success of this,' Jack cut in excitedly. 'We could put in a swimming pool and a games room, all that sort of thing.'

'Just one minor point,' said Alan with irony. 'How are we supposed to fund this project?'

'By my selling my cottage and you could either raise money on your share in the Cliff Head or use your savings and get a bank loan if that isn't enough, based on the reputation you will have built up from running the Cliff Head.' He'd worked it all out on the way into town. 'I know when we were talking once you said that your savings wouldn't be anywhere near enough to get your own hotel, but as there would be the two of us sharing the cost, and we'd be starting something from scratch with no goodwill to pay for, you wouldn't need so much.'

'I can't believe you'd sell your cottage.' Alan shook his head slowly. 'You love that place.'

'I do. Very much. But it is only bricks and mortar when it comes down to it.'

'That isn't what you said when you were doing it up,' Alan reminded him.

'I know what I said, but when an opportunity like this comes up, you have to adapt, don't you?' Jack told him. 'Anyway, the thing I love most about the cottage is that it's on the seashore at Gullscombe Bay. If I moved to the manor I'd still be on the bay and in an even better position.'

Alan couldn't help but be infected by his friend's enthusiasm but he had to be realistic. 'It's a nice dream, mate,' he sighed wistfully.

'It's more than just a dream.' Jack was deadly serious. 'This is a sound business idea.'

'It is, I agree. But it will have to stay just a dream for me,' he said. 'I can't come in with you on it, Jack. I couldn't do that to my folks. As I told you before, if I ever left the Cliff Head I would give them my share. But I still wouldn't do it because I know they'd be devastated.'

'I thought that might be your reaction.' Jack couldn't hide his disappointment. 'And the last thing I want to do is interfere in a family matter.' He paused, sipping his beer. 'But I will say this. You were my first choice as a business partner for two reasons. Partly because I believe we'd make a great team. And also because I know you're fed up and frustrated at the Cliff Head and need to do something in your own right, away from your parents. Well, mate, you'll never get a better chance than this.'

Because Alan wanted to seize this opportunity with both hands, he was beginning to delude himself into thinking it might be possible. 'Would it really be a viable proposition, do you think?' he asked.

'I'm as certain as I can be at such an early stage,' said Jack without hesitation. 'Obviously we'd have to find out what the reserve price is and work out some figures. But if we can get the finance side of things sorted, I don't see how the actual project can fail, not with us two at the helm, being both experienced in the hotel trade and having the same ideas for what we want in a hotel. Gullscombe Bay is a natural beauty spot badly in need of a hotel. Taking over the manor house would mean we could open one without spoiling the landscape. We'd keep everything as it is now as far as possible, with necessary changes inside done tastefully.' His enthusiasm was growing with every word. 'I could raise more money by selling my motorbike too, if necessary.'

'But that's your hobby – the love of your life,' said his amazed companion.

'It is, but I'd sell it to get this project off the ground,' Jack told him gravely. 'Harley-Davidsons fetch a good price, even old ones like mine.'

'I can't believe you'd be willing to sell your cottage *and* your bike.'

'That's how much I want to do this.'

'But you've never shown any interest in having your own hotel before,' mentioned Alan.

'I haven't thought about it until now, and I'm not interested in owning just any hotel,' he explained. 'But now that I've thought of this Gullscombe Manor thing, I can't let it go. The idea's too good.' He drank his beer, looking thoughtful. 'Anyway, I've been drifting for too long – going to work and coming home, messing about with the bike. I need a challenge in my life and I can't see a better one than this coming along – *ever.*'

'It's certainly got the makings.'

Jack put his pint glass down, looking at his friend closely. 'I want you to come in with me on this, Alan. But if you really don't feel able to, I'm still going to go ahead and bid for it at auction.'

'If things were different I'd jump at the chance of coming in with you on it.'

'I know you would, mate. But I'll have to find someone else as a partner.' Jack's thoughts were racing ahead. 'I won't be able to raise enough cash on my own. It's too big a project.'

Alan nodded.

'Still, I've got plenty of contacts in the hotel trade,' Jack continued. 'I should be able to arouse some interest.'

'I really wish it could be me.' Alan couldn't bring himself to let go of the idea completely. 'I'm long overdue a challenge.'

Jack looked at him. 'You wouldn't be going to the outback of Australia, you know,' he pointed out. 'You'd only be a few miles up the coast. You'd still be able to see your folks on a regular basis.'

'They wouldn't want to see me if I left their business,' Alan told him ruefully.

'*Their* being the operative word.' Jack didn't want to give up on Alan either. 'It's their business and not yours.'

'When they retire, things will be different. I'll be able to put my own stamp on the place then.'

'It'll still be a business they've built up,' persisted Jack.

'I'll just have to live with that.' Alan was resigned now. 'Because I just couldn't hurt them in that way.'

'We've been over this before and you know my feelings on the subject,' said Jack.

Alan sighed. 'It's easy for you to say but things aren't that simple when relatives are involved.'

'After leaving my family at the other side of the world, I think I know how difficult it is,' Jack reminded him. 'It's your decision, of course, but I wouldn't be a true mate if I didn't say that I think you're missing out on the chance of a lifetime. Not just because I'm certain that the two of us could make a go of it but also because I really do believe you need to break away from your parents' apron strings.'

'You're probably right,' agreed Alan. 'But it's actually doing it that's the problem.'

'I think you might be underestimating them, you know,' Jack went on sagely. 'They'll be upset at first, naturally, but they'd get used to it eventually. They might even be proud of you for having a go.'

'Sorry, mate, the answer still has to be no.'

Jack shrugged. 'OK. I've said my piece, I'll shut up about it now.'

'I hope it works out for you.'

'Me too.' His enthusiasm rose again. 'If it doesn't, it certainly won't be for the lack of trying. I've got a real good feeling about this one.'

'Keep me posted,' said Alan enviously.

'I'll do that,' said Jack.

During the winter months there was usually maintenance work of some sort in progress at the Cliff Head. General repairs, painting and decorating – bits of building work that couldn't be done when guests were around. It was Alan's sole responsibility to organise all of this. He decided what needed doing and when; he did the costings, found the tradesmen, did the hiring.

Or that was how it was supposed to work. But one morning a few days after Jack's proposition, Alan was given cause seriously to question his authority when he arrived in reception to find an argument in progress. The altercation was between his parents and the proprietor of the small building firm Alan had hired to do various jobs around the hotel.

'You were supposed to be here by nine o'clock this morning and you roll in now at turned ten o'clock,' Alan's mother was admonishing the man. 'It really isn't good enough.'

'Sorry we were a bit late, missus.' He was a stockily built, square-jawed man who spoke with a rich Devon brogue. 'But I had a bit o' trouble with the van this morning. I just couldn't get her going – had to get a mechanic out to her in the end.'

'Excuses, excuses,' she said.

'It in't just an excuse,' he protested, looking miffed but staying patient. 'It's the God's honest truth.'

'You builders are all the same,' Irene went on rudely. 'Unreliable, the lot of you.'

'Look, I've said I'm sorry,' he said, less patiently. 'I can't do more. So if you'll excuse us, me and the lads have to get on with our work.'

'My wife's right.' Gerald wasn't going to be left out. 'We want this job finished before this summer season, not next. The way you're carrying on, it still won't be done this time next year.'

'We'll be finished by the completion date we gave you,' the man assured him. 'We'll be out of your way well before you open for Easter.'

'I should damned well think so too, the price you're charging us.' Alan's mother was in her element. There was nothing she enjoyed more than flaunting her power.

And to hell with the consequences, thought Alan, observing the builder's annoyance which was increasing, understandably. Good jobbing builders were hard to find. They could pick and choose the work they took on in this age of prosperity, with so many people having property renovated and extended. If Alan's mother's vicious tongue lost them this one they wouldn't get anyone to finish the work before the start of the season because all the reputable builders were booked up for months ahead.

'It's all right, Mother,' Alan said, winking surreptitiously at the builder, whose name was Bill. 'I'll take over now.'

But she was in the mood for a battle and there was no stopping her now she'd got the taste. 'You're nothing but a bunch of layabouts, the lot of you,' she accused the man, whose two employees were standing quietly beside him.

'Here, you wanna watch what you're saying,' Bill objected, his brown eyes hardening as his anger grew. 'That in't fair.'

'As I'm paying your wages, I'll decide what's fair,' she argued. 'You come and go when you please with no consideration for us at all. You can't deny that.'

'I certainly do deny it.'

'Do you think we're blind or something?' Gerald put in.

'Do you think we don't notice what time you turn up for work in the mornings?'

'You obviously don't pay attention to what time we finish at night or we wouldn't be having this conversation,' Bill pointed out. 'Anyway, I'm self-employed. I don't have to account to you about time-keeping. As long as the job is finished by the specified date, I'm within my rights.'

'As we're paying you, we have a right to some kind of reliability,' Irene argued.

Now she'd pushed the man too far. 'Right, that's it,' he retaliated. 'As you're obviously not happy with our way of working, we'll get out of your way. We've enough work to last us for a year ahead. We're not staying here to be insulted by the likes of you.'

'Now you're being ridiculous,' said Irene.

'You listen to me, missus,' said Bill, observing her coldly. 'We've plenty of customers waiting to have work done, people who appreciate us and treat us with respect. So you can pay us for what we've done so far and get some other mug to finish the job for you because we in't doing it.' He paused. 'If you can find anyone who'll put up with your attitude.'

'Don't be hasty, Bill,' intervened Alan worriedly. 'My mother doesn't mean what she says.'

'Oh yes I do,' she made plain, undermining her son's authority completely. 'Never mind you walking out on us, you're sacked, the lot of you.'

Alan was so angry he couldn't speak. Hiring and firing building staff was his job and she'd ignored him altogether; behaved as though he wasn't even there. This sort of thing wasn't unusual and he normally accepted it as an occupational hazard. But in a sudden moment of clarity he saw it with a fresh eye.

He could now see with absolute certainty how right Jack

was when he said that Alan needed to break away from the family business. While he worked with his parents he would never amount to anything. He would always be twelve years old in their eyes, and he had had enough.

'Ignore my mother,' he said to Bill at last. 'I'm the one you deal with around here.'

'Really, Alan—' began Irene.

'Shut up, Mother,' he blasted.

'How dare you—' she began.

'Don't you dare speak to your mother like that,' added his father.

Had Alan not been so furious, he might have felt embarrassed at having to endure this public humiliation. But he was beyond that sort of sensitivity. He looked from one parent to the other. 'Fine, you deal with it then. I'll keep out of it altogether.' He turned to Bill. 'Sorry about this, mate,' he said.

Bill gave him a nod to let him know that he had no quarrel with him personally. He'd seen Alan humiliated by his parents too many times to bear a grudge.

'I'll leave you to it, then,' Alan announced to his parents, turning to go.

'There's no need for that,' said Irene, looking worried now. 'You can't just go off.'

'Watch me.' He paused, looking at them. 'And when you've finished with Bill, can you come up to my flat, please? I have something to say to you.'

And with that he headed for the lift.

'Your behaviour was utterly disgraceful, Alan,' reproached Irene, perched stiffly on the edge of an armchair in her son's flat a few minutes later. 'I was thoroughly ashamed.'

'I wasn't proud of your appalling behaviour, either,' was her son's unexpected response.

'What!' She wasn't used to having him answer her back

and it shocked her. 'In what way did I behave badly?'

'Apart from being unnecessarily rude to the builders, you went over my head completely with them,' he told her. 'And it just isn't on.'

'I had to step in and deal with the situation because you're too damned soft with people who do work for us,' she said. 'You let them do exactly what they like.'

'You have to let them know who's boss,' added his father, standing with his back to the window, dominating the room. 'You can't let them make the rules. You can't allow them to win.'

'But they have won, haven't they?' Alan pointed out heatedly. 'You've sacked them and now there's no one to do the work we urgently need doing. So we're the losers, no doubt about that. They're not bothered because they've got plenty of jobs lined up, like all decent builders these days. About the only people who aren't booked up are cowboys, and there are plenty of those about.'

'You'll soon find someone reputable to finish the job,' was his mother's confident answer.

'Oh, no. Not me,' Alan put her straight. 'You took over from me, remember.'

'Only temporarily,' she told him.

'It's a permanent arrangement as far as I'm concerned,' he informed her. 'The job's all yours from now on. You've humiliated me once too often.' He shook his head. 'But never again.'

'Don't be ridiculous,' rebuked his father. 'It's your job to sort this out.'

'Not any more,' he said. 'I quit.'

They stared at him in bewilderment.

'You mean you're going to leave the job of finding another builder to us?' suggested Irene nervously, at last.

'I'm leaving everything to you from now on.' He forced

himself to stay calm. 'I'm leaving the Cliff Head.'

Two pairs of eyes widened in horror.

'Now you really are being silly,' said his mother as though Alan was a recalcitrant child. 'Resigning just because you're in a temper because I paid the builder off.'

Alan looked from one to the other and when he spoke it was in a quiet, reasonable tone. 'That isn't the reason I'm leaving. That just forced me to take a close look at myself and my place in this business as well as my position as an adult human being. I'm not leaving the business in a fit of pique. I'm leaving because I need to do something on my own without the two of you looking over my shoulder the whole time.'

'We don't do that—' began his mother.

'With respect, you do, all the time,' Alan corrected firmly. 'Anyway, an interesting opportunity has come up for me and I've decided to take it.'

'You can't leave,' ordered Irene.

'I can and I will,' Alan told his parents in a definite tone. 'It's something I have to do. I need to prove myself.'

'And what are we supposed to do without you?' asked his mother aggressively.

'You won't have any trouble managing without me. You can run this place standing on your heads, as you've told me so often,' he reminded them. 'I wouldn't go if I wasn't absolutely certain of that.'

'You always have been selfish,' accused his father, hitting out unreasonably.

'I'm what you made me, which is one of the reasons why I have to get away,' Alan tried to explain. 'I'll never know what I'm really capable of if I stay here.'

'Rubbish,' said his mother.

'Absolutely,' supported his father.

'You'll be better off financially without me because I'm

giving you my share of the business,' Alan went on to say. 'You can take on a manager to replace me and you won't have to pay him a share of the profits as you do me. I'll be moving out of the flat so you can offer the manager accommodation, too. It'll be an attractive opportunity and you shouldn't have any trouble finding someone suitable.'

'Moving out of your flat,' gasped Irene, realising at last that he was serious.

'I won't be far away, though,' he assured her. 'Just a few miles down the coast.'

'Where, exactly?'

He outlined his plans.

'I see.' Her eyes were as cold and hard as stones.

'What will you use for money?' his father enquired coolly.

'I'll use my savings and get a loan for the rest,' he explained. 'It's such a good proposition, I should be able to persuade the bank to lend me what I need.'

'And get yourself into debt with huge interest charges,' warned his father.

'If I have to, yes,' Alan confirmed.

'And if you don't get Gullscombe Manor at the auction, you'll want to stay on here, I suppose?' his mother mocked.

'Oh no. Whatever happens, I'm leaving the Cliff Head,' he made clear. 'It's something I now know I must do. If the Gullscombe Manor thing falls through I shall find something else. I'll find a way to use my experience.'

His mother burst into tears. 'I never thought my own son would be so uncaring of his parents,' she said through dramatic sobs. 'I thought we'd brought you up to respect family values.'

'You have,' he said in a softer tone, because he wasn't an unkind man and he did love his parents. 'My striking out on my own doesn't mean I don't still respect family values. I'll still be a good son to you, if you'll let me. The only thing that will change is that we won't be working together.'

'We gave you everything a child could possibly want . . .' she went on woefully.

'Yes, you did,' he agreed. 'But as an adult I need something else – independence.'

'I've always prided myself on being a good mother.' She just wouldn't let go.

'And you have been,' he assured her. 'I wouldn't dream of saying otherwise.'

'The Cliff Head has always been a family firm,' she rambled on tearfully. 'We've worked hard to make it into a good business for you to eventually inherit. As soon as you were old enough we made you a partner.'

'I know all that and I appreciate everything you've done for me. But I've worked hard too, and I think I've made a valuable contribution to the business,' he asserted. 'But I've gone as far as I can here now. I need a new challenge, my own space, and the chance to see if I can succeed or fail in my own right.'

'You can do that here,' came his mother's muffled suggestion. 'We won't stand in your way.'

He chewed his lip, looking at them. 'You will, without even realising it,' he said. 'The original idea was for you to gradually stand back and leave more of the responsibility to me. But it hasn't happened. This place is in your blood. You just can't let go and leave things to me, which is why we had that scene downstairs just now and why you won't consider any of my ideas for the place. This is *your* hotel with your plans and opinions. You're a part of the place and it's part of you because you built it and made it what it is. I want to do the same thing with a very different kind of hotel from this. So why not let me go with your blessing so that we can stay friends? Wish me well and take an interest. I'd really like that. I'm sure any advice you have to offer will be useful.'

But Irene's tone hardened even more and her tears stopped as suddenly as they'd started. 'We'll have the accountant work out a reasonable price for your share of the business and you'll be paid what you're owed,' she announced through tight lips.

'There's no need for that,' protested Alan. 'I've told you, I don't want any money from you. You can have my share of the Cliff Head and welcome.'

'You'll get what you're entitled to,' she said in an acerbic manner.

'I don't want it.'

'As you were so keen to point out,' she went on coldly, 'you've worked hard and made a contribution. I'm not having you say that we've done you out of anything – that we haven't been fair.'

'Surely you know me better than that.' He was very hurt. 'I would never say any such thing.'

'To eliminate any possibility of that, we will pay you for your share of the business,' she insisted. 'But there'll be no question of us staying friends. You want to leave, so go ahead. But you'll be paid off and all ties between us cut.'

'Mother!' He was shocked. He'd known they wouldn't be pleased but hadn't expected to be banished from their lives altogether. 'Now you're just being vindictive.'

'Steady on, Irene,' warned Gerald.

But she was far too engrossed in her own self-pity to take any notice of him. 'As you've just said, Alan, your father and I can run this place standing on our heads so there's no need for you to stay around for a minute longer,' she blasted at him, her tone increasing in speed with the swell of her temper. 'You can get out of here right away, and any contact we have in the future will be through a solicitor. If you let us have a forwarding address, the money you are owed for your share in the business will be sent to you when the amount has been

384

decided. It will *not* be negotiable.'

Alan felt as though he'd been physically beaten. He looked at his father. 'Does that go for you too? Or are you going to stand up to her for once?'

Gerald looked at his wife. 'Don't you think you're being a bit harsh, dear?' he said in cautious admonition. 'They boy's entitled to a change.'

'You do what you like, Gerald,' she told him with a look that forbade disagreement. 'I've said my piece and I won't change my mind.'

'But, dear—'

'I've told you where I stand on this one, Gerald,' she confirmed. 'He's letting us down and I want no more to do with him. If you feel differently, that's up to you.'

Gerald studied his son's face, unable to hide a fleeting look of regret before saying, 'You heard what your mother said. We want you out of here right away.' His voice quivered slightly with emotion. 'So get yourself and your stuff out.'

Upset but not defeated, Alan said, 'OK. I'll go. I'm sure Jack will put me up at his cottage until something permanent can be sorted out.' He paused, looking at them. 'But aren't you just the tiniest bit proud of your son for finally having the courage to do something for himself?'

'You're no son of mine,' was his mother's parting shot before marching from the room, followed by his father.

For a long time Alan couldn't move; he just stood frozen in the centre of the room, so tense his limbs ached. He felt as though the heart had been ripped out of him; it was a terrible thing to happen between a man and his parents. But there was a new strength there too, a sense that he'd finally grown up. As much as he wanted to go after them, he knew he couldn't go back on what he'd said. To reverse his decision now would be the act of a coward.

Walking over to the window, he stared idly across the bay,

the sea black and choppy on this winter's day, banks of low cloud obliterating the horizon altogether. But this view always soothed him, however bad the weather. Thinking back on what had been said, he decided not to refuse the money his mother insisted on paying him. It would make them feel better about cutting him out of their lives, he thought miserably, because they could fuel their grudge by telling themselves that they'd given him something to which he wasn't entitled. Anyway, if he was honest, he reckoned he'd earned it for all the hard work he'd put in over the years, as well as the humiliation they'd made him suffer.

June came into his mind as she often did at odd moments because she was never far from his thoughts. He knew instinctively that she would support him in his current plans and wished more strongly than ever that she was here to go forward with him.

He turned back into the room, sad at the thought of leaving here but strong in the belief that he'd done the right thing. A fresh start was long overdue. The excitement of the new project was clouded by the rift with his parents, though. The last thing he wanted was them out of his life.

Maybe they'd have a change of heart when they'd calmed down and thought the whole thing through, he found himself hoping. But being realistic, he doubted it. His mother could be very stubborn when she wanted her own way about something, and he couldn't give in to her over this, as tempting as that was. He emitted a long sigh, sadly accepting the fact that this really was a parting of the ways.

Chapter Seventeen

Things moved fast in the Lionel Rivers case after Eileen Dodd's confession. Morris's arrogance earned him an early arrest. He was far too conceited to believe that his wife would actually go through with her threat to shop him so made no attempt to escape and was arrested at home later that night.

The fact that Eileen had obviously punished herself over the years and had finally come forward and confessed went in her favour and she received only a suspended sentence for perjury and conspiring to pervert the course of justice.

As for Lionel – his release wasn't immediate because the formalities had to be adhered to and his appeal had to go through the normal channels. Despite his daughters constantly badgering the authorities to hurry things along, it was February before everything was finalised.

On a bitterly cold morning with heatless sun glinting on the frosty rooftops of West London, Daisy and June stood at the prison gates, both dressed in warm coats and fur-lined boots.

'We've waited a long time for this,' said June, her breath turning to steam as she spoke.

'Not nearly as long as Dad has,' her sister pointed out, stamping her feet because her toes were turning numb.

'That's true enough,' agreed June, hugging herself against the cold.

'I feel nervous,' Daisy confessed. 'Excited and happy but a bit scared too. It's such a traumatic thing for anyone to deal with. It'll take time for Dad to adjust to life on the outside.'

'I feel churned up too,' admitted June. 'I hope we don't have to wait much longer because the butterflies in my stomach are multiplying by the moment.'

Just then the small door in the heavy prison gates opened and Lionel Rivers stepped out into freedom. Wearing the smart suit and overcoat his daughters had brought him for this occasion, he stood looking around him with a bewildered expression as the door slammed shut behind him.

Both feeling oddly shy, his daughters walked slowly towards him.

Daisy was too choked up to say anything coherent and only managed a tearful, 'Hello, Dad.'

'Hi, Dad,' said June.

He didn't speak; just looked at them, his eyes brimming with tears. 'Thank you, girls,' he muttered thickly at last. 'Thank you for making this happen.'

That did it; the barriers were down and with one accord they threw their arms around him, all three of them weeping with joy and relief.

'Today is your day, Dad,' Daisy said when she'd recovered sufficiently to speak. 'You can do whatever you like. Get drunk, paint the town red, anything. You deserve it.'

'The only thing I want to do is go home to your place for a cup of tea and the chance to get to know you better,' he told them.

Moist-eyed but smiling, they walked away from the prison in the winter sunlight, a proud father and his two beloved daughters.

One Sunday lunchtime several months later, Daisy said, 'More apple pie, Dad? There's plenty.'

'Thank you, dear, but I couldn't manage another morsel,' he said, patting his stomach. 'It was lovely, though.'

'Nora made the pudding today,' Daisy informed him. 'June and I were in charge of the dinner.'

'You all did very well,' he complimented in his gracious way. 'The whole meal was delicious.'

'It's all down to teamwork,' she grinned. 'I enjoy making Sunday dinner into a family occasion now that we're all together again. I hate to miss it when I'm working Sunday lunchtime.'

'It's good of you to put up with me every Sunday,' said her father.

He was far too self-effacing, in Daisy's opinion, and it upset her. Prison seemed to have robbed him of all his self-esteem. 'We don't "put up" with you, Dad,' she corrected. 'We enjoy having you.'

'We do,' confirmed June.

'Very much so,' added Nora.

'The whole idea of your getting a place just around the corner from us was so that we could see plenty of you,' Daisy reminded him. 'And if you get lonely living on your own, you're welcome to come back here.'

'It's kind of you to offer but you don't have room.' His soft brown eyes had had a worried look about them since he'd been out of prison.

'I suppose not,' agreed June, because she didn't want to patronise him by denying the facts. 'But we managed when you first came out of prison.'

'I wouldn't have imposed on you then if I'd had anywhere else to go.'

'You weren't imposing,' Daisy was keen to make clear.

'Perhaps not. But you and June had to share a bedroom because you gave yours up for me,' he reminded her. 'That's all right in the short term but not as a permanent arrangement.

Anyway, there's no need for it, thanks to my compensation money.'

'Just as long as you know that we always like to see you,' Daisy told him.

It was late summer and Morris Dodd was now serving a life sentence for the murder of Rose Rivers. Some people thought he'd got off too lightly, and should have been hanged as Ruth Ellis was last year for killing her lover. Daisy wasn't vindictive enough to wish that on him, or anyone. He was being punished and that was good enough for her.

As there had been no question about her father's wrongful imprisonment, his claim for compensation had been dealt with swiftly. He hadn't received a fortune, but enough to buy a small house in the next street. No amount of money could give him back what prison had taken from him, though: his confidence. He'd been shaky for ages after his release and was still finding it difficult to settle, though he didn't say much about it. Daisy thought it might help if he had a job more suited to him rather than the one in a factory he insisted on doing because there was nothing available in his own field.

Daisy, June and the girls made sure he never lacked for company, but it was Nora to whom he turned for friendship. Being such different types, Daisy didn't think they had much in common besides their age but they got on surprisingly well. Eager for him to be integrated back into the community, Nora had dragged Lionel off to various local associations, none of which he'd continued with except the gardening club, which he enjoyed, already having an interest because of the nature of his work before prison. Nora hadn't been a gardening enthusiast before but she went with him to keep him company and, typical of her, became keen. Between the two of them they kept his tiny garden and theirs a picture.

But now Daisy was recalled to the present by Nora, who was nudging her and saying, 'So what do you think, Daisy?'

'About what?' she asked, startled slightly.

'Cor, dear, oh dear, you're a dreamer today,' she said. 'I was just suggesting that we all go over to the park after dinner as it's such a lovely afternoon.'

'Can we, Mum?' urged Shirley.

'Go on, Mum, say yes,' coaxed Belinda.

'OK,' agreed Daisy absently. 'I'm on duty later on, though, so I won't be able to stay for very long.'

June gave her a studious look. 'Are you all right?' she asked. 'You seem very distant.'

'I'm fine,' she nodded, but there was something on her mind apart from her father, and she just couldn't let it go.

However, the subject of the job Lionel had taken in a factory because there were no vacancies in the council's parks department came up, and a discussion ensued on which she tried hard to concentrate. June pointed out that he didn't have to do that job. He could manage for a while on his compensation.

'I'm only fifty-two,' he reminded her. 'I'm not ready to be put out to grass yet. I need something definite to do, a proper purpose to the day.'

'But you hate it at the factory.'

'Yeah, but I'd sooner do that than be sitting on my arse at home all day.'

'You could afford to take some time to look for something more suitable,' June persisted. 'Isn't that right, Daisy? Daisy . . .?'

'What?'

'What *is* the matter with you?'

'Nothing, sorry. I'm listening now, honest.'

June repeated what she'd said and Daisy agreed. But she wasn't paying proper attention. Something about the shaft of sunlight pouring into the room through the window had set off a chain of memories about last summer and who had made that time, a year ago, so very special for her. Here the sun shining through the net curtains made dappled patterns on the wall. She recalled the effect of the same thing in Jack's cottage where there had been no need for net curtains. She remembered the feeling of fresh air and light and space, the prettiness of Gullscombe Bay. So vivid were her recollections, she could almost smell the air and taste the salt on her lips.

How ironic it had all turned out to be. She'd rejected Jack, only to have Nat betray her in the cruellest possible way. Dear Jack, just the thought of him made her feel warm inside. She must have been mad to turn him down.

She looked around the table at this cluster of loved ones, everyone interrupting each other in the way people do when they're close. It still gave her pleasure to see her father in their midst, her daughters sitting either side of the grandfather they'd taken to their hearts so readily. They all meant so much to her.

But there was something missing in her life, and it was that which dominated her thoughts all afternoon and right through her waitressing shift. By the time she got home from work that night, she had come to a decision. She asked June and Nora if they could do her rather a big favour this coming weekend . . .

The following Saturday her stomach churned throughout the train journey and she was visibly trembling in the taxi from Torquay station to Gullscombe Bay. What she was about to do was crazy; just to turn up at Jack's door without warning. It was a huge gamble but something she felt compelled to do. By arriving unannounced, she believed she would get a genuine reaction and know if he still wanted her.

It was mid-afternoon. Sunshine bathed the landscape and gave her a feeling of *déjà vu* because it had been like this when Jack had driven her to Gullscombe Bay that first time with the girls. Now, seeing the bay through the trees at the top of the hill brought tears to her eyes. It was so good to be back.

Her heart was pounding, partly with excitement, partly with nerves when she paid the taxi driver and walked up the path to the cottage, carrying a small overnight bag. With a shaky hand, she lifted the heavy metal knocker and let it fall with a resounding thud on the front door.

In all her agonising about whether or not he would still want her, she had never imagined the possibility of being greeted at the door by anyone but him. So her spirits plummeted when she found herself staring into the sparkling brown eyes of a youngish woman with honey-blonde hair and smoothly tanned shoulders gleaming beneath a yellow sundress.

'Yes?' said the woman, smiling enquiringly at the little woman with the big worried eyes. 'Can I help you?'

Daisy cursed her impulsive behaviour. Not only had she off-loaded her responsibilities for the weekend, she was now about to cause trouble for Jack by turning up on his doorstep. Having an ex of her husband's on the doorstep with an overnight bag would be about as welcome to this woman as a smack in the mouth.

'I was looking for Jack, actually, Jack Saunders.' She wasn't about to get into deeper waters by lying about it but she felt extremely awkward.

Just then two small children appeared, a boy and a girl. 'How long till we can go down on the beach, Mummy?' asked the little boy. 'I'm dying to go in the sea.'

Mummy – Daisy's thoughts went into top gear. These children were about the same age as her own daughters, and it was only a year since she'd last seen Jack. Surely he wouldn't have . . .? No, she couldn't believe that he'd had a wife and kids he hadn't told her about. Not Jack.

'I'll only be a few minutes,' the woman told the children. 'Go and wait for me in the back garden. Don't get impatient and go without me down to the beach.'

The children hurried away and their mother gave Daisy a conspiratorial look. 'The beach here is very safe but I won't let them go down there by themselves. They're not quite big enough yet. They might wander into the sea and go too far out.'

Daisy nodded in an understanding manner which, knowing the beach so well, she could do truthfully.

'So you want to see Jack,' the woman went on, seeming unconcerned.

'If he's around . . .' Daisy felt terrible.

'He isn't, I'm afraid.'

'Oh well, it doesn't matter,' she told her, anxious to get away under the circumstances. 'I just thought I'd call on the off chance that he might be in.'

The woman looked at the overnight bag and gave Daisy a querying look.

'I thought I'd look him up but as he isn't in, it doesn't matter.' She felt really embarrassed now, as well as having a horrible ache in her heart.

'It isn't that he isn't in,' explained the woman. 'It's just that he doesn't live here any more.'

'What!' Daisy couldn't believe it.

'My husband and I bought the place from him earlier this year,' she said. 'We live in London. This is our holiday cottage, our little bolt hole. The children and I have been down here for most of the school summer holidays. My husband just comes down at the weekends.'

'Oh.' Daisy felt weak with relief. On the heels of this glorious feeling came concern for Jack. Something very dramatic must have happened for him to sell the cottage he loved so much.

'You seem surprised.'

'I'm absolutely shocked,' she confirmed. 'This place was his pride and joy. I can't imagine there could be anything bad enough to make him sell up and leave here.'

'It wasn't anything bad – quite the opposite, as far as I know.' She gave Daisy a close look. 'But you've obviously been travelling and must be feeling a bit weary. So why not come inside and I'll tell you exactly where you can find him over a cup of tea.'

'But your children are waiting to go to the beach.'

'It won't hurt them to wait a little longer,' she said, ushering Daisy into the cottage. 'They're not exactly deprived.'

'In that case, thank you very much indeed,' said Daisy politely, and followed the woman inside, eager to hear what she had to say.

'It doesn't look much like the beginnings of a swimming pool to me, mate,' said Jack, grinning at the leader of the team who were installing a swimming pool in the grounds of Gullscombe Manor. 'It looks more like something from the Battle of the Somme, as though you're digging in for trench warfare.'

'Give us a chance,' defended the man, who was bare-chested and wearing shorts. 'We've only just started the job. It'll be lovely when it's finished. Just like the pictures in the brochure.'

'Yeah, I know,' sighed Jack. 'I suppose I'm getting impatient for things to be finished.'

'I told you at the start the pool wouldn't be ready for this season,' the man reminded him.

'You did. I'm just over-anxious to have everything in place so that when we start promoting the hotel we can truthfully offer a full range of facilities,' said Jack. 'My partner and I have put all our money into this project and we have to make it work as a commercial proposition.'

'Just as well to get the pool done now,' the man chatted on with a strong Devon accent. 'While you're in a state of chaos, having a few more workmen around and a lump of the garden dug up won't make much difference.'

'You're right there.' Dressed in shorts and a T-shirt, his skin deeply tanned, Jack looked towards the house. It had scaffolding all around it. The whole place was crawling with workmen and had been for the past few months. Builders were repairing outside walls, knocking down internal ones, fitting en suite bathrooms, making one of the downstairs rooms into a bar and another into a restaurant. And to add to all that, work on the swimming pool had just begun.

'Sometimes when I look at it I feel as though it'll never be finished. The renovations seem to have been going on for ever.'

'You're bound to feel like that,' sympathised the man, speaking with a cigarette in the corner of his mouth. 'You're having a lot of work done all at the same time. You can't do that without inconvenience.'

'My partner and I won't know ourselves when we're not tripping over builders' rubble every time we move about inside.'

'Living in the middle of it doesn't help,' he commiserated.

'We've no choice,' Jack confided. 'As we're paying the mortgage on this place it would be financial suicide to pay out for other accommodation as well.'

'There are worse places to live than this, chaos or no chaos,' the man commented. 'It's a lovely spot you've got here.' He looked out across the bay, the sea shining in the sun.

'It is.'

'If I didn't live around here I'd come here for my holidays myself,' the man chortled.

'Let's hope lots of people from the towns and cities feel the same way as you and me,' agreed Jack, following the other man's gaze and looking out to sea, shading his eyes against the sun.

A movement on the edge of the wooded area caught his attention. Someone emerged from the trees and was heading for the gardens. A woman carrying a holdall. That was odd because this was private property. This time next year hotel guests would be trailing up and down the beach path all day but whoever that person was, she was trespassing.

He stared, squinting at the slight figure struggling up the slope. Even at this distance there was something achingly familiar about the way she moved. Now he really was getting delusions, he told himself, imagining every woman he saw to be Daisy. But it really did look like her. She lifted her hand and waved and he knew that it was her. He didn't know how or why. *But it was her*. She'd come back. She really had come back to him.

Leaving the man staring after him, he tore across the garden to meet her, smiling fit to bust.

When Daisy saw him coming she dropped her bag on to the ground and ran to meet him, her laughter ringing out across the gardens. Everything she needed to know was there in his eyes. Words weren't necessary for either of them.

The swimming pool installer watched with interest as the couple clung to each other, making a romantic picture with the sea behind them. 'It's like something out of a bloomin' film,' he muttered to himself. 'Canoodling is all very well in its place but some of us have work to do.'

And he jumped down into the trench to talk to the men who were digging down there.

Alan was full of Jack's reunion with Daisy when he and Paula were dining in a Torquay restaurant that evening. 'Apparently she just turned up out of the blue, appeared on the beach path like a dream come true,' he told her excitedly. 'He thought he was seeing things at first. But no, it really was her. You should see him, Paula, he's like a ruddy teenager.'

She smiled. 'I can imagine. So what happens next?' she enquired conversationally. 'Will she leave London and come to live at Gullscombe Bay?'

'I don't know what their long-term plans are,' he told her. 'But he certainly can't up sticks and go to live in London now that we've taken on the manor, can he?'

'Not really, no.'

'So I suppose she will move to Devon,' he surmised. 'She's got to go back to London tomorrow, apparently, because of her two little girls. She's left them with her sister and her friend for the weekend, with her father helping out.'

'Her sister being your wife, of course?'

'Well, yes,' he confirmed, and went on to repeat what Daisy had told him about how they'd cleared their father's name.

'Quite a story.'

'Phew, I'll say. That's typical of June, though, to take on something like that,' he said in a tone of admiration. 'She's a very determined woman when she decides to do something.'

'Like when she decided to leave you,' Paula pointed out.

'Ouch, that's a bit harsh.'

'Yes, it was a bit bitchy,' she admitted, making a face. 'I'm sorry, Alan.'

He shrugged. 'That's all right,' he assured her. 'I'm the one who should apologise. I was going on about her, which is rude of me when I'm out with you for the evening, especially after what she did to me. I just didn't realise I was doing it.' He gave her a persuasive smile. 'Am I forgiven?'

'Sure.'

'Good.'

Breaking some bread to eat with her soup, she asked, 'Why are you so thrilled about Jack and Daisy getting back together?'

'Because he's crazy about her,' he explained. 'He's a good friend and I care about him.'

She gave him a shrewd look. 'It isn't because Daisy is your sister-in-law and her being together with Jack will give you contact with your wife, then?'

'Of course not,' he was rather too quick to deny.

Paula chewed her bread in thoughtful silence, then made an observation that took him aback. 'It isn't working out for us, is it, Alan?'

His soup spoon was poised in mid-air. 'Why . . . what makes you say that?'

'There's nothing there,' was her frank reply.

'I wouldn't say that.'

'As much as we both want it and as hard as we try, we just can't produce that magic ingredient.'

'That's just because we don't see enough of each other.' He was fighting against rejection even though he knew what she was saying was true. 'What with all the organisation for the manor and doing a job as well, I just never get any time as I only have the one night off a week.'

Both he and Jack still had jobs because they needed incomes until they opened the hotel for business next spring and got money that way. Jack had stayed on as restaurant manager at the Cliff Head since Alan's parents had no quarrel with him. Alan worked as a barman in a Torquay pub. It was quite a comedown after his previous position but it brought in enough cash for him to pay his way, and he actually rather enjoyed the job.

'It isn't just that, Alan, and we both know it,' came her candid opinion. 'I think if we'd been able to see more of each other we'd probably have ended our affair long before this.'

'Is that what you're leading up to, Paula?' he asked. 'You want to end it?'

She reached across the table and took his hand. 'I'm only doing what we both know is inevitable,' she told him in a tone of sad resignation. 'Let's finish it while we're still friends, which is what we should have stayed. Things were fine between us then.'

'And they still are.' He was reluctant to face facts because it would mean the awful loneliness of not having a female in his life again.

'No, they're not, Alan,' she disagreed, removing her hand and sipping a glass of wine.

'Is there someone else?' he enquired. 'Is that it?'

'Not for me,' was her cryptic reply.

'What's that supposed to mean?'

'You're the one with someone else.'

'I've not been seeing anyone else,' he denied hotly. 'I wouldn't do that to you.'

'I know. But you're still in love with your wife, Alan.' It was a categorical statement. 'That was what I meant.'

'June and I are finished, you know that.'

'You're still in love with her, though.'

'What makes you say that with such certainty?'

She gave a dry laugh. 'You should see yourself,' she told him. 'You light up when you mention her name.'

'Do I, really?' He hadn't realised his feelings were so obvious.

'Absolutely,' she confirmed. 'This probably isn't a conscious thing but I believe the reason you're so delighted about Jack's reconciliation with Daisy is because it brings June closer to you. Even if you don't see her, having Daisy around means you'll get news of her. It will give you contact with her again.'

'That isn't fair,' he protested. 'I am genuinely pleased for Jack's sake. You're making me sound selfish.'

'I don't mean to. And I'm not saying that your having a personal interest is intentional,' she explained. 'I know that you're pleased for Jack's sake. But I think that some of the pleasure comes from the reason I've mentioned, even if only subconsciously.'

He lowered his eyes for a moment because he couldn't honestly deny it. 'Even if it were true, it's only thoughts,' he pointed out. 'I'm not going to try and get her back or anything. June and I are history. I accepted that long ago.'

'You're not over her, though.'

'It isn't easy when you've been married to someone.'

'I accept that.' She looked at him over the small floral centrepiece of roses and sweet peas. 'Maybe there's a woman out there somewhere who can make you light up in the same way as June does. But that woman isn't me.'

Alan wasn't going to insult her intelligence by denying it. 'I'm so sorry, Paula,' he said, looking sheepish. 'You're a lovely person and I'm very fond of you . . .' His voice tailed off.

'The feeling's mutual so let's part while we can still do it in a civilised manner,' she said, to avoid any further embarrassment. 'We'll see each other around, as we always have, and I'll follow the progress of Gullscombe Manor Hotel with interest. But let's not try to force something that's never going to happen.'

He sighed. 'What can I say?'

'Nothing,' she said. 'Just finish your soup before it gets cold. Then you can tell me how the renovations are coming along at the manor.'

They chatted amiably over the rest of the meal but the atmosphere wasn't relaxed. They were both deeply disappointed. Disappointed because they had failed to find something they both needed and had hoped for in each other.

Daisy was extremely impressed with Jack's plans for Gullscombe Manor. 'I think it's a wonderful idea. It'll be fabulous when it's finished,' she enthused.

'It had better be after all the chaos and expense,' he told her. 'Though it is sometimes hard to imagine the finished product with all this mess everywhere.'

They were sitting on the veranda, surrounded by scaffolding and builders' materials, including a cement mixer and a mechanical digger. Looking beyond the incipient swimming pool, they could see the lights coming on all around the bay, a necklace glowing in the dusk. 'I can visualise it already,' she said. 'It's in such a wonderful position.'

'I hope you realise that you're to blame for all of this,' he teased her.

'Why?'

'When I saw that the place was up for auction I remembered you saying something about the possibility of someone buying it for commercial reasons,' he explained. 'That was my inspiration.'

'Let's hope it'll be a success, then,' she said, 'or I'll be in dead trouble.'

'I'm that pleased to see you I can't imagine ever being angry with you about anything.'

'I feel the same.' She paused. 'But I nearly died when I found out you'd moved from the cottage.'

'You couldn't have been more amazed than I was when I saw you coming up the path,' Jack said. 'You still haven't told me what actually made you do it.'

'Well, we were all sitting around the table last Sunday dinner time and I suddenly wondered what I was doing there when I could be here with you,' she admitted. 'I couldn't get it off my mind all day so decided to make the necessary arrangements to turn up on your doorstep. That way, if you'd found someone else at least I'd have known.'

'No chance of that,' he assured her. 'I still want to marry you.'

'I'd have been very disappointed if you'd changed your mind,' she said softly.

'On a practical note, though,' he began, 'one of us is going to have to move.'

'I'll come here.' Her smile darkened into a frown. 'It'll be hard leaving the others and I'll miss them like mad but you can't have everything you want in life, and the girls and I belong with you.' She shrugged. 'You're obviously not in a position to move to London now, are you?'

'Well, no.' He waved his hand towards the house. 'Anyway, I want you to be a part of all this, to work in the new business with me. If you'd like that, of course,' he added, because Jack wasn't the type to take anything for granted.

'I'd love it,' she was quick to assure him. 'But how will Alan feel about it?'

'He'll be all for it, I should think. We're going to need plenty of willing hands, and who better to fill the breach than a member of the family with a special interest in the place.'

'Family,' she echoed. 'It sounds lovely.'

'Husband and wife working together. I hope you won't find that too much.'

'I could never have too much of you.'

'Time will tell.'

'If I say it myself, I'm a good waitress,' she mentioned, her thoughts moving on. 'Or wouldn't that be a fitting job for the wife of one of the proprietors?'

'Daisy,' he said, leaning forward and holding her hands, 'we are all going to have to muck in to make this place a success. We will be taking on staff but there'll be times when

403

they're not around and we'll have to get on and do their work. I'll scrub the floors if I haven't got someone to do it. There'll be no standing on ceremony. We'll be part of a team.'

'Sounds great.' There was so much to think about and she did have to consider the girls' needs. 'Where will we live now that you've sold the cottage?'

'It'll have to be here at the manor somewhere. Even apart from the fact that I'll need to be on hand, I put all my money into this place so I can't afford to take on anything else.' He pondered for a moment. 'We're having the outhouses made into staff accommodation and making the attics into flats for management. Alan and I were going to have one of those each but that won't be suitable for us because of the girls.' He paused again, remembering something. 'There's an old gardener's cottage in the grounds that could be done up.'

'Sounds promising.'

'Leave it to me,' he assured her. 'I'll sort something nice out for us. The main thing is for us to set the date.'

'I can't wait.' She hesitated, looking worried suddenly. 'But I want to tell the others about it before I actually set the date, if you don't mind. I want to talk it over with them, you know. Obviously they'll be upset at the idea of me and the girls being so far away. I'm not happy about that aspect of it either. But I won't keep you waiting long because the sooner the better as far as I'm concerned.'

'Me too,' he enthused. 'I won't want you to go back to London tomorrow.'

'It won't be like when I left before, though, will it?' she pointed out tenderly. 'Because this time we both know that I'll be coming back.'

'So, what do you think of Daisy's news, then, Lionel?' asked Nora, a week or so later when they called in for a drink at the local pub after their weekly visit to the gardening club.

'I'm dead chuffed for her,' he enthused. 'This Jack sounds like a genuine sort of a bloke. I can't wait to meet him.'

'I'm looking forward to meeting him again too. I've only ever seen him once but he seemed like an absolute sweetheart when he came to the house before,' Nora told him, sipping a glass of stout. 'From what's been said, I get the idea that he's devoted to Daisy and the girls. You could tell they liked each other when he came to the house that time.'

'Sounds to me as though he's genuinely fond of her,' he said.

'I'm so pleased she's found someone decent at last,' Nora went on. 'She needs a bit of cherishing after the way that Nat fella treated her. As well as all the abuse she's had to endure as an unmarried mother.'

'Bad, was it?'

'Awful. It's disgusting the way people behave towards women in Daisy's position,' Nora declared. 'Even the midwife treated her like dirt when she had the girls. Wouldn't let her have anything to help with the pain because she wasn't married. I really gave her a mouthful over that.'

'I wish I'd been around at that time,' he said. 'I'd have given her what for.'

'Nat could have saved her from such a lot of pain by marrying her but he wouldn't do it.' She made a face. 'Still, it's just as well. He'd probably have been a lousy husband, anyway.'

'At least she's found someone nice now.'

'Mm. Although I'm pleased for her I'm devastated for myself,' Nora admitted, swallowing hard on a lump in her throat. 'She and the girls have been a part of my life for so long, their going away is bound to leave an awful gap. I've got so used to them being there, it never occurred to me that one day they wouldn't be.'

'We're all going to miss them and that's a fact,' Lionel

agreed in a sympathetic manner. 'I feel as though I'm just getting to know Daisy and she's going away.' He paused. 'It's a weird feeling having to get to know your daughters from scratch when they're grown women. I haven't always known how to handle it, you know . . . being a bloke.'

'You're doing fine.'

'I feel as though I'm beginning to get there.' He shrugged. 'And now Daisy's off.'

'It's a shame,' Nora commiserated. 'I wouldn't dream of spoiling it for her by telling her but I'm absolutely dreading her going.'

'Still, we'll keep each other company,' he encouraged, patting her hand in a friendly manner.

'I know,' she said, rummaging in her pocket for her handkerchief and sniffing into it.

'And we'll have June.'

'Yes, of course we will. I've grown fond of June,' Nora told him. 'But we're not as close as Daisy and I are. Me and Daisy have been together a long time, since before she had the kids, even.' She raised her eyes in self-derision. 'But what must you think of me, worrying about myself when Daisy's got the chance of a better life? She deserves a break and I couldn't be more pleased for her. I just wish she wasn't going to be so far away.'

'You wouldn't be human if you didn't feel as you do. And I certainly don't think bad of you for being sad about it. I'm grateful to you for being so good to her over the years. I was certainly no help.'

'Don't start beating yourself up about something that wasn't your fault,' she admonished kindly.

He gave her a lopsided grin. 'You're a good friend, Nora,' he told her in a warm tone. 'As much as I love my daughters, I need someone of my own age to talk to.'

'Same here,' she enthused. 'I didn't realise just how much

until you joined the family. However much we love the others, we are of a different generation and, as such, our ideas are different.' She paused thoughtfully. 'Of course, it doesn't always follow that you'll get on with someone just because you're in the same age group, but I felt comfortable with you right away, when I came to see you in prison that first time. Yet we're very different.'

'You're a lot brainier than I am, for a start.'

'Don't be daft,' she laughed. 'I'm curious about things so I take the trouble to find out more about them, that's all.'

'It isn't all down to that. You're an intelligent woman,' he insisted. 'But you don't shove it down my throat.'

'You'd soon tell me if I did.'

'Not half.'

A sudden commotion at the bar halted the conversation as a crowd of Teds came in and an argument erupted because the management were refusing to serve them with alcohol on the grounds that they were under age. The Teds denied it rowdily, even though the landlord was pointing out the undeniable fact that if they were eighteen they wouldn't have greased quiffs, long sideburns and a DA haircut but an army short back and sides.

'There's one good thing about Daisy going away,' Nora confided to Lionel as the Teds made a noisy exit. 'With all the trouble around here between the Teds and the immigrant community, with fights on the streets almost every night of the week, Daisy and the girls are better off out of it. At least she won't have to be out on her own late at night any more, travelling back from work.'

He nodded in agreement. 'You can feel the hostility simmering in the air, can't you?' he observed. 'As though violence is about to erupt at any minute.'

'I know what you mean.'

'Black and white don't mix around here, and from what

I've heard, all the trouble isn't only down to the Teds,' he confided. 'The older generation aren't blameless. There are plenty of fascists stirring things up.'

'And the Teds jump at the chance of an excuse for a fight,' agreed Nora.

'Exactly. After doing a long stretch in the nick, I reckon I'm pretty tough, but even I don't like being out on the streets on my own of a night in this area,' he confessed. 'And I hate to think of Daisy doing that journey.'

'I've worried about it for years,' said Nora. 'Even before we had a racial problem around here, the streets were full of dodgy characters after dark.'

'Thank God that's coming to an end for Daisy. She'll have someone to look out for her from now on.'

'Daisy will do her whack in that hotel business, though. She's been independent for too long to sit back and let a man keep her.'

'It'll be a better life for her, though.'

'Definitely.' Nora finished her drink, looking at him. 'You must have found London a very different place after all those years locked away,' she remarked chattily.

'I still do,' Lionel told her. 'Especially as I wasn't from around here, and Wembley was a whole lot quieter.'

'You wouldn't want to go back to Wembley?'

He shook his head vigorously. 'No fear. Even apart from the bad memories, there's nothing for me there now,' he said. 'Whereas here, I do have people. I know Daisy's going away but there's still June . . .' He paused. 'And you.'

'We all need people nearby who care about us,' she said. 'I think one of the reasons Daisy and I got friendly so quickly was because neither of us had anyone else, unless you count that waste of space, Nat.'

He nodded.

'Sometimes it used to seem as though it was just Daisy and

me against the rest of the world,' she went on. 'A spinster and an unmarried mum. Both outsiders.'

'And now you've got an ex-con in the gang as well,' he said with a grin.

She threw back her head and laughed. 'At least you can joke about it,' she chuckled.

'Just about.'

'Do you feel properly settled now?'

'No,' he replied without hesitation. 'I'm glad to be out of the nick, of course, and I value my freedom, naturally. But I still feel restless. I don't feel as though I belong.'

'Is that because you hate the job in the factory?'

'That doesn't help.'

'Can't you find something else?'

'No.'

'I thought there was supposed to be loads of jobs about.' She was puzzled. 'That's the impression I get from reading the paper, anyway.'

'There is plenty of work about but not in the parks department,' he informed her. 'There's nothing at all in that line at the moment. Still, beggars can't be choosers. So the factory will do me for the moment.'

'Hardly a beggar, Lionel, as you got your compensation,' she pointed out. 'Surely you've enough to live on until more suitable work comes up.'

'That money will soon fritter away if I sit on my backside all day doing nothing,' he said. 'I want to keep it in case of an emergency. One of the girls might suddenly need help, and if that happens, I want to be able to step in. Anyway, I want to give Daisy the best wedding ever. It's traditional for the bride's parents to shoulder most of the expense. Walking my daughter down the aisle is something I never thought I'd do. It'll be my proudest moment.'

'I can understand how you feel,' she remarked. 'But after

all you've been through, you're entitled not to have to do work you loathe.'

'I'll be all right,' Lionel assured her perkily. 'Don't you worry about me. The important thing is being free, and all thanks to my lovely daughters.' He smiled at her. 'With backup support from you, as well.'

'I was just baby-sitter and general dogsbody,' she explained. 'They did it all. You can be very proud of those girls of yours. They're fighters, both of them.'

'You don't have to tell me,' he said, his eyes soft with affection for them.

'I wonder who they get it from?' she grinned knowingly.

'God knows,' he said in his usual modest way.

Attracted by a sudden clatter, she looked towards the door as a couple of the Teds burst back in and swaggered over to the bar, insisting to the landlord that they were over eighteen and deferred from army service.

'Drink up, Lionel. I think we'd better get out of here, sharpish,' Nora suggested. 'It looks as though there's going to be trouble.'

'It does, an' all,' he agreed, draining his glass and standing up to go.

They hurried to the door and went out on to the streets that had such a dangerous feel to them lately.

Chapter Eighteen

Daisy's wedding was everything she'd always dreamed of and thought she'd never have: a long dress, bridesmaids, church bells, a reception with a four-piece band – the works. Even the weather smiled on her. Being early December it was cold, but one of those glorious winter days with a dry crisp feel to it and sunshine glinting on everything.

'Happy?' asked Jack as they smooched around the dance floor at the wedding reception in the functions room of the Gullscombe Arms.

'Need you ask?' She was radiant in an ivory satin dress of a simple design with a fitted bodice, long sleeves and a high neckline suitable for a winter wedding. Her hair was taken back into a chignon and adorned with cream satin flowers attached to a billowing veil. 'Are you?'

'Are you a Catholic?' was his answer to that.

She laughed. 'It's been a great day, hasn't it?' she said. 'Thank you.'

'You're thanking *me*?'

'I certainly am. Not only for marrying me but also for doing it the way I wanted it, in a Catholic church, and all that that entails.' As a non-Catholic, it had been necessary for Jack to take some instruction from the priest beforehand, during which he had agreed to allow any children of the marriage to be raised in the faith; standard procedure in a mixed marriage.

'I'd have married you in a phone box if it was what you wanted, and could be arranged,' he smiled. 'And the other stuff wasn't a problem.'

They'd chosen to marry in Devon rather than the church in London where Daisy and the girls attended Mass because they had both wanted the reception to be in Gullscombe Bay, where they had fallen in love, and would be living. Fortunately the parish priest here hadn't had a problem with Daisy having two children out of wedlock, and had been happy to marry them. She wasn't divorced – that was the important thing as far as the Catholic Church was concerned. The Manor wasn't quite ready to host a wedding reception so they'd decided on the village pub instead.

Shirley and Belinda had been bridesmaids, June a matron of honour and Alan the best man. Because Jack was so popular in the village, the wedding had turned into something of a community event and many of Gullscombe Bay's residents were here this evening. It was surprising the amount of people you could get into a village pub.

'It's been such a smashing day, I don't want it to end,' she sighed.

'There'll be plenty more good days for us,' he told her. 'This is just the beginning.'

'I know it is and I'm really looking forward to our life together,' she assured him. 'But today is so special I feel as though I want to hang on to it.'

'That's understandable and I hate to bring you down to earth but it'll be time to get changed out of your wedding finery soon,' he reminded her. 'We don't want to be too late getting away.'

'I'll go and get changed after this dance.' They were staying overnight in a Torquay hotel before travelling to the Lake District tomorrow for a week. June, Nora and Lionel were all taking time off work and staying on here to look after the girls while they were away. They were staying at Gullscombe Manor and making a sort of holiday of it. 'I'm still a bit worried about going away and leaving the girls, you know,' she confessed.

'They'll have a whale of a time with June and Nora and your dad,' Jack said to reassure her. 'They're so used to them they won't even notice that we're not around. Especially as they'll get spoiled rotten.'

'I know I'm being soft,' she went on. 'But I've never left them for as long as that before.'

'It's only a week, and we'll make it up to them when we get back,' he promised her.

'You're so sweet to them.'

'It's no effort, I can assure you, because I think the world of them. You and I need a honeymoon, a little time away on our own. But after that, whenever we go away it'll be all of us together as a family.'

'I love you, Mr Saunders,' she chuckled.

'The feeling is mutual, Mrs Saunders,' he said, holding her very close.

One thing that was casting a dark shadow over Daisy's perfect day was the thought of living so far away from Nora and June and her father. She knew she couldn't have everything and that Jack and the girls must be her priority now, but the thought of them not being close by gave her a tight ache inside.

'Brings tears to your eyes to watch them, doesn't it?' June remarked to Alan as they sat together watching the newly-weds dancing. June and Alan were alone at the table; everyone else in their party had gone off – some to dance, others to mingle. Shirley and Belinda – resplendent in red velvet bridesmaids' dresses – were bopping with Nora and their grandfather close to the band; they'd been at it for ages and

413

showed no sign of flagging. 'I've never seen a couple more right for each other than Daisy and Jack.'

'Just like us,' he said.

She forced a dry laugh to keep the tone light and hide the depth of her feelings for Alan, which were frightening in their intensity since seeing him again. Having been among the main participants in today's proceedings, they had been in each other's company for most of the time, albeit not on their own until now. 'Let's hope they don't end up the same way,' she said.

'It doesn't have to be like this, you know, June.'

'Alan, don't . . .'

'I still love you,' he burst out, unable to hold his feelings back.

She started visibly from the profound effect his sudden declaration had on her. But she daren't let a few sweet words allow her to lose track of the facts. 'Weddings have a romantic effect on people,' she said lightly, cheeks suffused with pink, folds of pale lemon satin so perfect with her dark colouring. 'They're known for it. It's got something to do with all the emotion floating about in the atmosphere.'

'I'd rather you didn't trivialise something that's so important to me,' he admonished.

'I didn't mean to trivialise it,' she explained. 'But this isn't the time to bring up our feelings for each other; not in a room full of people.'

'As far as I know, there is no special time to tell someone you love them,' was his simple answer to that.

It was what she wanted to hear so much, her good intentions weakened. 'Are you saying that even after the terrible thing I did to you, you'd still be willing to take me back?'

He met her eyes. 'Yes, that's exactly what I'm saying,' he affirmed. He had planned never to ask her back again but seeing her today, that resolution had disappeared.

414

'Alan, you don't understand—'

'Things are different now that I've made the break from the Cliff Head. I'm a different person, much more able to stand on my own two feet,' he cut in, having always suspected that his parents had been a contributing factor in June's decision to leave him, even though she'd denied it. 'It couldn't have been easy for you, working so close with my folks. I know my mother could be difficult at times.'

June felt like a different person too, since unburdening herself to Daisy about her past. The scars were still there but, bringing it out into the open had lessened the feeling of isolation and made her braver about her thoughts and memories. Being with Alan again was like being held in two loving arms and she wanted more of it, much more. That was all very well, she reminded herself, but nothing had changed as far as her reasons for leaving him were concerned.

Seeing the genuine warmth in his eyes, however, she felt a surge of hope and experienced a defining moment. There was only one way she and Alan stood a chance of happiness together and that entailed doing something that carried a huge risk. She decided to take that risk.

'Alan, we need to talk . . .'

'I'm all for that and the sooner the better—'

But at that crucial moment there was a noisy interruption.

'This is the best day ever, Auntie June,' announced Shirley, breathless from dancing, cheeks flushed with excitement. 'It's better than Christmas.'

'Mummy looks ever so pretty, doesn't she?' added Belinda. 'She looks like a film star.'

'I think so too,' agreed June.

'And you two look like little princesses,' said Alan, smiling at their shining faces, red velvet hair bands decorated with small white satin flowers adorning their heads. 'You're the prettiest bridesmaids I've ever seen.'

They beamed. This was their first taste of glamour.

'Come and dance,' urged Shirley, tugging at June's hand. 'And you, Uncle Alan.'

Nora and Lionel arrived back at the table just as the band struck up with 'Rock Around the Clock'.

'Phew, thank God for a sit-down,' said Nora, grinning at June and Alan. 'It's your turn now. Those kids will keep you at it until you're on your knees.'

June smiled at Alan and they allowed themselves to be led on to the floor to dance rock 'n' roll style. When they returned to the table the others were there so a private conversation wasn't possible. Anyway, Alan had to attend to his duties as best man, organising a send-off for the departing bride and groom.

Clouds of confetti showering the happy couple, they departed to cheers from the crowd gathered outside the pub. June stood beside Alan as they watched Jack's black Ford Anglia, with a 'Just Married' sign on the back, disappear out of sight. June was imbued with a mixture of emotions. She was happy for Daisy but sad that she was going to be living so far away. They would still see each other occasionally but it wouldn't be the same.

A hand holding hers recalled her to the present and she glanced down to see Shirley looking somewhat forlorn.

'What's the matter, poppet?' she asked.

'Nothing.' But she was brushing tears from her eyes with the back of her hand.

'They'll be back before you know it,' June comforted her, guessing what the problem was. 'And in the meantime, you and me and Nora and Granddad are all going to have such fun together.'

'Just because it's wintertime doesn't mean we can't go out and about,' Alan added. 'I'll take you all out in my car and you can help me show Nora and your granddad the area.'

'We have to go to school,' Belinda reminded him. Daisy had moved to Devon a couple of weeks ago so that she could be on hand for the wedding preparations. The girls had started at the village school right away. Daisy had wanted them to be settled in their new school before she went away on honeymoon.

'Yes, but we'll still have the rest of the weekend and the evenings,' June pointed out.

'Will you meet us from school?' enquired Shirley.

'Every day,' promised June, 'and I'll have Nora and Granddad with me.'

'And Uncle Alan?' asked Belinda hopefully.

'You'd better ask him,' suggested June, turning to him. 'But he does have to go to work.'

'I'm sure I can arrange things so that I can be at the school gate when you come out,' he told her.

This cheered both the children.

'Let's go and do some more dancing!' cried Shirley.

'Yeah!' added her echo.

And they all trooped back inside the hall.

'About that talk you were suggesting,' began Alan.

'That'll have to wait until they've all gone to bed tonight,' June whispered.

All the major structural work at Gullscombe Manor was done. Just the finishing touches were left to do before they opened for business at Easter: some of the decorating and the furnishings and fittings. June and her father and Nora were being accommodated in the rooms that were ready, albeit that the furnishings weren't complete.

What was to be the main visitors' lounge was more or less complete. It was a large, elegant room with huge bay windows, velvet curtains in a soft orange shade, wood-panelled walls, russet-patterned carpet and plenty of soft seating and subdued lighting. They'd had central heating installed throughout the building but had also had the original iron-work fireplace restored in the main lounge.

It was in this room, around midnight that same night, sitting either side of the dying embers of a log fire, that June told Alan everything.

'That was why I left,' she said in conclusion. 'Not because I didn't love you but because I didn't want to deprive you of the chance to have children. I just couldn't bring myself to tell you the truth. When you followed me to London, I had to pretend I didn't love you because I wanted you to give up all hope of my coming back so that you could get on with your life with someone else.'

He sat very still, his expression inscrutable. She felt physi-cally ill with fear – sick and giddy – because she wanted him back so much, but only if he still wanted her, knowing the truth. It was expecting a lot of any man and she wouldn't blame him for not having her back after what she'd done. But it was the only way they could go forward together.

'I feel so hurt, June,' he said at last, looking at her with a grim expression.

'I'm sure you must do,' she said. 'I'm not proud of what happened. But I was just a young girl and I didn't have any power over the situation.'

'I'm not talking about that,' he was quick to amend with emphasis. 'I'm referring to the fact that you didn't trust me enough to confide in me about all the terrible things that had happened to you.' He looked at her sadly, shaking his head. 'To keep it all to yourself and then just go off like that, leaving me worried and wondering what I'd done wrong . . .'

'It was unforgivable, I know.' She bit her lip so hard it hurt. 'But I just couldn't tell you the truth, Alan, I was too ashamed to tell anyone. I kept it all locked up inside until it all came pouring out to Daisy one night.'

'You couldn't possibly know how I felt after you left.'

'I think I can because I was equally as devastated,' she told him. 'Looking back on it, it was crazy. But leaving seemed like the only decent thing to do at that time. You were pushing for us to take medical advice when I already knew the reason we couldn't have a child. Had I known before we got married that I wasn't going to be able to get pregnant I would never have married you. I didn't want to stop you having kids.'

'And it never occurred to you, I suppose, that I married you because you were the woman I loved, not because I wanted a baby-making machine.'

'Come on, Alan, you were dead keen for us to have a baby when we'd been married for a while,' she reminded him. 'You must admit that.'

'Yes, I did want us to have a family, I admit it. It's a natural thing and I'm not going to deny it,' was his candid reply. 'But I didn't want children more than I wanted you as my wife.'

'Are you speaking in the past tense?'

'No,' he said. 'The same thing still applies. If it isn't possible for us to have kids, I can accept that.'

She couldn't believe how lucky she was. 'Oh, Alan,' she said, smiling.

He gave her a sharp look. 'There is a condition, though,' he began sternly.

'Oh, dear,' she uttered nervously, waiting for him to go on.

'There are to be no more secrets between us.' He looked very grave.

'There won't be—'

'I'm serious about this, June,' he cut in grimly. 'I need to know that you'll tell me in future when there's a problem. I can't cope unless I can have your word on this.'

'I promise.'

'Good. Now that that's settled, can we be a couple again?' he asked with a hesitant smile. 'Will you move into

Gullscombe Manor on a permanent basis, not just as a temporary guest?'

'Try stopping me,' she beamed.

'And as we're already married you can move in right away,' he suggested.

'I'll have to go back to London to clear up a few things, give my notice in at work and so on,' she said. 'But, yes, I can move in tonight, if you like.'

'Oh, yes,' he grinned, and as though of one mind they rose and moved towards each other.

'When you said you wanted me to tell you anything at all that's worrying me, did you mean everything?' she asked him later.

'Absolutely everything,' Alan confirmed.

'In that case, I have to tell you that there's one aspect of moving back to Devon that I'm not happy about.'

'What's that?'

'Being so far away from my father and Nora,' June explained. 'I don't want to leave Dad because I've only just found him and was enjoying getting to know him properly, and Nora because she's a true friend. She's already lost Daisy and the girls; with me gone as well she's going to be so lonely. I promised both her and Daisy that I would never leave them without a home so I'll have to work something out so that Nora's got somewhere to live.' She thought about this. 'I'll sell the house and get a flat or something for her because I won't leave her homeless.'

'And the fact that you're going to do the right thing by her doesn't make you feel any better?' he guessed.

'No, not really. The thought of leaving her and Dad makes me want to weep. We've all become so close, you see,' she told him. 'It's spoiling things for me a bit.'

He pondered the question for a while. 'Well, we can't have

our reunion spoiled, can we? Not when the problem can be easily solved,' he said mysteriously.

Gullscombe Manor Hotel was ready to open in March. The rooms were all furnished, the cocktail bar fitted, an alcohol licence obtained and they were fully booked for Easter, following an extensive national advertising campaign.

Both Nora and Lionel had jumped at the chance of moving to Devon and joining the team at the hotel. Lionel was in his element looking after the grounds and doing any small maintenance jobs that didn't need an expert from outside. Nora's sharp brain made her a natural for the office, June was in reception and Daisy was in charge of the waiting staff. Jack and Alan were at the helm as joint managing directors. Versatility was of the essence here. They all worked as a team and helped out wherever they were needed in the hotel, regardless of job titles.

Daisy and Jack and the girls lived in the renovated gardener's cottage in the grounds, June and Alan were in an attic flat while Nora and Lionel both had rooms at the back of the house. The family atmosphere was strong among this group.

The children thrived in the healthy environment with so much space to run and play, and a more personal atmosphere at the village school than they'd been used to in London. Daisy was able to work flexible hours that fitted in with their routine and they always knew where to find her if she was on duty after school hours.

All ideas were discussed and suggestions welcomed. Daisy's brain wave of having a reception in the new bar of the hotel just prior to its opening, for local businessmen and other hoteliers in the area and the local press, was greeted with approval by them all. So the invitations went out and the acceptances came pouring in. They were planning a prestigious event and were all very excited.

When there was no response at all to one particular invitation, however, June decided to take action . . .

'You,' gasped Irene Masters one afternoon when she answered a knock at the door to find June standing on the step. Being out of season she'd guessed she'd find her mother-in-law at home. 'I didn't think you'd ever have the nerve to show your face here again. I suppose Alan sent you.'

'Not at all. He doesn't even know I'm here,' she informed her in an even tone.

'Why have you come then?' she demanded, looking at June with hostility.

'I need to talk to you and Gerald.'

'Well, we don't want to speak to you.'

'Look, it really is important or I wouldn't have come, so may I come in, please? It won't take long.' This was a much more confident June than the one who used to inwardly quiver in Irene's formidable presence. 'Just ten minutes or so . . .'

Irene tutted and sighed, then with seething irritation she ushered June into the living room, a lavishly appointed chamber with deep-pile carpet and lace-curtained bay windows overlooking the sea. Gerald was sitting in an armchair reading the newspaper.

'Well, well, you're quite a stranger,' he said, looking up in surprise as June entered the room; he was noticeably less hostile towards her than his wife.

She nodded. 'How have you been, Gerald?' she asked politely.

'Not so bad, thanks.' He squinted at her over the top of his spectacles. 'We heard that you and Alan were back together.'

'The local grapevine is still in good working order then.'

'That's enough chatter,' intervened Irene, throwing June an

icy stare. 'Just say what you have to say and leave us in peace.'

June fixed her with a steady gaze. It felt so good not to be afraid of her. 'We have a mutual dislike of each other, and that's one thing we do agree on. Right?'

Irene nodded. Gerald made no comment.

'But we all care about Alan,' continued June. 'Well, I assume, as his parents, you must feel something for him even if you do have a funny way of showing it.'

This enraged Irene. 'How dare you?' she exploded. 'I won't be insulted in my own house.'

'I've come here to ask you to come to the reception we're having at Gullscombe Manor on Friday night,' she went on as though Irene hadn't spoken. 'You haven't replied to our invitation which probably means that you intend to hurt Alan by staying away.'

'Whether we go or not is our business,' snapped Irene. 'It has nothing to do with you.'

'I'm Alan's wife, which means it's everything to do with me,' June asserted. 'I'm not prepared to stand by and see him get hurt. Don't you think you've done enough of that already?'

'I think you'll find the boot's on the other foot there,' objected Irene. 'How do you think we felt when he told us he wanted to leave the family business?'

'Alan didn't do that to hurt you. He just needed to do something for himself and I admire him for it,' June replied.

'Yes, well, you're not a parent, are you? So you can't possibly know what it feels like to have your only son turn his back on you,' Irene went on.

'From what I've heard it was you who turned your back on him,' June corrected. 'You wanted to keep him at your beck and call indefinitely, and when he acted like a grown-up and showed some initiative, you were mean-spirited enough to cut him out of your life altogether.'

'We gave him what he was owed.'

'This isn't about money.' June was becoming heated. 'This is about Alan's right to make something of himself as a person as well as someone's son. It's a normal human desire. Anyway, you left him with no choice. You wouldn't give him the respect he needed here so he had to break away.'

'I want you to leave—' Irene began.

'Not until you've heard me out.' June was adamant. 'Alan hasn't said as much to me but I know that your approval of our new venture would mean a lot to him and I suspect that you're going to deprive him of that. That's why we haven't had a reply. You didn't even have the decency to decline the invitation. You're just going to let him keep on hoping that you'll be there and spoil it for him by not turning up on the night.'

'You don't know that,' was Irene's sharp response.

'I'm willing to bet on it.'

'He does actually want us to be there, then?' Gerald seemed pleased at the idea.

'Of course he wants you to be there. You're his parents, for goodness' sake, and you're important to him.' June paused, looking from one to the other, then continuing in a more conciliatory manner, 'Look . . . his leaving the Cliff Head had nothing at all to do with his feelings for you.'

'You don't betray people you care about,' announced Irene.

'He didn't betray you.' Her voice rose with exasperation. 'I wasn't around at the time but I know Alan and I know that that would be the last thing he intended. From what I can gather he was really upset about the rift between you. He didn't want it and still doesn't. He'd give a lot to be on good terms with you again.'

'Do you think we're enjoying it?' demanded Irene cuttingly. 'He's our only son, for heaven's sake.'

'And a son to be proud of, too. He's worked so hard to make a success of Gullscombe Manor,' June went on, 'serving in a pub to bring in money and organising all the renovations for the hotel at the same time. Both he and Jack have worked their socks off this past year or so. Between the lot of us we are going to make a success of it.'

'You don't need us then, do you?' said Irene miserably.

'No, we don't need you,' was June's frank response. 'And your being at the reception on Friday night will make no difference to the success of the hotel because that's going to happen anyway. But it would make Alan so happy if you were there.' She paused, feeling an unexpected surge of pity for them. 'Look, you've made your own success with the Cliff Head, now it's Alan's turn to shine. So why not come along to the party and give him your support? It will mean so much to him, even if you just stay for an hour.' Another pause and she heard herself say, 'I'd like you to be there too.'

Gerald looked at Irene. 'What do you think?' he asked.

'I'll give it some thought,' she said, looking at June. 'That's all I'm prepared to say.'

'Fair enough,' agreed June, and allowed Gerald to show her to the door without further comment. She'd done what she could. It was up to them now. But she hoped they would find it in their hearts to be there because Alan's happiness was the most important thing in her life.

Daisy had never been to anything as posh as the reception before, and she was enjoying every moment. Having always, until recently, had clothes that were years old and from a market stall, it was fun being able to have nice things and she felt good in a turquoise figure-hugging cocktail dress with a boat-shaped neck, which she was wearing with high-heeled shoes. With the hotel still being in its infancy, they couldn't afford to be reckless with money but, as Jack's wife, the standard of living for her and her daughters had risen dramatically. And as she worked hard alongside him, she wasn't troubled by the independent spirit she'd developed after so many years on her own.

'If my waitress friends at the hotel where I used to work could see me now,' she said to June as they sipped champagne together in between mingling with the guests, 'they'd be green with envy.'

'Full of admiration, more like,' corrected June, who was much more used to this sort of thing than her sister. She thought Daisy had coped brilliantly with the new etiquette required of her in her position as the wife of one of the principles. Making the transition from waitress to management couldn't have been easy but she'd slipped into it as though born to it.

This evening they had brought in their newly appointed staff to look after the guests so that they were free to socialise.

'I could get used to this sort of thing,' Daisy told her sister.

'That's just as well because there'll be more of it in the future,' said June.

'We've all been working so hard to get the place ready, we haven't had the chance to be glamorous.'

'You've made up for that tonight, though,' complimented June, looking approvingly at her sister's radiant face glowing with a dusting of make-up, her hair worn loose and casual.

'You look nice too.'

June was wearing a red satin dress with a low neck and short sleeves and a gently flared skirt, her hair taken back into a pleat.

'Thanks, kid.' She looked around to see Nora and Lionel engaged in conversation with the landlord of the Gullscombe Arms and his wife. Nora had splashed out on a green dress and jacket, her hair cut shorter now and properly styled for the occasion while Lionel looked spruce in a suit. 'It all seems to be going very well. Everyone seems to be enjoying themselves.'

Daisy nodded. 'I still have to pinch myself to make sure that this is all really happening to me,' she said. 'It's such a different life from before. And the best part is that we're all here together. The thought of living so far away from you all was spoiling it for me when I got married.'

'I think we're all relieved about that.'

'You and Alan seem to be getting on well,' Daisy remarked casually.

'Better than ever now that everything's out in the open,' June told her. 'Alan's changed too, now that his parents aren't pulling his strings.'

Daisy sighed. 'Everything's so perfect, I keep thinking that it's too good to last.'

'That's what years of trouble and hardship have done to you. Fearing the worst becomes a habit, I suppose. But you'll get more confident in time. Nothing's going to go wrong, Daisy. This is your life now, yours and the girls', here in Gullscombe Bay with Jack and the rest of us.'

'Yeah, I know.'

Jack appeared at Daisy's side, looking dashing in a dark suit and crisp white shirt. 'Come on, you two, get mingling. That's enough of all this sisterly nattering,' he joshed. 'This might seem like a night off but you are actually working. Socialising with all the local business people. Putting Gullscombe Manor Hotel on the map so that if they ever need a function or a conference, they'll immediately think of us.'

'All right, slave driver,' smiled Daisy. 'We were just taking a little break.'

'Just kidding,' he grinned. 'You carry on chatting if it makes you happy.'

Noticing that June was looking around anxiously, Daisy

427

asked her if anything was wrong.

'Some people I was hoping would turn up haven't done so, that's all,' she explained.

'There's bound to be a few who can't make it.'

June nodded.

'Anyway, enough of all this family rabbiting,' said Jack with a hearty grin. 'I must go and fly the flag for our hotel.'

Daisy watched him go, smiling affectionately after him. Nora and Lionel drifted over and the four of them talked about how well everything was going.

Jack appeared at June's side a little while later. 'Your missing guests have just turned up,' he informed her with a knowing look.

'Irene and Gerald?'

'The very ones,' he confirmed. 'Alan's talking to them in reception.'

'Thank goodness for that.' She shot him a look because she hadn't told anyone about her visit to Irene and Gerald. 'But how did you know it was them I was talking about? Have you added mind-reading to all your other talents?'

'Just a lucky guess. You and I have been friends a long time, remember,' he said, cocking his head and winking at her. 'I was hoping they'd turn up too, for Alan's sake. So now that they have, we can relax and enjoy ourselves.'

She nodded cheerfully.

'There's a couple of people over there looking a bit lost,' said Daisy, glancing across the room. 'I'll go over and make them feel welcome.'

'You're a natural for this sort of thing, a real asset,' was Jack's tender reply

Chapter Nineteen

Their first season surpassed all expectations and the hotel was fully booked right through until September. It was hectic, fulfilling and, at times, fraught with problems. Apart from the minor mishaps that arise in any business, a summer flu bug gave them a major staff shortage in the middle of high season, and a storm left them without electricity thus threatening to leave the guests without their evening meal. Fortunately, the power was restored at the eleventh hour and dinner was delayed rather than non-existent. But the experience was a salutary lesson and they had their own generator installed to avoid similar inconvenience in the future.

With a great deal of hard work, flexibility and an unflagging sense of humour on the part of the management team, they overcame these and other crises without the guests perceiving so much as a hint of the chaos that reigned behind the scenes.

Although they weren't planning to close for the winter, there were mixed opinions about Alan's idea of putting on a special Christmas programme. Mainly because they weren't sure if there would be sufficient bookings to make a party of it, Christmas being traditionally a time for hearth and home. In the end they decided to test the market by advertising, with the idea of not taking any bookings at all if there wasn't enough interest to make it financially viable and to create a festive atmosphere.

But the idea of a work-free Christmas with log fires, lashings of festive food, Santa Claus, a Boxing Day treasure hunt and various other social events appealed to a lot of people and the hotel was fully booked for Christmas and the New Year. Hosting the event was exhausting but enjoyable too, and a friendly atmosphere prevailed throughout the hotel.

In the quiet times during the winter they kept business ticking over by hosting conferences and seminars as well as keeping the restaurant open to non-residents all year. They also hosted special weekends for hobby societies and specialist groups. They had such enthusiasts as ballroom dancers, keep fitters, aspiring artists and writers, all of whom provided their own programme of events so only required food and accommodation. The introduction of the Gullscombe Manor Special Cabaret Weekends with dinner dances and first-class entertainment proved to be enormously popular too.

The following year, as their second frantic summer season advanced towards its end, they were quietly confident that their hotel was becoming established.

'I reckon we'll all be ready for the pace to slow down a bit when the busy season finally ends,' Daisy said to Jack one morning in September.

'You're not kidding,' he agreed. 'We're all shattered.'

They were finishing breakfast in the kitchen of their cottage, a warm and cosy, oak-beamed room where the four of them ate their meals, talked things over and generally congregated. A shaft of autumn sunlight was shining through the window and lying cheerily across the corner of the solid wooden table that used to adorn the kitchen at Seagull Cottage. This house wasn't yet such a triumph to DIY as the other one because Jack hadn't had time to get busy on it. But it had had a certain amount of refurbishment and was comfortable enough and very pretty with stone-faced walls and leaded-light windows. At the moment Daisy and Jack were enjoying a quiet few minutes alone together because the girls had finished their breakfast and were upstairs getting ready for school.

'We won't have time to take it easy for long, though, will we? Because no sooner will things have slowed down after the summer season than it'll be time to organise the Christmas programme,' she pointed out.

He nodded. 'The hotel certainly doesn't give us time to get fat and lazy,' he observed.

'I don't mind, though,' she told him. 'I enjoy being busy.'

'No regrets then?'

'You're joking.' She was emphatic. 'This is the best thing that's ever happened to me. Even apart from loving every minute of being married to you, I enjoy being part of a business. After all those years slogging away as a waitress, actually helping to run a hotel is really exciting.'

'Hard work, though.'

'Not half,' she agreed. 'It's certainly destroyed all my illusions about management having it easy.'

As they were finishing their coffee they heard the clunk of the letter box as the morning paper came through the door and dropped on to the mat.

'I'll get it, love,' offered Daisy. 'I've finished my coffee anyway.'

When she came back into the room, she was looking somewhat distracted.

'Something the matter?' he asked.

She handed him the newspaper.

'Blimey,' was his shocked response as he took in the violent scenes on the front page of race riots in the Notting Hill Gate region of London. 'Thank God you're out of that area.'

'I never thought things would get so bad,' she told him.

'I've noticed a few reports in the paper of racial attacks around there this past couple of weeks, but it seems to have escalated into a full-scale battle now.'

'This is shocking!' he exclaimed, reading on. 'They're fighting with anything they can lay their hands on. Cars have been torched, people knifed.'

'Let's have another look at the paper, please, Jack?' she asked with growing anxiety.

He handed it back to her and she read of a place she didn't recognise as the one she'd lived in for most of her adult life. This was a war zone, a place of petrol bombs, stabbings and fights with broken bottles, knives, sticks, iron bars and bicycle chains. Ordinary, decent people were confined to home because they were too afraid to leave their houses. In Paddington a house had been set on fire by a petrol bomb. 'It makes me want to weep,' Daisy said, her eyes fixed on the newsprint and pictures of policemen struggling with rioters. 'Who would have thought it would come to this, eh? I mean, trouble had been brewing for ages before I left there. Street fights between the Teds and the West Indians were par for the course around there. You couldn't not be aware of the racial tension if you lived there, even if you weren't involved, because it was all around you. But I didn't realise that feelings were running that high, probably because it was outside of my circle. Live and let live has always been my motto. And you only get to the heart of the culture of an area in so far as it affects yourself, don't you?'

'In a big crowded place like London that's probably true,' Jack agreed. 'Around here you only have to have a cross word with someone and the whole village knows about it.'

'Thinking about it, though,' she went on thoughtfully, 'the bad atmosphere was getting worse towards the end of my time there.'

'You must be glad you're away from it all.'

'I wouldn't want to still be living there, but I'll always be a Londoner at heart, wherever I live,' she told him. 'I have a special feeling for the place no matter how rough things get there. It has nothing to do with buildings or living conditions. It's an emotional thing. There's something about the place I can't shake off.'

'Oh.' He looked disappointed.

'Don't get all upset,' she said affectionately. 'Here is where I want to be. My home now is wherever you are.'

'That's all right then.' He seemed reassured.

'But I still miss London from time to time,' she continued. 'Don't you?'

'Yeah, course I do, sometimes. But not as much as you do, I suspect.' He gave a casual shrug. 'You know how attached I am to this part of the world.'

She raised her eyes, grinning. 'I couldn't fail to know that, and I'm very fond of it too,' she told him. 'But I think I'll always need to go back to London every so often to keep in touch with my roots, such as they are.'

'I can understand that.'

'And while we're on the subject of London,' she went on to say, remembering something, 'I've been meaning to tell you that June has asked me if I'll go with her when she goes to see the gynaecologist in Harley Street in a couple of months' time.'

'Has she got to go again?' He seemed surprised. 'Nothing wrong, is there?'

'Nothing new,' she told him. 'Still the same problem, the lack of a pregnancy.'

'I thought that was all in the lap of the gods now that she and Alan have both had tests and know that there's nothing wrong with either of them.'

'It is. There's no medical reason why June can't get pregnant. She's been given all sorts of advice about the right sort of diet, and told the most fertile times during her menstrual cycle and so on to increase her chances,' she informed him. 'This next appointment is just a follow-up.'

'I see.'

'I don't know if there's anything else they can do but if there is, June will jump at it. She'll do anything to have a baby, though she does try to accept that it might never happen.'

'Is Alan not going with her to the specialist this time?' queried Jack.

'He will if she wants him to,' Daisy replied. 'But she seems to want me to go with her instead. It's a woman thing, I think. She wants to make a shopping trip of it as it will be so near to Christmas.'

'She's still desperate to have a baby then?'

'God, yes. Everything's perfect except for that one thing. She and Alan are happy, the hotel's doing well and we're all here together. It's just that one thing that's spoiling it for her. And she knows that Alan would love a child, even though he keeps telling her not to worry about it.'

'Still, she's getting medical advice from someone who really knows their stuff.'

'Exactly. When she finally plucked up the courage to see a doctor, Alan insisted on the best, and this one is a specialist in fertility problems.' Daisy paused, looking at Jack. 'Anyway, love, do you mind if I go with her? You'll have to look after the girls but I'll only be away for a couple of days. And Nora will give you a hand.'

'Of course I don't mind,' he was quick to assure her. 'It'll be a nice break for you.' He paused, glancing towards the paper. 'As long as you keep away from Notting Hill Gate. It's too dangerous there at the moment.'

'We're not going until early December,' she told him. 'The trouble will be over long before then. The police have got it under control now, according to the paper.'

'Yeah, I expect you're right.'

'June suggested that we stay in the hotel where she used to work,' she went on. 'It's very central.'

'Good idea,' he approved. 'You go with my blessing and I hope you have a lovely time.'

'And in the meantime, I must take the girls to school.'

'I'd offer to take them for you but I know you enjoy going yourself.'

'You bet. One of the highlights of my day is that walk to the village school, especially on a glorious morning like this,' she said, glancing towards the window through which the sea could be seen beyond the hotel gardens. The cottage was tucked away at the far side of the tennis courts with just enough distance for its inhabitants to enjoy their privacy.

'On your way then, woman,' he joshed in the easy way they had with each other. 'Take your daughters to school and leave the old man to read the paper in peace.'

'You're gorgeous, do you know that?'

'You're only saying that because it's true,' he joked.

She brushed her lips against his hair then headed for the stairs. 'Time for school, you two,' she called up to the girls. 'So get yourselves down here sharpish.'

The West End of London was a seething mass of people when the Rivers sisters joined the crowds in Oxford Street one Friday afternoon in December. They'd got an early train from Devon and, as June's appointment wasn't until the next morning, they had the rest of today free for shopping, which they entered into with gusto.

'I don't know how we're going to get all this stuff back to Devon,' said June as they took a break for tea in Selfridges, piling their store bags on the floor beside them.

'We'll manage,' said Daisy, sinking her teeth into a buttered toasted teacake. 'Being in London at this time of the year is too good an opportunity to miss. I've certainly made inroads into my Christmas shopping list. I got some lovely things for the girls.'

'I've done well too,' said June, sipping her tea.

'That's a smashing wristwatch you got for Alan.'

'I think he'll be pleased.'

They fell into a comfortable silence. 'Aren't you going to eat your teacake?' Daisy enquired eventually as she made short work of hers.

'No, I'm not all that hungry,' June told her. 'I shouldn't have bought it.'

'It won't go to waste with me around,' grinned Daisy. 'But you ought to have something to keep your strength up if we're going to do some more shopping.'

June made a face. 'I hate to be a wet blanket but would you mind if I call it a day now?' she asked.

'Oh?' Daisy was surprised because they'd both been looking forward to doing their Christmas shopping. She squinted at her sister, noticing that she was looking rather pale. 'Are you OK?'

'I'm fine but I'm feeling a bit shattered after the early start this morning,' she explained. 'I'd like to go back to the hotel when I've finished my tea, if you don't mind. But you stay and do some more shopping if you like and I'll see you back at the hotel later.'

June hadn't been her usual self since they'd left home; she'd been quiet and preoccupied, Daisy thought. Probably had the doctor's appointment on her mind. 'I think I will wander around the shops for a little while longer,' she said. 'Though I won't be able to carry much more.'

'I'm sure you'll be able to manage a few more packages for those daughters of yours,' grinned June.

'Hello, Jack, it's Daisy.'

'Hello, love.' His voice was warm with pleasure and surprise to hear from her. 'Are you enjoying yourself?'

'I'm have a smashing time,' she told him. 'I'm just calling to find out if everything's OK.'

'Everything's fine.'

'The girls all right?'

'Good as gold,' he said. 'But you should be concentrating on enjoying yourself, not worrying about us.'

'I've got a few minutes to spare while June's in with the doctor so I thought I'd give you a call,' she explained. 'Just wanted to hear your voice.'

'It's lovely to hear yours. I've missed you.'

'I've missed you too,' she confessed. 'But I can't stay long because I'm in a phone box and the money I put in won't last long and I've no more change. I'll see you tonight.'

'I'll be at the station to meet you.'

'Can't wait.'

'Me neither.'

'Bye, then,' she said quickly as the coins were used and the line went dead.

She realised that she was smiling as she replaced the receiver. Just a few words with Jack was all it took to lift her spirits, she thought, as she crossed the road to the consultant's rooms. She'd been feeling a bit tense before the call. She hadn't wanted to worry Jack with it, but the trip had been rather a strain because June had been in such a strange mood. Her longing for a baby was really beginning to drag her down and Daisy was worried about her.

The waiting room was a far cry from the sort of doctor's waiting room Daisy was used to, she thought, as she went in and sat down on a sofa. Instead of hard chairs and well-thumbed, out-of-date magazines, here the seats were soft and the reading material new and of the thick glossy variety with photographs of beautiful homes and gardens.

She was immersed in a picture of a luxurious bedroom when the consultant's door opened and June came out. Oh Lord, she thought when she saw that her sister's face was wet with tears. She must have had bad news.

'June, love,' she said in concern, going towards her.

'Daisy, I've got the most amazing news,' she said shakily.

'Oh?' Daisy was wary.

'I'm pregnant.'

'What!'

'Isn't it wonderful?' She was smiling now and Daisy realised that the tears she'd seen were those of joy.

'But I thought . . .' The details could wait until later, she decided, hugging her sister, tears springing to her own eyes. 'That's the best news ever. Congratulations.'

Because their train didn't leave until late that afternoon, they had time to spare after lunch so decided on a nostalgia trip to Notting Hill Gate. Leaving their luggage at the hotel, they headed for Marble Arch tube station.

'I thought you'd seemed quiet ever since we left home,' remarked Daisy on the train, returning to the subject that was filling both their minds. 'I assumed you were fretting because you couldn't get pregnant when in actual fact you were preoccupied because you thought you might be. You're a dark horse.'

'I was dying to tell you but afraid that if I actually said the words out loud I would somehow be tempting providence. I know it's silly but I was scared to hope after waiting so long,' she explained. 'My periods have never been regular so being late is nothing new for me. I've been feeling a bit sick but that could have been anything.'

'I thought you were nervous about the doctor's appointment and that's why you didn't want much to eat.'

'That was part of it but I was feeling queasy too,' she said. 'Anyway, I told the consultant all this and he examined me and gave me the good news.' She shook her head, smiling. 'I still can't believe it.'

'You will do once you start expanding,' laughed Daisy, getting up as the train rumbled into Notting Hill Gate station.

It was a typical December afternoon: cold and still, a smoky haze hanging over everything. In contrast to the brightly lit West End shops and all the colourful Christmas decorations, the streets looked grey and dismal as they walked from the station to Larby Gardens, through run-down areas juxtaposed with pockets of affluence so characteristic of London. Passing through a shabby neighbourhood with the smell of poverty about it, it seemed to Daisy, who could now view the area from a broader perspective, having been away, that this bit of London had been forgotten by the affluent era.

In Larby Gardens, they stood outside their old house, staring at it like sightseers on their first trip to the capital. To Daisy's surprise she found the experience curiously unemotional, though they had had some good times there. Portobello market was as vibrantly vulgar as ever and evoked happy memories for them both. It also reminded Daisy of Nat, but she felt nothing more than a moment of sadness as she remembered the humiliating ending of a relationship that had once meant so much to her. He was her past, the same as this city. She would always want to come here to visit but she belonged in Devon now with Jack, and felt able to draw a line under her life here.

Thinking of her life in Gullscombe, a warm glow spread through her. As well as having her beloved Jack with her, she had all the other people who mattered most to her. The girls were thriving and her dad was happy and settled. She smiled, thinking of him and Nora, who were great pals and spent most of their spare time together. They sometimes reminded

Daisy of an old married couple, the way they teased each other and joked around, but there had been no talk of anything other than friendship. It might change at some time in the future – who could say? And if it didn't they still had something really special.

On the way back to the station, snatches of jazz and calypso music drifted out of the drinking clubs. The pubs were closing after the lunchtime session and people were straggling out and talking in groups in the street. A gang of Teds were congregated outside a seedy-looking café with filthy net curtains at the windows.

'I wonder if they're plotting another riot,' said June.

'Now, June, we don't know for sure that the Teds started the riots,' Daisy pointed out in a tone of gentle admonition.

'I didn't think there was any doubt about it,' was June's answer. 'That's what we've been led to believe.'

'According to the papers they were to blame but Dad reckons the Teds were just convenient scapegoats,' Daisy told her. 'He used to listen to what was being said in the pubs when we lived there. They were at the centre of the riots, no one can deny that, but it might not have been all their fault. Dad said they were used by the fascists to stir up racial trouble. The Teds jumped at the chance of a fight and got all the blame – that's Dad's theory, anyway.'

While they'd been talking some black youths had come out of a West Indian café and the atmosphere became threatening as the two gangs walked towards each other.

'Whatever the truth of it, the trouble obviously isn't over,' observed June. 'The riots have finished but the fighting hasn't.'

'You're right,' said Daisy, and they hurried away from a brawl in the making.

'It's quite frightening,' commented June. 'A relief to be away from there.'

440

'I'll say,' agreed Daisy. 'I'm glad to have got the girls out of that area before all the big trouble started. They love it in Gullscombe with Jack and me and the rest of the gang.'

'You only have to look at them to see that,' June remarked.

'Of course, your baby will know nothing of living in a place like this, will it?'

'Neither will it have to suffer any of the problems we had, Daisy.'

'No. Thank goodness.'

'Still, it turned out all right for us in the end, didn't it?' June reminded her cheerfully, linking arms with her sister. 'And the future is bright for us all.'

'Especially now that you've had such good news,' said Daisy.

'Yes,' June smiled, and they walked to the tube station, arm in arm, glad to be together and going home.

The Pride of Park Street

Pamela Evans

When Jess Mollitt gains a place with the famous Burton Girls dance troupe, appearing on the West End stage, it seems her dreams have finally come true. But then a family outing ends in tragedy, killing her mother and leaving her father a broken man. Jess is forced to give up the career she loves to look after her younger siblings and manage the newsagents her father is no longer capable of running.

Working in the shop is a far cry from the glamorous existence she has left behind and, unable to contemplate a life without dance, Jess searches for a way to bring a little of that joy back into her days. It's not long before she's running a hugely popular Saturday dance class for local children and this, combined with her blossoming friendship with neighbour Don Day, provides Jess with the saving grace she needs. But when the brother Don hates arrives on the scene, it seems Jess's problems may be only beginning . . .

'A good traditional romance, and its author has a feeling for the atmosphere of postwar London' *Sunday Express*

'The leading characters are finely drawn . . . crisp prose . . . a superb and heartwarming read' *Irish Independent*

'Very readable' *Bella*

0 7553 0041 6

headline

Part of the Family

Pamela Evans

Lizzie Smith became part of the Carter family when she was orphaned as a child. With four boys, Polly Carter sees Lizzie as the daughter she never had and it is only fitting that Lizzie should eventually marry one of her sons. But, much as she loves Stan, Lizzie knows that her husband has a dark side, and when he is involved in a work dispute with Philip Verne, at Verne's Silk Mill, Lizzie senses trouble ahead . . .

War intervenes, taking the Carter men away, but when Stan returns he is still bitter towards his employer. He confronts Philip late one night and their actions end in disaster. Lizzie and her three children are utterly devastated by the consequences, but it is Polly who cannot forgive Philip Verne for the tragedy that has occurred. Family loyalty means everything to Polly, and she insists that her other sons leave Verne's immediately, even though they cannot find work elsewhere.

Then Philip offers Lizzie financial compensation that would enable her to start a silk mill of her own. Lizzie is torn in two. As part of the family, should she accept Philip's kindness and rescue the Carters from poverty, or turn down his offer for the sake of Polly's pride . . . ?

0 7472 4835 4

headline

A Fashionable Address

Pamela Evans

The Potters of elegant Sycamore Square in Kensington take for granted all the comforts of their position in life, maintained by the large family drapery store. Then, one day, everything changes; Cyril Potter is a secret gambler whose debts have become so crippling that he resorts to suicide. Shocked, disgraced and left to clear the debts, his wife and daughters are forced to sell everything.

Young Kate Potter shoulders the responsibility for her pampered mother, Gertie, and frivolous sister, Esme, finding accommodation in the two dingy rooms of a dilapidated Hammersmith tenement house. Despite the dirt and poverty of their new lives, Kate is ever cheerful as she tries to rally her family to make the best of the situation, and she promises them she will move heaven and earth to make it possible for them to return to Sycamore Square.

As she labours long hours for low pay in Dexter's hat-making factory, Kate's dreams seem far away. The more so when she catches the lascivious eye of the factory owner Reggie Dexter and is left pregnant by him. Close to despair she is persuaded to have her son adopted so that he can enjoy a better life than she is able to offer. As she tries to come to terms with her guilt, Kate struggles to set up her own millinery business – and start on the slow road to achieve prosperity and a fashionable address.

0 7472 4313 1

headline

Now you can buy any of these other bestselling books by **Pamela Evans** from your bookshop or *direct from her publisher*.

FREE P&P AND UK DELIVERY
(Overseas and Ireland £3.50 per book)

Town Belles	£5.99
A Song in Your Heart	£5.99
The Carousel Keeps Turning	£5.99
A Smile for all Seasons	£5.99
Close to Home	£5.99
Always There	£5.99
The Pride of Park Street	£5.99

TO ORDER SIMPLY CALL THIS NUMBER

01235 400 414

or visit our website: www.madaboutbooks.com

Prices and availability subject to change without notice.